D0915275

LIGHT OF THE DESERT

by
Lucette Walters

authorHOUSE®

AuthorHouse™
1663 Liberty Drive
Bloomington, IN 47403
www.authorhouse.com
Phone: 1 (800) 839-8640

This is a work of fiction. All of the characters, names, incidents, organizations, and dialogue in this novel are either the products of the author's imagination or are used fictitiously.

Published by AuthorHouse 09/25/2015

ISBN: 978-1-4259-7748-1 (sc)
ISBN: 978-1-4259-7749-8 (hc)
ISBN: 978-1-4918-4256-0 (e)

Library of Congress Control Number: 2007903330

Print information available on the last page.

This book is printed on acid-free paper.

ACKNOWLEDGMENTS

To my dear friend **Victoria Dann**, NYU Professor, gifted teacher. I am grateful for her valuable advice and inspiration through the challenging years of writing fiction.

To **Crystal** for her endless love and support, and for sharing her creative gifts. I am deeply grateful.

To **Alain** for his love and support, and to Raya, light of our lives.

To **Ruth** and **Alvin Moss** for their inspiration, kindness and warm friendship and their professional and honest critique. I shall always miss them.

A heartfelt thank you to **Sara Held**. Great editor, patient teacher.

To **Katherine** and **Rod Russell**, for their incredible insights and spiritual awareness.

To my dear **Evie** and **Leonard Prybutok**, for their warm friendship and for sharing their wisdom which I will always cherish.

To **Nancy** and **Natasha Young**, for reading my manuscript until dawn, for their loving friendship and support.

To **Evelyn Cook**, dear friend, talented writer, many thanks for her honest critique, she inspired me through the tough writing process and taught me to cut, cut, cut!

To my dear sisters **Shelly** and **Spery** for their love.

To AuthorHouse's **Ron Bowles**, for his guidance, and to **Joel Pierson** for his editing support and sense of humor. To **Hilary Kanyi** for her kindness and patience.

To the great **Mario Puzo** who once gave me a job when I needed one, and who inspired me to keep writing. I will always remember him with blessings and heartfelt gratitude.

And mostly, to my dear husband, **David**, in loving memory, forever in my heart…

I DEDICATE THIS BOOK TO

MY BEAUTIFUL MOTHER,
SUZANNE
A WOMAN OF LOVE, A WOMAN OF FAMILY,
A WOMAN OF COURAGE.

IN THE SPIRIT WORLD NOW, SHE GUIDES ME

*****

TO CRYSTAL VICTORIA-HOPE
DAUGHTER EXTRAORDINAIRE, YOU MAKE ME PROUD

And
In Loving Memory of My Father

FARID FENDIL

BELIEVED HE HAD TO SAVE HIS FAMILY NAME

BEFORE HIS RELIGIOUS PEERS.

BUT A MAN CANNOT GAMBLE WITH

THE HAND OF FATE

OR OPPOSE THE WILL OF ALLAH.

THIS TRUTH, HE NEGLECTED TO HONOR.

AND SO BEGINS THE STORY OF HIS DAUGHTER NOORA,

LIGHT OF THE DESERT.

AL-BALLADI, JORDAN

MARCH 21, 1993

"I denounce you!"

He grabbed her by the hair, forced her to her knees, and kicked her in the face. He kicked her again. Blood squirted into her eyes, and before she could bring a hand up to protect herself, he kicked her a third time. She heard a cracking sound in her head and her vision blurred.

It had to be a nightmare. She must wake up now! But the horrific experience persisted. She was suffocating.

She tried to get away from him, but he caught her and dragged her down the long corridor by her feet. She heard screams and barely recognized them as her own. Blood from her fingers streaked the marble tiles. Men in gray suits stood like steel posts. She saw the man with the mustache.

The man from London.

She reached out a hand. Help me! *But he stood glaring at her, as her father dragged her down the pool steps and rammed her head beneath the water's surface.*

The loving hands that once taught her how to swim were drowning her.

The twenty-one years of her life flashed before her. The same pool sparkled beneath the sun-drenched crystal dome. Her father's arms were piled with presents. Ten illuminated candles were ready to be blown from her huge pink birthday cake …

Her sister Zaffeera, eight years old, stood at the edge of the pool in her red bathing suit, fists on her hips. "It's my turn to swim now, Father," *her voice echoed from the past.* "It's my turn!"

Please, God, keep her safe, Noora cried in her heart. For a brief moment, she could see the gold letters of her parents' initials etched in the marble, on the deep end of the pool. The undulating water turned murky with blood.

Her chest burned as her lungs filled with water. She needed to breathe, she had to breathe now! She had to beg for his mercy, for whatever the cause, she didn't know.

He pushed her down and would not let go!

If she could just reach the surface—and ask, WHY?

CHAPTER 1
NOORA

JULY 22, 1972

On a desert dawn,
Little light shines on ...

Yasmina Fendil rose from her bed, pushed her feet into her handmade *baboush* leather slippers, and stretched out her pregnant stomach. She had at least four more weeks to go, but she was anxious to hold the baby in her arms. *Little Light*—she remembered the dream song. She should tell her mother about it, Yasmina thought, making her way to the adjoining room. Most dreams had a message, but those of a pregnant woman had to have special significance.

She opened the door to her mother's bedroom and peeked inside. Beneath a silver satin comforter, Sultana Marietta, a petite woman in her late fifties, was snoring, her wiry gray hair spread wildly around her pillow.

Yasmina decided to let her mother rest.

The two women's bedrooms were connected by a nursery. Yasmina looked up at the blue-domed ceiling with painted white clouds and touched the dimmer switch. Tiny specks of stars brightened gently and changed hues as they sparkled overhead.

Yasmina's son, Nageeb-Gabriel, was asleep. They had recently celebrated his third birthday, yet it didn't seem so long ago that she was pregnant with him. She watched her firstborn and smiled. He probably had the longest, blackest eyelashes in the Middle East. And he was smart. *Inshallah,* if God willed, someday he would be an architect and a real estate developer, like his father. Carefully she replaced the blue satin down comforter he had kicked onto the floor. She bent to kiss him, but decided not to risk waking him.

Silently she returned to her bedroom suite and opened the glass doors to her verandah.

Lowering herself on a chaise longue, she sank into the billowy mounds of cushions. She had experienced mild abdominal discomfort during the night, and her ankles were swollen. She propped her legs up on two thick pillows and marveled at the deep, royal blue blanket of sky, dotted by sparkling stars. She inhaled the cool, fragrant air, sweetened by the rose bushes and plumeria trees in the garden below.

She knew that the day before, she had stood in the kitchen longer than she should have. But a good *molokhieh* took hours to prepare, and she could not disappoint her husband. The tasty spinach-like leaves that grew along the Nile were sent weekly from Egypt to Yasmina's kitchen. She had chopped the dark green leaves very fine and slow-cooked them in chicken broth seasoned with garlic, onions, coriander, cumin, and other spices fresh from her mother's herb garden. The mouth-watering aroma that wafted out of her kitchen every Friday drew the entire household, like children to candy.

As the stars faded with the indigo of night, Yasmina tried to remember her dream. She had a strong sense that this baby would not be a boy. The thought of a baby girl made her happy, even though she knew her husband would be disappointed. He wanted Nageeb to have a brother.

She dozed off. When she opened her eyes, she spotted a shooting star. Its brilliance lingered just as the brightening sky announced the sunrise.

A warm liquid flowed out of her. No, this could not be ... her water bag? Too soon. The contractions, if that's what they had been earlier, were mild. Certainly there was no need to worry or alarm anyone. But five minutes later, the next contraction became more painful.

"Ummy, Ummeee," she called out to her mother. No one answered. She began to breathe methodically, the way her mother taught her during the first pregnancy, but at that moment, she could not recall what else she was to do—except beg Allah for the pain to subside. She tried to relax before attempting to reach her mother's room, but the next cramp was long and acute, and Yasmina couldn't help but cry out. "Help me, *ya Allah!"*

Still no one heard. She checked her watch, determined she was not going to panic. *Babies didn't just fall out,* she reminded herself. *It could take hours.* But five minutes later, the cramps returned and they were unbearable. She felt great pressure, as if the baby was pushing down.

She screamed again. The maids were far away, in their living quarters downstairs by the kitchen, on the other side of the mansion, and her mother was still not responding. The only one who would come to her would be her little boy, and she did not want him to see her in such a state. All she could do now was pray.

"Ummy … Ummy!" Sure enough, Nageeb stood by the open glass door, holding his favorite blanket.

"Go call Nana. Please … Run, *ya ibni;* run, my son," Yasmina begged.

Nageeb rushed to his mother, placed his little blanket on her stomach, and ran back inside.

Finally, Sultana emerged on the verandah wearing a long white cotton nightgown, her silver hair matted and in disarray. Her sleepy eyes grew wide when she saw her daughter was about to give birth.

Less than an hour later, Sultana, who—by the mercy of Allah—was a midwife, cut the umbilical cord. *"Hamdallah!"* Yasmina's mother thanked the Almighty.

At the edge of town, the call to Morning Prayer by the *muezzin* on the minaret drifted with the desert breeze.

While the maids were busy tending to Yasmina, Sultana raised the baby to the sky. The sun was now above the horizon and cast a golden aura around the baby's head.

"May her life be as easy as her birth. *Allah Akk-barr!"* she chanted in her raspy voice. "God is great!" She wrapped the baby in a soft, hand-woven receiving blanket and stood fussing and cooing over the bundle.

"Praise to Allah. Bless you, Mother. Bless all of you," Yasmina said to the three maids. "Now let me hold my little girl!"

"She is ugly," Sultana said, introducing the newborn to her mother.

Yasmina gazed at her beautiful baby, and looked up at her mother. "Yes ... ugly," Yasmina agreed, uttering the untruth in order to banish ill luck and envy. "She arrived with *noor*—light... sunlight. If Farid approves, I would like to name her Noora," Yasmina said.

The maids put a sturdy blanket beneath Yasmina and swiftly carried her to her bed. The brass bassinet that had belonged to Nageeb when he was born was placed nearby. In no time, the housekeepers had changed all the ribbons and bows on the bassinet from blue to pink—except for the mandatory "blue bead" encased in a large solid gold medallion that dangled from a gold safety pin. The turquoise gemstone was the traditional protection to ward off evil spirits—*afreets*—and the dreaded "evil eye."

Nageeb, who had been kept away until his mother was ready to receive him, bounced excitedly into her room.

"Nageeb," Yasmina said, hoping he would not be disappointed, "you now have a baby sister ..."

"I want to hold her!" He climbed on his mother's bed and sat close to her.

As he held the baby in his arms, Yasmina said, "Promise me you will always take good care of your little sister, my son, and that you will always watch over her."

"I promise!" Nageeb said. "I will take very good care of my little sister." He never looked prouder.

When Sultana put the sleeping baby in the bassinet, the infant squirmed and opened her eyes slightly, revealing a flicker of turquoise blue that illuminated between her tiny, fine, dark lashes. Sultana raised the baby's head a bit more to take a closer look at those eyes. Most newborns had blue eyes, she reminded herself. But her granddaughter's were pale, more like those of northern Europeans. As far as she knew, everyone in Farid Fendil's family was Egyptian and had brown eyes. Sultana's grandmother had said some of their own ancestors who emigrated from Turkey had been beautiful, tall people with eyes shaped like almonds and pale turquoise like the Mediterranean seashores. But Sultana had always believed that the old woman exaggerated when she spoke about their "beautiful ancestors." Yet here was this baby, with those eyes. She hoped they would darken as she grew, because a child with such light eyes could bring envy or jealousy—even attention to the evil eye.

Clad in the traditional *gallabeya,* Farid Fendil shuffled to his wife's bedside. The housemaids disappeared silently from the room. He glanced at the baby girl, kissed Yasmina on the cheek, and turned to leave. He stopped at the door, returned to his wife's bedside, and stood gazing at the infant.

Carefully, he took the baby in his arms. He had just returned from the mosque, and needed to change into a business suit for meetings scheduled back to back in his office until sundown. Yet he did not feel rushed anymore. He took his time admiring the new bundle. He touched her tiny hands.

"So soft. Like silk," he whispered, his eyes mesmerized.

His infant daughter gazed right back at him.

"*Arusah, ya arusah anah,*" he chanted tenderly to his dear child.

Closing his eyes in prayer, he thanked Almighty Allah.

CHAPTER 2
ZAFFEERA

NOVEMBER 8, 1974

Sitting on the cool marble floor near the tall kitchen window, Noora was busy stacking up a tower of copper pans and bowls of all sizes, as high as she could. They eventually tumbled down, making a terrible racket. The toddler frowned in frustration, but persistently kept at it, stacking up each pan, only to watch it all crash again to the floor. Noora's almond-shaped eyes, shaded by long black lashes, remained a pale turquoise blue. Her thick brown hair already reached down to her shoulders, and every morning, Sultana looked forward to combing her granddaughter's soft curls. That morning, Sultana did not have the chance to fuss over Noora, because when she checked the calendar, she realized Yasmina was almost a week past her due date. She had to start preparations for the imminent childbirth.

Her tall, broad-shouldered daughter stood by the old wooden board, chopping a mound of *molokhieh* leaves. Her thick ponytail and curly black hair bobbed up and down as she worked. Farid Fendil had mentioned that he preferred lamb to chicken with his *molokhieh*, and of course, for Yasmina, nothing could be more important than pleasing her husband. The lamb was already cut up and braising on the stove.

From the beginning of her daughter's third pregnancy, Sultana worried about Yasmina's health. During the first months, she had experienced severe morning sickness. As she grew heavier, it was clear that at times, her discomfort became nearly intolerable, yet Yasmina hardly ever complained. Today, her face was more pale and puffy, and her ankles were so swollen, they looked like tree trunks. During the past few months, Yasmina had developed a strong appetite for salty and spicy foods. Sultana had warned her daughter about the dangers of toxemia, but Yasmina could not control her cravings.

Sultana often reminded herself that above all, it was the will of Allah, and Allah had been good to her. Yasmina, in truth, was not a great beauty, and Sultana had worried over her prospects for a good marriage. Her gentle disposition had, *hamdallah,* attracted a very good husband—a man she could compare to a prince or pasha of every Middle Eastern girl's dream.

Yasmina had not conceived after almost five years of marriage, and Sultana was aware of gossip starting around town—some families were planning to introduce their daughters to Mr. Fendil. Farid had told his wife he was confident she would eventually give him children and, like his father, he would not take on a second bride. To further show his respect for his wife, he invited her mother to live with them permanently.

Prior to marrying Yasmina, Farid had been a playboy who enjoyed the high life around the world. After their marriage, he continued to travel on business, and undoubtedly engaged young women who provided him with sensual pleasures. When he returned home, however, his arms were always filled with lavish gifts for his wife, and she, in turn, always had a feast prepared for him.

Farid Fendil had grown up in Egypt. During the sixties, as the regime of Gamal Abdel Nasser became more repressive, the young real estate developer had resettled at an oasis in a remote corner of Jordan, where opportunities abounded. Farid Fendil fulfilled his dream of building Al-Balladi, his new "homeland," a modern city of marble and glass buildings, with mansions surrounded by lush gardens.

Sultana knew her son-in-law was especially proud of the mosque he had designed. He had commissioned the best craftsmen to build it. Made entirely of limestone and hand-carved blocks of crushed crystals, the monument sparkled beneath the desert sunlight and cast an opalescent glow under the moon. Admired by princes and traveling dignitaries, Farid's mosque appeared to be blessed by the Almighty's hand.

Sultana watched Yasmina, who was vigorously mincing the *molokhieh* leaves finer and finer. She worked with a crescent-shaped *makratah* with alabaster handles, the same type used by their Egyptian ancestors. She rocked the sharp blade back and forth at least a hundred times. She could have minced everything in her French food processor in a matter of minutes, but she had to do everything the traditional way—as if her husband would know the difference.

Sultana brought a chair to her daughter. "*Bass ba'ah!* Enough! At least sit down and take a load off those poor swollen ankles!"

"No woman can cook sitting down," Yasmina said. "You're the one who taught me that, remember?"

"I taught you many things, but I didn't teach you to kill yourself fixing a meal. No man is worth that!"

"I'm almost finished."

Sultana shook an index finger at her daughter. "Your pasha can live without his favorite feast for one Friday!" When Yasmina didn't look up from her work, Sultana noisily pulled the chair back to a corner of the kitchen, plunked herself into it, folded her arms, and stuck out her tongue at her daughter.

The maids stifled their giggles. Sultana usually could cajole her daughter with a little humor, but this time, Yasmina just shook her head and went on with her cooking.

Abdo, Sultana's adopted son, walked in carrying a wooden box of shoe polish and brushes. He was followed by little Nageeb. Sultana wondered if perhaps she could get Abdo to distract Yasmina on some pretext.

Abdo went to his usual corner in the kitchen near the garden door, sat on a footstool, and pulled up another one for Nageeb. Together they began polishing Farid Fendil's shoes with a soft, worn cloth. Sultana knew Abdo would have preferred to spit-shine the shoes, the way he did when he was an orphan in Cairo. But Yasmina didn't like the idea of spit-shining, and Abdo respected her wishes.

Five-year-old Nageeb took pride in helping his "Uncle Abdo," the young man he now preferred to call "Big Brother." Sitting next to Abdo,

spotted her father sitting on a bench beneath the old mango tree. Dressed in the traditional garb which he reserved for prayers at the mosque, her father seemed engaged in a discussion with an older man who was also clad in the traditional *gallabeya*.

Zaffeera hid behind an archway by a pillar and leaned closer, eager to catch what they were saying.

She recognized the man, known as Sheik Abdullah Kharoub, head caretaker of her father's mosque.

"… sending your daughters to a foreign country alone. It is not done."

Her father defended his daughters, saying they were responsible, and added something about Nageeb, who had been in London studying medicine.

"Nageeb will be studying in Cairo now," the sheik objected. "Your daughters must have a bodyguard."

What business was it of his? Zaffeera wondered. Surely her father could handle his own personal affairs. But it looked like he had caved in, saying he would find a chaperone. The sheik insisted no, it had to be a man with the proper training.

Her father nodded patiently, saying he would look into it. She had never seen him meekly acquiesce to someone else's demands. And what did that sheik mean by "proper training?"

"I have elected Moustafa," the pompous old sheik said with finality.

"Moustafa? Your nephew?" her father asked.

"Yes. He is the proper man for the job."

Soon after the girls arrived in London, and on the first day of school, Zaffeera spotted Moustafa, the supposed bodyguard. "Proper man for the job?" The man was an imbecile. He was careless and conspicuous. She nicknamed him *homar,* Arabic for "jackass."

She had been tempted to contact the London Metropolitan Police and tell them she and her sister were being stalked by a terrorist type, then dutifully report him to her father. Wouldn't that embarrass the sheik! But after carefully calculating the situation, Zaffeera realized she could *use* him.

She noticed sometimes he carried a camera around his neck. She hoped he wore it today, ready to ogle Noora and snap pictures of her. It appeared that Moustafa had been lusting after Noora since the start of the school year. Zaffeera would use his passion to her advantage. Moustafa could provide proof that Noora was not the angelic girl her parents thought she was.

Noora was so engrossed in planning her wedding, so absorbed in herself, Zaffeera was convinced that her sister never noticed the *homar*. Her strategy would be that much easier to carry out if Noora didn't know someone from home was watching.

Zaffeera hugged herself and began to pace. In the distance, she could see Moustafa standing behind a bench near the pond, where children were tossing pieces of bread to a family of ducks. She slowed her pace, adjusted her huge Christian Dior sunglasses, and pulled down the rim of her hat so that she could observe Moustafa unobtrusively. He should be searching for Noora, but now his binoculars appeared to be directed at her. Kids were squealing with laughter as they tried to climb on the statue of Peter Pan. Zaffeera smiled for Moustafa's benefit, as if she enjoyed their shrieking. *I'll show him something to make his eyes pop out. Where the hell is that Noora?!*

Now in her senior year at the "LLC," the London Ladies' College, Noora sat in the last row of the empty classroom. She was embarrassed by the loud rumbling of her stomach. When the alarm rang at six o'clock that morning, she made the mistake of pressing the "off" button instead of the "snooze," and letting her head fall back on her pillow. She could not be tardy today. If it hadn't been for her sister, who came to her rescue by pulling her out of bed and starting her shower, Noora would definitely have missed the first-period exam. There had been no time for breakfast, and now, hours later, she was weak from hunger.

Her classmates finished their compositions and hurried out of the room the instant the bell rang. Noora kept finding weaknesses in the story she had written, and hesitated to turn it in. She found at least three misspelled words, and she knew Dr. Pennington did not tolerate errors. How many more misspelled words did she overlook? She could not take the time to proofread her work and check the dictionary. *How archaic,* Noora thought, *especially now that computers had spell-check.* Nevertheless, the school insisted on perfect spelling, perfect grammar, and perfect punctuation. It was hopeless.

To think, she had once fancied herself a writer, and had even dreamed of publishing a book of short stories in English. How pathetic. She sighed resignedly.

Her midterm assignment was to write a dramatic story, set during an important period in history. Noora chose to write a love story about a young couple separated during World War II, who found each other years later in Paris. Writing it had been a struggle. It was hard to focus on schoolwork—she couldn't stop thinking about her handsome Michel, their upcoming wedding, and most of all, their honeymoon.

She glanced at her watch and gasped. She remembered that her sister was waiting for her. Noora grabbed her overstuffed black leather backpack and hurried to the professor's desk, handing over her pages.

Dr. Pennington looked up from her pile of student manuscripts and put Noora's pages on top. A small, mousy woman in her sixties, she pushed her bifocals against her nose.

"I am looking forward to reading your composition, Miss Fendil," Dr. Pennington said, rising from her century-old desk.

She'll be disappointed, Noora thought.

"You have such a refreshing way with words," her professor said. She walked up to Noora and put an arm around her shoulder. "Always trust your imagination. You are a good storyteller."

"Thank you," Noora said, blushing. She was as surprised by the unexpected gesture of affection as by the fragrance of Je Reviens perfume, mixed with musty old wool, that emanated from her teacher.

"Miss Fendil?" Dr. Pennington called as Noora hurried to the door.

She turned, anxious to be on her way. Her sister was waiting out in the cold. "Yes, Dr. Pennington?"

"Have a nice vacation, and good luck!"

Why did she have to say good luck? Noora wondered as she rushed through the deserted, bleach-smelling hallway. Didn't she know it was bad luck to say good luck?

Tucked away amid a row of brownstones, the dark and dreary gray façade of the international school screamed for a facelift, but no modernization was contemplated. The unpretentious building was the perfect mask to discourage unwanted visitors, and one of the many reasons the school had remained a favorite among the very wealthy and the very private since it was founded in 1935.

The atmosphere seemed eerie now, without the usual resounding footsteps and the echo of female voices trailing through the halls.

As Noora exited through the heavy steel double doors, the wind slapped her flushed cheeks. Overhead, pink buds were beginning to burst open on the branches of the cherry trees lining the street. When she returned from her vacation, those trees would probably be covered with pink blossoms that would fill the air with their fragrance—*some consolation,* she supposed, *for having to finish the term.* Graduation was two and a half months away, and her marriage to Michel still an interminable three months and twenty-one days away! Noora could not stop dreaming of that moment when she would finally be in Michel's arms. *Honeymoon in Venice.* Her entire body tingled at the thought.

She had wanted to attend the college mostly because she would be near her brother, Nageeb, who had been studying medicine at the university just around the corner from the LLC. Nageeb always managed to take time from his busy schedule and dine with her on weekends. He also helped her with her studies.

Her fiancé was studying architecture in Paris. Though she was not allowed to see her future husband alone during the school term, Michel was able to fly to London for brief visits on weekends, always accompanied by his father. However, during his last year of architectural school, Michel had been too busy to travel. Still, it was consoling to know that Paris was not far from London.

Rushing up the sidewalk on her way to meet Zaffeera in the park, Noora passed a quaint bakery specializing in French pastries. Her mouth watered at the sight of huge, gooey Napoleons; but the shop was crowded, and she was really late. Something else in the window caught her eye: a crystal dish overflowing with white candied almonds—a sweet treat that she had loved since childhood. It reminded her of a wedding that was never far from her thoughts.

She was fifteen years old at the time. She remembered at least three hundred guests mingled at the lavish reception, near King Farouk's former summer palace, in the lush gardens of Montaza, in Alexandria. Noora would never forget the young bride who stood like a princess in a radiant white silk brocade gown. A violinist wandered through the crowd, playing Jacques Brel's classic, "If You Go Away ..." A big-band orchestra curtain suddenly lifted, surprising and delighting all the guests. Couples began to dance.

Noora stood next to her father by the huge atrium. Bridesmaids in pink tulle dresses handed each guest an elegant little crystal dish filled with white candied almonds wrapped in white tulle that puffed out like a fan—a gift from the bride and her groom. At that moment, a distinguished man about her father's age walked up to her father, and the two began to converse. Noora was admiring the heart-shaped crystal candy dish when she looked up and saw *him*. Dressed in a perfectly tailored tuxedo, he stood beside the man—obviously his father. When her eyes met the boy's deep-set green eyes, something so powerful passed between them, it seemed supernatural. To Noora's surprise, their fathers invited the young pair to dance together. The moment Michel put his arm around her waist, an electrical current ran through her body ...

"Careful!" someone yelled behind her as a black London cab made a sharp turn, brushing Noora's coat and jolting her out of her daydream, slamming her back to the present.

You almost got yourself killed! You have to live in the moment and stop being distracted! Noora reminded herself.

There was no traffic light at the intersection, and cars were not giving her the right of way. She managed to dart across the street, nearly getting hit. The rain had stopped.

In the distance, she spotted her sister. Standing alone in the park, Zaffeera seemed so small and frail, with that floppy black hat that reached down to her too-large-for-her-face sunglasses. Why did she want to meet her out there in the cold, when they would also have to wait outside the busy Hard Rock Café? Noora wondered. They could have met in that warm and cozy country French restaurant, with the little windows covered by lacy curtains, on Bayswater Road.

"Forgive me for being late," Noora huffed in Arabic, trying to catch her breath.

"You forgot all about me!" Zaffeera snapped in English.

"Please, Zee," Noora said in English. "I'm really sorry. I would never forget you..."

Zaffeera turned away to fold her Burberry umbrella and shake off the droplets of rain.

"I hope you didn't get here exactly at eleven o'clock!" Noora said, feeling guilty.

"I did."

"Oh, goodness, I apologize! Profusely."

"Let's go before the line gets longer."

Hurrying to the end of the park, they left through the black wrought iron gates and crossed the street.

Luckily, only a handful of people were standing outside the Hard Rock Café.

"Look, there's hardly a line," Noora said.

Zaffeera hated to be proven wrong, but masked her annoyance. She worried that someone would take that particular booth by the window. It was crucial that Moustafa saw them from outside, so he could easily follow them when they left the restaurant.

That morning, Zaffeera finished her exams effortlessly. The year before, she had requested—in a handwritten letter addressed to her father and mother—"the honor" of following her older sister's example and attending the LLC. Zaffeera knew her parents had been pleased with her decision.

Zaffeera prided herself on the knowledge that she was much smarter than her sister. But while she was blessed with brains, Noora was blessed with an unusual and beautiful color of eyes—pale turquoise—a rare phenomenon, especially in their Middle Eastern world. She was also blessed with a great, lean body. But worst of all, Noora had Michel.

Three inches shorter than her sister, Zaffeera had small breasts and large hips, and she always had to watch her weight. She liked her Egyptian brown eyes, especially when she accentuated them with makeup, but she needed prescription lenses. Her lips were actually her best feature—full and voluptuous. She especially enjoyed applying gleaming red lipstick, one of her evening rituals. She liked to stare at her lips in the mirror and she imagined being kissed. By him. *Michel. My darling Michel. I ache for your body; I wish she'd go to hell.*

He was meant for her and Noora stole him away ...

Zaffeera would never forget the first time she saw Michel—at a wedding in Alexandria, where her family spent most of their summer vacations.

Playing hopscotch in the garden with her little brother Kettayef, Zaffeera rapidly grew bored and went to the atrium, where the reception took place. As she stood by the entrance, praying that her father would finally signal the family that it was time to leave, she grabbed a glass of almond water from a passing serving tray. She nearly choked on the first sip when he walked in. The vision of Prince Charming just out of a fairy tale appeared right in front of her—in the flesh. Keeping a safe distance, she began to follow him around the reception area. A distinguished man, who had to be Prince Charming's father, accompanied him. Suddenly, the young man looked over his shoulder and saw her. Quickly she turned away, and as she did, she clumsily knocked a tray full of champagne glasses out of the hands of a white-jacketed server. Everything went splashing onto the floor. Zaffeera never felt more humiliated. While servants rushed to clean up the mess, a very flustered Zaffeera ran from the scene and out of the glass french doors, into the garden. She tripped and fell, luckily landing on the grass.

"Are you all right?" she heard someone say behind her, and a strong hand helped her up. To her horror, it was the young man. She thought she would surely faint, but he smiled at her. It was a warm, compassionate smile. He pulled out his white handkerchief and brushed away some dirt from her cheek.

"I hope you are not hurt," he said.

"I'm all right," she managed to utter. A whiff of his lemony, lightly sweet cologne mixed with fresh soap enveloped her.

"Thank you, I am fine," she said, never feeling more stupid.

Gently, he rested his deep green eyes on her, and during that brief moment, her heart skipped a few beats, and for the first time, she understood what they meant in French books by the *coup de foudre*. Two people met, and something struck like lightning, transporting them into a captivating feeling called True Love.

"That man with the tray was not careful ..." Prince Charming said, and Zaffeera noticed he had a brilliant set of white teeth—like perfect porcelain.

Blood rushed to the tips of her ears, and she prayed he did not notice her blushing. But he was a gentleman, and he had to be attracted to her as well. Why else would he go after her and follow her all the way to the garden?

"May I bring you some water?" he asked.

All she remembered saying was, "No, I'm fine, really ..."

He glanced over his shoulder, turned back to her, and said, "Excuse me, I'm being called."

She watched him walk away, and she nearly melted right there on the grass. She was only thirteen and a half years old. Even then, she felt the rush of desire to dance close to him. She even wished she could *kiss* him. She realized that she hadn't even had the presence of mind to ask his name. And she did not tell him hers. She had to regain some composure before she could properly introduce herself. She ran to the ladies' room. Her cheeks were burning hot. She splashed cool water, fluffed up her hair, and tightened the bow of her organza blue dress to give herself a thinner waistline. She locked herself in a stall and breathed deeply to regain control of herself.

When she returned to the ballroom in search of the handsome lad, she could not find him in the crowd of guests. Twenty long, anxious minutes later, with her heart sinking at the thought that he had left and she might never see him again, she spotted him—on the crowded floor, dancing with Noora! His eyes were on her and his arm circled her waist. But worse, Michel's father was conversing with her father while keeping a watchful eye on their children. The men smiled at one another, nodding with that awful, knowing look. Zaffeera understood the obvious: a future marriage—and a possible new business union for both fathers, as the result.

She wanted to tear Noora to pieces. Even if Noora was a little older, Zaffeera had met him first. She knew he liked her, before her father pushed him onto Noora. Always Noora before her. She stood in the shadow of a pillar, desperately trying to control her pain.

She kept her anger bottled up for almost six years. She was determined not to let that wedding take place. She would find a way, somehow, someday, to get Michel to fall in love with her. No matter what it took ... *No matter what.*

"... No matter what!" Noora's voice barged into Zaffeera's reverie, jolting her back to the present.

"What?" Zaffeera asked.

"Pardon?" Noora turned to Zaffeera.

"No matter what, what?" Zaffeera asked, annoyed. "What were you saying just now?"

"You didn't hear me?"

"I heard you," Zaffeera sighed. She didn't really want Noora to repeat whatever she was saying. *Always the same, always about herself.*

"I said I don't think I did well on my story."

"Oh, right. Don't worry."

"I'm just not going to."

Behind Noora, Zaffeera caught a glimpse of Moustafa walking toward the restaurant on the opposite side of the street.

"What does she expect?" Noora continued. "Two hours to write a story. It's crazy. Insane. Impossible."

"I thought you said she gave you the assignment last week."

"Actually, she gave us a week to think about it. That still isn't enough time to write a story ... in three scenes. Life is not in three scenes!"

"You mean three acts."

"Writers take years. It took Margaret Mitchell ten years to write *Gone with the Wind*. You know that?" She didn't wait for a reply. "I'm not talking about a novel here, but you'd think she'd give us more time ..."

Noora's endless complaints grated on Zaffeera's nerves. Only five more minutes, and that sexy American with the California surfer-boy blond hair would appear behind the double-glass entrance to unlock the doors. The line was now stretching around the bloody building.

"How were your exams?" Noora asked.

Moustafa had disappeared. *Where the hell is that idiot?*

"Zee? How were your exams?"

Zaffeera turned away from her sister and fiddled with her umbrella. She tucked it under her arm. "I'd rather not talk about it."

"I'm sorry. Was it grueling for you too?"

"No, it was not grueling at all," Zaffeera said, trying to keep calm. "We had a simple quiz. I didn't mean to sound short. I'm just hungry."

"Sorry ... I'm famished. They should open the doors any minute now."

Zaffeera dug in her latest spring fashion Louis Vuitton bag and produced a box of Altoids. "Here. Have one."

"Not those mint bombs," Noora said.

"These are different. Take this one. They help ease starvation," Zaffeera said, almost shoving the mint in her sister's mouth.

Noora chewed. "They taste weird."

"Weird?

"Well, different. A little bitter ..."

"That's because they're new. And improved. This new brand also freshens and kills bacteria. And ..." Zaffeera stopped. She shouldn't sound too eager to sell the mints.

Malibu Boy finally appeared behind the glass doors with his ring of jingling keys. Immediately, the line began to move inside. Zaffeera breathed in the warmth of the restaurant and looked forward to the mouthwatering whiff of charcoal-broiled burgers.

She guided Noora to the booth by the window. Elvis Presley's familiar thunderous voice boomed through the loudspeakers. "*It's now or never* ..."

Noora tried to flag down a waitress. A bubbly, gum-chewing server with a fiery eighties hairdo bounced in. Minutes later, she returned. "Didn't I just fill 'em, girls?" she asked, pouring ice water into the already emptied Coca-Cola-shaped glasses. "Where're you girls from? The Sahara?" She pronounced it "Sa-hair-ah."

Noora laughed. "Actually, we're not that far from there."

The waitress sauntered off to the next booth while Zaffeera glared at her. She leaned across the table and whispered loud enough for Noora's ears, "You don't have to tell everyone our business."

"Sorry," Noora said. "I think it went right over her Madonna hairdo," she giggled, lifting her glass. "To your health. And good grades!" She gulped down her second glass of water.

Zaffeera watched her sister and wondered how long it would be before the pill Noora thought was a mint took effect.

Preferring to eat something that had not endured the trauma of being slaughtered, Noora ordered a veggie burger. She was bothered by the undercooked meat Zaffeera always ordered.

Twenty minutes later, their order arrived. Noora looked away as Zaffeera hungrily devoured her bloody-rare hamburger. She spotted that man again—across the street. She had seen him before; she could swear he was watching them, even though he seemed to be waiting for the bus as he stood at the curb next to a lamppost. Noora was about to mention him to Zaffeera, but decided against it. *No need to alarm her unnecessarily,* she thought. It was probably just her imagination.

Noora's double-chocolate shake arrived with a slice of hot apple pie for Zaffeera. After a quick sip through the straw, Noora wrinkled her nose.

"I don't understand why Americans have to salt their desserts."

"Many dessert recipes call for a pinch of salt. It's to bring out the taste," Zaffeera said.

"I think that entire pinch of salt wound up in my one serving!" Noora said with a chuckle.

"I'll go pay the bill," Zaffeera said.

"But you haven't touched your dessert."

"I'm full. You can try my pie. Maybe they didn't salt that." Zaffeera took her wallet out of her purse. "Be back in a few. Wait for me here."

Noora tasted the apple pie, and turned to the window. The man was still out there across the street, and he spat on the sidewalk.

Noora recoiled with disgust. The bus stopped in front of the man and barred her view. She pushed the plate of apple pie away.

"Are you still working on that?"

Noora looked up. A yellow-haired busboy stood holding a stack of dirty dishes. "No, I'm finished. Thank you."

"You didn't like the pie?"

"Yes, well, actually ..."

"Tastes better a la mode, right?" he winked.

Noora laughed. "Well ... perhaps."

"If you like, we can get you a vanilla scoop. One scoop of chocolate and one vanilla would be even better. We also now have pistachio. You like pistachio?"

"I sure do, but no, no, that'll be fine, really."

"We also have the yummiest chocolate cake. Decadent. Deadly!"

"Really?"

"One of the customers here called it the Suicide Cake. That's 'cause once she tried one bite, she wound up eating the whole thing. Most people do! It's really heavenly." He winked again.

"Well ... I'm kind of full. But thank you very much, indeed."

"Hey, no prob. If you need anything else, holler. That's what we're here for, okay?"

"Thank you!" Noora said with a broad smile.

Moustafa spat again. The girl was flirting! A tease, she was. If he had not seen her with his own eyes, he would never have believed it. She was spoken for. That waiter in the restaurant was raping her with his eyes. Probably because she was taunting him with that smile of hers. Since last September, from the moment he laid eyes on her, Moustafa felt deeply attracted. Watching her, day after day, made him more and more frustrated. But he could only do his job. He was there for one purpose: to protect Mr. Fendil's daughters. He was an honorable man.

Inside the Hard Rock Café, Noora ventured a quick glance out the window, hoping the man had hopped on the bus. But the bus left and he was still there. He turned away and lit a cigarette. A sudden shiver ran through her. She grabbed her backpack and hurried to the cashier's desk.

Zaffeera was gone. Noora searched for her in the ladies' room, but she wasn't there, so Noora made her way to the exit. She leaned against the glass door for a moment to steady herself. She felt dizzy—not exactly sick, but lightheaded. Something in that chocolate shake did not agree with her. Perhaps she just ate too fast. *I hope I'm not catching the grippe,* she thought, chiding herself for not taking her daily vitamins. Behind her, she heard a couple of teenagers say to their friends, "Let's visit their logo shop around the corner."

The logo shop? Oh yes, Noora remembered. The restaurant had a gift shop, and Zaffeera had mentioned something about buying presents. She glanced across the street before venturing outside. Her heart was pounding faster now. She tried to calm down. Why was she feeling out of control? Thank goodness that man was not there. He must have taken another bus. How silly to imagine he was watching her. But where was Zaffeera? She walked around the corner and found the café's gift shop.

Inside, Zaffeera stood in line, studying a legal-sized piece of paper.

"*Hamdallah,*" Noora said, relieved. "Why didn't you wait for me?" she asked in Arabic.

"Noora, *English,*" Zaffeera whispered, giving her sister a reproachful stare.

"What's the difference? They're all tourists here."

"We're in England. We speak English."

"Okay! You don't have to be so stiff about it. We should be proud of who we are."

"That has nothing to do with it. Why didn't you wait for me in the restaurant?"

"I finished eating," Noora said.

"You could not have finished that pie so fast. You didn't like it."

"No, I ... okay, I didn't like it. Why didn't you tell me you were here?"

"Are you all right?"

"Well ... yes ... I'm fine, now. Is that a list you made for gifts?" Noora asked, looking down over Zaffeera's shoulder.

Zaffeera nodded toward a pile of gifts she had stacked on the counter by the cashier. "Keychains and little souvenirs for the maids ... I found that leather jacket ... and T-shirts. You should've waited for me in the restaurant."

"I'm sorry; I was worried about you."

"Why?" she asked, inspecting the price of the leather jacket, and raising an eyebrow.

"You're my sister. That's why. I'm responsible for you ... Besides, don't you want me to choose presents with you?"

"Of course. This jacket will look great on Nageeb, don't you think?"

"Oh, yes. You're amazing. I worried we wouldn't have time to find gifts for everyone, and here you are. With a complete typed list. Nageeb will love that jacket. As for little brother, you know he doesn't like to wear T-shirts."

Zaffeera smirked. "And we don't like those ugly striped pajamas our little Kettayef always wears around the house."

Noora laughed. "What about Shamsah? Sweet little sunshiny Shammoo-sah ..." Noora sang. She gave a quick glance out the window. That man was nowhere in sight, and indeed, she had been foolish. How silly of her to have imagined she was being followed. But she still felt a little unsteady.

"For Shamsah, I found this," Zaffeera said, inspecting a little denim top with white lace.

"But that looks more like for a seven-year-old. She's nine."

"I know. But it looks like it's her size. She's small," Zaffeera remarked. "I don't think she grew too much since the winter holiday."

"Three months ago. Last time we saw her ... Three whole months ... Seems like forever," Noora said, almost to herself.

Zaffeera walked out of the store carrying large shopping bags.

"Let me help you," Noora said in Arabic, following her sister.

"Once again, Noora," she chided, "we are in England."

"Yes, and we've been speaking British for months now. It would be nice to switch to our mother's tongue for a bit. What's the big deal?"

"We can do that tomorrow when we land," Zaffeera said.

"Oh, all right, *ya okhti* ... When in Rome, do like the British!" she said, exaggerating a British accent. She skipped along the sidewalk. Suddenly, for some reason, she felt like playing hopscotch or doing something fun and silly. "Sweet little Shamsah, I can't wait to squeeze her little cheeks!" Noora said, glad she didn't feel dizzy anymore. "Laugh a little, Zee. You are always so serious."

I'm not serious, I'm just angry! You bloody fool! Zaffeera wanted to shout. But it was essential to control her feelings, Zaffeera thought, stopping at the edge of a stoplight. And now there were no taxicabs for hire. Of course, they were never around when the weather turned miserable. Behind the lamppost across the street, she recognized Moustafa in his black rumpled trench coat. He was trying to light a cigarette with matches that would not catch in the cold drizzle. He would strike one again and again without success. Over and over, he repeated the nonsense. Why didn't the *homar* use a lighter? He should be paying attention, starting to wonder about Noora's silly behavior.

Quickly, Zaffeera turned and quickened her step.

"Why won't you let me help you with the bags?" Noora asked.

"I'm fine. And, guess what? Today is your day."

"What? Don't walk so fast ..."

"I said today is your day! Because anyone who has to look at old-maid Margaret Pennington every day deserves a break, if not a medal," Zaffeera remarked, slowing down a bit.

"You know, she actually put her arm around me and gave me a compliment this morning."

"I knew the old woman was a lesbian," Zaffeera muttered under her breath.

"What did you say?" Noora asked, chasing after her sister.

"Nothing!" She walked faster through the rushing crowd of pedestrians on the wide sidewalk.

"You said something. Did you say les…bian?"

"Noora!" Zaffeera stopped. "How could you say such a thing!"

"Whatever she is, she was being kind…"

"I said I knew the old woman was *intelligent*. Come, I have a nice surprise."

By the time they arrived at Allen Street, Zaffeera felt ready to collapse from carrying all the bulky bags for several blocks. They crossed the little landscaped courtyard, where a few roses were starting to bloom, and stepped up to the main door.

Noora rang the doorbell.

"Use the key," Zaffeera huffed, breathless.

"The concierge will buzz us in."

"She's on a holiday."

"Oh, that's right, I forgot." Noora rummaged through her backpack. "Come on, key. It's here somewhere …"

Zaffeera set the bags down, pulled her own set of keys from her purse, and unlocked the old wooden door.

"After you," she said. "Go ahead. I've got the bags." As soon as Noora entered the apartment building, Zaffeera waited a moment, and out of the corner of her eye, she caught Moustafa hopping out of a taxicab. *How did the* homar *find a taxi?* She noticed that the cab driver appeared Middle Eastern. Did Moustafa know him? Was the driver also connected to that sheik? As far as she knew, there was only one person following them, she thought, entering the building. Inside, Noora was persistently pressing the button for the lift—as if she thought it would arrive any faster—which annoyed Zaffeera even more.

Late one night, when Zaffeera took the trash out to the incinerator, she finally discovered where Moustafa lived. She spotted him as he scuttled into the apartment building across the street. She knew he had to live alone. One evening, she recognized his silhouette in the front window of the fifth-floor apartment, where he had a view of Noora's window. Zaffeera's bedroom was in the back, facing a wall in the alley—by the fire escape.

The girls squeezed into the one-person lift and rode up to the fifth floor.

"Who left the heater on? It's stifling in here," Noora said, entering their flat.

"I believe you did."

"Oh, sorry. Did I really? I don't even remember," Noora said, dumping her backpack on the living room sofa.

Inside her bedroom, Zaffeera opened a dresser drawer and removed a small sampler box containing a dozen chocolates. She inserted a needle into a syringe that she took from her purse, and filled it with a clear liquid from a small vial. She slowly injected about a half cc into two of the bite-size chocolate pieces.

"I can't wait to get out of those clothes!" Noora said, breezing out of the bathroom. "Why they insist on this stupid dress code is beyond me," she muttered, pulling her navy-blue sweater over her head. She unbuttoned the collar of her starched white shirt and made her way to her bedroom. "When are they ever going to get modern heaters instead of these awful radiators that get too hot and go tak, tak, tak all night long!"

"Right after we move out, no doubt," Zaffeera said, standing at the door.

Noora tossed her ankle-length skirt on her unmade bed.

"I have a surprise for you," Zaffeera sang, holding the box of chocolates. She waved the fragrant package.

Noora's eyes lit up. "Chocolate?"

"Swiss, if you please. They taste like silk, dahlin' ... A reward for getting through our exams," Zaffeera purred. "You know, when you wondered where I was that night? When you woke up and said you didn't find me? Well, I was out looking for the best shoco-lahs!"

"Oh my, Zee, you are so sweet. You shouldn't have gone through that trouble. But thank you, thank you."

"My pleasure."

"Which one of these sinful little devils should I pick?" Noora eyed each piece.

Zaffeera suddenly felt regret for what she was about to do.

Be strong, Zaffeera told herself. *But I don't really want to harm my sister,* a weaker voice pleaded within. The stronger one urged: *Just a little bit of ecstasy should do it. Chicken out now and you'll have to watch her marry your man. If she bears him sons, he'll have to love her. Then there will be nothing you could ever do ...*

"Take this one!" Zaffeera urged, sounding almost too anxious. Noora took one of the doctored pieces and popped it in her mouth.

Less than fifteen minutes later, Noora unbuttoned the endless little buttons of her shirt, and fussed impatiently over her cuff links. "It's too hot in here," she complained, peeling off her shirt and tossing it at the foot of her bed. "I can never open that stupid window!"

Zaffeera studied her sister. "Why don't we go out and finally enjoy the rest of our free afternoon. Let's go shopping! For your wedding night!"

"I haven't even started packing," Noora sighed. "Help me open this window."

Together, they managed to lift the window up an inch.

"Give it a few minutes, and it will be almost as cold in here as outside."

"I can barely feel the air. I can't wait to leave this place. Oh, I don't feel like packing—I feel kind of ... dizzy."

"I'll help you," Zaffeera said, faking a cheerful voice. "It's not as if we have to pack furs and heavy sweaters!" She laughed. "We're just going home, to the hot, blistering desert for a whole week!"

"Sounds wonderful. But I feel weird," she said, pushing the crumpled clothes on her bed to the floor, and falling in, grabbing a pillow and putting it between her legs.

"Maybe you can nap or watch a little telly while I change into normal clothes, instead of those silly school clothes. Oh, and I have another surprise. Something fun for you to wear," Zaffeera said, and returned to her bedroom.

She chose a mid-length black wool dress with scooped neck, and a black wool cape with fringes reaching to her low-heeled black leather boots. She pulled her hair back and topped it with a black felt beret. She studied her reflection on the floor-to-ceiling mirror. Not too stylish—a little matronly. She hoped it would not be difficult to persuade Noora to wear the sexy clothes she had purchased for her.

A half hour later, Zaffeera and Noora were on the sidewalk of a busy boulevard. Wearing a seductive low-neck pale pink knit top that fit tightly, and a short-to-the-waist butter-leather black jacket above body-forming jeans, Noora seemed to have popped off the cover of a celebrity fashion magazine.

They had no trouble finding a taxi.

On the first floor of Harrods department store, Noora admired the Egyptian artifacts on display. Unsteadily strolling through the aisles, gazing at the vases and gilded statues, she made heads turn and upstaged the exhibit.

Noora wandered into the food court and stopped to admire the assortment of wedding cakes.

Beyond the colorful tiled archway, Zaffeera spotted Moustafa. He was devouring a sandwich with all the grace of a hungry bear. She took Noora's arm and tried to pull her away from a towering wedding cake displayed in the center of the court.

"We would need a ladder to cut the first slice," Noora said, refusing to budge. "I wonder if those ... angels are edible." She acted more inebriated than drugged, and her eyes were glazed over. "Could they ship this ... wedding cake? How many people do you think it would serve? Is it *real?*" When she looked at Zaffeera, she seemed to have trouble focusing. "Wouldn't spoil, you know," she said, slurring her words. "It's probably mostly made of sugar. Sugar is a natural preservative. D'you know that? Of course! You know everything ... You're the brain in the family ... Unless they put custard filling. Right, Zee? Then it would be all messy ..." She moved closer for a better look and stumbled, nearly smacking her face into the twelve-tier wedding cake.

Zaffeera grabbed Noora before she made a terrible spectacle of herself (although that would have been perfect for Moustafa's eyes). "Perhaps we should wait after the spring vacation," she said, slowly guiding Noora away.

"*Aiwa, taba'an,* yes, of course. Sorry. No Arabic in London ... But we're at Harrods. And you know, it's owned by Mister... What's-his-name? He is from Egypt, too. Of course, you know that. Like Father. I do believe he is a cousin."

"Distant. Very distant."

"We're probably all related. Father should invite him to my wedding and I should add more swans made out of marzi...pan," she said. "I'll have none of those cheap plastic swans on my wedding cake."

"After our vacation, we'll order anything you want. That is, if you don't mind my help ..."

"I would be honored. Since you *are* going to be my maid of honor," Noora laughed.

Zaffeera gritted her teeth. She caught sight of Moustafa weaving through a crowd of Japanese tourists who had poured off a bus. She led Noora away, but not too far, hoping Moustafa had seen them.

On the second floor, Zaffeera maneuvered Noora to a display of lingerie.

"Feel the softness of this silk," Zaffeera whispered enticingly. She was checking out a long, skin-colored négligée on a mannequin.

Noora studied the fabric.

"Try it on!" Zaffeera urged.

Minutes later, Zaffeera paced in front of the dressing rooms.

Noora peeked her head out of a dressing cubicle and motioned to her.

"I don't believe it should be worn with a bra," Zaffeera said inside the dressing cubicle.

Noora unsnapped her bra and slipped it off. She studied herself in the mirror. "Oh my. I couldn't wear this, it's too ..."

"It's too dark in here," Zaffeera cut in. "They have a three-way mirror right outside."

"Are you crazy? I wouldn't dare. There are people out there."

"Don't worry. I'll stand right in front of you."

"Oh no, I couldn't ... I just couldn't ..."

"No one will see you. I promise."

Beneath bright lights, Noora gaped at her reflection in the floor-to-ceiling mirrors. Her figure was quite visible through the sheer silk. Zaffeera stepped aside, hoping to give Moustafa, and everyone else, a clear view.

"Goodness! I can't believe you got me out here," she giggled, embarrassed. "Don't you think it's way too risqué?"

"Not for a honeymoon. You look absolutely ravishing," Zaffeera said. If Moustafa was doing his job, he should have had an eyeful, she thought, as Noora rushed back to the dressing room.

Moustafa stood behind a rack of dresses, perspiration pouring down his back. *Sharmouta!* Because of that evil whore, he was painfully aroused. His little camera nearly slipped out of his sweaty hands. He fumbled with the gadget, trying to steady his trembling hands while snapping more photos. She had just paraded herself in that sinful excuse for a garment. Under lights, security cameras, and mirrors, no less!

She was unworthy of the Fendil name, and she was a curse on her family. Moustafa came from a very poor family, but his father prayed five times a day and they were respectful. Their women only wore long, dark dresses of thick material with the proper headdress, and kept their eyes down, never provoking, never *arousing* a man.

So what if he was the girls' bodyguard? He was not made of stone. He had feelings. He was a man. They had made him watch that beautiful young woman, day after day, until he could not sleep at night. He had found relief—shamefully—with the earlier pictures he had taken of that Noora girl. Though his job was to watch over Mr. Fendil's daughters, he had to remain invisible and stay out of their private business. But it was no longer private. She had behaved sinfully, in public. He wasn't sure before, but now he was convinced the girl was drunk. She had to be, and he should at least report her to the sheik.

First, he needed visual proof.

He checked for TV monitors. If he were caught taking pictures, they would arrest him or maybe accuse him of being a corporate spy, photographing the store.

She was now at the register, buying that bordello-wear, and God only knew what other filth! The short girl, the shy sister, stood behind with her head down, looking ashamed—as she should be.

*****   *****   *****

By three o'clock in the afternoon, Zaffeera exited Harrods with Noora walking ahead. Zaffeera was loaded down with large shopping bags. A two-tier sightseeing bus was waiting at the curb.

"I just bought the last two tickets for Harrods' bus tour," Zaffeera said, setting down the bags. "Look at this brochure."

While Noora read the information, Zaffeera noticed people were starting to queue up to get on the bus. "Let's go, so we can get a good seat on the upper level."

"I don't know, maybe we should do it another time," Noora said, staring blankly at the brochure. "We still have to pack ..."

"It's the only time we have," Zaffeera said, leaving the brochure with her sister and carrying all the bags. "They serve hot cocoa and chocolate teacakes. Should be enough caffeine to keep us going until midnight!" she added cheerfully. But she worried that they had the rest of the afternoon to kill, and her plan wouldn't go into high gear until the evening. Everything had to be just right. It wasn't going to be easy. That much she knew.

CHAPTER 4
THE VELVET CAVE

"Oh can't you see, I have a special hot dream," the lyrics of a popular song blasted from the disco's speakers.

Noora found herself standing on a crowded dance floor, wondering how she had gotten there. Around her, couples were moving dizzily to the thunderous beat. She couldn't find Zaffeera—she was nearby a moment ago, then she was gone. Noora managed to find her way off the dance floor.

She caught a glimpse of her reflection on a floor-to-ceiling gold-specked mirror. What was she doing wearing such a short skirt and a halter top that was so tight? Her hair was teased up wildly like a lion's mane, and her eyes were heavily made up. *That can't be me.* The last thing she remembered, she and Zaffeera were in her bedroom, applying mascara in front of her dresser mirror. They were having fun, like when they were kids and played dress-up. She remembered trying on a blonde wig. The hair felt like golden strands of silk—millions of them, flowing down below her waist. The elastic headband around the wig's cap was too tight to fit over Noora's voluminous hair. Zaffeera had tried it on, but she kept sneezing, with all those loose strands flying around. She did manage to fit into it because her hair was short and fine. But the wig looked ridiculous on Zaffeera, and Noora could not stop laughing. Could she have offended her sister? No, because she remembered Zaffeera holding on to her chest and begging her to stop making her laugh so much, for she would surely pee in her pants. This made them both laugh hysterically. Later, they caught a cab and headed to a disco, where friends from college were having a costume party. As soon as they arrived, Zaffeera said, "I don't know if we are in the right place." The music was too loud and the place was mobbed. Noora looked around but didn't recognize anyone from school. Zaffeera rushed away to stand in the long bathroom line. "If I don't go ahead of these girls, I'll surely make an embarrassing puddle," Zaffeera said, laughing.

A few minutes later, a girl with long blonde hair and a miniskirt appeared and began dancing around Noora—it was creepy, like some mixed-up dream. The air was getting stuffy and heavy with cigarette smoke. "Let's see if I can get us something cold to drink. Then let's get out of here." She heard Zaffeera's voice, but she didn't see her.

Lights flashed while the music continued. *How odd,* Noora thought.

Thunderous sounds vibrated like a thousand-piece orchestra. The neon lights made her hotter. She wished she could peel off her top. Her throat was burning and she wondered when Zaffeera would be back with cold drinks.

Someone sang along to the familiar disco song. His mouth was close to her ear. Too close. "Join me… Wild and wet…" he said. She turned. A dashing young man wearing a black tuxedo and a bright white shirt offered her a sparkling cold glass. The long-stemmed crystal flute shimmered invitingly under the multi-colored lights. She took the glass and drank it down.

The glass had a bright red strawberry in it; she tilted it until her tongue grabbed the sweet, juicy berry.

A handsome, dark-haired young man, also in a tuxedo, took the empty glass from her hand.

"Michel?" Noora couldn't believe her eyes. The young man's arms gently circled her shoulders.

"Yes, darling," he whispered close to her. "We are on our honeymoon, honey …"

Noora felt dizzy and terribly confused. "We're not married, and this dress … is certainly not a wedding …"

"Why do you hurt my feelings? I love you …" he said.

Gently, he lured her to a corner of the discotheque. He eased her to a low burgundy velveteen banquette. He massaged her back first. Noora began to relax. His tender but firm touch felt awfully good to her tense muscles. He moved his hands and caressed her breasts. The first man, the one who gave her champagne with the strawberry, sat next to her and nibbled at her ear.

"No. Don't," she whispered breathlessly while the first man's gentle touch started to arouse her. But this was wrong. "Go away, you're not Michel ..."

He reached under her short skirt and tried to pull down her panties, but the elastic band was too tight. Something inside her warned, *"No!"*

"NO!" Noora repeated aloud.

"I love you, I always will ..." he whispered while gently pulling down her strapless top, revealing her bare breasts.

She did not stop him, because with that tight top off, she felt cooler and free. She moistened her dry lips.

"I'm very thirsty and I want to get out of here right now!"

"Okay, honey. I'll get you out of here." He handed her another tall, cold champagne flute, and she drank it like water.

Her lips were moist now and he kissed them, his right hand fondling a breast.

"No, please," she said, trying to push him away.

"Make you feel good, Noora my sweet..." He slid his tongue into her mouth and practically down her throat while the music boomed from loudspeakers.

*****   *****   *****

Moustafa could not believe the spectacle unfolding only a few feet from where he stood. *Allah Akbar, those breasts!* His cigar almost fell out of his parted lips.

The crowd from the dance floor moved closer to the spot where the beautiful young woman was putting on an erotic show.

With trembling hands, Moustafa reloaded his camera, cursing under his breath that he did not buy more film.

"Sharmouta!" He pushed his way violently through the crowd to get at her.

What a body. He could hardly breathe.

He put the camera securely inside the breast pocket of his suit. When he looked up, he saw Noora being escorted by her two boyfriends through the crowded dance floor. He pushed his way through dancing couples and saw Noora disappearing toward the exit.

He tried to follow, battling his way through a crowd of newcomers. Once he was finally outside, he spotted one of the tuxedo boys putting her into a cab that was waiting in the no-parking zone. Moustafa shoved the man aside and tried to grab Noora. He almost had her when the other boyfriend jumped him from behind. Moustafa struggled with him.

"Hey! What's your problem?" the tuxedo boy asked.

Moustafa spotted the taxi pulling away. Sharply with an elbow, he shoved the other bastard who had fondled Noora. He wanted to smash his face, but there was no time. He ran across the street to catch the next passing cab, and hopped in.

Zaffeera's plan had unfolded better than expected. That evening, she had worn her long blonde wig, and once again, she knew she had been totally unrecognizable. She was sure Moustafa would be too busy with Noora to bother searching for her.

Zaffeera understood the desire for sex better than anyone. Her secret thirst could never be quenched. Ever since she was fourteen years old, Zaffeera had explored her sexuality. She learned to satisfy herself with a girl not much older than she was—her personal little maid, Gamelia, who was obliged to do whatever Zaffeera wanted without question and without ever revealing their personal affair to anyone.

When Zaffeera began her school year at the London Ladies' College, she had spent the first two months on a nightly search for the right club where she could fulfill her sexual fantasies.

She had chosen the two-bedroom apartment from the list recommended by the college. Their father had reluctantly approved, after much thought and the consideration that the flat was within walking distance of Kensington Palace, the London home of royalty.

Zaffeera had chosen the back bedroom at the end of the hall, with a fire escape—the perfect means to leave and return unseen.

Soon after the sisters moved in to the flat, the seemingly shy girl, dressed in black, silently climbed out of her room nearly every night. She left by the alley, where Moustafa—in his flat across the street—could not see her. Like a shadow, she wound through shortcuts, between Underground stations. In a public bathroom stall, she would put on a long blonde wig and wrap it tightly in a black scarf. At the entrance to the nightclub, she removed her scarf, and plain Zaffeera was immediately transformed into a blonde bombshell in four-inch stilettos.

The sleazier the nightclub, the better. There, she indulged in erotic pleasures. So loud was the music, no one heard lovers moan and cry out in climax. Zaffeera loved to watch them. X-rated videos seemed like family entertainment in comparison to what she saw live. If they spotted her as a voyeuse, they would invite her to join. But she looked for a special type of partner. Zaffeera's conquests kissed her long and hard. She was an experienced kisser, and knew how to make her lover-for-the-moment beg for more. Zaffeera did not wear panties, which gave her that extra charge, teasing herself as that burning part of her waited for someone's tongue to satisfy her. It didn't matter to her whether the lover was male or female, although at times she preferred girls.

"Harder!" was the only word Zaffeera ever said.

If the moment's lover was a guy, there was never penetration. Zaffeera was in total control of her priceless treasure, reserved for marriage—reserved for Michel. She never took chances. Every sense sounded out, like an alarm, if any male dared to go too far. After she climaxed, returning to a composed calm and gazing intently into space, Zaffeera would slowly smooth out her clothes and hair, stroking her long blonde wig repeatedly.

She returned to her flat at different times every night, always making sure the light was out in Moustafa's flat across the street.

If Zaffeera returned by midnight, tired but still too wound up to sleep, she lounged nude under her covers, which gave her that extra tease. She thought of Michel and masturbated to a gentle climax. Sometimes she felt relaxed enough to fall into a blissful sleep. Other times, she read murder mysteries until three in the morning, or finished her boring homework.

By 6:00 AM, when it was still dark, Zaffeera's alarm clock would sound. She bounced out of bed and immediately changed her Egyptian cotton sheets into a freshly laundered set and stuffed the ones she had used the night before into a special laundry bag—which she took that day to the cleaners. Resuming her regular morning routine, she made her bed, tucking the laundered sheets tightly around the mattress, and smoothed out her fluffy silk down comforter. She replaced her two huge shams that she kept every evening on a nearby chair, then aligned her six lavender-filled, heart-shaped throw pillows in an exact order, always the same way, one overlapping the other. She made it a rule to be organized at all times, alert, prepared, ahead of the game—whatever game she played.

But the most important rule was that she was to never be disturbed at night in her room. Zaffeera told Noora that if she were awakened by a knock on her door, she would be very startled and could never go back to sleep. She knew her sister would respect that request, because by ten o'clock in the evening, especially during the week, Noora went to bed. Luckily, Noora needed eight hours of undisturbed sleep in order to function, especially the next day, during the demanding school hours.

On her way home from the Velvet Cave, Zaffeera dumped her platform shoes, one at a time, in different trashcans, and replaced them with black Mary-Jane slippers. In the darkness of a deserted street, she removed her wig and hesitated. She really didn't want to discard it. It fit perfectly. Made of the finest human hair, it had cost her a fortune. But what if she was in an accident or someone rummaged through her bedroom and found it? *What if her father saw it?* There could be no trace or evidence, in case Noora remembered seeing Zaffeera in that wig. She tossed it in a dumpster down an alleyway, reminding herself that this part of her mission should be over. *It'd better be*, she thought, hiding in a dark corner to catch her breath. She turned the shiny red satin coat inside out. It was now a simple black coat. She unfurled the waistband of her miniskirt, letting the material down until it reached her ankles. She fluffed up her hair and covered it with the black, floppy beret she had hidden in her coat pocket. She removed her disposable, extra-light-blue contact lenses and extracted her black-rimmed glasses from her bag.

Hurrying through the streets, Zaffeera was back at her flat in record time. Only this time, she did not have to hike up the fire escape, very carefully and silently, fearing that someone might see her. She hoped she would never have to do that again.

She climbed the five flights of stairs, two at a time. The lift was much too slow. Once she locked herself in her flat, she leaned heavily against the door to catch her breath.

She checked her watch and calculated she was six minutes late, according to her timetable. The phone from the hallway rang, jarring every nerve in her body. After the third ring, and after a deep breath to regain her composure, she lifted the receiver.

"*Salaam,*" one of the maids said all the way from Al-Balladi.

"Good evening," Zaffeera said in a serene voice. "It is good to hear from you, and how are you doing this fine evening?" she asked in Arabic.

"Thank you, Miss Zaffeera, all doing well, *hamdallah*. We regret for being a little late calling. I am connecting you to your mother now," the maid yelled into the phone in Arabic, obviously not wanting to waste time on a long-distance line.

"Zaffeera, dear. Poor little Shamsah ..."

"What's wrong?"

"*Ya haraam*... She caught the chicken pox." Yasmina Fendil spoke to her daughter in Arabic. "I thought you and Noora should know ... It is better she has it now than when she is older."

"I'm so sorry. But do tell her I have a nice surprise for her."

"You are always so thoughtful, Zaffeera. We are giving her a bath with calamine lotion. We are trying to keep Kettayef away. He did not have the chicken pox, you know. Maybe he should have it too. But one sick child at a time is all we can handle ... aagh, how I miss your grandmother. She would have taken charge. She would have cured my little Shamsah in no time ..." She continued to ramble on, while Zaffeera rolled her eyes, waiting for an opportunity to get to the crucial matter.

"By the way," Zaffeera was finally able to interrupt, "they called this morning to confirm about the limo ..."

"Good. Do you know when you'll arrive?"

"They're picking us up at ten in the morning."

"Ten? But your father always arranges for you to travel earlier so you can arrive before sunset ..."

"Yes, but this time, I am glad they're coming a little later, Mother, because Noora ... well, Noora, I'll have to wake her up. And help her pack."

"Why?"

"Well, because, she is not ... home yet."

"*Allah! Fen okhtek?*"

"Well, mmm ..." She waited a moment, careful to deliver the next momentous line with seeming reluctance. Then, like a shot from a cannon, she said: "I don't know where my sister is; she went out."

There was silence at the other end. Zaffeera checked her watch again. According to her careful calculations, she still had a little time before the doorbell rang.

"What did you say? She went out?" her mother asked.

"Yes. She ... Noora went out for the evening."

"What do you mean, out for the evening? Where did she go?"

"I'm not quite sure. She went to a party with some friends ..."

"But it's too late there for a girl to be out!"

"Yes, but I'm sure she'll come home ..." She pursed her lips tightly. It was best not to say too much. She waited for tension to mount. She could hear her little sister whining in the background.

"Zaffeera, wait a minute, please."

The receiver clanked noisily on her eardrum, piercing her sensitive nerves like an alarm. Endless minutes later, her mother returned to the phone. "I have to go. Shamsah needs me. She is itching all over. It's even inside her ears now. *Zaffeera, ya habibti,*" her mother begged. "Please! If Noora does not return within the hour, you must call me!"

"Yes, I will. But please don't worry. I won't disturb you ... I am sure Noora will be home soon," Zaffeera said rapidly. "I love you, *ya ummy.*" She hung up.

A half hour later, Zaffeera was pacing nervously. She thought her heart would drum right out of her chest. The doorbell should have rung by now. What was taking them so long? With the drugs Noora had in her system, it should have been easy to seduce her, and it shouldn't have taken so long. Zaffeera didn't pay for those male prostitutes to enjoy themselves! Bastards.

Their instructions could not have been simpler: Put Noora in the taxicab that would be waiting outside the club. The driver was to drop her off in front of the apartment building and ring the doorbell. They all came from a reputable professional "escort" agency that supposedly offered the ultimate in privacy, at a high price. Cash in advance. She had saved her money.

At any rate, there would be photos—Moustafa had snapped pictures like some disgusting paparazzo. He could have been a little more discreet. But never mind about that, as long as there was proof enough to convince her parents that Noora was no angel.

What could possibly be keeping them? What if Moustafa decided to intervene, got in a fight with the love boys, or called the police?

Zaffeera planned to run down the stairs wearing her peignoir and house slippers. These guys weren't supposed to rough Noora up in any way, and the cab driver was part of her plan.

She almost forgot to change. She ran to her bedroom and grabbed her peignoir from the hook behind the bathroom door. She quickly rolled up a few pink sponge rollers in her hair. She put her glasses back on, but changed her mind and put them in her pocket. If Moustafa was to see her downstairs at the door, picking up her drunken sister, it had to be clear that Zaffeera had just gotten out of bed.

Zaffeera was rolling up the last sponge roller when the doorbell rang, piercing her nerves. The bell rang a second time, longer, more persistent. She began to panic. Where did she put her keys? Finally she found them, right where she had left them, on the hallway console. *Stop worrying,* she told herself, locking the front door.

Finally downstairs, she pulled open the main entrance door just as the taxi drove off, leaving Noora stumbling around like a drunken bimbo, balancing on one high-heeled shoe. Zaffeera glanced up while supposedly trying to help her sister inside. As far as she could see, the street was deserted.

Where the hell was Moustafa? Why was he not there to take more pictures?

"What happened to you, Noora?" Zaffeera purred, stalling for time.

Noora gazed at Zaffeera lovingly, then belched out a copious amount of vomit all over her sister's peignoir. Zaffeera shrieked, forcing herself to control the urge to slap the bitch's face, but the neighbors might have been watching from behind curtains. And still no sign of that *homar?* She heard a car drive up. Tires screeched to a halt around the corner. She prayed it was Moustafa's cab. It had to be. She held her sister up, at the same time trying to pick up Noora's shoe, which had fallen to the ground and down a couple of steps. It was full of vomit. She lifted it anyway, nearly retching. With her adrenaline pumping, Zaffeera lifted the dead weight of her sister's body without much trouble, though she couldn't help gagging from the stench.

She heard Moustafa running up the street. She also heard the click of his camera. *Only one picture?* She lingered a bit longer, displaying the difficult time she had. She put Noora down for a moment. Then, holding her by the waist, pretending to struggle, Zaffeera slowly pulled her sister inside. She would have preferred to remain out there a little longer, for Moustafa's sake, but she was satisfied that he had seen enough. As far as she was concerned, his job was done.

*****   *****   *****

Moustafa's job had just begun. By five o'clock in the morning, he had returned from the all-night photo lab. The enlarged prints of Noora at the Velvet Cave were strewn over his bedcovers. He had less than five hours before the Fendil limousine would come to take the girls to the airport. He was scheduled to leave later on a commercial flight that would arrive at Al-Balladi in the middle of the night—a bad time to disturb the sheik. But this was an urgent case. He should bring the originals personally, and as soon as possible. He picked up the phone. He had a difficult time tearing his attention from the provocative photographs, but he had to focus on punching in the right numbers to the main office. Surely they would have to put him through directly to the honorable Sheik Abdullah Kharoub.

CHAPTER 5
THE HOMECOMING

The flight from London's Heathrow to Cairo was turbulent. Zaffeera fell asleep minutes after takeoff and did not stir from the soft, kid-leather reclining chair. Noora had spent the last half hour of the flight vomiting in the lavatory. She did not understand why she felt so sick. Bumpy flights never bothered her before.

When they landed in Cairo, the Fendil private jet was delayed at the airport due to a *khamseen,* a sandstorm in the direction they were to take.

While the pilot waited for clearance, Zaffeera finished a lavish lunch of roasted lamb and soft-cooked vegetables on a bed of couscous that the hostess had ordered in advance and prepared for the girls.

Noora, who usually loved Egyptian cuisine, could not stand the smell of food, and the air in the jet was getting stuffy. She made another trip to the bathroom. When she returned, Zaffeera was savoring a small piece of honey-drenched baklava.

"I don't understand why I feel so ... squeamish," Noora said.

"Squeamish?"

"I've been throwing up. Sorry, I shouldn't talk like that while you're eating," Noora said.

"What's wrong?"

"I feel like I caught something. Are *you* feeling okay?" Noora asked in Arabic.

"Yes. I should think you'd be feeling good about going home," Zaffeera replied in English, licking the sweet honey from her manicured fingers.

"Yes, of course I'm very happy about that, but ... what happened last night? You disappeared all of a sudden."

"I disappeared?" Zaffeera asked, her eyes wide with surprise. "You're the one who disappeared. I searched all over for you, all over that noisy place."

"Remind me what happened exactly."

"You don't remember?"

Noora had to stop and think. *Oh my God, was that what alcohol did to people's brain? Made them temporarily lose their memory? Especially if one never had a drink before. God, forgive me ...*

"I had to run to the bathroom," Zaffeera explained.

"Yes, I remember that."

"It was mobbed with all these weird-looking girls, but I had to go, and when I ran back out to find you, you were gone," Zaffeera said. "I was sick with worry."

"You were?"

"Of course I was."

"I'm sorry. I know I was thirsty and I thought you went to get us something to drink from the bar. But after that, you went to the bathroom?" Noora asked, confused.

"Yes, didn't I just say that?"

"Please, Zee, just remind me again."

"Before waiting to get drinks, I went to the bathroom. As I said before. Then I went to get us a lemonade, but the line was too long at the bar, and when I came back to find you, you were gone. What happened? Don't you remember?" Zaffeera asked, pushing her tray aside.

"No ... I ... I think I was foolish enough to accept someone's drink."

"Then what happened to you?"

"I drank something that had a strawberry in it. I remember the strawberry."

"You remember the strawberry, but you don't remember the rest?"

"I'm not sure. I think it was champagne that I drank, because it was in one of those champagne glasses."

"You mean ... like a flute?"

"Yes. I'm afraid it was champagne that I drank. I think they offered me another one ... But that wouldn't make me ... What *did* happen?"

"You're asking *me?* You left me. When I finally found you, I called a cab."

"Wait. Let's backtrack a bit."

"Backtrack? Noora, forget about it. It's in the past. We're going home."

"Okay, but wait. Just a moment. Just tell me … Where was I when you found me?"

"What do you mean? You were … sitting in a booth near the dance floor. You said you were hot, and that you wanted a breath of fresh air. I wanted to get out of there, but you wanted to stay."

"I did not. I wanted to go to that other place—the restaurant where the girls from school were meeting to celebrate … you know, by the carousel. We were there once before. Before the winter break. I can never remember the name of that restaurant. A little college hangout. We told the cab driver … Wait a minute. I remember now. The driver said he knew where it was, and you said something about a cave, and we wound up somewhere else."

Zaffeera looked deep into her sister's eyes. "What cave, Noora?"

"I don't know," Noora said. She shouldn't be blaming Zaffeera when she herself was the one at fault. "When we arrived at that place, somebody offered me a drink. I was so thirsty. I think I drank two of them. And …" Noora sighed and let herself fall onto the seat next to Zaffeera.

"Maybe you drank alcohol," Zaffeera said. "Made you sick. Okay. You should've waited for me. It's over now. Forget it."

"Zaffeera, something went wrong. I feel terrible."

"Relax. I'll give you some Tums. You like Tums. You'll feel better soon."

"I feel terrible because I drank *alcohol*. How could I have done such a stupid thing? Oh my God!"

"Shh," Zaffeera said, leaning closer to her sister. "The flight attendant doesn't need to hear us."

"Sorry," Noora whispered. "I thought it was water." She breathed a deep, guilty sigh. "No wonder I feel so sick."

"If you keep talking about it, you'll make yourself sicker. Forget it, Noora. Let's never talk about it anymore. It's our secret," Zaffeera whispered. "Maybe they'll let you deplane and get some fresh air. I'll go with you, if you like. I'll ask the pilot." Zaffeera unbuckled her seat belt.

"Zaffeera ... thanks."

"Of course."

Moments later, Zaffeera returned from the cockpit.

"The pilots said we can't deplane at this time because of some political commotion on the outskirts of Cairo."

"What happened?"

"Nothing to worry about, they assured me." Zaffeera sat down and buckled herself in. "They're just taking extra precautions. But good news, they said the *khamseen* is blowing in another direction. We should leave in a half hour or so. Don't worry anymore, Noora. Soon we'll be home."

Noora tried to relax on a reclining seat in the rear of the plane—close to the lavatory. Wearily, she gazed out through the porthole. A thick, golden haze veiled the city. She watched as the sun sank lazily behind a horizon of old buildings and minarets. She had visited Cairo on many occasions, but she never spent enough time to appreciate the city.

Before moving to the rented flat she occupied with Zaffeera, Noora had lived with a stern older couple. They had originally attended the LLC when it first opened and were now both part-time math teachers. Nageeb used to rescue Noora every Friday night and take her to dine in Middle Eastern restaurants, with the valid excuse that they both missed their mother's cooking.

It just wasn't the same with Zaffeera, though she liked having her sister with her—and she was pleased that their father had given them the trust and liberty to live in their own flat without a chaperone. But Zaffeera was always so prim and proper, so mature and organized. Noora sometimes thought her sister took life too seriously, especially when it came to her schoolwork.

Noora remembered how sad she had been when Nageeb announced that their father wanted him to take his residency in Cairo. She had missed him during the eight long months without him in London. She couldn't wait to see him, and he most likely had many new *noktas* to tell her. Those clever and funny Arabic jokes always made her laugh out loud. And he would probably know the right medicine to give her for her weak stomach.

The family's white stretch limousine was parked in its usual spot when the private jet landed at the Al-Balladi airstrip.

The sisters stepped out onto the portable stairway. Noora looked around for Abdo but he was not there. She had looked forward to his warm welcome. He always ran up the jet's steel steps, practically trampling all over his floor-length traditional white garb, and after bone-jarring hugs, he would carry their luggage to the car.

This time, there was a straight-faced chauffeur.

"We should have dressed up," Noora remarked. She wore form-fitting designer jeans and a snug T-shirt with the Hard Rock Café logo.

Behind her tinted, gold-framed Christian Dior prescription lenses, Zaffeera studied the new situation. The driver was dressed in a dark gray business suit and stood in front of the limousine. Her gaze fastened on the man's crimson necktie with a golden emblem in the middle. She recognized the insignia: "MOFHAJ." Her heart began to race. Quickly, she reached in her Louis Vuitton travel bag and extracted a large black silk scarf. She was glad she had had the good sense to change into a long skirt and black long-sleeved blouse just prior to landing. She draped her scarf around her head and covered her mouth. She cast her eyes downward and walked to the limo.

Noora filled her lungs with the familiar warm air. She felt instantly revived, and tossed her long brown hair, letting its waves dance around her shoulders, as she breezed her way to the car.

The chauffeur grudgingly held the door open for Noora. When she climbed in, he slammed it so hard, he barely missed hitting her from behind.

She was shocked by his disrespectful behavior.

One of the airport assistants handed the chauffeur the girls' luggage, and he carelessly dumped the pieces in the trunk.

As soon as he sat behind the wheel, he closed the glass partition and switched on the ignition. Noora thought the new chauffeur had the personality of a camel. He did not even say *welcome*, did not speak to them at all. Actually, he did remind her of a camel, because a few times, he grunted loudly as if he had something stuck in his throat. *As long as he didn't spit*, she thought, opening the small refrigerator; to her surprise, it was empty. That driver did not think to put spring water in the limousine. Not even a soda? Abdo always made sure the limousine's little built-in fridge was stacked with bottled water and soft drinks.

She was feeling sick again. Perhaps she should have some ginger ale. If she told the chauffeur she had been dreadfully ill on the plane ride since they left London, and that she was about to throw up all over the limo, perhaps he would speed up a bit.

She leaned over and tapped on the glass. *"Min fadlak?"* she asked respectfully in Arabic to get his attention.

The man gave no reply.

She turned to Zaffeera who was curled up against the door, her shawl wrapped tightly around her head and mouth. She had fallen asleep. She seemed unusually exhausted and preoccupied about something. Perhaps she didn't do well on her exams. Zaffeera was a very bright student, and if she ever did have any difficulty with her studies, she never complained. She would never burden anyone with her problems, Noora thought. That's how Zaffeera was.

Beneath a moonless sky, the Fendil limousine slowly made its way through the gleaming white iron gates. The royal palms lining the wide circular driveway did not stir in the faint night breeze. The exterior lighting barely illuminated the steps that led to the large Tiffany front doors. Noora hopped out of the car while the chauffeur put the luggage next to the doors. Zaffeera stumbled out of the limousine groggily and covered her head and mouth with her veil as she climbed the front steps.

The chauffeur returned behind the wheel and quietly rolled the car out of the driveway. Noora turned and watched the limousine as it drove out toward the service entrance behind the house, where their father had his sixteen-car garage.

Inside their parents' home, Noora felt strangely uncomfortable. "Where is everybody?" she asked, shivering with the chill of the air conditioning.

"Asleep, I'm sure. It's very late," Zaffeera whispered.

"Mother must be exhausted."

"Yes, she would be. She's been up for several nights, taking care of Shamsah."

"Poor Shamsah," Noora said quietly. "I feel so guilty. I didn't even call her when we were in London."

"I know. I did."

"I hope she is better."

"Me too. Let's not disturb anyone."

"Right. We'll see them in the morning. Aren't you going to your room?" Noora whispered.

"I need some chamomile tea."

"I need some water. I'll just get it in my room." Noora waved a weary hand, slung her backpack over her shoulder, and entered another corridor. *At last we're home!*

As Noora headed to her room at the end of another long hallway, a shadow passed.

"Hello?" Noora called, trying to keep her voice low. No one answered. "Hello, hello?" she said a slight tone louder.

It was perhaps a new maid working the late shift and too shy to respond, Noora thought, *or probably Gamelia, Zaffeera's little maid, who was always painfully timid.*

Yes, it was very late—but something didn't feel right, Noora thought, wishing they could have arrived earlier to enjoy their usual warm welcome. Finally in her wonderful bedroom, Noora turned on all the lights and locked her door.

She dove into her sumptuous bed amid mounds of fluffed-up pillows. "Ah, so good to be home, my own room. I missed you so much," she said, looking up at the pale pink chiffon and lace that draped around her four-poster bed. She found a crystal carafe filled with water on her nightstand. The ice had melted long before, dampening the embroidered linen napkin under the carafe. The maids must have prepared everything hours ago, knowing she would need water for the night. *How nice to be pampered again,* she thought, gulping down more than half the carafe. She dropped her sneakers on the floor. With her toes, she peeled off each sock. She sank her head into one of the billowy pillow shams and luxuriated beneath the cool down comforter. Sliding a cheek against the silk pillowcase, she fantasized about Michel kissing her. She felt blessed. Blessed to be home and blessed for the chance to live in such luxury, which she especially appreciated after the gloomy apartment in London. Above all, she felt especially blessed because soon she would be married, and she would never have to sleep alone; and with that, she fell into a blissful sleep.

Bright sunlight flooded the bedroom through the sheer drapes, waking Noora. Moaning with delight, she relished the thought that she was not dreaming. She was indeed home. But the seams of her tight jeans were cutting painfully at her skin. She had fallen asleep before she could undress. And her body ached all over. *God, I hope I'm not catching some kind of a flu,* she prayed, stumbling stiffly out of bed. To her surprise, she found her luggage inside her room, near her closed door. She thought she had locked it the night before.

Under massaging shower sprays that came from all directions inside the wide pink tub of her marble bathroom, Noora's aching muscles began to relax.

Wearing her soft, thick peignoir, she pushed into her cushiony slippers and padded across her shaggy lamb's-wool rug. She dropped her luggage on top of her bed and began to unpack. She lifted some kind of sheer undergarment and examined it with surprise. *Where did that come from?* She checked the luggage tag to make sure it was hers. Indeed it was, but she certainly didn't remember owning such a sexy-looking négligée.

A loud pounding on her door startled her.

"Who is it?"

"Your father needs to see you in the living room," came a harsh female voice from the opposite side of her bedroom door.

Noora did not recognize the woman. It must have been a new housekeeper. But the new ones usually used more discretion. Maybe they tried to get her attention when she was in the shower for almost an hour, Noora thought, dropping the négligée in her open luggage. She tightened the belt of her peignoir. Brushing wet hair strands away from her face, she ran to the door and opened it wide.

No one was there. She stepped out on the corridor and heard footsteps. "*Sabbah El Noor,* good morning!" Noora called happily. No one answered. Why didn't her father buzz her on the intercom? she wondered, closing the door behind her.

Searching through her huge walk-in closet, Noora wondered what she should wear after such a formal request. She couldn't make up her mind. She was too excited. Could it be that Michel was there waiting?

No, he was spending the spring holiday with his father in Switzerland. She had to rush and not make her father wait. Her heart tingled with excitement.

Something was definitely going on. What was the surprise? She chose a classy, round-necked black dress with a delicate silk shawl to match. Black was always fashionable, especially lately, and smart when one didn't know what, or whom, to expect.

CHAPTER 6
THE SILENT BOY

"Take off your shirt!" the elementary school nurse told Mr. Fendil's youngest son.

Not waiting for him to refuse, the nurse removed it. Kettayef had never been more embarrassed. The male nurse lowered the waistband of his pants and examined to see if there were any lesions of chicken pox that might have flared up on his stomach.

That morning, Kettayef felt ill the moment he arrived at school. He prayed that by lunchtime he would feel better, but he felt worse. His schoolmaster suspected it could be the start of chicken pox and sent him to the infirmary. The headmaster said Kettayef had a fever and could be contagious. He was just flushed from being ridiculed, standing with his bare chest where other classmates could see him. For the first time, he wished he could speak. But he said nothing; Kettayef never said anything. The nurse called his mother. One of the maids must have answered; Mrs. Fendil could not come to the phone.

"His little sister has a bad case of the chicken pox," Kettayef heard the nurse say to his headmaster. Quickly, Kettayef buttoned his shirt. He saw the two adults give each other a worried glance. "We need to send him home," the nurse said, scribbling something on a pink release form.

A heavy hand gripped Kettayef's shoulder. "I'm taking you home," a lanky young man announced with authority. He was the principal's son.

Kettayef's clothes stuck to his sweaty skin. He knew he wasn't all that sick, but he was glad to be going home.

He sat in the back seat of the school's silver Mercedes van. The mobile phone rang.

"Another one with chicken pox? This is terrible," the driver said, stopping in front of a mansion. He opened the door for the boy.

Blistering desert air engulfed Kettayef as he stepped off the van.

The driver turned to Kettayef. "I have to drive another sick kid home. Are you able to walk to your front door by yourself?" he said, enunciating each word carefully as if speaking to an imbecile. Kettayef hated it when adults did that to him. But he just nodded, showing his pink release slip.

The van drove off, creating a cloud of dust, leaving Kettayef standing alone, in front of a wrought iron gate. The golden sign on the gate read:

27 Aswan Street

Kettayef's house was at 27 Anwar Street, the next block over.

He began to walk home, telling himself he wouldn't get sick. His older brother Nageeb was home from Cairo. Nothing could please him more than seeing him. Even if Nageeb was there for only a few days, his brother was sure to spend time with him. The last thing Kettayef needed was to be sick with chicken pox.

His older sisters might have arrived in the middle of the night. He wasn't sure. His mother said they had been delayed in Cairo. The girls were surely going to bring him more T-shirts that he didn't need. At school, he was only allowed to wear a uniform, and at home, he preferred to lounge around in cotton pajamas. Why did they always bother him with T-shirts?

Someone was mowing the lawn beyond a tall filigree fence. The fragrance of fresh-cut grass reminded him of his grandmother, who often preferred to mow the lawn herself. She didn't think gardeners did a good enough job. She looked pretty funny, his little grandmother, roaring around on that big mowing machine. Kettayef always admired her strength. When he was smaller, she used to let him ride on her lap, and together, they mowed every inch of grass. He could feel her presence as never before. Like the rest of his family, he missed her terribly. But he was sure he missed her more. She never tried to make him talk. She just accepted him the way he was. If he had a fever, his grandmother would have taken care of him, giving him one of her miracle cures.

He stopped in front of his father's mansion. A navy blue car was parked on the horseshoe driveway. *Those horrible men were at Father's house again?* They were always there these days. They were supposed to be doing business with his father, but they looked suspicious in their dark gray suits. Like sharks. The man who was their leader wore the *gallabeya* and headdress. Kettayef did not like him either. They probably wanted money, and he thought they were taking advantage of his father. He loosened his shirt and blew onto his feverish chest.

Kettayef sneaked through the rear entrance and ran through the garden. He jiggled the old handle and it opened. He made his way through long corridors, and reached the huge atrium, where the Olympic-sized pool sparkled beneath a glass-domed ceiling. He knew no one swam at that hour, and he couldn't wait to remove his sweaty clothes and finally enjoy a cool swim. When he heard footsteps echoing throughout the area, he quickly hid under the diving board. A man dressed in a dark gray business suit was opening the double glass doors. He stood erect at the entrance, as if waiting for someone. Now these terrible men were invading his father's pool, too? Kettayef worried that he wouldn't be able to get out of there without being noticed.

CHAPTER 7
IN THE NAME OF HONOR

Noora rushed through the corridors. Meeting her father in the family's living room was odd, but he always surprised her with something new, something special from abroad, including boxes of chocolate.

At first, she felt a burst of excitement, but when she arrived in the grand living room, she stopped. She had almost forgotten how gaudy it was, with gold-leafed marble pillars, Louis XIV-style furniture, and high, painted ceilings. Crystal chandeliers hung heavily, illuminating an unusual scene.

Her father wore the traditional white *gallabeya,* which he usually reserved for religious occasions. He was pacing upon one of his prized antique Turkish rugs like a caged cougar. His hair was unusually unkempt.

At least five men in shark-gray suits stood behind her father. They all wore the same attire the chauffeur had worn the night before. An older, leathery-faced man in a *gallabeya* hovered in the background. The moment Farid Fendil caught sight of his daughter, his kind brown eyes flashed fiery daggers. He groaned something in *Nahaoui,* a literary Arabic the younger generation did not bother to learn.

The words were familiar to Noora, but she did not comprehend them. First they sounded like words from a prayer, and then vile insults.

He ran up to her...

"I denounce you!"

He grabbed her by the hair, forced her to her knees, and kicked her in the face. He kicked her again. Blood squirted into her eyes, and before she could bring a hand up to protect herself, he kicked her a third time. She heard a cracking sound in her head and her vision blurred.

It had to be a nightmare. She must wake up now! But the horrific experience persisted. She was suffocating.

She tried to get away from him, but he caught her and dragged her down the long corridor by her feet. She heard screams and barely recognized them as her own. Blood from her fingers streaked the marble tiles. Men in gray suits stood like steel posts. She saw the man with the mustache.

The man from London.

She reached out a hand. *Help me!* But he stood glaring at her, as her father dragged her down the pool steps and rammed her head beneath the water's surface.

The loving hands that once taught her how to swim were drowning her.

The twenty-one years of her life flashed before her. The same pool sparkled beneath the sun-drenched crystal dome. Her father's arms were piled with presents. Ten illuminated candles were ready to be blown from her huge pink birthday cake …

Her sister Zaffeera, eight years old, stood at the edge of the pool in her red bathing suit, fists on her hips. *"It's my turn to swim now, Father,"* her voice echoed from the past. *"It's my turn!"*

Please, God, keep her safe, Noora cried in her heart. For a brief moment, she could see the gold letters of her parents' initials etched in the marble, on the deep end of the pool. The undulating water turned murky with blood.

Her chest burned as her lungs filled with water. She needed to breathe, she had to breathe now! She had to beg for his mercy, for whatever the cause, she didn't know.

He pushed her down and would not let go!

If she could just reach the surface—and ask, WHY?

Too weak to struggle, Noora was pulled into a dark vortex.

Moustafa thought he deserved a medal. Was it not all thanks to him, as faithful member and employee, that the *sharmouta* was finally getting what she deserved? He stood at the edge of the deep end of the pool, guarding the area in case the whore should try to get away. Not that she ever could. It was exciting to watch her father, the honorable Mr. Farid Fendil—the one they also called Abu Nageeb Fendil—kick her and drag her down the pool. In case she did attempt to escape, he would catch her. Actually, he wished he could. He would strangle her—watch her beg for her last breath. He was the one she had belittled. He glanced across the opposite side of the pool, toward the shallow end. Four of the other men, also in dark gray suits and red ties, were watching. Like himself, they were members of the MOFHAJ, the newly formed association named after the street in a rural town outside Cairo where the sheik was born. The letters also stood for Men of Faith, Honor, and Justice in English, words Farid Fendil and the sheik strongly believed in and followed. Their committee now had more than thirty men, and Mr. Fendil proved that he was a morally ethical and religious man when he allowed the chosen ones to assist in the execution.

The one thing that bothered Moustafa, however, was that he had not yet been acknowledged—not even a word of praise by any of his peers for his deed.

Crouching under the diving board, Kettayef trembled so hard, his teeth were chattering. He prayed that the man who stood like a secret agent didn't notice him. But he had to do something to save his sister. He wanted to scream but couldn't. He held his knees tightly against his chin.

Was that really his father? Impossible. It had to be a nightmare, and soon he would wake up. But the nightmare persisted, and the boy couldn't bear it anymore.

"Enough, Father!" Kettayef said in Arabic, breaking out of his silence and articulating each word clearly.

He realized a miracle just happened. He actually spoke.

No one heard him.

"*Kefaya, Abuya!*" the boy repeated louder.

Still no one heard. *Nageeb! Do something. Why was his brother just standing there?*

Nageeb had been briefed by two or three men he had met once before, in his father's office. He didn't remember how many there were, or who they were. He had assumed they were men from his father's mosque. He was shocked when these strangers informed him that his sister, Noora, had committed an immoral crime.

"*Immoral crime?*" Nageeb asked.

"We have proof … pictures," one of them said.

The other man put a heavy hand on Nageeb's shoulder. "*Unless action is taken to resolve and erase the shame immediately, what your sister did will dishonor your family name … Will defame your father… and you, forever …*"

Their words punctured his heart like a knife.

Nageeb had worked around the clock at the hospital in Cairo so he could finally fly home and enjoy a few days off with his family. Now he felt dizzy, disoriented, and his mouth was dry. Like a sleepwalker, he'd found himself being escorted by those men from his father's office to the indoor pool, at the opposite end of the mansion.

Standing at the edge of the pool, watching helplessly while Noora struggled for her life, Nageeb's blood drained from his face.

"*Kefaya, Abuya,*" said Kettayef. Nageeb *heard* him. His little brother had never spoken before.

The pitiable plea galvanized him into action. Without removing his trousers and shirt, or even his shoes, Nageeb slipped into the pool before these men could stop him.

"Father, with all due respect, we can't kill a dead body!" Nageeb declared loudly, standing waist-deep in the pool and carefully approaching his enraged father.

His father did not stir.

"She is already dead," Nageeb said with authority. "Please allow me to confirm it."

An endless moment of stillness followed.

As if coming out of a trance, Farid Fendil at last released Noora. He rubbed his hands on his clothing beneath the surface of the water, as if he had touched sin.

Noora's limp body, wrapped in black cloth, slowly floated away toward the deep end.

"*Mayetah,*" he announced. "She is *dead.*"

Everyone heard it.

"MAYETAH," Nageeb repeated louder.

Silence reigned. Everyone waited for Mr. Fendil's next move.

"Take it away," he said. Pale and trembling with fury, he waded up toward the side of the pool. He stumbled on the shallow steps. Sheik Abdullah Kharoub offered Farid a hand, which he accepted with a grateful *"Shokran."*

Farid Fendil walked with the sheik through a long corridor that led to the men's wing. His sandals squished with every heavy step he took, and left wet imprints on the marble floors. Sweat dripped into his eyes, blurring his view, but he had a mission and continued ahead. He made his way through another maze of tall arches and white pillars.

Like a procession, five men followed Farid, the sound of their expensive Italian footwear echoing through the halls of the west wing, where no woman ventured.

Noora's father opened the tall double doors to his private office. The walls were paneled with floor-to-ceiling mahogany shelves and lined with leatherbound books written in Arabic, English, and French, which he was proud to own, but never took the time to read. A tall window opened to a huge verandah surrounded by potted palms and facing the mansion's circular driveway below.

He did not care that the prized Turkish rug he had received from a Jordanian diplomat was getting soaked.

Breathing heavily, he moved behind his huge oak-carved desk and sank into his massive high-back leather chair. He leaned over, opened a drawer, and pulled out a thick folder.

Out in the hall, Moustafa was the last man in the procession that followed Mr. Fendil to his office. He suddenly slipped on the slick wet floor and went flying, landing heavily on his behind. Quickly, Moustafa looked around, straightened himself up, and smoothed out his trousers. It would have been terribly embarrassing if any of his peers saw him. He knew they always thought of him as being clumsy and not as bright as they thought they were. Luckily, they had all gone inside Mr. Fendil's office. He rushed to join his companions and entered Mr. Fendil's office, as one of the partners was about to close the heavy mahogany double doors.

Farid Fendil selected the twenty-four-karat Dunhill from his desk and flicked it a few times, to no avail. He reached in the deep pocket of his garb and produced another solid-gold lighter. He flicked the wet lighter several times in frustration. Standing to his right, the old Sheik Abdullah Kharoub offered him his cardboard matchbook. Mr. Fendil accepted it, tore out a couple of matches, and in one stroke, a tall flame ignited while everyone watched.

Mr. Fendil set fire to some papers he pulled out of a folder. Moustafa knew they must be his daughter's documents—birth certificate, perhaps pictures he had once treasured—all proof of her existence.

Standing behind his partners, mesmerized by the flames, Moustafa watched with clenched teeth.

The sinful girl was where she deserved to be—in hell … and he was free.

CHAPTER 8
THE RESCUE

Nageeb lifted his sister's body from the pool and rushed through the women's wing, down to another corridor and through a hallway. Noora's head swayed from side to side inside the black veil, and one arm dangled limply.

Nageeb headed to the room that had once belonged to their grandmother, the beloved Sultana, who had died in her bed six months before.

Kettayef appeared behind Nageeb. With a trembling hand, he turned the knob and pushed the door open for Nageeb and their sister, while his eyes darted in all directions to make sure no one saw them.

"Lock the door!" Nageeb commanded as he laid Noora on the rug at the foot of their grandmother's four-poster bed. Despite the chill in the room, he was sweating profusely.

Kneeling beside his sister, he unwrapped the bloody black shawl from her face while his little brother stood behind him, sobbing.

"Get my medicine bag. And dry clothes. Hurry! Let no one see you."

Kettayef was already out the door.

Noora's face was unrecognizable. Her nose had been smashed. Her beautiful eyes were now swollen shut. The badly bruised lids were turning a grisly purple color.

How could he have allowed this to happen? He prayed to Allah for mercy. He held his sister's limp hand to his chest, unwilling to believe his beloved Noora was gone. He thought he felt a pulse.

Do something, a voice urged deep within his soul.

He began to perform CPR.

She did not respond. He tried again. Again and again, more aggressively, desperately trying to get her to breathe. It was hopeless. *No! She had to live.* Still she was not responding.

Kettayef returned with an armful of clothes and his brother's medicine bag. His chest heaving from running so fast, he dropped his load and locked the door.

Hopelessly but persistently, Nageeb tried to resuscitate his sister. He thought he heard his brother speak. Again.

"*Sh-shokran, ya Allah…*" the boy whispered.

Nageeb turned briefly to his little brother. "Why are you thanking God?" he asked bitterly. Faintly at first, Noora groaned, and finally coughed and vomited a large puddle of water onto the floor.

"Yes, yes, *ya Allah!* Indeed … Thank you, God. Thank you for hearing our prayers … thank you for saving our sister …" he sobbed.

Sultana's room had a private door with stairs that led down to the kitchen. The passageway had been built for her convenience, so she would not have to take the long way around the mansion. Abdo used to meet her downstairs and drive her, usually in the middle of the night, when she was needed to assist a woman during childbirth.

Nageeb had almost forgotten about the staircase. He had watched the carpenters build the addition when he was a boy.

Kettayef opened their grandmother's armoire and removed a few folded sheets. Nageeb wrapped the sheets around Noora and gestured at an ornate chair across the room. Kettayef had never before noticed the doorknob above the embroidered chair. He quickly pushed it aside and turned the knob.

"The light! Should be on the left!"

Kettayef switched it on.

Nageeb quickly carried her down the stairs. Kettayef followed, glancing around in disbelief. He had never seen this passageway before.

Nageeb rushed through the kitchen, while Kettayef switched off the light and closed the door behind him. He'd always thought this door was for one of the broom closets. Two maids with their backs to them were engaged in a lively conversation. One was washing dishes while the other was on a stool, carefully stacking china platters in a high cupboard.

Before the maids could see what was going on, Nageeb and Kettayef had run out through the kitchen service door and halfway across the large sun-drenched cobblestone courtyard.

Under the shade of the huge mango tree, not far from their father's garage, they found Abdo, who had just finished polishing Nageeb's black Mercedes. In the bright sunlight, the car sparkled like a tinted mirror.

Abdo looked up and saw Nageeb. At first glance, he smiled, but then his face fell.

"Open the trunk!" Nageeb whispered breathlessly. There was no time for explanation.

Abdo opened the back door.

"The trunk, the trunk!" Nageeb begged.

Abdo reached under the driver's seat and popped the trunk open.

Nageeb laid his sister inside. He lowered the lid but did not snap it shut. He moved close to Abdo's ear while Kettayef dumped a load of dry clothes and his brother's medicine bag on the passenger seat.

"Pray for me," Nageeb urged with a trembling voice.

Still surprised, Abdo nodded.

"Nageeb ..." Kettayef was standing behind Abdo.

Abdo turned and stared at Kettayef in disbelief.

The reality of his little brother's newfound voice finally sinking in, Nageeb grabbed Kettayef by the shoulders. "You can speak," he whispered, his voice thick with emotion.

"*S-s- ... save her ...*" the boy stuttered shakily.

"I promise," Nageeb managed to say.

With tears cascading down his cheeks, the trembling Kettayef nodded. "*Allah ma'ak ...*"

Abdo watched in a daze as Nageeb drove away from the mansion's service entrance. The trunk lid flapped, and the car disappeared in a thick cloud of dust. He turned back toward the kitchen door and noticed the maids chattering nervously. Abdo guided them back inside.

"Everything is fine," he assured them.

The maids nodded respectfully.

"What was Nageeb carrying?" one maid asked.

"I don't know. Was he carrying something?" Abdo asked.

"He came through so quickly," another maid replied.

"Nageeb is a doctor now," Abdo said sternly. "He will have emergencies to run to ... It is not our place to question. You understand, of course, right?" he said to all the maids.

"*Tab'aan,*" they all agreed and nodded respectfully.

On the opposite end of the mansion, one by one, the Men of Faith and Justice were kissing Mr. Fendil's hand.

Farid invited the sheik to remain in his office while the other five men were told to dispose of the body, clean the mess—erase all evidence.

They knew everything that was going on in the Fendil household—at least they assumed they did. They knew that Mr. Fendil's wife, Yasmina, was busy taking care of their youngest daughter, who had a severe case of the chicken pox. They knew the boy was in a special school—an educational institution for children with some kind of disability.

The other daughter, Zaffeera, was with her mother, tending to the youngest child. Zaffeera's behavior was reported as respectful, and she was seen always with her head covered and her eyes kept low. She was the exact opposite of her shameful sister. They had all seen the photos of Zaffeera in London, her face contorted with embarrassment, the night she tried to get her drunken sister inside their apartment building.

When Farid Fendil retired to his private suite to change into dry clothes, the MOFHAJ men assumed his son, Nageeb-the-doctor, did the same.

Sheik Abdullah Kharoub went out to the royal blue Lincoln Town Car that waited by the entrance of the Fendil mansion.

The chauffeur and a stocky woman named Magda were stationed at the front door. She wore a dark brown suit with a long, straight skirt that reached the floor, and masculine brown leather shoes. Her short-cropped hair was covered by a scarf. Formerly a nurse and a prison guard, she was the only female associated with the MOFHAJ group.

Sheik Abdullah Kharoub nodded to his two protégés as he walked out into the bright sunlight.

Someone handed him his sunglasses while the chauffeur hurried to the MOFHAJ car and drove it right to the front steps. He then hurriedly opened the back door for the sheik. Magda stood behind the chauffeur, respectfully asking him to wait for the others, who were bringing the body.

On the opposite side of the house, Kettayef flew up the private stairway, as Abdo followed. Bath towels were neatly folded in a linen closet in their late grandmother's bathroom. Kettayef tossed a few towels to Abdo. Quickly, they wiped away the bloody smears and puddles along the pathway of Nageeb's escape, through the corridors where adult men usually never ventured. Kettayef closed the sliding door, which led to the entrance of the women's wing. That door was normally left open. When it was closed, it became part of the wall. It was not a secret door, only an architectural afterthought, to give the women privacy.

Kettayef and Abdo finished cleaning the floors as footsteps were heard rapidly approaching from another corridor. The moment Kettayef closed the private women's sliding door, the MOFHAJ members arrived at the indoor pool. Fearing the men may have seen him, the boy ran back up the stairs to his grandmother's room with Abdo behind him, and they locked the door.

Fiddling with his cellular phone, Moustafa stopped a few feet from the pool. His phone seemed to be out of power.

"Give me your battery!" he demanded of one of his partners, without looking up. He frowned as a thought crossed his mind. "Did you bring the bag?" He was handed a new battery. He had a difficult time fitting the charged battery into his cell phone. He looked up at his partner. "How do you think you can take out a dead body without the proper body bag?!"

The other two men looked at each other blankly.

"We need towels!" Moustafa huffed. "Do I have to be the only one who has to think of everything?!" He punched buttons on his cell phone and pressed the receiver against his ear. "Magda!" he said with authority. "Get the body bag from your trunk. Bring towels. And find me bed sheets. I'm sending someone over to you right now." It felt good to give orders.

As one of the men rushed out, Moustafa and his other partner approached the pool, where they were astonished to find no trace of Noora's body.

***** ***** *****

Nageeb took every shortcut he knew through the old section of Al-Balladi. He stopped at a deserted, narrow alleyway, where dilapidated structures awaited bulldozing to make way for new construction. He knew that area well. His father had bought this four-acre lot, where Bedouins had brought camels to sell since ancient times. A gust of dusty wind whistled through the narrow passageway, as if spirits were chanting eerily. Nageeb hopped out of the driver's seat and raised the trunk lid, then lifted his sister in his arms. The white sheets that were wrapped around her were splotched with blood. He placed her across the back seat of the car and checked her pulse, blood pressure, and pupils again. All were as good as could be expected—except one pupil was dilated. He carefully palpated her face, mouth, head, and neck. Nothing except her nose was broken, and one tooth was chipped. But her mouth, face, and head were cut, swollen, and seriously bruised. He cleaned her wounds and rolled a towel to form a pillow under her head.

He quickly changed into the dry clothes Kettayef had left in the front seat. Nageeb was amazed at his little mute brother, who had acted with such calm intelligence at this terrible time of crisis. Thanks to Kettayef, he would be able to pass through town, and if anyone saw him, since he was well known in their town, there would be nothing unusual or suspicious about his appearance. He realized he was still in his wet loafers and socks. From the glove compartment, he retrieved the kid-leather driving shoes Abdo had once given him. Nageeb never thought he would need such decadent luxury. He was thankful now, but as he drove, he wondered where he should go. Where would there be a place to hide and take care of his sister? A hospital was out of the question.

The cellular phone in his Mercedes chirped, jarring every nerve cell in Nageeb's body. He hesitated. But he had to answer it. He prayed it would be Abdo.

"Allo?" he asked, sweating heavily.

"Nageeb?" His father's voice came sharply through the static.

Nageeb's blood drained to his toes.

"Where are you going? Where is the body?" his father demanded.

The body?! She's your daughter! "I am taking it to the desert where we buried Grandmother," he said, keeping his voice as steady as he could.

"Whaaat?!" his father's voice bellowed through the receiver. "Not there! It is a holy site. Listen, my son! You ... you must return. Immediately."

"Yes, Father." *Like hell I will!*

Noora began to moan in the back seat.

Nageeb was about to enter into the downtown traffic. The business section of town consisted of just two blocks of immense limestone and marble buildings. Sounds of motorcars and motorcycles helped muffle Noora's moans.

"I ask you please, Father, this is a family matter that needs to be addressed by the men of our family, in all due respect," Nageeb said, speaking a language his father would hopefully understand.

There was a long silence at the other end of the line. Finally, Farid Fendil said, "Yes. It is a family matter."

Nageeb sighed. He heard his father muffle the phone.

Nageeb assumed that at the other end of the line, his father was being interrupted by the sheik, that self-proclaimed leader of the fundamentalist group.

"Since you are already on the highway," his father said after an endless silence, "go to the airport. We want you to ..." he paused. He was breathing harder into the receiver.

Nageeb could tell he was puffing on his pipe, probably trying to figure something out.

"Who's in the car with you?"

"I beg your pardon, *Abuya?*" Nageeb asked. He made a sharp turn and entered an alleyway to avoid the traffic jam on the main boulevard. In the one-lane alley, he found himself stuck behind a shiny Jaguar that had stopped for a flock of goats. The flock was led by an ancient-looking shepherd in a ragged gray garb, and he was obviously in no hurry.

"Nageeb! Answer me!"

"Pardon me, Father, what did you say?" Nageeb asked, searching for some valid excuse. He pressed all the buttons, rolling down all windows, hoping the outside noise would muffle Noora's moans.

"Who's in the car with you?"

"Goats! I mean, out there. Ahead of the traffic." He turned on the radio. "Yes. That's right. There's ... up ahead, a flock of goats!"

"What street are you on?"

"I took shortcuts to avoid the traffic and here I am. I was just heading out of the city. And now I'm stuck behind a bunch of goats."

The shepherd up ahead had difficulty controlling his bleating, frightened goats, while the metallic green Jag in front of Nageeb's car began honking impatiently.

Nageeb tucked the receiver between his ear and shoulder to free his hands so he could grab his medicine bag.

"*Ibni*. Answer me, son. Where are you exactly?" his father demanded.

"Well, let me see exactly ..." Nageeb stalled while Noora moaned louder. He jabbed a syringe into the rubber seal of a small glass vial. "I ... I am, ah, just outside of the boulevard."

"Which boulevard?!" Farid Fendil sounded impatient.

"El-Khartoum, Father," Nageeb lied.

"You're already that far?"

"Yes, that's right."

"What are goats doing in the middle of El-Khartoum Boulevard at this hour?"

"Not in the middle, Father ... just beyond, outside of ..."

"Hold ... hold the line." Farid Fendil muffled the phone again. Apparently, he was interrupted once more. After a moment, he returned to the phone: "All right. Go straight to the airport. By the time you arrive, a helicopter will be waiting for you. He'll take the load, and you will be flown to Aqaba."

"The goats are going crazy, Father. I can barely hear you. Let me get out of this traffic jam and I'll call you in just a few minutes."

"*Ya ibn*," he said, sounding more eager. "I'm calling you from my private line. So listen."

"Yes, Father."

"Someone will be waiting for you. You will be flown to Aqaba," he repeated. "Is that understood?"

"Yes, Father." Nageeb replied, understanding absolutely nothing.

The goats finally trotted out of the way, and the Jaguar zoomed off, coating Nageeb's windshield with a layer of yellow dust.

"I am on my way," he said, feeling like a robot responding to an incomprehensible command.

"When you get to Aqaba, you will see a black limousine. A man whose name is..." Farid muffled the phone then spoke again. "His name is Youssef ... YOUSSEF, the chauffeur in that limousine will be there, waiting for you. When you arrive, they will take it from you."

It?! His sister was now an *IT?* He cleared his throat and somehow kept his composure. "What do they plan to *do with it?*"

"They'll know," Farid Fendil answered sternly.

Nageeb had never trembled as he now did.

"Ma'a'l salaam," he heard his father say before he finally hung up.

God had better be with me! If there is a God! Nageeb saw the last goat, zigzagging, searching for the rest of his flock. Suddenly, he felt like the animal—lost and confused.

He drove toward the airport on the newly paved road that stretched for ninety miles along desert land. He remembered an incident that had occurred two years before. A young Jordanian woman right in Al-Balladi had been accused by someone—a family member or neighbor, he wasn't sure. He had known the family briefly. The young woman, they said, had had a relationship with a man while she was engaged to another. Nageeb's grandmother had protested vehemently to save the girl. He knew his father had strongly opposed the practice of "honor killing." After hearing of the accusation, he said he had tried to talk to the family, but they assured him the matter was already resolved. He seemed genuinely upset when they heard that the girl had been executed, by her own brother—supposedly to erase the shame—and Nageeb remembered that his grandmother had been devastated by the terrible news. His father had said he could not control who moved into Al-Balladi. What bothered Nageeb most was that the majority of the families were wealthy and educated, yet it appeared—especially lately—that some had returned to practicing ancient ways. Nageeb had read in a local newspaper that in fact, the law of Jordan had no punishment for honor killings except two months' probation. The man who executed his own sister had been interviewed on television, and had expressed no regret, and even believed what he did was a rightful deed!

I'm not that type of brother, he thought bitterly. He never would have believed this could ever happen to his own family!

He pulled to the shoulder of the road, praying no one he knew would pass by. Most of all, he hoped no one would stop to see if he had car trouble. Locking the door, he climbed into the back seat, injected Noora with a sedative, cleaned her wounds again, and put on temporary dressings. There was a nasty cut beside her right eye. She needed stitches, but that would have to wait.

Hitting the road again, he called the operator and asked to be connected to the Al-Balladi Morgue.

Sweat pouring out of every pore despite the air conditioning running full blast, Nageeb was glad his friend answered after the first ring.

"*Salaam,* Moharreb. Nageeb Fendil speaking," he said, putting on a jovial voice. "How are you, my friend? ... *Hamdallah.* It's been a long time indeed ... Yes, very busy ... How is the family?" He glanced over to check on Noora while Moharreb chatted. She was asleep. Blood trickled from the corner of her mouth. "*Hamdallah,*" Nageeb said. "Glad everyone is doing well. Listen, I have a big favor to ask ... It is for an important and confidential cause."

"I have no doubt it is for a very good cause," Moharreb said.

Nageeb had known Moharreb since elementary school. He was a kind-hearted, trustworthy, and hard-working young man who had a weakness for American cowboy movies and Pepsi-Cola. Because he drank gallons of the soda, his childhood friends nicknamed him "Pepsi."

"We are in need of a young body for research."

"We have two bodies ..."

"We just need one, thank you, Moharreb."

"The one that just arrived last night was of a young woman. Did you need a man?"

"No, a woman. How old?"

"Only twenty years old. *Ya haraam,* what a shame. Poor thing."

Please don't tell me another victim of honor killing! Nageeb thought angrily.

"Luckily, the deceased had no children," Pepsi continued. "But the family has no money for burial."

"Can you tell me what was the cause of death?"

"Pancreatic cancer. She went quickly."

"Moharreb, I am most grateful ... Can you meet me at the airport, with ..."

"For you, *ya habib,* anything," he said. "But I'm wondering about something important, *ya Doctoor.*"

"Oh?"

"Why you don't call me Pepsi anymore."

"Pepsi, Pepsi. My apology. Do you know the Beau Rivage Café?"

"Do I know the Beau Rivage Café? *Eh Paisano!* Too much studying makes one forget, you know!" Pepsi teased.

The Beau Rivage had once been a favorite local hangout where loud Arabic music blared and travelers met for Turkish coffee, a smoke, and a few rounds of backgammon. Over the years, the Beau Rivage Café had lost its clientele to busy lives–the regulars became involved in business and daily prayer times at the new Al-Balladi mosque, leaving little time for leisure.

"Are you going back to Cairo today?" Pepsi asked.

"Yes. What I'm asking is confidential, so keep it under your Stetson, cowboy."

"*Habib,* that goes without saying. Coming from you, it must be for a great humanitarian cause."

In front of the Beau Rivage Café, a hand-painted Arabic sign read, "Closed for Remodeling." Nageeb pulled in behind the establishment. He covered Noora with a clean white sheet.

It didn't take long for Pepsi's truck to appear, out of a thick fog of desert dust.

Nageeb remembered his grandmother's words: *"In the face of disaster, an angel always appears."* He could have fallen to the ground and prayed in gratitude.

Moharreb's yellow American GMC pickup pulled in, enveloping the area in a cloud of dust. The door to the truck creaked open. Tattered and dusty snakeskin boots landed on the dry gravel. Clad in worn-out blue jeans, a Western shirt, and a leather belt with a large silver buckle, Pepsi appeared out of the yellow fog. A cigarette dangled from his lips. He approached Nageeb with a smile. Wearing a cowboy hat, he looked like a young, darker version of Clint Eastwood. A wavy black strand of hair dangled over his forehead. He removed his cigarette long enough to hug Nageeb.

"*Habib,*" he said, then opened the tailgate of his truck and slid out a black body bag.

Nageeb opened the trunk of his car.

Pepsi carried the corpse in his arms. He did not dump it in the trunk. He held the body bag with respect and lowered it gently.

A gusty wind blew more desert dust around the two men. Nageeb shook Pepsi's hand. "Thank you, my brother," he managed to say, trying to swallow the lump stuck in his throat.

When Nageeb arrived at the airport, he could see the helicopter was waiting. Dressed in the customary MOFHAJ gray suit and red tie, a man paced impatiently, squinting at the highway, glancing at his watch. He appeared relieved when he spotted Nageeb's black Mercedes-Benz S600.

Nageeb was unsure how to handle the situation. He knew Noora could not be seen through the heavily smoked windows. Still, he could not take chances. He slowed his car, and with trembling hands, he reached in the back seat and covered Noora with another bath towel and some of his wet clothes.

He drove around the chopper and stopped several meters away. He popped the trunk open and jumped out of his car, immediately clicking the door locks. The man in the gray suit ran up to Nageeb, introduced himself as Youssef, and they shook hands. Grimly, they loaded the body bag into the helicopter.

Yelling over the roar of the whirling helicopter blades, Youssef told Nageeb he had orders from Mr. Fendil to have his son ride in the helicopter.

Nageeb shouted back over the helicopter noise that he just spoke to his father, and that he was going to drive. He shook the man's hand vigorously and thanked him several times.

Nageeb's Mercedes flew across the desert road at over a hundred miles an hour. He adjusted the rearview mirror so he could keep an eye on his sister as he dialed his mobile phone. To his relief, Abdo answered after the first ring.

"I'm on my way to Aqaba. Thank you for fine-tuning my car. Everything is going well; I am pleased, yes, *hamdallah,*" Nageeb said in one gulp, trying not to give out too much information, in case someone was listening to their conversation.

Inside Farid Fendil's museum of cars, Abdo stood numbly next to the wall phone and slowly replaced the receiver. With his shirt sleeve, he wiped his sweaty brow and walked out to the courtyard, beyond the mango tree. Stepping further out into the brilliant sunshine, Abdo looked up, closed his eyes, and whispered a prayer: "*Hamdallah.*" Praise be to you, O mighty God.

CHAPTER 9
AQABA

Before three in the afternoon, Nageeb checked into the Hotel de Mer near the Red Sea. It was an ancient little inn, catering to students and clandestine travelers from distant shores. He had heard about the establishment when one of the interns in Cairo had boasted about an unforgettable fantasy-filled night with a belly dancer, where he did not have to show a passport or any identification, as long as the room was paid for with cash in advance.

He found a parking space near the entrance. He hated to leave Noora alone in the car while he registered, but he had no choice.

From the dark old lobby of the hotel came a pungent odor of stale tobacco mixed with mold—a scent that seemed to impregnate the weave of the ancient tapestries on the walls. In Arabic, Nageeb scribbled "Mr. and Mrs." in front of a fictitious surname on the faded pages of a dusty ledger.

"It's our special honeymoon suite," the boy behind the counter—who could not have been more than fourteen—informed Nageeb with a wink. He handed him an ancient copper key with the number five etched on it. *Khamsah*—five—a good-luck number in the Middle East, Nageeb thought as he rushed back to his car. He found a few teenagers admiring it. He didn't think the youths could see Noora through the smoked windows. Still, he was concerned the luxury car attracted too much attention. As soon as the young strangers spotted Nageeb, they took off. Nageeb climbed in the driver's seat and swiftly pulled out of the parking space, hoping the same spot in front of the hotel would still be available when he returned. Driving along the main street, he searched for a fabric store. It seemed everything closed for lunch—and the traditional afternoon nap. He chided himself for not stopping earlier. Stores probably didn't open again until three or even four. He drove around a few blocks. Fifteen minutes later, he found a parking space near a small fabric store. Leaving the windows slightly open, Nageeb rushed inside and found two men sitting in the corner on layers of Turkish rugs and mounds of cushions. Sleepy-eyed, the vendors were sipping coffee from demitasses, and they didn't appear in a hurry to sell their goods.

"Do you have tulle?" Nageeb asked.

The two men looked at each other. "Tulle?" the man wearing a red fez asked his partner.

"White veil," Nageeb said, glancing over at his car outside.

"We have silk. We have also rayon and acetate. Many types, many colors," he said, pointing up to a far wall.

Bolts of tulle of all colors, from white to yellow to red were aligned on the very top shelf, just below a cracked and moldy ceiling.

"This one," Nageeb said, pointing to a white bolt of tulle.

"*Ya Wallad!*" the vendor with a red fez yelled out. A sleepy-eyed young man in a *gallabeya* appeared from behind a curtain. The man yelled something in a different dialect. Taking his time, the boy picked up a ladder from a corner and pulled it to the bolts of fabric. Slowly he climbed. For a moment, Nageeb was sure the boy was going to fall off the wobbly ladder. He ran to his help. The boy pulled out the bolt and let it fall to the floor, nearly hitting Nageeb. The vendor with the fez finally rose, not happy about taking time away from his coffee. Holding on to his back and giving a groan, he picked up the bolt. "I hope you want more than one yard after all this trouble. We are not open yet," he huffed.

"I am very sorry. I'll take the whole thing," Nageeb said.

"The whole what?"

"The whole bolt. How much?" Nageeb said, pulling out large bills from his wallet.

"There are at least twenty yards here. How many girls are you marrying?"

"We are decorating a hallway at a hotel."

"Oh?" The man grinned at the money in Nageeb's hand. "Sounds like a very big wedding." He took Nageeb's paper bills and, after analyzing their authenticity, his smile grew wider. "Let me see, I'll have to calculate. I may not have the change ..."

"Keep the change. Sorry for disturbing your break time," Nageeb said, grabbing the bolt and rushing out.

Pulling away from the curb, he whispered, "Luck is on our side, Noora." *Please God, let it continue this way.*

Back at the Hotel de Mer, the same parking spot was still open.

Nageeb unrolled the yards of fabric until his entire car was filled with white fluff. He tried to tear the material, but it was too strong. He searched for his scissors, which he found in his medicine bag, and cut the veil. Though he was covered in sweat, he put on the black suit jacket Kettayef had left for him. Grabbing at least a half dozen yards of the veil, he wrapped Noora with it. Her head resting on his shoulder, he locked his car. Quickly, he carried her inside like a lifeless mannequin, covered by their grandmother's white satiny sheet hanging below her feet, several yards of white tulle floated behind.

When Nageeb returned to the lobby, the boy behind the counter had been replaced by a chunky old man, about as wide as he was high.

A cardboard sign taped to the faded, flocked golden wallpaper indicated room numbers, handwritten in black felt-tip pen. Nageeb's room was at the very end of the dimly lit hallway. By the time he reached his door, the old man from downstairs was breathing down his neck.

"Excuse me, sir ..." he said, his mustache fluttering while he cleared his throat. "I am Otto, the owner," he added, stepping on the veil that trailed down the hall. "Oh, so sorry." He picked up the tulle and awkwardly stashed it closer to Nageeb and Noora.

"Thank you. We're fine," Nageeb said as he fumbled with his key.

"Allow me, please. You have luggage? My nephew did not offer to help ... He is lazy ..."

"Thank you, we can manage."

"Very lazy ... Allow me," he said, looking down at his wide metal ring that carried at least a dozen large, old keys.

"I have the key," Nageeb said impatiently, lifting Noora up and placing her head closer to the crease of his neck. He brought more of the veil up to conceal her head. As he was doing so, he noticed blood oozing out of her mouth again, staining the veil. "We have the key," he repeated firmly. "We've had a big wedding, many relatives, celebrating all night, we want to be alone and get some rest!"

The man took a step back. "Of course. Allow me. Aha, here is the key," Otto said, stepping around Nageeb and unlocking the door. He pushed it wide open. "Best room in the hotel. Beautiful, with view!"

"Thank you," Nageeb said, entering the room with Noora. He tried to close the door behind him, but the veil trailed out a few feet. The man gathered the long tulle and pushed it all inside the room, with a grin. "My, I think they say the longer the wedding train of the bride's dress, the longer the marriage. I am honored you chose my hotel ..."

"Thank you, yes," Nageeb said and closed the door. Sighing deeply, he noticed a drop of blood had dropped down to the sheet below Noora's waist. He prayed the man didn't notice.

The moldy smell that filled the room made him wrinkle his nose and sneeze. At least the bright red comforter on the queen-sized bed looked new. He laid Noora down and unraveled the yards of tulle away from her face and body and pulled the bedspread out from under her. *If any blood should stain the comforter, it probably wouldn't show,* he thought thankfully. She moaned. Beads of sweat formed on her forehead. He turned on the air conditioner.

Sitting on the floor by the bed, he watched his sister with increasing sadness and anxiety.

Resting his head on her arm, he dozed off. An hour passed. The little beeper in his wristwatch went off, startling him and pulling him out of a dream about his grandmother. She had smiled, that same gentle expression, he recognized. She gave him some kind of a message, something he couldn't quite decipher.

This tragedy would never have happened if his grandmother were alive. Somehow, things began to change after the death of Sultana. He wasn't sure how. He wasn't sure about anything right now. *How odd,* he thought, feeling dizzy from the faint fragrance that enveloped him. He could swear it was Sultana's Joy perfume. He remembered how she used to keep the perfume in a little antique crystal bottle festooned with tiny pearls. He had once disliked that scent. Now he wished he could linger in it. If only Sultana could materialize and make everything all right.

Leaving the "Do Not Disturb" sign on the door, Nageeb returned to his car to get his bag of medical supplies. He noticed a small café at the edge of the street, and hesitated. He didn't want to leave Noora too long, but he felt dizzy. He had to eat something to nourish himself and gain his strength. For Noora.

The old television set in the lobby was turned on when Nageeb returned to the hotel carrying a bag of food. The evening's movie broadcast featured *All About Eve*. In a young woman's clear, dubbed voice that sounded absolutely unlike Bette Davis, the classic American actress announced in Arabic:

"Fasten your seat belts, it's going to be a bumpy night!"

"Fasten that seat belt, it's going to be a bumpy *life*," Nageeb mumbled bitterly. He trudged up the steps, which creaked no matter how silent he tried to be, while behind the counter, the hotel owner was dozing off on a stool and shrinking into his balloon belly. His mustache fluttered to the rhythm of his loud breathing.

Relieved to find Noora in the same position he had left her, Nageeb began organizing the medical supplies he had bought. There was a nagging feeling in the pit of his stomach. Wasn't he supposed to call Uncle Fellous, his father's brother, who lived in Aqaba? He'd worry about that later. Right now, he had to take care of his sister.

He bandaged her face, carefully taping it to protect her broken nose. She needed hospital care and X-rays. But he'd have to fill out insurance forms. How would he explain the cause of her injuries? He could claim she was his wife and give false names. No, he could not afford such a risk.

He began to eat the warm falafel sandwich on pita bread, chewing without tasting. His tired eyes drifted to a large painting of a young woman that hung on the wall near the bed. The woman had shiny black hair, short and teased up in a bob—a style that seemed in vogue in the sixties. He stared at the picture until he couldn't keep his eyes open and began to drift into a light snooze. He thought of Noora and Zaffeera in London, before the winter holiday. He remembered their brunch at the Dorchester Hotel. Noora had been chatting happily, but Zaffeera appeared annoyed. Something about her eyes reflected perhaps ... jealousy? He was tired and probably imagining something nonexistent. Zaffeera loved Noora. Perhaps she didn't like her new school. Perhaps she felt uncomfortable in a foreign city. But Zaffeera was the one who had begged their parents to study in London and be with her older sister. She had even written their father the nicest letter ...

With that last thought, Nageeb fell into a deep sleep.

He dreamed of a newspaperman standing on a sidewalk in London and waving the latest edition. When Nageeb passed him by, the man opened the newspaper and showed him provocative pictures—of Noora! But when he looked closer, the girl in the picture had blonde hair and looked like a pop star. "*Undeniable proof!*" the man shouted angrily. He resembled one of the fundamentalists Nageeb had seen at his father's office. Zaffeera appeared from the corner of the street, holding a book in her hand.

Nageeb woke up with a start. His eyes drifted back to the painting of the black-haired young woman holding a yellow flower about the size of a daisy. He rose from his chair to better read the handwritten insignia on the bottom of the painting. "*Admire ma fleur de la passion.*" Admire my passion flower? Nageeb thought there was something odd about this picture. Her eyes were beckoning, almost hypnotic. He gave a shiver. Somehow that glance reminded him of Zaffeera. But he remembered how at times she appeared so shy and removed. She used to slouch and hide behind her books.

What happened in London? What impelled Noora to do whatever it was that she supposedly did? It wasn't like Noora to venture to a foreign disco at night. She loved music and dancing, but she never went out on her own. Unless she was lured out by one of her classmates? Had someone given her drugs? Who took those pictures? Did their father hire a bodyguard without their knowledge while they were in London? He was aware that his father wasn't too happy about leaving his daughters unchaperoned after Nageeb left London. But he knew the school's reputation and all their professors; plus, the girls were safe, living in a quiet, posh neighborhood, and Noora was a responsible young lady. What could have happened?

Nageeb felt dizzy and sick to his stomach—too many unanswered questions. He was sorry he ate that sandwich. He went to the bathroom, poured a glass of water, and sipped it slowly. No use trying to figure out what happened. He had to focus on Noora and her serious wounds.

*****   *****   *****

In the confines of her bedroom, Zaffeera stretched and yawned on her low-to-the-floor, billowy, down-filled sofa surrounded by mounds of silk pillows.

From a platter on the glass cocktail table in front of her, Zaffeera picked up a half mango with the pit still in it. She sucked out most of the juicy flesh, revealing the whole long seed, which now looked like a stiff tongue. She closed her eyes and slowly began to twirl the pit around and around in her mouth, sucking on its juice, imagining it was his tongue.

"Michel," she whispered. She would give him such pleasure, he would be on his knees, begging for more! She smiled at her fantasy. The flame of the almond-scented candle on top of the cocktail table cast shadows of erotic figures on the wall. Her head resting on a large pillow, she slowly opened her Christian Dior satin robe. She ran the tip of the juicy mango seed down to her breasts. She loosened the robe, twirled the mango around her erect nipples. *Patience, my dear*. She would make Michel the happiest man on earth. She grinned at the thought, separated her legs, and imagined *him* there. "Aah, ooh! Yes ... Yes!" She moaned with the unbearable pleasure of it. She shuddered as one exquisite explosion after another shook her from head to toe.

Resuming her composure, she tossed the mango seed back in the platter and pushed it away. With eyes blazing, as in London after her evenings of satiation, she pressed a switch on the remote control next to her. The entire room lit up. She slipped her robe back on, then rose and glided to her bathroom.

A faint chime sounded on her bathroom phone. She grabbed the receiver.

"*Ya mazmazelle Zaffeera ...?*" a young woman's voice ventured timidly.

"Where the hell have you been?!" Zaffeera snapped, turning on the golden faucet of her tub to its maximum force.

"A woman told me to stay in my room until now ..."

At that moment, Zaffeera thought she heard something. She turned off the faucet. Someone banged loudly on the locked door of her bedroom.

"Stay where you are until you hear from me," she barked. She hung up as the pounding continued.

"Who is it?!" Zaffeera shouted. She would have to talk to her mother about hiring such incompetent maids. She tightened the satin belt of her robe as she marched through her bedroom.

"Your mother wants to see you in her bedroom," came a gruff woman's voice.

"Who is this?" Zaffeera demanded without opening her door.

"Magda," the woman answered. The sound of thick heels clacked on the marble floors and echoed away through the corridor.

CHAPTER 10
THE PROMISE

Noora was drifting in and out of consciousness. Nageeb improvised an IV stand from a wire coat hanger and coat rack from the rickety armoire. He attached an IV bag to the hanger, connected the tubing, and inserted the needle in Noora's left hand, taping it carefully in place so it would not tear loose. For now, he would keep her sedated. He had enough supplies to feed her intravenously for a day or two. He turned on the light in the bathroom and kept the door ajar.

He remembered when he was a little boy and Noora was just born. Their mother had looked like an angel, sitting up in bed, surrounded by pillows as if she were floating on clouds. Sultana had stood next to his mother. Three generations of women—the most wonderful women in his life. *"Promise me you will always take good care of your little sister ..."*

The words echoed painfully in his heart.

He knelt at her bedside and kissed her forehead. *"Allah ma'aki okhti anah,"* he whispered, invoking God to be with his dear, wounded sister.

Nageeb locked the door, leaving the "Do Not Disturb" card dangling from the doorknob. He tiptoed out into the dark corridor. Downstairs, the boy was watching the news on the black-and-white tube in the lobby. He did not notice Nageeb.

Sitting in the sun-heated leather seat of his Mercedes, Nageeb dialed his mobile phone to check his messages. His father's male secretary had left an urgent request to call the office at once. Nageeb was aware that his father never spoke personally into recording machines, because it was beneath him.

He thought of his mother. Why didn't he simply dial her private line and tell her what happened? But if he did, she would never be the same. It would not be the right thing to do. He would regret it later. What about the other children? Would there ever be a right time to tell them the truth? He wished he were a boy again, so he could pour his heart out to her. She always knew how to console him. His father never knew that soft part of his son—that was something only between him and his mother.

"*Ummy anah,*" he whispered to his mother, "I will keep my promise."

In the rearview mirror, he caught a glimpse of himself. His eyes were bloodshot. "He will regret it," he said, grinding his teeth. He found his sunglasses on the passenger seat and put them on.

He dialed his father's number.

*****   *****   *****

"Nageeb? *Ibni,* I have been waiting for your call."

"Yes, my father."

"Where are you? *El arabeya?*"

"*Aiwa,* my father," Nageeb answered in Arabic. "I am in the car … Good evening. I met the gentlemen at the helicopter, and they left for Aqaba. I'm calling from Aqaba. I had some mechanical problems with the car and I had it checked. It was the fuel injector …" Nageeb spoke rapidly, knowing his father understood nothing about cars, except where to purchase them for his collection.

"*Esma'a menni.*" He enunciated each word softly and with such patience, it seemed he was talking to Nageeb the boy, instead of his grown son. "Listen to me. I wanted you to go with … *esh esmou …*"

Nageeb knew his father never remembered names. "His name is Youssef …" he said.

"What?"

"I believe his name was Youssef, Father."

"You were to fly with him in the helicopter. I didn't ask you to drive."

"I am terribly sorry. I misunderstood. I've had the night shift at the hospital. I was not thinking straight. I know it's no excuse, and I …"

"I understand you have important duties. That is why I wanted you to fly."

"Father, there was no room for me in the helicopter, and ..." Nageeb almost lost control of his anger. He wanted to shout "*MURDERER!*" He wanted to scream out every insult he knew, in every language ever invented. He reminded himself he must handle this terrible situation very carefully—for Noora's sake. "I'm sorry I interrupted you, Father." He kept his voice as calm as possible.

"What is it you want to tell me?"

"Just that ... I am on my way to see Uncle Fellous," Nageeb mumbled, feeling defeated.

"Good. That is very good, my son."

Uncle Fellous did not own a telephone. Nageeb understood why his father wanted him to pay a visit to the aged uncle who had just undergone heart surgery. But ... did his father truly expect him to go with those fanatics out on the fishing boat and watch them dump ... *the body?*

The thought of the poor girl being shredded by sharks made him ill. How could he possibly allow such a terrible thing to happen? He remembered how Moharreb had treated the black plastic bag containing the young woman's body. How he had eased it in the trunk, with such respect. If his trusted childhood friend had found out the truth—Nageeb shuddered—he never would have believed that he, Nageeb Gabriel Fendil, would stoop so low and tell such a lie to Pepsi.

Nageeb found himself trapped, and he was suffocating in his father's web of lunacy. Their last conversation was something out of a nightmare.

In his office at Al-Balladi, Farid Fendil was puffing on his pipe. He knew that Nageeb never cared to fly, especially in helicopters. His son preferred to drive. That was the reason Farid never bothered to purchase a helicopter in the first place.

"That's fine," Farid said on the phone. "*Yallah,* go and give Uncle Fellous my very best. Let him know I will be seeing him soon, *inshallah,*" he said. "God be with you, my son," he concluded and hung up.

Farid Fendil's mind was on other matters now. Earlier, he received word from the head man of the MOFHAJ, the sheik Abdullah Kharoub, that the helicopter landed in Aqaba. The chartered fishing boat was there, waiting. Two MOFHAJ members were given the orders to take the boat out to sea at two in the morning. The sheik assured him that "the girl's shamefully contaminated body" would be obliterated.

Farid's anger mounted. He wished he could have ripped her apart with his own hands. From the day she was born, he had loved her. He had given her everything her heart desired. She had been his little girl. She had been his pride. She had been ... How could she have betrayed him?!

The sexual images of the photographs the sheik showed him that fateful morning kept appearing vividly in his mind again and again, torturing him until he could no longer stand it. He felt sick to his stomach. Sick at the thought of men touching his daughter—fondling her body, naked for the world to see. She had dishonored and violated his name. She had *shamed* his entire family. She had ...

He staggered to the bathroom in his office, barely making it to the toilet, and threw up, then leaned on the sink and glanced at his reflection in the mirror. He had to regain control of himself, so he ran the faucet full force and splashed cold water on his face. He held a hand towel to his face as he stumbled back to his desk and let himself fall heavily in his armchair. He breathed deeply; never had he been so out of control. Nausea? Even vomiting? Those were signs of weakness. He was a man!

He made the mistake of raising his daughters too liberally. He had been influenced by Western ways, but he should have known: A man must never have a close relationship with a daughter; it leads to evil. He rose from his chair and thrust his fist into the nearest wall, feeling no pain—just a little relief.

Farid had one more task to complete; it was his duty as the head of his household and as a husband. "I must *protect!*" He rubbed his bloody knuckles on the white cotton of his garb.

Earlier, he had been introduced to Magda—the only woman connected to the MOFHAJ group, a religious and respectful relative of the sheik.

Magda was to inform his wife of their daughter's "accidental death," the sheik had wisely advised. Farid agreed that Magda would watch over Mrs. Fendil during the mourning period—in case Yasmina started screaming and crying, falling apart, like most women did.

*****   *****   *****

Standing at the Al-Balladi airport, where a row of private jets gleamed impressively beneath the bright desert sun, Moustafa ground his teeth in anger. He should have been on the fishing boat in Aqaba, instead of boarding a private jet. *He* should have been the one to see to it that the girl was dumped into the Red Sea. He had brought a flashlight to watch as sharks yanked pieces off her. How many times he had dreamed of devouring those breasts! He saw them in person only too briefly, the beautiful breasts those vile young men at the disco fondled with their filthy, sinful hands. He would never forget the disdainful look she gave him behind the window of that restaurant in London. *You thought I was beneath you. Look at you now!*

The call came from the sheik himself. It was, of course, an honor. But he was told instead of heading for Aqaba, he had a new assignment: to guard and protect another wealthy man's daughter, who was studying at the university in Egypt. He was to remain in Alexandria for a year. The sheik gave him bonus money for his work on the Fendil girls, and an advance for the upcoming assignment. He would be staying at the luxurious Cecile Hotel for the duration of his new job. Better than the dreary flat in London. But the sheik had not given him a single word of praise. That would have been worth more than the bonus money.

CHAPTER 11
THE SEARCH FOR A SANCTUARY

Uncle Fellous was the brother of Farid's father. As he lay dying, the old sultan had whispered his last wishes to his only son, Farid Fendil: "Visit my grave once a year. But promise to see my young brother several times a year."

Farid kept that promise. Nageeb never knew what Uncle Fellous really did for a living. After a failed venture as an antique rug dealer in Istanbul, Uncle Fellous worked for a cotton mill in Alexandria. A few years later, he ended up in Aqaba with his doting wife, Zouzou. They had lived for twenty years at the edge of the city, in a small dwelling he called a villa. It was a dilapidated house surrounded by a low stone wall, festooned with dried weeds. Nageeb's uncle was nicknamed *Uncle Fellous,* which meant "Uncle Money," probably to compensate for the fact that he never had any.

Uncle Fellous and Aunt Zouzou had no children of their own. They only visited Al-Balladi after the birth of each Fendil child. They knew Nageeb quite well, because Farid made it his duty to bring Nageeb every time he visited his uncle in Aqaba.

Nageeb wished he did not have to leave Noora a moment longer than necessary, but he had been brought up never to go to anyone's house empty-handed. He could not take the time to find a florist. Luckily, he found one of his uncle's favorite treats on his way to the house.

When Aunt Zouzou opened the door and saw Nageeb, she burst into joyful tears. Nageeb-*el-doctoor,* as she proudly called him, had come to see them. It was a wonderful surprise.

An ancient kerosene lamp barely illuminated the living room. Nageeb found Uncle Fellous sitting cross-legged on the low divan, like a Bedouin.

"*Ahlan wosahlan,*" Aunt Zouzou welcomed him.

The tang of incense, cumin, coriander, and other herbs engulfed Nageeb's senses, and for a brief moment brought him back to his happy childhood.

He was glad he came to pay a visit at night. If they noticed that his eyes were bloodshot, even though the living room was dim, he would explain that he had been studying hard for his medical exams and working nights at the hospital in Cairo.

The old grandfather clock chimed, vibrating every nerve in his body. He had been away from Noora for almost twenty minutes.

Nageeb cleared his throat. "Uncle Fellous, I wanted to come and see you after your operation, but this is the first time I could get away," he said in a voice he prayed would not betray his feelings.

Handing Aunt Zouzou the treats he had brought, Nageeb sat on the couch near his uncle. While Uncle Fellous chatted on about the rising costs of food and all the pills he had to swallow, Nageeb kept nodding compassionately. He was trying to decide if this house could possibly be a safe hiding place for Noora.

"Oh, Nageeb, Nageeeeeb," Uncle Fellous whined, "if you only knew what the doctors put me through." He blew his nose into his handkerchief as if blowing into a musical instrument. He wiped his eyes with the sleeve of his *gallabeya.* "Why didn't you tell me they were going to crack my ribs open?"

"You know you are fifteen years younger!" Nageeb turned to his aunt. "You see, Auntie Zouzou? Now he is as young as you!" he teased.

"Look, our Nageeb, *el doctoor, o'ombri anah,* he brought us *Loukoums!* Turkish delight with pistachios too! Your favorite. Your favorite!" She turned to Nageeb. "You always spoil us so much. Too much! But we are very grateful. How is the family, *ya* Nageeb?"

"Why do you always bring us gifts, when you know you are our gift?! *Ya ibn,* you are our angel!" Uncle Fellous sniffled. "Yes, how is the family?"

"*Hamdallah*," was all Nageeb managed to mutter.

"And tell me. How are the children?"

"*Hamdallah*." Nageeb nodded.

"Let me see. I know their names all in their proper order! I don't forget," he said proudly. "First of course, there is you," he chuckled. "And, after you, there is Noora, ah, the beautiful Noora ... with those eyes. *Mashallah!* Then the next daughter, Zaffeera." He tapped his temple with two fingers. "Smart one, she is. She will be a teacher. You will see. I know. And then, there is Kettayef. A son we must bless ..."

"Yes," Aunt Zouzou said, raising both hands up. "May Allah bless him and protect him."

"Someday he will speak. You mark my words. And then there's our little Shamsah. The little *arusah*. Little doll! She is sweet like honey, right?"

"That's right." Nageeb nodded, trying to keep a steady smile.

"You see, I know all the children like they were my own. Allah bless them."

"Each and every one of them," Aunt Zouzou added.

"I expect everyone is happy and in good health. Right?" Uncle Fellous said, apparently forgetting his surgery for a moment. He smiled broadly.

"Yes," Nageeb said, watching the two of them—the frail man and his anxious little wife. *No. This would definitely not be a hiding place for Noora.*

***** ***** *****

Night had fallen on Al-Balladi.

Farid Fendil did not bother to turn on the lights in his office. He had not moved from his leather "throne." He leaned back and rocked himself as he studied the new handmade pipe the MOFHAJ men had given him. He was using the cardboard matchbook Sheik Abdullah Kharoub had left for him. *To hell with the fancy lighters,* Farid Fendil thought. From now on, he was going to use only matchbooks. The old ways were better. He would make sure from now on, traditional laws would be enforced.

The phone on his desk broke the silence. It was Nageeb calling from the car, informing him about Uncle Fellous and the state of his recovery.

"Stay at the hotel tonight. It's too late for you to drive."

"Yes, Father."

"Come back tomorrow. I have meetings scheduled all day. I will see you tomorrow night. *Ma'al salaama.*"

Relieved by his father's decision, Nageeb pressed the gas pedal, impatient to get back to the dingy hotel.

In the middle of an unpaved one-lane road, his car died without warning. Angrily, he pressed on the gas pedal. Nothing happened. He was out of gas. He pounded on his steering wheel, furious for not taking a moment to notice the gauge. He jumped out of his car and looked up and down the street. In a city filled with gas stations, why was there no station in sight? Luckily, no car was behind him and he was at the edge of a brightly lit, store-lined street. He shifted into neutral, jumped out, and began pushing his car to the nearest parking space. At that moment, even though he was indeed a Muslim, somehow, he could not help but think of a movie he saw that touched him as he watched Jesus Christ bearing the heavy, wooden cross through the street. It felt as if he too had a weighty burden to bear. As he glanced up, a few onlookers were actually watching him from the sidewalk, while the wheels of his car moved forward, the tires crackling upon the gravel. No one made any attempt to give him a hand. Once he got the car rolling, it was not difficult to maneuver it into a parking space. He had no choice but to leave it there overnight.

Up ahead, he saw a small clothing store. He locked his car and went inside, where he found a black sack dress and sandals for his sister. As he was about to leave the store, a long black shawl on a mannequin caught his eye. It would work well to help conceal his sister's wounded face.

With the clothing he just purchased, Nageeb rushed back to the hotel. He prayed Noora hadn't awakened to find herself alone.

Thank God, Nageeb thought when he was finally back in the room. He found Noora resting in the same position he had left her. No doubt by dawn, she would awaken in pain, especially from her broken nose. He would have to augment the pain medicine.

He took the telephone to the bathroom and dialed the five-star hotel where his father stayed when he visited Aqaba. Using his father's platinum credit card, he reserved a room for one night. When the bill arrived in his father's office, he and perhaps even those fanatics would surely believe that Nageeb had spent the night there while in Aqaba.

He hated having to go out again, leaving Noora alone, to check into that hotel. He would figure out what to do later. He felt like a criminal trying to cover his tracks.

Whom could he trust? he wondered, stretching on the bed next to his sister. Where would she be safe? Abroad? Perhaps somewhere like Greece? Noora loved the Mediterranean. He could rent her a small villa somewhere in a village by the sea. How could he smuggle her out without a passport? With money, he could *buy* a passport. It would mean searching around town and probably dealing with sleazy people. What else could he do?

Feeling restless, he walked to the window. He wished for a cigarette, even though he had stopped smoking more than a year ago. He longed for the soothing effect that would spread from his lungs to his brain, dulling his pain. He had noticed there was a cigarette machine downstairs, but again, he would have to leave Noora.

He opened the gaudy taffeta maroon drapes of the small window and realized the room actually had a nice view. He gazed out at the twinkling lights that danced off toward the hazy horizon. *Wasn't that …? It had to be.* Shimmering there, across the Red Sea. *Eilat?* He had promised himself he would visit Eilat someday, one of the most beautiful resort towns in the world, where people from all over the globe came to vacation. Eilat. A resort haven for honeymooners, pleasure-seekers, leisure-lovers, and maybe … a place where Noora could be safe?

Nageeb thought of Shlomo Moghrabi, who had quit medical school to get married. As far as he remembered, Shlomo had taken a job managing a timeshare resort in Eilat.

"Shlomo…" Nageeb whispered his friend's name while staring out at the lights on the horizon.

An ex-classmate and good friend who always seemed to carry that certain *joie de vivre*, Shlomo always knew how to brighten the gloomiest situation when he attended med school in London.

Nageeb closed the drapes and shuffled wearily to the opposite side of the bed, where Noora lay motionless. As soon as his head hit the flat pillow, he fell into a disturbed slumber.

A few hours later, a shaft of sunlight cut through the open crack of the curtain and shone into Nageeb's eyes.

"The Crystal Resort ... Coral Beach!" That was the name of the resort where Shlomo worked. He had sent Nageeb a postcard the year before, inviting him to visit. Now he regretted that he had never taken a moment to reply to his friend.

He glanced over his shoulder at the sleeping Noora. Soon he would have to change the IV bag. He rose and walked groggily to the bathroom, while wondering if Shlomo was still working at that same resort in Eilat. He opened a bottle of aspirin and popped three pills. *I must call Abdo,* he thought, swallowing the aspirins all at once. He searched in his wallet for his international credit card. The bills were sent straight to his med school address in Cairo.

*****   *****   *****

Abdo had spent the day in the garage, polishing Farid's Mercedes four-by-four, the one he named the Popemobile. With each stroke of polish Abdo applied on the new paint job of the twelve-year-old metallic-green Benz, he prayed: "In the name of Allah, most gracious, most merciful... I beg of you, I am *pleading* with you, *ya Allah,* please, send me good news from Nageeb. *Inshallah. INSHALLAH.*"

An endless hour later, as Abdo stared at the polished car that gleamed under the sun, the phone rang.

"I'm in Aqaba," Nageeb said. "I'll need that document to travel. Pass' Passing through, you know. It's in my attaché case. I'll be traveling."

Abdo looked to the sky and murmured a grateful *hamdallah.*

While Nageeb was on the phone with Abdo, he did not see that Noora opened her eyes again. She could hear her brother's voice now. She watched him as he ran his hands through his hair and paced on the wooden floor that creaked with every step he took.

She tried to shift her weight but couldn't. Her back was itching. Her body ached, her face hurt. She couldn't bear the needle sticking in her hand. She tried to yank it out.

Nageeb hung up and turned to check on Noora. When he saw she was awake, he ran to her bedside, kneeled, and gazed at her as if witnessing the rise of a prophet. "*Hamdallah, hamdallah,*" he whispered. "We are going to make it ..."

CHAPTER 12
BY THE GRACE OF ABDO

Abdo made his way through his grandmother's rose garden toward the little limestone house that served as a utility shed. He went in, and a few moments later emerged carrying a plunger and a metal toolbox.

Inside the Fendil home, as he walked through the corridors of the men's wing, a chilly feeling loomed.

A man dressed in a tailored gray suit and red tie appeared from behind one of the white pillars.

"Where are you going, Abdo?" the man asked, looking at him disdainfully.

Abdo froze. How did the stranger know his name? He thought of his uncle in Cairo who used that same tone of voice prior to sliding out his leather belt; the scars from his ruthless whippings still marked Abdo's back.

I am Abdo Fendil, legally adopted son of Sultana's family. And you, sir, are an ibn el kalb! *Son of a dog!* Abdo thought.

"I asked you a question. Where do you *think* you're going?"

Abdo replied as if he were mentally slow. "*Sabbah el noor, ya Fendi.* Good morning, sir. I have come ... to fix ... Nageeb's plumbing. If you'll excuse me for saying the word, I have to unplug the toilet."

"What's inside the box?"

"Tools. A toolbox, and a special gift from my legally adoptive father, Mister Farid Fendil." He accentuated "legally adoptive" and opened the metal case. He held it up, showing an organized array of shiny tools.

"You may go." The intruder motioned Abdo away, as if he were nothing more than a smelly dishrag.

As he headed to Nageeb's room, Abdo listened for footsteps in the hall behind him. He knew he was being watched. How many more of them were there? He never imagined that he would feel threatened in what had once been a loving and secure home.

Inside Nageeb's room, clothes were scattered. It appeared the young doctor must have begun to unpack his suitcase when he arrived from Cairo. It was still open on top of his bed. A few gift-wrapped boxes were on a chair. At least these MOFHAJ men respected Nageeb's privacy—they did not seem to have entered the room.

Nageeb's open attaché case was on the floor, next to his desk. Inside a brown folder, he found Nageeb's passport. He hid the document in the deep pocket of his *gallabeya*.

Abdo returned to the kitchen. Two maids were busy at work. One was plucking feathers from a just-slaughtered chicken; another was kneading dough. The usual happy hubbub in the Fendil kitchen was gone. Word had leaked of Noora's terrible "accident," but no one knew anything more. Even Bijou, the fluffy family cat, seemed to know something had gone dreadfully wrong. Under the kitchen table, the Persian feline sat up like the Sphinx, its ears perked at attention, watching everyone's movements.

Abdo casually whistled his way through the courtyard and out to his orange Mercedes 300 Diesel. If Nageeb needed his passport, then *what about Noora?* She had to be alive. Otherwise, Nageeb would not have so readily said *Hamdallah*, giving thanks to the Almighty.

Abdo had to find a way to get to Noora's room and locate her passport. But he feared someone would question him, and he had no idea where to look first. Sweat poured out of him as he rushed through the garden door and another side entrance behind the kitchen. He opened another door and ran up his grandmother's private stairs. He checked both doors—the one that led to the stairway where he had come up and the regular door that opened to the corridor of the women's wing, near Sultana's private suite. Silently, he turned the locks. Once he was sure no one followed, he opened the antique armoire, where a stale fragrance of Joy perfume still lingered. Vivid recollections of happy days returned.

He realized how much he was missing the woman who had saved him from his uncle, the woman he called "Ummy." He often wondered why her daughter Yasmina had insisted on keeping the room intact after Ummy passed away. Now he could not have been more grateful.

He opened the fourth little drawer inside the armoire. He found everything just the way she had left it. Her passport was still there, beneath sepia-toned pictures. He remembered the day he drove her for her passport picture. Several years before, the family had persuaded her to take a trip to Europe. She didn't like to travel by plane and never went on any trips, but she kept her passport in her drawer.

His heart hammering nearly out of his chest, Abdo leafed through the passport. He was relieved to see it had not yet expired. He studied Sultana's picture. Looking serious, her face framed in black by the traditional headdress, she appeared more like a washed-out nun than the cheerful, fun-loving lady she had always been. He pocketed the passport and quickly searched for anything else Noora might need. He grabbed a long black dress and a black shawl with golden fringes he remembered Mr. Fendil had brought back from Italy. No, he'd better not take that shawl; too ornate. He took the old, soft afghan she used to wear when she had to leave at night to deliver babies. She called it her good-luck shawl. He smelled it deeply and tears immediately welled in his eyes. He rolled it up tight, tucked it under his arm, and rushed out.

***** ***** *****

Nageeb stood by the bank counter against the window and pretended to be busy doing his business. Abdo was late. The huge wall clock indicated the bank would close in just minutes. The knot in his stomach tightened. A security guard jiggled his keys annoyingly. *Abdo, please hurry*. Did he misunderstand where they were to meet? Without money, Nageeb was finished.

Noora had been alone for too long. Nageeb wiped the beads of sweat from his forehead.

The security guard was now holding the glass door open to let the last customers out. Abdo bounced in past the guard, with a cheerful grin. He tapped his watch with his finger. "We have two more minutes!" he declared.

Oh, thank you, God, Nageeb thought.

"Why didn't you take the four-by-four?" Nageeb asked when they walked out of the bank.

"Some people might recognize your father's Popemobile. But he knows I never drive my old Benz too far. He won't suspect I drove it all the way to Aqaba."

"What if he's looking for you?"

"If he can't find me, he'll think I went to the movies. The Academy Awards are going to be on television Monday. Your father will assume I've gone to the Odeon. They're having a marathon of all the nominated films. He knows my routine. If I'm not working on his cars, I'm at the movies."

"Good thinking," Nageeb said.

But as soon as they were inside the old Mercedes, Abdo burst into tears.

"Abdo ..." Nageeb had never seen him cry before and realized the terrible pressure Abdo had been under—the horror, the danger—the grief. "*Ya akhouya* ... she's alive. She *is* alive, and she will be all right. You'll see."

Abdo nodded and started the car. He remained speechless, tears flowing down his cheeks. "I'm sorry ... I don't understand why this had to happen."

"I am sorry too," Nageeb said, taking a deep breath and fighting back his own tears. "Let's hurry."

When they reached the side street where Nageeb had parked, the black Mercedes Benz S600, loaded with everything, was gone.

"Are you sure that's where you parked it?"

Nageeb nodded. He was sickened by the realization that someone had actually *stolen* his car.

"It's only a piece of machinery." It was Abdo's turn to console Nageeb.

"I know," Nageeb managed to utter through a deep, painful sigh. "I feel... violated."

"Do you remember if you left anything important in the car?"

"I don't think so. Except the mobile phone."

"Now you have a valid excuse. Your father can't reach you."

Nageeb cracked a bitter smile.

Abdo had to park at the end of the long block, and around the corner because there were no parking spots near the Hotel de Mer.

"What name should I use?"

"They'll be more interested in your money than your name," Nageeb said.

At the check-in counter, Abdo registered for a room. Nageeb, who had waited outside for a few minutes, anxiously entered the lobby and headed for the stairs. The hotel's owner stood at the landing, barring his way.

"When is the *bride* going to remove that Do Not Disturb sign so we can clean the room?" the man asked, his chunky hands resting on his wide hips.

Nageeb was too weary to think of a clever lie. "After we leave tomorrow morning. But if you prefer, we can check out today. Then you can clean the room. Only I'll need a refund because I paid you in advance."

"Take it easy. Just making sure you and your wife are comfortable. That is all, *monsieur.*"

The man's nephew was busy counting the cash Abdo laid out on the counter, when everyone's attention turned to the television set that was prominently displayed in the small lobby. They could see the television from the stairway as the newscaster announced that a 7.1 earthquake had just hit Cairo. The concierge gasped and forgot about Nageeb. He brushed past him and rushed down the stairs to get a closer look at the television.

Soon after Abdo checked into his room at the opposite end of the hall, he rushed back to Nageeb's room.

"I hope the owner didn't see you come in our room," Nageeb said, locking the door. "He'll think we're doing something kinky."

"Don't worry about him. He's glued to the television, scared that the earthquake will travel to Aqaba," Abdo said. Then he saw Noora—in bed, with the IV bag hanging from a makeshift hook. He kneeled to her bedside and watched her bandaged face in disbelief. "Why?" he whispered. "Oh, Allah. *Why?*"

He hesitated to touch her. Gently, he pulled a hair strand away from her face. Tears streamed down his cheeks. *How could this have happened?* He was not religious, but found himself reciting a silent prayer from the opening passage of the Koran, the only one he knew, the one he was once told was the most significant of all: "*In the name of Allah, most Gracious, most Merciful... Praise be to Allah, the Cherished...*" He continued to pray silently. He added: "Praise be to Noora, for having the courage to survive."

Downstairs in the lobby, Nageeb rushed to the phone booth in a dark corner. The sound on the television was turned down, and the hotel owner stood behind the counter, watching him.

"Any more news about that earthquake in Cairo?" Nageeb asked.

"It's terrible. Many people killed! Many trapped under buildings! It is horrible! I pray to God to spare us. My building is very old." He nervously wiped his brow with his soiled handkerchief.

"We're really far from Cairo."

"Earthquakes travel far, *monsieur*. Have you ever been in an earthquake?"

"Yes ... in Alexandria. A small one, nothing serious ..."

"You don't know how damaging ... Only Allah knows our destiny," the fat little man said with a shiver, as he glanced nervously at the ceiling.

"My bride and I have family in Cairo. I need to call and find out how they are doing. Does this phone work?"

"Aah, you have family in Cairo? Oh. That is something to worry about. But ... you have a phone in your room."

Nageeb could not chance calling from the room. He needed a public phone so that hopefully his call could not be traced as easily. "We need to leave the line open in case our relatives want to call us."

"Ah, yes, but of course! That is a good thing. You need change?"

"Thank you. I have plenty."

Inside the dusty phone booth, Nageeb dialed home. His father's office voicemail kicked in before he had a chance to think of a believable message. So he hung up, took a deep breath, dialed again, and spoke to the answering machine.

Before sundown, Abdo had gone out to purchase a wheelchair, and now Nageeb was feeling sleepless and anxious. He leaned against the windowsill, watching the twinkling lights on the horizon.

"How can we transport Noora out of here without this guy poking his fat nose at us every second?"

"It'll be easy ..." Abdo said, tearing off the price tag from the wheelchair, "if we leave now."

"Now? But that's impossible. She's in no condition, and certainly not at this hour."

The antique grandfather clock from the hotel's lobby struck three. Abdo and Nageeb silently rolled the dark figure in the wheelchair through the main exit door. Instantly, the alarm went off, blaring like a fire truck siren.

Nageeb rapidly wheeled his sister along the dark sidewalk and searched for Abdo's car. Covered in black from head to toe, Noora slumped over with her head reaching her knees. He grabbed her by the back of her dress, just in time to keep her from tumbling out of the wheelchair.

He turned a corner and finally spotted Abdo's orange car across the street. There was no way to get the wheelchair down the high sidewalk unassisted. He headed for an intersection where the sidewalk slanted to the road. Luckily, all the stores were closed.

Carefully avoiding potholes, he took his time wheeling Noora along the road until they finally reached Abdo's car. He fumbled with the key and realized the keychain had a small flashlight. With sweaty palms and trembling fingers, he turned it on, found the keyhole, and unlocked the car door. He placed Noora in the back seat and tried to be silent as he stuffed the wheelchair in the trunk. A light from an apartment window above popped into life, and a curious silhouette appeared. Nageeb slid behind the steering wheel, silently closed the door, and slouched.

What was taking Abdo so long? He didn't want to switch on the ignition. Diesel engines, especially this car with over 250,000 miles, made a racket. It would surely wake the entire neighborhood. He hoped no one was calling the police about the suspicious figure seen stuffing a body in the back seat of an orange Mercedes.

Abdo stood on the sidewalk, trying to justify his action to the furious concierge. "I just wanted to go out for a quiet smoke," he explained.

"It's three o'clock in the morning. This is a respectable hotel!"

Abdo coolly lit a cigarette, a la Humphrey Bogart. "I never claimed this is not a respectable hotel," he said. *Nageeb should be in the car by now,* he calculated, but the money and passports were in the black travel bag he was clutching under his arm. He watched the little fat man as he flailed his arms, screaming, "You made my alarm go off! I thought we were having an earthquake!"

"No, sir. I simply went out for a smoke."

"Anyone who sneaks out of my hotel in the middle of the night must have intentions!" the concierge screamed.

"Intentions?"

"Unlawful intentions!"

"No, sir. I assure you ..."

"My alarm goes straight to the police!"

"That's very good and comforting. My apologies if I caused a problem."

"We have a special section for smoking! Can't you read my signs?"

Abdo offered the concierge a cigarette, which he quickly took and placed behind his ear.

"Do you also have a special section for cockroaches? Because I found one right on top of my nose when I was sleeping on one of your flat pillows. I should get a refund for tomorrow night and the night after, which, as I am sure you know, I paid you in advance."

"What is this with refunds?!"

Abdo began to walk away. The concierge chased after him.

"We'll spray your room," he offered.

Abdo stopped and turned. "So that all the other roaches come out for air? No thanks."

The concierge mumbled a few insults and stomped back inside.

Abdo parked his car by the water's edge. The two young men sat silently while Noora slept in the back seat. Nageeb was glad he would never have to return to that dreary hotel. He had cleaned the room, even making the bed before leaving, so there would be no trace of blood. He had rolled the soiled tulle up tight and stuffed it in a paper bag, along with their grandmother's sheet he had used. Abdo had discarded the bags in public trash bins along the way.

Nageeb thought of the dream he had had in the room—a dream evoked by that eerie picture of the girl above the bed.

"Have you seen Zaffeera?"

"No," Abdo replied. "Why?"

"I … was just wondering. How is she doing?"

"I heard the maids in the kitchen talking about how wonderful she's been, tending to her mother around the clock, without even taking a break."

"I see," Nageeb said, frowning.

They watched the calm Red Sea shimmering like glass. The first ferry to Eilat would open for business at seven o'clock in the morning. In four hours, Abdo and Nageeb had smoked two packs of cigarettes. Still, they had not come up with a solution.

Where would Noora be safe?

"Something will surely come up," Abdo said.

Nageeb dropped his head back on the headrest and finally allowed his lids to close, but only for a few minutes. He opened his eyes and rubbed them, then grabbed the pack of cigarettes on the dashboard. Empty. He crushed it.

"We have a week reserved at the timeshare resort where my friend works. By tomorrow, Noora should be better. I should get her started on solid foods. Where can we get more cigarettes?"

"I have gum. It's better for you anyway."

"What's better for me doesn't matter anymore," Nageeb said bitterly.

CHAPTER 13
EILAT, ISRAEL

While crossing the Red Sea on the ferry to Eilat, Abdo leaned against the railing and studied a tourist brochure and map he had picked up at the dock.

Wearing her grandmother's black traditional garb and slumped over on the wheelchair, Noora's face remained concealed.

When they arrived at Israeli Customs, Abdo showed their grandmother's passport. Nageeb was impressed by Abdo's ease and confidence when he told the authorities that because of religious beliefs, the woman could not allow them to see her face. But the three of them had to wait over an hour in the hot sun until a female Customs authority finally came to check Noora's passport—and Noora.

When the security woman unveiled Sultana's black shawl that Noora wore around her head, she saw the "old woman's" face was bandaged.

"I cannot let you through Customs unless I see her face."

Nageeb began to sweat. Profusely.

"My grandmother's been in a serious car accident," Abdo explained. "She lost a lot of blood, and now she has pneumonia. We are taking her to the best hospital we know."

"Ben Gurion Hospital," Abdo said to the taxi driver a few minutes later. Sitting on Abdo's left in the taxicab, with Noora in the middle,

Nageeb shot Abdo a sharp look. The white lie he told the authorities had surprised him—and hospitals were out of the question.

What was Abdo up to now?

Nageeb settled uneasily in the back seat. He rested Noora's head on his chest, keeping her face covered. She was beginning to moan discernible words. He knew her pain medication was starting to wear off.

The taxi dropped the trio off at the curb.

Abdo wheeled Noora to the main hospital entrance. "Hurry! The military police put us in that cab," Abdo explained in a low voice. He wheeled Noora through the handicap door. Nageeb turned to look back at the cab—it was still waiting at the curb.

In the huge hospital lobby, hundreds of people were milling about. Nageeb felt safer in the crowd.

Abdo wheeled Noora through one corridor, then another, as if he knew where he was going. Nageeb was starting to feel dizzy, until Abdo finally stopped inside a busy emergency waiting room.

"Wait here. I won't be long," he said, rushing out of the double glass doors.

Nageeb sat close to Noora's wheelchair and rested her head on his shoulder. Abdo was still gone. He said he wouldn't be long, but more than an hour must have passed. Nageeb didn't want to attract attention, sitting there with Noora in a wheelchair, and with her head concealed. Luckily, so far, no one had come to ask him if he needed assistance.

He glanced up and spotted a maroon-colored van with dark tinted windows that had just pulled in, in front of the emergency street entrance. The driver's door opened and Abdo bounded out. Wearing white shorts and a peach-colored golf shirt, he looked like a tourist. He gestured to Nageeb.

"I had to do a lot of bartering to rent this cheap piece of machinery. They told me I had to reserve a car in advance. They gave me the worst van on the lot!" Abdo explained once they were on their way. "The brakes scream like a rooster, but it's drivable."

"Where did you get those clothes?" Nageeb asked, wondering why in the world Abdo had taken the time to go shopping.

"The car-rental office. They try to sell you their logo clothes."

"You don't look like yourself."

Noora moaned painfully in the back seat. Nageeb and Abdo exchanged worried glances. Nageeb wondered if his sister would ever look like—or even be—herself again.

Abdo drove the van through dusty, unpaved roads, until he reached a deserted hill and parked under a lone tree. He walked outside while Nageeb stayed in the van to finish changing Noora's bandages. Later, he joined Abdo, who was perched on a large red rock a few feet from the van.

In the distance, they watched a Bedouin, who sat cross-legged in the shade of an olive tree, his camel nearby. The Bedouin was motionless in his black garb, seeming completely undisturbed by the scorching heat.

A crescent-shaped turquoise lagoon was nestled between burned orange hills beneath them. The Red Sea gleamed on the horizon. Motorboats, appearing out-of-place in the ancient setting, sliced across the sea.

Nageeb and Abdo gazed numbly at the beauty before them. They watched silently as the sun cast its last glow and stars began to appear in the darkening, cloudless sky.

"I guess we could go to the resort and check in now," Nageeb said.

"Maybe we should wait until dark, when everyone is out to dinner, so we can wheel her in without an audience," Abdo suggested.

Nageeb lit a new cigarette from the embers of the one he was smoking.

"Time. In time ... Like a bad wound, slowly it will heal," Abdo offered.

"This feels more like an amputation," Nageeb said bitterly.

Nageeb opened the sliding doors and stepped onto the balcony of the fully furnished, one-bedroom condominium at the Crystal Resort and Spa. He leaned on the railing and gazed at Eilat's coral reef in the distance.

Far across the sea, barely visible on the hazy horizon, was Aqaba.

God bless Abdo, Nageeb thought, allowing his weary body to relax on a lounge chair. Two days had passed since Abdo left to catch the evening's last ferry back to Aqaba.

"Make sure Kettayef understands that Noora is fine, and recovering well," Nageeb had reminded him. Abdo nodded, giving him a somber look.

"He must know this is going to be a secret he will have to live with for the rest of his life."

"No," Abdo had corrected, "a secret he will have to carry for the rest of *Farid Fendil's* life."

Nageeb closed his eyes. If he could sleep for a few hours, he would be able to think clearly. Time was running out. He must call his father soon and leave more messages filled with lies. He wished he never had to face that man again.

"He is no father of mine," he muttered to himself.

Only a few days before, Nageeb could not wait to go home and be reunited with his family. He never had the chance to see his little sister, Shamsah. Shamsah, meaning *sun,* was born at high noon and delivered by their grandmother. Shamsah, who had caught the chicken pox. Shamsah, who loved Noora so much.

Murky reflections of his future raced through his mind. He liked Cairo and the hospital where he worked. Devoting his life to healing the sick and saving lives was what he had always dreamed of doing. Eilat was not easily accessible from Cairo, but still not too far, an airplane ride away. Most of all, Noora would be safe here. He could not imagine his father having any reason to travel to Eilat in Israel. But Noora needed to be with a relative. Someone they could trust. *Who?*

He could rent her a charming little villa. Like their grandmother, Noora loved to grow flowers. Gardening would keep her busy. She would need to change her name—of course—and accept the fact that she could *never* go home. He would have to convince her ...

What about Michel? He had almost forgotten about Noora's fiancé. What lies had his father told Michel? *I must contact him and tell him the truth! Would he believe in his heart that Noora did not betray him? If he truly loved Noora, he would know ... Or would this always hover in their life like a dark cloud ...?*

He fell asleep and dreamed he was weaving his way through a field of daisies that danced beneath the brilliant sun. Sultana was standing at the crest of a hill. She was smiling and opening her arms wide, welcoming him. His dream was shattered by the sounds of a crash, as if someone just tossed a rock through a window. Noora screamed. Nageeb rolled off the lounge chair and ran to the bedroom. The bed was empty. The door to the bathroom was closed.

"Noora!"

He opened the door. Hair sopping and a towel wrapped around herself, Noora looked blankly at her brother. The crystal vase, which held a bouquet of peach-colored roses, lay smashed on the white tiled floor. Jagged pieces of razor-sharp cut glass were strewn around her bare and bloody feet.

"Don't move!" Nageeb begged.

Noora gave her brother a peculiar blank stare.

"Don't move!" he repeated. "Stay right where you are, Noora!" He ran back to the living room to slip on his shoes. Broken glass cracked under his soft leather soles as he made his way to Noora. He pushed the dangerous debris out of the way and carried Noora to the bedroom, laying her down at the edge of the bed.

After he cleaned and bandaged her feet, he kneeled next to her.

"Just a couple of minor cuts," he said, forcing a smile. "Nothing serious." He pulled the blanket to her.

"I should kill myself," she murmured, her eyes downcast.

"You have a long life ahead of you," he said, holding both of her hands in his.

She pushed him away and pulled at her hair hysterically. The towel loosened away from her. Nageeb quickly pulled up the comforter and tried to wrap it around his sister. He tried to hold her and calm her down.

"I don't deserve to live! I should be punished. I am so, so sorry. Look what I am putting you through! You don't deserve this … I … Oh God, I don't know … I have wronged you and everyone else …"

Nageeb wrapped his arms tightly around her.

Noora finally stopped thrashing and went limp. She stayed in that position for a few minutes without moving.

Finally, breaking the unsettling silence, she repeated: "I should be punished."

She needed another sedative, Nageeb thought, but he wasn't sure he could leave her alone, even for a moment. The medicine was in the living room, and right now, that seemed too far. A voice within him said "*Ediha hodn*—give her a hug."

He held her in his arms and finally she fell asleep. He let her lie in bed with the comforter wrapped around her. He tiptoed out to get her the sedative but decided against it. No need to bombard her with any more drugs—she was asleep.

The phone rang. He prayed it was Abdo as he picked up the receiver from the kitchen.

It was Shlomo, inviting him and Nageeb's "girlfriend" out to dinner with his new wife. Nageeb was grateful Shlomo was so gracious in providing a condominium at a time when the entire town was sold out. Shlomo probably had to juggle guests around at the last minute, after Nageeb called him asking for a condo. Shlomo must have given him the best unit available—it had a magnificent view.

"You called me at the right time when I have great news! My beautiful Orly, she is three months pregnant! Don't tell anyone. We haven't announced it yet. I am the happiest husband!" Shlomo sang out on the phone.

"Congratulations. *Mazel tov!*"

"Thank you, *habib.*"

"Listen, Shlomo, we are here incognito because, well, I know this sounds crazy, but my girlfriend just had her nose fixed. She's got her face bandaged and her eyes, well, you know how women are; she feels kind of self-conscious ... she doesn't want anyone to see her ..."

Shlomo laughed loudly on the phone. "Agh, ya, ya, you keeds just want to be alone. *Nakhon. Habib!* I understand," he chuckled.

"Maybe tomorrow night we can get together ..."

"Tomorrow we are busy. My mother-in-law invited us to dinner. This I couldn't cancel. Even if I am completely seek and dying in the hospital, aii, I would steel have to eat her cooking!"

Nageeb was relieved.

"How about the night after?" Shlomo asked.

"Dinner on me."

"No way, *slackhlee. You crazy?* You are our guests!"

"You're letting us stay in one of the most spectacular condos and you expect me to let you pay for dinner? I wouldn't think of it."

"We'll fight over *l'addition* another time, *ya doctoor,*" he laughed with his delightful Israeli accent. "You keeds enjoy yourr-selves! It is an order! *Nakhon?*"

"Understood."

Nageeb opened his eyes, realizing he had fallen asleep on the couch. He tiptoed to Noora's room and found her asleep. Leaving the bathroom door slightly ajar, he took a quick shower. After dressing, he walked to the balcony. Classical music wafted from the café below. In the distance, a magnificent yacht was moored before an ornate white villa.

He heard a shuffle and turned. Noora stood, wearing a peignoir provided by the resort. Her voluminous hair was in disarray. Her eyes were swollen.

"Look out there, Noora," he said as he put an arm around her and led her to the balcony. "Isn't it beautiful here?"

"Yes," she said, watching the radiant colors of the day's end.

"How would you like to live here?"

"What do you mean?"

"I mean stay in Eilat. For ... a little while?"

She seemed puzzled by his question. She looked deep into her brother's eyes. "I ... can't go home?"

He had to look away. How could he possibly answer such a question? It was too soon to make her face the truth, a truth too painful to hear.

CHAPTER 14
THE AGREEMENT

In the Fendil mansion, Michel Amir studied the intricate designs of the antique handmade Egyptian brass table. Plates of dried fruits and nuts had been placed before him. Absently, he picked up a hazelnut, cracked it with the heavy silver nutcracker, and popped the shelled nut in his mouth. He chewed rhythmically without tasting, his mind on Mr. Fendil. Why did his father want them to meet there today?

He felt very uncomfortable. All he really wanted to do was run away from this home and these people. He wanted to be left alone and cry without anyone judging his weakness. He closed his eyes and tried to take a deep breath. He had a difficult time breathing. He needed fresh air.

On the opposite side of Mr. Fendil's lavish living room, the fathers were talking. He could not hear what they were saying. He knew this time they were not discussing business matters. What more could be said?

Noora was gone.

He thought of his mother, who had died of cancer when he was twelve. A beautiful, modern, and aristocratic woman of French and Egyptian descent, she had been educated in the best schools in Switzerland, and spoke seven languages with ease and grace. She never revealed her disease, and his father blamed himself for not noticing his wife's illness. Michel was aware that his father still mourned her loss. He never remarried. A respected Egyptian citizen and renowned real-estate developer,

Alexander Amir built private villas in Egypt, France, and Italy. Together, Michel and his father had begun plans to build a modern mansion at Al-Balladi, where Michel and Noora were to have lived. Where he and his fiancée had planned to raise a family. Now all was in vain and his life was over.

He chewed on an apricot. It tasted sour. Earlier, he had asked if he could see where Noora was buried. Michel's father said the family had already buried her out in the barren desert where her grandmother had been put to rest. But he could not rest until he at least placed flowers on her grave. It appeared the Fendil family had gone back to the old Muslim tradition of burying the dead within twenty-four hours. Mr. Fendil apparently prayed five times a day. Perhaps he had returned to ancient ways after having lost his daughter.

Alexander asked Michel a question, most of which did not even register with him. "You …" he heard his father begin, and the question ended with "do you agree?"

Michel nodded out of habit and respect. "*Oui, c'est d'accord.*" He was beginning to feel more comfortable speaking French. It was easier to just say yes to whatever his father wanted, so that no further questions could be asked of him.

He saw the two men rise and shake hands. He realized the meeting was over when his father touched his shoulder. Finally, it was time to leave. Mr. Fendil extended his hand. Michel shook it numbly.

When they left the mansion and sat in his father's Lincoln Town Car, driven by their longtime chauffeur, Monsieur Amir turned to Michel.

"I am proud of you, my son."

Proud of what? Michel wanted to ask, but stared ahead at the road and remained silent.

CHAPTER 15
A PLACE FOR NOORA

Against a balmy royal blue night sky, disco music floated up to the balcony where Nageeb and Noora sat. There was some kind of a hot calypso dance contest going on. They could hear vacationers clapping and cheering.

Luminous yachts rocked in the distance. For most people in this region, it was a magical night, where time flowed gently with the warm breeze.

Nageeb had gone out earlier to stock up on food. Noora promised she would not harm herself. She seemed calm and content, engrossed in watching *The Sound of Music* on television. But he worried about what was going on in her mind—how much did she remember? When he hurried back, he was relieved to find Noora sitting on the floor in front of the television, humming along with the movie's score as the end credits rolled.

Nageeb broke the crusty French bread he bought from a nearby delicatessen, and slapped mustard on top of imported cheese. But Noora had a difficult time chewing the sandwich because of her sore jaw. Nageeb watched her from the corner of his eyes and chided himself for not buying something soft like mashed potatoes or better yet, cream of chicken noodle soup.

Noora's eyes seemed to have found a new gleam. "You see, I kept my promise," she said.

"Your promise?"

"I was a good girl and waited for your return when you went to fetch us some food."

"Thank you."

"I'm the one who should thank you, for everything you are doing for me."

The lump in his throat kept him from replying.

Nageeb found a selection of tea bags on the counter, and made hot chamomile tea for his sister. He tried to talk about happy times—their trips to Europe when they were younger, funny incidents, and the unforgettable vacations in Alexandria, Egypt.

"Remember the French ball game we used to play? What was it called?"

"*Ballon Prisonnier?*"

"Yes. It was fun."

"Uncle Khayat taught us what he called the Middle Eastern version of Prison Ball," Nageeb said, remembering how Noora and Zaffeera—and even their grandmother—had teamed up against the boys, proving that they could play the game even better than their male opponents.

Remembering *Montaza*—the magnificent promontory where they used to picnic near the former royal gardens of King Farouk's summer palace, Nageeb sighed. Those were beautiful days—times when he would never have believed their lives could take such a drastic turn.

"Someone threw the ball too far, and it rolled all the way down the ravine, remember?" Noora said.

Nageeb nodded, reliving that happy day. "I think it was Zaffeera who threw the ball real hard because she was angry at the boys," he said. "Uncle Khayat's houseboy nearly killed himself trying to fetch the ball. And when he climbed back up without the ball, his *gallabeya* had those little things stuck all over."

"Hitchhikers. Poor guy. Remember how we tried to pull them out one by one?"

"Yes, and then Uncle Khayat drove away in his new convertible Jaguar and came back with treats for the children and a new ball. Those balls were leather, handmade. They weren't cheap. He always came to our rescue," Nageeb added thoughtfully.

"Remember the play we put on?"

"Hmm ... I don't. But I do recall we wanted to become movie stars ... as big as Omar Sharif."

Noora chuckled. "Yes."

Nageeb smiled at the memory. "He moved back to Cairo. I saw him less than a month ago at Justine's restaurant."

"You saw Omar Sharif?"

"I did. He still looks pretty good."

"Does he really look like Father?"

Nageeb nodded. Why did he have to mention Omar Sharif? The film star actually did look like an older version of their father.

There was an unsettling silence.

"You know what?" Nageeb said. "I forgot to bring chocolate."

"You can't forget chocolate."

"What was it that Grandmother used to say?"

"We must always sweeten our mouth with something sweet after supper," they sang in unison, and they both laughed.

It was good to see his sister laugh. The sparkle in her eyes returned, but not for long.

"Tonight, I'm taking you somewhere special," Nageeb said.

"Where?"

"It's a surprise."

"How can I go out looking like this?" She brought her hands up to hide her bruised face.

"They'll think you just got nose surgery. Believe me. It's quite dark in there, and no one knows us."

Elegantly dressed couples, mostly European tourists, crowded the trendy French café. As they were guided to a table in the corner, Nageeb realized Noora must feel out of place in their grandmother's black shawl and the oversized black dress he bought for her. To his surprise, he saw a few men in traditional Arabic garb along with others in business suits seated near the entrance of the restaurant.

"I didn't know Arabs came to Israel," Noora said.

"Not all Arabs are at war with the Israelis." He forced a smile. "Business is still business."

"Wouldn't it be wonderful if everyone lived without wars?" Noora said. She scraped off the twirled chocolate design of her pastry. "Without boundaries ... without enemies."

If there is no peace in the family, how could there be peace in the world? Nageeb thought sourly as he lifted his demitasse to sip his cappuccino.

That's when he saw two of the men from MOFHAJ. He recognized them. What the hell were they doing there? If they spotted Noora, they would take her to their father ... there would be no mercy.

Had they examined the body and realized later it was not Noora's? He should have taken Noora's bloody veil on that horrific day and wrapped it tightly around the poor dead girl's face.

"What's the matter?"

"Matter? Nothing. Too much caffeine," Nageeb said, trying to keep a steady smile.

"It's probably the smell of those cigars. They stink like, if you'll pardon the expression, *khara,*" Noora said.

"Yes, real shit."

"This place has an interesting history," she said, leafing through the restaurant's brochure. "Look here, it says it's a sad story of medieval times. One sister betrayed the other over a man they both loved ..."

"Medieval times?" he asked, keeping a watchful eye on the men with gray suits and red ties—the members of the so-called Men of Faith Honor and Justice. "I think it's more of a myth," Nageeb said. But he went cold all over as he saw the two MOFHAJ men being guided to a table close—way too close—to theirs. One of them was the guy he had met at the airport. They must have followed him.

The men appeared preoccupied with themselves, but Nageeb feared it was all an act—while they were watching Noora and Nageeb's every move. They didn't like the table that was offered to them by the silver-haired maitre d'. They seemed to know the host. One of them said something close to the maitre d's ear and slipped some bills in his hand. The maitre d' took a quick glance at the bills and smiled. He led the men to a table near another group of Arabs in headdresses and traditional garb.

Nageeb threw a generous amount of Israeli currency on the table, thankful that Abdo had thought of exchanging money on the ferry. "Let's get out of here," he said, and wrapped an arm around Noora. He led her outside.

"What's wrong, Nageeb?"

"Nothing."

He took her down shadowy cobblestone streets and finally led her back to the resort.

They climbed the three flights of stairs and stood in the breezy open-air hallway of the resort, while Nageeb nervously fumbled with his key. What if someone was inside the condo, waiting to arrest them? Cautiously, he unlocked the door.

They had left the lights on. Inside, everything seemed normal and in place. Once satisfied that all was well—at least as far as he could see—Nageeb locked the door. Noora was tired from the climb—Nageeb didn't feel safe taking the elevator. He sat with her on the couch for a moment, then propped up her feet and let her head rest on a few throw pillows. He dashed to the bathroom.

Studying his reflection in the mirror, he saw that his face must have paled several shades, and he was even trembling. He hoped Noora didn't notice his concern. He wondered if those monsters had been watching them, laughing at him while they waited for the right moment to throw out the net. *Wasn't Eilat known as a trade hub between different countries because of its key location?* He turned on the faucet and splashed cold water on his face. Didn't the ad in the *Travelers'* magazine state that the *Grotte des Deux Soeurs*—"Grotto of Two Sisters" restaurant—was world-renowned? He grabbed the last clean towel from the rack and dried his face. It was merely a coincidence—it had to be—that these men were at the same café; nothing more than simple coincidence!

He should never have taken Noora out. He switched off the faucet and heard a sound. Voices! He ran out and found Noora talking to someone out in the hallway. *Why did she open the door?!*

Noora stepped away from the front door as two women entered.

"Housekeeping. They want to turn down the bed," Noora explained.

Did they turn down beds at night in timeshare resorts? He thought that service was only done in luxury hotels. "No! We're fine."

One of the housekeepers said, "Okay," but she did not move away, and stood in the middle of the living room, making no attempt to leave.

The other maid went out to the cart. Nageeb saw her reaching under a pile of towels.

He grabbed Noora's arm and stepped in front of her to shield her. This was a setup. *What if they had a gun?* They were trapped.

"We don't need anything!" Nageeb shouted. *Why didn't I think to buy a gun?!*

"More towels?" the housekeeper asked in Hebrew. "Towels?" she repeated in English, pointing to the bathroom.

"No!" he said in Hebrew. "Go! We are fine."

The maid was still standing in the living room, looking curiously at the two of them.

Nageeb didn't know how to get them to leave without alarming Noora. He quickly grabbed a wad of bills and gave them to the housekeeper. "Please go!"

The maid looked at the money and smiled. She said something in Hebrew to the other maid, who dropped a pile of towels on the table by the door. Nageeb closed it quickly and turned the lock.

Noora looked puzzled. "They just wanted to bring us towels, Nageeb. We hardly had clean ones left."

"Sorry. I didn't realize ..." Nageeb said.

While Noora slept in the bedroom, Nageeb sat on the couch, keeping a watchful eye. What if those men really knew what was going on? Would they kick in the door, with guns in their hands? Would he really kill if he had to? To protect his sister, he would not think twice. He had to get back to Cairo. Noora should go with him. For now.

Their father traveled to Cairo a few times a year and always stayed at the Mena House. Noora could live at the opposite end of the city. He would never run into Noora in such a dense city. Perhaps Nageeb could get her an apartment near the Bazaar, where he knew his father never went. But Farid frequented most of the popular restaurants, and many people knew him, Nageeb thought, watching the front door. *What if those housekeepers mentioned seeing an injured Arab woman?* Did they know the pair were not Israelis?

As dawn neared, Nageeb fell asleep on the couch.

As if from a great distance, he heard Noora's voice. When he opened his eyes, she was looking down at him and smiling.

"What time is it?" he asked.

She glanced at her watch. "After nine."

"Already?"

"I didn't want to wake you. You were mumbling. I wasn't sure if you were sleeping," she said, walking to the window. She opened the drapes, and bright sunshine flooded the room.

"I was really awake," he said, rising painfully and squinting. He wished she had not opened the drapes.

"I wanted to know if I could do some shopping ... I'll need sunglasses. Can I use yours for now?"

"Yes."

"I'll also need some personal things ..."

"Of course, of course." He couldn't believe he had slept so long. He experienced weird dreams—celestial dreams. He saw beautiful, brilliant pastels that turned into crimson, shiny red like blood ...

"Last night, I noticed there was a small gift shop right downstairs."

"Where's my wallet? Oh yes." It was under the sofa pillow he had slept on. "Here," he said, opening his wallet. "Whatever you need." He handed her a few Israeli bills. He looked up at her and saw that her eyes were clearer now. But she had removed the bandage from her nose; he wished she had not done that.

"I doubt I'll need more than that."

"That's fine, Noora. How are you feeling?"

"Fine, but you don't look very well, I'm sorry to say."

"No, I'm doing well." In truth, he had never felt worse.

"Wasn't that a great movie?" Noora asked.

"What movie?"

"*The Sound of Music.*"

"Oh yes ... yes."

"They don't make movies like that anymore," Noora remarked, folding the Israeli currency. "There are too many violent ones these days. We have enough violence in real life. They should have called it *The Sound of Happiness.*"

"Sounds good to me," he said with a smile. How safe was it for them to leave the condo?

With the black shawl partially concealing Noora's face, and wearing his sunglasses, they took the elevator down to the gift shop. Noora stood in front of the store and admired a pretty yellow dress with large pockets on the mannequin in the window. Nageeb pressed a few more bills into the palm of her hand.

"I have the feeling this dress will bring you luck. It's a sunny, bright color," Nageeb said when Noora argued that she didn't need the dress.

"I insist," Nageeb said. "Try it on."

While he waited outside, he wondered again about those men in the restaurant. Eilat no longer seemed so magical. The benign, warm climate for which Eilat was known was now stifling and hot. The fresh, balmy breezes became annoying winds to Nageeb and carried too much dust. He could not wait to leave.

"I really like it," Noora said, modeling her new dress when they returned to the condo. "It's cotton and very comfortable. You were right ... Thank you."

They sat on the floor and had an indoor picnic. Crudités, pâté, and caviar were laid out on the glass cocktail table, and they ate as the sun slowly set. Noora went to the kitchen and found candles in the cupboard. "We'll have dessert by candlelight," she said.

"Alexandria!" Nageeb said, out of the blue.

"What?"

"I don't believe Father would want to go to Alexandria."

"What are you talking about?" Noora asked, clearing some of the paper plates from the table.

No, Nageeb did not want to bring up the subject of their father again, but how else could he convince Noora that Alexandria might be the right place for her safety?

"Remember how frustrated Father became with Alexandria, how he never could get approval on anything he wanted to build, or even repair, after the Jewish developers had to leave, and Europeans for that matter. The business situation became too unstable and too risky for Father."

"Yes, I remember him talking about that."

"And then there was the problem with Uncle Khayat."

"Oh yes. But why was Father so mad at Uncle Khayat?"

"Because he didn't want to help Father build Al-Balladi."

Noora put the food on the kitchen counter and sat at the edge of the couch near Nageeb. "Wasn't Uncle Khayat an architect before he decided to retire when he was still so young?"

"Yes. He was brilliant. A visionary. He could have helped Father, but Uncle Khayat didn't want to leave Alexandria."

"He loves the sea," Noora said, looking out at the balcony. Why should he want to build something in the middle of the desert? There's nothing like the cool breeze of the Mediterranean Sea. You know how intensely hot and dry it can be at Al-Balladi. Really, he was right about that."

"He used to say, *lazem el bahr*."

"We must have the sea," she sighed pensively, remembering. "I miss those summers in Alexandria. With Uncle Khayat ... and his wonderful little villa."

There was a long silence.

"I know you would be safe there, Noora."

"What do you mean?"

"You loved Alexandria."

"We all did," Noora said.

"You can stay there."

"That's a good idea. I am sure Uncle Khayat wouldn't mind. Perhaps I can stay there awhile. When things settle down, we can call Father and let him know I am all right."

Nageeb was thunderstruck. *Was she that much in denial?* "Listen ... Listen to me," he said. "You cannot go back."

"Maybe not for a ... a while ..."

Nageeb shook his head. "No, Noora."

"Two or three months ..." she said, her eyes filling with tears. "I know Father will be glad that I am okay."

"Noora ..." Nageeb took her hands in his. "Please. You must understand ..."

"Understand what? That it was all a horrible mistake, a terrible misunderstanding? I'm not saying it wasn't my fault ... I had no right to drink alcohol. I must have been terribly drunk. I'm sure it didn't take much for someone like me who never touched alcohol ... I thought it was water ... I made a terrible, horrible mistake, and maybe he can hold a grudge like that with Uncle Khayat, but I'm his daughter ... and ... Father is the one who always taught us to forgive." She was talking faster now. "Remember at school? Whenever we got mad at a classmate or a teacher, Father always said, 'Let it be. Forgive.' Do you hear that, Nageeb? He's the one who always taught us to forgive … Nageeb, please, don't tell me I can't go back …"

Silence.

"Nageeb? Answer me. Please, tell me what you said is not true."

"Noora, there were pictures. Proof …"

"Pictures?"

"You can't go back."

"But that's impossible! What do you mean, pictures?"

"You must promise me. You won't go back, you won't contact anyone."

"No. No!"

"You must promise to stay away. I believe Uncle Khayat is the only one who can protect us now …"

"*Protect?*" Noora said, looking at him blankly. She rose and walked to the balcony, staring out at the deep blue shades of the Red Sea.

"Uncle Khayat will welcome you," Nageeb said, following her. "Please, Noora, promise you won't call Father. Promise."

Noora continued to stare at the sea. Finally, she turned to her brother. "All right, Nageeb," she murmured, her eyes blank. "I promise."

Nageeb woke before dawn, anxious to call the first helicopter company open for business, so he could charter a chopper that would fly them to Alexandria. After leaving Noora with Uncle Khayat, he would need to rent a car and drive to Cairo. Somewhere on his way back to Cairo, he would have to stop at a public phone and call his father. He dreaded the thought of speaking to him again, but he could not raise any suspicion. He also dreaded the thought of returning to the hospital in Cairo. He wished he could stay with Noora and Uncle Khayat at his peaceful seaside villa.

CHAPTER 16
THE PEASANT GIRL

Young Gamelia came from a small village between Assiut and Menya, along the Nile River, an area known as Lower Egypt.

Her mother, Um Gamelia, had worked for the Fendil family for more than a decade. Um Gamelia had been a devoted and loyal maid, and probably Mrs. Fendil's favorite. She was bright and quick, and understood Mrs. Fendil's needs. She was also very personable. To reward her for her loyalty and hard work, Mrs. Yasmina Fendil allowed her maid to return home every three months. Um Gamelia spent two weeks with her aged mother, and her daughter, Gamelia. Bent Gamelia—daughter of Gamelia—was Um Gamelia's only child. Um Gamelia had lost her husband to another woman when her daughter was just a baby, and she never heard from him again, which suited her very well.

Bent Gamelia had been a happy child, carefree and comfortable in her home village, where she used to play along the banks of the Nile. She was surrounded by friends and neighbors, and had grown accustomed to being away from her mother for three months at a time. When she was not playing with other children and young teen girls, weaving baskets or selling fruits, she would lose herself in the picture books her mother sent her from Al-Balladi. She lived with her grandmother in a safe world of innocence and simplicity.

Until one night when she was thirteen years old.

She had gone to fill her clay water jug with cool river water, a chore she always did before sunset. This time, she was late. Engrossed in a wonderful new book of fairy tales her mother had mailed her all the way from Al-Balladi, she kept procrastinating until it was almost dark. It was late October, when the days grew shorter. Even so, Gamelia had never felt frightened alone in that part of the village. It was her world.

Returning from the river, he appeared like a tall shadow and said something in a foreign language—English, French, German, or maybe even Russian—she didn't know foreign languages enough to understand the difference.

He wore dark pants instead of the traditional *gallabeya,* and unzipped them in the middle. She thought he had some sort of a large knife when he pulled this big thing out of his trousers. She feared he would hit her. She wanted to run but he barred her way. He spoke to her in a gentle tone. With his other hand, he pulled out a candy bar with shiny wrapping from his pocket, while stroking what she realized was his member. She refused to take the candy, even though she knew it was the most expensive treat sold in the marketplace—a foreign chocolate bar with a crisp wafer in the middle. The water jug became heavy, slipped out of her hand, and fell on the muddy riverbank. When she tried to retrieve it, he grabbed her. She froze. She felt something hard poking against her stomach.

"*Hellwah, enti bente hellwah,*" he repeated in broken Arabic.

No one had ever told her she was pretty before. "Pretty girl," he repeated in a heavy accent, breathing nauseating smells on her—stale cigar smoke and alcohol.

For a moment, she thought she could run from him, and when she tried, he wrapped one strong arm around her waist tightly. Suddenly, her undergarment was down and his hand was probing between her legs. She struggled and managed to break away, but his hand grabbed her skirt and she fell on the grass close to the riverbank. He threw himself on top of her, one hand over her mouth and the other forcefully pulling up one of her legs. He thrust himself into her but finally he let go of his hand over her mouth.

The pain was so intense, she wanted to scream, but she was terrified he would strangle her. "Please don't kill me," she managed to mutter while he continuously whispered how beautiful she was.

"*Aiwa. Aiwa!* Yes. Yes!" he panted in Arabic.

"No, no!" she begged, and bit her knuckles until she tasted her own blood.

"*Hellwah,* pretty ... *Ahhh Aiii-wah* ..." he panted. " ... aaah so pretty ..."

She felt very wet suddenly—to her horror, she was sure he was urinating inside her. As she was about to scream as loud as she could, he held his hand to her mouth again.

Finally, he stopped moving but remained on top of her. He continued breathing hard close to her face, like the hot desert wind that sent odors from the livestock nearby. At last, he moved away from her. Slowly, he rose to his feet. While she tried to hold her breath for fear that if she moved he would kill her, she heard the creak of his metal zipper. He sighed deeply and groaned. Then he laughed. She saw his teeth shine under the first moonlight. He tossed the candy bar next to her. Her heart was pounding so hard, she thought it would burst out of her chest. She wanted to crawl away into a nearby bush, but she was in so much pain, she could not move. As she silently prayed to Allah that the man would spare her life, the tall figure slowly walked away, like an *afreet,* an evil spirit of the night, a dreaded ghost dragging his long shadow with him.

Stifling her sobs, Bent Gamelia managed to rise to her feet and wade into the river. Slowly, the pain inside her began to subside. Shuddering with horror and disgust, she scrubbed away the sticky substance he had left between her legs. But she felt that a part of him was still stuck to her. She waded deeper and scrubbed herself until she was sure there was no trace of his stench or any other thing that came from that devil man.

As she waded back to the riverbank, she wiped her face with her drenched skirt. Shivering from shock and the cool night air, she searched for her undergarment. It was too dark, and she panicked at the thought that if anyone found her panties in the morning, they would surely suspect what happened. Perhaps she would even be blamed and accused of selling her body to a stranger for a candy bar. Searching frantically, she finally found the garment near the bushes and stuffed it in her skirt pocket. As soon as she had the chance, she would burn it. She found the candy bar with the shiny wrapping on the ground and as she tossed it in the river, she stumbled on her jug by the muddy soil. She filled it quickly, her eyes darting fearfully, worried that the devil man might return. Silently, barely able to walk, she finally made her way home.

Later, when her grandmother asked to help her lift the water jug for cooking, Gamelia noticed it had a chip on the top rim. Under the kerosene lamp, she could see a deep hairline crack running from top to bottom of the jug.

"Let me do this. It's too heavy," Gamelia said, and she kicked the jug, pretending it was an accident. The jug split in half.

"Forgive me," Bent Gamelia said to her grandmother. "But we still have water in the other jug I filled this morning. I will bring you clean water from the well first thing tomorrow morning."

"*Ma'alesh*, it is fine," her sweet grandmother said.

In the traditional way, the peasant woman believed accidents happened for good reason.

That water was contaminated by the devil. How could Bent Gamelia ever drink from the Nile River again? She promised herself she would never reveal her horrible secret.

A month later, when Um Gamelia returned home on her regular vacation, Gamelia begged her mother to let her work for the Fendils. The timing was perfect. Um Gamelia wanted to stay in the village to take care of her mother, who was growing weaker.

Mrs. Yasmina Fendil had readily agreed to have the young Gamelia work for her and her family.

At the train station, Um Gamelia had instructed her daughter on what was expected of her, and reminded her several times that everyone wanted to work for the Fendils because they were good and generous.

"They will treat you like an employee and not like an animal. They will give you a nice, clean room with a television. And they will even let you use the phone to call me!"

Bent Gamelia was well aware of the Fendils' generosity.

"Always be at their service," her mother tried to whisper in her ear as her daughter was switching the old luggage from one hand to another.

"Yes, Mother."

As she rushed to climb on board the crowded train, her mother stopped her, looked into her eyes, and said, "Listen, Gamelia. Do anything they ask. Even if they ask you to *lick their behind*, you *lick it!* I know it sounds strange, but you know what I mean."

"Yes, Mother," Gamelia nodded. Quickly, she kissed her mother and boarded the train, promising her mother she would be a good servant, follow her mother's instructions—and secretly promising herself that she would never return to that village again.

Zaffeera was fourteen years old when young Gamelia went to work for the Fendil family. Soon, Zaffeera recognized there was something different about the girl with the pink *medawara*—a chiffon scarf that she always wore wrapped around her short, frizzy hair. The little maid was painfully shy and shamefaced. Zaffeera noticed whenever she accompanied her on a shopping trip, or any family outing, Gamelia showed an irrational fear at the sight of men who wore trousers instead of the traditional *gallabeya*. Every time Zaffeera questioned her about her fear, the maid blushed, looked away, but never gave a response. Zaffeera judged by her servant's face—and body language—that it was possible someone had been at her. No one else guessed such a thing, but Zaffeera was convinced and began to have fantasies about her maid being raped by a man in trousers, a thought that aroused her.

One night, Zaffeera was bathing in her bathroom, and as usual, the young Gamelia helped her with her bath. After Zaffeera was done, the girl routinely took her towels and soiled clothes out to the laundry room to wash them separately, because Zaffeera was allergic to regular detergent. That night, a few weeks after her fifteenth birthday, the routine changed. Zaffeera told her maid that she was exhausted from all the hard work at school and she needed a massage. She casually asked Gamelia to lick her "down there," so she could really relax until she could fall asleep.

Remembering her mother's instructions, which she took literally, Gamelia did what her mistress commanded. From that moment on, Gamelia became Zaffeera's very personal maid. No one ever knew or even suspected what her "work" involved.

*****   *****   *****

Zaffeera was playing the role of devoted daughter. She spent two days standing at her mother's bedside. She comforted her, changed the compresses on her forehead, and spoke to her softly.

"Ummy, ya ummy anah."

She read to her mother passages from the Koran, and old poems she knew her mother liked.

Magda remained in Mrs. Fendil's room throughout the time that Yasmina refused to leave her bed. Standing next to the door like a prison guard, Magda seemed like a robot and never sat. Every four hours, she injected Mrs. Fendil with a sedative.

On three occasions, Farid Fendil came to visit his wife. He held her hand. He whispered her name several times, but she refused to even acknowledge his presence.

The last time he paid a visit to his wife, Farid spoke to her in a low voice, while Zaffeera stood respectfully several steps behind him. Her eyes cast to the floor and her face covered by a sheer black veil, she heard her father say: "Allah blessed us with other children. We must not neglect them. It is our duty to take care of them so they do not go astray. They need *you,* Yasmina. They need you."

Yasmina Fendil had finally opened her eyes and turned from her pillow. She looked straight up at her husband and said, "Tell that woman who looks like a man never to touch me again."

That evening, Magda left Yasmina's room, never to be seen in the Fendil household again.

CHAPTER 17
LEAVING EILAT

As the first rays of sun shimmered across the Red Sea, illuminating Eilat's beaches into a sparkling gold, Nageeb sat leaning against the front door of the condominium, clutching the phone in one hand and leafing through a phone book. Finding what he had been searching for, he dialed the number of a private limousine service that apparently catered to dignitaries and celebrities.

"You didn't have to go to all this trouble, Nageeb," Noora told him once they were in the rented limousine. Under her large black dress, he was glad she wore the yellow dress he had encouraged her to buy. It would take two or three weeks for her bruises to disappear. *She would heal faster in Alexandria,* he thought.

He hated the idea of having to stop before boarding the chartered helicopter, but he could not forget his good friend. He asked the chauffeur to take them to a delicatessen. He chose a large basket of international delicacies, and a magnum-sized Dom Perignon for Shlomo and his wife.

An endless hour later, through heavy traffic, the dark-tinted, bulletproof limousine arrived near the airport and pulled to a helipad where their chartered flight awaited. In no time, and to Nageeb's relief, the three-passenger chopper, piloted by a young Israeli, lifted off. Destination: Alexandria, Egypt.

The weather was clear and bright—a perfect day for a beautiful flight.

Noora's heart lifted with hope as she watched the beautiful resort city of Eilat below at the edge of the shimmering turquoise sea. Soon she would be in Alexandria with Uncle Khayat, where she would swim in the sunny aquamarine Mediterranean. She would miss Nageeb, but Cairo was not that far after all.

He promised he would visit her every chance he could, and in turn, she promised him that she would not contact their father and she would stay with Uncle Khayat. She should never break that promise. *Time would wash away the pain,* she reminded herself. And then, perhaps in time, her father would ... Well, perhaps, he would forgive her. *Would he?* She would think about that later.

In the meantime, Uncle Khayat would help her decide what was the right thing to do. Obviously, she would not be able to return to school in London. But how would she explain her absence?

Nageeb, who was in the front seat next to the pilot, turned and gave her a broad smile.

"Don't you think we should call Uncle Khayat and announce our arrival?" Noora asked.

He couldn't hear her with the roar of the helicopter.

She mimed a telephone receiver. "Uncle Khayat! We should call him!"

The sun was bright and she squinted. Nageeb bent over, searching for something in his bag. He handed her a pair of sunglasses and nodded. "Okay! When we land! Okay?"

"O-kay!" she yelled back and put on the sunglasses. But she didn't need them for long.

Less than thirty minutes into the flight, the sky turned dark. A sudden *Khamseen,* a powerful sandstorm, appeared from the distance and quickly engulfed them.

The pilot tried to gain altitude and rise above the storm. Nageeb gave Noora a nod that all would be okay. But before Noora could pray, the chopper tossed around, shuddered, and shook violently. Rapidly, it plunged down, down.

The sandstorm finally subsided, and the desert sun blazed above her. She felt as if her feet were on fire. Her left leg was scorched, and the hot sun intensified the burning pain. She had a difficult time opening her eyes, but when she finally did, she saw Nageeb a few feet away, flat on his back, unmoving, one leg bent in a bizarre position.

"Nageeb! NAGEEB!" She tried to crawl to him, but she couldn't move. The sand stuck to her flesh like burning powder.

Pulling herself on her elbows, she cried out in pain, but she had to reach Nageeb, and when she finally did, she saw his chest was covered in blood.

"No! God, NO!" She pressed her hand on his chest to stop the bleeding. One deep cut ran alongside his right eye, oozing blood. He was struggling to breathe.

"I'll get help." She looked around. She began to crawl away, trying to figure out where they were. Not far from them, the pilot lay still, his body nearly covered by sand, next to the twisted and demolished helicopter.

"Run, Noora," Nageeb whispered.

"NO!" She tried to get back closer to him, and she felt a stabbing pain on her left leg.

"Run, Noora," he murmured.

"I'll never leave you, Nageeb! I beg of you … please … Oh God, somebody help!" She pulled herself closer to her brother.

"Promise …" He whispered as she attempted to clear the sand away from his bloody lips.

"Okay," she cried, wrapping her arms around his body. "Nageeb … please … I love you!"

"*Run. Runnnn!*" his voice echoed in her brain.

"I'll never leave you." Somehow, against her wishes, she began to crawl away while Nageeb's commanding voice rang in her ears with the sounds of the wind.

"Nooorrraaahhh," the wind called, no longer Nageeb.

A thunderous explosion sent a hail of flying debris from the helicopter. Something heavy slammed into her head.

*****   *****   *****

Noora heard a loud bleating and wished the annoying sound would go away. Her eyes were crusted shut. She finally managed to open one eye slightly, then the other. Her vision slowly came into focus.

An eyeball with a horizontal pupil stared down at her. *A goat?*

When her vision cleared a little more, she saw tall, dark bodies looming above her. Their billowy black robes flapped loudly like flags in the wind, their shadows shielding her from the scorching sun. But her body felt like it was on fire, and she was in great pain. If those looming shadows had been angels, they would have worn white and they would have had wings.

She must have gone to hell. She fainted into darkness.

CHAPTER 18
THE SEDUCTION

Zaffeera sat on an embroidered wing chair, staring at the intricate weave of her father's carpet. She wore the traditional black dress. A black veil covered her face—the same style Mrs. Jacqueline Kennedy had worn during President John F. Kennedy's funeral. She had carefully planned her attire for its mourning effect. She cast a quick glance at Michel, who was not far from her, a low copper table between them. He seemed lost in his thoughts. His face was pale, but he still looked so good. What was he thinking about? Sex? He probably desperately needed it. She would give him all that his heart desired. He needed sun too. They would surely honeymoon by the sea in a luxurious resort. *He had been in "gray Paree" too long—the winters of Paris could be too cold, and cloudy,* she thought. Her entire body tingled, just looking at him. *Michel, darling, you were meant for moi.*

She stole a quick glance at her father, who was on the opposite side of their huge living room, beyond other antique furnishings and Turkish tapestry. Sitting across from each other on ornate Louis XIV furniture, next to the fireplace, the two men seemed engrossed in a serious conversation. She would give almost anything to hear what was being said. Did Michel have any idea what the topic of their conversation was? She hoped they were discussing their children's future. Together.

Michel had no idea why he had to sit and keep Zaffeera company while his father met with Mr. Fendil. Unless they told him where Noora was buried, he saw no reason to be in that house.

It was not fair to make Noora's sister sit across from him. She hardly ever spoke to him, and surely she had to feel as awkward as he did.

He glanced across the living room at the men. Earlier, his father said Mr. Fendil hinted that, *"Since Noora passed away, it would be advisable to marry her sister."* Wasn't that what they did in biblical times? When the wife died, the husband married the sister. Mr. Fendil must have gone temporarily insane. He noticed he had become much more religious and wore the traditional garb. But who was he to judge a man who had lost his daughter? Well, he too had lost someone he loved so much. His chest tightened and he could barely breathe. He wanted to run outside and cry, but that would surely belittle and embarrass his father. He picked a walnut from the huge bowl on the cocktail table that separated him from Noora's sister, and with hidden strength he didn't realize he had, he cracked it with his bare hands. He glanced again at his father. *This senseless meeting had to end. Now.*

He rose from his chair, ready to head over to his father, when a houseboy appeared and began serving the men tea from a tall silver carafe. Michel sat back down, but on the edge of his seat, ready to jump up the instant the houseboy left.

Noora's sister whispered something.

"What?"

"I know where she is buried."

Michel pulled his chair closer and leaned across the copper table. "Excuse me?"

"I know where she is buried," Zaffeera repeated slightly louder behind her veil. She threw a quick glance at her father. He was staring blankly at his demitasse and shaking his head.

"I can take you there."

"When?" Michel searched for Zaffeera's eyes through her veil.

"Tomorrow. After lunch."

"Anytime will be fine ..."

"Shh ..." She lifted her veil. "Don't let our fathers know."

"Why?"

"Tradition … Women here are always buried in the desert. In unmarked graves. I'm sorry … you didn't know?"

"No. I … I am sorry. I did not know …"

Tossing restlessly in his king-size bed, Michel's father glanced at the clock on the nightstand. Past midnight. He had to be up by five in the morning. If he did not get enough sleep, he would be too tired to think clearly tomorrow. He and Mr. Fendil had scheduled meetings back-to-back, starting early in the morning, with bankers, attorneys, and executives to go over plans for the new hotel in Egypt. Switching on his bedside lamp, he sat up, grabbed his attaché case next to the bed, and began to sort out some folders. But his mind kept drifting back to his son. Surely Michel was upset with him. How could he blame him? He had made a selfish decision. He had nearly forced—and perhaps even bribed—his son to marry Noora's sister. Just because he was doing business with the girl's father was no reason for him to talk Michel into marrying someone he didn't really know, let alone love.

"They need some time. They're still young," he had said earlier when he met with Mr. Fendil. In truth, he didn't have the nerve to tell him that just that morning, Michel had a change of heart and even denied agreeing to propose to Noora's sister.

But Mr. Fendil had apparently made up his mind. "They will have plenty of time after they are married," he said. Mr. Fendil had not been the same since his daughter's fatal accident. When Michel's father offered his condolences, Farid changed the subject. Everyone had his way of dealing with death and grief. He understood the pain of losing a loved one as well as anyone. He was still grieving the loss of his beautiful wife, who had passed away many years before. But nothing could be more devastating than a parent losing his child. He heard a light knock on his bedroom door.

"Father?"

He was surprised to hear Michel's voice. "Come in, come in," Mr. Amir said, propping himself up against a couple of pillows. He hoped his son was not upset with him.

"I didn't want to disturb you," Michel said, standing at the door. He tentatively ventured into the room, still dressed in his suit. His tie in his hand, he appeared weary.

"You never disturb me."

"I saw the light under the door; I thought it would be all right ..."

"I was just getting ready for tomorrow's meetings."

"Yes. Congratulations," Michel said.

"We are only in the very beginning stages. There is so much to do."

"I'd love to see the architectural design."

"As a matter of fact, we are getting the revised ones tomorrow, as well as the scale model. I can't wait to show them ..."

"I'm looking forward to it ..." Michel cleared his throat. "By the way ... regarding tomorrow ..."

"Sit down," Michel's father said, pointing to a nearby chair.

"No, that's all right. I'm on my way to bed. But I was wondering ... perhaps ... I could meet with Noora's sister? Maybe after lunch ... for a lemonade?"

The moment his son left his room, Mr. Amir wanted to phone Mr. Fendil and give him the good news: It was time for courtship. But it was late. Instead, he picked up the phone and dialed the direct extension to his private chauffeur.

Shortly after the Morning Prayer and his first meeting with Mr. Amir, Farid Fendil marched to his office in the high-tech building where he occupied most of the penthouse floor. One of his world-renowned architects had somehow dropped the ball during Farid's absence, claiming he never received the fax Farid had sent him with all the important changes.

Cement for the two-story waterfall feature had been poured into concrete blocks; tons of imported coral rocks had already been intricately fitted into it, according to the original plans—which had been changed! The oversight was going to cost an easy quarter of a million dollars to undo and restructure. The grand opening of the office building was scheduled in a few days. *We'll never make it now!* Farid had thought he was done with that project, and he needed to focus on the new 300-suite hotel and spa at Sharm El Sheikh.

As he searched frantically through a pile of file folders on his huge black granite desk, he realized, to his horror, that he had never dictated the urgent changes. He had written them down on legal-sized paper, something he often did before dictating to one of his male secretaries. Such an oversight had never happened before. He was furious. How could he possibly have made such a costly error?

It was *her* fault—the one who shamed him. The one who made him lose control enough to lose it all. The one whose name he had to erase forever! He pounded a fist on his desk. He could not afford such an oversight. It wasn't the money. It was the fact that he could lose face in front of the investors and his employees. He decided from now on, it was imperative to do nothing else but immerse himself in business.

Early that morning, he received a message from Mr. Amir—his son had finally come to his senses. He scribbled a note to liquidate the London flat and dictate a letter to the LLC. As far as he was concerned, Zaffeera was finished with college. Education was not for women. The wise sheik had warned him. He should have listened.

He was, however, pleased to learn, from the written reports brought to his desk by the sheik himself, that Zaffeera had remained close to her mother's bedside, doting on her tirelessly around the clock. His wife Yasmina should recover soon, and he would have her so busy planning a huge wedding, she would have to forget about ... about everything else. He pressed his intercom and shouted for his secretary.

The Lincoln Town Car, driven by Monsieur Amir's longtime chauffeur, made its way through the outskirts of Al-Balladi. Zaffeera sat close to the door, and Michel was on the opposite side, to her right. Her acrylic nails were painted with a gentle coral-pink polish. The fragrant cream on her hands had a sparkling glow. She rested her right hand on her knee for Michel's view. If he were not going to look at her, he would surely rest his eyes on her hands. Noora's hands were certainly not as lovely as Zaffeera's, because she never bothered with manicures and she had dry, ugly cuticles.

On her index finger, Zaffeera wore a delicate ring with tiny diamonds and a small, round turquoise stone in the middle. Michel was still staring out the window. Finally, his weary eyes turned, he blinked a few rapid times, looked down, and rested his gaze on Zaffeera's hand. He looked away again.

"Excuse me, please?" Zaffeera asked.

"Yes?" Michel finally looked at her.

"Ask your chauffeur if he would not mind to make one more right, then stop at the end of the street. At the corner."

Once they arrived at the place Zaffeera designated, she opened her own door and began walking down the sidewalk without saying a word.

"Wait for us here," Michel told the driver. He ran after Zaffeera.

She entered an outdoor bazaar on a long, narrow street. She stopped at a kiosk where fresh-cut flowers were on display. A bouquet of peach-colored roses and baby's breath were handed to her. Zaffeera paid for the flowers.

When Michel realized Zaffeera was buying flowers, he wished he had thought of doing that. Peach-colored roses had been Noora's favorite. Zaffeera walked up to him, her black veil over her face, and handed him the flowers. She turned away, walked out of the bazaar, and crossed the street. He followed. Zaffeera finally stopped, turned, and slowly ventured closer to him.

"*Min faddlak,*" she whispered. "May I ask permission for an important favor?"

"Yes, anything," Michel answered numbly. Holding the flowers to his chest, he bent closer to Zaffeera so he could hear what she had to say.

"Please don't let anyone know where I am about to take you."

"You have my word."

"Not even your father, in all due respect. No one, please."

"You have my word of honor, Miss Fendil."

There was a long silence before she finally spoke. "Where she is, only women can visit." She lowered her eyes some more.

It was getting harder for Michel to control his tears. He had to turn away because he didn't want her to see him cry.

"I am terribly sorry; are you all right?"

"Yes," he answered, his voice breaking. He wanted to run through the empty field and break free from the pain in his chest that imprisoned him. He hadn't cried when his mother died, except when he was alone. Even then, he had hidden his tears under his blankets when he was certain no one could see him. Now he felt out of control.

*****   *****   *****

Zaffeera had the burning desire to touch him. Finally, she was alone with him. She could smell his mild, lemon-scented aftershave. She admired the form of his strong, V-shaped back. *Patience, my dear.*

Just touch *him. Noora's gone. He's mine.*

"Maybe we should come back another day?" she asked in a gentle voice.

"No, I'll be fine." He sniffled, unable to find a handkerchief. His eyes were red and wet. "I'm sorry. Men aren't supposed to cry," he chuckled nervously.

"The man who allows himself to cry has a good, kind soul. If a man does not cry, it means his heart is cold," she murmured, looking at the sky, thinking, *Get over it!*

She walked on, a few feet ahead, while he searched in his breast pocket.

Zaffeera faced a rocky hill in the distance. She made imaginary calculations, observed the jagged formation of a rocky hill lining the horizon. The sun shone brilliantly just above the tip of the mountain. She called out to Michel. He immediately ran to her. The scent of his cologne made her dizzy, and her body tingled all over. She had to control her feelings.

She pointed to the ground. There was an elevation, and the sun shone on it.

"There must have been much wind last night," she said in a quivering voice. She stared at the ground, closed her eyes, and cupped her hand to her forehead. She walked away from Michel. A gust of wind picked up. "You see, the sand must have swept away the mound of her grave last night. Like Allah swept away her life that night."

She did not run, and she did not sob like they did in the movies. She did not make a scene—or any dramatic motions. Instead, she slowly walked away from Michel, just a few feet, and then she let her knees drop on the sand. Her back to him, she remained motionless.

Behind her, she caught a quick glance at Michel as he kneeled by the mound that looked like a gravesite and placed the bouquet of roses on top.

"My sister. She was my sister!" she sobbed. "We played together. We slept together, we laughed together. She taught me every ... everything. How can I go on without her ..." She wept into her hands, slowly curling herself into a fetal position.

Finally, she felt him close. He held her in his arms. Together, they cried.

He cried for Noora.

She cried for joy.

CHAPTER 19
THE BEDOUINS

Noora lay in agony. Her legs burned as if they were on fire, but she could see no flames. Whenever she tried to stir, pain ripped through her chest and left shoulder.

She was lying on a bed. Or was it on the floor? She was sure she was not in a hospital. She felt around with her fingers. The mattress was like a large sandbag.

Dark shadows loomed around her. Someone was chanting nearby. Earlier, she heard a familiar song. Someone was putting cold compresses on her legs.

A powerful aroma of incense made her drowsy, and the excruciating pain began to ease. She thought she heard a goat. She drifted off to sleep.

When she awoke, a brilliant shaft of sunlight cut diagonally in front of her. She watched as thousands of minuscule specks of dust danced inside the luminous shaft—like sparkling stars. A dark figure, followed by a long shadow, passed through the light beam. A couple of flies buzzed by Noora's nose. Someone shooed them away. She managed to turn her achy head to her left and glanced up. A boy with glowing bronze skin wearing a white *gallabeya* stood above her, staring down with large dark eyes. He smiled.

Who were these people?

"My name is Dweezoul," the boy said, sitting on the floor by her bedside. "It is a pleasure and a privilege." He spoke with a soft voice, in

Arabic, but with a different accent, almost singsong. He crossed his legs and turned his attention to a small black box he was holding. He looked back down at Noora and smiled, as he held the box to his ear. *Was that a transistor radio?*

Behind the boy, Noora saw an ancient woman standing with her back to them. Covered in black from head to toe, the woman chanted in a low, soothing voice and seemed busy mixing something.

"She is my adopted great-great-great-grandmother," the boy explained. "She possesses many gifts. She will make you well again."

Gifts? Noora wondered.

"From the Source," he said. "Naturally."

"Why didn't you let me die?" she whispered. The boy didn't answer. She wasn't sure if she spoke loudly enough. She did not have sufficient strength to repeat herself.

The woman shuffled over to Noora's side, lifted her head a bit, and helped her drink a lukewarm, fragrant tea, sweetened with something that tasted like clover honey. The boy helped raise Noora so she could drink more easily. She sipped the fruity tea from a thick earthenware cup. It soothed her burning throat.

She was anxious to get up and walk, but her body felt like lead, and her eyelids were even heavier. She wanted to ask about Nageeb. She was too drowsy to turn her head to the two of them, and she couldn't lift herself, not even an inch. Her right arm was bandaged. Her left hand was being gently lifted. At least she could move her fingers. The old woman smiled down at her. She had only one tooth.

She stroked Noora's wrist. In her singsong voice, she said something to the boy about a line on her wrist that was like a bracelet.

I'm not wearing a bracelet, Noora thought. Maybe they meant her wristwatch?

"She is one from the light, all right," Noora heard the woman whisper. "She must keep her physical body for many more years. That is her contract in this life. It is her destiny."

Noora feared she would fall asleep at any moment. She needed to stay awake and hear what they were saying. She opened her eyes again, but everything appeared blurry.

"Are you listening to me?" the old woman asked the boy. "Or are you still playing with that music box?"

"I'm listening," he whispered. "What about this line that looks like a bracelet?"

"Well. Hmmm. Ah ... yes."

Noora wished she could pull her hand away.

"She doesn't want us to bother her more than necessary."

"The tea will sedate her. Let me read this. I see ... It is an indication and an explanation why she was given an extra thirty years of life, above the expected lifespan."

"You have that bracelet too, *Ummy*."

"This is true, the reason I am still in the physical, talking to you," the old woman chuckled.

"What else do you see, Um Faheema?"

"Her soul contracted to take on great challenges on this earth, in this life. Says it right here," she said, tracing Noora's palm. "It is *maktoub*. You can see the lines ..."

"But she is suffering."

"It is not for us to question."

Noora wanted to hear what else they had to say about her, but her eyelids grew heavier ...

When Noora awoke, all was ink-black. Her eyes were wide open, but she couldn't see a thing. She brought a hand to her chest. She was clothed in a very soft material. Her right arm was still tightly bandaged. The pains she had felt in her chest and left shoulder were more tolerable. She touched the material that covered her. It felt silky and light to the touch, like a comforter.

Was she still on that sand-filled bed? She could not tell. Her mouth was dry as cotton. She tried to inch her way out of that bed, but as she moved, the pain of her shoulder returned, excruciating now. *Wasn't anyone around?* It smelled moist. Like ... wet earth? There was complete silence. The old woman was not there chanting or humming a tune. Noora had difficulty breathing. Where was she? In a cave? *Or a grave?* No, NO! Panic-stricken, she yelled, "HELP!"

No answer.

"My God! Oh my God. SOMEBODY HELP ME!" Noora sobbed and began breathing faster and faster. They must have put her in a coffin!

She managed to rise a bit and tried to get out of that bed, but her feet were too heavy and her legs were bandaged.

They thought she had died. They must have buried her.

"ALLAH, YA ALLAH!" Noora shrieked louder. "HELP! Dear God, forgive me, somebody. AAAAGH." Soon she would run out of air. Soon she would suffocate.

There was a tiny speck of light in the distance. Slowly it grew brighter. A shadow loomed above her. Noora screamed louder yet.

"Little dear, do not fear us."

Noora recognized the old woman's voice. But she couldn't stop yelling. "GET ME OUT OF HERE! Please, oh God!"

A flicker of light followed, growing brighter, and the silhouette of the old woman took shape. She was holding a lantern. Another light behind her glowed, then another. Noora realized she was in the same bed as before, but she could not stop wheezing and screaming. She let herself fall back on the bed, crying from pain—her shoulder, her chest, her entire body.

At least there was light.

Brightly lit lanterns were all around her now, held up by women in black, surrounding her bed. They looked eerie. She was relieved when she recognized the boy who ventured closer to her bedside. She had stopped screaming, but her heart was hammering.

"We are your friends," the boy said.

"Forgive me. I thought you ... Oh, I ... I hurt so much. Thank you. Oh, thank you for coming to my rescue."

More women appeared, young and old, murmuring comforting words.

"Thank you ... please ... I don't mean to sound ungrateful ... I just ... can't bear all this pain."

"Ointment. Compresses! More tea ... my tea potion," the old woman urged. "And bring us more lanterns!"

Noora was helped up to drink. The tea was soothingly warm, sweet, and tasty.

*****   *****   *****

I must have fallen asleep, Noora thought after opening her sticky eyes. The pain in her shoulder was bearable now, but she had to try and stay awake, and not fall asleep again. A faint light streamed through one of the little windows nearby.

She was in the same mud hut with round windows, covered by colorful drapes that appeared to be hand-woven. A few brightly lit lanterns were hung around the perimeter of the hut, even though she could see that soon the sun would brighten a new day.

Everyone was gone except for the old woman, who was sitting on a mat, her profile to Noora. She was hunched over a low wooden stool, humming a song. Noora watched her as she squeezed juice out of a variety of fruits, while mixing some kind of a potion in a large black kettle over a small fire, where steam was rising. The old woman picked up a carved copper ladle and poured some of the concoction into a small earthenware bowl. With little effort, but not much considering her age, the woman rose to her feet and wobbled over to Noora's side.

"I'm so sorry," Noora said.

"Why?"

"For waking you in the middle of the night ... for disturbing everyone."

"Your presence is our gift," the woman said. "Take a little sip of tea and tell me if it is sweet enough."

Noora tried to lift herself up. "I'm not hurting as much. Thank you."

"I know," the old woman grinned. She brought the cup to Noora's mouth.

"It's very good," Noora said, after the first sip. "I love apricots."

"The Source brought the doves that brought the seeds, and we now grow the tastiest apricots and the juiciest *mish-mish*," she said. "We were gifted with many, many trees that bless us with many fruits." Her voice was old and raspy, yet somehow musical.

"Very good indeed, thank you ... What else is in the tea?"

"Special healing herbs and honey, with dwarf-tree tangerine peels and lemon juice. Slowly cooked. I added orange blossom and essence of almonds ... fermented, of course, and well, a recipe I learned from the Source. Our boy Dweezoul will be here soon."

Dweezoul. He had introduced himself. She had tried to remember his name. He had a kind, soft-sounding voice.

"I see you like his energy."

"Yes."

"He is making more pillows for you. His pillows feel like resting on clouds, don't they?"

"Yes."

"He has many gifts."

Gifts? The boy had said the same thing about the old woman. "Why didn't you let me die with my brother? Is ... he still out there?"

"*Ya habibti anah,* their true selves returned to the Homeland. And the air police came to find the bodies of your brother and the pilot. They were returned to their earth fathers," the old woman explained. "And how could we leave you there on the sand? Not after I read what was *maktoub* in the palm of your hand."

"I'm sorry. So sorry," she cried, with another fit of tears. "I don't understand ... What do you mean ... *written* in the palm of my hand?"

"The energies around your aura were muddled, so I read your palm," she said, smiling. "And with the assistance of the Source, I found out who you are."

Noora didn't know who she was anymore—or why she had been put in such a horrible predicament.

"You are a child of the light who wants to live," she said, widening her eyes brightly.

My brother Nageeb wanted to live! Noora wished to say. *And the pilot. They did not deserve to die.* Instead, she asked, "Who are you?"

"I am known as a lady of knowledge. *Alashan Anah n'efham.* Because I understand. Beyond the eyes, where the deep soul lies," the old woman said. "I earned my name, Um Faheema, Mother of Understanding. But in the beginning, things were different. Many decades ago, the people of other desert villages thought of me as a sorceress. And I was stoned."

Stoned? Noora was trying to digest what the old woman was telling her.

"I was only twelve years old. But old enough to be sentenced to stoning." She handed Noora a large, soft cotton handkerchief. "When they left my body for dead, someone picked me up and took me away. I don't know his name to this day. He took me to this village. Far from the place where I was born, where people were filled with anger and fear and had dark auras around them. That was almost eighty-nine years ago. Here, in this village, we are part of the light, at one with the Source of All That Is. It was in this village that I came upon the realization that I was born to heal. When you heal others, you love unconditionally. We all have a direct line. Alas, many choose to turn away. Until something powerful happens."

"Powerful?" *More like terrible,* Noora thought, wiping her tears.

Dweezoul bounced in. "They are very light," he grinned proudly. "And really soft." Holding two huge pillows, and wearing his long white *gallabeya,* he looked like an angel with a billowy white cloud on each arm.

"They will feel like you are floating on feathers. Allow me." He eased one pillow behind Noora's back and another under her bandaged right arm.

Indeed, her achy body felt better with the light support of the pillows.

"I'll make you another one. Smaller, for the back of your neck."

A tear fell from Noora's eye. Then another, and like a fountain, the tears flowed again and she couldn't stop. "Please forgive me ... It's just that ... you are so good to me ... I know you said I shouldn't say I am sorry, but I *feel* sorry. Sorry for myself. Sorry for putting you through all this trouble. I'm so sorry for what I have done."

The old woman glanced at the boy and nodded. He sat at the foot of her bed and crossed his legs while Um Faheema held Noora's hand for comfort.

"Nageeb, Nageeb ... Please, God, I beg of you, forgive me!" she cried into the night while Um Faheema and Dweezoul remained nearby, comforting her, at times holding her hands, gently pulling away wet hair strands from her face, drying her tears. They remained silent, allowing Noora her time to grieve.

Two days later, Noora woke up as the early morning sun shone through a small window in the mud hut. As she shifted her body for a more comfortable position, she realized she could now lift her arms a little more, and without pain. Um Faheema was again sitting on the floor by a low table, happily humming her familiar tune.

"Today you are feeling better," she said, without looking at Noora.

"Yes. I am. What date is it today?"

"April 13 on the calendar," she said. "For us, it is a day of celebration!"

"What are you celebrating?"

"You."

After a breakfast of mixed fruit compote, *ae'egga,* a fluffly little omelette with herbs and goat cheese, apricot juice, and a little cup of hot tea, Noora fell asleep again, a gentle, restful morning nap. When she opened her eyes, she found a group of older women, their heads wrapped in black veils, some with tattoos on their faces, sitting cross-legged around her bed, rocking themselves, softly humming prayers.

"Angel with sea-color eyes is awake. She is not used to seeing women like us," Um Faheema whispered, shooing them away.

But Noora wasn't frightened of them anymore. They all seemed gentle and kind.

"You told me who you are, but who are they? And where are we?"

"We are all Bedouins of an old tribe named *Bayt Nabbi Jebbelia.* We are many days away from the next oasis," Um Faheema explained. "Time is of no essence here, except to remind us when it is time to learn and when it is time to end our journey on this planet. We know time from the movement of the stars ... the change of seasons ... Even in the desert, we have our seasons, hmm?" she said, smiling.

CHAPTER 20
YASMINA FENDIL'S DREAM

More than a week went by before the helicopter wreckage was found in the desert. The authorities had informed Yasmina's husband that their son had perished along with the pilot.

There were no survivors.

"Don't cry for me, Mother," Nageeb's voice echoed in Yasmina's dream. He had appeared like a vision—vivid. He was handsome. She could almost touch him. "I am happy. I have accomplished what I came to do. I will always be with you, walk with you ... walk with Noora, too."

Walk with Noora? What did he mean?

Why, oh why did this have to happen? Not one of her children but two.

Yasmina had never seen Noora's body. They had told her she was in the burial site out in the barren desert, "where Sultana-Marietta was laid to rest." That sheik and his men who believed they owned the rights of women never knew her mother. Sultana-Marietta could never "rest," and her body was merely remains. She had heard the voice of her mother time and again. "Don't go searching in the desert, *ya benti,* daughter of mine. While my spirit soars, Noora is walking the land."

Nageeb had given her just about the same message. *What did that mean?*

After the dreadful news of Nageeb's accident, she had stayed awake most of the night. In the early morning, as dawn neared, just as the muezzin was heard chanting the Morning Prayer that echoed from the minaret through the town, *"Allah Akbar..."* Yasmina Fendil heard a gentle knock.

"Go away," she begged in a weak voice.

The door opened slowly. It was Zaffeera, dressed in a traditional long black dress.

She looked tired, pitiful, and frail. "I love you, mother of mine," Zaffeera said as she walked a few steps to her mother, looking at the floor. She broke down crying. "Allah blessed you with other children who ... who need you. They need you to care for them. They need you now more than ever, *ya Ummy*."

Yasmina Fendil rose from her bed and hugged her daughter.

Zaffeera was right. Indeed, since Noora's death, she had neglected her other children.

"I am proud of you," she said to Zaffeera. "Proud of your good reasoning and of your strength."

Yasmina sent Abdo to tell her husband that she intended to go with him and see Nageeb's body as soon as they flew him back to the Al-Balladi airport. If Farid had to go with the sheik and those men who always hovered around him, Yasmina would have Abdo drive her. She would not allow those men to prevent her from seeing her own son. Her dream—her vision of Nageeb—had given her a sense of strength, but she wasn't sure how she would react to seeing her son's body.

When she arrived at the airport, Abdo was told to stay in the car. He was not a member of the Fendil family. Yasmina stood a step behind her husband. She did not collapse. She did not shout or pound at her chest or rail at the Almighty for robbing her of her beloved son. Instead, she held herself straight, ignoring the disapproving murmurs and stares of the sheik and his men.

They had apparently cleaned Nageeb's lifeless face. There was no mark on it except for a slight cut by the side of his right eye.

He looked like a prince. Instead of grief, she experienced a prolonged moment of inner harmony and warmth, such as she had never thought possible. Words ringing like a melody from some celestial plane penetrated straight to her heart: *"To the Almighty we belong, and to Him we return."*

After viewing Nageeb, Yasmina saw that it was her husband who needed her help. Remembering Nageeb's words, Yasmina firmly took hold of her husband's arm, just as he was about to collapse, and led him back to the car. Together, they rode home.

Later, Farid sat alone in his quarters and mourned his son. Yasmina knew men cried silently in their hearts, more for the loss of a son than the loss of a daughter.

During the next few days, Yasmina went to care for her little girl, Shamsah. With Zaffeera's support, they spent hours helping Shamsah to accept the fact that her brother and sister had returned to heaven.

One night, Yasmina went to Kettayef's room to read to him, something she had not done in a long time. Her boy looked into her eyes. Articulating each word, still with a certain degree of effort, he said: "Mother, Nageeb ... said I must ... speak ... now."

When Yasmina heard her young son's voice for the first time, she grabbed him, cried, and kissed him all over his head. "Kettayef! You can speak!" She screamed and wailed as her cries of joy echoed through the corridors, announcing to everyone that a miracle, an act of God had just occurred.

From that moment on, the Fendil family decided it was time to put their misfortunes behind them. They were going to care for the other children God had given them, and Yasmina knew it was time to appreciate them—every moment of every day, and give thanks to the grace of Allah, because like Zaffeera—who had been strong for them all—they were also in good health.

Yasmina Fendil had even thought perhaps it was time to spend private moments with her husband. No one could ever replace the children God took away. But she was still young enough to conceive. She could bear another son. Perhaps one more daughter as beautiful as Noora, if that were possible. It was too soon to bring up the subject, and she felt embarrassed to discuss her feelings with her husband, who was too busy with his business—and his grief.

But then, another unexpected event occurred—something extraordinary that only Allah could explain—which helped Yasmina close the heavy doors of sorrow: Michel Amir honored the Fendil family by asking Zaffeera for her hand in marriage.

CHAPTER 21
OASIS MIRAGE

Several weeks had passed since the helicopter crash, and Noora was able to lift herself up in bed—but she still felt dizzy, unless she moved very slowly.

She started eating more solid foods: fresh-baked pita bread with goat cheese, mixed with cut-up tomatoes and sprinkled with dried fragrant herbs, luscious cookies and date cakes. Slowly, as she began to regain her strength, she took small steps around the bed at first, and later with Dweezoul's help, she walked around inside the hut.

One morning, Dweezoul walked in and took Noora by the hand. This time, he guided her outside. She was unsteady and a bit frightened. The sun shone so brightly, she couldn't see. She wanted to crawl back into her sand bed, but Dweezoul encouraged her to hold on to his arm and continue. "You can do it, Noora, you can!"

Dweezoul stood patiently with her, and waited as her eyes slowly adjusted to the bright daylight. Rows of mud huts, baked by the sun to a pale peach, began to focus into her view as she walked slowly farther and farther from Um Faheema's main hut at the top of a small hill. Other huts in the village were smaller and surrounded by pink-and-white miniature picket fences, overflowing with flowers—mostly pink and purple bougainvilleas. There were apricot trees, orange trees here and there, short and tall date palms, shading her way. Noora looked around in wonderment.

Such a lush oasis in the middle of the desert?

Women, young and old, dressed in black, came out of their homes, some holding babies, others passing by balancing a water jug on their head, waving at her. Everyone was smiling, greeting her as she continued down the palm-shaded path. Children scampered around, laughing and cheering, and even Saloush came to her side, followed by other goats. The soft grass massaged her feet as she walked. She continued down a pathway bordered by a long row of dwarf citrus trees. Dweezoul remained by her side, holding her hand, guiding her along. Further down, beyond another row of small palms and brush, a vision of turquoise slowly took shape.

Tiny waves of clear, transparent water gently lapped on a powdery, golden shore. *A pond?* Noora blinked several times to focus. No, this was more like a lake. Surely it had to be a dream—or a mirage, for nothing could be so beautiful.

Slowly, she walked along the smooth, wet sand lining the water. She dipped her feet in. It was cold at first, but she quickly grew accustomed to the cool, refreshing liquid. She made her way down deeper in the water and gradually sank in. She was dreaming, and wished she could remain there—as long as possible. When she began to move her limbs—carefully at first—she felt rejuvenated. She was not worried that the water might be too deep. But when it reached her neck, she swam closer to shore and let herself float. She must have entered some kind of a blissful state; all her senses were renewed.

She wanted to remove the white cotton garb she wore so she could feel the cool water caress her entire body. Dweezoul had disappeared by then, and only the village women were standing at the edge, cooling their feet, happily watching her.

When Noora slowly waded to shore, the women followed. Forming a tight ring, they slipped off her dripping cheesecloth gown. Noora did not feel threatened by them, but she wondered what they were about to do to her. They were all smiling while they dried her off with large colorful woven cloths that were as absorbent as towels. Over her head, they slipped a black traditional robe similar to the ones they wore. One by one, they introduced themselves by name. The first one pointed to her chest and said her given name was Ouahdah. The second one pointed to herself and said, "Tneinah." The third one said, "Ashrah," and so on.

Noora wondered why their names sounded like consecutive numbers in Arabic.

They guided her to the shade of a short palm with a fat trunk. They all bowed as if she were some high priestess, then shuffled away, leaving her alone.

Dweezoul, Um Faheema, and a tall, thin woman appeared, carrying large copper platters of apricots, dates, and something that looked like teacakes, covered with powdered sugar. They placed the trays in front of her.

"This is our aunt Zeinab," Dweezoul said. "She can bake whatever it is you want, and later, if you like, she will be proud to show you the ovens that she built herself. With my help, too, of course."

Noora was speechless. The only thing she could mutter was, "*Shokran* ..."

"You are welcome," the tall woman mumbled humbly, "*Bent el Noor*."

Daughter of light? Why would she call me that?

"Her *aagwas* are the best. Like what you would expect to eat in the best bakeries in the world, or even in heaven," Dweezoul said.

Aunt Zeinab bowed her head, and following Um Faheema, she walked away.

Dweezoul flopped down across from Noora and wiggled himself into a comfortable position on the sand.

"I bet you think I am much older than I really am."

"How old are you? If I may ask?"

"I am eleven years, and you are welcome to ask anything you want," he said, his eyes resting on the tray of goodies. "How can you look at the *aagwas,* smell them so close, and not want to devour at least one?" He picked up the tray. "Please, try one."

Noora took one of the round teacakes and began to eat. "Mmm ... melts like butter."

"Indeed." He served himself one of the cakes. He popped the entire thing in his mouth. "Dee-licious," he said, his mouth stuffed. "You are sitting under the tree of energy," he remarked, puffing out some powdered sugar as he spoke.

The boy was so lively, Noora couldn't help but smile, watching him as he smacked his lips and licked his fingers. She noticed that when it came to sweets, Dweezoul acted like a typical kid. But there was something about his eyes. When he was quiet and looked straight at her, they seemed older, reflecting much wisdom.

"Eat, eat. Um Faheema's *mish-mish* are the sweetest."

She picked an apricot and passed its smooth surface across her cheek. She inhaled its sweet fragrance and took a small bite. Juice squirted down her chin. Indeed, she had never tasted apricots so sweet.

"You see? I told you," he said, smiling. "Rest your back on the tree. It will bring you peace and energy. Now you are not sick anymore," he announced. He looked up and squinted at the sun. "It is naptime." He rose to his feet. "Enjoy the sweets. Um Faheema will be back with more treats!" He shuffled off.

Noora looked around. All was quiet now. Not even the sound of children's laughter or even Saloush's bleating. Was everyone in the village napping? The gentle rustle of palm fronds above soothed her, and she was lulled to sleep.

CHAPTER 22
A MISSING PIECE OF THE PUZZLE

Farid Fendil sat in the darkness of his office. The gloomy atmosphere matched his mood.

"Father, it's Nageeb. Cairo had a strong earthquake, as you probably heard. The hospital suffered no damage. But they need me to help with casualties. I … I have to fly back to Cairo immediately …"

He detected the uneasy pause in his son's voice on the answering machine. *"I'll call you when … Inshallah, I'll call you soon, when the phone lines are not overloaded. Ma'al salaama…"*

He had heard the same announcement at least a dozen times—the last message received from Nageeb before the helicopter crash. He had made a copy of the tape and kept it on the top drawer of his desk. He pressed the instant replay and listened again to his son's last words.

There was something about Nageeb's message that did not feel right—something just didn't add up. The Tiffany clock on his desk chimed. Three in the morning already, and he was still filled with questions. Nageeb had seemed evasive. He was definitely hiding something … *What was he concealing?* Frustrated, Farid rose from his chair.

He took the service elevator down to his sixteen-car garage.

On yet another sleepless night, Abdo decided to go to the garage and polish Nageeb's car. Privately grieving over the loss of Nageeb and the fact that there were too many unanswered questions, he found that waxing and polishing the black Mercedes helped him deal with his sorrow and his troubled mind. Nageeb's car had been recovered in Aqaba, and luckily, when it was towed back to Al-Balladi, Farid was not home. Abdo had cleaned away Noora's bloodstains in the back seat, but there were a few stubborn ones on the carpet that he was unable to remove. The hubcaps, phone, and sound system had been stolen by vandals. They were all replaced, as per Mr. Fendil's orders. No one mentioned the stains to Abdo. If anyone said anything to Nageeb's father when they found the car, Abdo was not told.

Was there a chance that Noora survived? Was she still in Eilat? He had called the timeshare resort where Nageeb and Noora stayed. They had checked out. There was no report of a woman in the helicopter, he reminded himself yet again. There were two casualties, the authorities had said—the pilot and the passenger. So where was Noora?

Abdo was startled when his surrogate father appeared, approaching him. Dressed in his traditional *gallabeya,* Farid Fendil—who never came to his garage in the middle of the night—was now shuffling heavily in his leather house slippers. He put a heavy hand on Abdo's shoulder and shook him slightly. "It's yours," he murmured, blinking his eyes nervously. "Nageeb would have wanted it that way." He shuffled away, leaving Abdo dumbfounded. "I'll sign the papers over to you tomorrow," Farid added over his shoulder. He pulled out a handkerchief and blew his nose, sounding like a foghorn echoing through the huge garage. He headed away and stopped in front of the white Rolls-Royce convertible Corniche that gleamed under the recessed lighting. He turned to Abdo and asked, "Is the Corniche ready?"

"Yes, Abu Nageeb," Abdo replied, calling him Father of Nageeb out of habit. He was glad that the part for the air conditioner had finally arrived from England, and he had decided not to put off repairing the Rolls, even though Abu Fendil hardly ever drove that car.

After years of dealing with mechanics who were unable to keep his cars in perfect condition, Farid Fendil had awarded Abdo the job of full-time mechanic. He did not expect Abdo to wash and wax his cars as well—he had a special team to clean and detail his Al-Balladi cars, but Abdo enjoyed the process. He was meticulous about keeping Farid Fendil's cars all in perfect condition and waxed to a mirrored finish. The process of washing and waxing cars actually helped Abdo think. And at times, it helped him not to think.

Nervously folding the soft polishing cloth into a small square, Abdo watched Farid from the corner of his eye, as the weary man climbed into his Rolls-Royce. One of the garage doors clicked open, bringing a whiff of cool desert night air. The car made its regal way out of the garage and into the night. As the door slowly slid back down, Abdo wondered why Farid Fendil would want to give him Nageeb's car. He did not need it, even if it was worth a fortune. *Nothing seemed worth anything anymore,* Abdo thought bitterly. Besides, he had his own four-by-four Jeep, in addition to the twenty-year-old Mercedes 300 Diesel. With over a quarter of a million miles to its credit, the old Benz still handled just fine. He was thankful, however, not because of Abu Farid's generous gift, but for what was probably a gesture of gratitude.

But why did he decide to drive the Rolls at this time of the night, and in his house slippers? Where was he going at this hour? As much as it concerned him, Abdo knew it was none of his business. It was certainly not up to him to question Farid Fendil's outings. Perhaps torment over his son's death left him restless. Perhaps he was headed to the mosque to pray?

Farid stopped his car at the intersection of two major highways. The roads were dimly lit and there were no cars in sight. He pressed the lighted buttons of the tortoise-shelled, gold-trimmed mobile telephone receiver.

"Is this the magnificent Madame Medina?" For the first time in a long time, he found himself smiling.

"Yes, it is," the sleepy female voice answered.

"This is Farid Fendil," he said, making a sharp turn onto an unpaved highway and heading away from the mosque.

CHAPTER 23
LIFE IN THE DESERT

As the weeks and months elapsed, Noora was more at ease with her Bedouin friends. In the beginning, she had a difficult time understanding their dialect, even though many of their words and sentences were similar to the Arabic of Egypt. Now she could easily understand them.

Noora spent most of her days helping the women in their daily chores. They taught her how to care for the goats, sheep, and chickens. But under the blazing sun, Noora quickly tired. Um Faheema tried to give Noora easier chores, but Noora wanted to keep up with the rest of the women, who seemed tireless and efficient in their tasks. After the midday meal, Noora usually napped, as the children did. After their nap, they drank the cool apricot juice the women brought them. Noora looked forward to this time each day, when all the children gathered to sing songs and play games, always with Saloush tagging along.

In the late afternoon, Noora helped Um Faheema crush and put away the herbs that had dried in the sun.

Soon after sunset was their suppertime. They ate a simpler meal than the one at midday. They had goat cheese, omelettes and hard-boiled eggs, tomatoes, just-baked pita bread, and fruitcakes filled with sweetmeats. They drank aromatic sweet herbal teas, served in shiny silver vessels, which their ancestors had made centuries before. The children enjoyed foot-long lollipops made from molasses and sugar and ground almonds—probably the most succulent treats Noora had ever tasted.

Later in the evening, the women gathered outside and sat around an open fire while knitting intricately designed sweaters, scarves, and *tala'eyahs*, beanie-like hats. Made of fine sheep's wool, the garments kept them cool in the summer and warm in the cold desert winter. Patiently, the women had taught Noora how to knit. She found it soothing to sit in the late evenings, knitting while listening to their captivating tales and myths, many of extraterrestrials who had come to Earth eons before and helped build the wonders of the Earth, the huge statues and temples; some of those stories were filled with enchanting characters. The smaller children listened attentively until they could no longer keep their eyes open, and fell asleep all curled up, close to their mothers. The older ones sat out with the men and listened, wide-eyed, transported by the beautiful tales and poems of legends and lore passed on by their ancestors. Dweezoul had told Noora he loved all the stories told by his elders and none of them ever grew tired of hearing them.

After everyone retired back to their huts, the eldest of the tribe—who believed they were nearing the final destination of their life's journey—sat out alone and meditated. Others marveled at the celestial show of stars in the dark desert nights, while contentedly puffing on their water pipes.

On the first day of September, Dweezoul left on a caravan ride to another oasis across the desert with two other men he called his uncles.

"We're going to the *souq* and bring back cane sugar and molasses, wood planks, oil, grains," Dweezoul had told Noora. "Guess what else I will bring back! Batteries! Batteries for my radio!"

Noora worried and wondered how he and the two men who traveled with him could survive crossing the treacherous desert for many days and nights.

"They're used to it," Um Faheema said.

But they were still human, Noora thought. And she had heard about mountain lions and desert bandits who carried huge daggers and killed without mercy to steal their victims' camels and goods. But it was best to trust as the villagers did. No one knew exactly when they would return. And Um Faheema would only tell her to trust they would show up when it was the right time.

But Noora missed Dweezoul terribly and prayed daily for his safe return. The village was not the same without him—especially at night, when everyone was asleep, Dweezoul would venture away from the village, out to the high sand dunes. Noora accompanied him almost every time he went out there. They sat on his large hand-woven blanket at the top of a dune, and imagined they were gliding on what he called his "magic mat."

It was then that he turned his radio to its highest volume and rocked to the rhythm of "The Oldies-But-Goodies." The voice of Casey Kasem trailed in, all the way from the United States, broadcasting straight into Cairo and other cities in the North African region. Never mind that Dweezoul did not always understand the words the American DJ was saying. After two or three years of listening in, he began to get the gist of what was being said. Thanks to that little radio, Dweezoul was tuned in to the modern world of news, sports, international weather changes and current events.

But the people of Bayt Nabbi Jebbelia did not rely on the radio. They followed the moon, stars, and the direction of the wind, especially when it came to the weather in their region. Aside from their lagoon, where the sweet water oozed up from the bowels of the earth, the village was blessed with two wells that never ran dry.

Once or twice a year, Dweezoul told Noora, the village endured powerful sandstorms. Um Faheema could always tell the day and exact time a *Khamseen* would come sweeping through. "She is the only one in the village who knows before it comes, and we all prepare for shelter. The storms never come at the same time, but she can see them coming in her mind's eyes—and she is never wrong."

One month to the day after Dweezoul had left the village, shadows of a caravan were spotted on the horizon.

Noora was under a tent with the other women, preparing the children's evening meal, when one of the elders rose and pointed west. Slowly approaching from the distance, in front of the huge orange ball of sun that had dipped halfway down the horizon, the caravan came into view. Everyone in the village jumped at the sight.

Um Faheema wobbled down the path, holding a large silver carafe of cool apricot juice and strings of plumeria necklaces hanging down her arms, ready to receive the traveling trio who were returning with their camels and provisions.

"They're back! They're finally back!" Noora cried.

"Of course they are back," the old woman said with a happy grin.

There was so much rejoicing in the village, Noora realized indeed how much Dweezol and his two older companions had been missed by everyone.

"We didn't sell as many goods as I had hoped, so I could not buy as many batteries as I wanted for my radio, but certainly more than I had before!" Dweezoul said when Noora ran to the boy, lifted him up, and hugged him.

One night, after the storytelling, Dweezoul came bouncing into Um Faheema's hut. "Time to go dancing," he said, inviting Noora to another night of music and fun.

Noora joined Dweezoul on his "magic mat" and there, while listening to an American station, they lay on their backs and gazed at the brilliant show of stars.

"Some of the stars sparkle to the rhythm of the music, you notice that?" Dweezoul said. "Like a heartbeat. It's their way of communicating with us, telling us they are alive and well, and that they know we are in harmony with them."

On the radio, the Bee Gees began their song "Night Fever." Dweezoul slid down from the high sand dune and rocked to the upbeat rhythm.

When the song ended, he climbed back up to the top of the dune and fell breathless on his mat. "I like the Bee Gees, but I still prefer tearjerkers," he said. He stretched out his arms and watched the sky. "Life's good."

Noora found Dweezoul more entertaining than the show of stars, though they were indeed an incredible sight, especially when she spotted so many shooting stars. And to her surprise and delight, some of the brightest stars did pulsate to the rhythm of the music from the transistor radio.

"Dweezoul? What do you mean by tearjerkers?"

"That's what they used to call them in America. They were supposed to make you cry. For a few decades, music was good in the United States. I especially enjoy the 1950s songs," he said, turning on his side and facing Noora. "Now they have that rap music. It's all right ... but not as good in the musical sense, because who can dance to that? Unless you have many nervous tics," he laughed. "They think it's got rhythm but I think it lacks soul."

"How do you know so much?" she asked, pulling a warm blanket over herself.

"We have lived before. Some things our deep mind remembers. The earth is filled with treasures, as is the night sky. A feast for the eyes. Nourishment for the soul. It all began out there ..." Dweezoul said, seeming to lose himself in his own thoughts. "We come from there; we are made from those stars. If you watch them for a long time, they become part of you again. Part of your heart. And you are never alone."

After Dweezoul turned off his radio, he removed his batteries and secured them in his pocket—his nightly routine. "Good night," he said, and fell asleep almost immediately.

During the past several months, Noora had grown accustomed to sleeping under the stars. She wasn't sure about becoming a part of the stars, but she knew she had become a part of the Bedouins.

What about Uncle Khayat? How could she forget the promise she made to Nageeb? She must find a way to contact him. She could not believe time had gone by so quickly.

She snuggled close to Dweezoul and curled up under his large blanket. Usually Saloush leaned right next to her, keeping her warm; but that night, the goat stayed in the village with the children. Noora dozed off and on.

The air became too chilly for comfort. She decided to head back to the village. She knew Dweezoul would not mind. Um Faheema's warm hut, with its cozy fireplace and her own bed with the soft blanket the Bedouin women had woven for her seemed inviting.

She dropped her feet deep into the soft sand dune. Still warm from the day's heat, the sand massaged her legs. The stroll back to the village was illuminated by a brilliant half-moon. She watched the sparkling sky and thought of what Dweezoul said about the stars. Her mind drifted back to Uncle Khayat and his lovely villa by the sea. Alexandria was so far. She would have to cross the desert for many days.

She heard a hoarse cry and looked up. A black horse, with a tall dark rider, was galloping straight at her. The horse and rider stirred enormous clouds of sand, like a gusting sandstorm, stinging Noora's eyes. She could barely see.

She tried to run. Somehow, she couldn't. The ground seemed to hold her feet like heavy weights. The sand in her eyes burned horribly. Forcing herself to open her eyes, she saw the dark figure in a black cloak that flew behind him like huge wings of a devil. He raised his curved sword; the blade glinted in the moonlight. She was sure he was going to cut her in half with that terrible weapon. As she tried to run, the sand gave way beneath her feet and she sank with every step she attempted to take. And yet the horse was able to gallop with great ease, even grace. She yelled for Dweezoul. The village was close—why did it seem so far?

The black shadow on the horse had grabbed Noora, lifting her up like a rag doll. As he was about to take her away, Dweezoul was suddenly there, vaulting up on top of the man's saddle. The boy grabbed the assailant's throat and would not let go. The dark shadow was forced to drop Noora, and she fell to the sand. The devil on horseback threw Dweezoul, who went flying after her. The boy bounced up and ran to Noora. By that time, the Bedouin villagers were running to the rescue, holding torchlights and daggers.

With his black cloak billowing behind him, the assailant galloped into the night and disappeared in the darkness. His sword lay on the sand, glowing like a mirror, reflecting the moon's light.

Noora finally reached the village. Her heart raced so fast that the pain in her chest became unbearable, and she fainted.

She found herself in Um Faheema's hut, on the sand-filled bed. The Bedouin men had gathered inside. *What was the cause for this assault?* they all asked.

"He'll be back," someone announced.

"Desert raiders pass through all the villages," an old man said. "They come through here once a year but they never stop."

"They do not disturb us because they are afraid of our spiritual powers," Um Faheema said.

"Why did that stranger ride alone? They usually travel in pairs," another man said.

In the dim light of a candle, one of the wise elders analyzed the sharp blade of the aggressor. "He will return ... He will return to claim his weapon," he said, studying the sword's ornate hilt made of solid silver with brilliant jewels. It had intricate designs, and Arabic writing etched elaborately into it. "It has a message," the old Bedouin said. But he could not read it because most of the words had been worn away by time.

"He will return because he saw the girl ... *He'll be back for Noora!*"

Noora screamed.

"Noora!" Dweezoul called.

She opened her eyes and saw she was on Dweezoul's mat on top of the dune, trembling and drenched in perspiration.

"Wake up!"

Noora realized she had just experienced a nightmare. But it had felt so real. Relieved, she grabbed Dweezoul and crushed him in a hug.

The next morning, in Um Faheema's mud hut and in her cozy bed, Noora woke to find the wise old woman and Dweezoul standing by her bedside. Holding an earthenware cup of aromatic tea, Um Faheema smiled. Dweezoul held a plate of *aagwas*.

"I am sorry," she said, rising painfully from a stiff sleep. "I have brought you enough trouble."

"On the contrary, my child." Um Faheema smiled. "You have brought light to our village."

"Light. That's what my name was supposed to mean."

Um Faheema nodded.

"Looks to me like I have brought darkness. Every path I've crossed ..."

"No, *ya benti,*" Um Faheema said. She began to hum a lullaby while handing Noora the earthenware cup of hot tea. The familiar melody soothed Noora, bringing her calm, as the tea did when she began to savor it.

So very old, Um Faheema's dark bronze face was marked by lines of a century. To a stranger, she might seem ugly, perhaps even frightening, there in the shadows of her hut—yet, to Noora, Um Faheema was beautiful, with eyes filled with splendor.

"*Ya habibti,*" she said, "through the voice of your soul, you told us your story."

"What did I say? Forgive me, I must have been delirious."

"No, you revealed only what your heart wished us to know."

"All I know is my brother died because of me. How could I ever forgive myself?"

"Your brother left his body because he was done on this planet."

"What do you mean? He was going to be a doctor. Probably the best. He wanted to heal the sick and save lives!"

"He was pledged to save *your* life. This is why he never sought a young lady's hand in marriage."

What was Um Faheema telling her? Noora thought for a while. Indeed, Nageeb never had a girlfriend. At least none she was aware of. "But … it's because he was always so busy."

Um Faheema sat watching Noora. She turned to Dweezoul. "Go outside and listen to your music box, *ya ibni anah,*" she said.

"You don't like it when I listen to my radio. And I am well-informed about adult matters," he said, helping himself to one of the last cookies on a tray.

She picked up a large earthenware water jug. "We could use some water."

"You have plenty of water," Dweezoul said, his mouth full. "Look, I just brought you a jugful."

She picked up a large platter. "Go and ask Aunt Zeinab to give us more *aagwas*. Soon we won't have any left."

"Now that is more like it!" the boy said, grinning. He ran out with the platter and his radio.

Um Faheema sat at the foot of Noora's bed. Bringing the cloth of her long black dress around her legs, she said, "When you are in the flesh, there is always time for love. Nageeb was not different. But if he had made any contact, the young woman would have fallen in love with him. That was the energy your brother gave. He did not want to grieve another person when it came time for his passing into the higher dimension. His subconscious was aware of that, and that is why …" She stopped and watched a moth dance around the flame of her candle.

In her mind's eye, a vision appeared. Someone in Noora's life had mourned the loss of Nageeb, but only too briefly. It was clear to her now that the disappearance of Noora had brought rejoicing. There was even an evil spirit pursuing Noora. She was surprised that she had never before felt this dangerous energy around Noora. There was something hidden and mysterious hovering around the girl. Even now, after Um Faheema had made *Boukhour,* the powerful incense to ward off evil spirits, there was still something she could not quite understand. She shuddered.

"What is it?" Noora asked. "Are you feeling cold?"

The old woman quickly dug under the collar of her garb. "No, wait. This ... you must wear it. It will protect you," she said, displaying a blue bead strung on a copper chain. She brought Noora's head closer to her and whispered a silent prayer and put the copper chain around Noora's neck.

Um Faheema knew that Noora was not mentally prepared to accept, or even understand, evil deeds caused by someone as close to her as her own flesh and blood. It was up to Noora to make this complicated discovery, and only when she would be ready. She closed her eyes in thought and prayer for the safety of Noora.

"There is much learning and healing to be done first," Um Faheema murmured. She opened her eyes and looked straight into Noora's.

"When it will be time for you to wear a Western dress, where the necklace will show, then put another piece of jewelry that will be more suitable for the dress. But you must *always* keep this close to you, maybe under your pillow, and at night, try to remember to put it back around your neck when you sleep. It will help ward off evil spirits. *Be'eed min hinnah*, may they always remain away from us. But this piece I am giving you is also to remind you of courage. With courage, you can conquer all. Do you understand?"

Courage? Conquer all? "Thank you very much," Noora said, staring at the blue bead. "I will always cherish it."

Dweezoul returned with a large platter full of *aagwas*.

"Did I give you enough time for girl talk?" he said with a wink.

"Afreet, enta!" Um Faheema said, picking herself up, not without a degree of effort. She wobbled her way to Dweezoul and tousled his hair. "Little devil, you are!"

Noora did not believe a blue stone could chase away evil spirits. She never really believed in good-luck charms. She thought the whole idea was silly superstition. A talisman was something similar to the feather in the Disney movie *Dumbo* that made the young elephant believe he could fly. She was glad Um Faheema did not give her something that had once been alive, like a rabbit's foot. How could killing an innocent creature and keeping a part of its body bring luck? If anything, it should bring *misfortune*. She thought of Zaffeera, who always carried a rabbit's foot on her keychain.

That night, in the hut, after supper and story time, Noora picked up her blanket, ready to join Dweezoul where the high sand dunes undulated and formed gentle peaks. She could clearly hear Casey Kasem from Dweezoul's radio.

Um Faheema was brewing yet another fragrant concoction. But this time, she was not humming a tune, she was seriously mumbling.

"Is something the matter, Um Faheema?"

The old woman turned. She motioned for Noora to sit on the rug next to her. She cleared her throat.

"Your phantom of the night came on a horse in your dream?"

"Yes," Noora said, bringing her blanket and sitting close to the woman.

"Horses don't come through this part of the desert. We're too far from other villages. And their hooves would sink too deep. Sand's too hot. Travelers never come through here except on camels, unless you're watching a movie, hmm?"

How did the woman know about movies?

Um Faheema rose. Spreading her arms out wide and looming above Noora, she said, "Your dream was a message that you must continue on your journey."

My journey? Noora bit her lip and put a hand to her scar by her eye. How could she leave the people who had become her family? Now that she was finally strong enough to help with the village chores, she had to leave? She could plant seeds, harvest, feed and care for the children. The young ones depended on Noora's nightly story time. She also learned how to make pita bread, and even knit—from shawls to blankets to little booties for the newborns. She had even assisted the village midwife in two childbirths. It was not right to leave now. But then she thought of Nageeb's urging, and the promise she made to him the last time she saw him. A strong shiver unconsciously shook her entire body. She hugged her blanket.

***** ***** *****

The first time Noora rode a camel was on a short visit to the pyramids of Giza with her family. She was twelve years old. She had had a rider with her and someone on foot holding the reins. She had been so scared of the camel she and Zaffeera were riding that she could not wait to jump off. Zaffeera had been more courageous, but not Noora. Now she was holding her own (but just barely), sitting on a grouchy creature with a mind of its own and doing a great job convincing Noora *it* was in charge. Dweezoul and the man they called Uncle Omar rode ahead. Their camels were certainly more tractable.

Uncle Omar had once been a desert bandit, Dweezoul told Noora, and no one could feel more comfortable in the desert than when accompanied by Uncle Omar. But like Um Faheema, could he predict weather changes in the desert?

She turned to bid her beloved Bedouin family adieu. Far in the distance now, all the villagers she had grown to love stood, forming a long line of well-wishers. Tears welled in her eyes, but she had to be strong.

"He will always be with you ... in spirit," Um Faheema had said.

Being with the Bedouins in that part of the world had made her feel connected to Nageeb. Noora's chest ached as she thought of him. Um Faheema had also assured her that she would always be close, and she would send Noora soothing thoughts. Noora would miss her. She would miss the children and their melodious laughter. She would even miss Saloush, that silly, stubborn goat, who every morning licked her toes to announce that breakfast was ready.

As the camels plodded across the desert, Noora turned and gazed at the smooth domes of the golden clay huts sparkling beneath the sun. From a distance, the village seemed mystical, unreal. The glowing aquamarine pond reminded her of a precious jewel. She looked back until the village slowly dissolved into a haze on the horizon.

Um Faheema stood with the villagers as they waved a blessed *Ma'al Salaama*, a farewell to Noora—the one they named Light of the Desert.

Someday, Noora would return. Um Faheema would be waiting for her. By then, she herself would have taken on a different form—a lighter one, in the higher plane of existence.

Noora soon learned that the Bedouins had remedies for virtually everything that might go wrong. Before venturing out into the desert, she had been instructed to rub her body with a pungent herbal ointment that would keep her cool during the hours when the desert's scorching heat reached as high as 126 degrees. Their camels were laden with all the necessary provisions. The large clay jugs they carried kept the water cool.

Aunt Zeinab had filled sacks with her baked specialties, including her luscious *aagwas*. Um Faheema had loaded the camels with fresh lemons stuck full of cloves, sacks of dates, and sun-dried fruits.

High upon a rocky mountain now, Noora, Dweezoul, and Omar faced an endless sea of golden sand—an awesome universe spread out before them. As they descended into the desert, Noora's camel suddenly picked up speed and launched into his turf, like an animal that had been set free. From that moment on, to her own surprise, Noora no longer feared the animal she had named Camelot. Camelot was certainly in harmony in his own element, and soon became as docile as a friendly horse.

Static drowned out Casey Kasem's station on Dweezoul's transistor radio, but they could hear modern Middle Eastern music. Noora, Camelot, and her traveling companions made the three-and-a-half-day journey through the desert to the swinging rhythm of lively Arabic songs.

CHAPTER 24
THE SOUQ

The sun rose high above a citadel that loomed over the dilapidated buildings of an ancient marketplace.

Noora had not seen such a dense and noisy crowd since she had visited a souq in the outskirts of Cairo when she was a child. Here, it seemed as if she had stepped back into the Middle Ages. Hundreds of men, women, and children milled about in traditional dress on one long, narrow street.

The air was heavy with smoke from grilled lamb, incense, and spices. Noora realized that at Um Faheema's Bedouin village, she never saw or smelled the roasting of lamb—or any meat. The animals of Um Faheema's oasis were their pets and gave milk, but were not eaten.

Omar and Dweezoul had left their camels in a campsite where vendors were setting up their tents for the cold nights.

At the edge of the souq's narrow strip, Dweezoul helped Omar put up their kiosk. Noora watched with amazement as her companions rapidly unrolled bolts of canvas, nailed wooden sticks, spread out colorful tabletops, and in no time assembled a large kiosk with an extending tent. They laid out their finest goat cheese, the diversity of Aunt Zeinab's luscious baked goods, Um Faheema's essential oils in a variety of tiny ornate alabaster jars—their best sellers; plus aromatic dried herbs in small, hand-woven pouches.

Noora's traditional long garb and veil were far too hot in the midday sun. Um Faheema had advised her to wear the complete attire so she would not attract attention. But Noora had to drop her veil so she could at least breathe.

Dweezoul prepared a tall glass of cool lemonade and added a few drops of Um Faheema's condensed oil of chrysanthemum, other herbal nutrients, and stevia to sweeten the drink. He dipped in mint leaves and offered it to Noora, who gladly found a spot in the shade.

"Thousands of years ago," Dweezoul said, seemingly unaffected by the heat, "The Source of All offered seeds to a hawk, who flew above our land and dropped them for our ancestors to plant. The herbs grew fast, and our people grew healthy and disease-free."

"May Allah bless you," she said, savoring the cool drink. "This is really refreshing."

Covered in black from head to toe, except for their eyes, women of childbearing age lined up in front of Omar and Dweezoul's kiosk. Some were carrying their babies wearing bright bonnets with strings of blue beads sewn into them. Noora wished she could hold one of them. By now, Noora thought, she could have had one of her own. She and Michel ... *Don't think about that, Noora. You must help your friends and not be a burden to anyone anymore.*

"Here, Noora! Inhale this," Dweezoul said cheerfully.

She buried her nose in one of the sachets and breathed in a lungful. "Thank you, Dweezoul, thank you and may Allah ..."

"Most welcome! You know, if kids from the ghett-ohs inhaled these, they would never need drugs," Dweezoul sang. He gave a customer a colorfully wrapped treat for her toddler.

"Where did you learn that? From your radio?" Noora said, helping Omar with the long line of customers.

"I learned from Elvis Presley's song, 'In-the-ghett-oh!' Come, my sister. Unfortunately, I see it is time for us to leave," he said, fetching her bag.

"But Omar needs our help. We can't leave him with all these customers."

"Omar loves the chaos. Don't worry about him. He's cool."

Omar turned to Noora and bowed low. Noora bowed back while shaking his hand. "Thank you for all you have done for me. May Allah keep you and bless you."

He smiled. His teeth were brilliantly white, like the turban that appeared permanently planted on his head. In Arabic, he murmured, "May we see your face in happiness, daughter of light."

Noora spotted a tear escaping from the corner of his eye. "May God bring light upon you," she replied in kind.

As Noora and Dweezoul headed for the train station, Noora was amazed.

"This is more like a city, not an oasis."

"Most oases are vast. Except for ours. We are from a different energy."

"Different energy?"

"Yes. I know a good shortcut to the train station. It's through another souq. Come, let's hurry."

The Bedouin women had washed and repaired the yellow dress Noora had bought in Eilat. They managed to salvage it somehow, patching or reweaving the torn material and removing the blood stains. It looked practically new again. Noora was embarrassed because she did not remember if she thanked the women for their hard work. Noora would be able to wear the dress in Alexandria—in honor of Nageeb.

You see, Nageeb, I am keeping my promise. I am going to be with Uncle Khayat.

As they walked in the scorching heat, Noora unconsciously removed her headdress and pulled up her sleeves. "What happened to that cool cream we used in the desert?"

"It's in your bag." Dweezoul pulled out a small earthenware jar with a cork. "You must remember to always keep your face covered up to your nose and your arms must be covered too. All the way down to your fingers."

"Yes, my brother," she teased in Arabic, rolling her eyes.

"Hey, I didn't make the rules. If it were up to me, I'd have all the girls in a bikini! Like in France. And America!" He switched to English and mimicked a perfect American accent. "It was an *itsy-bitsy, teenee-weenee polka-dot beekeenee...*" he sang, guiding her away from the passing crowd of men who were giving Noora a disapproving stare.

"This man-made tradition, and I doubt it is really a tradition, is ridiculous. It's too hot," Noora complained as they stood on a narrow street with rows of medieval structures. She rolled down her sleeves. "We could get so much more done if we didn't have to cover up our arms."

That's when Noora realized it had become such a part of herself, she had forgotten. "Oh my goodness."

"What?"

"My watch!"

"Yes?"

"Dweezoul!" she grabbed him by the shoulders and shook him. "I can't believe I didn't even think of it."

"Better not think of it. Whatever I think you're thinking."

"I can sell it!"

"Oh no!" He pounded his forehead. "I was afraid that's what I thought you said … and no, no, you can't …"

"Don't you understand what this means?"

"It means forget it."

"I can buy my own train ticket. And you can buy all the batteries you want. Don't you see?"

"I don't see it, and I don't even want to think it."

"Why?"

"It's gold. It belongs to you. It's of a personal matter."

"It is impersonal if you can't buy anything with it, and if I can sell it, we can even buy all the sugar from here to Hawaii," Noora said, stroking the solid-gold watchband under her sleeve.

Dweezoul didn't want to hear any more about the watch. He rushed ahead of her. "Please, Dweezoul. Please?"

"Souq El Kanto is less dense than Souq El Mogharba, where we left Uncle Omar, and it's not far from the train station," Dweezoul said.

Noora realized a richer clientele frequented the area. Men in turbans rode donkeys, and there were even a few Volkswagens, Toyota trucks, and noisy little motor scooters.

"First a medieval marketplace. Now it looks like we have entered into the late twentieth century," Noora said. "I feel dizzy from it all."

"You're dizzy because you are hungry. And I am famished."

"Yes, indeed, we must eat something. Something healthy." With the thought of selling her watch, Noora insisted on going to the café across the street.

They took the table in a corner, and a waiter served their favorite Arabic food: spicy brown fava beans, strained the way Egyptian mothers prepared them for their children because of the high content of iron. They sprinkled their bowls of *fool medammes* with bits of hard-boiled eggs, and like kids, they dunked warm pita bread into the hot brown soup and licked their fingers with great delight.

Dweezoul finished his plate before Noora and set it aside. "It's not right," he said.

"I want to sell the watch. Do it for me, please."

He pulled out something from his pocket. "Do me this favor, Noora. When you get to Alexandria, let go of this in the middle of the sea."

"The middle of the sea?"

"Yes."

Noora stared at the pebble he placed before her. How would she get to the middle of any sea?

"Every time you think of something sad, remember it is not so bad, but the wonder of the journey. When you return, and this you will do," he said, placing the pebble in the palm of her hand, "this pebble will drift back to shore, and never again will you face a closed door."

"You lost me, Dweezoul. Did you just recite some lyrics from a song?" She studied the pebble. What was so special about an ordinary little polished stone?

"No, it's from our friends of the spirit world."

"I'm guessing you don't mean the radio."

"A different radio. One that doesn't need batteries," he grinned. "It's getting late," Dweezoul said, standing. "Let's give the good man a *bakshish*, and hurry. The stores will soon close."

Noora dropped the little pebble in her pocket while Dweezoul placed a generous tip on the table for the waiter.

They had spent half the money Dweezoul and Omar had brought with them, on Noora's one-way train ticket and on the restaurant. When he leafed through the information booklet about the train ride to Alexandria, Dweezoul found out the trip would take sixteen hours because it made many stops. Trains to Alexandria left only once a day, and always at noontime.

Noora realized they would need a lot more money than just the train fare. As the brilliant ball of orange sank beneath the horizon, so did her morale.

"We'll have to return to Omar," Dweezoul said. "No worries, he has made quite a bit by now from all the goods he sold today."

"That money is for your village, Dweezoul."

"Actually, we at the village get by very well without money," Dweezoul said. He flipped on his radio. Sarah Vaughn's "Broken Hearted Melody" played. He raised the volume and held the radio to his ear. "I love that song. Don't worry. Remember, things happen for good reason. They always do."

Noora agreed this time, because she would have time to sell her watch and pay back Omar and Dweezoul.

The campsite was teeming with lively Arabic music and the scent of open-air cooking. "*Ahlan. Ahlan wasahlan!*" Omar said, putting his hands together in prayer, then clapping.

"We missed the train," Noora explained.

"Things happen for good reason," Omar said. He turned away, smiling, and kneeled to resume his cooking. He served the two of them lentil soup, rice, cooked vegetables, and a delicious chopped salad. "*Hamdallah,* you were meant to share this meal with me," Omar said, pouring aromatic mint and honey tea in demitasses.

After their supper, Noora rested her head on a pillow that still carried the scent of Um Faheema's herbs. Under a dimly lit lantern, she studied her watch, read and re-read the tiny inscription on the back.

My Arusah
Happy 16th
Your Father Forever

Forever? Tears welled in her eyes.

She still was not clear about what happened or why. When she told her story to Um Faheema, the wise woman had appeased her fears and anxiety. But Um Faheema didn't encourage her to go back to her father.

Did that mean that she could not go back? Not yet or not ever? She reminded herself again of her promise to Nageeb—she would not get in touch with their family. She had to remain in exile and stay with Uncle Khayat. If she could only remember what happened in London. But what good would it do? She had been drinking and someone photographed her at a disco. Someone may have framed her—that man with the mustache? Still, it was her fault. She drank alcohol. She danced with strangers. She had shamed her father and everyone. The memory of the beating flashed through her body—he had hit her. He had *kicked* her. Tears flowed like a fountain now, and her stomach cramped. She pulled up her cover to her eyes. She couldn't let Dweezoul see her in this condition. She wanted to fall into a deep sleep. *Push away the feelings. The pain. Forget. Uncle Khayat will know what to do ...*

As the sky began to show its first light, the men rose with the raucous pre-dawn chorus of distant roosters. Noora woke to the inviting aroma of Turkish coffee. It appeared everyone was awake, hunched over the fire, sipping their demitasses and talking to each other. Arabs of all tribes must have passed through here for centuries, en route to distant shores. They seemed to know one another. *In an endlessly changing world,* Noora thought, *this land remained unchanged.*

Early in the morning, Noora and Dweezoul returned to the souq.

"Look at this modern little store. Looks like it's open." She pointed to a shop displaying a variety of modern jewelry.

"I was hoping you changed your mind."

"I've made up my mind, Dweezoul, I'm sorry."

Dweezoul pointed to a fruit cart across the street. "Okay. I'll wait for you over there."

A bell jingled as Noora entered through the opaque glass door protected by filigree ironwork. Like a whiff of cool air on a seashore, Noora felt immediately revived by the store's air conditioner—a nice refuge from the stifling heat outside. She hadn't imagined that modern amenity existed in this part of the world. But somehow and all too soon, Noora began to feel uneasy.

Behind a glass counter, the jeweler closed his display case against the wall and finally, he turned to face his only customer.

"Yes?" he asked in Arabic. He was not dressed like most men in the area. He wore black trousers and a short-sleeved white shirt.

Noora was pleased to notice a large sign in Arabic and in English stating that they buy and sell estate jewelry. "Hello, sir. I ... see that your store buys jewelry. I should like to sell my watch ..."

"You'll have to show it to me first," he interrupted, scrutinizing her with disdain, above his bifocals.

She reached beneath her sleeve and removed the watch from her wrist. But something wasn't right. She hesitated. The diamonds around her Rolex sparkled brilliantly beneath the store's recessed lighting, and Noora found herself unsure about letting go of the last thing that linked her to her father. Overcoming her doubt, she handed the jeweler her watch.

Pushing his glasses closer to his eyes, he checked the watch carefully for what seemed like an endless moment. Noora wished more customers were in the store. An unconscious shiver ran through her body.

"I'll have to go in the back and test if it's authentic," he finally said without looking at Noora.

"Never mind. I changed my mind ... You see, it was a gift."

"Oh, yes. And I'm King Farouk reincarnated, and they're giving me back my throne."

Noora was shocked. "I beg your pardon?"

"Do you have a receipt or proof of purchase?"

"Proof of purchase? It was a gift!"

"You stole it, didn't you?" he sneered, checking her out, from top to bottom with disgust. "You *stole* that watch!"

"I most certainly did not! My father bought it for me." She was suddenly unable to say another word. The mention of her father made her feel weak—and defenseless.

"I'm giving you a chance to leave right now. Or I'll call the police!"

"What?"

"You heard me."

"Please, give me back my watch."

"Out! Or I'll have you in jail." He put her watch in his pocket and moved around the counter toward her. "You know what they do to people like you?"

"That watch is mine."

His eyes flashed. "They cut off the hands that steal."

"It's mine!" The watch was rightfully hers. But she was starting to collapse inside. Her father gave her that watch. Since he didn't love her anymore, since he denounced her …

"There is no mercy for thieves. If you don't want to lose your hands, you'd better get on your feet."

Noora retreated as fast as she could and pulled the door open. The bell jingled wildly. Across the street, Noora spotted Dweezoul, who was busy enjoying an enormous mango, juice all over his face, licking all fingers. He didn't see her. While the store's bell continued to jingle, sounding more like an alarm, something snapped in her brain. Feeling more anger than fear, Noora stepped back inside.

"Get out! THIEF!"

"I am not leaving without my watch."

"I am calling the police."

"The serial number matches a famous jeweler in Switzerland, with my family's name!"

She was the one now moving closer to the storekeeper. He began retreating.

"Give me back my watch now!"

He ran behind the counter, lifted the phone, and began dialing furiously.

"Go ahead." Her eyes glared, turning icy. The jeweler saw their color and gasped.

"Who are you?" He dropped the receiver back in its cradle. He was about to press a red alarm button by the phone when the doorbell jingled again and Dweezoul bounced in.

"Queen Noor … ah …Your Highness! The limousine's waiting for you," he shouted.

While the jeweler was distracted by Dweezoul, Noora dug in his pocket and took out her watch.

She pulled away the veil that concealed her mouth. "Insulting a queen is a costly offense!"

She marched out, followed by Dweezoul. Once outside, they flew down the winding streets, mazes, and narrow alleyways. Finally, with hearts pounding, they stopped in a deserted alleyway and fell on each other, laughing.

"You should … have seen … oh, you should have seen … his face when you put your hand inside his pocket!"

Noora had not laughed so hard in a long time. It actually felt good. So good. Especially because she had stood up to that jeweler. She wouldn't allow herself to be a victim. Never again—this she had to promise herself.

Twenty minutes later, Noora and Dweezoul walked away from the train station. This time, they were serious.

"There is always a reason," Dweezoul said, holding Noora's bag.

"Yes, the reason is that it is my fault we missed the train."

"It is not your fault. In life, there is no coincidence, and also in life, there are no accidents."

"Well then, if this incident is no accident, perhaps you can sell my watch."

"Oh, you clever one. This incident is different. I mean, this *instance* is different. Ah, you're making me all confused, and I don't think I can sell your watch. I'm not good at that sort of thing."

"Maybe *you* would be more successful. They don't seem to have much respect for women around here."

"I'm still a kid in the eyes of man, and men here don't respect kids."

"Still easier than being a woman. Please try, Dweezoul, please."

Noora waited on the bench of a small square with a large fountain in the middle where women washed clothes. At the edge of the stone wall, women pounded their laundry, while children played nearby. However dirty the water was, Noora still wished she could jump in the fountain to cool off.

When Dweezoul finally returned, she barely recognized him. He wore a sultan's outfit, with a bright red fez, a tad too large for his head.

"You look so … handsome." She didn't have the heart to ask where he could possibly have found such an ancient Ottoman costume. He did look handsome, actually, as if he had jumped out of some exotic fairy tale novel. *But what about the watch?*

He guided her away from the crowd. In an alleyway, safe from dangerous eyes, he pulled out a wad of money.

"You sold it? You did!"

"You won't believe how much I got for it," he whispered, barely able to contain his pride. "The owner of the pawn shop even gave me this suit," Dweezoul said, modeling it for her. He spun around. "Free." He rearranged his fez, which tipped a bit too far down to one side.

"Fancy threads," she said, anxious to see how much he got for the watch. She looked down at the money and quickly counted it. "A ... thousand pounds?" she whispered, while her eyes drooped.

"Pretty good, even I didn't think I could. Wait a minute. You have changed your mind."

Silence.

"I knew you would regret it. I'll get it back, I will. I don't care about the 'fancy threads,'" Dweezoul said, removing his fez and his bright red jacket with golden fringes all around.

"No! No, Dweezoul, you are wonderful. We ... we can go back to that restaurant. And we can order all the food we want! Dessert, too. And you can buy batteries for a year. For *two* years! You can even get a cassette player! And earplugs. I mean ... earphones. For you. Earplugs for Um Faheema, and ... and you can listen to your music all night, as loud as you want! And tonight, we can stay in that nice little inn so that we can bathe and be close to the station." She was searching for all sorts of positive reasons why she was glad he sold it, because she did not have the heart to tell Dweezoul the watch he pawned for a thousand was worth more than twenty thousand pounds.

CHAPTER 25
JOURNEY TO ALEXANDRIA

At the edge of the expansive oasis, Dweezoul rushed along the tattered boardwalk of the Zaggah-zig railroad station, which was brimming with a colorful crowd of people and families en route to the city.

The train known as the *Masbout,* "punctual," earned its name by having always been on time for more than fifty years, Dweezoul told Noora.

Dust combined with the *Masbout's* fumes created a hazy film that reminded her of old-time sepia photographs she had seen in library books, and for a moment, she felt transported into a bygone era. The train had five cars with wooden banquettes for passengers who would soon rush to fill every seat. Security guards in dusty uniforms were everywhere. Noora could not help but wonder if the train would make it all the way to Alexandria. The ancient machine seemed more appropriate for a museum display.

The stench of incense, livestock, and body odor sickened her.

"As soon as you get your seat, open your bag. You'll find a small bottle of rose water with lavender," he said. He was still wearing his red ottoman jacket and fez. "Put a couple of drops on one of the herb sacks we gave you and inhale. After that," he said, with a wink, "even if someone puts camel poop in front of you, you won't smell it!"

He led Noora to the *Masbout's* third railroad car. She climbed the high steel steps. In a moment of hesitation, Noora turned to Dweezoul. She wasn't ready to let go of him. Suddenly, she felt unsure.

"Hurry, Noora. Get to a seat, or you'll have to stand for hours," he said, handing her the heavy bag.

It was too late. Too late to change her mind ...

Dweezoul yelled something else. She could barely hear him over the crowd that pushed into the car, searching to find empty seats. A security guard blew a whistle to restore order.

A conductor grabbed Noora's ticket and punched it. Someone tried to get ahead of her, but Noora managed to rush through the aisle of weathered old banquettes and found a window seat. She attempted to open the murky window for some air, but it was stuck. A woman came from behind and in a swift jerk, managed to open the window, then took a seat behind Noora in a banquette loaded with wooden cages full of chickens. Feathers were soon flying all around.

The station master blew his whistle. Another shrill sound echoed from the next car. Noora peered out the window, desperately searching for a last glimpse of Dweezoul. If she could just see him one more time ... But the *Masbout* jerked forward. She realized they had not exchanged addresses. Where would she write to Dweezoul? And Um Faheema! They certainly didn't have mail delivered in their village, except maybe she could have arranged for her letters to be delivered to the oasis where Uncle Omar sold his goods. Why didn't she think of such an important detail earlier? She bent out of the window as far as she could, searching for the boy, unable to control her tears, as a thick lump grew in her throat. Finally, she spotted his head. Springing up and down, he was waving his red fez.

The train coughed and spit out black smoke as it jerked forward. As Dweezoul diminished in the hazy crowd on the boardwalk—the vision of a little prince from long ago—slowly at first, and faster now, the *Masbout* picked up speed, screeching over rusted rails.

Dweezoul stood at the station and watched while the crowd around him began to dissipate. Amid a dense cloud of smoke, the *Masbout* shrank into the horizon, diminishing to the size of a toy. He remained there, still, until the train that carried his dear Noora slowly disappeared from view behind a thick gray and yellow dust. Looking at his fez now, Dweezoul slowly turned and made his way to the rear of the dilapidated railroad station. He held his fez to his heart and faced the hundred-year-old stone wall of the train station. Tears streamed down his cheeks, and he could not stop them. "I will miss you, *Bent el Noor,*" he murmured. She wanted to stay ... He wished she could remain with them, in their village, but they would not stand in the way of her fate. Like a bird with a broken wing, once healed, it must be set free and resume its destiny.

*****   *****   *****

A young woman with two small children and an infant at her breast sat on the banquette that faced Noora. They were all staring at her.

Noora forced a smile until she realized it was pointless. How could they see her mouth behind the veil?

The woman was very young—a child herself. Her little girl, perhaps five years old, continued to gaze at Noora. While chickens clucked behind her, and people sneezed and coughed, Noora looked out the window and thought of the timeless Bedouin village she had left, as if it had all been a dream. She touched her chain with the blue bead. It gave her a sense of hope and the knowledge that she was not alone. She had people who loved her. And soon, she would be reunited with her uncle. She watched as the villages of mud huts, sad and decrepit, flashed past the window—donkey carts filled with garbage; peasant women balancing earthenware water jugs on their heads; endless rows of date palms flew by. Blindfolded water buffalo turned around and around water wheels in a pattern, unchanged for more than two thousand years.

Noora's eyes began to sting. She had stared out the window too long. She felt dizzy and groggy as the train raced along, passing villages, townspeople, and animals, all rolled into one image like a fast-paced movie. She had to close her eyes.

She was startled awake by the weight of her head dropping toward her chest. For a moment, she forgot where she was. Her mind swirled with questions and confusion, and her body felt stiff.

Suddenly feeling fearful and alone, she clutched her bag. She remembered Dweezoul's words: "The watch that belonged on your wrist is now the money that belongs in your pocket," Dweezoul told her when she tried to give him half his share of the money and he had refused. When he wasn't paying attention, Noora managed to put the five hundred Egyptian pounds in the deep pocket of his *gallabeya*. It wasn't easy, because he had his bright red ottoman jacket over the robe.

The *gallabeya* pockets were a great invention that foiled pickpockets who found it difficult to pull valuables out.

Again, she wished Dweezoul could have accompanied her on her journey to Alexandria. She had become attached to him, and relied on him—and his wise words. But he belonged in his wonderful world and uncomplicated life.

What a sneaky little guy, she smiled, pulling from her bag the pita bread and falafel he had wrapped in handmade wax paper. She dug deeper and found the delicious goat cheese she had grown to love, plus the succulent dried apricots, the sweet dates, and so many almonds. Dweezoul even included a small pocketknife! She couldn't wait for him to find his own surprise. What would he say when he found the money she'd left for him? He would probably be upset. But it would certainly help. He will be able to buy more batteries and enjoy the music of his little radio for … maybe even up to two years, driving Um Faheema crazy! Thinking of her dear friends, her newfound family of the Bedouin village, made her smile and brought her a warm sense of joy. Before she knew it, the train had reached the fourth stop. She noticed here that the women boarding the train seemed more westernized in their appearance. Some even wore colorful dresses. Noora was finally able to remove her veil. Freedom. *What a wonderful feeling*, she thought, as she busied herself cutting the goat cheese in small pieces.

Three pairs of brown eyes bore down on her. She drank the cool water from her earthenware jug. As she swallowed, her eyes met the young mother's, who by now had also removed her veil. The woman quickly darted her gaze out the window.

Noora prepared another sandwich and extended it to the little girl.

The child immediately looked up at her mother, who refused Noora's generosity. The little boy, who was not more than four, grabbed Noora's offering, quickly stuffing in a large chunk way too big for his hungry little mouth. The mother gasped in shock at her son's bold behavior. She immediately removed the rest of the sandwich from his hand and returned it to Noora.

"Forgive my son; he did not mean to take your food," she said in Arabic.

The child held his hand to his mouth so he could finish chewing.

"Please, please, let him eat. I have plenty," Noora said, afraid the boy would swallow too quickly and choke.

"*Ummeee?*" the little girl looked up to her mother with pleading eyes.

It was obvious the children were hungry.

The woman nodded to her little girl, venturing a shy, grateful smile.

"Thank you..." the young mother said. She looked away for a moment. Noora saw she was fighting back tears.

In time, Noora and the young mother began to converse, while the children consumed Noora's sandwiches with great gusto.

As the night quickly fell, the train cars were barely lit—most of the light bulbs had burned out. While the passengers slept, Noora took advantage of the darkened railroad car and slipped on her yellow dress, beneath her Bedouin garb.

As the *Masbout* forged on through the starry night, Noora tore off pieces of her Bedouin dress to use as diapers for the young mother's baby.

By the time the train arrived in Alexandria in the early morning, Noora had learned all about her young traveling companion.

Her name was Yasmina. *Yasmina? Like my mother's name,* Noora thought, immediately feeling the need to cry. But she listened intently to the young woman's story so she would forget her own.

Two years younger than Noora, Yasmina was the only daughter of a woman whose husband had left her. When she was fifteen, Noora's traveling companion married the son of a doorman, who was a handsome eighteen-year-old Prince Charming. He promised Yasmina a house in the country, and once they were settled, he assured her that he would pay for her mother's train fare and she could live with them. The house in the country turned out to be a filthy cardboard hut, and Yasmina had to work twelve hours a day in the cotton fields. After the children were born, and with the demanding work in the fields, Yasmina was too tired to cook anything but the simplest meals. Her husband began to beat her. He took on another wife, a village girl with a fat dowry.

"He abandoned us," Yasmina said. With babes in arms, begging on the streets, she managed to scrape up enough money for train fare home to Alexandria.

Alexandria was more crowded than Noora remembered. There were cars everywhere, honking incessantly, driving daringly. At Noora's insistence, Yasmina and her children climbed into the chill of an air-conditioned taxicab.

Yasmina's mother lived thirty-five minutes from the train station, in a section called Camp Caesar.

"Less than thirty years ago, Camp Caesar was a beautiful, modern district, my mother told me."

"Yes," Noora sighed, "I know." Her grandfather had been involved in the architecture and planning of the once-beautiful apartment homes with large balconies and marble interiors. Now the buildings were old and shabby.

The taxi pulled up in front of a dilapidated stone building on the Rue Naucratis—one of the few streets, Noora noticed, that kept its French name after Gamal Abdel Nasser became president. Noora pressed paper bills in Yasmina's hand.

"Oh no, no. I cannot accept," Yasmina said, blushing.

"For the children. Please."

Yasmina looked at the money in shock and burst into tears. "I didn't know how I was going to survive without food. I knew I would be too weak to walk all the way to my mother's house, so far from the train station. My breasts were dry. I was scared to beg on the street. They beat me before with a stick because I wasn't covered enough for them, there in the village ... and ... I was afraid someone would take away my children. I prayed so hard. Allah must have heard me," she cried. "You came to our rescue." She looked up at Noora and stared deeply into her eyes. "You brought us *light*. Allah sent you to us. You must be an angel."

"No, God gave me the opportunity to help you. For this, I am grateful," Noora said, remembering Um Faheema's words when she herself had been destitute.

The children rolled down the taxi's window and peered out in awe at their grandmother's apartment building, so huge to their little eyes. An old woman appeared at the front door, slapped her cheeks with both hands, giving the traditional cry of joy. Her cries echoed throughout the overpopulated neighborhood, announcing that her daughter had returned.

Noora could no longer hold back her tears. Soon she would also be reunited with a loved one, her uncle Khayat.

As the taxi sped along the Corniche, Alexandria's seacoast road, Noora inhaled the *tarrawah*, Alexandria's incomparable aromatic salt air that came singing from the Mediterranean, caressing her face.

She closed her eyes and inhaled the savory smell of *dora*, grilled fresh corn, sold by vendors on the sidewalks facing the beach. She hesitated, but the aroma from her childhood made her weak with hunger. She asked the taxi driver to stop. The meter had already reached double the pounds she had expected to pay for taxi fare, and she was not even halfway to Uncle Khayat's villa. She paid the driver and added a *bakshish*, but was ready to apologize for not giving him a healthier tip, when he jumped out of his car and ran to open her door.

"*Shokran, shokran*," the driver nodded a few times gratefully, as if he did not expect a tip.

Waiting at the bus station on the seacoast road, Noora took that time to enjoy an ear of grilled sweet corn. She spotted a public phone booth across the street, but hesitated because she might miss the bus. Perhaps she could find her uncle's name in the phone book, she thought, when out in the distance, she spotted the bus heading her way.

When she climbed in the bus and inserted the required coins, she barely made it to a nearby empty banquette before the bus took off. Young students, not more than twelve or thirteen years old, in black-and-white uniforms, were clutching heavy school attaché cases. They sat giggling and telling each other secrets. They seemed happy and carefree. When they got off, Noora moved to a vacated seat by the window and watched the girls as they skipped down the street. They were probably going home, where parents were waiting for them, welcoming them with a warm meal. Soon, she would also be welcomed by a loving relative. *We are almost there, Noora. There is no need to envy anyone or worry anymore.* But her heart was beating hard and she felt anxious.

CHAPTER 26
PARIS

On the Rue De Castiglione, in a fashionable upper floor apartment of the Intercontinental Hotel, Michel woke to the annoying drumming of rain that echoed through his fireplace. Another rainy Parisian morning, he thought, staring morosely at the hundred-year-old ornate marble-and-porcelain mantelpiece.

Everybody loved Paris. Hundreds of books and poems and songs were written about the most romantic city in the world!

Michel loathed Paris.

Once, when he believed life was beautiful and he was immortal, he had wanted to know everything about Paris.

His romance with the city was now over. The weather was cold and damp during the fall and winter, when he attended L'Ecole Des Beaux Arts. Spring was too short, and summers were too hot. Paris was dirty, and some parts of it even stank like a sewer. Everyone around him smoked, polluting the air even more. Some of the waiters were rude, and people on the street rarely smiled. He preferred to stay in the darkness of his apartment.

He reached for a bottle of tranquilizers on the nightstand. Only six five-milligram pills left? The doctors never seemed to prescribe enough. He remembered the unopened bottle of wine on the mantle. If he washed ten milligrams down with wine, it would perhaps make his morning bearable. But his mind would be like gelatin during one of his most challenging classes.

"Il ne faut pas se laisser aller, Monsieur Amir, la vie continue," his professor had preached just the week before, when Michel was called in to the private office. One must not let oneself go? What did the professor know?

His teachers showed their disapproval, making it clear they had sympathized with him long enough. "Life goes on," they all said. *Does it?*

Missing Noora was a pain so deep, at times his chest felt as if it might cave in. Noora died before her life began. How could he explain that to anyone?

To comfort himself, he toyed with the idea of a suicide plan. He would go to several doctors and have them prescribe tranquilizers. He would swallow them all with a tall glass of whiskey. He didn't have to go through this pain. He would join Noora. If it weren't for his father, who had also lost the love of his life, his beautiful wife, Michel would not hesitate. But he could not hurt his father, whose only reason for existence was his son, his heir, and his hope for a brighter future.

He closed his eyes and imagined a villa by the sea, and Noora by his side. The *tarrawah,* the incomparable fragrant sea breeze of Alexandria beckoned. He remembered how they had danced on the terrace by the beach. He even remembered the music …

He had planned to surprise Noora and take her to Alexandria, for the first part of their month-long honeymoon. He had inquired about a summer cottage, not far from where she used to vacation when she was younger. He crunched his pillow.

What date was it? May 15 or 16? You'd think it was still the middle of winter. April in Paris had come and gone, but the dreary winter refused to make way for spring. Everything was still dead. No sign of rebirth. Like his future. He put the new goose-down pillow over his eyes.

"MERDE!" he said aloud. He never used to swear—it was against his principles. But he could not bear his life, gloomy-gray Paris, and the miserable rain.

The only one who understood was Zaffeera. She had lost her sister *and* her brother.

In a recent telephone conversation, Michel had mentioned to Zaffeera that he had a stiff neck and a sore back. She responded by sending him a contoured neck pillow and a European featherbed to match. On a monogrammed note card, Zaffeera had written that she hoped the bedding would help. Her penmanship was graceful, even similar to Noora's. He had not yet responded or taken the time to write back. He noticed the two sisters were in some ways alike, though they didn't resemble one another at all. Like Noora, she was thoughtful and kind. But she was not Noora.

He tossed in his lonely bed, grabbed the goose-down pillow, punched it, and threw it across the room. He had to be strong. He would get no sympathy from his professors, and graduation was around the corner. He had to concentrate on his finals, strictly because he did not want to disappoint his father. But one thing was for sure: There was no point in trying to get his average up to where it had been. No point working so hard when death was inevitably there, always waiting in the end.

CHAPTER 27
UNCLE KHAYAT'S VILLA

The seaside villa was freshly painted in white, with peach-colored trimmings around the windows and forest-green wooden shutters. Except for the large window upstairs—the one in Uncle Khayat's study leading to his verandah—all the shutters were closed.

Noora pushed open the four-foot wrought iron gate—the same one she remembered running through when she was a child, with her brothers and sisters, when they first arrived for summer vacations at their uncle's villa. She rushed through the brick pathway bordered by rose bushes. The same purple roses! She never forgot the pots of overflowing purple, yellow, and white pansies surrounding the front porch, and the bright red bougainvillea climbed so much higher than before, they reached around the two white pillars that separated the front door. *Finally, finally!* she sang in her heart. She felt as if she were ten years old again, anxiously running up the steps to greet her uncle, then change into a bathing suit and run to the beach with her siblings. She did not see the raised brick in front of her and she tripped. As she got to her feet, she noticed blood pouring out of her scraped knee. Never mind. She looked up. The front door opened and she recognized Mohammed, Uncle Khayat's houseman, who ran down the steps. Except for gray temples and more lines on his face, Mohammed had not changed. He was holding a baby, about eight or nine months old.

"*Ezayak!* How are you, Mohammed? I am Noora Fendil ..." she managed to say, out of breath from excitement. "Remember me?"

"*Noora!* Daughter of Mr. Farid Fendil. *Ezayek!* What a wonderful surprise!" he said, happy to see her. "How are you? It's been so long. How is the Fendil family?"

"Fine. *Hamdallah.* Fine. I'm here alone … I mean I'm not right now with my family," she blurted out quickly.

"Are you with … a husband?" He looked out to the street to see if there was a car or someone waiting.

"No! I'm … still in … school."

"*Ahlan wasahlan,* welcome! Please forgive me, how rude of me; let me find a bandage for that knee. I am so sorry you fell"

"I'm fine, really."

"*Hamdallah,* it does not look bad," he said, looking at her wound.

"It's nothing, nothing at all," Noora said, eyes welling, and unable to hold back her joy at finally being there.

He guided Noora inside, and still holding the baby, who squealed and gurgled, he rushed down a long corridor.

The interior of the house was dark. Noora wondered why the green shutters weren't open. Inside, the atmosphere seemed different.

"How is everyone?" Mohammed asked again when he returned. He handed her a wet hand cloth. "Sit down, please. I'll get you the first aid kit. It's in the drawer in the kitchen."

"I'm fine," she said, patting her wound. "Please, no need for that. You see? The blood stopped," she laughed. "Silly me. I wasn't looking where I was going, I was so happy to finally be here!"

"Are you on vacation?"

"Yes. No, well, on an expedition, with … school. " Maybe she would tell him the truth after she saw her uncle.

"That's wonderful. Are you staying far from here? I didn't see a car," he said, turning to open one of the closed windows.

While Noora tried to think of another lie, the houseman made his way back to the vestibule and closed the front door.

When he returned, the baby in Mohammed's arm gurgled happily and made saliva bubbles.

"I took a cab to surprise my uncle. We're staying in town … at the … Cecile. The hotel."

"Ah … beautiful hotel. Far away."

"I hired a taxi driver. Is the baby … a boy?" Noora asked to change the subject. *Whose baby was it? Where was her uncle?*

"Yes. *Hamdallah*, a blessing. Miss Fendil, it has been many years since we had the pleasure of a visit from your family," he said, staring at the right side of her eye.

Noora felt self-conscious. She forgot to remove the elastic band that tied her hair back in a ponytail, and revealed the scar that ran from her right temple down to her cheek.

"May I offer you a glass of lemonade?" he said, guiding her to the drawing room.

Noora did not recognize the gaudy furniture, and the room looked more cluttered than she remembered. There were few toys in the corner of the floor.

"Oh, no thank you. I'm sorry, I should have called first. I … didn't think he would mind my visit. Where is my uncle?"

When Mohammed told her, Noora had to hold on to the sturdy wing chair next to her.

"Your uncle sold the villa and moved to France about two months ago, to be close to his doctor. I am very sorry, Miss Fendil; I thought maybe he had corresponded with your father. I was never more sad than when Mr. Khayat left. I am still here because *hamdallah,* your uncle gave the family that bought the villa good recommendations and they invited me to continue to work here, for them. They are from Cairo. They're all at the beach right now. I'm sure they would love to meet you. I expect them back soon …"

Noora could no longer hear what the house-man was telling her, except for the words that echoed like an alarm: *Your uncle sold the villa and moved to France.*

Tears inundated her face as she ran through streets of Aboukir—streets, alleys, boulevards she no longer recognized. Pollution had taken over. What did it matter anymore?

Uncle Khayat had left Alexandria.

She hopped on a moving tram and found a seat by an open window. The strong wind slapped her face, and she wished she were someone else in a faraway place.

In less than a dozen or so years, the elegant villas all over the outskirts of Alexandria were now overpopulated apartments. Manicured lawns became dried-out weeds on cracked sidewalks filled with trash.

Noora stepped down from the tram at the last station that took her downtown. Feeling numb, she walked along the crescent-shaped Corniche. The once-famous seacoast road, with its turquoise shores, had lost its glow, and everything appeared dusty and dim.

Miles away from Aboukir, Noora found herself at Ras El Tin, the Alexandria pier. She gazed at the cargo ships that bobbed on the horizon.

"God is punishing me," she said to a pigeon that had landed nearby. The pigeon jerked its head and flew off.

She sat on an old stone bench and watched as waves crashed against the square cement rocks that protected the sea wall below.

Um Faheema would not like it if she lost courage and faith. Maybe things would be better in France. She remembered Dweezoul's words: "Things always happen for good reason."

As she stood at the pier where she had once fished with her uncle, she imagined Uncle Khayat fishing in the South of France. Perhaps he was sipping his favorite tea and smoking his cherry tobacco pipe on a verandah, in a lovely villa, like the one at Aboukir.

"*Lazzem El Bahr.*" Uncle Khayat's words rang in her ears. *We must have the sea.*

Holding her bag, she rocked herself. After a while, she set it down next to her feet and smoothed out her piece of paper on which the house-man had written the address.

Again, she read the address Mohammed gave her.

46 Rue Charlemagne, Antibes

He had also scribbled the phone number. She looked up. She had to change her paper bills to coins. She needed to find a public phone. How much would she need to call Antibes?

She was exhausted. Perhaps she could lie down, but the bench was covered with dried pigeon droppings. A soft bed with a pillow would feel wonderful right now.

Her eyes wandered tiredly and rested on a fishing boat docked nearby. Aboard was a fisherman weaving his fishing net. She realized that while he worked, he was also watching her under the visor of his navy blue cap.

She looked away and wondered if she had enough money to stay at a hotel for one night, or maybe two. But the hotel would ask for her passport and a credit card. A woman alone in this part of the world probably looked suspicious. She thought of her new friend, Yasmina, from the train. She wondered if she could stay with her and her mother for one night. But she could not impose. She sighed and closed her eyes, thinking of the Hotel Cecile, where she could luxuriate in a bubble bath.

Mohammed seemed concerned about Uncle Khayat, who Noora learned had cancer. She regretted not asking Mohammed how serious the cancer was. Uncle Khayat had no wife or children. She could take care of him.

But why did he sell his villa? Did he not plan to return to Alexandria? Perhaps he needed the money.

Noora looked up, startled by the voice of the fisherman, who was now standing a few feet away.

"Good day. You need assistance?" he asked in broken Arabic.

"No, thank you. I was just leaving," she said, but her tired body could not budge.

A pigeon landed on the man's left shoulder, then another on his right. He pulled out some seeds from his pocket and tossed them as the pigeons launched after their meal. He sat on the opposite end of the bench. More pigeons gathered around the two of them. He extended an index finger and a pigeon rested on it. Slowly he turned his hand, opening his palm full of seeds. The pigeon ate out of the man's hand. Noora could not help but smile.

"Where do you need to go, Miss?" he asked in Arabic.

"Nowhere. I am just ... enjoying the sights."

"Do you speak Greek?"

"No."

"*Fanransawee?*" he asked in Arabic.

"*Oui, je parle un peu Francais,*" she answered.

"I can speak English better zan French," he said in English with a strong Greek accent.

"I can also speak English better than French," she replied with a smile.

"I like to practice English," he said. "See over dere? All the boats?"

"Yes."

"Men digging big statues of Cleopatra."

"Really? Divers?" Noora asked, staring out to sea.

"Divers. Yes. Lots of people out dere. They are gone for now. They be back tomorrow, early."

"That's good."

"No. Eez terribileh. Catastrophique. Too many people. Photographers. Movie cameras. Too much agitation. Bad luck. Bad for fishing. That's why we leave sooner."

A white dove landed on the Greek's lap, and he caressed its back nonchalantly. The dove did not appear the least bit frightened. The man stuck his finger out and the dove balanced on it for a moment before flying off serenely into the sunlight.

Noora wanted to stay awhile longer, watching the fisherman feed the birds, but he stood up.

"I have to go back to work, my friends," he said to the pigeons, "if I want to make it to Marseilles!" He lifted his cap to Noora, nodded a polite adieu, and began to walk away.

"Excuse me, sir, did you say you were going to Marseilles?"

"Yes. First stop in Athens. Then Marseilles."

"How long does it take to sail to Marseilles?"

"About four days, not long." Again, he lifted his cap to Noora, clicked his heels, and headed back to his fishing boat, the *Lydia*.

Noora studied the boat, wondering idly if this rusty old bucket could get her to Nice. Wasn't Marseilles near Nice?

Noora paid the taxi driver and climbed out of the car, dazed at the sight before her. She scarcely recognized the façade of the Cecile Hotel, because the structure was in the midst of remodeling. She entered through the revolving doors into the familiar marble lobby, decorated with tapestries. A group of tourists had just arrived by van. They looked like Americans, but spoke animatedly in French and Arabic. Luggage was stacked in the lobby, and the bellmen were busy attending to the new arrivals. Noora stood in line at the registration desk. She should have called first to find out if there was a room available. If she paid for one night in advance, perhaps they would not insist on a credit card. She could concoct a story that she was waiting for her brother, who had been delayed and was on his way. She had enough money.

That's when she saw him. *The man with the mustache!* The same man she had seen in London. Her heart began to race. He was sitting in the lobby with two other men, holding a demitasse midway to his mouth. From across the lobby, he stared at her.

Oh God! She turned away and looked down, holding her bag tightly.

"May I help you, please?" Noora heard the clerk behind the counter say.

"Oh. Thank you ... I ..." *Why hadn't I thought of wearing a veil to conceal my face?*

Hands grabbed her by the shoulders from behind. He jerked her around to face him.

"You!" he said, and spat right at her face.

Another man rushed up and screamed in Arabic, "Moustafa! What are you doing?"

As Moustafa turned to the other man, Noora managed to break free. Holding tightly to her bag, she ran out through the revolving doors. She flew down the sidewalk and made a quick left around the building to the seacoast road. Nearly getting hit by the oncoming cars, Noora dodged her way across the boulevard. Cars honked furiously. She heard the sounds of screeching brakes and angry drivers shouting.

She ran faster than she believed possible. A few minutes later, as she mingled in a sea of pedestrians along the wide sidewalk, she slowed down to catch her breath. Narrow cement steps led down to the beach. As she was about to take the stairs, she ventured a quick glance over her shoulder. To her horror, the Arab man, in his shark-colored suit and red tie was rapidly gaining speed, getting closer.

"Stop! Thief!" she heard him shout.

Trying to escape, she bumped into a tall man in a white garb, who grabbed her. Hitting him with her Bedouin bag, Noora managed to push him away and break free just as her pursuer was about to jump on her. She spotted a bus passing by on the street.

Two boys in traditional striped pajamas were happily riding on the bus's rear bumper. She chased after the bus. Behind her, cars honked, and people screamed for her to get out of the road.

"*El ha'ooni!* Help me!" she yelled out to the kids over the noise of the traffic.

The two youngsters reached out their hands. But the bus was going too fast, and Noora could not touch even the tips of their fingers.

"Throw your bag," one of the boys yelled. Noora hesitated then threw it and he caught it like a ball. He grinned with pride. The other boy stretched out one arm to Noora while his friend held on to the elastic band of his pants.

The bus picked up speed, and the Arab man was gaining on her. Noora did not think she could go on. The bus suddenly slowed as it neared an intersection, and Noora was lifted up on the ledge by the surprisingly strong arms of the boys. Moustafa ran faster, furiously trying to grab her off the rear bumper. Noora sat on the wide bumper between the boys, supported herself by their arms on each side, held her legs up, and kicked her pursuer in the face.

Passengers on the bus were watching from the back window above Noora. Her kick incapacitated him, but only for a brief moment. He came after her, faster, angrier, reaching out to yank her off. The bus crossed the intersection. Picking up speed, it spewed out black fumes. Her pursuer was out of view, hidden by a noxious cloud of black smoke. More cars were honking. When the exhaust fumes began to dissipate, Noora spotted him coughing, at the edge of a sidewalk. Not seeming to care why the girl was being chased, the boys who rescued her whistled at the pursuer, jeering and waving their arms as if they had just won a race. The man disappeared behind heavy traffic.

Noora was out of breath. *Moustafa*. Now she knew his first name. She put a hand to her chest and felt a sudden cooling sensation from the blue stone on the copper chain Um Faheema had given her.

CHAPTER 28
THE SEA VOYAGE

Sailing through an unusually rough sea, the *Lydia* creaked, and everything not nailed down banged and bumped in the night. Noora thought the old fishing boat would split apart and she would surely drown. The way she was feeling, death seemed like a preferable alternative.

Three more days, and Yorgho—the man who communed with pigeons—would dock his old, smelly fishing boat in Marseilles. He had given her a nice little cabin with a tiny but private bath, where she spent most of her time. He had told her she should sleep out on the bridge if she was so sick. Noora felt safer locked in her cabin. She was not sure she could trust the man, though he seemed harmless and was constantly busy with his work. Finally, Yorgho convinced her to get some fresh air. He brought a lounge chair on deck for her. Even though it was the middle of May, the cold wind howled as if they were in the middle of winter.

"Is just a passing storm, nut'ing serious."

Serious or not, she barely missed his shoes when the next bout of nausea struck.

"Please forgive me," she cried.

"Is okay," he laughed. "You get used to it, Bebba."

He went downstairs, leaving her alone on deck in her misery.

She must be the only woman on board. How could she have been so naive? A Greek fisherman and the Italian seaman who had helped her upstairs could do anything they wanted with her. She would be at their mercy, she thought, as she dragged her way to the rail and vomited again, though there was nothing now but bile in her stomach. Yorgho said she should eat something and watch the horizon. He appeared bored with her. He seemed, however, to have a decent disposition. If not, those pigeons would never have gotten so close to him. Pigeons, she thought, instinctively knew the difference between good and evil. Like all animals.

Resting on a teak deck chaise with shredded canvas upholstery, Noora nodded off into an exhausted sleep. She dreamed she was on a white horse, galloping along the seashore. She was the only one riding, while everyone else lounged beneath blue-and-white-striped parasols. Beautiful couples, dressed in fine clothing, were watching her, smiling, as her white stallion galloped gallantly along the beach. She heard the music of Dweezoul's favorite song, Sarah Vaughn's "Broken Hearted Melody." Somehow, the dream brought calm to her torment. The wind began to feel cold again, waking her to consciousness. Slowly she rose and made her way back to her cabin, while the *Lydia* headed north, rising upon the swells, then slapping hard into the troughs.

Soon she would be in Nice. There, women could wear a bikini and swim wherever they pleased. Girls could even go topless. In Alexandria, women could not even wear bathing suits—they had to keep their arms, legs, and heads covered. She remembered again Dweezoul's wise words: *Maybe things do work out for the best.* Holding on to her Bedouin blanket, Noora fell asleep on the narrow cot.

She was awakened by a heavyset woman, holding a tray of food. Noora sat up. *A woman on board?*

The woman said something in Greek to Noora, showing her a tray with hot cereal and a tall glass of steaming milk. She placed the tray at the foot of the cot, smiled, and left. Noora tried to go after her, but the woman disappeared behind one of the cabin doors. Noora returned to her cabin and closed the door. She stared at the hot cream of wheat, inhaling the inviting aroma.

Later that evening, Noora managed to wash under the showerhead that sent down intermittent blasts of cold and hot water. Splashing water on her face, she caught a glimpse of her reflection in the stained chrome mirror of her tiny bathroom. She scarcely recognized herself. Her face was a grayish green. Her eyes were puffy. The scar that ran down her right eye seemed more prominent. She dried her body with a small hand towel.

There was a persistent knock on the door. Unable to find something clean to wear, she slipped on her soiled yellow dress.

"Good morning," Yorgho said. He removed his cap. "How are you doing, good?" he queried in Greek, then switched to English. "You look more better."

Noora ventured a smile.

"Good morning," she nodded. *Let him think I'm English. Anything but who I really am.*

"You like the breakfast, yes?" he asked as he replaced his dust-encrusted cap, hiding his greasy, thinning hair and bald spot.

"Yes. The woman who brought me breakfast," Noora ventured, unable to contain her curiosity, "is she your wife?"

"*Ohhy, ohhy, ohhy!* No, no, no!" he said, as if he had been insulted. "She belong to Yanni!"

Noora thought Yanni must have been the handsome seaman who helped her on the bridge the night before.

"Yanni is Italian who work for me!" He knocked on his chest boastfully. "Obleevia, she work for both us two! She cook a lot. She eat a lot too!" He chortled. "May I come in, pleeze? I need to see some-ting leaking."

Already brushing past her, he headed straight to the wall next to her cot and pointed to a slight trickle dribbling down the wall and collecting in a little puddle on the flimsy carpet at the foot of her cot.

"Aha! I feex it. No problem. Obleevia, she has good eyes." He turned and looked at Noora, who grabbed her Bedouin blanket and wrapped it around herself. She knew her yellow dress smelled like vomit.

"Eef you need wash clothes, Obleevia she wash for you. She hang laun-dree in boiler and every-ting dry very queek. Queeker than sun."

He himself did not smell too grand, reeking of a mixture of stale tobacco, fish, and some kind of musk cologne that failed to conceal his pungent body odor.

"Where did you learn to speak English so well?" she found herself saying, then immediately regretting it, because it would keep him longer in her cabin.

"I speak seven languages! And you don't speak Greek?"

"Just a couple of words actually, like *tee kannes,* how are you, and goodbye. And also, *oppa!*" She laughed nervously, wishing she had kept her mouth shut.

"Ah, *tee kannes. Kalla.* I am fine. Very good. Greek is the prettiest language in the whole wahrld," he said, gesturing with his hands to form an imaginary sphere. "You change an' go upstairs. Nice day. Storm is passed. Fineesh. Sun is good and hot now. Sea is no more agitated."

"Where can I find Olivia?"

"No, no. Obbleevi-a. Obleevia-blimp. You know what eez blimp? Like zat." He mimicked a gorilla. "I go get her."

"Thank you," Noora said, quickly closing the door behind him. He probably had a key to her cabin. He'd be back soon to repair the leak.

After the terrible first night on board the rusty old *Lydia,* the trip improved. Noora began to enjoy standing by the rail as the wind slapped her face and the ship cut through the sea. She spotted schools of dolphins, one after another. Multicolored fish streamed beside the *Lydia*. By now, the boat was laden with tuna. Noora had not realized so many fish could be caught in one afternoon. The men handled nets expertly, and in no time, mounds of shimmering fish were packed as tightly as sardines into steel containers filled with sea water. As soon as they were full, the containers sank like elevators down to refrigerated compartments. *Poor fish,* she thought. Um Faheema and Dweezoul would not have liked to have seen that.

In time, Noora began to feel less apprehensive about her four companions, and she was grateful they left her alone. Yanni, the good-looking Italian, had pumped muscles and a navy-blue-and-white-striped T-shirt that he seemed to never change. Despite his powerful build, Yanni looked puny next to Obleevia. Yorgho appeared intimidated by the woman and stayed well out of her way.

There was another seaman, a little chunky fellow who was never introduced to Noora. He was a dwarf, a little over three feet tall. She tried not to stare. He seemed an unfriendly little character, with large, black, deeply set piercing eyes.

When the *Lydia* arrived in Athens, Noora felt happy, anxious, and impatient. She was getting closer to Nice.

"You can leave ze boat. Come back before nighttime. Take tour to Acropolis, eef you like. Eez very old," Yorgho said. "We sail to sea very, very early tomorrow. Before the sun comes up. Very bee-zy now. Much work to finish."

When Noora set foot on the Athens dock, she felt dizzy. The dock seemed to be swaying. Was it an earthquake? She was about to rush back on board when it occurred to her that she had been at sea for four days and she had lost the feeling of her "land legs."

Up ahead, a crowd of seamen and travelers from other cargo ships that had just arrived began forming a line into Customs. Noora had forgotten a critical detail: She had no papers. How was she ever going to get through Customs at Nice? How could she have been so stupid? She wanted to run back to the *Lydia*, but the gangplank was removed. She could not find Yorgho, his crewmen, or Obleevia.

A seagull landed nearby.

"If I were a seagull," she thought as tears welled, "I would fly to France."

"Eh, Bebba!" Yorgho called as he pushed his way through a crowd of dockworkers. The seagull flapped its wide, majestic wings and flew into the vast blue sky.

"What you doing? You need to go over dere!" He pointed to the Customs building.

"I changed my mind. I need to get back on board."

"Ah, *les filles*. They change mind all de time. Okay. Come."

"You took away the gangway," she said, rushing after him.

"What?"

"The bridge."

"We take away because we want no monkey business and pirates on my *Lydia! Capisce?*"

"Pirates?"

"Thieves." Yorgho whistled shrilly up to the deck. From the *Lydia*, the dwarf's large head and serious face appeared out of a small porthole.

"Marius, he weel help you. No changing of mind so much," he said, moving closer to her.

She could see the beads of sweat that dotted his forehead under the hot sunlight. He smelled like fish and major body odor.

"Yes. Sorry."

The dwarf began to roll down the gangplank while Yorgho spotted other seamen and walked off with them, rambling on joyfully in Greek. He seemed well-known and well-liked.

Once on board, Noora searched for Obleevia. For the first time, she ventured everywhere, discovering many cabins, mostly tiny, and a cozy one that looked like a living room. There was no sign of Obleevia. She found the kitchen, where a fresh-baked braided loaf of bread was on the counter.

Noora caught a glimpse of the dwarf in a dark corner of the narrow hallway. He faded silently back in the shadow.

She lay awake that night, worrying about a passport. What could she do? There was no solution. She drifted into an uneasy sleep.

The *Lydia's* engines woke her before dawn. They were underway. Destination: Marseilles.

She made her way up to the deck, and found Yorgho sitting on a stack of thick ropes, staring out to sea. As Noora approached, he jumped up, putting on a toothy smile, so wide that she saw the gleaming golden teeth in both corners of his mouth.

"Ah, good morning. You had a good rest?"

"Yes, thank you," Noora replied, noticing the sky, glowing with pink, orange, and blue hues. She was relieved to see there was no storm and the sea was calm. "Where is Obleevia?" she asked.

"Busy with Yanni." He formed a fist with his left hand and thrust his middle finger in and out, suggesting they were fornicating.

"Oh ..." she said, trying to appear nonchalant. She turned and headed back downstairs. Up to now, he had been polite. This surprising gesture made her terribly uneasy. *Just because pigeons responded to him did not mean he was to be trusted,* she reminded herself.

When she reached her cabin, she found Obleevia carrying away her food tray. "Thank you!" Noora said in Greek.

Obleevia turned and smiled at Noora.

The next day, as the *Lydia* glided on calm seas under a gray sky that sent a steady drizzle, Noora stayed in her cabin.

Late in the afternoon, there was a knock on her door.

"Obleevia say I am insolent, because I should invite you to captain's table. Join me for supper, please," Yorgho said, the second Noora cracked the door open. He stood two feet from Noora, breathing hard. He stank of stale tobacco and strong mouthwash.

The dinner table was nicely set, with a yellowed but clean tablecloth. Yorgho sat without his cap, his hair combed back, sticking to his scalp and perfectly parted to one side. Noora realized "supper" was going to include only the two of them.

"Who is navigating the boat?" Noora asked.

"Marius."

She wondered where Yanni and Obleevia were, but this time, she had no intention of asking.

Yorgho offered her rolls in a red plastic basket. The Greek was being a little too gallant, she thought. She nodded politely and took a roll, wishing she could be off the ship. She wondered if she could slip away tomorrow in Marseilles and hitch a ride to Nice. Or call Uncle Khayat from Marseilles?

Yorgho was chatting away, telling her about the art of fishing, and boasting that he was the best on the Mediterranean. Noora sat up straight, trying to look as if she was paying attention.

He lifted his wine glass. "Drink, drink. Eez good wine."

She had taken a couple of sips a few minutes before. The wine tasted like sweetened vinegar.

"Good, yes? I buy by the case," he said proudly, and swallowed his entire glassful, which he replenished immediately, and poured more for Noora. "Good for blood circulation," he said, watching her. "You don't like?"

She took a sip and nodded politely. "Yes. It's good."

He was talking faster now, shifting in his chair, and not making much sense.

Obleevia entered, bringing a tray of fresh-baked macaroons. She said something in Greek to Yorgho, removed her stained apron, and then left the cabin.

"What did she say?" Noora asked, putting down her wine glass.

"She is going out dancing." He frowned. "You don't like wine?"

She picked up her glass, put the wine to her lips, but didn't drink.

"Drink! Eez good."

"I am drinking. Very good indeed."

Dinner was actually quite good. Obleevia had made pot roast and potatoes. Yorgho talked wildly while gobbling down his food. Now and then, he stopped talking, laughed, and stared at her oddly, his eyes seeming to bulge. Was he drunk? She caught him a couple of times staring at her breasts. After he ate the last bite, he tore a chunk of bread and wiped his plate clean. Oil glistening down his chin, he smiled. "Eat, eat," he said. He put both hands under the table and shifted rhythmically in his chair.

"Feenish wine. Eez too expensive to waste," he said. He seemed out of breath—almost panting now, his hands still under the table.

"You enjoy food?" he asked, leaning toward the table. "Good, yes?"

She began to feel threatened but tried to appear at ease. "I'm enjoying the food," she responded, taking a bite of the potatoes.

"I like to see you with mouth full. Aakh," he said, his eyes rolling. He shifted in his chair again. He poured another glass of wine for himself, drank it like water, then rose abruptly and left, barely saying good night.

What was that about? Noora wondered. She heard music coming from above. She took the plates to the kitchen. When she returned to finish clearing the table, she felt faint. A bit tipsy, perhaps. She grabbed a macaroon and ate it quickly. She wondered what kind of wine could have such a strong effect. She needed fresh air. She ventured up on deck. The wind cooled her flushed cheeks. She saw Yanni and Obleevia's silhouettes as they danced to the music of Edith Piaf from a small tape recorder nearby. Obleevia and Yanni were graceful on their feet, he so light, and she following his every step as if weightless.

Noora leaned on the rail and watched the waves slapping against the hull. She felt revived. She did not want to think about Yorgho and his odd behavior. Luckily, he was not on deck. He always seemed to stay out of Obleevia's way. The song changed to a slower beat. Noora did not want to disturb the couple's private moment, so she sat in a hidden corner. Yanni and Obleevia danced so close, they were almost one. She thought of Michel, and their first dance. She remembered every moment of the first time they met, at the beautiful wedding in Alexandria—and the next time when they danced at San Stefano beach terrace during a summer vacation in Alexandria. She closed her eyes and relived the moments when he held her in his arms. She, snuggling in the curve of his neck; he, loving her. Tears began to flow. She ran down to her little cubbyhole cabin.

When Noora awoke the next morning, she heard pots clanking outside her porthole and men's voices shouting in singsong French. Distant horns and the call of seagulls sang in her ears.

Noora rolled up her blanket and stuffed it in her Bedouin bag and groggily made her way up into the bright sunlight of the old port of Marseilles.

An elegant cruise ship, large as a city, glowed under the Mediterranean sky. *Le Cristal Turquoise* looked out of place in the old, dilapidated port of Marseilles. Noora stood mesmerized by the enormous ship that floated jewel-like in the blue water, making the *Lydia* and other fishing boats look like rusty bathtubs. She noticed a dozen or more French coast guard boats patrolling the harbor waters.

When she disembarked, Noora found the port swarming with policemen. *Were they checking passports?*

"They say maybe there is bomb in fancy boat," Yorgho said, standing on the dock right behind her. "Vat a mess."

"I need to make a quick phone call. I have someone who can pick me up. I just misplaced my passport. That's all."

"Oh, that eez all? Come."

She followed him. Her heart began to pound when he marched right up to a police officer. They seemed to know each other. After exchanging small talk, Yorgho turned to Noora and guided her just before Customs to an area with rows of public telephones. Noora was impressed.

"I have, shall we say, a few friends in right places," he grinned, clicking his heels and lifting his dusty cap to Noora.

He moved a few feet away to allow her privacy and waited; but he was not far enough. She checked the piece of paper with Uncle Khayat's number. She had memorized it in Alexandria, and now she could not remember anything. While dialing, she made a mental note never to forget his phone number, in case she lost the paper. Her heart skipped a beat when she heard his voice.

"Nous regrettons d'avoir manqué votre communication. Prière de nous laisser un message.»

Uncle Khayat! His voice on the electronic answering machine brought tears to her eyes. Except for his slight melodious Middle Eastern accent, his French was impeccable. He sounded a bit like Omar Sharif, the actor. But even more, he sounded like her father.

She had to hang up and take a deep breath. Her hands were trembling. Trying to keep her index finger steady, she redialed but quickly hung up again. What a fool. She had always dialed long distance without a second thought, using her father's credit card number. She knew the long numbers by heart. She still remembered them. But she could never use the privilege again.

Yorgho curiously inched a few feet closer.

"I need some more change," she said, trying to sound calm. She was perspiring, and the palms of her hands were clammy.

"No problem, I have lots of French coins. *Ah, les sous, les sous, j'en ai plein de sous! Mais une Maume pour m' chauffer les couilles, ça c'est une autre histoire!*" Yorgho rambled on in southern French slang. He pulled out a handful of French francs. "Vatever you need, I have, Bebba."

Noora understood the first French words Yorgho said: "Money, money, I have plenty of money." *But what else did he say?* she wondered uneasily. Soon she would not have to worry about figuring out what he was constantly mumbling in French or Greek or whatever other language he knew she didn't understand.

She counted the francs needed to make her call. As she dialed, she prayed her uncle would finally answer in person. The answering machine clicked in. She heard his voice again. She almost spoke but realized she could not leave a message, since he could not return her call. She would have to wait until he answered in person.

Yorgho stood right behind Noora now, breathing garlic in her ear. "I invite you to best sandwich of smoke fish and *moutarde de Dijon,* with deeh-luscious cornichons. Shoor-lee, you cannot say *non, n'est-ce-pas?*"

"Thank you. I'm fine," Noora said, wishing she could just wait by the phone. She had to keep trying until he answered.

"I in-seest," Yorgho said. Without waiting for an argument, he guided her to a nearby greasy-spoon restaurant built on the water.

Sitting across from Noora on a sticky wooden bench, Yorgho dug into a huge fish sandwich that dripped mustard and oil onto his tin plate.

"Okay, Bebba. I take you vere you vant to go," he mumbled, his mouth full.

Yorgho took her across the sea and never asked her for a passport or ID or anything. All he asked her for was what he claimed was the going rate for the journey, in Egyptian pounds—the equivalent of two hundred dollars. All that was fine, but she saw how he looked at Yanni and Obleevia with envious eyes. Now she noticed the way he watched her as she nibbled on a pickled baby cucumber. She looked away.

She thought of escaping—hopping in a cab and going to Nice. How difficult could that be? But she had no papers. "Since you're so well-known here, maybe you can help me get through Customs without all the formalities," she ventured. "I have some money left." She gulped down her Coke and nervously played with the bottle.

"Formalities," he said, watching her toy with the bottle of Coke. He wiped his mouth, dug in his pocket, and pulled out a thick wad of money. He rose and shuffled over to pay the cashier.

"Please let me pay for my drink," Noora said.

"No, no. Eez my pleasure," he grinned. "Too bad you did not eat."

"I wasn't hungry. But thank you. You see, I lost my passport. If I could just get in the country without formalities," she tried to explain as they were leaving the restaurant.

"I can do any-ting, Bebba."

Noora sighed. "Good."

"Any-ting, I can do. Ask ME! I do." He walked ahead of her.

"Okay. Thank you," Noora said.

"But this thing, this formality," he said, obviously liking the word, "this formality, I can-NOT do."

"No?!"

He stopped and stared at Noora. "My *Lydia* is waiting. But take it teasy. I figure some-ting. Later on."

Noora quickly glanced around the port.

"Come, Bebba," he said, patting her on the arm.

She could do it. She could just act as if she needed to make a phone call again, then simply go around the area, passing Customs. Yorgho was marching ahead of her. She could still make a fast dash, she thought, but froze, realizing the dock was swarming with *gendarmes* and armed military personnel.

When she was back on board, she noticed Marius the dwarf giving Yorgho a disapproving stare.

Noora sat forlornly in her cabin and waited for the crew to unload their fish and go about their regular routine as they did at the Port of Athens. There seemed to be more commotion here, probably because of the bomb scare.

What did Yorgho mean when he said he'd figure something out later? When was *later* going to be? She remembered the needlepoint pillow Uncle Khayat used to keep on his favorite wing chair in his drawing room in Alexandria.

"Don't Wait For Your Ship To Come In. Swim Out To It."

CHAPTER 29
THE STONE AND THE SEA

Yorgho could not contain himself any longer. It must be tonight. During the past few months, he had not had the need for a woman, thanks to the cheap brothels where he had contracted herpes. The painful sores took a long time to heal. As soon as the herpes became dormant and Yorgho believed he was finally cured, he found himself craving a woman again.

His pretty young passenger was the ideal girl of all his sexual fantasies. He did not care who she was or where she came from. He was sure she was a virgin. That thought alone made him quiver.

She had appeared at the Alexandria quay at *Ras El Tin*—an angel—there to fulfill his needs.

While navigating his *Lydia,* Yorgho gently caressed his crotch. Soon, he would find relief and finally satisfaction with real, young flesh. He unbuttoned his fly but spotted a shadow moving below. What the hell was Marius doing down there?. *Get lost, shrimp,* Yorgho thought as he quickly rebuttoned his fly. But Marius was already standing nearby, and Yorgho hoped the dwarf didn't notice what he was doing.

Marius noticed. Nothing passed by him. But he said nothing. He watched the world go by; he watched people make fools of themselves, and he said nothing. At the entrance to the dimly lit navigating cubicle, Marius motioned to Yorgho that he was being relieved from his shift. Yorgho nodded without looking at him and faded into darkness.

Marius, who originally frowned at the idea of stopping at Nice, was glad now about the change of course. A feast for his eyes lay out there, where the most beautiful yachts appeared at this time of the year, in their luminous glory.

Marius loved yachts. Especially the ones owned by Greek magnates and Saudi kings and princes. He watched through the darkness as twinkling lights began to form on the horizon. A yacht glided smoothly and luminously over the water.

Noora heard a knock but thought she was dreaming. After all, there were many knocking noises coming from the old *Lydia*. There was another knock. This time, she was certain someone was at her cabin door. She had difficulty pulling herself out of her cot. Sleepy-eyed, she slowly cracked the cabin door open.

Yorgho was standing at the door, smiling.

"Are we getting close?"

"Not yet. But soon." He removed his cap and tucked it under his arm. "I invite you to talk to me in my living room. Over good tea and cake."

Noora hesitated.

"Very good cake," he smiled. "You will like."

"Well, okay ... I guess. I'll be there in a minute."

"I will wait," he said with a broader smile. He bowed and turned on his heels.

Noora sat in the small dining room as Yorgho poured tea into a demitasse. There was a plate of almond butter cookies. Noora did not have the desire to eat. She was waiting anxiously for their arrival in Nice.

"Yorgho," she started, stirring her tea in her chipped teacup, "you said you would be able to help me."

"Yes. I can do any-ting," he said, sitting across from her and slurping coffee from a tin mug.

"I *do* have a passport; it's just that it's not with me right now."

"I understand," he said.

She wasn't looking at him. She was thinking about how to approach the subject of her problem. An idea flashed.

"Can I phone Nice from the boat? Do you have that kind of equipment?"

"Equeep-ment," he said, rising. "Equeepment, I have, Bebba. I can do any-ting."

"Well then, if I may use ..."

"First, let me show you *thees* equeepment! Eez wonderful. And then, I can *buy* you a passport!"

Noora searched in her pockets for the piece of paper with Uncle Khayat's phone number. How could she have forgotten it again? She must have left it on the bed in her cabin. *Did he say, "BUY ME A PASSPORT"*? She looked up.

"Bebba, look at this!" he said.

He had pulled out his erect penis, and he was flaunting it for her view.

He licked his lips and his eyes were bulging. "How fantastic you will feel when I put inside of you, Bebba. Oh, ah, *Dio mio, DIO MIO!*"

Noora jumped from her chair and let it crash on the floor in the narrow space behind her. She tried to open the same door she had entered—he had locked it!

"Oh, Bebba. Pleeezz. I will make you feel goo-hood. Look at it!"

She couldn't help but stare. She felt herself drift away strangely, as if she were in a movie, watching something that was happening to someone else.

"Come on, boobby Bebba. Lift up dress. Pull down panties slowlee ... Den show me. *Montre-moi ta jolie chatte, ma ... oh mamma mia ma petite,*" he panted, stroking himself rhythmically. "Show me your pretty little pussy!" he shouted. Shoving his other hand in his pocket, he displayed a thick wad of money. "I give you any-ting you want."

"I just wanted a passport, you bastard," she said, her eyes darting around in search of a way out.

"Fuck de passport. I buy you dresses. I buy you dress store. You must let me ..."

She frantically tried another doorknob behind her, but it was a narrow closet.

"No bother to run. Ship not very beeg! I can always find you!" he said with a hideous laugh. "Oh, my sweet little pussy, my little beetch. Oh, ah!" he heaved as he stroked himself faster and faster, like a locomotive. "I luh-v you, Bebba."

She pushed the last door and made a fast dash out through the kitchen. *Don't wait for your ship to come in. ...* She flew up on deck.

Noora climbed over the ramp and dove into the blackness of the sea. The water was icy, but she did not feel it at first. She could have been chewed up by the *Lydia's* churning propellers, but with her adrenaline pumping, she swam furiously away from the *Lydia's* hull. The dwarf's silhouette appeared on deck, standing erect like a short mast. He tossed a life preserver in Noora's direction. Noora swam toward it as the *Lydia* faded into the night.

She thought the huge swells would surely engulf her before she could grab the floating white life preserver. Sucked beneath swell after massive swell, Noora didn't know how long she could hold on. *Somebody help me!* she cried and pleaded in her heart. *Help me— I will never make it.* The salt water was burning her throat, and her lungs were about to give in and breathe in the sea.

Ride with the waves, a voice urged. The life preserver bobbed up and down, seeming far out of reach, floating on huge dark swells. A towering swell loomed over her, rising higher and higher. It crashed down, dragging her under—too dark to see the surface. Which way should she go? She had to get air now!

"*I denounce you!*" Her father's words echoed through her soul while the sound of water filled her ears. She would no longer fight to survive. He wanted her dead. She felt herself being pulled up, but the surface was too far and her lungs could no longer sustain the pain. There was nothing left but despair. *I will die now Father... God! Let me die!*

Her dress had ridden up against her face. She pushed the material away from her, suddenly feeling Dweezoul's pebble that had been lodged in the pocket. She held it in a tight fist—her last link to Dweezoul. If she let go of that pebble, it would sink down to the depths of the sea, where she would soon be. But she realized she had reached the surface! There was air. She gulped a lungful.

A cloud passed, revealing the moon, which offered enough light for Noora to see the life preserver floating a few feet away. If she made one last effort to reach for it, she might be able to grab it. But she had no strength left. A wave floated her closer, and Noora was able to grab it while violently coughing up the salt water she had swallowed. She held on to the life preserver until her hand cramped. Shivering uncontrollably, she managed to slip it over her head and shoulders.

The ocean seemed calmer now. Twinkling lights on the horizon appeared and disappeared as she rose and fell with the swells. She could swim toward that direction thanks to the life preserver that kept her afloat. But the salty sea burned her eyes, and her weary vision could deceive her. The luminous dots on the skyline could be miles away.

Her dress was not allowing her to swim freely. She managed to slip it off and wrap it around the life preserver.

Up ahead, a lighted yacht floated.

"Hey! Help!" She waved her exhausted arms.

There was no response. She realized there was no way anyone could see her from the boat.

Rest. I must rest, she thought. *Then maybe I can scream.* She did not want to close her eyes, for fear she might fall asleep and the yacht would sail away from her view. She nevertheless drifted into sleep.

She was slammed back to reality when the sounds of a motor approached. She couldn't tell where it was coming from. The yacht was much closer now. A speedboat full of passengers was racing toward it.

Noora paddled closer, but she was still too far away to be heard.

Music drifted from the deck. By now, the yacht was close enough and she could see blue-and-white-fringed awnings dancing in the night's breeze. Again she waved wearily.

There was a party going on. She could even hear glasses clinking and people laughing.

Guests from the motorboat were being helped on board. As she swam closer, she could see them clearly. Couples—men in tuxedos, women in shiny evening gowns.

The shrill laughter of a young woman wearing a bright red sparkling dress pierced the air as she was being helped on board by a few men.

If they should rescue me, what story would I tell them? Her chest tightened. Warm tears cascaded down her cold cheeks.

Noora swam closer to the yacht, out of sight of the approaching motorboat. She wrapped her dress around her neck and pulled herself up the anchor chain. In elementary school, she had been the fastest rope climber in gym class. She had practiced a system. Midway through her climbing, her dress slipped off and fell into the sea, floating rapidly away with the current. Noora hesitated, but decided to continue her climb. Exhausted, she didn't think her arms could support her weight. Twisting her feet around the rope, slowly she climbed. The party was taking place at the opposite end of the boat. She fitted her foot into one of the yacht's hanging lifebuoys, and with one last effort, heaved herself on board.

Wearing only underpants, she crouched in the shadows and waited while catching her breath. She crossed her arms around her bare breasts and sat shivering, waiting to gather her strength and her courage. She heard sounds of someone approaching above deck. She darted through a narrow passageway, in search of an open door, wishing she could find a towel or something to cover herself. She jiggled every door in her path. The fifth door opened and she stumbled inside.

She was in a large, luxurious cabin, dimly lit by candles everywhere. Soft music played from hidden speakers. A magnum-sized bottle of Cristal was chilling in a sparkling silver bucket, on a bright white tablecloth, with two place settings of gold-and-white china.

Keeping her breasts concealed by her hands, shivering even more from the air conditioning, Noora made a fast dash through another door, into a sumptuous powder room. She heard footsteps.

A large, shiny black marble bathtub was surrounded by thick, tall glowing candles on the marble ledge, along with a bottle of Dom Perignon champagne, which was nestled in a Lucite bucket filled with fresh ice cubes.

Noora reached for one of the monogrammed towels from the golden rack and quickly dried herself. She folded the towel and replaced it the way she found it. Two white peignoirs were hanging on electric racks. Too cold to resist, she grabbed a robe and slipped her shaky arms into the soft, warm terry cloth. She crouched in a corner behind the door, hugging herself. Her body shook uncontrollably and her teeth chattered. The warmth of the robe felt soothing, and slowly she was able to calm her trembling body.

She was startled at the shrill sound of someone whistling. A man began humming a happy tune. Noora realized she must have dozed off for at least twenty minutes, because the tall candles had burned a good way down. She had not heard him come into the stateroom. He popped a cork. It flew past the bathroom door and ricocheted on the wall not far from where Noora hid behind the door. The cork hit the tub, bounced a couple of times, rolled around and around, and finally landed next to the bathtub drain. The man came into the bathroom and turned on the light. Noora huddled closer to the wall behind the door. Spotting the cork, he bent to pick it up from the tub, his back to Noora. Clad in a white tuxedo jacket, he resembled the movie star, Cary Grant, at least from where she hid. He paused for what seemed to Noora like the longest and most uncomfortable minute. Finally, he turned on the faucet, selected one of the nearby jars of pink bath powder, and sprinkled some in the tub. He stopped, looked at the tub, and poured the entire container into the rushing water. He tossed the cork back in the tub and whistled off, shutting the door behind him.

Noora couldn't believe he had not seen her. She could hear a phone ringing out in the stateroom.

"Hello? Yes! Good. Have Stefano escort her," the man said.

With the slight rolling of the yacht, the bathroom door creaked open a few inches. Through the crack between the hinges, Noora could see what was going on in the stateroom.

A tall female appeared. Noora recognized the young woman in the shimmering red dress she had seen in the motorboat. Her stunning gown had a side slit that reached nearly up to her hip. Her golden hair was styled in a classy French twist.

Searching for a way to escape, Noora noticed the porthole above the tub. It was too small.

"You had to send me some fucking foreigner to greet me on board," Noora heard the young woman say loudly. "Too big to do it yourself, huh, honneee."

"Ah, Ana-leaze, please," the man said.

Noora peeked through the hinges and saw the man putting his arms around the young woman and kissing her neck.

"Screw you."

"With pleasure, my love."

"Ooh, champagne. And caviar canapés? Surely you didn't go through all this trouble for *moi*," she sang out.

"Who else but you, *mon amour?*"

"*Who else*, you have the *nerve*."

"I have another surprise for you, darling," he announced, taking her by the hand. "Step into my powder room."

She stopped him midway and wrapped her arms around him once again. "I love it when you spoil me. Turns me on."

They kissed wildly.

"All right," he said when they finally unplugged from one another. "We will keep my surprise for dessert. I've been yearning to have you all to myself. Most of all, darling, I've been yearning to taste you ..."

Noora shrank behind the door. Trembling, she waited. Her throat tightened. What was she going to do now? Maybe she could pass for one of the guests. But how? What clothes could she steal and from where? Her hair was all matted. She probably stank like rotten fish. Perhaps she should just tell these people the truth: She had fallen off a fishing boat on her way to Nice. She wished she could shower. She wished she could die.

She knew her only option was to crawl out of the stateroom and hope the couple would be so wrapped up in each other, they wouldn't notice her. As she began to make her way to the door, she was astonished by what she saw on the black satin bedspread.

The woman in the red sequins was on her back, her legs spread out, her dress pulled to the waist. The man had his face planted between her legs.

Noora tried to crawl out while the couple was thus occupied. The young woman suddenly rose and rested on her elbows. Noora quickly shrank back to her hiding place behind the door.

The golden faucet continued its gentle cascade and the water now reached the edge of the bathtub. Mounds of pink foam started flowing down the sides of the tub, drowning out the candles' flames. Soon the man would have to switch off that water.

The lovers seemed too busy. Noora sprang and turned off the faucet, then dashed back to her hiding place. The moaning from the stateroom got progressively louder. The woman let out a few yelps. Moments later, she heard the woman chuckling.

"Careful!" she giggled.

"You do it, then."

"No, you do it ..."

He was trying to help her remove her gown. It seemed they could not decide whether to slip it from the bottom or from the top.

"I wouldn't want to mess your perfect chignon, darling. Your queenie hairdresser would never forgive me."

Giggling like teenagers, they managed, and now the young woman was proudly displaying her nudity. She stretched her arms over her head and purred with lusty delight.

Noora recognized the woman whose face had graced magazines all over the world. She was Analissa Nielsen, the American movie star.

While the lovers were busy in the stateroom, Noora could no longer keep her eyes open. She nodded off. Um Faheema was humming a tune and smiling. Saloush the goat appeared behind her, bleating loud, louder.

She was slammed back to consciousness when the bleating became a loud shriek.

The movie starlet had sat on the black porcelain toilet when she discovered the stowaway crouched snugly behind the door.

Noora's eyes popped open, and she found herself staring back at Analissa. Caught in the middle of relieving herself when she spotted Noora, the nude celebrity was unable to rise fast enough from the toilet, because she wasn't done. She was screaming while pointing at Noora, as if she had discovered a mouse. Finally, Analissa Nielsen sprang to her feet, grabbed Noora by the hair, and pulled her out of her hiding corner and dragged her to the stateroom, shrieking all the while.

"Son of a bitch!" she yelped at the surprised lover who was stopped short of pouring champagne into a crystal flute.

The star's long, red acrylic nails dug into Noora's scalp. "*This* was my surprise? *This* is what you call dessert?!"

Noora screamed with pain.

"I'm no lesbo and I don't *share* my men!"

With a burst of adrenaline, Noora managed to twist the starlet's arm and break free. The furious Analissa lunged after Noora, grabbing her by the collar of the peignoir. Noora peeled out of the robe and tore out of the stateroom.

Clad only in her underwear, and in a moment of desperation, Noora climbed over the ramp.

Out on the main deck, guests were dancing to a hot Latin rhythm.

She hoped no one saw her silhouette diving overboard.

CHAPTER 30
YASMINA FENDIL'S REQUEST

The Fendil household was buzzing with excitement. Yasmina and her husband Farid set the date—July 6—for the marriage of their daughter Zaffeera to Michel. Gifts were already pouring in to the mansion's delivery entrance.

Zaffeera stood on the verandah of her mother's suite and watched the setting sun. She wore a long, black traditional dress, and a black veil covered her head.

Mrs. Fendil was resting on a lounge chair, her tired legs propped up. They were quite swollen at this time of day. She was hemming a dress for Shamsah.

"Out of respect to my dear sister Noora, I would like to keep my wedding simple and religious," Zaffeera said, her back to her mother.

The evening's call to prayer wafted from a distant minaret.

Mrs. Fendil sighed. *Inshallah.* If it were the will of Allah, a small, traditional wedding it would be. She had never been religious herself. Somehow lately, the whole family had turned to religion—Zaffeera most of all. Mrs. Fendil understood that religion was a comforting way to heal the pain one felt at the loss of a loved one. *No,* she corrected herself, *two loved ones.*

She put down her sewing and studied her daughter. She realized she had never known her as well as her other children. When Zaffeera was an infant, Yasmina had given her all her time because she was frail and needy; but she had neglected Nageeb and Noora. When Kettayef was born and Yasmina had been so preoccupied with her boy's mysterious muteness, taking him from one specialist to another, she had neglected her other children. Especially Zaffeera who was quiet and shy, and had grown apart from the other siblings, and from Yasmina herself. Zaffeera was very intelligent and independent—in fact, she seemed to need nothing from her mother. After Noora's accident, Zaffeera became more attentive toward Kettayef and Shamsah. She read to Shamsah every night. Zaffeera had also been the one who convinced the Al-Balladi Primary School principal to enroll Kettayef, who was now miraculously starting to form sentences.

Yasmina wondered what was on her daughter's mind. Was she worried about becoming a wife? Did she know what would be expected of her? Perhaps Zaffeera was too embarrassed to ask questions. But she had received a modern education. Surely she would know what she was to do on her wedding night.

Zaffeera did not wish to face her mother, for fear that her eyes would reveal the lusty excitement and triumph she felt over finally conquering Michel. She swallowed hard before answering. *"Aiwa, Ummy?"* she said, turning slightly, and casting her eyes to the floor.

"I would like to ask a favor of you."

"Yes, Mother, anything."

"When you have a daughter, nothing would please me more than if you and Michel name her Noora."

"Yes ... Yes, Mother," she replied, her voice breaking. She stood a calculated moment before rushing out of her mother's room.

By the time she finally made it back to her room, Zaffeera was boiling.

"I shall never!" She said between clenched teeth. She made her way to her bathroom and locked the door.

"Over my dead body!" she growled at her reflection in the mirror. Besides, she would give him only sons. She would make sure of that.

CHAPTER 31
RESCUE ON THE RIVIERA

On a seashore filled with more pebbles than sand, Noora lay face down. Waves lapped at her bare feet. She was experiencing bizarre dreams—voices muttering, faces fading in and out of focus. Um Faheema's face appeared. She was smiling, offering comfort.

Was she back at the village with Um Faheema? Noora wondered. Was she waking from a dream on her sand-filled bed? She could hear one of Dweezoul's favorite songs. Did he have his transistor radio turned on? No, not possible. The only way she was back in the desert was if she were dead. Her eyes felt sticky. She remembered that earlier, she had felt a light drizzle falling on her achy back. Now her back felt warm and dry.

"Dis donc, excuse moi, mais tu vas t'faire brûler," said the voice of a young woman, in a strong Parisian accent.

Keeping her face turned away, Noora tightened her arms around her head. The girl's shadow felt unpleasantly cool on her back. She wanted heat.

When Noora didn't respond, the woman continued in English. "Soon we'll be able to fry an egg on your back!" Noora peered an eye out from under her arm. The girl's shadow was still shading her. Standing about three feet from Noora, she was holding what looked like a bottle of suntan lotion.

"J'ai besoin de soleil," Noora muttered, glad she still remembered some French. She wanted warmth. She *needed* SUN. But the young woman would not budge.

"Vous êtes Anglaise ou quoi?"

I'm not English! Why would she think that? "Go away, *s'il vous plait,*" Noora whimpered.

The girl remained planted in the same spot.

Noora managed to pull herself up a bit and ventured another quick glance. She couldn't quite see the girl's face in the sun's glare.

"Whaat happen to you?!"

Noora squinted up and fell back to the sand. "Leave me alone."

"*Pardon* ... I mean no offense."

Noora took a quick look around the vicinity. Further down the beach, young couples were sunbathing. The girls were topless.

Was she nude too? Horrified, Noora quickly felt her bottom. She was relieved to find she was still in her underwear—the yellow stretch knit pair she had bought in Eilat.

"Where are you from?" The young woman persevered. "Are you here for ze *festival?*"

When Noora gave no response, the girl walked back to her beach mat. Before long, she was again at Noora's side. She dropped her canvas bag, her towel, and herself three feet away.

"I am here early this morning to look at the beautiful Greek yacht zat just arrive. You were in same *pozee-seeon*. I go to work and when I come back after *le dejeuner de midi* and soon it will be sunset, and you are in same *pozee-seeon*. Surely something eez wrong ... Did you lose your things?"

Noora opened her mouth to speak, but no voice came out. The ball in her throat was too large and she needed to cry.

"Maybe you should like a good after-sun low-seeon? Or *une couverture* ... *euh* ... *une* ... towel?"

Noora could hear the honking of cars and the growling of motor scooters from the busy road above the beach. A French sixties song wafted faintly from somewhere nearby, reminding her of the happy times when she and Michel used to dance to old, romantic songs. *Michel.* She could still feel him close as the two of them swirled around the open-air terrace of San Stefano Beach.

"I like your aura," the French girl said.

Noora turned to see who this person was. The girl wore a pale pink-and-white polka-dot bikini bottom and a white tank top. She stood about five feet seven inches. Her hair was brown, cut short *à la gamine*, with wispy strands framing her face. She had large, honey-brown Bambi eyes.

My or-what? "What did you say?" Noora had to ask. She could now feel the terrible aches all over her body.

"Your aura. It's pink. And violet. Like a … rhain-bow. *C'est joli*. Pretty. Euh, I would say, like a crown almost. Interesting. Sounds cray-zee, *non?* But I can see auras. Sometime. Eet is a light. Eet comes from the top of our head."

Noora's head was pounding.

"Where are you from?" the girl asked her.

Water. If the stranger could perhaps be kind enough to let her have a little water. Noora managed to raise an achy arm and pointed to the sea. "There."

"*Oh la, la!*" she exclaimed. "*Eh ben dis donc,*" she murmured to herself then remained silent for a long moment before speaking again. "I *knew* it. I *saw* it! Always because of men." She plopped herself back down on the sand. Hugging her legs, she rested her chin on her knees and rocked herself. "He beat you up?"

Noora didn't answer.

"Did you catch him with anozer girl? So you had to … escape and jump in the sea? Yes?"

"Amazing," Noora said, squinting against the glare.

"All of life's creation is amazing."

"You know Dweezoul?"

"*Pardon?*" asked the French girl.

Noora realized she was not thinking clearly. "Sorry … I don't know. I just … wish I could have some water."

"Yes, yes, I have," she said digging in her beach bag. She stopped and looked up. "Oh, *pardon*. Annette Bonjour," she said, extending her hand to Noora.

"*Bonjour*… And *au revoir*," Noora said without taking the girl's hand.

"*Non, non. Je m'appelle Annette Bonjour*. Eez my name. And you?"

Noora pulled herself up from the sand just a bit. She hesitated, then accepted the girl's hand, keeping her other hand over her breasts.

"Oh …" Noora stammered. She realized if she showed her bare breasts when she sat up, she would not look out of place in this part of the world.

"Here. Have good fresh water," the girl said, extending a large bottle of Evian. "Wait. I have a glass, even."

"I don't need a glass ..."

"Yes, yes." She dug in her beach bag again and produced a plastic wine goblet. She poured water and offered it to Noora, who gulped it all down in a matter of seconds. "You are so thirsty, *pauvre chérie*. One would sink you came from the desert." The girl took the goblet from Noora, refilled it, and handed it back to her.

"Thank you," Noora said, hunching over to keep her breasts low to the sand.

"What is your name?"

"Ouch. My back is burning." Her entire body ached more.

"Let me poot some cold water in your back. It will ... how eez the word? It will seezzle. But it will cool your hot skin. Zen we can poot a low-seeon."

"Thank you," Noora said. The girl slowly poured water on Noora's back and patted it gently.

"That does feel better, thank you," Noora said, starting to wonder why this stranger was so friendly.

"Eef you go to the police, they will make you feel out all kinds of formalities, and believe me, it's a waste of time," she said, dropping her bottle of water in her bag. "*Les hommes!* Testicles of shit ... Sorry. I get agitated when I sink how some men treat women. No respect. It is diss-grace-fool."

Noora wondered if the girl had an extra bottle of water ... Perhaps she would not mind lending her just enough money for a local phone call and perhaps some clothes?

Annette extracted a cigarette from her beach bag and lit it. "We flush our men down the *toilette*, and then we regret later. Why? Because ... we *need* them later. Tsk, tsk," she grumbled, shaking her head. She drew deeply on her cigarette, as she contemplated the yachts and slowly exhaled. The smoke drifted into Noora's face.

"*Oh, j'm'excuse.* I forgot, I queet!" Annette said, burying her cigarette in the sand. "I am asphyxiating you. I know you don't smoke."

"How did you know?"

"I am learning to be, how shall I say, *une clairvoyante*. It is a geeft, you know, but many don't know it."

Noora turned and looked around, trying to figure out the map of her surroundings. Over her shoulder, she glanced inland and spotted international flags in the distance. They graced the façade of … the Carlton Hotel?

I'm in Cannes?

The fog lifted from Noora's mind.

Swimming with the tide toward the blinking lights on the horizon, she had actually landed on French soil … *without a passport.* Memories of her ordeal flashed. She escaped the actress who could have scratched her eyes out with those long fingernails. Noora remembered when she dove off the yacht and when a strong wave slammed her closer to shore, where strings of lights grew brighter and she could see cars moving along a seacoast road, giving her temporary hope. But the waves claimed her, dragging her out again. In the darkness, she had feared that surely she would be thrown toward the barrier of rocks that rose like jagged teeth waiting to crush her bones. She remembered she could barely lift an arm to swim. A shark could have easily attacked her. She slammed into one of the looming rocks, begging God for mercy that she would die quickly without suffering, and discovered it was a buoy. Somehow, she had avoided death—again.

She reached for her neck. To her relief, Um Faheema's amulet was still there.

"I was saying zat you can borrow my towel," Annette said, breaking into Noora's thoughts.

"Thank you so very much," Noora muttered and took the warm, dry towel. "Forgive me. I did not mean to be rude. My French is not so good." Slowly and painfully, she managed to rise a few more inches from the sand.

"Eez better zan my English. But I need to practice very much, for my work. I am … how shall I say … *une femme de chambre* … a chambermaid at the Majestic Hotel, and they have many American people for the next two weeks because of the film festival, and most of the big shots, they don't speak French … And your name is?"

"Oh … Pardon?" Noora asked stalling for time. She had to invent.

"Your name."

"My name?" The first thing that popped into Noora's mind was Monaco, and the movie star princess. "Kelly," she mumbled quickly.

"Eet's Kell-ey?"

"Uh ...yes. It's Kelly."

"And your surname?"

"My what?"

"*Nom de famille...* Your family name?"

"Oh ... Uh ..." Noora stammered, slowly turning her stiff neck to her left. She could see the Carlton Hotel in the distance. She was about to say *I do not have a family,* but thought better of it. "Carlton ... Kelly Carlton." She nodded slowly, running a shaky hand through her matted hair.

"Kelly? Do you have any relation with the Carlton Hotel, by chance?"

"No."

"No, I thought not."

"Karlton is spelled with a K. And Kelley ... with an e-y at the end," Noora found herself lying. She wondered how she even came up with such a spelling, but then she needed to add some quick originality here and perhaps now the girl would leave her alone.

"Eef you go back to that yacht, the man who beat you up, I don't want to scare you, but ..."

"It was just a fishing boat. It's gone now. To Marseilles."

"Marseilles?"

Noora nodded mournfully. "I left all my money. And my bag ..."

"I am not surprised. He probably toss all your belonging to the sea. Pouf. He took your money, *bien sûr!* Men. They have no heart."

"It was nice talking to you," Noora said, trying to rise to her feet. She feared that she may have broken something, but all the parts were moving, however stiff she felt.

"Where are you going with no clothes?"

"May I please borrow your towel? I have family ... I need to find a public phone."

"Ah, *ben non,* we mustn't bother family with our personal *problèmes.* Everyone must follow their destiny ..."

"I have an uncle. He's like ... a father to me." She burst into tears. She tried to stop but couldn't.

"Oh, *mon Dieu!* I am sorry. It is my fault. I had no business to talk so much. I have a beeg mouth."

"Just go away," Noora managed to say. She gave the towel back to the girl. She didn't care if her breasts were bare. *God made them, a decent job at that,* she thought angrily, plus she was on the beach in the South of France! She was unable to stifle her sobs, and all she could do was hide her miserable face in her hands.

By the time Noora regained some control of herself, Annette had gathered her beach gear. She picked up her towel and handed it to Noora. "Please keep it. A gift. I did not mean no offense. Very sorry." She started to walk away.

Noora wrapped the towel around herself and stumbled painfully after Annette. "Please. I am the one who should apologize. I didn't mean to be rude ... It's just that ... you see, I *must* find my uncle."

"Maybe I can help you?"

Annette lived behind Cannes' prestigious Majestic Hotel, across the narrow alleyway.

"We pass through *l'hotel de luxe* where I work, cross this little *ruelle* and *voilà—chez moi*. You can shower in my bathroom. I poot new tiles last week. I did a better job than that shit, Bruno," she said. "Come. I have a telephone."

"Thank you. Thank you so much."

Annette made a fast dash across the busy boulevard. Noora held the towel in place, took a deep breath and every ounce of effort she had left, to follow Annette.

She had a terrible time keeping up with her new acquaintance. Her stomach was churning, and her head was pounding harder now. They passed by rows of colorful pastries and croissants displayed in bakery windows. Noora was not only weak from her recent ordeals, but she was weaker yet from hunger.

"*Voilà*, my best friend, Micheline. You like?" Annette asked proudly. Micheline was a rusty, beat-up lemon-colored Renault, with a shredded convertible top.

Annette drove like a maniac. *If God spared me last night,* Noora thought, *I'll surely die now from a collision.* But somehow, the cool sea breeze that slapped her face revived her. Annette found an impossibly small parking space on one of the side streets from the Croisette, and to Noora's surprise, she maneuvered the jalopy expertly into the tiny slot.

"I leeve on the seventh floor," Annette Bonjour explained as they started up the first flight of stairs. "Zey built zis building much before elevators were invented," she said, laughing. Noora wondered how she would ever make it up. The narrow stairs creaked under her feet. She dragged upward slowly as Annette sprinted on ahead. By the sixth floor, Noora thought she would surely pass out.

Annette waited patiently for Noora until she made it to the last step.

"Now can I faint?" Noora managed to say, breathless.

"You get used to it; good for the legs!" She said, barely out of breath. She unlocked the door. "It's a leetle bit messy, so don't look too closely."

Noora sat down on the first chair she found and closed her eyes while she caught her breath. She heard Annette lock the door. She opened her eyes and saw her picking up newspapers and magazines from the floor next to a love seat in the tiny living room. A tall rooftop window was covered by sheer, lacy drapes with pink-and-white-striped curtains tied back with pink satin ribbons.

Annette opened the floor-to-ceiling white shutters, revealing a kitchenette. "I just painted them. You like?"

"Yes," Noora forced herself to answer.

"They were ugly brown when Bruno lived here. Now they make the apartment look bigger, more bright. White opens the eyes."

There was a large black pot on the old two-burner stove. Annette lifted the lid and inhaled the cooking aroma. "I was not tired last night, so I cooked. I bought different fish and shrimps and clams from the fish market, on sale. I had to cook them right way before they ... how shall you say, spoil. I make the best bouillabaisse! I made eenuf for ten people. I wanted to send some to my *grand-mère* in Paris, but eet would spoil too soon. I am happy I can share wiss you."

"May I please have a glass of water?" Noora asked, her eyes searching for a telephone.

"But of course!" Annette opened a tiny refrigerator jam-packed with food and bottled water. "*Qu'est-ce que tu préfère?* Perrier *ou* Evian?"

"Just water from the faucet."

Annette took out a bottle of Evian. "*Pas potable!* Not good for you from the faucet. Here. Good water, fresh from the French mountains."

Annette brought the phone, attached to a long, twisted cord, while Noora gulped down the entire bottle of water.

Next to the window, Annette set a small round table with a white lace tablecloth.

"I just bought this porcelain china. Beautiful, yes?" she said, holding up two plates she removed from a small wall cupboard. "It is very expensive. Slowly, I buy one piece at a time. One or two every year. I have almost enough for a set for two. Next year, I will buy the *sucre* and *crème* sets."

"It is beautiful," Noora said, holding the phone and listening to Uncle Khayat's message again. She hung up. She was not sure what to say to the machine. She would try him again in a little while. Looking down, she noticed she had sand stuck between her toes. Her feet felt itchy and the skin of her heels was dry and cracked. She hoped soon to be soaking in Uncle Khayat's bathtub. He probably had a comfortable guest bathroom like the one in Alexandria. "May I please leave your phone number on my uncle's answering machine?" The room began to spin. "He … is still not home …"

When Noora opened her eyes, she was lying on Annette's loveseat.

"You fainted," Annette said, placing a cold, wet towel on Noora's forehead. In her other hand, she held a bottle of cologne.

Chabrawichi! Noora sat up, remembering the clean, lemony scent of her uncle's aftershave. She could see him vividly in her mind's eye, smiling at her.

"I should have offered you something to eat before I made you climb up all the stairs … I am very sorry. When did you eat the last time?"

"I'm not sure."

"That is too long ago if you don't remember." Annette helped her sit up. "Chicken soup good when we break a fast. Only I have fish soup. But you must eat."

The best bouillabaisse she ever tasted was devoured with crusty, warm, buttered bread. Later, Noora felt better and began to think more clearly.

"I drive you to your uncle later," Annette said, while clearing the table. "I think it is thirty minutes, more or less, from here. They have beautiful villas where your uncle lives. I used to drive there with Bruno and dream that someday … I think first you need to shower, yes? Comb your hair?"

Noora rose to take a look at her reflection on the small mirror by the front door and stumbled.

"Rest now. I put good *crème medicinale* on your sunburn back. We go tomorrow."

Noora didn't think she could wait until tomorrow. She was still wearing Annette's towel. She wished Annette would lend her a dress or something appropriate to wear, but felt uncomfortable about Annette's hospitality. She never heard of anyone who picked up a stranger on the beach, took her home, and fed her dinner—especially in a foreign country. Unless ... she had ulterior motives? She wrapped herself in the bath towel, stepped out of the tiny bathroom, and immediately reached for the phone, dialing her uncle again, praying he would finally answer.

"Still not home?" Annette asked, searching in her armoire among the small selection of clothes.

Noora held Annette's telephone against her chest. "He's home! His line is busy! Oh my God!"

"I will drive you," Annette said, pulling out two dresses on hangers.

"Thank you so much. I will repay you ... ten times, this I promise."

"Oh, silly, it eez my pleasure." She held up the dresses for Noora's perusal. One was sleeveless yellow and the other was sky blue with short sleeves and deep front pockets. "I think the blue one to match your eyes?"

"That is, if you don't mind ..." Noora said, wondering where her yellow dress had drifted by now.

"You have not seen your uncle for a long time?"

"A very long time."

Uncle Khayat's villa was minutes away from Cap D'antibes at Eden Roc. Night had fallen, and all was dark and quiet at the villa on the Rue de Charlemagne. Not as large as the one in Alexandria, his villa was nevertheless lovely, from what Noora could see. There was a large verandah with clay pots of red bougainvillea that climbed up and flowed over the banister—like the ones she remembered in Alexandria. A dim light illuminated a shiny green front door.

Annette kept the motor running. A vicious-sounding dog barked next door.

Noora knocked on the door a few more times and waited. Ten minutes later, she returned to Annette's car.

"Maybe he went out to dinner," Annette suggested, switching off the ignition. Her car was making a racket and spewing out too much smoke.

"Maybe he's in the backyard, and he can't hear the door," Noora said hopefully. She was looking forward to daylight, when she would see his roses and other flowers that were giving off such a lovely fragrance. There was no doubt this villa was Uncle Khayat's. "Maybe he is asleep." It could not be more than eight thirty.

The girls passed through a narrow pathway by the side of the house, where orange trees were in full bloom. Noora wondered why he had not picked all the ripe oranges, many of which were rotting on the ground. Under the thin crescent moon, she could not see them too well, and had squashed a couple of oranges on her way. A sinking feeling came over her.

"You are crying?"

"No, no," Noora said, holding a sniffle and making her way silently back to the front yard.

Annette followed. "We can wait longer if you like," Annette offered. "It is not like I have someone waiting for me."

"You have to work early tomorrow," she said, heading for the car.

"*Et alors?* So?" she shrugged.

Leaning against Annette's car, they waited while watching the villa, as frogs called to each other, echoing through the cool night air.

"Annette, I don't know why you are being so nice to me."

"Why wouldn't I?"

"Someday, I shall reciprocate."

"It is the Almighty Source of All That Is that takes care of that," she whispered. "It … How shall I say, is good karma. You know what means karma?"

"I've heard the word."

"The more good we do, more good returns. From the Source, not from the person where we give, *tu comprends?*"

"Yes. I understand," she said, remembering Um Faheema's words. She wanted to say to Annette that she knew someone dear to her who talked like her. She would tell her when the time was right. "I would like to stay and wait for my uncle, if you don't mind," Noora said, feeling more anxious and even a bit nervous now.

"Okay. Telephone me. Don't forget." Annette reached in her bag. She scribbled her number on a piece of scrap paper.

"How could I ever forget *you,* Annette?"

CHAPTER 32
FINAL DISCOVERY

At six o'clock in the morning, the front door to the villa on the Rue de Charlemagne opened. Noora had fallen asleep on the narrow wooden bench on the front porch. Her eyes popped open. There stood a stylish woman in her early forties perhaps, wearing a marabou-trimmed white peignoir. She glared suspiciously at Noora.

"Is Uncle ... I mean, is Monsieur Khayat Fendil home?" she managed to utter in English, smoothing out her dress and feeling awkward. "I mean, *est-ce-que Monsieur Khayat...*"

"Is this a joke?" the woman responded in British-accented English.

Noora was stunned. "Excuse me, Madame?"

"Who the hell are you?"

Noora glanced up at the number near the front door. This was indeed the right address. "I am Monsieur Khayat Fendil's niece, and I am here to see him."

"Monsieur Khayat did not *have* a niece."

"What? Of course, he does. I was like ... his daughter," she said, on the verge of tears.

"Khayat is deceased! And you are trespassing."

Noora had to steady herself against the brick wall next to where she stood. "What did you say?"

"Khayat is deceased," the woman repeated coldly. She stood guarding the door, studying Noora with an air of superiority. "If you don't mind, I am very busy. Where is my newspaper? Did you take my paper?"

Noora took a deep breath, trying to regain her composure. "No, Madam," she managed to say. "My Uncle Khayat cannot be dead!" She swallowed hard. "And who are YOU?"

"I am his widow."

Noora gasped. "Oh my God. But he never said ... Wait a minute. How long has my uncle been married?"

"That is none of your business."

"But we used to visit him in Alexandria. Every summer. He had a villa there, and ..."

"We had to sell it to pay his medical bills, if you must know," the woman said, staring down at Noora. "Now go away."

"Look. Please. I've come a long way ... a very long way. You see, I know he came to Nice to be near his doctor..."

"I'm the one who took care of him."

"For God's sake, please, I beg of you ... tell me where he is!"

"Honey? What's going on?" a male voice drifted from the living room.

"Coming," the woman replied, planted at the threshold, without removing her eyes from Noora.

"Honey?" the man's voice persevered with a British accent. "That answering machine. We have a million hang-ups. The outgoing message won't erase. Bloody piece of shit!"

"Be right there!" the woman said louder, her eyes still on Noora.

"Please tell me, when did it happen?" Tears were now pouring out of Noora's cheeks and she could not stop them. "For the love of God ..."

The woman softened briefly. "Over a month ago."

"Where is he?"

"I told you, he's *deceased*. Do you have identification showing me who you are?"

"Well, not with me, but ..."

"I didn't think so."

"Please. Is he ... buried in Alexandria? In Egypt?"

"He's buried in Grasse," she said and closed the door.

Noora walked, dazed along cobblestone streets lined with ancient buildings. Reaching the highway, exhausted, hungry, and thirsty, she decided to hitch a ride. She wasn't sure if it was allowed. She figured if girls could sun themselves topless in this part of the world, surely they could hitch a ride. A red scooter driven by a young man sporting a white skull emblazoned on his black T-shirt slowed close to Noora. She turned away and continued her walk. The scooter followed her for a long moment. He said something in French, but she didn't understand and headed up toward one of the stone villas. Finally, the young rider took off.

More than four hours must have passed since Noora left that dreadful woman at the villa, who claimed she was Uncle Khayat's "widow." It must have been early, because the tall gates where Noora stood and waited were locked. Surely someone would come soon and let her inside the cemetery.

Her mouth was pasty, and as dry as cotton. She had munched on rose petals along the way. Remembering her grandmother's garden, she picked a few fragrant rosemary leaves she found growing along picket fences. They briefly helped moisten her dry mouth, but she was thirsty for something refreshing, like a large bottle of Annette's cool Evian.

"God bless you, Annette Bonjour, for lending me your dress," she mumbled to herself. She should be grateful; at least she had a nice dress to wear. She found bobby pins in the pockets and pinned her hair away from her face. And thank goodness Annette's old leather sandals were comfortable, even on cobblestones. She wished she had a purse to carry. *A woman carries a purse when she leaves her house,* Noora thought. Beggars and runaways looked like she did. She stuck her hands in the dress pockets.

She tried to remember the French words for what she needed to say: "*Je cherche la tombe d'un membre de ma famille. Pouvez-vous me diriger? S'il vous plait?*" She had to remember to add "*S'il vous plait.*" Or she should say, "*Pouvez-vous me donner la direction?*" She wasn't sure how she should phrase her request for directions to her family member's grave, and practiced the sentences a few times, hoping she would not be misunderstood. She spotted an old man hobbling up the sidewalk, carrying a tattered attaché case in one hand and a set of dangling keys. He walked as if one leg was shorter than the other. Stopping in front of the huge wrought iron gates, he unlocked and pushed them open.

Noora peered inside. Stone and marble tombs were lined up ahead. The cemetery was small and peaceful, built on a hill surrounded by stone walls and tall, shady trees. Birds were chirping. The air was fragrant with a potpourri of flowers and herbs. She spotted a water fountain nearby.

"Je cherche la tombe d'un member de famille," Noora said, feeling her heart racing faster.

"Par ici." The old man beckoned her toward a small building. He unlocked a narrow door.

"Do you speak English?" Noora asked.

"Yes, mademoiselle. A little. Come. This way."

He limped past a wall of floor-to-ceiling filing drawers. The place had a musty smell, like that of an old library. He turned on a small desk fan.

She stood just outside the door, and heard voices coming from behind her. She turned and saw a handful of people entering the open gate, some holding armfuls of flowers, climbing up the steep hill.

"What was the name of the deceased, Mademoiselle?" Without waiting for an answer, he handed her a small card and a pencil. "Print the name in large letters so I can read it. Sit. Sit down."

Holding back tears, Noora sat at the edge of a chair and printed the name

Khayat Anwar Fendil.

As she wrote, she prayed that the woman at the villa had lied, and this man would tell her no one with such a name was buried there.

Wandering among the gravestones, Noora clutched the small brochure and map the old man gave her. Beneath an olive tree, she found a simple slab of dark gray marble inscribed with his name—Khayat Anwar Fendil—and the years of his birth and death. She recognized his birth date—July 8. They always celebrated his birthday when she and her family visited him in the summer. She could still see him blowing out the candles from a huge cake they ordered from his favorite bakery on the other side of the city near the Hotel Cecile ... She sank to the ground and sobbed uncontrollably.

Why! Why was he buried here? Shouldn't he have been in Alexandria—resting next to his parents? She remembered Nageeb had told her that their uncle's mother had been Jewish, and that she had married Uncle Khayat's father, who, like all their forefathers, were Egyptian Muslims. Perhaps because of his mother's religion, it had been Uncle Khayat's request? She would never know.

Nearby, she spotted another water fountain connected to a small hose and turned on the faucet. She drank the cool water and washed away her tears. She dried her face with the hem of Annette's dress.

"I am so sorry, Uncle Khayat," she said, clearing away dust and a few fallen leaves from the tombstone. *Nageeb, you see? I kept my promise. Where did it get me? All for nothing. Nageeb, your death too, for nothing. Nothing, nothing! Oh God, what have I done?*

Something warm and furry brushed against her. She gasped at the sight of a large sheepdog with woolly gray fur and patches of white. The animal was panting, sending his warm breath straight into her wet face. The huge dog settled comfortably next to her. Someone whistled.

"Baldo? *Ou es-tu, Baldo?*" a man's voice called.

She heard footsteps crunching on the gravel and swept her tears away with the back of her hand. She heard the crinkling of cellophane and smelled the flowers before seeing them.

A young man kneeled and placed the bouquet at the foot of the tombstone in front of Noora.

"*Bonjour,*" he muttered, nodding a polite good morning. He was obviously surprised by Noora's presence.

Noora looked up. She wanted to run, far away, but her legs would not budge.

"*Excusez-moi mademoiselle…*" the young man said.

Noora ventured another glance.

"*Vous connaissiez le décédé?*"

She wrapped her arms around the huge dog and caressed its fur in long strokes.

The man spoke in French, but she couldn't find the words to respond to him.

"What a beautiful dog," she muttered in English, almost to herself, thinking the man must have placed the flowers on the wrong grave.

"Thank you," he said in English.

"What's his name? Bardot?" she continued in English."After… Brigitte Bardot? She likes dogs … too …"

"Actually, it's Baldo."

"Oh. What kind is he?"

"Bouvier des Flandres." He pronounced it beautifully in French.

"A sheepdog?"

"Yes. He needs to be groomed," he said, studying her.

She noticed his large hazel eyes. They looked sad. She looked away.

There was an uncomfortable silence.

"Did you know Monsieur Khayat?" he asked.

"What?" she responded, looking up at the stranger.

"Monsieur Khayat Fendil ... The deceased ..."

Deceased? That terrible word again. "Yes. You ... you knew him?"

"I was his doctor."

"You were?"

"Yes. Are you ... were you perhaps a relative?"

Noora nodded. "Yes, yes, I was." She looked away. He bent closer to Noora and extended his hand. "I am Alain Demiel. *Enchanté*. Pleased to meet you."

The weather had changed to cloudy and windy. Noora sat on the cold, wet sand by the receding tide. She began to write in the sand.

Uncle Khayat is gone.

I ran along French shores

I ran till I could run no more.

She needed a pen and paper, but couldn't even afford that. She owned nothing. "Writing is an extension of the soul," she remembered Dr. Pennington say. *What soul?*

She cleared another area in the sand and continued to write.

What have I done?

What dreadful thing?

Uncle Khayat is gone ...

She read the words again. With a stroke of her hand, she wiped away what she had written.

She hugged her knees, rocked herself, thinking, wondering. She rocked faster, faster, jumped to her feet, and ran to shore. She glared at the sky. "Why?" she asked defiantly. She kicked the sand and screamed. "Why?! What have I done?! Answer me! "ANSWER MEEE!" she shouted, attracting people on the beach, some shaking their heads at the madwoman. Noora did not care anymore. She was speaking to her father—as if he were standing right above her.

"Kelley?"

Noora heard the call but ignored it because she really wanted to tear her dress off. It wasn't even hers! She wanted to remove it. Yes, that's what she had to do. She had to dive in the water and swim far out until she would finally drown. "You wanted me dead. DEAD! Okay! I'm gone. Finished! Whatever the reason, I'M DEAD! See? Watch me! Watch me, Father! *KHALLAASS!*"

"Kelley! KELLEY!" Annette reached Noora just as she was about to remove her dress. "Kelley! It's all right. It is okay ..."

Noora wanted to scream, *My name is not Kelley, it's Noora!* "Can't you understand?" she shouted at Annette.

"Yes, please, come with me. Everything will be all right. I promise," Annette said, gently pulling Noora away from the water.

"I'm sorry. Oh my God, I am so, so sorry!" Noora sobbed, her entire body shaking.

"Let us sit for a moment," Annette said, taking Noora's hands and guiding her further away from the shore.

She let her cry, gently pulling Noora with her to sit on the sand. When Noora finally regained some control of her sobs, Annette said, "I telephoned you at your uncle's house and a woman answered. I had the feeling you were here."

"Oh, Annette, I am sorry." *I am destroyed* was what she really wanted to say. *Détruite!* All hope was gone. And now she had nothing.

"What happened? Your uncle?"

Noora nodded.

"Please say to me what happened."

Noora managed to tell her story through her tears.

"*Mon Dieu.* This, I did not predict," she said, looking out to sea. "Everything has a reason ... You know? A ... a purpose. We must believe. We must have faith, you understand?"

Faith? Noora touched her blue bead. Um Faheema, she cried in her heart, *what's my journey now?*

They sat side-by-side on the sand, watching the yachts, some more luxurious and elaborate than others, bobbing in the expanse of gray to dark blue as the clouds slowly dissipated. Annette turned her attention to Noora. "*Pauvre chérie*. Tell me the rest. The doctor."

Noora sighed. "He invited me to lunch."

"The *docteur* invited you to lunch?"

"Yes. I was very grateful, because ..."

"He *paid?*" Annette asked incredulously.

"Well, I had no money. I wasn't hungry, but he insisted I eat. I ate everything he ordered. I didn't think I could. But I did. He must have felt sorry for me."

"He has a car?"

"Yes, a Citroen. His dog, Baldo, occupied the entire back seat. He panted in my ear all the way, but I didn't mind."

"*Le docteur?* The jerk!"

"No, silly, his dog," Noora couldn't help but chuckle at Annette's comments. "It's a Bouvier des Flandres."

"What was his name?"

"Baldo."

"The doctor's name is Baldo?"

"No, Annette." Noora said, chuckling again. "*Non, le docteur.*"

"*Ah, le docteur. Et lui, comment s'appelle-t'il?*"

"His name is Alain Demiel." She returned to her serious mood. "He gave me his business card and said I can call him anytime."

"*Vraiment?*"

"Yes, really. He probably felt sorry for me because I couldn't stop crying. I cried before and after lunch, and in between."

"I am sorry. I am glad you ate. That was good. Is the *docteur* married? He must be married."

"His wife died two years ago. He told me he goes to the cemetery every week and puts yellow roses on her grave. Today he also put flowers on Uncle Khayat's grave ... he was not only his patient, he said they were friends."

"How old is the *docteur?*"

"I couldn't tell."

"I mean, twenties, thirties, forties? Fifties?

"Maybe mid-thirties. Maybe almost forty. Not sure."

"Aah. Did he say what happened to your uncle?"

"Prostate cancer; he said an advanced case. But he said my uncle had responded well to treatments. He also talked about his wife. She had ovarian cancer."

"Terrible disease. Very sad."

"He said if it hadn't been for Uncle Khayat, he would not have become the specialist that he is today. He was an old friend of his family."

"Your uncle was an old friend of the doctor's family?"

"Apparently. But I never heard of him before. The Demiel family ... I asked him if my uncle died in the hospital. He said no, he died sitting on his rocking chair, in his verandah, facing the sea ... Sounds like my uncle," Noora said, her voice breaking as tears rolled down her cheeks. "He died with his pipe still clutched in his hand ..."

The sun had set, leaving an array of purple and pink in the horizon. Annette and Noora remained sitting together in silence.

"The doctor drove me back to the beach where you and I met," Noora finally said. "He had to go back to his clinic, so I told him to leave me here. I didn't know what else to do. Thank you for coming to find me. You see, I was really not ... being myself ... Well, anyway. How did you find me?"

"I heard you."

"I'm so sorry. I didn't mean to make a scene and scream."

"I heard you in my heart. We need some good hot *shocola,*" she said, rising and dusting off sand from her skirt.

Noora managed a bitter smile. How could one buy hot chocolate when there was no money for even a breadcrumb?

"Now zat I don't have to buy expensive wine for Bruno, I can afford good *shocola!* I know exactly where to go!" Annette said, helping Noora up. "Come, *ma chère amie.*"

Inside Annette's apartment, after consuming a box of chocolate-covered marzipan treats, luscious petits fours, and a chocolate éclair they had split in half, over a bowl of café au lait, Annette talked about her life. Sitting on Annette's cozy loveseat, Noora held her second bowl of café au lait with both hands for warmth and comfort. She could see the rising moon from the window.

Annette had lost her mother when she was a teenager, and she lived with her grandmother in Paris. When she was nineteen, Annette left

Paris to live with Bruno in Cannes. Her boyfriend had chosen the rooftop apartment behind the hotel because he could walk through the luxurious lobby, acting as if he were a guest. He frequented the bar nightly, and made everyone believe he was a wealthy *bon vivant*. Every night, when the evening was over and he ran out of money, Bruno stumbled drunk through the back door to the alley and the apartment he shared with Annette.

"I left my grandmother to realize the dream of my life. I met him in a summer camp. I was fifteen years old. *Grand-mère* did not approve, but she believed I needed to live my life. As long as we were free. With no war. I loved Bruno too much to think with my head. I thought we were going to be married as soon as we had a little money. Have a family. I wanted to prove to *Grand-mère* that she was wrong. But she was always correct. Bruno had big dreams. But too lazy to work. He wanted me to work and buy the food, make dinner, clean, everything. Food is expensive. And all the wine ..."

Noora felt embarrassed that she was eating Annette's food. She showed such generosity and trust. How would she ever repay her? In the meantime, the aspirin Annette had given her was starting to take effect, and Noora was sleepy.

"Bruno wanted sex all the time," Annette went on talking. "Sex every day, every night. I went to work bow-legged," she giggled. "Funny now. It wasn't funny before." She removed her dress, and wearing only transparent lacy underwear, she crossed the room to a little dresser drawer. She took out a long white nightgown and put it on.

"I was pregnant one time, you know?" she said removing her makeup with a wet cloth. "He made an appointment for an abortion, but I lost the pregnancy. It was God's will. But then, he made an appointment to tie my tubes so I would not get pregnant anymore," she said. "Can you believe how cruel some men can be?"

"Well, yes ... perhaps," Noora mumbled, thinking about her father. She would not go to that time, that painful past.

"Oh my goodness! I am sorry. You must be exhausted. You are so polite. Tell me to stop talking. You are a good listener. I never tell about my secrets to anyone before," she said, putting the dishes in the sink and closing the sliding doors of the kitchenette. "You can sleep on my bed if you like. My little couch is very comfortable for me," she said, opening her armoire and pulling out a pillow and blanket.

"I like your little loveseat," Noora said. "It's cozy. May I sleep here?"

"*Ah mais oui*, and even when I become rich one day, I will always keep this loveseat," she said, handing Noora the bedding.

"I'm sorry," Noora said, curling up on the sofa, covering herself.

"About what?"

"About your being forced to do that operation."

"Operation?"

"Tie your tubes."

"*Ah, non, non!* I went to the *clinique*, yes. But nothing more. I waited a few hours across the street and then I took the bus home. I told him I had the operation, but I did not do it. I took birth control pills and I put them in my locker at work."

"Good for you. That was very smart."

"But I was still stupid, because Bruno was drinking more and more and I had to work to pay the hotel bar. Then I heard Bruno was seeing a girl who had a yacht. I left work in the middle of the day and I rented a ... a how you say, *barque à moteur*."

"Speedboat?"

"Yes, and I saw him with the girl. She was wearing nothing, only a *ficelle*, up her *cul!*"

Noora didn't recognize the words.

"A G-string, you know, up her derriere. When I saw my Bruno caress that derriere, I became crazy. I climb on the stairs on the yacht. There was a party. All the rich people with perfect bodies and perfect tans eating fancy foods; I even saw a mountain of caviar on the buffet table, and ... Bruno did not see me because he was busy kissing zat beetch! I screamed, 'Stop! Bruno is mine!' I was screaming so loud, Bruno ran to me and grabbed me by the hair. He slapped my face and said he was going to call the police. Like he didn't know me. Arrest me for trespassing ..."

"What did you do?" Noora asked.

"So I jump in the water and swam to the beach. Even I didn't know I could swim so fast. It was because of the ... how you say ..."

"Adrenaline?"

"Yes."

Noora recalled how she also dove off the yacht, that night the actress nearly clawed her with her nails, and how she was able to swim to shore like she never thought possible.

"I hated my life. Mostly, I hated me! I wanted to run back to Paris and hide. I believed I became a crazy person. But I did not want to worry my grandmother. She has … how shall I say, she has endured many, many horrible times in her life. She was a survivor of a concentration camp. It was not fair for me to worry her … you know?"

"I am so sorry," Noora said. So much suffering in this world, she thought, as Annette continued. But Noora's eyelids were becoming heavier.

"I was ready to commit suicide. But I could never, because I could never hurt my *Grand-mère* anymore. Then, *par chance,* I found a wonderful store with incense and there I read a book called *Take Charge of Your Life*. And so I did."

"Take charge of your life …" Noora murmured, trying to stay awake.

"Yes," Annette answered, yawning. "I am sorry. I should stop talking. We should sleep now. *Bonne nuit. Beaux rêves.*"

The small cuckoo clock by the front door chimed twice. Noora was thrust out of a deep sleep, wondering where she was. *Two o'clock in the afternoon?* Realizing she was in Annette's apartment, she groggily stumbled for the bathroom, and discovered a note tacked to the bathroom door.

> *"I went to work. Back at six. I left un croissant au chocolat et une bouteille d'aspirine. Annette"*

Another note on the table gave instructions on how to use the coffeepot. Annette had also left two chamomile tea bags on a plate. Next to it was a small bottle of aspirin and a tube of after-sun lotion. Noora was amazed. God must have sent Annette, an angel.

It was almost too good to be true.

CHAPTER 33
LIGHT OF THE DESERT MEETS ICE OF THE JUNGLE

Noora pushed the heavy cart through the hotel hallway.

"Housekeeping," she said timidly, after tapping on the fourth door.

She had gratefully accepted the job. How could she refuse? They did not ask for any "formalities." No need for any of that here, thanks to her friend Annette. The pay was miserable, but she could never think that way anymore. She would be able to help Annette pay for groceries and perhaps, eventually, she could help pay the rent—if Annette would allow her to stay.

One day at a time, she reminded herself. One moment at a time. You have a new name; you are a new person. No one ever has to know who you once were.

She tapped on the door to room 224. No answer. She ventured inside and found the door to the bathroom wide open and a man sitting on the toilet.

"Oh, so sorry," Noora blurted out, blushing. "*Je m'excuse...*" She hustled out of the room, and as she closed the door, she heard the man's thunderous voice.

"Come in, come in. I'm done!" he said, over the sounds of flushing toilet. "COME IN!" he yelled louder. He sounded like an American.

"*Pardon, Monsieur!* Housekeeping. I ... I shall return later."

"NO! Now. Clean room right now."

Noora hurried through the small vestibule and straight to the large, sunny suite. She heard the man run the faucet in the bathroom. She grabbed the two trash baskets that were overflowing with discarded mail and crushed-up balls of paper. That was the first thing you did, Annette had instructed: remove the trash. Noora had to pass through the bathroom again, where that man was. Never mind. She was to do her job and think of nothing more. She nearly bumped into him as she tried to make her way out to her cart in the hall.

"So sorry, sir," she said in English, getting a good look at him for the first time. He had gray hair, gray-blue eyes, like ice, and a stocky build. He appeared to be her height or about an inch shorter.

The head of housekeeping had warned her in advance about the guests at this time of the year. "Most of the British in the film business speak French. The Germans also. But the Americans from Hollywood, aiii, Cary Grant and Grace Kelly, they are not!"

"Do toilets first. Bathroom. *Capisce?*" the belligerent man demanded as he brushed past her.

"Yes. I understand. I can come back, sir ..."

"Hallelujah, Hollywood! Someone speaks English. I'm gonna do cartwheels."

"Yes, sir," she managed to mutter, as she moved toward the door. "I shall return at a more convenient time."

"This is the *only* convenient time. Bathroom first. And bring more towels. Don't forget. More towels!" The phone rang. He rushed to a desk piled with magazines, books, fat binders, mail, and a huge basket of fruit. "Get rid of this," he said, indicating the basket.

Noora dumped the trash in the cart's trash bin, and rushed back inside to return it to its proper place. She took the pretty basket out to the hallway and made her way to the bathroom to resume her task.

He snatched up the phone and barked, "Ian Cohen!" Pressing the phone to his ear, he moved around the desk and sat. "Where the *hell* have you been, Arnie? I left a million messages, and God forbid you return one of my fucking phone calls!" He listened for a moment, then yelled louder, "Hey, Arn. Don't bullshit me!"

Soiled towels were piled high next to the tub in the luxurious marble and mirrored bathroom. Several towels were smudged with red lipstick, as if a woman had deliberately wiped her lips on them instead of using tissue. Noora had forgotten to put on her rubber gloves. "You must wear them or you will catch AIDS," Annette had warned as if talking about catching the common cold. In the other room, the man was still yelling on the phone. She had heard he was a prominent producer. She wondered if all wealthy American men were so loud and undignified. She wished she could find an excuse to leave. There were two more rooms she could clean. Noora slipped on her gloves. She would have to remove them when she made the bed, even though Annette insisted she should wear gloves at all times. But she found it too difficult to work wearing rubber gloves.

"... So FIRE him!" came the man's growl from his suite. "I ... don't ... care! No sound man's gonna FUCK UP MY MOVIE!"

He was yelling so loud, Noora's heart fluttered.

"I *AM* calm! Get Shawn O'Shaunessy. I told you to get Shawn in the first place ... I told ya!"

There was silence finally. But not for long.

"WHAAAT?" He sounded fully capable of crunching the receiver in half with his teeth. "I never said that! I never, NEVER said that! Goddamn it, Arnie. The hairdresser's sister sucks your dick, you screw the stand-in, you *fuck* with the DP's wife, and-don't-tell-me-you-don't, and now you're fucking up my picture! You've got your head up your ass! Don't you think I know what's goin' on out there on location? Just 'cause I'm in friggin' Frogsville doesn't mean ..."

In the corridor, Noora dropped the soiled towels into the portable laundry bin and brought in clean ones. Didn't that man care that with the windows open, he was probably being heard all the way down the Croisette Boulevard?

Back inside, Noora felt sickened as she stared into the tub she had to clean. There was so much hair stuck in the drain that hardly any water could run—gray soap scum, mixed with coarse dark, curly hair. *Pubic hair?* Her stomach churned. But she was to clean, not think. She had a job. She had a place to live. She was a maid. But in a very luxurious, world-renowned hotel. As long as she did not allow herself to think about her past, she was fine. As long as there were no people from her homeland, she was safe. The man continued to yell.

"I *saw* the dailies! THEY SUCK! They're out of fuckin' focus. What's with all these extras?"

A short-lived silence, then: "Yeah? No. NO, I don't think we need all that atmosphere!"

She tried to avoid looking at her reflection, but every wall presented mirrors. She had pulled her hair up into a ponytail and twisted it to form a doughnut, secured by a hairnet. Her scar seemed more pronounced and her nose bent to the right. She had lost so much weight, she looked scrawny. But never mind about her appearance.

At last, she was done with the bathroom. Maybe she could have done a better job. There was no time. She had two more rooms to clean before break time. She had mastered the way to fold towels, just as Annette had taught her. She had stayed up late practicing until she finally got the hang of it. Down to every detail, no matter how silly it seemed. Did these Hollywood people really notice? Weren't they too busy partying, being interviewed, and having their pictures taken? Annette had laughed. "These movie people don't notice anything until you do not do it exactly right," she'd said. Folding the toilet paper into a crisp design seemed the most ridiculous thing to have to do, but the finished effect showed this was no ordinary hotel.

When she tiptoed into the suite to make the bed, the man was fuming.

Noora's heart began to race.

"I'd like my room done ta-day. Not ta-morrow!"

"Yes, sir." She removed the old pillowcases. One was stained with lipstick smudges. The producer must have had a wild night. She came around the bed to finish the other side. Aside from the lipstick stains and hair strands here and there, nothing showed a missus was sharing the man's suite.

What business was it of hers? *Make the bed, dust, vacuum, do your job, leave.*

She removed all the soiled sheets and dashed out of the room with her load, returning instantly with fresh, folded bed linens. The first guest she personally encountered had to be this uncouth American. She felt degraded. If he tossed one more sarcastic remark, she would have to walk out of the room—but then he would certainly complain about her.

He was now furiously scribbling something on a legal-sized yellow pad. He tore out some pages then got on the phone again.

"Get me my secretary," he huffed, out of breath. Then he slammed the phone back down.

Noora could swear he was watching her. The blood rushed to her face and she could feel a cascade of perspiration flow down from under her arms. He marched to the hallway that housed the mini-bar, opened the small refrigerator, and extracted a bottle of Perrier. Then he went to the bathroom. She heard him run the water.

She folded the sheets under the mattress exactly the way Annette had taught her. Fold one side this way, and then take the other, form a point, and tuck under the mattress. She had never bothered watching her maids make her bed.

She noticed a small pair of lacy women's underwear on the floor, next to the bedside table. She had almost stepped on it. She would have to remove the underwear and place it on the chair as she started to vacuum. Annette had warned her about soiled underwear—either men's or women's. "If you find used undies on the floor, use plastic gloves and put in the special plastic sack marked 'for your convenience' and leave on the *chaise*," Annette's words echoed in her ear. *Okay, Annette, I shall.* What chaise? The room had no chaise. Oh yes, now she remembered. *Chaise* meant "chair" in French, and not one of those lounge chairs.

As Noora rushed silently out of the room to get the plastic bag and slip on her gloves, she again nearly bumped into Monsieur Ian Cohen.

He did not excuse himself, and headed straight to the phone. He watched the receiver for a moment, then noticed the underpants on the floor. This seemed to displease him greatly. He was about to cross the room to pick up the underpants when the phone rang. He picked up the receiver. "Ian Cohen!" he barked. "What? No…NO! Absolutely not, do not send him in. I'm in a meeting. No. I'm NOT here, *capisce? Comprendey?* I am NOT here!" He slammed down the phone. The phone rang again. Ian snatched it up. "I said, I'm not! … Oh … Roz. Glad it's you. I got a coupla letters to dictate. They have to be sent A.S.A-mmediately …"

Out in the hallway, Noora was searching for plastic bags. She was sure she had put some in her cart. She was going to have to talk to that man and say she could come back later to vacuum, because the noise would surely disturb his phone conversation. *A-ha, there they were, the bags, hidden under shampoo bottles,* she thought with a sigh of relief. She returned to the suite and noticed that the throw pillows on the bed were crooked, and that she had forgotten to flare out the quilted bedspread the way Annette had shown her. She fixed the pillows and bedspread.

The producer had rattled her—what else was she forgetting? After the final touches, and just as she was about to remove the underpants, a tall, handsome young man clad in casual Gucci pants and perfectly tailored silk shirt appeared.

"You *sonnomabeetch,*" he growled, his eyes afire.

Noora recognized him. He was the Italian movie star she had read about in magazines in London. Wasn't he the one who just married ... *Oh my God!* Noora gasped. *This was the guy who just married that girl! The movie star who threw me out of the yacht!*

"I just arrive from location and I find out why my wife is not in penthouse because you *screw* her?" He pointed his finger like pointing a knife. "*You*... FUCK my wife? *SONNAMABEETCH*. I sue you! I should *keel* you!"

Noora thought this could not be happening; but she could smell his strong cologne, and he was altogether too real, blocking the exit.

Ian Cohen immediately glanced over at the underpants on the floor.

Noora caught his glance as the young stud continued to wave his arms and threaten the producer. Noora picked up the underpants and thrust them in her pocket. She excused herself loudly, and nearly brushing her right shoulder against the Italian movie star, she rushed out of the suite.

Trying to get far away from that wild episode in Mr. Cohen's room, Noora pushed the cart down the corridor. She shoved it out of view in the housekeeping storage room and ducked in after it. She had to get rid of the underwear. If she were caught, they would think she was some kind of a pervert. What a stupid thing to do, run with a woman's soiled underpants and put them in her pocket! But if the Italian movie star saw them ... So what? What business was that of hers? She thought of the way Mr. Cohen looked at the underpants next to his bed—and the way he shot a quick glance toward her direction. "*Get them out of here,*" she could swear he wanted to tell her.

What should she do with them? She threw the underpants in the trash, realizing she might have saved that man's reputation. She pushed her cart back out into the corridor, ready to tackle the next room.

That night, Annette's eyes were clearer than usual. She seemed happy, even after a long workday at the hotel.

"Tell me more about the *docteur!*" Annette asked for the third time. "A widower? And, he is *Juif?* A Jewish *docteur,*" she murmured dreamily. "He must have liked you very much. A man never invite a girl he just meets for lunch in a nice restaurant, and pay. *Jamais! Les hommes pareils, ils n'existent plus.* Men like that don't exist anymore. They always want something more in return," she rambled on in French, talking to herself. She drowned a chunk of buttered French bread in her homemade lentil soup. "Only please don't forget *moi,* your friend, yours truly, when he *proposes.*"

Noora nearly choked on her food. "You've been reading too many romance magazines, Annette." She broke off a chunk of warm, crusty baguette and piled on some creamy butter. She dunked it into her soup, popped it into her mouth, and closed her eyes to better savor the luscious taste. Annette was a true culinary artist who delighted in mastering the most challenging French recipes, using the least expensive ingredients; she had a gift in turning any cheap meal into a feast.

"There are no accidents in life," Annette declared.

Noora did not want to think about her encounter with *Docteur* Demiel, because she could not bear to think about Uncle Khayat. She rose to clear the table.

"What happened? You were so hungry, and now, *non?*"

"Thank you, it's very good. I enjoyed it. It's just that ..."

"You need food. You are skinny."

"I will pay you back for all you have done for me. If it weren't for you, I don't know what ..."

"For the love of God, you are my friend. We have known each other in another life. We were friends before this lifetime. I had a dream before I meet you ... now I am sure it is true! I know I sound like a crazy girl right now, but I believe inside my heart we died in a concentration camp together. We were little. Maybe ten years old. We promise each other ... We promise ..." Tears began to well. "... One day, we would find each other. If it did not happen, why I feel so much strong energy when I first see you on the beach? We lived another life. We suffered very much. This time we are going to make up a good life."

"I don't know about another life. Perhaps it's because we have both experienced a degree of hardship in this life."

"*Non*, it's much deeper. We need to help one another."

So far, Noora thought, *Annette was doing all the giving.* How could Noora ever think to repay her?

Parallel to the Croisette, Cannes' popular seacoast road, was a little side-road café, where starving painters had once traded their *chef d'oeuvres* for meals.

La Poulette, a quaint and eclectic hideaway, had served lovers, foreigners, and people-watchers for decades—a perfect place, especially during the film festival.

Noora's hair fell loosely around her shoulders. Her bangs were too long and annoyingly covered her eyes. She needed a haircut. She sighed at the thought that she did not possess one franc to pay for a visit to the beauty parlor. Payday was in five days. The money was going to be barely enough to help Annette pay for food. If she was lucky, perhaps she could buy flowers for Uncle Khayat's grave. Money for a haircut was a selfish thought. She looked at her luscious *baba-au-rhum*. Annette was devouring her second chocolate éclair. They had so much in common. They loved sweets and did not have to worry about putting on weight. Stress took care of that.

A crowd gathered outside on the street. Screams and whistles were heard, and within minutes, photographers exploded out of nowhere, as cameras flashed, blinding everyone.

Analissa Nielsen was walking alone, wearing a wide-brimmed hat and Chanel sunglasses. She had a low-cut white halter top, revealing cleavage that probably made men drool and women envy, and a red-and-white polka-dot chiffon skirt that flared out two inches above the knees. She walked and swayed in slow motion.

Analissa decided she had to get some fresh air. Her penthouse suite at the Majestic Hotel was lonely. Her new husband of four months, the world-famous movie actor, the one and only Sergio Maggiamore, had recently returned from location. He was out again, this time attending some kind of a serious meeting with producers, accountants, and attorneys. She loved the movie business but hated the business of movies. Sergio made it quite clear he did not want Analissa in his business meetings. He said she would be bored. What he really meant was her presence would distract the little horny idiots with balding heads, small penises, and ugly wives. Their attention would not be on Mr. Maggiamore.

Well, Analissa thought, she needed attention, and stroking too! Lots of it. Why did she become a star in the first place? She decided to give her favorite friends, the paparazzi, a run for their money.

Two nights before, Analissa had dumped Bob Brockman, the producer who had the nerve to hide some bitch in his bathroom. He wanted to surprise her, he said. She was no lesbian. The bastard. Furthermore, the so-called big-shot producer was either too cheap or probably not rich enough to own his own yacht. He rented one. And he was married. With too many ex-wives and spoiled kids! He was losing his hair, and he was really a lousy lay. The price she had to pay for stardom. She had won the lead role in his upcoming movie. She had earned that part! The script had called for great locations: *Streets of Beverly Hills*. Every starlet would have *killed* to get the chance to work on that film, and she got the lead role. After that fiasco night in his chartered yacht, Bob Brockman had called her time and again, begging her forgiveness and swearing that he had no idea there was a young chick hiding in his cabin's bathroom. *Yeah, right! Some clandestine girl happened to be there by mistake*. Did he think she was that stupid? After the movie, she would not need the jerk anymore.

She had called her agent in Beverly Hills and told him Bob Brockman was a pervert and enticed her to a ménage-à-trois.

"This is Hollywood, honey; you don't burn your bridges," the agent had the nerve to tell her. She would have dumped him on the spot if he hadn't been one of Hollywood's top agents.

The thought of how she had been used and abused made her furious. She had to do something to gain more respect. Ian Cohen was more powerful than all of them. Mr. I.C., the untouchable. Well, she finally *touched* him. In more places than one. It had been a great challenge to get the old mogul's attention. She had tried for more than five years. Why did he not show interest? Because she was married? That never stopped a big shot movie producer before! To be in one of his action-packed movies would make her a bigger star. The opportunity might even win her recognition in the *Guinness Book*, as the highest-paid movie star—at least for that year! Perhaps her wish would come true. Only a few hours before her husband arrived in Cannes last night, she had wangled her way into Ice's hotel room, into his bed, in his arms, and even beneath his balls! She had left her underwear on the floor. On purpose. Of course. She was going to cry in her husband's arms as soon as he walked through the double doors of their hotel suite, and she would tell him how Ice tried to seduce her.

Sergio would not doubt her one bit, and Analissa was going to get her revenge. No one ignored Analissa Nielsen. Not even asshole Ice Cohen.

This is how she made it happen: It was late. Ice had a few drinks and he looked beat. He had hosted the first film festival press party at the Hotel du Cap. And he had *not* invited her. She had waited for him downstairs in the garage when his guests had all gone to their rooms and he was on his way to his rented car. She had convinced him he was too drunk to drive. She drove him to the Majestic—it was not out of her way since they stayed in the same hotel—and together they had stumbled into his suite. She had made him laugh and did not talk about movies. At dawn, during the thunderous sounds of his snoring, Analissa Nielsen sneaked out, leaving lipstick smudges on the towels—he should never forget their bath together—and she had left her underwear on the floor next to the bed, before returning to her suite, a few floors up.

Exiting through the rear door, trailing perfume and knowing full well she would attract fans, Analissa strolled down the avenue.

"It's Analissa!" fans roared to her delight. The paparazzi called out to her for a better pose, a better picture. Soon, she would be in all the French magazines.

Sitting at a small round table with Annette at the little sidewalk café, Noora turned pale. Analissa, who was spotted gathering fans at her heels, may have recognized her. While cameras flashed, the starlet stopped dead in her stilettos and actually glared at Noora. Noora almost choked on her *baba-au-rhum*. Fans were shoving papers and pens for Analissa's autograph, cameras flashed blindingly, but Analissa pressed closer, obviously trying to get a better look at the dark-haired young woman sitting at the café.

"You!" Noora heard her yell. A gleaming white convertible honked as it glided around the bend toward Analissa Nielsen. More fans gathered around her. She turned and immediately put on her famous smile, sent air kisses to her fans, and was helped by two men through the growing crowd and into the car.

"Did you see that car? It is a Rolls-Royce. I think a Corniche! Why all those stupid movie stars receive so much admiration and have gorgeous cars!" Annette said.

Noora nodded, looking away. Her father had a white convertible Corniche. He wasn't stupid or a movie star ...

"I don't know, but I think she recognized you!" Annette exclaimed.

"Me? No," Noora said nervously, turning her back a little more to the street.

"You know who she is?"

Noora shook her head no.

"She is the biggest *vedette!* The new Brigitte Bardot of the American movies, and now even of the world! But you will never believe me when I tell you," Annette said, leaning closer to Noora. "I clean her room at the hotel."

"You *do?* She's ... in the *hotel?*" Noora's heart began to pound. That woman could have her arrested.

"Yes, and not only that, but eef only everyone know what a dirty person she is, *oh la, la,* maybe they all be more disgusted and not so goo-goo, ga-ga about her," Annette snickered. She took another sip of her hot chocolate. "I cannot even tell you how dirty she is, because I don't want to ruin your appetite."

If only people knew what a sharmouta *she really is,* Noora wanted to say.

CHAPTER 34
THE MYSTERIOUS BIRTH ANNOUNCEMENT

Al-Balladi's most prominent *hakim*, the family physician, shook his head. He was unable to convince his patient Mr. Farid Fendil that he was digging his own grave.

"I'd like to refer you to a nutritionist and a personal trainer. They are both excellent. I use them myself."

Farid Fendil was sitting up in bed. He respected Doctor Hamid, but how could he possibly admit that he had spent the night fornicating like a young Arabian stallion with Madame Medina? It had nothing to do with his cholesterol. When you're older, you are a little out of practice, and you just can't do it as much, and for as long, even though he actually had. And without the help of that latest blue-pill craze.

"*Esmaa, ya Doctoor Hamid,*" Farid Fendil said, smiling humbly. "I just exerted myself."

"Exerted yourself?" The doctor studied his patient curiously.

"Yes. With work, and I have not had much sleep."

"I advise you start swimming at least fifteen minutes every day. Then graduate to twenty minutes. I know you've got a great pool ..."

"The pool is closed!" Farid Fendil interjected, slamming a fist on the bed, surprising the doctor with his sudden outburst.

"Perhaps it is a good time to reopen it," the doctor replied, looking straight into Farid Fendil's eyes, showing he was not intimidated by his prominent patient.

"I can't," Farid Fendil replied weakly, avoiding the doctor's eyes.

"Mr. Fendil, you have built a wonderful spa for our community."

"I did, didn't I?" He recalled how hard he had worked at getting the most qualified team of men. His world-renowned spa had graced the latest magazines, even in Europe.

"I am a proud member," the doctor said. "I frequent it once a week. I advise you do the same. It would be a pleasure to see you there."

"Have a good day, Doctor." Mr. Fendil waved him off.

"One more thing," the doctor said, seriously. "I need to schedule you for an angiogram. How would next Monday be?" he asked, checking his book.

"What for? I'm busy."

"When can you make time?"

"I'll call you."

The doctor shook his head as he scribbled something in a notebook, then snapped it closed and replaced it in his attaché case. He opened a new manila folder and scribbled some more information. "I wouldn't wait if I were you. It's a simple procedure."

"All right. I'll phone you after the sixth of July."

The doctor understood. "Fine. It's only a few weeks away. We have just received the invitation to your daughter's wedding. My wife and I will be honored to attend. My wife is sending you a written reply, probably as we speak. I will call you on the seventh of July, to remind you of your angiogram."

"God willing. *Ma'a Salaam*," Farid murmured, sinking into his pillow, pretending he was going to get some sleep.

He heard the doctor leave. Today, he had to hire a new chief financial officer. The one he had had for many years just keeled over right at his desk—a sudden heart attack. He had other problems, too. His comptroller wasn't coming up with the right numbers. One of his best architects had accepted a job to build a hotel in Shanghai without consulting with him first. So many problems. So much happening at once; some of his best people quitting on him.

But first and foremost, he needed to get to the bottom of an important matter, the one concerning his son.

Who was Shlomo? A friend of Nageeb, who had sent a birth announcement from Israel. *Israel?* Apparently, Nageeb had seen this man before the ... *crash*. Allah! *Why did Nageeb go to Israel?*

The authorities had never said his son's ill-fated helicopter flight had originated in the resort town in Israel, until months later when he read the accident report. All this time, he had believed the chartered chopper had flown from Aqaba and was on its way to Cairo, not Alexandria. Then again, perhaps he could not get a helicopter that would land in Cairo due to that earthquake. But Farid had done some research and found out there was no damage reported at the Cairo airport after the quake. Did his son plan to drive from Alexandria to Cairo? He knew Nageeb preferred to drive, but it would have taken too long to get to Cairo, since he needed to be there as soon as possible.

He had to stop torturing himself with all these questions. His head was pounding. He had heartburn and shortness of breath. And now his doctor insisted on an angiogram. What did that entail? How long would it take? He would have to ask his secretary to do some research on angiograms. Better yet, he would make inquiries himself. He did not want to raise any questions about his health.

Why didn't the dictionary he kept next to his nightstand, with his Koran, not have enough information on angiograms? Impatiently he leafed through the thick book and found the word *angioplasty*. Something to do with repairing or replacing damaged blood vessels. Nageeb would have known all about that.

Wasn't that what his uncle Fellous recently endured?

Farid crawled out of bed, pushed into his leather slippers, and shuffled to his huge, hand-carved dresser. He opened the middle drawer and took out the cards that had been sent to Nageeb from Israel—Shlomo's post card and birth announcement. He read them for the sixth or seventh time. He weighed every word of the note his son's friend had written—the card thanking Nageeb for the gift basket and Dom Perignon that apparently Nageeb must have sent before leaving Eilat. Another piece he could not fit into his puzzled mind.

Nothing made sense anymore. Everything seemed more confusing. His chest felt tight and his heartburn intensified.

CHAPTER 35
THE DOCTOR AND THE DOG

The balmy Riviera night brought everyone out, beneath the starlit sky, especially Hollywood celebrities. The evening was spectacular; film festival electricity charged the air. Only winners of this game, those who made millions per movie, could afford to be there in their proud splendor—top studio executives, independent producers, world-renowned directors, and international film distributors. The Carlton terrace sparkled with the brightest celebrities the world had to offer.

Annette was not going to miss this evening. She was going to stargaze at the American male stars. Tonight, once and for all, she would forget Bruno.

"I am no more *victime d'amour*. I am in control." She hooked her arm around Noora's and guided her to the Carlton terrace. The girls found two chairs and claimed them before anyone could take them away.

They ordered one café au lait to share.

"Hot. I am feeling hot. Look, look! It is Tom Selleck, *non?* He is even taller and more good-looking," Annette squealed. "Look. That is him, *en personne*."

She spotted Johnny Hallyday, the blond, green-eyed singer and guitarist who had become a Parisian pop artist since the sixties. "I don't believe it. It's him! You know, he is still trying to make it in America!"

In his younger years, the Parisian rock star, now in his fifties, had once been referred to as the Elvis Presley of France. Proudly, he strolled by, only a few feet away from Annette, with a voluptuous young blonde by his side. "My mother knew him when he used to sing during intermissions at the neighborhood cinema near the Rue Caulaincourt in Paris. She knew him even before Sylvie Vartan!"

"Who?"

"His ex-wife! She was also a well-known singer. Look at him now. Johnny Hallyday. Stealing the cradle!"

"You mean, *robbing* the cradle?"

"Yes, and I am not interested in French men! I am not even interested in Italian men. Give me a good, juicy *Americain*. A big, tall muscle hunk! Like the one in cigarette commercials, but who doesn't smoke! A *coy-boy*."

"A cowboy? You'd have to find him in America, and I don't mean New York," Noora said with a deep sigh. She was tired and wished she had some of Um Faheema's special potion to soothe her sunburned back, which still ached and started to itch.

Beyond the promenade, on the sidewalk, Noora saw a familiar figure. She rose from her chair for a better look.

Uncle Khayat's doctor, Alain Demiel, was following the leashed shaggy, huge ball of fur. "Baldo?" Noora said. With his eyes concealed by a curtain of matted fur, the Bouvier des Flandres led the way, while the doctor stumbled around people, barely able to keep up.

"Who eez that?" Annette asked.

"It's him. The doctor I told you about."

"No!"

"Yes."

"*Ce n'est pas possible*. He eez handsome!" Annette exclaimed, surprised. She rose to get a better look above a crowd of lively patrons. A tall, heavy-set man with a fat cigar, sporting a Stetson and a pot belly, tried to take Annette's seat right from under her.

"*Non mais dis-donc, c'est ma chaise!*" she growled, defending her chair. "*Espèce de con*... crazy *producteur Hollywoodien de merde*," she cursed under her breath, snatching the chair back.

Docteur Demiel disappeared in the crowd.

"Where did he go? Oh no! Do you still have his card?"

"I think so."

"You must find an excuse to fall sick and call him. We must invite him to dinner. We must not lose him."

"I thought you were through with men. He is not American, you know," Noora teased.

"Yes, but something eez boiling inside. A good sign."

Noora remembered the cemetery. She plopped herself back down on the wicker chair. Baldo's fur brushed against her leg and the big dog flopped down next to her feet. Surprised, Noora laughed with delight.

An hour later, Noora, Annette, the doctor, and his dog sat together in Annette's apartment. Annette had opened a new bottle of red wine. An old Dalida song played on the radio—"Bambino."

"Dalida ... That was my mother's favorite song when I was growing up in Egypt," the doctor said.

"My mother loved that song also. Dalida could sing in every language. Did you know her?" Annette asked.

"Yes. My mother used to buy all her records. I don't know why Dalida wanted to end her life so soon. Sad. Very sad."

"I read she believed that life had nothing further to offer her," Annette said.

"She was wrong. Life is always filled with new beginnings," Alain Demiel said.

"And new hopes." Annette's Bambi-brown eyes grew larger.

Though she was exhausted, Noora did not want the evening to end. It appeared that her new friends had a lot in common. They liked the same music, the same artists, the same food. Baldo was now curled up cozily next to Annette's feet, as if he approved of her.

Doctor Demiel's pager beeped just after midnight. Excusing himself, he pressed the buttons from his mobile phone. A moment later, the doctor closed the flap of his phone and rose.

"Sorry, I must leave right away. I'm being called at the hospital in Nice. I need to call a taxi."

Noora suggested that Annette drive the doctor. She watched Annette's eyes light up when the doctor readily accepted.

"Baldo can stay here if you like," Noora said to the doctor, but the dog was by the door, anxiously wagging its tail.

"I don't mind taking care of Baldo while you are at the hospital," Annette offered. I am sure Baldo will like my Micheline."

As soon as the doctor, Annette, and Baldo left the apartment, Noora curled up on the old, soft loveseat and pulled the blanket to her eyes, because she was too tired to get up again to turn off the lights. She prayed that Annette and Alain would realize they were meant for each other. It seemed Baldo already did. The moment she rested her head on the small pillow, she fell asleep.

Annette was evidently trying to be quiet as she unlocked the door and entered her apartment at four in the morning, but Noora was a light sleeper. She opened her eyes and smiled. "You had a nice evening. I can tell."

"After I drove the doctor to the hospital, I walked Baldo," Annette said, starting to undress. "*Docteur* Alain came out of the hospital one hour and a half later and invited me for brioches and *café-au-lait* in the all-night bistro across the street. And he *paid!* He opened my door, even. He is a true gentleman. He comes from another era. My kind of time."

Annette left for work just before eight in the morning. She sang a Dalida song in the shower and was bouncing with energy, even though she had had less than three hours' sleep. As soon as Annette left her apartment, however, Noora began to feel morose. She stood in the tiny bathroom. A sharp-pointed pair of scissors was on a nearby shelf. She picked them up and studied them. These scissors had powers. They could alter her existence. They could do her a great favor and take away her life, or they could do something as small and as simple as change her appearance. She began to cut her bangs. She cut them in a straight line but when she combed them, they looked crooked. The more she tried to straighten her bangs, the worse they looked. And now they were too short. What was so difficult about cutting hair in a straight line?

She grabbed a chunk of her voluminous locks that fell down her back, and chopped them off above the shoulder.

With every strand of hair that fell to the floor, Noora separated herself from memories of the past. The hair Michel had touched and stroked once upon a lifetime ago, the hair that had lived with her and still carried her past was now going to be flushed away.

Noora made her way through the service access and punched in her time card five minutes before 12:00 PM. She ran a hand through her very short hair. She hoped her new, badly chopped hairdo wouldn't attract too much attention.

When she entered to clean Mr. Ian Cohen's suite, he was at his desk, barking on the phone.

"Basis the above, I expect an immediate reply ... Sincerely, et cetera. Enclose two copies of the script ... Wait a minute, Roz." He snapped his fingers for the chambermaid, indicating that he wanted her to clean his suite.

Noora nodded and headed straight for the bathroom. She had no desire to face that belligerent man again. She noted that today, only one towel had been used.

"Enclose another copy of that letter. With the script!" Noora heard him shout. "Yes, yes!" he continued, louder. "The same copy we sent last week. That asshole said he never got it. Messenger it immediately, back it up by registered mail, return-receipt-requested! From now on, Roz, everything gets messengered first thing in the morning. They have martini lunches at Le Dome, screw their brains out in the afternoon with their assistants, and they wonder why they forget the head between their shoulders ... Whaaat? Roz, damn it, I'll relax soon as I hear they got the stuff. You've been with me too long to let those morons bullshit you."

Noora returned to her cart in the hallway to toss out the trash. There was even more rubbish than the day before—trade papers, copies of scripts, crumpled papers, as well as unopened gold-and-silver-trimmed invitation envelopes addressed to Mr. Ian Cohen in handwritten calligraphy.

Returning to his room, Noora pulled the sheets off the bed. The covers were barely used. Her task should be easier today. Suddenly, she could feel him staring at her. She tried to focus on her work by moving around the bed to tuck in the sheets. She felt herself blush. Was he really staring at her or was she imagining it? She glanced up. Sure enough, he was *glaring* at her.

"You! Aren't you the maid from yesta-day?"

"I beg your pardon, sir?"

"No English?"

"No, sir! I mean yes, sir. I was here yesterday," she managed to say.

"Jeez, Loo-eez. What'd you do to your hair?!"

Noora self-consciously ran a hand over her hair and took a deep breath. His rudeness was unbearable. She wanted to scream—*it is my hair! I have the right to do any bloody thing I want with it!* Instead, she took a breath and said in a small tight voice, "I cut it."

"What?"

"I cut it. Would you like more towels, sir?"

"No." He started to leaf through his thick stack of messages. "Listen, uh ... what you did yesterday was smart," he said without looking up. "Quick and clever," he muttered low. He picked up the receiver and punched in numbers.

"Pleasure, sir," Noora replied. What a stupid thing to say. It wasn't her *pleasure!* She finished tucking the sheets under the mattress. She still had to clean the bathtub. She had to do that stupid fan detail on the toilet paper and mop the bathroom floor. And she had to vacuum.

"Sir, shall I return later for the vacuuming?" she asked, hoping he planned to leave the room.

"No. You can do it now," he replied, slamming down the phone. As soon as the phone hit the cradle, it rang. He snatched up the receiver and growled into it.

Noora cleaned the bathroom. She was glad that at least today there was less soap scum, and hardly any hair around the bathtub drain. Cleaning dirty bathtubs made her want to vomit. Annette did not seem bothered by that type of mess. Perhaps Noora would also get used to cleaning other people's dirt. She made her way out into the hallway as she peeled off her rubber gloves. She dreaded the idea of having to vacuum in his presence. He was still yelling on the phone. Something the caller was saying must have irritated him enormously.

When she returned to the suite, pulling the vacuum cleaner behind her, Noora found Mr. Cohen banging his fist on the desk and breathing heavily. She thought it was a good thing the person on the opposite end of the phone call was not standing in front of him, because he looked enraged enough to kill.

She decided to drag the vacuum cleaner out of that room and start cleaning the next room—before the man turned his anger on her.

She heard him wheezing, and she turned. He was desperately motioning to her, waving a hand frantically, trying to get her attention.

Was he asking her to close his door? *Try another tactic,* she thought.

The cart out in the hallway was barring the entrance. When cleaning rooms, doors were to remain open.

Mr. Cohen was crouched over the desk, his face turning an odd greenish shade. He clutched his chest. Gasping for air, he motioned frantically to his jacket on the chair across the room.

Something was terribly wrong with this man—it did not seem to be an act. Noora grabbed the jacket and handed it to him. He thrust a shaky hand into the breast pocket and produced a small bottle, then began to panic when he couldn't open the childproof lid. He looked at Noora with beseeching eyes.

She took the bottle, opened it, and thrust it back to him.

With trembling hands, he pulled out a pill and put it under his tongue.

Was he all right? No, he was still wheezing. She loosened his shirt and helped him into bed.

"Sir, I shall call for a doctor."

He shook his head. "No!"

"You need a doctor, sir."

"No!" he whispered, struggling to breathe. "No friggin' doctor!"

She noticed the receiver on the desk was still off the hook.

"Close my door, put your cart away… next room or something. Just don't let anyone see me," he said as she dashed over to his desk to hang up the phone, when she heard someone still on the line. "*Ian! What's going on!?*" a male voice shouted.

Placing the receiver to her ear, Noora put on a professional voice. "This is the hotel operator," she announced in her best British accent. "We are experiencing minor technical difficulties due to overloads … Yes, that's right … No, I cannot say when the lines will be cleared," she found herself saying. "We apologize for the inconvenience. Please try your call later. *Merci, Monsieur*." She hung up.

"Be right back. One minute," she said and ran out and pushed the cart to the next room in the corridor. "Housekeeping," she announced a few times while gently knocking on the door. There was no answer. She left the cart in front of that door, as if ready to clean the next room, and rushed back to Mr. Cohen's suite. She dashed over to the desk and, replacing the cap on the medicine bottle, she checked the label.

He watched her in action. Lying back weakly, he asked Noora if he could hold her hand. Noora hesitated. She walked over to his bedside and propped up a couple of pillows for his comfort.

"Don't tell anyone … about this," he whispered, squeezing her hand a bit too hard.

His face was a deathly hue and his skin felt clammy. He was indeed sick, and was not faking it. It was possible he was seriously ill. A thought came to mind. *The doctor! Where was his business card?* Had she left it at Annette's apartment? No, she had taken it with her because Annette had begged her to call the *docteur* and invite him to dinner. With her free hand, she dug in her pocket, found the card, and checked the private number the doctor had scribbled on the back.

The phone rang.

"Don't answer, don't …" Mr. Cohen begged, squeezing her hand.

"I pressed the *private* button, so that your calls would be referred to your voice mail, sir," she said. "I hope you don't mind." She wished she could free her hand from his tight grip.

"You're s- smart, kid… Why isn't this nitro shit working?"

Noora managed to release herself from Ian Cohen, and picked up the phone on the nightstand next to her. As she began to dial, Ian Cohen took her hand again and squeezed harder.

"Don't call anyone. I just need a coupla minutes' rest. I'll be fine …"

"Doctor Demiel is a personal friend. He might give you a new prescription. Yours has expired, sir. And it says 'no refills.'"

"Oh, shit."

Docteur Alain Demiel had barely knocked on the door to Monsieur Cohen's suite before Noora opened it. "Thank you so much for coming so quickly," she said, realizing he had not recognized her at first glance under the dim light of the hallway. She unconsciously ran a hand through her chopped-up hair.

"I wasn't far when they paged me," he said, following Noora to Mr. Cohen's bedside.

"I'm sorry," Noora said. "I have to clean the next room. I can't stay …"

"Fine, I'll let you know …" the doctor said.

Doctor Demiel checked the producer's blood pressure. It was sky-high. "We will need to run some tests. Can you make it to the hospital?"

"What? There's no way I can go to any hospital at this time."

"Okay. Tomorrow morning. I would advise we schedule you for an angiogram ..."

"Can't you just give me something until I get back to the States?"

The doctor read the label on the nitroglycerine bottle. "Your prescription has expired several months ago."

"I know."

Doctor Demiel handed Mr. Cohen a few samples from his case and recommended that he remain in bed for the rest of the day.

"I'll be back to see you tomorrow morning, Mr. Cohen," Doctor Demiel said. "I'm going to write you a new prescription," he said, pulling out a pen and scribbling on a pad. "You may call me on my personal line or at home," he added.

Doctor Demiel caught Noora in the hallway as she was picking up clean folds of towels for the next room. Quietly, he briefed her on Mr. Cohen's situation. "He should not be left alone," he concluded.

Noora didn't know what to say. She could not leave her position and stay with the guest in his room. She would have to contact Annette. "Yes, I ... By the way, Annette wanted to invite you to dinner at her apartment," she said, realizing she had probably chosen an inappropriate time. But Annette had asked Noora several times to please call *Le Docteur*.

To Noora's surprise, the doctor actually seemed pleased. "Thank you. When?"

"When? Well, if you're not too busy, how about ... tonight?"

"Please tell Mademoiselle Annette I would be honored."

"Really?"

"Yes."

"All right then... Good. Oh, and Baldo too, of course."

"Thank you. In the meantime, I would suggest you keep an eye on Mr. Cohen," he said, extending his hand to Noora. Then he gently gave her a kiss on each cheek. He headed for the stairs, instead of waiting for the elevator.

Later that evening, Ian gave Noora several names and numbers and asked her to cancel all his meetings. He also canceled a tennis game for the next morning with other producers at the Mont Fleury Hotel.

"I never missed a tennis match since I started coming to the Cannes Film Festival in 1971." He changed his mind several times about the excuse he would need to use. "Leave a message with the concierge and say I had some emergency. No, say I had to attend an urgent meeting. No, just tell them I am canceling due to emergency rewrites."

Later, Noora sat on a chair by Ian's bedside and watched over him with concern.

"I'd like you to come to Los Angeles with me and be my personal assistant," Mr. Cohen said.

Noora was speechless.

"How about it? I see you're quick on the phone."

Silence.

"I'm offering you a job, kid."

"Thank you."

"Good."

"But I am sorry, sir; that will not be possible. However, I am grateful and honored for the offer," Noora uttered, thunderstruck.

"If you need a part, I may be able to help you. Later on."

"A part?" Noora did not understand.

"In my upcoming picture ... Christ, you deserve it," he murmured as he slowly lifted himself from the bed and sat at the edge, his hair messed up, his eyes glazed and half-open.

"I am not an actress, sir," Noora said, standing a couple of feet away from the bed now.

"All girls are actresses." Cohen rose and headed groggily to the vestibule. "Not an actress? I've never heard *that* line before," he muttered, wobbling to the bathroom.

Noora heard him urinate. *Didn't he believe in closing doors?* She wasn't sure how to take this rude behavior. He was a strange man. He had a terrible temper, but somehow she didn't feel threatened. In fact, he was rather intriguing.

"I need someone I can trust," he called from the bathroom.

She rubbed Um Faheema's blue stone and replaced it under the lacy white collar of her black uniform. He was facing her now. He had splashed water on his face, and was drying himself with a hand towel.

"Where's my jacket?"

"On the chair, sir."

He sat on the edge of the bed. "Stay with me."

"I'm sorry, sir. I have to go and finish cleaning …"

"I would never say this to anyone, but I'm scared shitless. Wish I could get back to L.A. right away, but everyone here will know I'm a sick man. Why'd you chop off your hair? There's no script in development for a concentration camp survivor. I don't do *Sophie's Choice* genres."

"I beg your pardon, sir?" Noora ran her hand through her hair again, nervously.

"Never mind. I'm just rambling on. Probably that medicine under the tongue. Listen, I'll make you a deal: I'll pay you anything you want if you could just stay with me tonight."

"Sir, that is absolutely impossible."

"Christ, you can see I'm in no condition to make advances. Stay with me in case I get another attack."

Noora stood speechless.

"I don't beg."

"It's just that it's not allowed. I must abide by the hotel rules. Doctor Demiel will be here anytime you need him; he assured me of that. He left you his card. I'll write down the direct number where you can reach him this evening. He won't be far, actually," she said, glad he had accepted Annette's invitation. She needed to let Annette know right away.

"Does anyone know a doctor came to see me?"

"I doubt it very much, sir. He left by the service stairs."

Noora had volunteered to take over one of the maids' evening shifts to give Annette and the doctor some space—and earn a little extra money.

At midnight, Noora ended her second shift. She felt bad about refusing to stay with Mr. Cohen, but she could not jeopardize her job. Should she check on him before leaving? Ask if he needed anything? What if he was asleep? What if someone saw her in his room? She took her employee card and punched out.

Under a glowing royal blue Riviera sky, the Croisette was bursting with lights and music. Noora wished she could sit in an outdoor café, order a *salade Niçoise* perhaps, or even a warm, crusty baguette with butter, anchovy paste, and slices of tomatoes with *cornichons* and *moutarde de Dijon*. Or maybe even something as simple as feta cheese on pita bread.

Or toast with caviar, and an icy glass of Coke with lemon. Her mouth watered and her stomach growled. She had not one franc to her name.

She ventured near the Palais du Festival, where a crowd of fans had begun to gather. A huge banner stretched above the marquee:

IAN COHEN *PRESENTS:*
"FROM HERE TO HELL"
Written and produced by Ian Cohen in association with
IAN COHEN ENTERTAINMENT (I.C.E.)

Electricity filled the air. The area was swarming with movie stars making their staged exits from the theater. They paused and posed for the photographers, and glided out upon the red-carpeted steps, all in resplendent finery. Thousands of fans cheered on the street. Throngs of photographers swarmed the entrance to the Palais du Festival. Blinded by flashbulb bursts, Noora became dizzy and disoriented.

Analissa Nielsen's name was called. The crowd roared and cheered, and began to surge along the sidewalk. Noora was engulfed like a sheep in a stampede.

The crowd became rowdy. The fans aggressively pushed for a better view of the movie stars. Noora felt the noisy crowd press closer around her. High-pitched whistles assailed her eardrums and she began to push her way out of the crush. A group of gendarmes finally arrived and struggled to restore order.

Everything began to spin around her. *Please God, don't let me faint*. If she wound up in the hospital, how would she explain her existence?

She managed to make her way out of the chaos. She hurried away, grasping her heaving chest and passing the Carlton Hotel terrace.

She passed by the brightly illuminated Martinez Hotel. A few blocks further on, the crowd had dissipated, and she began to breathe easier. She headed down to the beach, where she saw a few couples locked in close embrace. She unlaced Annette's work shoes and eased her sore, blistered feet out of them. It had been a long, exhausting day. The sand soothed and massaged her feet with every step she took. The salty Mediterranean air revived her. She walked down to the edge, letting the cool water ripple over her feet. She heard music from the beach restaurant nearby. She closed her eyes and imagined she was back in happier days.

Noora leaned next to Annette's door to catch her breath after climbing the seven flights of stairs. She had to be quiet and not wake Annette. Silently, she turned the key Annette had given her. As she cracked the door open, she was surprised to find Annette, and *Docteur* Alain Demiel, cozy in her love seat, with teacups on their laps. Baldo was curled up at Annette's feet. The romantic voice of Dalida, singing a French fifties song, trailed from Annette's little cassette player.

"Where were you?" Annette said, her face flushed.

After the doctor left, Annette insisted on warming up dinner for Noora. "It's the least I can do." Annette looked uneasy. She poured some hot chamomile tea for Noora.

"You are so good to me. How will I ever repay you ..."

"*Moi?* I thought you would be mad."

"Mad? Why?"

"Because I was entertaining *your* friend. I called the hotel. You were kind to take Martinelle's place, because her little girl was sick with a *terrible grippe,* and oh, that was so thoughtful of you. I hope you didn't mind. I mean, for Alain... *le Docteur*. He told me what happened to his family. His parents and grandparents had to leave their country, Egypt. They were thrown out. His grandfather was even put in jail because he was Jewish. They escaped on a small fishing boat to Italy, and ... he told me so much about his life, and ..."

"I think you two would make a wonderful couple," Noora cut in.

"You do?" Annette blushed deeper.

"I do," Noora smiled.

"You are not mad?"

"*Au contraire,* Annette. I am happy for you," Noora said. "Very happy ... By the way ... something happened today on the second floor."

"You can use my passport," Annette said after Noora told her about Ian Cohen.

"I don't believe I heard you correctly," Noora said.

"You can use my passport. I have a new one!" Annette said proudly while slicing into a crusty baguette. "I got a new passport when I thought I was going to go on my honeymoon to Venice with Bruno. *L'imbécile.*"

"I'm not sure I understand ..."

"Well, it is the balance of life. When one door closes, always a window opens."

"Annette, it's very kind of you. But it is absolutely not possible."

"Everything is possible."

"But Annette, it's *illegal*."

Three days later, Noora stood at Charles de Gaulle Airport, waiting to board the Concorde.

Annette had reshaped and fixed Noora's choppy haircut, and coiffed it to look similar to the style in the passport picture—a short bob *à la gamine*. The stark picture showed Annette with eyes half-closed and a crooked smile—convincing enough. With makeup, Noora managed to conceal the scar that ran down below her eye. The French passport listed the color of eyes as *marrons*, brown. Noora prayed no one would look at her closely.

Noora feared if they discovered her deception, she would be deported. But where? To France? *What if they found out the truth?*

Every ounce of energy drained out of her when the uniformed security officer opened her passport. She kept her eyes lowered. At that moment, another uniformed official appeared behind the man at the customs counter and whispered something to him. The official holding Noora's, alias Kelley Karlton's, alias Annette Bonjour's passport, barely glanced at the document's picture. He methodically leafed through to the last page, stamped it, and handed it back to Monsieur Ian Cohen, with a respectful salutation.

CHAPTER 36
NEW YORK, NEW LIFE

A chauffeur welcomed Ian Cohen at Kennedy airport. The luggage was placed in the trunk of a black stretch limo.

At the check-in counter of the Plaza Hotel, Mr. Cohen was greeted with the respect usually accorded to royalty. Noora followed him down the corridor toward his reserved suite. He seemed tired but wouldn't let anyone carry his leather attaché case, heavy with file folders and scripts. In his other hand, he carried a canvas tote bag advertising his latest movie, *From Here to Hell*.

Noora was not sure what Mr. Cohen expected of her. It had all happened too fast, as if destiny was thrusting her ahead, somewhere, but she didn't know where or why. Mr. Cohen had refused to take no for an answer. It was clear that he needed her. She remembered an Arabic poem her grandmother used to quote: *Elleh maktoub fel gebben, ye shoufou el ein*—"what is written on the forehead can be seen in the eyes."

In the eyes of Ian Cohen, she saw an honest plea for help. He offered her a job. She would probably live in his luxurious lifestyle. How bad could that be?

"You must follow the journey of your destiny," Um Faheema had said. This journey was all too uncertain. She missed Um Faheema more than ever now, and Dweezoul, and even Saloush the goat.

The bellman opened the door. She followed as he entered the lavish penthouse suite. She was relieved when Mr. Cohen pointed to another room and informed the bellman where to put her one small piece of luggage. He sat wearily on the couch, when the bellman left the room, closing the door behind him.

"I'll be in meetings starting at six o'clock in the morning. I'll be back at six in the evening. At six thirty you can come with me to see the rushes. They'll bring sandwiches."

"Yes, sir," she said, wondering what he meant by "rushes."

He pulled himself wearily off the sofa, loosened his tie, and slowly removed his jacket. His sleeve was stuck in his cufflink. She hurried over to assist him. After hanging his coat in the closet next to the front door, she stood uneasily a few feet away. He pulled out a thick wad of hundred-dollar bills and tossed five of them on the cocktail table.

"Get yourself a raincoat, and maybe a nice dress," he said, then turned and trudged to his room. "I'm gonna take a shower. I'll knock on your door when I need you," he said and walked to his room, closing his door.

Noora stood in the living room, wondering. *What did he mean by that last comment?* If he did expect any sort of intimacy, she would fly back to France. She entered her room and locked the door. At least there was a lock. She immediately slid beneath the luscious down bedspread of the queen-sized bed. She did not touch the money he tossed on the table. Why would she need a raincoat? How cold could it be in New York at the end of May? So far, they hadn't discussed a salary, and she didn't feel at ease taking his money. She wondered what Annette would have said if she had seen all this money tossed at her by a man who wasn't a father, or even a husband—or ... boyfriend? He must have ulterior motives, even if he was a sick man. She would undress and shower after he left for his meetings ... Her eyelids could no longer stay open.

She dreamed of Alexandria. Beautiful San Stefano Beach Club. On the marble terrace, where everyone used to dance. Dweezoul was standing by the banister, fiddling with his transistor radio. It was a new gadget, much larger than the one he carried around at the Bedouin village. Annette was dancing with *Docteur* Alain Demiel. But when he turned, the young doctor was Nageeb, and he danced with her to the tune of Sarah Vaughn's "Broken Hearted Melody."

"Where is Michel?" Noora asked her brother.

"He can't be here."

"Why?"

"He is ill," Nageeb replied, twirling Noora as they danced. He was twirling her around and around until she felt dizzy.

"Stop," she said. "When can I see him?"

He stood and stared at her with a smile and a nod. "Not for years. But don't worry, it's up to the patient ..." She heard the roar of an airplane flying in, getting close, too close. Nageeb shielded her. She looked up and they both laughed at the sight of a small airplane dropping hundreds of candy bars wrapped in shiny golden paper. Like children, they ran after the candy. She looked closer and realized the candy was inside little crystal bowls wrapped in white tulle, with long strings of silver ribbons. She was dressed like a bride, but with no veil. Someone was coughing loud, louder. Suddenly everyone was gone and she was in the desert, her dress soiled, the helicopter burning in the distance.

Her eyes popped open, and her heart was racing. She was drenched in perspiration. The room was dark, except for a shaft of light that came from the bathroom door she had left ajar. She realized she was at the Plaza Hotel—in New York. The green lighted numbers on the nightstand clock showed 3:33 AM. Still wearing Annette's blue dress, she rose out of bed and walked slowly to re-orient herself. What a weird dream she just had. Her dear grandmother used to say dreams were filled with messages, she thought, opening her door cautiously. She ventured out into the living room. On a table by the window was a huge basket of fruit. If she could dig into the cellophane without messing up the wrapping, perhaps she could grab an apple or a pear. The floor lamp next to the tall window was dimly lit, and Noora was startled to find Ian Cohen sitting on a loveseat, reading a script. He looked up.

"Jet-lagged, eh?" He smiled, removing his bifocals and tossing the script aside.

"Well, actually ... I'm a bit hungry," she said, trying not to look surprised to find him there.

"Me too." He rose from the sofa and grabbed on to his back. "Ooh, I'm stiff." Wearily he walked to the fruit basket on the desk and removed the cellophane. "Want an apple? Or an orange?"

"Either one, thank you."

"They even have mangoes and ... papayas? Who gave me that?" he asked, searching for a card. "Ah, bet ya it was the hotel manager."

"I have not had a mango in a long time," she said, taking a step forward.

"Here!" He tossed her a fat mango.

She barely caught it.

"I don't know how to eat mangoes," he said, biting into a red apple. He pointed to the phone. "Dial room service. Order anything you want. They got twenty-four-hour service. Great, huh? Almost as good as the Majestic." He winked.

She was glad to see he was in a good mood.

"Order me three eggs, bacon, sausage, and rye toast," he said. "There's the menu, by the phone. Why didn't you take the money?"

Money? "Oh ... thank you ... I have enough warm clothes."

"You'll need a raincoat where we're going."

Where are we going? She wanted to ask, but he walked to his room.

Room service arrived within minutes. She had ordered hot cream of wheat with raisins. When she convinced him to try some, he wound up eating the entire bowl, saying with great surprise, "This is really good. Reminds me when I was a kid. My mother used to make that every morning. I haven't had that in a hundred years."

She showed him how to cut up a mango.

"You slice it in the middle, then slide the two pieces back and forth, and now you can spoon away the sweet meat ... like so."

"How 'bout the pit? You gotta get your hands full of the juice to get the pit out, don't you?"

"No, you just pick it out with the spoon, like so, and it falls off its nest. See? Easy. Then you hold it like a small bowl and spoon the second half ..."

"Ingenious," he said.

They talked about food and the fruits they liked. He mentioned the pies downstairs at Palm Court, which used to taste better. "Things have changed. Even their cream puffs don't taste as good as they did in the seventies. Maybe they have a younger chef. I remember especially in '73 and '74, when I used to come here a lot more often..."

Noora noticed he often talked about things being better in the seventies. By the time they were through eating, cutting fruit, and talking, it was after five in the morning.

"I believe it is time for your medicine," she said.

"I'm fine. I ate fruit."

"Doctor's orders, sir."

"Yeah, yeah." He opened the bottle and popped the medicine Dr. Alain Demiel had prescribed in Cannes.

"If you would please drink water, the medicine will dissolve better."

"Okay, nurse."

He rose and grabbed the script he was reading earlier, then tossed it at Kelley Karlton. "Read this and tell me what you think."

She caught the hundred-or-so-page manuscript bound by copper fasteners.

"When you leave the hotel, check messages so I'll know where you are. In case I need you."

"Yes, sir," she said, rising with the script in her hand. She began to leaf through it. She had never read a movie script before.

Relieved to be alone in the suite, Noora took her time luxuriating in the bathtub—with the bathroom door locked and keeping an ear out for Mr. Cohen's return—in case he knocked on her door.

At two in the afternoon, she decided to venture out. She left a note in the suite letting him know she had gone downstairs to shop for a raincoat.

In the lobby, she browsed through the small clothing store next to the luxurious entrance of the hotel. On the rack by the wall, she found a few London Fogs. They were too large and way too expensive. She made her way to a delightful little gift shop she found at the end of the hallway.

Annette had lent her two hundred dollars. Noora refused her generosity, but Annette insisted and swore she would not write to her (for a long time) if Noora did not take the money. With Mr. Cohen's money, she had seven hundred dollars in her pocket. None of the cash was hers, even if it was in her possession, she reminded herself. She stood by the magazine rack and leafed through a *Paris Match* magazine. Already there were a couple of interesting articles on the Cannes Film Festival. There was also an article on Alexandria. She wanted to return to the suite, lie in bed, and read the entire article on Egypt while enjoying the chocolate bars with marzipan filling that she just couldn't pass up.

She heard men speaking Arabic behind her. Instantly her heart skipped a beat and she replaced the magazine on the rack. Two men were discussing the difference between one brand of cigars and another. Their accent was all too familiar—they were definitely from Jordan! She ventured a look. The men, one of them with a bushy mustache, stood almost barring her way as they sniffed cigars and made idle conversation. She managed to squeeze through a narrow aisle between two bookshelves and made her way out of the store. What were those men doing there? *Well, why not,* she reminded herself. *Didn't a prominent Arab recently buy the hotel?* Could her father be there as well? That was possible. He had made numerous business trips to New York. *Oh my God! He used to stay in this hotel!* If he wasn't there, someone she knew—or worse yet, someone her father knew—could easily have recognized her. Like that man who chased after her in Alexandria. Shuddering, she ran up the stairwell, two steps at a time. She could have sworn someone was rushing up the stairs behind her. Horrified, she ran faster. Those men! Could they be chasing after her? As soon as she reached Mr. Cohen's suite, with trembling hands, she inserted the key and locked the door behind her.

She had to do something about her looks. Anything so she would no longer look like Noora. From that moment on, her name would have to be Kelley Karlton. She would find a way to acquire her own identity, her own passport. She would change her hair color—bleach it blonde—and maybe even get plastic surgery. No one should ever know who she once was. Besides, wasn't she supposed to be dead?. She ran to her bathroom, turned the lock securely, and sank to the floor, supporting her back to the door. She was unable to shake away her fear. *Um Faheema,* she thought, her eyes tearing, *why didn't I stay in your village? I felt safe there.* She pressed Um Faheema's blue bead against her chest. *With this amulet, we shall never be apart. I will regain my courage and never lose faith.*

Six o'clock that evening and not a minute later, Ian Cohen entered his hotel suite. Noora waited for him by the door.

"Ready?" he asked as he hurried to his room.

"Yes, sir." She clutched Annette's hand-knitted sweater.

"I'll be a coupla minutes," he said, disappearing behind the double doors of his master suite.

At six thirty sharp, Noora and Ian passed through the Palm Court on their way out of the hotel. She noticed a woman wearing a black veil and a long black dress, walking a few feet behind a stern-looking Middle Eastern man.

"Don't get why they make 'em dress like that," she heard Ian say.

Distracted, Noora tripped on the raised small marble square and almost fell. Ian grabbed her arm and looked down at the floor. "Careful! They'd better fix that!"

"I'm all right, sir, thank you."

"They're letting this place go to hell," he muttered, gently taking her by the elbow and guiding her ahead of him through the revolving doors. She was impressed by this unexpected gallantry. But as he followed her through the revolving doors, she could swear that she heard him say, *"Fucking rag-heads… They're takin' over."*

The limo dropped them off by a delicatessen. Ian went inside and was greeted by storekeepers as if he were the Godfather. Noora followed him down on narrow steps behind the restaurant into the large, well-lighted lobby of a screening room. Inside, where the smell of fresh paint lingered, five men waited for Mr. Cohen. They all settled in reclining red velvet chairs.

Ian introduced Noora as "Kelley Karlton, new apprentice from France."

Apprentice? Noora wondered, but nodded politely.

A couple of the younger men, in their mid-thirties, shook Kelley's hand. She recognized the man who barely acknowledged her presence, seemingly busy in his own thoughts. He was the film director, Bernie Berkovitz, also known as BB Gun. She was sure he was the man she spoke to on the phone at the Majestic Hotel. She remembered him from television talk shows in London, where he was interviewed for some kind of an action, cult-type movie he'd made several years ago. The young director had a distinct voice and a quintessential New York accent. Noora thought it was best not to speak, because he might recognize her voice—but perhaps she was just being silly. Still, she could never be too cautious. While the men were busy conversing and settling into their seats in the front row, Noora found a seat in the back. They all carried legal-sized note pads and flashlight pens that they used as soon as the theater lights dimmed to black and the screen came to life. She thought they were going to project a movie, a new feature, perhaps not yet released.

After ninety minutes of painfully boring scene after excruciatingly rough-cut scene, without sound, Noora understood what he meant by "rushes." She found the whole process so monotonous, she wished he hadn't brought her along. Worst of all, practically every scene was bloody and violent.

When the rushes were finally over and the lights came up, Ian stormed out of the screening room. Once outside, the men separated in different directions. BB Gun had his own limousine waiting. The other men walked away without saying anything to Noora.

She was glad to be out in the fresh air, and hadn't noticed when Ian approached her.

"So, Mrs. Lincoln, how'd you like the play?"

Play? "Pretty violent, I'd say." The words left her mouth before she could stop herself.

He chuckled and walked ahead of her. "I like that answer," he mumbled almost to himself.

A taxi went by, and Ian waved until he saw the off-duty sign lighted.

"Shit! God forbid taxis are around when we need 'em. Let's get outta here," Ian Cohen said. He started walking fast down the block, grumbling to himself. "Asshole, BB Gun ... Not worth another heart attack."

Noora had to hurry and keep up. Less than two blocks later, he began to slow down. He seemed out of breath.

"Young directors! They get lucky for a sec and think they're hot. What they really got is rabbit-shit for brains!" he muttered. He turned to Noora. "You look beat."

"Yes, Mr. Cohen, I am kind of tired, sir," Noora said. Actually, she feared his anger might give him another attack.

"Okay, let's go home. Hey!" He waved down a taxi. "We're in luck!"

They settled into the cracked back seat. The cabby looked Middle Eastern. He turned a corner, maneuvering as if they were on a roller coaster.

"Slow down, we're trying to carry on a conversation back here!" Ian shouted, and turned to Noora. "So you thought some of those scenes were a little too violent?"

"Well, actually perhaps ... Yes, they were." Now he would surely be mad.

"Good, because we focus on male audiences age fourteen to twenty-four. They're the moviegoers. Immune from TV violence. We gotta give 'em something more on the silver screen. More fun. Faster scenes, more shocking. What worries me is BB Gun's direction. Sucks. Thank God I got a decent editor beside me!" he said, watching the taxi driver, who drove carelessly.

The taxi made another quick turn and she nearly fell on top of Ian.

"You can hold on to my arm."

"Thank you," she uttered, feeling for the handle on the door. It was torn off.

"Hey! Slow down!" Ian shouted.

"My driving eez the safest in the city. You don't like eet, get anoder cab!"

"You got it!" Ian retorted.

The cabby screeched to a halt, nearly sending both Ian and Noora into the semi-closed glass partition.

Ian gave the driver his money. No tip. The taxi took off.

They stood by the Peninsula Hotel. Ian looked around. "It's freezing. I told you you'd need a raincoat. Let's grab a cup o' coffee. Forget the cabs. I'll call for the limo. Freakin' ragheads," he mumbled. "I swear ... City's full of 'em! God protect us!"

Ragheads? She knew the taxi driver was from somewhere in the Middle East. Mr. Cohen's remark hurt her. What would he do if he knew she was from the Middle East herself? A Muslim, no less.

CHAPTER 37
BEL AIR

The plane ride from LaGuardia to Los Angeles was uncomfortably turbulent. Ian Cohen's pilot flew the private jet at different altitudes, trying to avoid rough air caused by storms in the vicinity. Still it bounced around like a paper airplane in the wind. Ian realized he wasn't going to get much reading done. At times, the motion was so severe, it was making him uneasy. He watched his new companion, Kelley Karlton, who sat a few seats away, across from him. She appeared composed, as if she'd flown on private jets before. Staring out the window, she seemed lost in her own thoughts. He wondered what they were. Not that he cared. She probably left an abusive boyfriend who beat the shit out of her. But she didn't look that stupid. Although pretty girls usually were, when it came to men. Whatever her past, it was good to have her along. Her genuine indifference about her surroundings actually started to make him feel more at ease.

When they finally landed, Sam, Ian Cohen's personal driver—and butler—waited at the gate.

At five o'clock in the afternoon, the San Diego Freeway was creeping along, bumper-to-bumper, giving Ian an opportunity to work on his notes and sign letters that had been faxed to him in New York.

At last, the gleaming royal blue Rolls Royce made its regal way through the imposing Bel Air West gates.

Turning on to Bel Air Road, the Rolls Royce entered through a wide-open wooden gate and stopped beneath the porte-cochère at the top of the circular driveway. Mr. Cohen's house was a combination of a mansion and a huge hacienda. With Spanish-tiled roof and peach stucco walls, the house was surrounded by perfectly trimmed, tall Italian pines. Mediterranean-style windows with flowerpots made her feel as if she was either in Spain or Italy.

Ian Cohen flung open his door and bounded out of his car.

"Finally!" he mumbled.

Sam jumped out of the Rolls and opened the front door of the house for Mr. Cohen.

"You know, Sam? Never thought I'd make it back. Sure glad to be home."

"Yes, Mr. Cohen," Sam replied, apparently glad to see his boss as well.

Mr. Cohen crossed the large foyer with a wide sweeping staircase to one side, and headed straight to his office. He sank into his brown leather wing chair, took a cigar from a carved wooden box on his Hawaiian koa desk, and flicked his black-and-gold Dunhill. He sighed and coughed. Wasting no time, he dialed his secretary's voice mail and dictated a letter while fumbling through the pile of mail stacked high on his desk.

Sam stood at the door and cleared his throat. "Where shall I put your guest's luggage, Mr. Cohen?"

Ian looked up. "Oh, yeah. Why don't you show her to the guest house. Wait. On second thought, put her in the upstairs guest room. Next to mine."

Noora was delighted with her room. A tall window opened to a charming little balcony. As the sheer drapes billowed and the cool California breeze caressed her, she stood there, hugging herself. *It's beautiful here.* Below her balcony, she saw a tennis court surrounded by perfectly trimmed, tall Italian pines. A few steps down, beyond trimmed bushes, was a gleaming aquamarine oval-shaped pool. Chilled by the evening air, Noora stepped back inside and removed her shoes to better feel the soft peach carpet. Everything in the room seemed new. Even the walls looked like they had recently been painted—all in peach tones.

Coincidentally, her favorite color. Surely there had to be a catch. No man would offer all this without expecting at least something in return.

Noora was still resting snugly beneath the down comforter when the sun was already high in the hazy sky. She had fallen asleep with her dress on. She was grateful no one disturbed her during the entire night.

But when she opened her eyes, she realized someone was knocking gently at her door. She heard a woman's voice.

She jumped out of bed, and when she opened the door a crack, she was surprised to find a Spanish- or Mexican-looking woman, in a starched white uniform with a pink organza apron. Smiling, the woman showed silver caps on her two front teeth.

"*Buenos dias,*" the maid said. "My name is Cessi. When would you like breakfast?" she asked in Spanish.

"Oh ... uhm, later ... I need to dress," Noora said in English, trying to figure out how to repeat the words in Spanish. She had learned some Spanish when she visited Madrid a few years back, but she forgot most of it. The maid lingered for a brief moment then left.

"Miss Karlton, I'm sorry," Sam, the lanky African-American butler said when Noora came down the stairs, freshly showered, wearing another one of Annette's dresses. "Cessi doesn't speak much English. She didn't mean to barge in your room while you were still asleep. I told her not to disturb you."

"Oh, it's perfectly fine, thank you. You see, I'm just here ... visiting ...," Noora said, feeling awkward about this situation.

"It is our pleasure to be at your service, Miss Karlton," Sam said. "Mr. Cohen wanted you to know that he'll be busy all day at the studio. He said you needed to do some shopping?"

"Well, no ... I don't ..."

"Mr. Cohen said I should take you to the Beverly Shopping Center and pick you up before six o'clock, because he'll need the car by seven for his dinner meeting."

Cessilia entered the large foyer holding breakfast on a white wooden tray. There was a bright glass of orange juice, a mound of scrambled eggs, toast, small jars of jam, and a tiny basket with steaming miniature muffins.

"She baked those muffins this morning. We hope you would like them. Would you like breakfast in your room or the dining room?"

"Oh ..." Noora was speechless. The butler and the maid patiently waited for her answer. "Thank you ..." Noora thought surely she should eat in the kitchen—wasn't that where she belonged? They didn't offer the kitchen as an alternative, though. "If you don't mind, I guess ... in my room?"

Sam drove Noora to the mall in West Hollywood and parked the Rolls-Royce in the valet parking space on the bottom floor.

"By the way ..." he said as they walked to the elevators. He handed her an envelope. "Mr. Cohen asked me to give you this. When would you like me to pick you up, Miss Karlton? Or would you prefer that I escort you and help you with your shopping bags?"

"I'm really not here to do any shopping. I came here to work for Mr. Cohen."

After a pause, Sam said, "Of course." He pressed the elevator button for the fourth floor.

The elevator doors opened and Noora stepped into a shopper's fantasyland. Beautifully displayed windows graced brightly lit shops everywhere she looked.

Sam gave her a moment to take it all in, then he politely cleared his throat.

"When would you like me to pick you up, Miss Karlton?"

"I don't know," Noora said, worrying about getting lost in such a maze. "How about in an hour?"

"Miss Karlton, are you sure an hour would be enough time?"

"How long does one need to shop in such a wonderful place, would you guess, Mr. Sherman?"

"It's hard to say. Perhaps three hours, Miss Karlton. At the very least." He smiled, showing a brilliant set of bright whites against his coffee-brown skin.

The moment Sam left, Noora opened the envelope and found five hundred-dollar bills. She gasped and shoved the money back in the envelope. There was a letter written on Ian's personal letterhead.

"Buy a nice suit. Dinner's at eight sharp. Sam will drive you."

Mr. Cohen had a very distinctive signature.

For a brief moment, she felt carefree. She found a classic gray suit on sale for less than two hundred dollars. *Annette's white blouse would look smashing under the jacket,* Noora thought. She would wear her friend's blouse for good luck. As she breezed past store windows, she caught her reflection and stopped. Her hair looked like she had been through a hurricane.

Ian Cohen returned home from the studio at seven sharp in a miserable mood. Sam had Mr. Cohen's gin and tonic waiting for him.

"I don't feel like going out tonight," he said to Sam. "But even on my deathbed, I'll have to go. Can't say no to a Japanese billionaire, now can I?"

"No, sir," Sam replied.

"I hope you convinced the girl to get something decent to wear for tonight …"

When the girl he brought from France met Ian in his study, he was speechless. She wore a simple and classy gray suit. He did not realize such simplicity could make a woman look so attractive. Her short brown hair and bad haircut had been trimmed and restyled, with sunny blonde streaks, obviously by professional hands, giving her skin color a healthy glow. Wispy fringes softly framed her high cheekbones and oval face.

The faux-Chanel earrings she wore looked as exquisite on her as if they were genuine.

"I can change …" she said, blushing.

"You look perfect. We match … Don't we?" He grinned. He was also clad in a dark gray suit and white shirt.

Sam drove them to the Beverly Regent Hotel.

At the hotel's posh Gardenia Room restaurant, Mr. Cohen introduced Noora simply as Miss Kelley Karlton, with no further explanation.

Kazumi, Mr. Okata's wife, an attractive, tiny Japanese lady in her late forties, and their daughter Takako, a shy eighteen-year-old, sat next to Noora in the circular booth.

Although the hotel served excellent Japanese cuisine, Mr. Okata and his family all ordered prime rib with baked potatoes.

"Ice" Cohen had begun to relax and enjoy himself. He was glad he had decided to bring Frenchy, who seemed at ease with the Japanese. But his comfort didn't last; his stepson Kennilworth, clad in a designer suit, accompanied by his current blonde-for-the-moment, had just walked into the restaurant.

Mr. Massa Okata nudged Ian and said close to his ear, "My wife and my daughter are having a nice time with Miss Karlton."

"Yes. It sure looks that way, Okata-san," Ian replied.

Kennilworth and the tall, buxom blonde, who was wrapped in a stunning sable stole, approached the table.

Looming above his stepfather, Kennilworth extended his hand.

"Mr. Okata, it is always a pleasure to see you."

Mr. Okata lifted himself from the booth and shook Kennilworth's hand while bowing traditionally.

"Good to see you, Ian!" Kennilworth said, a bit too enthusiastically. "I have been looking forward to our next meeting, Mr. Okata," he said, turning to the Japanese investor. "Sorry I missed you in Cannes," he said, louder than necessary. Spurred on by the girl pinching his arm, he cleared his throat. "And I'd like you to meet Miss Francine Papillon. She just landed the lead role in a new television series, and we are celebrating her success," he said all in one breath.

"How do you do!" Francine chirped cheerfully and waved to everyone like a high school cheerleader.

"Congratulations!" the Japanese family sang out in unison.

Puckering her artificial and overinflated lips, Francine Papillon whispered: "Ooh, *thangyooh,*" then pulled Kennilworth away to their waiting table.

Kennilworth was the son Ian Cohen had legally adopted when he married his mother, Beverly Hillard-Cohen. The boy had been nine years old. Beverly was the love of Ian's life. They had almost twenty happy years together. She died of cancer five years, two months, and three days ago, to be exact. Ian never stopped missing her. He wished they had had a child together, someone just like his darling "Bevvy," someone other than Kennil-worthless.

As the dinner plates were cleared, the conversation at Ian Cohen's table became livelier. Noora nevertheless kept a serious eye on her host. She noticed he barely touched his food. She wished he did not smoke, but he stubbed out his Camel cigarette before it ended. Perhaps he had shortness of breath again. Perhaps he was feeling ill. She watched as Ian loosened his tie. She saw the beads of perspiration on his forehead.

She could see that he wanted to remove his jacket, and appeared uncomfortable about having Kennilworth a few tables away. If she could just convince him to see a doctor before it was too late. But she was just a new employee and could not suggest anything. So she feigned fatigue, put a hand to her mouth, and gestured a yawn.

"I am sorry. I must be jet-lagged," she said. Knowing yawning was contagious, she hoped the other ladies would do the same.

Mrs. Okata also yawned and giggled. "Good food too, make us tired," she said.

Ian signaled to the waiter for the check.

Beneath the Beverly Regent Hotel's porte-cochère, Kelley bowed to the Japanese family and said, "*Oyasumi Nasai,*" wishing them a restful sleep.

Mother and daughter, as well as Mr. Okata, were visibly impressed. They repeated the words a couple of times, giggling happily and bowing, before finally crossing the cobblestone driveway and heading to the private penthouse elevators beyond the glass doors. *There was something wonderful about that family,* Noora thought. She liked Mrs. Okata and their daughter. She liked the Japanese people she had met over the years. They were kind, respectful, intelligent ...

"I didn't know you spoke Japanese," Ian said, visibly impressed.

"Just a few words."

"Sounded fluent to me. Where'd you learn it?"

"Well, I learned it ... at the hotel ... where I worked, sir." Noora did not dare admit she had been to Tokyo with her family five years before, where they had visited Tokyo Disney and she had learned basic Japanese.

Sam pulled the Rolls-Royce up to the curb and got out to let Noora and Ian in. She wondered if he was aware of Mr. Cohen's heart condition.

The butler must have been his confidant. So what did Mr. Cohen need her for? She still had no clear idea what he expected from her, what kind of work he wanted her to do. Why did he fly her all the way from France when he could easily hire someone from Los Angeles to look after his personal needs?

The moment Sam stopped the car in front of the Bel Air mansion, Ian opened his own door and climbed out. He mumbled a quick "good night" and hurried inside just as Cessi opened the front door.

At the Beverly Regent, Kennilworth left the restaurant and got into his car, forgetting to open the door for his date. His mind was busy with other matters. First, he wanted to dump Francine Papillon. The only problem was, she now lived with him. Kennilworth had done everything, short of (God forbid) marrying the high-maintenance starlet, just so he could get into her pants.

He had conquered. Now he was bored.

He waited for the valet to hurry up and close the passenger door after helping Francine into the car. He never should have invited her to move in with him, he thought, zooming out of the restaurant driveway. That bitch was taking over his closets, his kitchen, his house, and now his life! Luckily, she had an early call the next morning and lines to memorize. Good excuse for him to slip out of his house tonight.

He couldn't stop wondering how the old man could have had dinner with one of the world's biggest investors, without inviting him. His own stepfather had deliberately avoided him during the entire Cannes Film Festival. Something was definitely going on. He switched gears furiously, while his Maserati Ghibli screamed up the hill, toward the street he dreaded.

He never took Cielo Drive up to his house. He stayed away from that street at all costs. From Benedict Canyon, he always took Angelo Drive up the winding road to his house, which was on the private street called Angelo View, just below the cul-de-sac.

But tonight, he had been so engrossed in his thoughts that he had somehow missed Angelo Drive. He never missed his own street before. He should have made a U-turn and gone back to Angelo. Too late; he would have to take the next street up. He was too anxious to take Ms. Papillon back to the house and get her off his back so he could turn around and head to his father's house in Bel Air, which was only fifteen minutes away. He had to give the old man a piece of his mind and find out why he had been ostracized. Something fishy was going on. He was determined to find out.

As he continued up the hill on Cielo Drive, his luxury sports car stalled and died. Just like that, and he was not even low on gas. Kennilworth felt the sweat pour out of every pore in his body. Right in the middle of Cielo, the just-renovated $100,000-plus Maserati Ghibli decided to stall. *Why?*

It was the street. Cielo was cursed. It was damned with bad luck. Bad omen. Bad shit.

"Shit!" he shouted.

On the dark, unpaved road, left of Cielo, was the house where Sharon Tate had been brutally murdered by the Charles Manson Family back in 1969. Kenni had been eight years old and living with his mother in Sherman Oaks, down in the San Fernando Valley. He never forgot how terrified he had been, glued to the television reports of the grisly murders. More than twenty-five years later, Kennilworth thought he was going to get sick when he found out, just two months after purchasing his beautiful glass house on Angelo View Drive, designed by a renowned architect, that right below the hill of his new home was the residence Charles Manson's followers had raided, where the horrible killings had occurred.

"Take it easy, honey," Francine purred.

How easy would she take it if she knew *anything?* The girl was not even *born* when the *Helter Skelter* horrific tragedy happened, just up to the left of that street he was on. He switched the ignition for the third time.

"You're going to flood it, babe."

Thank God he hadn't married her. "Why don't you get out and push, honey?" Kennilworth sneered just as the engine screeched back into action.

"Excuuse me?"

"Nothing!" he yelled, relieved that his Maserati was back under his command. He swore to himself that no matter what, he would never take Cielo again.

He made a sharp left onto Davies Street and down to Angelo View, where a splendid show of the city's multicolored lights appeared before them. It was a crystal-clear night. From the horizon, they could see airplanes descending, one behind the other, like stars in succession, into the Los Angeles airport.

"Wow. What a view," she said. "Takes your breath away, huh, honey? I love it here. Too bad the house is so screwy. Can't wait to remodel. Right, baby?"

He winced as a nerve began to throb on his right temple. He floored it down the one-lane driveway and finally to his wide, circular courtyard.

The three-car garage was separate from the main house. The light bulb outside had burned out. "Shit," Kenni cursed under his breath. He hated to walk through the darkened walkway to the house. Carefully sliding his car into the garage—because she had her ridiculous BMW parked too close to his space—he had to open the door for the bimbo. Francine never could figure out how to open his sports car door. It was just as well. Her nails were too long. She would surely scratch the handle.

Down the walkway to the house, she clung to his arm, as she clippety-clopped her stiletto way. He had forgotten to turn on the pool light when they left the house earlier, and it was so dark, he could barely insert the key to the door. The alarm was not always working—mice had long ago chewed on some of the wires through the crawlspace.

It was unfortunate that John Lautner, the renowned architect who had originally designed the house thirty years ago, had recently died. He would have to start looking for an architect who could finish the plans for the remodeling, Kennilworth thought. He had been so busy at the studio, plus traveling and attending the Cannes Film Festival, that he had neglected his dream house.

Tonight, he would find out what was going on with Ian Cohen, why his stepfather had been so secretive. Angrily, he pushed the door open. The ear-piercing alarm sounded. Cursing under his breath again, he ran into the house and turned on the switches that partially lit up the courtyard and the oval-shaped pool. He rushed back outside and pressed the code buttons. The alarm finally stopped. All was quiet again. He knew the alarm was a joke. It wasn't even connected to the police. The service had been canceled months before, because of his plans to remodel.

"Good to be home," Francine sighed, kicking off her shoes, swinging her way to their bedroom. "We should have a dog, honey. It's more fun to be greeted by a little pooch than by something that could damage my eardrums," she said, removing her dress, letting it fall at the foot of the bed. She tossed her bra across the room and it landed on the carpet near the row of closet doors. She sighed delightedly as she sank into a pile of plush leopard pillows propped against the headboard of his king-size bed. She picked up a script from the floor by her bedside and began to leaf through it.

Kennilworth loathed a messy house. Francine always dropped everything on the floor. He grudgingly picked up her dress and hung it in the closet.

"Honey, when did you say we were going to start remodeling? I like to share with you. But a closet, well, a girl needs her space." She yawned again.

"Darn it. I forgot to pick up that new script from my father. I won't be long," he said, carefully closing the sliding doors of his closet, where one of the hinges had lost a screw.

"You can't leave me. Not at this hour ..."

"I won't be long."

"It's creepy up here by myself." She puckered her lips, slowly running her hand down to her crotch.

"A girl like you shouldn't be afraid of anything."

She threw a pillow at him. He caught it. "You are perfectly safe here. You have the alarm and the phones. You can call me on my cell. Besides," he said as he crossed the room, keeping his distance from the bed and replacing the pillow, "we wouldn't want your director to blame me for not knowing your lines."

She leaped up, grabbed him, and wrestled him onto the bed. "My memory clears incredibly well after a good fuck."

Before he could break free, she was kissing him hard while her hands yanked his shirt out of his pants.

"You win! I surrender!" he said, pretending to be happily seduced. He would give her twenty minutes of his time. *Tomorrow, she would definitely get her walking papers,* he thought, rolling over in bed, imprisoned by her arms and legs.

*****   *****   *****

In the quiet walls of Ian Cohen's mansion, Noora sat numbly at the edge of the bed and stared at the doorknob. *What if Ian decided to get fresh?* She wasn't sure if the lock worked. Sam the butler was off that night. Cessi, the Guatemalan maid, had a nice little room decorated in pink-and-white lace that perpetually smelled like a mixture of garlic and gardenia. The maid's room was downstairs, a few feet away from the kitchen. At least there was another woman in the house.

On their way home, Mr. Cohen had asked Noora again if she finished reading the script he had given her. She had told him yes, but she was embarrassed to admit she had a difficult time reading such a terribly bloody and violent script. She had counted nine"F" words just in the first two pages. She had forced herself to read it, the way she used to read difficult books when she attended school in London. But she did not understand all the abbreviated words, apparently movie lingo, and she did not dare ask Ian.

She wanted to write to Annette. She knew Annette was waiting to hear from her, and she wanted so much to tell her all about her new life and Ian Cohen's Bel Air mansion—and that so far, Annette had been right: Mr. Cohen was still a gentleman.

She undressed in her lovely, small bathroom and carefully hung up her new suit, then slipped into Annette's blue dress. She caught a reflection of herself in the bathroom mirror. *Is that person really me?* The hairdresser had layered her short hair perhaps a bit too much. And the streaks were really blonde. She no longer looked like Noora. But that was exactly what she had wanted. She was now Kelley Karlton. *Kelley Karlton,* she repeated to herself. She felt a draft on the back of her neck. California nights were colder than she had imagined. She practically dove between the sheets and turned up the dial on the electric blanket that Cessi had tucked between the comforter and top sheet. Tomorrow she would write to Annette and tell her about her dinner with the Japanese family. And shopping at the Beverly Center.

Loud voices came from downstairs. A man was shouting. Ian's voice loudly retorted. Then she heard shattering glass, like an explosion. A door slammed hard, vibrating the walls of her room. *An earthquake?* She jumped out of bed. More doors slammed, jarring every nerve cell in her body. Then, an eerie silence prevailed.

After a few moments, she heard sounds of a loud motor rumbling close to the house and tearing up the road; a sports car. When all was quiet again, she ventured to the door and put an ear into it. Should she go out on the corridor and see what just happened? She heard nothing more. Shivering, she returned to her toasty warm bed. Moments later, someone was knocking softly. She hoped it was her imagination, but the gentle knock persisted.

"Kelley?" Ian was calling from the other side of her door.

Noora slipped on Annette's sweater and grabbed her purse, making sure she had her money and passport. If he tried anything, she would be ready to run.

"Kelley, please ..." she heard Ian Cohen's pleading voice. His distress sounded genuine. She opened the door.

Ian Cohen was breathing hard. His face was pale and covered with beads of sweat.

Under the fluorescent lights of the hospital's stark waiting room, Noora sat on a cold plastic chair. The wall clock displayed two o'clock. What was taking so long?

Chilled from the air conditioning, Noora wanted to go outside, into warmer air. But if Mr. Cohen were discharged or needed her, she had to make sure he didn't think she left him. She decided to go through the double doors, and she ventured down the hallway where he had originally gone in.

While searching for Mr. Cohen, she wondered if perhaps she should have told Sam about his employer's health. Shouldn't the butler be the one to take Mr. Cohen to the hospital? Maybe Sam would have called an ambulance. Instead, Mr. Cohen drove to Cedars Sinai Hospital himself. He was so secretive about the state of his health, he probably thought an ambulance would have brought too much attention.

But that was more dangerous. She feared he might have a stroke while driving, but he drove with ease, even though he was breathing hard. On their way to the hospital, the only thing he revealed was that he had just had an argument with his stepson, and heart palpitations started again.

As Noora ventured down the hall in the emergency ward, she overheard a conversation between two nurses.

"You know who he is?"

"Is he that big-shot producer?" one of the nurses behind the counter asked loudly while glancing down at a ledger.

"Ian Cohen," the other nurse said.

"Ian Cohen? No way."

"Yeah. Can you believe it? Himself. He wouldn't give my boyfriend a chance to read for him. He's a bastard. I hear he screams at everyone who works for him."

"What's he in here for?" She opened a file folder. "Overdose?"

"Over-sex, I'm sure," another nurse said.

Noora took a step back to avoid being seen. She heard giggling.

"Heart condition … Too much you-know-what, I'm sure …"

More giggling.

Noora walked further down the hall. Through a glass partition, she spotted Mr. Cohen lying on a bed, wearing a hospital gown.

"Mr. Cohen?"

"Thank God it's you. I've been here with my head up my ass, waiting for my damn doctor to show up. I don't know what the fuck's going on. Help me up. See if you can get me a nurse who can speak English. I need to take a whiz."

"Mr. Cohen, sir, I'm sure this is a great hospital, but I don't think …" Noora blurted before she could stop herself. She bit her lip.

"What're you saying?"

"I'm sorry. I'll … find you someone who …"

"No, wait a minute. What did you mean exactly?"

"Well, I may be wrong, but … the nurses recognized you, and … well …"

"Get me my clothes." He pointed to the chair.

From the reflection of the glass wall behind him, she could tell he was nude. She kept her eyes to the ground as she handed him his clothes.

"Do me a favor," he said. "Go out there and tell 'em it was just a bad case of gas. I'm now feeling a hundred percent better, and thank them very much. I'll meet you in the car."

In the parking lot, as he drove out of the hospital gate, Ian seemed suddenly energized.

"Kennil-worthless," he mumbled. He turned to Noora. "Let's grab a bite, kid. I know a great place. Open all night. You'll love their chocolate cake." He turned his attention back to the road and made a sharp left. "God, I hope you're not a vegetarian."

At the Hamburger Hamlet on Beverly Drive in Beverly Hills, Ian Cohen devoured a juicy rare hamburger, along with a large order of french fries drenched in ketchup, and a tall glass mug of draft beer to wash it all down.

Noora was enjoying a triple-layer chocolate cake with a mug of hot chocolate—hopefully it had enough caffeine to keep her awake.

"You didn't really respond when I asked you if you finished that script."

"I'm sorry; I should have returned it to you …"

"I got more copies. Did you read the entire thing?"

"Yes, sir."

There was a long pause.

"That good, huh?" He poured salt over his ketchup.

"Well, it was all right, really …"

"Quit the B.S. Tell me how you *really* liked the script."

"Well, I found it a bit too … Well, too bloody. Gory … I'm sorry."

"You didn't like it.

"Well … In my opinion, and that is strictly my own opinion, sir …"

"I won't get mad if you finally get to the point." He took a big bite of his burger.

"There were some scenes I found …" She stopped herself.

"Some scenes you found what?"

"Perhaps a tad too far-fetched," she said before she could stop herself.

He stared at her for a long, uncomfortable moment. She was sure he was going to explode.

Instead, he swallowed his food and said, "I see. Tell me everything that's bothering you about the story, and I'll give you a good reason for it, because I've been through this property a zillion times with a gazillion writers."

But Ian Cohen knew he was running out of creative juice. Good material didn't come by like it used to. There was a time when he could doctor any script, or if he had a story idea, he could assign a writer. In a few weeks, they practically had a shooting script. Not anymore. There were so many scripts floating around Hollywood, but none of them moved him anymore. He spent a fortune on rewrites. Maybe he should just shelve the damn script. What the hell did she mean by "a bit too far-fetched"? What the hell did she know? "Kids love things that are far-fetched," he said.

"I don't believe the antagonist should be killed by the protagonist. The antagonist should be killed as a result of his own actions."

"Screenwriting 101," he mumbled.

"Pardon?"

"Never mind."

"And Michael the antagonist ... Michael Mancuzo, that's his name, isn't it?"

"Yeah," he said. At least she remembered the character's name. Most readers didn't remember names of characters. That was one positive point.

"The character of Michael Mancuzo is all bad. Nobody's all good or all bad. There's no depth to his character."

"He's a mean bastard who kills. A cold-blooded murderer. How much depth does he need?"

"He is not a robot."

He's a fucking moron and a damned killer! Ian wanted to say, but he was in the company of a lady. "All right, even if he's a killer, he's still human," Ian admitted.

"He was once a child," Noora continued. "And innocent ... before he started to go bad. I'm sure there was someone he had to care about, still cares about."

Ian chewed on that idea. "So?"

"It would give the reader ... I mean the audience ... a moment to think ... to have a little compassion," she said, thinking he was surely going to tell her to go back to cleaning rooms.

Ian stopped eating. "Then what?"

"That's it."

"C'mon. Tell me more."

"I'm sorry, this is only my opinion."

A waitress slung a platter of onion rings on their table.

"That was a good observation," he said. "I'll buy you another piece of cake. What else about the story? I didn't write the script. You wouldn't be insulting me."

"It's just that the characters hardly speak to one another. They are not robots."

"We established that. They are actors. What's the difference?"

Noora shot him a look.

"Okay, maybe I'm kidding. Guess I shouldn't insult 'em. Damn actors. Wait till you work with one."

"Mr. Cohen, sir, to me, the story seems … well, monotonous."

"You must be joking. That movie's a rollercoaster ride."

"Perhaps … but the plot is predictable. You always know the kind of thing that's going to happen next."

"Yeah, but it's the fun of how the predictability comes out at the end, and of course, the special effects."

"Yes, but where are the unexpected twists, the ones that fool you, that grab you? There's nothing … I mean, not enough to make the ride fun and interesting … then … it's … the end. Like the French say, it ends *en queue de poisson*. In a fish tail."

"Give me a for-instance."

She blurted out what she thought of the plot, her ideas about how the characters could be given more depth, how she would want to see the story evolve—beginning, middle, and end.

Ian stopped eating and stared at her. The kid made sense. "Ever been to Honolulu?"

CHAPTER 38
PRENUPTIAL PREPARATIONS

In the Fendil mansion, the household staff prepared Zaffeera's favorite dish—lamb chops, extra rare filet mignon, saffron rice, and steamed vegetables, always served on a shiny silver tray with embroidered linen. But Zaffeera barely touched her food.

Um Gamelia, the mother of Zaffeera's personal maid, had returned to help with the wedding preparations. It was unusual for all the maids to be in the kitchen at the same time, but there was so much to do, and they were all genuinely concerned about the health of the young bride-to-be.

"You know what she said?" Mona whispered aloud to another maid named Khadiga.

"No," Khadiga said with eyes wide as an owl.

Um Gamelia, who was preparing a lunch platter for Mrs. Fendil, shook her head. She was well aware that gossip was dangerous. It could easily cost those two maids their jobs, however genuine their concern was for Miss Zaffeera. They had both been with the Fendil family for five years and had been sent by a renowned employment agency. They were trained to respect their employers' privacy at all times. Um Gamelia did not want to lose focus and began to work faster, putting the final touches on the platter. If she forgot something, like a condiment or the special sea salt Mrs. Fendil required, Um Gamelia would look like a fool, and she would have to return to the kitchen, a long and unnecessary trip, including a waste of time.

"Miss Zaffeera never says anything," Aziza, the laundry maid said, heading for the ironing room, her arms laden with the family's white linen.

"That is true. But this time, she probably couldn't help it and needed her mother's reassurance," Mona said.

"Zaffeera spoke to her mother in front of *you?*" Khadiga asked, surprised.

"Yes," Mona said.

"She usually closes the door when she's with her mother," Khadiga noted.

"What did she say to her mother?" Mona had to ask.

"She was crying. She said she felt guilty, and that Mister Michel should have been her brother-in-law, not her husband. I never saw Miss Zaffeera cry like that."

Um Gamelia cleared her throat loudly. A long silence fell in the kitchen. Everyone returned to their respective chores.

"She's been through a lot, poor thing," another maid dared to break the silence.

"There is nothing abnormal for a young bride to be scared before her wedding day," Um Gamelia said, staring at everyone firmly. "I would appreciate it if we tend to our own business and never speak about our employers' personal affairs," she added sternly. Everyone lowered their eyes and nodded.

Um Gamelia lifted the heavy platter she had just prepared and marched down the long corridor.

Oh my God, oh my God, oh my God! What is going to happen to me now? Um Gamelia's daughter wondered again. Bent Gamelia leaned wearily against the kitchen sink, drying a porcelain platter. She kept drying that same platter absent-mindedly, knowing her face was white, and if anyone should see her, she would raise suspicion.

Would her mistress still need her—after she was married? Would she continue to use her, *that way?* She prayed that would not be the case. Zaffeera and her new husband would be away for a month-long honeymoon. Bent Gamelia looked forward to that time of rest. But what then? She knew Zaffeera was going to live in Mr. Amir's mansion. Would she still be Miss Zaffeera's personal maid? *Only Allah and time would tell,* she thought with a shudder. She was exhausted. Zaffeera had kept her up until dawn.

The night before, Bent Gamelia had committed a sacrilege, an unforgivable sin. But she was given no choice. *Choice* was not a word she could ever consider. She was a servant.

She wanted to crawl into a corner of the kitchen. Perhaps she could confide in her mother? *No!* Zaffeera would surely find out and she would certainly kill her. She would take the small, thin, sharp knife she used for her mangoes, and without a second thought, she would slit Bent Gamelia's throat. Her body would be thrown in the Red Sea for sharks to shred her to pieces. She had heard about this happening. She had heard it from Mona, the inquisitive maid, who had seen a report on television. The newsman said that girls from neighboring countries in the Middle East who did not behave properly, or shamed their families, were no longer stoned or beheaded, but thrown alive to sharks in the middle of the Red Sea. *Was that why they called it the Red Sea? Because it was infested with hungry sharks and stained with the blood of sinners?* But the Red Sea was quite far from where they lived, she tried to remind herself, feeling her stomach starting to cramp.

"Poor children," she heard Mona say.

"She is now an angel and she must have brought the two of them together. We must pray for their happiness ..."

"The Good Lord works wonders ... *Hamdallah,*" another maid said.

"*Hamdallah,*" Mona said, sitting in the corner of the kitchen and plucking feathers from a just-slaughtered chicken. "They will soon be husband and wife. He is a respectable man. Handsome too!"

"That young man is as good as a prince," Khadiga said. "It is a blessing indeed for the Fendil family. The devil came one night, *be'eid min hinnah,* far, far away from us, ptoo!" She mock-spat. "But, *hamdallah,* the Good Lord arrived in time to restore the misfortune of the family, by having the sister marry the young man. We have so much to be grateful for."

"May Allah the great, the Almighty all-powerful grant the new couple many healthy sons!" Khadiga said.

"Gamelia? Are you sick?" Mona asked.

Gamelia had to control her trembling and say something quickly. But words refused to form out of her lips.

"What is the matter with you, *ya Bent?* You have not said a word, child," she said, resting the now-nude hen on the marble counter. She began to carefully fold the flying mounds of feathers in sheets of newspaper.

Did it show?! She could feel her blood draining to her feet. *Oh my God, they know!*

"Listen, young lady ..." she heard Mona say.

"Yes?" Gamelia's voice came out weakly screeching. She stared at the dead chicken on the counter.

"It would be best if you go and rest now. The bride-to-be will soon require much attention," one of the maids advised.

"If you need assistance with her washing or ironing, don't be embarrassed to ask. It will be our pleasure to help you," Aziza the laundry maid assured her.

Pleasure? "No, really, I'm fine, thank you ..."

Hopefully, these women would never imagine the "pleasures" Zaffeera required, or rather commanded. She shuddered again.

In the past few months, Bent Gamelia had begun to see things more clearly; it was not normal to do what her mistress demanded of her. Worst of all, something more horrible had occurred the night before.

She had gone to prepare the nightly bath for her mistress. Afterward, Miss Zaffeera had settled in bed and decided to read. It was another one of those big, thick science fiction-type books all written in English. As usual, Bent Gamelia had gathered Zaffeera's wet towels and soiled clothes to be washed separately in the special hypoallergenic soap. Zaffeera asked lazily, and in a half-yawning voice: "Fluff me up two more of those pillows for my back."

As Bent Gamelia obliged, Zaffeera suddenly grabbed her and kissed her hard on the lips. She held her tight and pulled her onto the bed—the way a man might subdue a woman. She did not struggle. She froze. Perhaps it was shock. Perhaps subconsciously, she knew that was what she was to do in a situation such as this. To her surprise, she actually found herself being aroused by her mistress's hungry kisses. Zaffeera's expert hands traveled under Gamelia's starched pink-and-white uniform, under her brassiere, and a second or so later, she was fondling Gamelia's left breast. She squeezed both nipples so hard, Gamelia could still feel the pain.

Gamelia's body had responded with an involuntary quiver of pleasure, while at the same time, she wanted to scream, "No, please ..." but Zaffeera had rolled on top of Gamelia and pulled down her panties. At first, Gamelia was terribly embarrassed. This time, it was Zaffeera who was separating her maid's most personal spot—that sacred place of hers which had already been violated, "down there," the one where only a husband should touch in darkness for the sole purpose of conception. Zaffeera licked her fast and furious, in hard, circular motions. For the first time in her life, the maid experienced a certain deep, delicious feeling as her body shuddered like warm electricity running through her entire being, one spasm after another. She had to bite the back of her hand, to the point of drawing blood, so she would not scream with a mixture of pleasure, pain, and shame.

Zaffeera, who was breathing hard like a man, tore off her peignoir and rubbed her nude body wildly against her maid's. They thrashed around in bed together for what might have been an eternity, kissing, thrusting fingers and tongues on each other's sacred place.

When Zaffeera was done with her maid, she gave her a tall glass of cool, sweet almond juice that she had kept in her small bedside refrigerator.

Soon after she drank, Bent Gamelia felt dizzy and disoriented. Everything around her began to blur.

Zaffeera ordered her to gather the laundry and leave.

"Go straight to your room. Speak to no one. Wash my clothes at dawn before everyone else's clothes. Come back at eight in the morning."

When Bent Gamelia stumbled through the halls, her arms full of wet towels, she prayed she would not run into anyone. Zaffeera's perfume was still lingering over Gamelia's entire being. It was a new fragrance. Zaffeera frequently changed perfumes. Bent Gamelia didn't remember how she managed to make her way to the laundry room. It was a miracle she had not fainted in the corridor. She dumped everything in the special laundry machine. She then washed her face and arms in the gushing warm water of the washing machine's gentle cycle.

"*Speak to no one,*" the words of her mistress echoed. Did she tell her to wash her clothes in the morning so they would be fresh and not sit overnight in the washing machine? Too late. She would have to wait until the cycle was complete. But that dreadful dizzy feeling intensified. For a moment, she thought she was on a boat in the middle of a stormy sea. Zaffeera must have drugged her. She must have put something in that almond water; she was now sure of it. A feeling of panic overcame her. She could not wait to be in her own room so she could throw up and clean her stomach of any drug that would destroy her. She had managed to quietly rush through the service exit and outside to the garden. A few yards away, she entered the small building of the servants' quarters. After she closed the door to her tiny private room, grateful that she had her own little bathroom closet, and even more grateful no one saw her, she hugged the toilet and vomited everything she could before letting herself fall into her narrow bed. She heard the dawn chant from the *Muezzin,* the distant Morning Prayer voice that came from the town's minaret. She prayed desperately through her silent sobs: "Please, Allah, I beg you forgiveness. Once again, I have sinned."

Two days prior to the wedding, on July fourth, America was celebrating Independence Day, broadcasting the parades and celebrations on the international news channels—in major Hollywood production style.

In the women's den, Zaffeera was being fitted into her wedding gown. Last-minute stitchings were being done by the French seamstress, Madame Solange, along with her two assistants. Zaffeera finally allowed the head seamstress to add a few pearls and tiny silver beads around the edge of the skirt and around the borders of the long train.

Shamsah was on the floor, watching the American parade on the modern large-screen television.

"Shamsah! See, over there, right on that street ... can you see the colorful awnings?" Zaffeera pointed to the TV. "That's the hotel where we'll be! Michel and I will be right there in just about a week from today."

"*Inshallah,*" their mother was quick to say. "God willing."

"I want to go with you," Shamsah said to her sister.

"You can't, it's their honeymoon, *ya habibti,*" Yasmina said with a smile.

"Next time, Shamsah, I promise I will take you to Los Angeles, and we'll stay in that hotel," Zaffeera said. "And guess what! Disneyland is only an hour away from there."

"I'd rather go shopping with you in Beverly Hills and visit Rodeo Drive."

Everyone was surprised at Shamsah's comment. They all laughed.

"Tell them where else you're going on your honeymoon," their mother said. She was painstakingly stitching tiny needle points of shiny white silken thread into a silk handkerchief. "That is, if it's okay with you, Zaffeera. It's not a secret, is it?"

"No, no," Zaffeera answered slowly, turning for the seamstress to finish with the hemming. "I spoke to Michel yesterday morning. He just came back from Paris, you know ... Well ..." Zaffeera took a deep breath, trying to contain her excitement. "He wanted to keep it a surprise, but he had to tell me. I believe his father suggested it, and I am most grateful ..."

Everyone stared at Zaffeera. Yasmina Fendil was glad her daughter was more talkative. She seemed even happy for the first time in so long.

"Yes, and?" Shamsah asked impatiently.

"I am most grateful to the Good Lord ..."

"All right, already, my sister. Stop the suspense!" Shamsah pressed. She punched the mute button on the remote control.

"He is taking me to Honolulu," she proudly announced.

Everyone looked at Zaffeera with surprise.

The assistant seamstress turned to Madame Solange and whispered, "Where is Ana-lulu?"

CHAPTER 39
THE WEDDING

They held hands while the sheik prayed in front of them. Farid Fendil had originally wanted his daughter and Michel to be married by the wise man who had originally married him to Yasmina almost thirty years before. But the old mullah was now in his eighties and somehow, Farid had accepted the offer of Sheik Abdullah Kharoub, the head of the MOFHAJ group, to perform his daughter's wedding. Of course, the MOFHAJ men were honored. They were all standing around him now in a circle. Farid Fendil tried to concentrate on the prayer. He needed to repeat some of the words from the Koran. He could not allow himself to be distracted by thoughts of the past. He felt dizzy and his mouth was dry. He promised himself he would take care of his health as soon as the wedding and the festivities were over.

Sitting on the low ottoman, Michel kept his head bowed. He was holding Farid Fendil's hand. Nodding his head at times, eyes half-closed, he tried to understand what the sheik was saying. If he had known, he would have called the whole thing off. It was embarrassing. He was told that the ceremony was going to be "traditional." He thought he would walk down the aisle, and it would be short and simple—but it was turning out to be this tedious ceremony in which the women were not even participating. And his new bride was not even with him! No one had told him it would be this type of old-fashioned, or more to the point, ridiculously archaic wedding ceremony. There was a roomful of men in traditional dress, and endless prayers. The lengthy ordeal made him feel awkward and terribly uncomfortable.

The hand of his future father-in-law was becoming clammy, and Michel could feel him tightening his grip.

They asked him to repeat the verse of a prayer. His French and his English were better than his Arabic. The sheik patiently repeated for Michel, who uttered each word like a parrot. *Pay attention,* Michel chided himself. He could still change his mind. Couldn't he? "I was not told it would take so long," he would tell them. His old, wise professor in Paris had once told him that it did not take him long to get married, and he was married a long time. So what was the point of this pompous fanfare? *I am deeply regretful! I made a dreadful mistake, don't you see?*

Instead of speaking what was on his mind, Michel repeated the next verse he was asked to say. He looked up. All the men around him nodded in agreement. He glanced at Noora's father. ... No, he had to change his way of thinking: *Zaffeera's father*. What was Mr. Fendil thinking now? A moment ago, he seemed quite uncomfortable. Now he appeared content. No, perhaps more like satisfied. Michel could have sworn that Mr. Fendil's eyes were tearing now, although it appeared that he was trying to conceal it.

He wished he could just get up and run. It would be dishonorable if he did. Especially to Mr. Fendil. He also suffered the loss. His daughter. With this wedding, Michel believed that he would bring hope to the Fendil family. Zaffeera would be good for him. She was smart. She possessed a certain degree of strength, especially at this difficult time. Whatever he needed, she ordered it for him, and it was at his doorstep within twenty-four hours. Like the pillows. And great books on losing a loved one ... and on architecture. Yes, he would immerse himself in architecture, his true passion. He would let his new bride take care of everything else.

The old sheik barged in on his reverie, asking him to repeat another verse. Michel did. His Arabic was lousy and the sheik did not seem pleased. *Too bad,* Michel thought. That old man was lucky he didn't just get up and leave.

*****   *****   *****

Farid Fendil was uncomfortable holding Michel's hand under the embroidered handkerchief his wife had sewn for the wedding. He did not realize the ceremony would go on for so long. He needed air. *Dear Allah, I plead with you, help me ease away that awful feeling of nausea.* Beads of perspiration formed. His abdomen began cramping. Cold sweat poured out of his body. Everyone was too close. Oh, mighty Allah …

His head hit the ground first, with a loud thud.

When he opened his eyes, everyone was staring down at him. First the sheik with intense dark eyes, expressing disapproval. Then Michel, who looked at him with great concern—and two other men from the religious group, who stared at him with steely eyes.

"Mr. Fendil, are you all right?" Michel asked, helping his new father-in-law up.

"Yes, yes," Farid Fendil nodded, sitting back down. Someone brought him a glass of water and he took a sip.

"We must call the doctor."

"No. Please, gentlemen. I just needed some water. I am terribly sorry…"

"*Hamdallah*. He is regaining color," someone said. Everyone was nodding. "*Hamdallah*."

"Gentlemen, let us forget this incident. I am feeling better," he lied. "*Shokran* … to you all. Thank you."

Ten minutes later, and what had seemed like an eternity to both Farid Fendil and Michel Amir, Abdo (who was chosen as the messenger), rushed out to announce to the women that Zaffeera and Michel were officially husband and wife.

From the opposite end of the Fendil mansion, where the women had waited impatiently to hear the good news, ear-piercing ululations suddenly broke forth with such volume, the men could clearly hear the joyful cries.

In the grand ballroom of the new Al-Balladi Prince Hotel, the reception was a feast none of the guests would ever forget.

Crisp white brocade tablecloths covered the round tables in the grand ballroom. Each table had a work-of-art centerpiece of tall topiaries, decorated with densely filled red roses and fresh lilies of the valley from

Switzerland. From the food to the thousands of imported flowers, everything had been planned by Zaffeera. No detail was overlooked, and nothing had been left to chance.

Except her honeymoon.

CHAPTER 40
HONOLULU CITY LIGHTS

The L1011 departed Los Angeles on time. Ian Cohen briefed his new young companion about the purpose of the trip.

"I gotta get an angiogram. Whatever the f... the heck that means," he said. "It shouldn't take more than a coupla hours. There's only one doctor I can trust. Used to be my war buddy out in slant-land. I don't think anyone knows me in Honolulu. I'm sure they don't give a rat's ass about Hollywood. They'd rather surf. Well, I'll be mostly at Straub Hospital..."

Noora tried to take notes, but he might as well have been speaking ancient Chinese. Did he say "Strowb Hospital?" It sounded more like "strawberry hospital." What did he mean by "slant-land?" She had an idea, but she wasn't going to ask.

Five and a half hours later, they landed in Honolulu.

At the busy airport, Noora followed Ian Cohen out of Gate 22, through the open-air walkway. Sweet tropical fragrances enveloped her. The memory of Uncle Khayat's garden of plumeria, frangipani, and roses rushed in on her entire being. Noora felt transported to the age of ten, arriving in Alexandria on the first day of summer vacation. She experienced a sudden burst of joy, a feeling that had been so dormant, she had almost forgotten what it felt like to be happy. Reality struck when she realized Mr. Cohen had moved on far ahead of her. She hurried after him. *Stay in the present; you must not think of the past!*

In the terminal, bare-chested young men and lovely long-haired women in colorful muumuus held up handwritten signs with the names of passengers they were meeting. *The only thing missing,* Noora thought, *was live Hawaiian music and hula dancers.*

"The last time I was here, they didn't have all this cement," Ian Cohen said, setting his attaché case down. Some passengers walking ahead of him stopped to pull out carts for their carry-ons. Ian dug in his pocket in search of some change. He slid several quarters into a slot and released a cart. He'd never used one before, and he wondered why there were no porters like in the old days. It seemed a sad lifetime ago since he had visited Honolulu with his wife Bevvy. He put his carry-on and attaché case on the cart and pushed it ahead of him. After a few steps, he realized he was out of breath, and a tremor of fear moved through his gut. "Shit," he said.

He felt his hair stirring in the warm trade winds. He smelled the plumeria. Maybe it wouldn't be so bad if he died here.

Once outside of the baggage claim, Noora followed Ian Cohen to a limousine. They were whisked down the freeway ramp and onto Kalakaua Boulevard, where traffic nearly crawled. Noora was mesmerized by the scenery, marveling at the indigo ocean along the wide boulevard. As soon as they entered the Waikiki strip, she felt overwhelmed and confused. It was like something out of Asia, yet it was American, Honolulu was like nothing she had ever seen before. And yet ... there was a feeling of déjà vu. Because of the beaches, perhaps? There were so many tall buildings facing the long stretch of beaches.

The limousine made a sharp right at the end of Waikiki and to the entrance of the imposing white porte-cochère.

"Welcome to the Moana Surfrider," a white-clad Hawaiian valet said sonorously as he opened the door.

On the front verandah, gleaming rows of white wooden rocking chairs faced the main Waikiki drag.

A Japanese bride wearing a bright white traditional wedding gown with a Cinderella skirt brushed by Noora as tourists snapped pictures of her. The bride nodded a few times shyly, hiding her mouth with her white-gloved hand.

Noora followed Mr. Cohen down the hall of the second floor—the one she heard the clerk at the counter call the Historical Section. She was carrying Annette's small black suitcase, Annette's hand-knitted sweater that felt too warm around her arm, and Annette's purse—God bless Annette.

Ian stopped.

"You know this hotel was the first one built here? It was named The First Lady of Waikiki. See? I'm a good tour guide. Here's your key." He handed her a small envelope with two plastic cards. "Let's see... Here's my room. I think yours is across the hall. They said they can change us to adjoining rooms tomorrow ... Come in for a minute."

The heavy door to the room slammed after them automatically. He gestured toward his garment bag and let himself fall into a wicker chair. Noora left her luggage near the door and began to hang up Mr. Cohen's clothes.

"Call the bellman or someone and ask 'em to fix this shit."

Fix what? Noora wanted to ask.

He was pointing angrily at a mechanical box on the nightstand.

"Ask for a bigger room, damn it. This is too small!"

Noora fiddled with the buttons on the box.

Soft music wafted from somewhere below on the beach. The clinking of silverware and china, children's laughter, along with the gentle lapping of ocean waves upon the shore, made the melody of the outdoors quite inviting. Ian Cohen was looking out at the scenery. Noora followed his gaze. Beyond the verandah, surrounded by white pillars, a young woman in a long, flowing dress was strumming a harp.

"Without health, money means shit," Ian mumbled as if talking to himself.

Noora tried to understand how the lights in his room worked. After she tried several buttons, the television, floor lamp, and air conditioner kicked into life.

At least she accomplished something for Mr. Cohen. She still couldn't understand why a man in his position would want her around—except that ... well, at that moment, he seemed genuinely exhausted.

In her room, Noora opened the white shutters. Looking out at the ocean, she thought perhaps she could start another life right there in

Honolulu. Perhaps she could find a job and get a little corner flat with one of those balconies in one of the many high rises.

Mr. Cohen wanted her to be ready by six o'clock—Hawaii time, he had added. She checked the digital clock by the bed. Hawaii was three hours earlier than California. She had three bonus hours to rest her tired body and mind. She flopped gratefully on the bed. With a weary hand, she pulled the folded comforter by the foot of the bed up to her eyes.

The jingling phone jarred her out of a dream. She stumbled around the bed searching for the phone. She had been dreaming of the Bedouin village again, and thought she was being awakened by the little bell that used to hang around Saloush's neck. She knocked the receiver off the hook and quickly picked it up.

"Did I wake you?" Mr. Cohen's voice asked.

"Oh no," Noora lied.

"What are you doing?"

"Well, I ..." She turned to the window. "I was just admiring that ... banyan tree."

"It's a fake."

"Oh?" Noora tried to focus.

"Why don't we go and find out? Are you dressed?"

"Yes!"

"I gotta make one more phone call."

Noora hopped out of bed, combed her hair, brushed her teeth, and smoothed out her dress. A few minutes later, she heard a light knock.

"Ready?" he said when she opened the door. He seemed out of breath as he stood at the threshold, making no attempt to enter her room. He had changed into a blue short-sleeved Hawaiian shirt and wrinkled gray trousers.

At the Banyan Verandah restaurant, Ian sat across from Noora at a table near the shore. A Hawaiian band strummed ukuleles, and two young hula dancers moved gracefully. But the music and the dancers did not seem to change Ian Cohen's foul mood.

"I'll be happy to bring you something from the buffet, sir," Noora offered.

"I'm not hungry. I'll just have coffee. Screw them. Why can't they just serve from the menu?" he grumbled. "Anyway, we're only here for a couple of days. Then you can bet we'll blow this Popsicle joint."

A white-gloved waitress served Noora passion fruit iced tea.

Ian had a double gin and tonic.

As Noora studied the lavish array of foods on the buffet tables, she was surprised to find Ian Cohen standing right behind her, awkwardly holding a plate, like a brooding kid. He served himself hearty portions of salad, sushi, and beef.

A young, petite Chinese woman replaced the Hawaiian band and played on a white grand piano near their table. The Hawaiian melody she played seemed to help appease Ian's mood. As he ate his meal, Noora noticed his shoulders starting to relax.

She felt her own anxiety begin to dissolve. She tucked some loose strands of hair behind her ears. As she dug a fork in her salad, she heard Ian: "Where did you get that scar?"

Ian's question was so sudden, Noora didn't think she heard right. "Excuse me, sir?"

"I said I gotta get something from the bar. Stop saying *sir*," he said and motioned to a passing waitress.

"Yes, sir ... Sorry." As soon as Mr. Cohen looked away, she brought back strands of hair closer to her cheek.

Six o'clock in the morning—Noora and Ian headed for Straub Hospital in a rented limousine.

"They say an angiogram is nothing more than a fancy X-ray. Shouldn't take more than fifteen minutes. They want me to hang around till noon. They'll have to show me that machine first."

Noora sat in a dimly lit waiting room. *Why must they keep it so cold?* An hour later, when her nose felt as if she'd been walking in the winter streets of London, a nurse arrived.

"Miss ... Cohen?"

"Karlton," Noora answered, jumping to her feet.

"Are you Mr. Cohen's daughter?" Obviously, the nurse didn't hear Noora's correction.

"Well, I am his ... Yes."

"He asked me to give you his jewelry." She handed Noora a chain with a Hebrew letter in gold, and his wedding band. "He wants to see you."

Noora found Mr. Cohen in a hospital gown, lying on a gurney next to the wall. Two male nurses were ready to wheel him to X-ray.

"Wish me luck, kid," he said.

"Yes, sir. Of course." She did not want to say "Good luck." She feared it might bring him *bad* luck. She would have preferred to say *Allah ma'ak*—God be with you.

Slowly, she walked out to the waiting room and put his jewelry in her pocket. Nageeb used to say he felt comfortable in hospitals. She never felt more uncomfortable.

Noora sat downstairs in the cafeteria, nursing a second cup of hot cocoa from the vending machine. Two hours had passed, and she thought she would soon pass out. What was taking so long, and why did they have air conditioning, when the island was blessed with trade winds perfumed by plumeria trees? They were everywhere in the city and in full bloom.

From the loudspeaker, she heard the name. A female voice on the intercom repeated "Kelley Karlton" twice. *Are they calling me?* She was actually being paged?

She found the stairway and took the stairs three at a time. There should be no reason to summon her, unless something serious happened to Mr. Cohen.

Behind a curtain, she found him lying back in the same place, and he was shaking uncontrollably beneath white sheets.

"Kelley ... Where the hell'd you go? I thought you were gone."

"No sir."

"Look at me. The big-shot prick. I'll be a stiff on a slab if I let 'em touch me."

"No, sir. Not at all," she said. They had removed his lower denture plate. Suddenly she wanted to laugh. Nervous reaction? She couldn't help it.

Until then, Noora had not realized he had false teeth. He looked so different. Old. Helpless. She had to turn away and stifle a chuckle. She started to laugh. But she wanted to cry. Stubborn tears escaped, yet she wanted to run out to the corridor and laugh out loud. Such a mix of emotions ... What was wrong with her?

The doctor walked in, giving Noora a quick glance at first, but then he did not acknowledge her presence. With his back to her, he began to talk to Mr. Cohen. He was holding a plastic form in the shape of a human heart. There was another doctor now, and two nurses stood nearby. Slowly, Noora began to take a few silent steps away. Miss Nobody needed to make herself invisible. They caught her laughing at the wrong time.

"Kelley!" Ian Cohen called. "Come back. She needs to hear this too, Paul."

The doctor turned and extended his hand to Noora.

"Dr. McGratten."

"Kelley ..." she nodded, taking the doctor's hand, then looked off. Why did this doctor make her feel uneasy? She walked to the opposite side of the bed. Ian Cohen reached for her hand and held it tight.

"You said it was going to be just an X-ray. You can't make me stay!"

"I can't force you to do anything. But you must know what is going on with your heart and what the angiogram shows."

"If you can't give me a drink, then give me a Valium. Why's it so friggin' cold?!" He squeezed Noora's hand harder.

"You have a badly diseased heart, Ian," the doctor said with intense eyes. "We can operate on you tomorrow."

"Tomorrow?!"

The doctor turned to one of the nurses and gave her some quick instructions. She hurried to one of the desks across the room and picked up the phone.

"Paul, you don't understand. I've got a company to run. Hundreds of people ..."

"Yes, Ian," he said. "If you weren't my friend, I wouldn't talk to you this way. You could have a major heart attack at *any time*. You were lucky that time in France. You could be permanently ..."

Noora could not listen anymore. Mr. Cohen was squeezing her hand so hard, it hurt. She wanted to cry. Why did she care so much about this man, who was little more than a stranger? Perhaps he had been her last hope? She could always go back to France. No, it was Ian Cohen himself—for some reason, she felt a sense of compassion. She could *feel* his pain. He was in great danger.

"Quadruple bypass?" Ian shouted.

"We remove arteries from your leg to replace the diseased ones," the doctor said.

It all seemed complicated. And frightening. Nageeb would have explained it all to her if he were there at that very moment.

"I didn't expect that," Ian Cohen said. "This is total shit."

"You'll have a younger heart," the doctor said, cracking a quick smile.

"This is not a good time. We're about ready to go into production."

"I wouldn't wait if I were you," the doctor said.

Ian let go of Noora's hand. "Kelley, get me my clothes."

"Mr. Cohen, you heard the doctor ..." Noora said timidly, afraid to disobey, but even more afraid of what would happen if she helped him leave.

"I'll do some homeopathic crap and I'll be fine. I know what these guys do. They'll *saw* open my damn rib cage!" He turned to the doctor. "You'll slice me up like a butcher."

The doctor gave Ian a serious look.

"What about my movies? My studio?"

"You'll have more years to make better movies," Doctor McGratten said.

"My movies are very successful, asshole."

"At least you haven't lost your sense of humor," Noora heard the doctor say as she made her way out of the ward. She leaned against the wall. She should stand nearby in case he called for her. But who was she supposed to be? How would she introduce herself? Kelley Karlton, Mr. Cohen's personal assistant? Just what exactly was a personal assistant?

Moments later, to her surprise, Mr. Cohen was dressed and walking toward her. "Come on, kid. We're outta here."

The pair took a cab to the hotel. They waited for the elevator, and when it finally arrived, a group of Japanese piled inside, barely leaving room for Noora and Ian. "Let 'em go," he said. "I'm no sardine. Listen. It's too nice a day," he said, watching the elevator door close. "How about we go for a walk along the beach. Maybe stop at the Honolulu Zoo down the street or something. Would you mind?"

"No, sir." *There was a zoo nearby?* Noora loved the idea. Perhaps later she could talk to him and change his mind about his operation, although he seemed pretty stubborn about it and made up his mind that he would not do it.

They walked the short distance to the tip of Waikiki, crossing the street to the park. A huge old tree shaded the entrance to the zoo.

"Ah, wouldn't you know it, wouldn't you know it!" Ian said.

A large sign displaying the words "Temporarily closed for renovations" blocked the wrought iron gate.

"Of all times. Shit, it was fine the way it was before," Ian whined. "Where do you suppose they stashed all the animals during the supposed renovation? I mean, they had elephants and lions here, and the neatest monkeys. Bevvy loved to come here. What a shitty day ..."

"Look at this tree," Noora commented. "It's incredible. Why I don't recall ever seeing such a ... What kind do you suppose ..."

"It's a banyan," he grumbled.

"I think it's a monkey pod. A very old one. Must be over a hundred years old," Noora said, admiring the old tree branches.

"Well, if it is a monkey pod, where the hell are all the monkeys?"

"Mr. Cohen!" Noora giggled.

"*Don't tempt me*," they heard someone growl.

Startled, Noora turned and saw a homeless man in baggy, dirty pants and a cut-up, soiled tank top, staring past them angrily. He began walking away rapidly, mumbling to himself. He stopped abruptly. "Don't tempt me!" he repeated. Shuffling away from Noora and Ian, he seemed oblivious to anyone around him, except perhaps the imaginary tempter.

"Perhaps we should give him a few dollars," Noora suggested.

"He'll use it for drugs."

"Oh?"

The man came around again to their view and passed them by. He stopped suddenly. "Don't tempt me, *kimosabe!*" He walked away and crossed the street to the beach while mumbling away to himself.

Noora saw that Ian was amused. "What did he say? Wasabi?"

Ian burst out laughing and couldn't stop. "I ... I'm sorry, kid. I didn't mean to laugh at you."

"Oh, it's all right, sir," Noora said, glad to see him laughing—whatever the reason.

"Not wasabi ... Wasabi is that green paste you put in your soy sauce. For sushi!" He laughed again. "It's *kimosabe*. Ever watch *The Lone Ranger?*"

"Excuse me?"

"A television show."

She gave him a blank stare and looked off.

"Never mind. You'd have to be American. And a lot older."

But Noora knew what he was talking about. Nageeb, Abdo, and Kettayef used to watch *The Lone Ranger* with their father—among other old American television shows. But she was not going to think about those days. No, she wasn't going to even think …

"When I used to come here in the sixties," Ian continued, walking away from her, apparently expecting her to follow him as he spoke, "and even in the seventies, I never saw homeless people." He stopped, kicked a nearby pebble, and plunged his hands in his pockets. "Everyone was rich," he said as he continued to walk, Noora following by his side. "And I'm not talking about the tourists. I mean the Hawaiians. The authentic ones, not the Happas. The *real* locals. They fished all day and strummed ukuleles at night. They had that *ohana* spirit. Family. Strong, spirited families that stuck together. Who needed money when everyone looked out for everyone? Now it's cement city. Look at this place. High rises, fancy hotels … and freaks. Hey, wait a minute. Maybe there's still one place that didn't change very much. God, I sure hope not."

Under the canvas umbrella of Honolulu's famed Outrigger Canoe Club, Noora and Ian Cohen waited for their order to arrive while they silently watched the dazzling orange sun as it sank on the horizon.

The ocean reminded her of Alexandria's sea—calm and turquoise, turning to indigo as it spread out to the slightly curved horizon. Again, she felt the need to lose herself in her own reverie. Dreams of happy times. An old fifties song came to mind: "Whenever I want you, all I have to do is dream …" In dreams, she could imagine herself in the arms of the man she would never stop loving. But she had to face reality, because the man sitting across from her was playing Russian roulette with his life. He could have a heart attack at any moment. *Allah! Protect this man …*

"What are you thinking about so hard, lady?" She heard Ian's grave voice.

"Well, just that …" She looked out at the ocean. "It's beautiful here."

"It sure is. Life can be sweet. It would be hard to leave it."

"Then, Mr. Cohen ..." This time she turned and looked straight at him. "Please, have that operation."

He didn't seem to hear her. He watched the boats bob gently in the distance. A brightly colored catamaran drifted majestically to shore.

"I've been a member of this club for over twenty-five years. I used to come here with Bevvy. We used to order liver n' onions. Now they have nothin' but *nouvelle* frog food."

"Bevvy?" He had mentioned that name before.

"My wife. Beverly. Beverly Hillard-Cohen. She was wonderful. She was beautiful," he said, looking off. "God took her away from me. Son of a bitch."

"Sir, please be careful what you say ..."

"Why?"

She pointed to the sky. *There you go again,* Noora chided herself, *putting your foot in your mouth!*

"You mean you believe in God and all that stuff?"

"Well, sir, maybe not 'all that stuff,' but I believe there is an Almighty one."

"Why?"

Noora shrugged.

"Why would you believe in someone or something with the power to bring so much injustice? So much suffering in the world. So much crap ..."

Her eyes filled with tears.

"Sorry, kid. Don't mind me. I'm just a grouch." He turned and stared back at the ocean.

The Hawaiian waiter bounced in with platters of teriyaki beef on a skewer, and a large platter filled with a mountain of nacho chips blanketed by a thick layer of melted cheese.

Ian Cohen wondered about the girl who saved him in Cannes. She had substance. She had depth. *What was her story?* She was not one of those whiny types of "take-me-show-me-buy-me" chicks. Or one of those with some kind of brought-upon-yourself traumatic, trivial oh-brother story—like most people he knew. Sure, everyone had a story. As far as he could see, this girl had *history*. Maybe she came from a broken home. No, it had to be something less common. Definitely some kind of tragedy happened to her. But why should he get involved? As long as she stuck around and didn't gossip, her business was none of his.

He remembered the dream he had had the night before. He was lunching at the Peninsula Hotel in Beverly Hills, eating alone. Bevvy was sitting at another table across the restaurant of the hotel, which he didn't think was even built when she died. In the dream, she was holding the receiver of an ornate golden telephone to her ear. He could hear her voice—as if on a phone line—and she was talking to him. But there was no phone at his table. He forgot what they talked about. He remembered the last thing she said before getting up and leaving. Something like, "Take care of the kid, she'll take care of you." For some reason, the dream kept nagging at him.

When the taxicab pulled out of the Outrigger Canoe Club parking lot, Ian Cohen had a sudden change of heart. Instead of telling the driver to head back to their hotel in Waikiki, he asked him to drive to Kahala, in the opposite direction.

"I really didn't want to come back here ever again," he admitted to Noora as they rode through Kahala's residential streets lined with ornately gated mansions. "However..." he said, then remained silent.

"However?" Noora asked.

"If I'm gonna croak, I might as well see the old place. One more time."

"You will live a long time, Mr. Cohen."

"How would you know?"

"Because your friend, Doctor McGratten, really cares for you."

At the entrance of the newly renovated Kahala Mandarin Hotel, two valets opened their doors.

"Come, I want to show you something. Have you ever heard of this place before?"

"No, sir."

"Quit calling me *sir,* kid."

"Quit calling me *kid,* sir."

Ian Cohen laughed. The girl was all right.

Noora followed Ian to the hotel's lagoon and stood next to him on the Japanese bridge. Two dolphins jerked their heads, showing their permanently smiling snouts. As they twirled beneath the surface, Noora squealed with such obvious delight that Ian was glad he had decided to come back to the hotel in Kahala after all. He thought he would never return to the special hideaway he had shared, year after year, with his beautiful wife, Bevvy. A place with happy memories was a trap for him. But now, somehow, his grief had been appeased.

"Enjoy the dolphins," he said to Noora. "I'll be in the bar."

He was already dialing on his cell phone.

"Roz!" Ian Cohen shouted into his cellular while heading toward the outdoor café nearby. "Listen, I'll be away for longer than I thought."

CHAPTER 41
FARID FENDIL'S FIRST VISION

As the festivities continued at the Al-Balladi Prince Hotel grand ballroom, Mr. Farid Fendil was back shaking hands, accepting good wishes from his guests.

After recovering from the fainting episode, he had to excuse himself several times. He was convinced it was a case of stomach virus or the flu. At his back, always shadowing him, was the man he was beginning to think of as the Nosy Nuisance. Sheik Abdullah Kharoub did not have the courtesy to leave him long enough to relieve himself in private in the men's room.

Almost two hours after the marriage ceremony, and after the second dinner course was served, a group of belly dancers performed an outstanding spectacle to Middle Eastern music, as the newlyweds sat on high-backed gilded chairs upon a podium ornately decorated with red and white roses. While the guests were enjoying the food and the spectacular show, Farid Fendil managed to disappear through the crowd at a moment when the sheik was distracted.

He spotted Abdo standing near an exit door and maneuvered him outside. He asked Abdo to drive him home. Abdo seemed quite surprised, but Farid also knew Abdo never asked personal questions. The mansion was not more than twenty minutes away. Neither the sheik nor his men would suspect Farid to ride in such a clunky, undignified vehicle, especially during his daughter's wedding celebration. Farid crouched in the back seat of the ancient orange-colored Mercedes, as Abdo quietly drove him out of the hotel.

As Abdo pulled into the Fendil driveway, worrying more than wondering why he was asked to drive him home, Farid said, "If Sheik Abdullah Kharoub or any of his men should come here and ask where I am, tell them I said it's none of their business!"

Abdo was surprised by Mr. Fendil's comment. Surely they would not believe him.

As if Farid read Abdo's mind, he added, "If they don't believe you, you can tell them to go to hell!"

Abdo was stunned. Was he really talking about the MOFHAJ men, whom he always seemed to want to impress? The men whose values Mr. Fendil had so much embraced recently? "Mr. Fendil," Abdo found himself saying, "in all due respect, they might become more suspicious."

"Tell them I'm ... at the reception. And absolutely do not allow them in my house. Wait for me, *ya ibni*. I may take a while," he said, opening the door to Abdo's car.

In the privacy of his bathroom suite, a good half hour later, Farid felt much better and could breathe more easily. He splashed cool tap water on his face and patted it dry. Opening the large mirrored door of his medicine cabinet, he noticed the bottle of cologne that was still sealed. He stood for a moment and hesitated. Finally, he took the bottle and unsealed it, splashing a large amount on his face and neck. The lemon-scented Egyptian Chabrawichi cologne had been a birthday gift his cousin, Khayat, had sent him more than two years before from Alexandria. Farid Fendil had never sent a thank-you, or acknowledged that he received the gift. Perhaps he should have sent his cousin a wedding invitation. He had heard rumors that he moved to the South of France and married a European actress. Khayat had told Farid years before that he would never leave Egypt. He had criticized Farid for leaving Alexandria to rebuild the poor, run-down oasis, far out in the middle of the desert.

Farid studied his reflection on the gilded mirror of his bathroom. He saw dark circles under his eyes. *You're the fool, Khayat Fendil, you are the jackass!* Farid thought. He picked up the bottle of cologne and spoke to it: "You said you'd *never* leave Egypt and then you did. One should never say *never.* It couldn't have been for money. Must've been for that European pussy. You couldn't settle down with one of our own. You lied, *ya* Khayat."

Never mind about my cousin, Farid thought, tossing the bottle of cologne in the trash nearby. *Everybody lies.*

Would Khayat have declined his daughter's wedding invitation? he wondered, running a comb through his graying hair. He inserted his comb on top of his brush and, hesitating for a moment, he picked up the bottle from the trash and put it back in his medicine cabinet.

Returning to his room, he removed his ornate *gallabeya* and laid it on a nearby chair. He would rest for fifteen minutes. The wedding festivities should last a few more hours, and he would not be missed, he thought, dimming his bedroom lamp low. He would take care of his health after the wedding ceremonies. Maybe he should have that angiogram. If they found clogged arteries, it would mean heart surgery. His health was fine. He was simply stressed, he thought, stretching on his bed.

He dreamed he was in Khayat's villa, resting on a hammock with the gentle breeze swaying him to the *tarrawah,* Alexandria's own sea breeze, the one he had missed when years ago, he vacationed with his wife and children. He could smell and *feel* it now. He turned his head to the breeze. The vision of Noora appeared. *"Look at me, Father, I am here,"* her voice echoed with the sea breeze. She wore a yellow dress. With the sun behind her, illuminating her, Noora looked breathlessly beautiful. Her long brown hair shimmered in the bright light and floated around her shoulders, glowing like gold, as she approached her father in slow motion. She headed straight to him, her arms opening and reaching out to envelop him. He stretched out his arms to her and suddenly fell off the hammock. The grass beneath him, to his horror, became an abyss.

His body jerked from the dream and he jumped, finding himself in his bed with cold sweat pouring out of him.

He had never dreamed about Noora before. It was too real. Did he oversleep? He checked the illuminated digital clock on his nightstand. To his relief, he realized less than fifteen minutes had elapsed. *He must immediately dismiss that dream from his mind!*

When Farid Fendil returned to the grand ballroom, the bride and groom were just leaving for their romantic horse-drawn carriage ride that would take them around the hotel before returning to cut the cake. A crowd of well-wishers began to cheer.

As Farid Fendil returned to the grand ballroom, Sheik Abdullah Kharoub walked up to Mr. Fendil. "Ah, you look more relaxed now that your daughter is in the hands of a husband," he nodded, smiling for the first time.

"We are very grateful for the blessings Allah has bestowed upon us."

The sheik nodded again. "Indeed. *Hamdallah*. Alas, it is getting late ... It is time to gather my family."

"The evening is young. The bride and groom have not yet cut the cake."

"Save us each a piece," he said. "It is too late in the evening for my wives. They have done enough celebrating. Thank you for bestowing on me the honor of marrying the children."

"The honor is ours, *hag* Abdullah Kharoub," he replied respectfully.

Farid Fendil's youngest daughter, Shamsah, bounced between the two men. "Father!" she squealed excitedly, skipping in her pink dress that fell just above the knees.

"First excuse yourself, Shamsah. As you can see, I am busy ..."

"But Father, you promised you would dance with me at least one time. You promised..."

"First, what do we say, Shamsah?" Farid Fendil said, his voice soft.

The girl turned to the sheik and batted her eyes shyly. "Excuse me for interrupting." Turning back to her father she whined, "Father ...?"

Farid noticed the sheik's posture had stiffened and his eyes widened. It was obvious his daughter's intrusion had irritated him.

"I'll be with you in a little while, my daughter. Go dance with your brother."

"All right, Father," Shamsah said. "Don't forget, you promised to dance with me."

The two men watched as Shamsah scurried off to the dance floor. A young man approached Shamsah and asked her if she would dance with him. She shook her head timidly, then ran to the sweet table, where Kettayef was biting into a huge chocolate éclair.

Sheik Abdullah Kharoub took Shamsah's father aside and whispered, "I would assume she is not circumcised."

Farid raised his eyebrows. He was shocked. He thought he had misunderstood the sheik's request until the old man stepped shoulder-to-shoulder and whispered his request closer to Farid's ear.

Moments later the sheik gathered his entourage of wives, a dozen or more children, and countless grandchildren. They all left the grand ballroom, while a long, shiny ring of black limousines waited outside.

When they were all finally gone, Farid gave a deep sigh. He headed straight to the hotel bar and ordered a strong drink. The old sheik would have fiercely disapproved. Farid Fendil only drank occasionally, when he was abroad. At home, he respected his custom and wanted to be a good Muslim—alcohol was not a good idea right now, but would not Allah, the all-merciful, forgive him this time, knowing how badly he needed to calm his nerves?

He sat in a corner of the grand ballroom and observed his daughter Shamsah dancing with Kettayef. He smiled as he watched his handsome son, barely recognizable in an elegant white tuxedo. He turned his gaze back to Shamsah. She had thick and lustrous brown hair, styled in long ringlets. He brooded glumly on the terrible duty … the obligatory request the sheik commanded that Farid owed to his vivacious young daughter.

CHAPTER 42
THE RING AND THE CURSE

Outside the Al-Balladi Prince Hotel, two white horses pranced gracefully as Zaffeera and Michel exited through the lobby's revolving doors. The newlyweds were greeted by yet another cheering crowd of well-wishers, and a downpour of gold coins was tossed for good luck. The horses were hitched to a beautiful white carriage, festooned with golden ribbons and hundreds of red and white roses.

Zaffeera knew she had never looked more beautiful. Her eyes, brightened by honey-colored contacts, had been expertly made up by a renowned French makeup artist. She kept one layer of her double veil in front of her face, while the other fell behind her delicate tiara and flowed down her back, to her waist. This, too, had been carefully planned so that the groom would view his new bride through the sheer veil, allowing her face to glow with a slightly out-of-focus radiance.

Zaffeera glanced around, looking for the four photographers she had hired to snap pictures as Michel gallantly helped his bride onto the carriage. Had the photographers taken enough pictures with her glowing tiara in virgin white? There could never be enough wedding pictures, as far as she was concerned. She had instructed the photographers to shoot as many pictures of the bride and groom as they could, but in a discreet manner. Now the world would see he was legally hers. They were both laughing delightedly, for the first time, as they tried to dodge the endless gold coins and birdseed thrown at them. Once the couple nestled inside the carriage, the white mares pranced and whinnied, then set off in a rhythmic trot. It was a glorious night, the midnight blue sky spilling a glittering jewel box of stars. In the distance, however, clouds had gathered and flashes of lightning grew closer, heralding the approach of a thunderstorm.

Back at the hotel, the women's quavering cries of joy continued to echo through the hotel's hallways, all the way to the streets and the grand ballroom. The loudest cry, it seemed, was her mother's, who could not stop herself from trilling in joyous ululation. She followed a group of musicians playing their instruments as they danced their way back to the grand ballroom, where the celebration was to continue for their guests until dawn.

Inside the horse-drawn carriage, for the very first time, Michel took Zaffeera's perfectly manicured hand. Upon her left ring finger, he placed a gold ring laced with baguette-shaped diamonds designed to look like a bow, and in the center of the ring, six prongs held a single sparkling blue diamond.

Zaffeera gasped. She recognized the ring immediately. Michel had designed it for Noora. The stunning piece of jewelry was called the "Forever Ring." When Michel had given it to Noora during a family engagement ceremony two years before, the ring had been a bit large for Noora's finger.

Later, after reading about the quality of diamonds, Michel had decided to replace the original stone with a blue diamond for Noora. He had taken it back to Paris for a better fit and mostly for a finer diamond.

Now the ring sparkled on Zaffeera's finger, and her entire body tingled.

She had cursed that ring when Noora wore it for the first time at her engagement announcement. Noora had shown it off to the whole family, including all the household help. Zaffeera had hidden in her room, searching for a book about witchcraft. She needed to find a curse to bestow upon that ring in order to mar the wedding of Noora and Michel. She could not find anything that fit the circumstances, and decided to improvise. At dinnertime, Zaffeera dropped twenty milligrams of Valium in Noora's soda. Later that night, after everyone retired, Zaffeera went to Noora's bedroom. While Noora was sleeping soundly from the effect of the Valium, Zaffeera removed the ring from her finger and tried it on. The ring's original size had actually been a perfect fit on Zaffeera's finger.

She had spent a good half hour admiring the ring that was now on her own finger. She remembered murmuring low, "You see? The ring fits my wedding finger. It was meant for me.." How she wished she did not have to put that ring back on Noora's finger. "I curse that ring for all times," she said, removing it. "And may the Evil Eye bring you misfortune and as you wear it, may you never have sons," she said, replacing the ring on Noora's finger.

Zaffeera smiled at the memory. Her plans had evolved quite well.

Perhaps too well. She had not expected their father to kill Noora for the shame she had brought. Noora *had* dishonored him through her own sheer stupidity and selfishness. Noora had shamed everyone in the family because she had been weak. She could have been stronger and said no! It wasn't Zaffeera's fault. It was not she who killed her sister. That was not at all what she had planned. She just wanted her parents to know that they had been wrong about their favorite daughter, Noora, and that indeed she was the wrong choice for Michel. No, she definitely had nothing to do with the killing of Noora. Everyone believed she drowned the night she arrived with her sister. It was possible. She could have gone for a quick dip and drowned because there was no one there to rescue her. She arrived late, was fatigued from the long trip, and had a cramp. Zaffeera knew it wasn't likely. Cramp or no cramp, Noora was an excellent swimmer. Zaffeera suspected something dreadful might happen when she saw how the chauffeur glared at her sister that night after they landed at the Al-Balladi airport. There was hatred in that man's eyes. Word had obviously gotten to the men who were followers of the old sheik. The pictures of Noora in the disco undoubtedly had been shown to her father. Undoubtedly he had been dishonored. Everything happened the way Allah had wanted it. Her brilliant scheme could only have succeeded with the help of Allah. And now the brilliance of the ring that bound her to Michel, the man who was always meant for her, sparkled brightly on *her* finger.

Michel had actually given the ring to *her!* Out of the love he had for *her* and only for *her!* He must have always really loved her, because now they were married. Married! She started to weep with joy and relief. She threw her arms around Michel and hugged him so tightly, she nearly dislodged her headpiece. Never mind; she wouldn't need it anymore!

The horses trotted back to the hotel. Inside the white fairy-tale carriage festooned with flowers, Zaffeera inhaled the fragrance of her husband's aftershave mixed with his own dizzying scent that transported her into a frenzy. She couldn't wait for their marriage to be consummated. They would have sex every morning and every night—at least! She would surely make him the happiest man.

On the penthouse floor of the Al-Balladi Prince Hotel, minutes before midnight, the newlyweds entered the luxurious honeymoon suite.

Zaffeera stood at the foot of the sumptuous bed before her. Her entire body tingled at the thought of the sexy night that awaited them.

Michel, in his handsome tuxedo, walked straight to the bar and studied the large selection of drinks in crystal decanters.

"There's juices, soda water, 7-Up, Coke. I don't think they forgot anything. This is quite an incredible variety," he said, stifling a yawn. "Perhaps we should have a little champagne." He pulled a magnum-sized bottle of Cristal out of an ice-filled silver bucket.

"All right," she whispered.

"Would you like a strawberry in it? There's a whole bowlful here." He opened a blue Tiffany box and pulled out two sparkling crystal champagne glasses. "Wow," he said, bringing a glass to the light. "Beautiful."

"Strawberries in champagne. How clever," she said, inching her way closer to the bar. She wished they would both inch their way closer to the bed.

"I saw that in a movie once. Nice touch. Look at all the strawberries they left here for us," he said, sounding rather awkward. "My, they thought of everything."

Zaffeera was the one who had thought of everything. "Perhaps I should change," she said, batting her eyes.

She stood in her wedding gown, feeling stupid. She had removed her veil and draped it on the couch. She was glad the hotel's management remembered her strict instructions to keep the lights dimmed low, and to place two lit vanilla-scented candles by the bar, and two almond-scented candles on each side of the king-size bed. She had thought of requesting a smaller bed, so Michel would have to sleep close to her, but decided she did not want to appear too forward and demanding in front of the hired help or the wedding planners.

She had also requested soft music.

Didn't he hear what she just said? *Perhaps I should change*, she wanted to repeat, but thought she had better wait.

She watched him as he slowly unwrapped the golden foil from the top of the champagne bottle, unwinding the wire fastening from the Cristal, pulling the cork with some difficulty. Finally with the loud pop, *"Voilà!"* he said, with what she could have sworn was a nervous chuckle.

He poured champagne into the tall, delicate crystal flutes and dropped a strawberry in each glass. Bringing a glass to his new bride, Michel looked uneasy when he briefly met Zaffeera's eyes.

"Thank you," she murmured, taking the glass.

"My pleasure," he said, watching the bubbles rise to the surface of her glass.

Why is he looking so … melancholic? Zaffeera wondered, feeling suddenly insecure. He should be happy. *What is he thinking about? Why isn't he looking into my eyes, telling me how beautiful I look? He hasn't even complimented me on my dress! This is our honeymoon, dammit.*

"Come, let's go out on the balcony," Michel said without looking at her.

The balcony? The bloody balcony?! That would be farther from the bed!

Michel had already opened the tall french doors. The sheer curtains billowed out in the breeze. He held the doors open for Zaffeera. In her wedding gown, she stepped outside, feeling awkward.

Zaffeera stared at her stunning ring. Under the recessed lighting that shone from the archways surrounding the balcony, blue light shot from the diamond. She reminded herself again that Michel had actually given *her* the ring—with the "better diamond." She wondered how many carats it had. She would have to have it appraised. Not that it mattered. She would never forget how he gave it to her, looking at her with such kindness. *Yes, he must have always loved me,* she thought, gazing now at the sky. Why was he wasting time out here? It was time for lovemaking. He was leaning against the rail, sipping champagne and gazing at the stars. He should be gazing into her eyes, for crying out loud! Perhaps he would make her pregnant tonight, and nine months from now, she would give him a precious son. *No. Too soon.* Maybe her pregnancy would be a difficult one. She must not allow negative thoughts. But what if expecting a child took away the joy of sex? She doubted that. She read in magazines and books that couples could have sex up to the ninth month, or at least till the end of the seventh month. She would surely put on more pounds around her waist the minute she conceived. *Pregnancy could wait!* What she needed was to have him all to herself. Her mother did not get pregnant for five years after her marriage. Their father was fine with that. He had even kidded that Allah had given them more time to enjoy each other before all the children came. She would wait three years. Three glorious years of sex, day and night! Her entire body tingled at the thought. And after that, when she gave him a son, he would forever be tied to her. But he was tied to her now, she thought. *Silly me.* One thing for sure: He would never look at another woman after she gave him an offspring. Or two sons. He would never think of … Noora? No! Their marriage was now a bond like blood, a bond that could never be broken—especially after the birth of their first son.

Twenty long and uncomfortable minutes later, while Zaffeera was occupying herself with thoughts of their future, he was still standing there, in the same position, his back to her. He had finished his champagne, and he was toying with the glass, running his index finger around the lip of the crystal, making that ringing sound—while she sat on one of the chaises, like an idiot, waiting for his first move! Wasn't he supposed to carry her in his arms through the threshold, and weren't they supposed to be kissing by now? Maybe she should say something.

"I'm going to …" she said while at the same time he said, "Would you like some …"

"Sorry!" she said.

"Oh, sorry," he said.

"You first. Sorry."

"I was just … going to ask if you would like some more champagne."

This is a catastrophe, Zaffeera thought. She lifted her glass, showing it had barely been touched.

"Sorry. We didn't have to have champagne," he said.

"Oh, no. It's very good."

"Would you have preferred Coke?" he asked.

Noora would have preferred Coke. Zaffeera lowered her eyes. "Yes, actually, I like Coke. But I do like this …" she said demurely.

"Are you sure?"

"Yes. We rarely ever have champagne. Except on very special occasions. And this sure is one ... Well ... I think I'd better change," she said softly. "The night air is making me feel a little chilly. I'm also tired."

He finally turned and looked straight at her. "I'm so sorry. How selfish of me. Of course, you must be exhausted."

"Aren't you?" she asked, lowering her eyes.

"No."

No?! What did he mean by "no"? On second thought, that meant he could keep it hard all night. She felt like a kid waiting impatiently to open the last and largest birthday present. She couldn't wait to *feel* him. She wondered how big he was. She closed her eyes and wiped the sweat that formed on her brow. What did he really look like? How many professional women had he had? One? Two? More? She felt a twinge of jealousy. She supposed his father had followed the tradition of taking his son to a brothel, to have sexual experiences with a professional—a man must learn these things, so he would know what to do on his wedding night. But were there any others?

"Come, let's go inside," she heard him say finally, his words drifting into her ears like music.

Zaffeera took her time in the bathroom. She would have preferred it if he had torn off the wedding gown and thrown her in bed. *Be cool,* she thought, *control yourself.* The first night was always the one couples remembered most. She was going to make his wedding night memorable.

After her shower, she rubbed her entire body with a pheromonic lotion she had ordered from abroad and had read so much about its effect—the fragrance alone was supposed to drive the groom wild in bed. *Oh, I can't wait!* She slipped into her long, white, thin satin nightgown.

A renowned beautician from France had been flown to Al-Balladi the day before the wedding, to do the expert hair extensions. He spent four hours painstakingly adding strands of human hair by intricately weaving the strands with Zaffeera's own. Zaffeera removed the last pins that had supported her tiara, and gently combed her hair. The hairdresser had done a superb job. Michel would never know that the thick, silky hair was not all hers, when he ran his fingers through it. As for the hair on her body, it was gone. Her skin was still tingling from the *hallawa,* the wax job she had endured the night before. There would be no way Michel could possibly resist her hairless, silky skin. But what about her small breasts? He did not have to see them. *Nothing to worry about,* she thought as she inspected her reflection on the floor-to-ceiling mirror. *Look at you. You never looked so good. Wait till he tastes your lips ... and the rest of you!*

The hotel's Imperial Honeymoon Suite had separate his-and-hers bathrooms, located on opposite sides of the bed. She wondered if he was also taking a shower and changing into something more comfortable, preferably into nothing.

When she opened the bathroom door and made her grand entrance, she found him sitting at the edge of the bed, facing the door to his bathroom. He had his back to her and he was *still in his tux?!* Staring at the floor, with a newly opened bottle of champagne in one hand and an empty glass on the other. He filled the glass.

"Are you feeling all right?" Zaffeera asked, as she slowly moved closer to his side of the bed. She prayed he would look at her and get aroused.

He jumped to his feet, turned to her, and smiled uneasily.

She glanced downward, then at him. To her dismay, there was no sign of any bulge. This was a catastrophe. Gently, she lifted the bedspread and held a pillow awkwardly. She slid between the white satin sheets.

She did not remember if it was a tradition, but it seemed a family custom that the bed sheet for the honeymoon night be blue. It was to bring luck for the bride to conceive a male child. Zaffeera wanted white sheets, so he could better see that she was a virgin.

"You look very nice," he said.

She smiled. It was about time he gave her a compliment.

"More champagne?" he asked, looking a tad drunk.

"I'd better not, thank you," she said, pulling the comforter to her chest. An awkward moment passed. She couldn't stand it anymore. *What was wrong with him? Didn't anybody tell him what to do?* She hid her face in her hands and began to sob.

"What's wrong?" Michel asked, dumbfounded.

"Forgive me."

"What is it?"

She shook her head, her hands hiding her face.

"It's those men, isn't it? They talked to you too?" Michel asked.

She was about to say something about Noora, how she missed her, how she regretted ... what would she regret? No, too dangerous to make him think of her. She was crying because she wanted sex! Right now. *Give it to me, I'm starving, can't you see?* She wanted him! And he wasn't getting a fucking clue!

"Did they have their women talk to you?" she heard him say.

She looked at him with surprise.

"I knew it!" He jumped to his feet, paced a moment, and then sat back down next to her.

There was a box of tissues by the bedside. Michel took it and placed it on her lap.

"Men?" she asked, taking a couple of tissues.

He looked embarrassed. He put the box back on the nightstand. "Nothing. It's nothing. I'm sorry."

"It's just that it's so hard ..." Zaffeera said.

"Hard?"

"I just wish my brother ... and my sister ... were with us ..." she said, her tears cascading now. She hoped the waterproof stage makeup she ordered all the way from New York would not fail her. The makeup finally arrived the day before the wedding. Otherwise, she would never have been able to allow her tears to fall so freely.

Finally, he reached across the bed and held her in his arms. She felt dizzied by his scent—a mixture of cologne, soap, and fresh sweat. She put her arms around him and hid her head against his shoulder. His muscles were wonderfully firm.

He patted her on the head. "It's all right."

She didn't like the gesture. She wasn't a dog.

"I'm in such pain," she cried, longing to rub against his vital part.

He pulled away from her. "I am too."

What did he mean? Was he still in love with Noora? How could he be in love with a dead person?

"I am grateful we have each other, and that we are friends. We have much in common. We share the same grief. In time ... time heals, they say."

Zaffeera was ready to explode. *Friends?*

She cleared her throat. "Friends?" She busied herself folding her tissue and patting her nostrils.

"Yes," he said, matter-of-factly.

"You could say we are … friends. But now, we are also married," she said.

"Yes," he said. "It was a nice wedding."

"We made our families happy," she said.

"But … I would have preferred to hold *your* hand instead of your father's. We were in that stifling room surrounded by those … religious fanatics. I don't understand why your father would allow them around. And that … sheik."

She shrugged. She was not prepared for this type of an evening. She couldn't respond, sitting up in bed, holding a tissue crunched tightly in her hand.

"Are you afraid of … because it's our wedding night?" Michel asked awkwardly.

"Oh, no."

He rose with his back to her. He stumbled, caught himself, and sat back on the bed, staring at his shoes.

Zaffeera realized he must have had more to drink than she calculated.

He ran a hand through his wonderful, thick, dark hair, then removed his bow tie and his cummerbund. He loosened his collar; he still had his jacket on.

"You don't have to worry about me. I won't do anything."

Do anything? "Well, there is one thing I'd like you to do."

"Yes?"

"You can remove your jacket," she said coyly.

He removed his jacket, tossed it on the nearest chair, and removed his shoes. He moved around Zaffeera's opposite side of the bed, fell in, and stretched out.

There was an endless, awkward silence. Zaffeera took a deep breath and looked away. He took her hand and toyed with her ring.

"You have pretty hands."

"Thank you … Thank you for the most beautiful ring I ever saw." Their eyes met and held there for a long moment, for the very first time.

Michel let go of her hand. He looked away and closed his eyes. "I'm tired," he said, rising from the bed. "I'm going to freshen up."

She heard Michel in the shower as she sat in bed, feeling numb. If he was washing, did that not mean he was planning on having sex?

Twenty long minutes later, they lay in bed. Three feet apart.

Patience. We have an entire life, she reminded herself, turning, facing Michel. He wore light gray cotton pajamas. *Pajamas! Tops and bottoms,* plus he pulled the covers to his waist and he lay on his back, his arms behind his head, staring at the ceiling.

"Is anything wrong?" she had to ask.

He turned to her and rested his head in his hand. "I wish I could go for a run."

"I'll go with you."

"Really?"

"Yes," she said without moving.

"I can still hear the music downstairs," he said, while sitting up in bed.

"They must be having fun," she murmured.

He lay back down and propped his pillow behind his head.

"They may be partying till dawn. If they see us jogging, they may wonder ..." she hinted.

"It's those men," he whispered.

"I beg your pardon?" Zaffeera whispered back.

"Do you mind if I turn on the light?"

"No."

He got up, flicked on the lamp on the nightstand, walked to the balcony, came back in, stood by the window staring out, paced again for a bit, walked to the nightstand, switched off the light, and lay back in bed, leaving Zaffeera totally confused. The candles had already burned out, except for one. The last flame flickered and sputtered, struggling to stay lit.

Zaffeera was angry. She hadn't expected such behavior—especially on their first night. She'd been sure that as soon as they walked in, they would timidly approach one another, perhaps experiment a bit by kissing gently, softly. He would kiss her again until he couldn't resist her anymore. He would unbutton her wedding gown, lift her into bed, both naked finally, and they would devour each other and climax together. A hot, furious, simultaneous climax. But she should make sure they would be in the middle of the bed, the one she would stain after he entered her, so she could prove her virginity to those men and to everyone. She would kiss him again. No, he should be the one kissing her. Together, they would remove the proof-of-virginity sheet, carefully fold the blood stain. While she would shower and make herself pretty again and ready for another round of lovemaking, he should be waving that sheet from the banister, where the guests below would be whistling, trilling ululation, and applauding.

She had imagined every luscious moment. But no, he had to go out on the bloody balcony and get drunk, and she had to cry, wasting precious time, just so that he would finally show some compassion.

"I should tell you what happened," he said.

"Happened?"

He took a deep breath. "The guy downstairs, the one who married us..."

"The sheik?"

"Yes. He ... t- took me aside, said that ..." Michel stuttered.

She had seen the sheik whisper in Michel's ear during the festivities, and when the two of them walked out of the grand ballroom. She had figured the man gave Michel an envelope with a check for a wedding present.

"You would never believe what he asked me to do."

"What ...?" Zaffeera said, inching her way closer to Michel. "What did he say?"

He was silent.

"Tell me, please."

"They said tomorrow there was going to be a luncheon in our honor."

"It's for the out-of-town guests. They don't expect us to show up. Besides, our flight leaves at two o'clock, right?"

"Yes."

She lay near him, facing the ceiling. "It's going to be a wonderful ..." she wanted to add *honeymoon,* but changed her word to "trip." For some reason, she felt too embarrassed to remind him it was their honeymoon. She hoped he would correct her. She waited. He didn't say anything. "What did the sheik say?" she asked, trying to move past the uncomfortable moment.

"He said he would have one of his men phone from downstairs, to signal that they were all waiting. I should go down to the mezzanine and stand by the banister, and …" He stopped.

"And?"

"There's something wrong with that man. And his entourage."

"They have been tremendously supportive to my father and our family during this time …"

"But what they asked me to do was appalling. Humiliating. Not only to me, but to you," he said, turning away from her.

"What did he ask?" she said, inching closer to him.

He turned back to her and put his arms around her. The flickering flame on the last candle finally sputtered out, and now there was total darkness. She had to hold on to her breath so that she would not appear too anxious.

"He said after our wedding night, I must save the sheet … wave it from the banister … as proof I married a … virgin. Forgive me. I did not mean to sound disrespectful."

He remained motionless. Zaffeera was silent.

"I should've told him to go to hell. Sorry. I don't mean to swear. I was just too shocked."

"They will think I'm not a virgin."

"If he should get near me again, I swear I'll punch him."

Obviously, he did not hear what she said. "I'm afraid my mother had to go through that. I'm not sure. But I do believe so."

"I can't believe it," he said, removing his arm from her and rolling on his back.

"I'm afraid it's true," she whispered.

"But that's terrible! We read about these things, and watch documentaries on television … I don't want to sound naïve, but we're not like that; we don't come from that cloth. We're *educated*."

"I know." She propped up her two pillows, folded her arms, and stared up at the dark ceiling. "But what can we do? It's the old custom."

A sudden flash of lightning, followed by a deafening sound of thunder, made Michel jump. In that split second, the entire room lit up.

"Are you afraid? I mean of the thunder?" he asked.

"No. Well, to tell you the truth, I am." It started to pour. "I'm not used to thunder. It's very unusual," she said. But she was more afraid of not having sex on her wedding night than of the stupid thunder!

"Unfortunately, I haven't spent enough time here to know. I'm looking forward to building the house. When we get back, I'll work on the scale model. I can't wait to show you those books I ordered on Frank Lloyd Wright. I want to build a house like 'Falling Water,' but I'd also like to have a major waterfall facing the great room ..."

"The great room?"

"Yes. The living room. I know a guy who builds incredible waterfalls. There's also a couple of houses in Los Angeles I can't wait to see ..."

Lightning struck again. This time, Michel caught Zaffeera hiding her face in her hands.

"You *are* scared."

"I'm sorry," she said, keeping her face hidden. "I don't remember the last time we had such a terrible storm." If she showed fear, surely he would have to hold her in his arms and protect her. At last, he did. He held her tight. *Delicious.*

Zaffeera woke up with a start. She felt the chill of the air conditioner, and looked to her left. Michel was asleep, his back to her, softly snoring. It was after four in the morning, according to the digital clock on the nightstand. The rain had stopped. She must have dozed off in his arms. How could she have allowed herself to fall asleep? She stepped into her white satin, marabou-trimmed slippers and padded to the glass door. A crescent-shaped moon began to appear through dissipating clouds.

This was truly a disastrous night. Dawn was imminent, yet they still had not made love! At least the storm had subsided.

Silently, she made her way to the bathroom, brushed her teeth again, combed her hair, freshened her makeup, put drops in her eyes, and rubbed on some more of the love potion that had so far been worthless. She returned to bed and slipped back between the sheets. Slowly, she approached him. "I'm cold," she whispered as she snuggled closer to him.

Half-awake now, Michel put his arm around her. With one hand here, another there, one thing led to another, and before he knew it, he was on top of her. She helped him pull down the elastic band of his ridiculous pajamas. His early morning hard-on felt like a baton. *How exquisite,* she thought, closing her eyes. She guided him, and with a short squeal from her and a groan from him, he jerked back and forth a few times and exploded inside her.

A moment later, he fell on his back, leaving her wondering, *Was that it?*

But they did it! She had felt the brief, sharp pain, but she was too excited about the *act* of lovemaking—was it lovemaking? She didn't even reach orgasm. A warm liquid oozed out of her. *He had to have been a virgin. What a disappointment. What a lousy lay. Never mind.* They had a lifetime to practice…

In the meantime, how could she convince Michel to wave the bloody sheet, and show them all that his lovely bride had indeed been a virgin?

***** ***** *****

Zaffeera called her mother from the privacy of her bathroom and spoke softly, to make sure Michel would not hear. The first thing she did was assure her mother that all was well and they were very happy.

"Michel and I, however, feel rather embarrassed about … you know, about his having to stand over the banister … and wave the bed sheet. He refuses to do it. Says it's disrespectful."

She could tell her mother was shocked by what Zaffeera told her.

"Who would ask Michel to do such a barbaric thing?"

"The sheik, Mother, the sheik."

"But Zaffeera, they must have been joking. Men, between themselves, they can be quite crude. As long as what they talk about is not repeated to the women …"

"Michel said the sheik was quite serious. Michel and I have grown close. He talks to me … He told me about this embarrassing thing because he did not want me to hear it from other sources …"

"You have a good man, *hamdallah.* I am sure your father would feel the same way. We are lucky to have respectful husbands. I will discuss this matter with your father. Don't worry, my daughter."

"I love you, *ya ummy anah,*" Zaffeera whispered close to the phone. "If you don't mind, however, I will put the bed sheet in a large Tiffany box—it *is* our own embroidered sheet. I'll write 'special for Mrs. Yasmina Fendil, the bride's mother' on top of the box, so you won't mistake it for a wedding present. I'll have the sheet with proof of my virginity delivered to your attention at home. Would that be all right with you, Mother?"

There was a pause at the end of the line. Finally, and after some hesitation, Yasmina said, "There is no need to put you, or myself, through such embarrassment, Zaffeera."

"Yes, but still, if you don't mind, please, for the sake of tradition, Mother dear? Just in case they bother us about it."

CHAPTER 43
FATE AND THE WRITTEN WORD

Noora stared at the pale blue-gray wooden shutters that allowed horizontal rays of sunlight into her hotel room. She had turned off the air conditioner during the night, and now she felt hot. She glanced at the digital clock —5:43 AM. She glided out of bed and opened the shutters, seeing the waves gently lapping the shore. She felt revived by the ocean breeze and the gentle whiff of gardenias. She made a special prayer for Ian Cohen before rushing to get ready, for today, he would drive to the hospital and go ahead with the heart surgery. She hoped he didn't change his mind. Most of all, she prayed nothing would go wrong.

They had removed his false teeth. His eyes were barely open. She held his hand. "Stay with me," he whispered as he was about to be wheeled to the operating room.

She pecked a kiss on his cool cheek, assuring him she would stay as close as the nurses would let her. She doubted that would reassure him. "I won't leave you. I promise," she said.

She sat alone in the waiting room, wishing she could talk to someone who knew something about "coronary artery bypass surgery" and about what to expect next. The nurse had given her pamphlets on the subject. "Everyone recovers from surgery at a different rate," one of the booklets said. He may need three weeks to recover. She would have to move out of the hotel. They told her she could stay in the hospital, upstairs where they had rooms for families of patients. She would, at least, have a place. Most of all, she would have a purpose. The admired Hollywood producer needed her. *Not for long,* she reminded herself. Soon he should be well again, ready to return to his life. Soon he'll realize he won't need her anymore.

Noora paced in the hallway. She wished she had a notebook or a small hardbound journal like the ones she spotted in the gift shop of the hotel. She made a mental note to check out the hospital gift shop, and dug in her purse—Annette's purse—and pulled out a pen and a couple of letterheads she had taken from the hotel. She returned to the waiting room, where she would write down her thoughts and record Ian's operation and recovery period, but now every chair was occupied and the television was on.

She had four hours to kill. Four hours of worrying and wondering, while praying the doctors could repair his heart.

The day before, Ian had told her he was sick of seeing her in the same beige blouse. He gave her two hundred-dollar bills and said, "Buy yourself something Hawaiian. Something colorful." Perhaps she should go find something bright and cheerful to greet him when he got out of the operating room. *What if something went wrong and he didn't make it?* She remembered the way the cardiologists looked at each other. They didn't seem too happy about the results of that angiogram.

Noora sat in the far corner of the cafeteria with a cup of hot cocoa before her. *Writing is good for the soul,* she thought, remembering Professor Pennington. She left her cocoa on the table and rushed to the gift shop. She didn't care if someone took her cup or cleared the table—she had to find a journal or a notebook.

Her bowl of cream of wheat became a glob of paste. The wall clock showed eleven thirty, more than four hours since she left Ian Cohen. Noora had lost track of time, writing in her new journal. It had cost twenty dollars, but she had to buy it. On the first pink pinstriped page of the cloth hardbound journal, using the hotel's pencil, Noora wrote "Kelley Karlton" and the date. "This book begins with all my prayers for my father's speedy and successful recovery." She erased "my father's" and wrote Ian Cohen's name.

"Kelley Cohen, please report to I.C.U. North," a female voice came from a nearby speaker. Her heart skipped a beat. Leaving her food and thrusting her journal in her purse, she took the stairs two at a time to the third floor.

Ian Cohen was hooked up to a maze of tubes. White tape held a large mouthpiece, and to his left, she saw a blue screen monitoring his heart. She couldn't stand watching him in such a pitiful state. He looked small and helpless. When he opened his eyes, he did not seem to recognize her. She searched for a nurse, but they were all busy tending to other patients. So many patients were moaning. So much suffering. Noora had to walk out in the hallway. She pressed her forehead against the wall as tears flowed.

"Are you Mr. Cohen's daughter?"

Noora turned. "I'm sorry," she said, drying her tears. She stared at the young Asian nurse, who spoke with a melodious accent.

"He's doing well. The operation was successful. Are you the only family member present?"

"Yes ..." What else could she say?

"Are you Mr. Cohen's daughter?" the nurse asked again.

"Yes," Noora had to give a satisfactory answer. "My name is Kelley."

"Miss Kelley?" the nurse asked, extending her hand.

"Yes," Noora said, shaking the nurse's hand.

"Pleasure; my name is Felo. Doris, the social worker will be in shortly. She can answer any questions you have."

"Thank you," Noora said. Watching the nurse return to her station, Noora thought that she should place a call to Sam the butler. She knew Mr. Cohen phoned him the night before and briefed him on his bypass surgery. Sam wanted to hop on the first plane for Honolulu, but Ian said it was best to keep the routine the same, and let everyone think he was on vacation.

The social worker sat Noora down and explained what was to be expected. "Mr. Cohen will probably stay in the hospital for seven days. Of course, every patient is different," she added. "Then he can be moved to rehab."

Noora's tears flowed. She couldn't stop herself. She wondered why she felt such anguish.

The next morning, Noora checked out of the Moana Surfrider. The night before the operation, she had not been able to convince Ian that

Roz should be informed about his surgery. "You tell one person at the studio, and the world will know. I won't tell her, and lay off my case about it, or you can go back to Frogsville, for all I care," he had said.

Noora tried not to take his remark personally. He had every reason to be nervous about his surgery. But that morning in the hospital, after he was weighed and given a sedative, he said, "I did call Roz last night. Work things out with her."

What did he mean by that? Noora wondered.

"Day two since the operation," Noora wrote in her journal. "Ian Cohen is still not responding to painkillers. He was angry about the tubes and tried to pull them out. I cannot say I blame him. The nurses had to tie him to the bed, like a madman."

Finally, on the third day, Ian, still in ICU, began to show progress.

Noora's tension eased. She was grateful there was a vacant little room upstairs that she could rent as a family member. Only days before, she had worried about Mr. Cohen making a pass at her. Now she wondered if he would survive. She thought of Michel, and she closed her eyes. With a tear falling from her nose to her pillowcase, she dozed off.

The next morning, Saturday, Roz landed in Honolulu. She brought his mail, along with trade papers and three or four screenplays to read—and approve—in a separate suitcase. But when his secretary approached Mr. Cohen's bed, on the ICU floor, Noora could see the woman was shocked. "Oh my God. He looks so ... helpless ... old ... What have they done to him?"

"Actually, he's much better," Noora whispered cheerfully. "This morning, they removed his mouthpiece."

"Mouthpiece?"

"He had to have oxygen. But now he's breathing on his own. They even put back his denture plate. It's major progress."

"Dentures?" Roz asked, appearing horrified.

Ian Cohen had been rather glum and unresponsive in Kelley Karlton's presence. But later that day, when Roz approached his bed, he recognized her and smiled. But it was a short-lived smile that quickly switched to reproach.

"What're you doing on the set? You got letters for me to sign? Why all these extras?"

"Oh my God," Roz whispered, her eyes widening. "What have they done to you, Mr. Cohen?"

Over caesar salads at the restaurant across the street from Straub Hospital, Roz kept shaking her head. "I don't know what to think. I'm very concerned about Mr. Cohen."

"Yes, of course," Noora said.

"I had no idea …"

"But his operation went well," Noora said, trying to sound encouraging. "You heard the nurse. He just needs time to recover." She liked Roz—her honesty and intelligence. She wore her graying hair up in a neatly combed chignon. Her granny glasses were held by a string of oyster-shell pearls. Her clear complexion revealed that she was probably younger than she appeared.

"I'm also concerned about the fact that he won't get to read the script, let alone dictate changes."

"What script?"

"The violent piece of junk called *The Lord of Doom.*"

"Oh. Yes."

"Don't tell me he made you read it," Roz asked, chewing on her lettuce.

"He suggested that I read it … Didn't you?"

"Just because I work for Mr. Cohen's studio doesn't mean I have to read such crap."

"That's what sells … I hear."

"Yes, and who am I to complain? Puts bread on my table. But frankly, and this is between you, me, and the wall, I don't know how I'm going to explain this whole thing to the writers," Roz said, drinking down half her glass of white wine. "No one will believe Ian Cohen is too busy to make script changes because he's vacationing in Hawaii with some bimb …" She bit her lip. "I'm sorry … I … I shouldn't have had so much wine," she said, picking up her glass of water. "But people like to gossip. They always imagine the worst."

"Mr. Cohen has been very respectful. I do believe you and I have this in common. We're probably the only women close to him who aren't …

well ... romantically involved with him," Noora said, to make sure Roz understood her message.

Before flying home, Roz told Noora they would have to put her on the payroll. Noora did not argue. She would need money. In Ian's wallet, Roz had found almost two thousand dollars, which she told Noora to use for expenses during his recovery. When Noora refused to take the money, Roz took one of the studio's letterheads from her attaché case, and in her own handwriting, she confirmed permission for Mr. Cohen's "personal assistant" to spend the exact sum of $1,882 on expenses and incidentals during Mr. Cohen's stay in Honolulu, as per his request. She signed it and drew a line next to it.

"Get Mr. Cohen to sign right here. For now. When I get back to the office, I'll type it up and fax it to you, so it's all legal and no one will accuse you of stealing his money," Roz said. "Oh, and by the way, I like you; I appreciate your honesty."

"Day 5: Ian Cohen is still in the ICU ..." Noora wrote in her little journal.

After a wakeful night, and still shivering from the air conditioning in her little room, Noora was still in her dress and Annette's sweater. She decided to hurry back down to ICU and check on Mr. Cohen before she took her shower.

She found him sitting upright on a high-back vinyl reclining chair. He appeared to be in a trance. His hair was combed and he had been shaved. He had his teeth in. "Ah, it's you," he said. His voice sounded raw, like the Godfather's.

"Mr. Coh—" Noora stopped herself, remembering she was supposed to be his daughter. "How are you feeling this morning?"

"All these people running around. Where's Roz?"

"She ... had to go back to the office."

He grunted. "Tell craft services if they don't shape up, they'll have to be replaced."

"Craft services?"

"Food's lousy. How'd they expect anyone to function?"

"You're in the hospital. And you've just had a very successful operation."

"I know. Nice dress. Yellow's good. No tacky muumuu Hawaiian shit."

"Thank you ..."

"It's time for your blood pressure, Poppa!" a nurse sang cheerfully.

"When will the doctor be in to see him?" Noora asked.

"He already came to examine your father."

"I was hoping to be here when ..."

"The doctor said tomorrow Poppa is ready to be moved to a hospital room. Right, Poppa? You heard what the doctor said. Good news, huh?" she said, bending to Ian's eye level.

"About time," he grumbled.

On the sixth day after Ian Cohen's operation, Noora received a call from Roz.

"Did you get the script we sent overnight express?"

"Yes."

Obviously, Roz did not understand that her boss was still in no condition to read or sign anything. Returning to his room, Noora saw a male nurse tending to Mr. Cohen.

"Are you his daughter?"

"Yes," Noora sighed, wishing they'd stop asking her that question. But she was getting used to the lie.

Mr. Cohen was asleep, and his breathing sounded ragged and labored.

"He had a rough night," the male nurse explained.

"What does that mean?" Noora asked. "What happened?"

The nurse shrugged.

"Why didn't anyone call me? I have a room upstairs."

"He's resting now. We put a foam mattress for his back, and we gave him a sleeping pill," the nurse said and left to tend to his next patient.

At ten o'clock the next morning, Ian Cohen was still asleep. Noora had to get up several times and adjust the air conditioner for his comfort. At times, he shivered; other times, he perspired profusely.

"How is he supposed to get any sleep in this hospital? The constant interruptions by nurses checking on Mr. Cohen's blood pressure and IV bag can't possibly help his recovery," Noora wrote in her journal.

Writing helped her pass the long, frustrating hours. The waiting, the worrying. She should complain to someone—Ian Cohen was not getting the proper care. She went to the nurses' station and asked, "Where is Mr. Cohen's ... my father's doctor? I must speak to him. He has been avoiding me long enough. I must speak to that doctor right now!"

The nurse looked up from her computer screen. Her eyes were glazed over. She stared at Noora for a moment. "Whose daughter are you again?"

"Mr. Ian Cohen. He had bypass surgery, and Dr. McGratten is his physician."

"Oh yes. I will leave him a message ..."

At eleven o'clock, a nurse came to Mr. Cohen's door. "There is a phone call for you, Miss Cohen."

"Is it the doctor?" Noora asked hopefully.

"No, long distance. You can pick up the phone at the nurses' station."

"How is he?" Roz asked the moment Noora picked up the receiver.

"He's had a restless night ..."

"Get Mr. Cohen to give a response on the script. By the way, I express-mailed some more paperwork for you to sign."

"Me?"

"Yes. As of today, you're officially hired. We'll just need you to fill out the employment application I sent you. Do you have a green card?"

"No."

"We'll put you in as a temp."

Noora felt the blood drain to her feet. What if they found out she was a phony with someone else's passport? She looked up and spotted Mr. Cohen's doctor.

"Put your passport number if you don't have a social security number yet," Roz continued. "The form I'm faxing is self-explanatory."

Passport number? Why would she ask me for such a thing, Noora wondered. "Excuse me, Roz, the doctor just arrived. I'll let you know what he says."

"What?"

"The doctor is here; I must speak to him before he disappears again."

"Okay, but make sure Mr. Cohen makes those changes, and ..."

"Yes, yes, sorry, g'bye," she said and hung up. Noora was not going to miss that doctor again.

"The doctor is pleased with your progress, Mr. Cohen," Noora sang out when he finally awoke in the early afternoon. She wanted to add, *He is also quite pleased with himself!*

The doctor's visit had been rather unpleasant—he had treated Noora with a patronizing air.

"Roz is waiting for you to approve these changes," Noora said later, trying to appear cheerful. She placed a document on Mr. Cohen's portable tray.

"Nurses think you're my daughter," Ian said, coughing.

"Here, Mr. Cohen, hug the pillow," she suggested as Ian coughed louder. She gave him the flowered cotton pillow shaped like a baby whale.

"I'd rather hug the teddy bear ... one you got for me. Looks like me. Don't you think?" He said, coughing louder yet. "God, I hurt ..."

She found the teddy bear on the chair and gave it to him.

"They think you're my daughter," he repeated.

"I'm sorry. I ... didn't know what else to tell them ..." Noora said, embarrassed.

He waved a hand attached to intravenous tubes. "Tell 'em you're my wife," he said, laughing now while coughing.

"Mr. Cohen ..."

Keeping the teddy bear snugly against his chest, he said, "Okay. Tell 'em you're my assistant."

"I tried ..."

"... and my daughter. My assistant and my daughter. We're a team," he said, coughing louder.

When his cough began to abate, she handed him a small paper cup filled with juice. He sipped slowly through a straw, turning to Noora with droopy eyes. "As long as they don't think you're my granddaughter."

"Oh, no, no, Ian. You are way too young!"

Closing his eyes, he dropped back on the pillow with a deep sigh.

"Roz called and said they'll need some script changes and your approval ..."

"Gimme my glasses," Ian said.

Noora fitted them on him, then pressed the button to raise his bed a little higher toward a sitting position.

"Roz wanted you to sign this letter first," she suggested hopefully, sitting quietly while he read. He signed a few letters and a document. Minutes later, while Noora prayed he would not be interrupted, Mr. Cohen picked up the *Lord of Doom* screenplay and leafed through it for a long while. Finally, he put it down and sighed.

She knew he would soon be too tired to go on.

"It's worse. They didn't change anything. Just page numbers and swapped scenes. They must think I'm a moron. I liked your ideas."

"My ... ideas?"

"What you told me at the Hamlet."

Two staff workers walked in with a lunch tray—a small piece of grilled chicken breast, mashed potatoes, and sad-looking green beans. There was also a small can—some kind of a nutritious milk drink.

Another nurse arrived to change his IV bag. "The doctor said if he drinks three of these cans a day, it's equivalent to the nutrition he needs," the nurse said, unhooking the plastic medicine bag.

"You call those nutritious drinks? They're shit. Plaster of Paris in a colorful can," the patient said.

"They come in flavors. Strawberry and chocolate," the nurse recited with a broad smile.

"Go tell that to another patient," he murmured.

"Okay," the nurse said, smiling and walking out.

"Directors ... If I'd known, I would've told that ... son of a bitch BB Gun to go and ..." Ian sighed. He closed his eyes and whispered, "I feel like shit ..."

"Try to eat a little something, please," Noora said.

"Let's wait until tomorrow morning."

"All right," she sighed.

Once they were alone again, Ian whispered, "Stay with me. That night nurse might poison my IV."

"Mr. Cohen, they're nice here."

"Not the one at night. Hitler's twin. She'll knock me off my bed if I dare look at her knockers ..." he murmured before drifting into sleep.

His condition seemed worse. Noora decided to spend the night in his room; she would ask for a cot. If only he could swallow some of that nutritious "plaster of Paris."

"He's making progress," an exhausted Noora lied when she spoke to Roz, who called the nurses' station. "But he's still too groggy from the pain pills to look over the script you sent."

"Buy a small fax machine and install it in his room," Roz said coldly. "Call me tonight at home. I'll fax you more pages, and some letters Mr. Cohen must sign." There was a short pause. "Listen," Roz added, "I'm sorry if I'm hard on you. I'm getting a lot of pressure from the writers and that egomaniac director. Mr. Cohen couldn't have picked a worse time to get sick. Glad to hear he's improving. You're doing a good job. Better get him back on his feet ASAP. We need the script changes and approvals sooner than that or the whole project is kaput."

***** ***** *****

Returning from the cafeteria downstairs with a cup of hot cocoa, Noora spotted Ian Cohen's cardiologist walking out of his patient's room, looking quite serious. The second she decided to leave Mr. Cohen for a few minutes, the doctor made his visit. What terrible luck—when she had nerved herself to confront him with all her questions about Mr. Cohen's condition. She watched Dr. McGratten as he made his way around the nurses' station, with his back to her. He sat on a stool behind the counter and scribbled inside a manila folder. She approached the doctor. He picked up his folder and rushed down the hall. She had to talk to someone. The nurses? Or Doris, the social worker?

"The doctor ordered a colonoscopy for Mr. Cohen," Doris informed Noora. "Why? He has been through so much already."

"I know," Doris replied compassionately. "The doctor wants to check for a possible tumor in the colon," Doris said, guiding the worried Noora to the waiting area by the elevators, where they could sit and talk privately. "Just to rule it out. More likely, I would say, it's impacted poop that needs to be flushed out."

"*Impacted poop?* You mean ... he is constipated?"

Doris nodded. "Very likely. I've seen many cases like that. Usually it's caused by antibiotics and sometimes painkillers."

"It's my fault. I'm the one who constantly begged the nurses for painkillers."

"Kelley, it's not your fault," Doris said. She touched Noora's shoulder. "Mr. Cohen is very lucky to have such a devoted daughter."

Noora put up a hand to hide her face. She wanted to cry. What would Doris say if she knew the truth?

CHAPTER 44
THE HONEYMOON

Zaffeera and Michel returned to the Beverly Regent Hotel, where they occupied a luxurious honeymoon suite. She enjoyed walking arm-in-arm with her handsome husband. They had strolled along Rodeo Drive, shopped in Century City, and lunched in one of the trendy restaurants. Everywhere they went, she could tell she was the envy of the women who saw her husband. *If only he could fuck like he looked, life would be heavenly,* Zaffeera thought. *Soon, things would have to improve.*

On their way back to the hotel, Michel talked about a house on the hill designed by some famous architect. It belonged to a young Hollywood producer who had not yet returned Michel's phone calls. Zaffeera wanted to shout: "Forget about famous architects and the damn houses! And the renovated hotels! This is our honeymoon!" But she decided not to offer suggestions at this time of their life together.

When they returned to the hotel, Michel began examining the ceilings of the newly renovated lobby.

"I hope you don't mind," Zaffeera said as sweetly as she could, while Michel stared at the ceiling, "I am tired ..."

"Oh, I'm sorry," he said, setting their shopping bags down and removing the plastic keycard from his wallet. "I'll join you in just a bit ... hope you don't mind. I just need to see something."

"Not at all," she said, minding very much.

Alone in the elevator, Zaffeera punched the Penthouse button a few frustrating times. Married six days and five nights. Sex once? Okay, they cuddled. *But doesn't honeymoon mean SEX?* She wanted to punch every elevator button that would light up, but she had to control herself. She had to find a way to satisfy her needs while gradually molding him to her desires.

That afternoon, Michel received the awaited phone call.

"I can see the house tomorrow morning," he said gleefully, the moment he hung up the phone. "Would you like to come along?"

Zaffeera sat on the edge of the king-size bed, her eyes cast downward. "All right," she murmured.

"What's the matter, are you upset?"

"Me?" Zaffeera looked up at Michel and batted her eyes.

"I'm sorry," he said, sitting next to her. "I've been very selfish."

Zaffeera twisted her wedding ring and watched the huge diamond sparkle in the sunlight streaming from the tall window behind her. "No," she said, looking down at her perfectly manicured hands, which she rested on her lap.

"If you'd rather go somewhere else, back to Neiman Marcus ..."

"No," she said, wishing she could tear off his clothes.

She hid her head in the crease of his neck.

He put an arm around her. Now they were starting to get somewhere, Zaffeera thought.

If she could just push him down onto the bed. They sat in that same position for the longest time. She was beginning to feel a cramp in her leg.

"I would love to see that house with you," she finally said, with a deep sigh.

"I don't want to make you feel like you have to come."

"No, I would love to *come,*" she murmured. *Cum, cum, cum!* Merde! *Can't he get a clue? Shit!*

But her double entendre went right over his head. She was about to explode.

CHAPTER 45
A MATTER OF HONOR

On Friday afternoon, Farid Fendil asked his wife to meet him in his office. Mrs. Yasmina Fendil assumed that a week after the beautiful wedding of their daughter, her husband wanted to share an evening with her. After all the recent events, especially during the past year, Farid had not asked Yasmina to see her for the purpose of being together as husband and wife. Usually, he came to see her in her room.

Eagerly, she walked to his office in the men's wing. She realized she had not been there in two years.

"It was such a beautiful wedding," she told her husband, smiling. She had forgotten how sumptuous his office was.

He asked her to close the door and sit down.

She was looking forward to reminiscing about the wedding. But Farid Fendil stood in front of his desk and looked at his wife seriously.

"Is there something wrong, Farid?"

"Actually, no," he said, picking up his pipe and lighting it.

Yasmina coughed lightly from the smoke, but pretended she was not bothered by it.

"I wanted to ask you an important question."

"Yes?"

"Is Shamsah circumcised?"

"What?" Yasmina could not have heard her husband correctly.

"Is Shamsah circumcised?" he asked matter-of-factly.

"You ... know we don't ... None of our daughters ... And you know I never was, thanks to my mother ..."

"Don't you think it's high time we should?" he interrupted.

"What are you saying?" she asked, bewildered.

"Don't you think it would be to everyone's interest ..."

"*Interest?* No, I don't believe our ancestors should ever have started this terrible thing in the first place. That's like butchering ... It's mutilating a child, Farid ... *please*."

"Nonsense. Not nowadays, when it's performed by trained people."

"*Trained* people?"

"Due to modern conditions, our daughters have forgotten their traditions. It has been decided that the old traditional ways are still the best. We must obey our customs, our beliefs," he said with authority. "Now that Zaffeera is in the hands of her husband, we no longer need to worry about her. However ..." he enunciated each word very calmly, "in the case of Shamsah, who is probably due to become a young woman any month now ..."

"Why do you think my mother became a midwife?" Yasmina said, her face turning red.

"You interrupted me," he said.

"Why did she want to travel to so many rural towns to deliver babies?"

"I don't know, and that's not the issue!"

"Farid, it wasn't just for her to be a midwife! It was to *teach*, to inform young mothers exactly that ... that it was wrong! You ... You can't! Not your own daughter ..."

"Your mother was wrong."

Yasmina jumped from her chair. She wanted to hit him. Instead, she bit her index finger as hard as she could, drawing blood. She slapped her own cheek hard and clawed both cheeks with her nails until they bled.

Farid Fendil's eyes widened in shock as his wife began to tear at her clothes. She grabbed her blouse with two hands and ripped it off.

"Woman! You stop that right away!" he demanded, and rapidly retreated behind his desk. He reached for the phone, as if to call for help.

Yasmina grabbed her long skirt and tried to tear it off with her teeth.

Her behavior left him too stunned to call anyone.

"Here, heeere! Take it! TAKE IT ALL, WHY DON'T YOU?! Tear me apart!" She grabbed the shiny silver letter opener from his desk. "Here! Stab me, why don't you! Tear my heart out! Go ahead! Like you've torn our family apart!"

"Woman, you are crazy."

"And who made me crazy?! What happened to you?! You! The pasha! The decent ..." she said, hitting her chest, "decent man ... you once were. What happened to him? What *really* happened ... to our child? What did you do to our Noora?! Aii, my NOOR ... AGH!" she sobbed.

"What?!"

She dropped the letter opener on the floor. "You never grieved for her! You never ... Why?" She grabbed her hair and tried to yank it out of her scalp. "WHY! *Bentak!* Your daughter! *Aiii, benti anah!* Oh, daughter of mine!"

"STOP!"

She fell to her knees and began banging and pounding on his antique Persian rug.

"STOP IT!" He came around his desk and kicked her on her side.

"Good, good! Kick me, KICK ME SOME MORE!"

"Stop it right now or I'll have to say the words!"

"You can kick me. But you can never touch my children again! Not ever! You'll have to kill me first, but even from the grave, I'll haunt you day and night and send the *devil* after you! THIS, I PROMISE!"

He snatched his letter opener from the floor and rushed back behind his desk, as if to protect himself from this madwoman.

"I DIVORCE YOU, I DIVORCE YOU, *I DIVORCE YOU!*" he screamed. After a few moments, he solemnly repeated the words for the world to hear, "I divorce you, I divorce you, I divorce you!"

There was silence.

"Now I have said it," he announced. "It is done."

They both knew that when a man repeated these words three times, the marriage was considered dissolved.

He lifted a hand. "You are to leave my house!"

Yasmina slowly rose and stood erect before him. Her chest heaving, she stared at her husband for a long moment. "The women's wing belongs to *me*. I will leave when *I* decide," she said as firmly and as calmly as possible. "You can leave your wing, if that is your wish. You will hurt us no more."

Farid Fendil's eyes blazed. "What do you think you're saying?!"

"You know perfectly well."

"You have gone insane!"

Yasmina opened the door and walked out.

He tossed the letter opener angrily on his desk, fell into his chair, and buried his head in his hands.

CHAPTER 46
HOLLYWOOD HONEYMOON

The black limousine glided regally up Benedict Canyon, passing the Beverly Hills Hotel.

Zaffeera wore a tailored St. John sapphire blue knit suit with delicate pink borders around the neck and cuffs of the exquisitely designed jacket. She had seen it featured in a fashion magazine months before the wedding, and had ordered it. It took weeks to have it fitted and blocked just the way she had to have it, to complement her pear-shaped body.

"Could we go to the Polo Lounge sometime?" Zaffeera purred as the limo passed the Beverly Hills Hotel.

"As a matter of fact, I made reservations to have lunch there today!"

"You did? My goodness. I've been thinking about going there and seeing how it looks since they remodeled," she lied.

"You have?" He looked pleased.

"Yes," she said. She really didn't care to see it. But that morning, while Michel was in the shower, she had peeked in his Gucci calendar in his attaché case. He had written *"Polo Lounge. Maybe lunch?"* and scribbled the hotel's phone number. "I've been wanting to see the unusual circular lobby," she said, knowing he would be pleased at her interest. She had read about the Beverly Hills Hotel in an architectural magazine, only days before their wedding. "I would also *love* to see the new tapestry and furnishings ..."

"The owner of the house said if we should miss Angelo Drive, we'll find ourselves on a street called Cielo," Michel interrupted Zaffeera.

She sank in her seat, realizing he didn't really care what she had to say. *He was more interested in finding that fucking house.*

"He said we shouldn't take Cielo Drive, or Cielo Street, because it's the service entrance and there's no view. Oh, there it is, there's Angelo ..." Michel pointed as the chauffeur turned up the street.

"I've never been this far up; looks quite secluded," the chauffeur said, slowing the limo to negotiate the steep turns and narrow uphill climb.

"We need to go down the private driveway," Michel told the driver as they reached the end of a cul-de-sac.

The limo took the drive down, between geometrically shaped huge cement blocks that served as pots for royal palms.

"That definitely looks like a John Lautner design!" Michel exclaimed, sounding like a kid discovering Disney's Futureland.

As the limo drove down, the narrow driveway opened to a wide circular parking area, large enough for a dozen cars. The driver pulled to a stop, away from the three-car garage's doors.

A bright red BMW convertible was parked in front of silver-painted wrought iron doors.

Michel climbed out of the limo just as a woman's voice shouted "Fuck you!"

The wrought iron door flew open and a young woman with a Barbie-doll figure exploded out of the house. Her arms hugging a mound of clothes on hangers, the woman shouted: "YOU'RE A SON OF A BITCH!" She dumped her entire load on the back seat of the convertible. "Bastard!" She wore skin-tight leopard-design stretch capris, black heels at least four inches high, and a silk-sheer beige blouse so transparent, she might as well have been topless.

Michel turned to Zaffeera and nudged her back in the limo. But she would not miss such a scene, and pressed the button slightly to open her darkly tinted window. *First excitement in days.*

"Honey, it's not what you think!" A man's voice was heard.

A tall, good-looking, dark-haired man appeared, wearing black trousers and a charcoal silk shirt opened to below the chest. He carried a few pieces of Louis Vuitton luggage. *Wow,* Zaffeera thought, *a live Hollywood show.* She pressed the window button slightly further down. Michel was standing outside, his back to her and partially blocking her view. But she could see the man as he set the valises by the trunk of the

BMW. "Darling, you won't like it when construction workers are here. You said so yourself."

"We could've moved out together!"

"Honey, remember ... I'll have to stay with my stepfather ..."

"Lots of rooms in his castle."

"It's not a castle!" the man retorted, obviously irritated by the young woman's remark.

"A mansion. Same shit!"

"It won't look right. I don't think that he ..."

"He's not even there!" she barked. "Shacked up in Hawaii with some bimbo, I'm sure!"

She stormed back in the house.

The man ran around the BMW and popped open the trunk. He dumped in all her luggage and slammed the trunk shut. As he started back for the house, he noticed Michel and Zaffeera's limousine parked in the shady corner. Zaffeera watched as the man put on an exaggerated smile and headed over to greet Michel.

"Hello, I'm Kennilworth Cohen," he said extending his hand.

"How do you do ... I am Michel Amir," he said, shaking Kennilworth's hand. "We had an appointment ... We can come back another time," Michel uttered awkwardly.

"This is a perfect time, actually. Just wait here for a couple more minutes. Be right back."

The blonde exploded again out of the wrought iron door, holding yet another mound of clothes, which she threw on top of the previous load.

Kennilworth ran to her and opened the driver's door.

Shouting something else at the man, she slid behind the wheel and slammed the car door, screaming, "Fuck you!"

Tires burned on the hot cement as the fire-engine-red BMW rocketed up the hill.

The man appeared rather glad to have been left by the young woman in the red convertible, and eager to show off his property. He led Michel and Zaffeera to his front door.

"You came here all the way from Paris to see my house?" the owner said, visibly impressed. "Did you say you're ... originally from Egypt?"

"We're Egyptians, but we live in a small town in Jordan called Al-Balladi."

"Is that like near the ... the Sahara Desert?"

Zaffeera narrowed her eyes. She would have loved to thrust a knee really hard into his crotch and watch him dance.

"No," Michel replied politely. "Actually, it's not at all in that region. It is a beautiful, modern town, with gardens, office buildings, lakes, and monuments. We are in the process of building our new home there."

Kennilworth checked out Zaffeera. "How interesting," he said.

On the granite counter of the oblong kitchen, next to floor-to-ceiling glass sliding doors, Kennilworth proudly unrolled the new plans of his house, as well as John Lautner's original blueprints. "I'm going to keep Lautner's ideas. That architect was incredibly gifted. This is the last house he ever designed, you know."

"Would you consider selling it?" Michel asked.

"Selling this house? Oh, well, I'm not sure," Kennilworth said. "However, anything can be bought. Right? That is, if the price is right."

That night, in their hotel room, Zaffeera stared fixedly at the ceiling, hoping and praying for lovemaking.

"I'm so sorry," Michel said.

"Why are you sorry?" she asked hopefully. She inched closer to him.

"Because I have subjected you to such unruly behavior."

"Forgive me, but I am not sure I understand."

"That woman. This morning."

"It is not your fault, Michel."

"I brought you there."

"I closed my ears. I heard nothing."

A long moment passed as they lay side by side in darkness.

"I don't think that guy is very much attached to that house," he said. "I think I may be able to make an offer."

"It could be a great house ... if you remodeled it ... with your own vision."

"I couldn't change anything structurally. The design is ...wonderful. Fantastic."

"The view is beautiful," she said. She had to say something positive. *What was so great about that house? Floor-to-ceiling glass everywhere, barely any walls except steel sticks to hold an oddly shaped roof?* She could tell that a man designed the house. It had small bathrooms and hardly any closets—no provisions for even one servant—merely a glorified bachelor pad.

How many nights would she lie in that same position, wishing he would make love to her? She could not keep waiting for Michel to make the first move. *This could not go on!* She wanted sex. She *needed* it. He was her bloody husband!

She cuddled close to Michel and began to caress his chest, then down below the elastic band of those bloody damned blue pajamas he always wore! She wanted to hold his most precious part and rub it and feel it grow. Her hand stopped right below the elastic band. Why did he make her feel shy? How much could she do to him, without his thinking she was perverted or ... whorish? He seemed so inexperienced. She was about to gently move her hand away when he turned to her, and very slowly at first, he kissed her.

Here we go finally, Zaffeera thought. It was a pretty good start. His lips felt wonderful. There was potential. As they continued to kiss, she searched for his tongue. She slowly wiggled her way beneath him. They would do it old-fashioned style—for now. She didn't want him to suspect she was an expert at this pleasurable game. She could feel him against the thin satin of her nightgown and the thick cotton of his pajamas. He was so wonderfully hard! *Oh my,* Zaffeera thought, arching her back. The moment seemed endless when, yes ... YES! At last, she guided him inside her. Aaah... Her entire body trembled at the sensation. Michel's penis was completely inside her now. She helped him through his awkward movement. *In and out. Not too far out now. Keep doing this,* she sang to herself. She was on the verge of screaming, *"I love you! Don't stop! Stay there, I-want-you-all-night... I command you!"*

He reached a silent orgasm.

She bit her lip. *Shit!*

Zaffeera was asleep, her head on Michel's arm. Slowly, he eased his stiff arm away from her and crept out of bed. He tiptoed to the desk and opened his attaché case. He pulled out something from one of the pockets and silently went into the bathroom. The early-morning sunlight streamed through the bathroom window. He sat on the steps of the whirlpool tub and bent to stare at the picture he held in his hands.

"Forgive me, my darling," he whispered to a small portrait picture of Noora.

CHAPTER 47
RAINBOW RIBBONS OF HOPE

Twelve days after Ian Cohen's bypass surgery, Noora decided she must talk to Mr. Cohen's doctor. She could not allow him to intimidate her. Mr. Cohen had suffered yet another terrible night. She had waited, but the doctor never showed up in the morning, or after lunch. Mr. Cohen could no longer eat, and the state of his health was deteriorating. By three o'clock that afternoon, Noora was informed that Dr. McGratten had left on an emergency.

"Where?" Noora asked a male nurse she had never seen before.

"The mainland. His father had a stroke," he said.

"I'm sorry to hear that," Noora said. "But I need to know who's replacing Mr. Cohen's ... my father's doctor. No one came to see him today."

"I'll find out for you," the nurse said, heading to the next room on the floor.

Which direction was Mecca from Honolulu? Noora knelt, facing the window, and touched her forehead to the floor. *Allah Akbar,* she whispered ... *What is God's will now? Um Faheema, you said you would be with me always, in spirit.* Looking to the sky, she clenched her copper chain with the blue stone. In the name of God ... please, *guide me.*

She wondered why the nurse asked Noora if Mr. Cohen had a living will. What did he mean? Was Mr. Cohen dying?

As Noora gazed out the window, she saw a glorious rainbow forming behind the hill in the distance. She gasped when ribbon rays of color appeared, forming a second rainbow, outside the first, appearing more luminous and ethereal.

"What'sa matter?" she heard Mr. Cohen ask gruffly behind her. "What're you doing on the floor?"

"Mr. Cohen, you're awake … look! Outside …" Noora said, rising stiffly. "There is a double rainbow!"

"Where?"

"Right there, in front of your window!" She held his head up for a better look, and arranged the pillow for him to see.

"Oh," he said, showing a certain degree of interest through his droopy eyes.

"So beautiful," she said, pressing the button a notch and raising his bed so he could have a better look.

She walked to the window. "I've never seen that color of lavender on a rainbow before …"

"Violet."

"Pardon?" she turned to him.

"It's violet," he said, his eyes closed.

She turned to admire the rainbow again. "It *is* violet." She turned back to Mr. Cohen. He was silent. She moved closer to him. A tear slowly rolled down on his left temple.

"Rainbows are a sign of good luck," Noora whispered.

"*You* are my good luck," he murmured.

His eyes were still closed. His breathing seemed shallow and labored. Even though they said the X-rays showed no tumor in his colon, his stomach looked larger than it had been that morning.

At three o'clock in the morning, Noora was jarred out of a dream. She had fallen asleep under double sheets in her cot next to the window in Mr. Cohen's room. He still had difficulty breathing; he wanted water, and his stomach seemed to have grown to double its previous size. She gave him water in a small cup, which he drank like a thirsty man in a desert. He wanted more. She wasn't sure if that would aggravate his situation.

Noora left his room with the excuse that she would find ice water. She ran out to the nurses' station and demanded to see a doctor.

"First thing in the morning, Doctor Ferguson, the doctor on call, will be here to see your father," a nurse said calmly.

"First thing in the morning? He's having trouble breathing now! We need a doctor right now! IMMEDIATELY!" Noora commanded, surprised at her own forcefulness. "No doctor came in today *at all!*"

Doctor Ferguson, a tall, handsome young man, walked into Ian's room not more than twenty minutes later. Noora watched as he tapped on Ian's stomach, which sounded like a hollow drum.

"It's going to take a few more days to get all this inflammation down," Dr. Ferguson said. "At least."

I must get Roz back here, Noora thought, rushing out to the public phones next to the elevators. She began to dial and realized it was just about 6:30 in the morning in Los Angeles. She hung up, paced for a moment and dialed again, leaving an urgent message for Roz to call her back. She knew Roz would be at the office just before 8:00 AM, Los Angeles time.

An endless hour and a half later, Roz finally returned Noora's call at the nurses' station. "It's impossible for me to leave the office at this time," she said to an exhausted Noora. "And between us, Kennilworth-less is getting more and more demanding. He has his own secretary, but he wants me to transcribe his letters and do everything. And the writers are demanding the changes now … They have no clue regarding Mr. Cohen's condition."

"But Mr. Cohen did make—is still making the changes on the script, you know," Noora found herself saying.

"He is?"

"Yes. I'll send the changes as soon as I can."

"I knew I could count on you. Just fax everything ASAP. What's your fax number?"

"Oh. Sorry, I never had the chance to leave the hospital …"

"Get with the program, dear. This is the film biz. We don't waste a second, even if we're on our deathbed."

"I'm sure the nurses will let me use their fax machine. I'll get that number as soon as the changes are done."

Mr. Cohen was in no condition to *think,* let alone dictate anything. All he could do at that time was fight for his life while trying to breathe through his vaporized-oxygen mask.

In the afternoon, after the lunch tray was removed, and the nurses stayed away for a good two hours, Noora had a chance to read through the script. She asked one of the nurses for a small portable lamp. Lowering Ian's food tray—which she used as a makeshift desk—to a workable level, Noora settled on the plastic recliner in his room. While Ian Cohen slept, breathing through his oxygen mask, Noora picked up a pencil and studied his notes. Tracing over his handwriting and signature, she practiced until she could imitate his unusual scrawl. She would be in deep trouble if anyone found out. But Roz was pressuring. No, she was *demanding*. What else was Noora to do?

Luckily, there was a postal substation downstairs, next to the hospital's gift shop. Before changing her mind for fear that she might get into even more trouble by forging Mr. Cohen's signature, Noora mailed the first part of the doctored script to Roz—Overnight Express.

Noora had begun to get used to the dreadful sight of what the nurses told her was a catheter, a rectal tube that had been inserted to release the toxins from Mr. Cohen's abdomen. The transparent tube snaked down to a pouch beneath the foot of his hospital bed.

Today, Ian was too weak even to speak, and Noora wondered if there was any hope for him. But while she waited and prayed for his recovery, she continued to make script changes on her own. What else was there for Noora to do? Except to keep mailing out the edited pages. Roz said the writers were pleased with what she had sent so far. Apparently, everyone assumed he was on vacation. No one suspected Mr. Cohen was in the hospital and that he was in no condition to keep his eyes open long enough to read anything.

More than two exhausting weeks had elapsed since Mr. Cohen's operation.

"Sitting morning and night, worrying, is unhealthy," Doris told Noora. "That's what *we're* all here for. Take a walk on the beach. Waikiki is a great diversion. You need a little sun and fresh air, Kelley."

"If something happens to him while I'm gone, I'll feel like I've abandoned him."

"We all know you would never do that. Here is my card. It's got my pager number. You can call me from wherever you are."

"Please don't misunderstand. It's not that I don't trust you, Doris. You and the staff here are doing a good job. And you're an angel."

"You are the angel, Kelley. Your father is lucky to have a daughter like you," the social worker said. "It's obvious he's proud of you."

"Thanks … Thank you." Noora turned and hastily made her way to the elevator, and punched the button down to the lobby. The doors opened. She was alone. "My father is not proud of me," she said to the mirrored elevator. "My father is *ashamed* of me."

CHAPTER 48
CHANCE ENCOUNTER

Michel and Zaffeera landed at the Honolulu airport in the early afternoon. As they made their way out of Gate 22, they were greeted by a chauffeur holding a sign:

"Mr. and Mrs. Amir"

Through the open-air walkway, the fragrance of plumeria flooded Michel with memories of his younger and happier days. He remembered the plumeria trees that grew in abundance in Alexandria, around King Farouk's gardens, where he had first met Noora with that bright smile, eyes like the Mediterranean seashores, golden bronze skin ... soft ... if he could just touch her. Once more. And her hair ... Lustrous brown. Silky ...

Maybe choosing Hawaii for his honeymoon was not a good idea. He had looked forward to visiting Honolulu. Most of all, he wanted to be on the other side of the world, completely away from anything that would remind him of his lost love. He had forgotten that Hawaii also had plumerias. He didn't know their fragrance would ignite his memory in such a way, the trade winds bringing him that same perfumed air, like the *tarrawah,* the sea breeze of Alexandria. Next year, he would have to venture out to Asian cities—Hong Kong—cement city. Great buildings. Shanghai. Bangkok, dense with incense and smog. In Hawaii, he should not think about Alexandria! He would focus on visiting the historical buildings—and the renovated hotel in Kahala where he and Zaffeera were scheduled to spend their honeymoon. But first, Michel had reserved a suite for two nights in the historical section of one of the oldest hotels along Waikiki's famous Kalakaua Boulevard.

A white limousine drove them to the Moana Surfrider at the end of Waikiki. Under the white column of the porte-cochère, as Michel and Zaffeera were greeted by two friendly valets, a beautiful Hawaiian maiden winked at Michel as she placed a lei of purple and white orchids over his head first, and another for Zaffeera.

Michel admired the tapestry and the early century's architectural style. "Look at that," he murmured almost to himself. "Interesting design. Embossed fleurs-de-lis on the façade, giving it a French regal look, yet keeping the original British tone of old Hawaii."

Later that day, as the sun began to set, casting a brilliant glow above the ocean, Michel sat with Zaffeera, to dine at the Verandah Restaurant. They were serenaded by the pianist, whose fingers danced across the keyboard, making the melody seem like a gentle waterfall.

"I think we should have a white grand piano for our new home," Michel said, watching the young pianist. "Do you play?" he asked Zaffeera.

"I used to. Unfortunately, I dropped piano lessons when I was fourteen. A white grand piano would be lovely," she murmured demurely. "Do you play, Michel?"

"Not very well. I'm a bit rusty."

Zaffeera smiled and lowered her eyes. He was making plans for their future. His words, "for our new home," sounded more melodious than the piano music.

She was hungry and turned to the buffet table. She didn't like the idea of having to serve herself. They had to stand and wait in line, holding their plates—as if they were beggars! *How utterly repulsive,* Zaffeera thought. She turned to Michel. He was now gawking at walls and ceilings—not looking at her.

After they had made love in Los Angeles, he had been polite toward her, but during the entire five-and-a-half-hour flight, Zaffeera recalled, he had not even looked into her eyes. He never complimented her on the long, flowing navy blue dress with delicate little flowers that she had ordered from Paris. The fitted dress actually gave her a slim line. It cost more than a thousand dollars and was worth the price. Her navy blue high-heeled Bali shoes gave her height and made her feel even slimmer. *Stand up straight when you walk,* she reminded herself every minute. She had felt like a model walking down a ramp. Her lustrous dark brown hair fell down to her shoulders, thanks to the best products available. She had spent half a day in a Beverly Hills salon just the day before, while Michel was busy sketching ugly old buildings in the dreary parts of downtown Los Angeles.

All this high-maintenance work on her appearance was for him, so that he would love her. Instead, he was interested in buildings! But he did sleep in her arms the night before, and they *did* have their entire life together, she tried to console herself yet again.

***** ***** *****

Noora walked out of Straub Hospital and stood at the intersection. She eyed the colorful red-and-white awning of the restaurant across the street where she had had lunch with Roz. *It would be a nice change to eat something other than hospital food,* she thought. Perhaps eating at a restaurant by the beach would help her feel less tense.

When she left Mr. Cohen, he was resting with a vaporized oxygen mask.

She noticed a taxicab waiting at the curb and thought, *why not?*

At the Moana Surfrider's porte-cochère, a valet opened the cab door for Noora. She climbed the steps to the hotel and took in a deep breath of the sweet-scented open-air lobby. The fragrance of plumeria mixed with the ocean breeze reminded her again of Alexandria—and Michel. One of the valets looked at her and smiled. "Aloha! Welcome back."

"Thank you ... *Ma-halo,*" Noora replied. Did he recognize her? It had been two weeks, yet it had felt like a year since she had enjoyed dinner there with Mr. Cohen ... and that wonderful pianist.

Noora remembered the caesar salad she had with Mr. Cohen. Her mouth watered; but a small line had gathered at the front desk of the Verandah Restaurant, and every table appeared occupied.

She would wait for that same table, not far from the pianist.

"It'll be about a twenty-minute wait," the hostess said regretfully.

She checked her wrist—Mr. Cohen's watch was running slow. On her index finger, she wore his wedding ring. She had made it tighter with a thick piece of adhesive tape—keeping it for her employer while he was in the hospital.

"Is there a public phone nearby?"

"If it's a local call, you can use this one." The gracious hostess pointed to the white phone next to her.

"Thank you."

Noora began to dial. She would have to make sure and say she was Miss Kelley Cohen, Mr. Cohen's daughter. She could have said Mrs. Kelley Karlton, she had married a Karlton, but her maiden name was Cohen. They knew at the hospital she wasn't married, but if the social worker asked, Noora was prepared to say she was divorced. That's why it was easier to say she was Miss Cohen. She should have been Mrs.…

"I didn't get your name," said the hostess.

"Amir," Noora said watching the phone, lost in her thoughts.

The hostess checked the appointment book.

Why did I say Amir? "My goodness," Noora said, quickly replacing the receiver in its cradle. "I'm sorry, I meant to say …"

"We do have you…" the hostess said, looking at the name written on her ledger.

She picked up a menu, ready to escort Noora to the Amir table.

"I'm so sorry. I meant to say Cohen … Cohen," she laughed nervously. "I made a mistake … I … was busy dialing …"

"Cohen? Oh, I thought you said …" the confused hostess said.

"Sorry. Last name's Cohen," she repeated definitely. "I don't mind waiting. I need to call my father. It's local; he's at Straub Hospital."

"Oh sure. Just dial nine first." The hostess turned her attention to the next waiting customer.

Noora looked away and ran a finger down the scar on the right side of her face. She was tired, hungry, flustered, and most of all, she was embarrassed. People were waiting, and she was taking her time, confusing the hostess. She hurried down the steps away from the verandah toward the open court under the banyan tree. What impelled her to say Amir? She probably needed nourishment—like a hearty bowl of chicken noodle soup and vegetables. *Fool Medammes*—fava beans and pita bread would've been better, but never mind. After dinner, she must get some rest. Fatigue and stress could play tricks on one's already fuzzy brain.

For years, she had enjoyed thinking of herself as "Mrs. Amir." She had written it in cursive and drawn flowers around it while doodling on her school notebooks—but that was a lifetime ago, and she had to focus on the present!

Every table under the banyan tree was occupied. Noora decided to return to the lobby area. Passing the elevator doors with art deco motif, she caught her reflection in the mirrors that framed the elevator doors. No makeup, dark circles under her eyes, she was a mess. She tucked loose strands of hair behind her ears. For the first time, she was glad to have light-colored eyes. With lighter strands of hair, her olive skin gave her a tanned appearance, and with the proper foundation, no one would guess she was from the Middle East. Perhaps she should streak her hair lighter ... then she might pass for an American—a California girl. One thing was for sure: With short blonde hair, she did not look like the old Noora.

Standing at the lobby entrance, the smell of savory dishes from the nearby buffet just beyond the potted palms wafted straight to her nostrils and her stomach growled, demanding food. She peered into the restaurant. She would wait ten minutes more and ask again for the same table where she had sat with Mr. Cohen.

But the whiff of food was beckoning—and that wonderful piano music she could hear from the lobby made the ambiance feel heavenly. Yet something felt wrong. She couldn't figure out what. Perhaps she was still uneasy about having said "Amir."

She decided to head back to the restaurant and take the first available table. She walked back to the polite hostess, who informed her that a table would be ready for her in just about ten minutes. To keep her mind off food, Noora stopped and admired Tiffany's exquisite window dressing. She felt as if eyes were bearing down at her. She shuddered, remembering the dreadful man with the frightening eyes and the bushy black mustache who chased her in Alexandria. There was no way he would know she was in Hawaii!

Michel stood by the buffet table, perusing the trays of Japanese dishes, and the colorful variety of international specialties. He stopped in front of a huge bowl of caesar salad. As he began to pile his plate, he looked up and saw a young woman in a yellow dress walking beyond the partition of potted palms that separated the lobby from the restaurant. He craned his neck to get a better look. The attractive young woman was far from view now, but he had caught a quick glance—a glimpse of her profile and the way she walked.

Standing behind Michel, Zaffeera wondered what on earth he was trying to see that would nearly cause him whiplash. She followed her husband's gaze and also caught the girl's figure, just as she disappeared to the right, down the hall.

This time, it was not architecture that Michel was watching. It was a woman! Something hissed inside her, like a gush of boiling lava about to erupt—*How dare you look at anyone but me! You're a married man. You should be ashamed!* Zaffeera wanted to shout. She felt a sudden need to grab his face with her two hands and run her nails down his cheeks until he bled. He was looking at another woman—on their honeymoon!

Michel returned to their table without even waiting for her. He seemed totally preoccupied. She loaded her plate with a mound of lettuce. That was all she would eat.

Returning to his table, Michel gazed absently at the ocean and the colorful catamarans gliding back to shore. He was thinking about the girl beyond the palms, beyond his reach. A profile though barely glimpsed. That same regal walk. That ballerina back. That slight wiggle, even. And the base of her neck. Like Noora's when she had her hair up in a chignon. The girl he couldn't see had very short hair —Noora would never have cut hers, and that girl had lighter hair. They say when you often think of someone, you think you see them everywhere.

You are married now, he reminded himself. *God, what have I done?!*

A waiter asked him something.

"I beg your pardon?"

"Would you care for a drink?"

"Straight vodka," Michel said. "Thank you."

Zaffeera arrived at the table. The waiter helped her to her seat. She gave Michel a reproachful glance.

"Would you like some wine?" Michel asked, hiding his face behind the long wine list.

"No, thank you. I'd like a Coke with a slice of lime, please," she said to the waiter. She studied her husband. He seemed off in some world of his own. A world that excluded her. And he was drinking. *A true Muslim does not touch alcohol. He spent too much time in France, drinking too much wine, no doubt! What else did he do in his spare time?* Zaffeera wondered, feeling a painful stab of jealousy.

Ten long, silent minutes later, Zaffeera excused herself and headed to the ladies' room. At least Michel had politely risen when she stood up. She walked straight with a slight sway, just in case he was watching.

They had made love twice. Twice! She pushed open the door to the restrooms. The second time they had sex was better. *I must be patient. He just needs practice, lots of it.* She entered one of the bathroom stalls.

Around the corner from the hotel lobby, inside Tiffany's, Noora leaned against the glass case and admired the display of perfumes. A saleslady showed her the new fragrances for men and women, explaining which ones had a "gift with purchase." But Noora was not listening. She wanted to return to the restaurant, eat, be lulled by the piano music, watch the ocean. Had ten minutes elapsed?

Noora stood at the restaurant entrance.

"We have a table available right here." The hostess pointed to a table near the buffet, in a corner by a palm tree.

Nice and private, Noora thought. "Thank you," she said.

"It'll be just a minute; they're setting it," the hostess said.

"Thank you. Where's the ladies' room, please?"

Noora entered the powder room and caught her reflection on the floor-to-ceiling mirror on the wall facing the entrance. She noticed her wrinkled dress. She had slept in it. Luckily, she did not need to impress anyone.

Noora looked for an empty stall. From her cubicle, she could see the person's feet in the stall next to hers. *Pretty pumps,* Noora thought. *Is there a Bally shoe store in Honolulu?* Noora could no longer afford such luxurious footwear—that was long ago, she thought in Arabic. While sitting on the toilet, Noora bent a bit more to see the shoes better. Didn't she once have a pair like those? The shoes weren't Bally. They were

Ferragamo. Definitely. Those had much higher heels than the ones she used to have. Perhaps she should ask the girl. Would it be impolite if she inquired?

Noora unlocked her door and headed to the basin. As she washed her hands, she listened to the piano music that wafted in through hidden speakers. Drying her hands, she removed the wet adhesive tape she had wound around Mr. Cohen's ring and wiped the band clean. She noticed there was an inscription inside his wedding band. She was not going to read it; it was his personal property, and he trusted her with it. He must have loved the woman he called Bevvy very much. Perhaps she and Ian didn't have anything in common, but one thing was for sure: They had both lost a loved one. Tears welling in her eyes, she slipped the ring on her middle finger, and inserted a small dry piece of tissue paper. *I must stop feeling sorry for myself,* she thought.

The toilet flushed again. If she didn't get back out there, the hostess might give her table away. She would wait a little longer, hoping the girl with the pretty shoes—the pretty, expensive shoes—would come out of that stall. Never mind, she could never afford them anyway.

Roz said she would call her this evening. Noora was to fax more changes. This time, she had even risked changing some of the dialogue. The hostess would probably prefer to give that table to two people instead of just one. It was time to return to the hospital before Ian started calling for her.

Zaffeera opened the door to her stall. In that instant, and from the corner of her eye, she glimpsed at a familiar-looking back and part of a profile, as a girl in a yellow dress left the ladies' room, closing the door behind her. *Was that the same girl Michel had been staring at?*

Zaffeera approached the sink and stared at the mirror.

No. It could not be. She looked at the exit door then turned back to the sink, turning on the faucet at full force, splashing water on her face several times.

Now look what you've done, you idiot! She would have to re-apply eyeliner and pat some heavy foundation under her eyes. The eyeliner, she had realized too late, was not waterproof, and with the humidity, her eyes started to look as if she had dark circles!

She carefully patted her face with one of the cloth towels from the wicker basket on the counter. Would the vision of Noora keep haunting her forever?

She continued to stare at her reflection in the mirror. *Everyplace we go, it's like the ghost of Noora is following … May Allah curse her soul!* Zaffeera thought, her eyes glaring furiously at her reflection.

She took a deep breath and slowly exhaled. *I must relax.*

I must already be pregnant!

She smiled. *So what if he looks at another woman? I'm the one who sleeps with him. Every night—for the rest of his life! Wait until I give him a son. He will surely adore me.*

Leaning his chair back against the column, Michel gazed at the ocean. A waiter placed a glass of wine on the table.

"Thank you," he said, looking up. From the corner of his eye, he caught the girl's lean figure just as she was gliding through the restaurant and out to the hostess's desk. He looked in shock at the familiar figure. The young woman's back was to him. She stopped and talked to the hostess. Other people waiting for a table barred his view for a moment. If she would only turn a bit so he could see her. He had to go after her and see her up close.

He jumped to his feet and weaved his way through diners going to and from the buffet tables. He had to see that girl's face.

He bumped into Zaffeera as she was coming out of the ladies' room. Michel and Zaffeera stared at each other, speechless. He did not dare even move his eyes in the direction where the young woman had been standing.

"I … I was just looking for the men's room," he managed to say, feeling the blood rush to his face.

Noora walked out to the lobby and stood for a brief moment under the porte-cochère.

"Are you waiting for your car, Miss?" one of the valets asked.

"No … but thank you," Noora said.

"Would you like me to call a taxi?"

"No, thank you. I … Well, I'm going to walk." She turned left and headed for the Royal Hawaiian shopping center. There, she found a hot dog stand, and decided, *why not?* She'd never had an American hot dog before. With tomatoes and relish, it tasted pretty good, actually. But she couldn't finish it.

She spotted a bookstore nearby and went inside.

"Would you happen to have anything on screenwriting?" she asked the clerk, who showed her to the back of the store. "We don't get much call for these," he said, "but ... here we are." He pulled out two books from the shelf.

Screenwriting for Those Too Shy to Ask, and *Screenwriters and Other Strangers,* Noora read.

"Silly titles, aren't they?" the clerk said.

"I guess I'll buy the silly things."

Returning to the hospital with her new books, Noora heard Mr. Cohen's voice the moment she set foot out of the elevator. "Water! Morons! Water is the source of life!" She ran to quiet him down, and the second he spotted her, she shouted. "Where ya been? They're tryin' a kill me!"

He lifted his head and looked at Noora with bulgy, watery eyes. His stomach still looked swollen. His teeth were soaking in a plastic cup nearby. He looked like one of the poor beggars she had seen in a souq, only his skin was a shade too white.

"Where the hell were you?"

I should never have left the hospital, Noora thought, feeling guilty.

A nurse appeared.

"Where is Doctor Ferguson?" Noora asked, while she held Mr. Cohen's hand.

"He'll be back tomorrow morning."

"Pain does not wait until tomorrow morning!" Noora heard herself say.

The young nurse ran out of the room. Moments later, Doris came rushing in.

"I'm sorry, but your father can't have anything more than a little shaved ice for now," the social worker explained, apparently a little out of breath. "The doctor ordered that we only give him a little ice water from time to time, and nothing more."

"Well, can I give him the shaved ice or a little ice water every now and then, or do I have to wait for a nurse to do it?"

"No you can. But please again, not too much until we hear from the doctor."

As soon as they were left alone in his room, Mr. Cohen whispered with darting eyes, "I'll give you all my money. I'll give you the lead in *Lord of Doom,* I'll sign the contract now. If you could just bring me a large glass of ice water."

"Mr. Cohen, please. We're going to get you well again. I promise you."

She was determined to get Mr. Cohen to accept the shaved ice in small spoonfuls to keep his furious thirst quenched, even if she had to keep at it all night, and hopefully his bloated digestive tract would start functioning on its own.

Noora was sitting exhausted in her chair when Doctor Ferguson arrived shortly after eight the next morning. He wore a white shirt with thin blue stripes, and gray trousers. He was tall and his eyes were chocolate brown. For some absurd reason, Noora felt like hugging him.

The doctor was talking, but she could not concentrate. She averted her eyes, trying to listen to his words. He said something about "a central line that would nourish ... bypassing the digestive system ... Hyper-elementation." *Or was it hyper-alimentation? Whatever that meant.*

Words bounced into her exhausted brain, medical words she did not know. *Pay attention, Noora.* "I'll try to convince my father ..." she heard herself say. The room began to spin.

Noora found herself on the couch by the elevators; the doctor, along with a couple of nurses, were making her smell something strong.

"She'll be all right," Noora heard the doctor say.

"I'm ... fine, really," Noora explained, embarrassed. She must have fainted. One of the nurses sat next to her, holding her hand. Another gave her a glass of water, which she sipped. "I'll be all right, really," she assured them.

"Don't worry, Miss Cohen. These things take time," the doctor said.

"I'm sorry," she blushed, "I'm so sorry."

"I suggest you go home and get yourself some rest, all right?"

She nodded.

"I'll be back tomorrow," Dr. Ferguson said, stepping into the waiting elevator.

She watched as the elevator doors closed and took him out of view. *But I have no home, don't you understand?*

Noora walked down the stairs and out of the hospital, crossing the street to the small park shaded by an enormous monkey pod tree. *So beautiful,* she thought, sitting down under one of its wide, protruding branches. She leaned back against the trunk, closing her eyes. She remembered what Dweezoul had told her: *Sit under a tree... It will bring you peace and energy.* She needed every ounce of energy. Some peace would sure help too.

"Should I have stayed in the desert? At the wonderful village?" Noora asked a white pigeon that ventured close to her feet.

Perhaps Mr. Cohen would have had a heart attack ... and perhaps Annette would not have met Docteur Alain ... She had to trust that there was a reason, a purpose behind everything that happened to her, she thought as she watched the pigeon take flight, its wings flapping so gracefully, white feathers against the blue sky. *So pretty. So free.* She dozed off.

She awoke feeling she must have slept a long time. She actually felt refreshed. Walking back to the hospital, she spotted a little health food store.

Night had fallen as Noora stood by Mr. Cohen's bedside, applying a poultice of fragrant herbs on his forehead. She massaged his arms and hands, humming the same hymn that Um Faheema had sung to her.

A tear rolled down the side of his eye, to his temple and onto the pillow. "I love you, little girl," Ian Cohen whispered, looking up at Noora with eyes filled with gratitude.

"I love you too, Mr. Cohen," Noora murmured.

Two days later, Noora finally had a fax machine. Doris helped Noora set it up in the small conference room near Mr. Cohen, and Noora called Roz, who wasted no time faxing script pages for Mr. Cohen to edit and approve.

"If anyone at the studio finds out about Mr. Cohen, we're deep in elephant manure," Roz wrote Noora in her memo. "Rumor has it he is in Haiti with a very young woman. I don't know where they got the Haiti part, when last week it was Hawaii. It's like a broken telephone around here. Of course, working for Mr. Cohen means total confidentiality.

Fortunately, the writers are satisfied with the recent changes you mailed . . ."

They are? Noora couldn't believe it.

"Not that they have a choice in the matter. Mr. Cohen's words are as good as gold."

Noora was astonished. *If they knew I was the one who made the changes without his approval, God knows what they would do.*

"Keep up the good work, Ms. Karlton," Roz concluded in her memo to Noora.

What did Roz mean? Did she suspect Noora was the one making the changes?

CHAPTER 49
SAVING SHAMSAH

Farid Fendil decided to pick up his daughter from school in the white Rolls-Royce Corniche convertible. He arrived fifteen minutes early, before the long line of Mercedes four-by-fours and SUVs queued to pick up the other children.

A sharp bell rang out. Four women, clad in long black dresses and sleeves, with their heads covered by the traditional veil, opened the tall black wrought iron doors, and the little girls walked out in a procession, two by two. Farid Fendil was surprised. The children used to burst out of those doors chattering and giggling as they ran to their parents' cars or chauffeured limousines. Now there was no talking. It had been a long time since he picked up his daughter from the private elementary school, Farid realized.

He could not help but wonder, was the change due to the sheik's Men of Faith, Honor and Justice? They were everywhere these days—enforcing old traditions and religious observance in the town, which had once followed a more westernized lifestyle.

He spotted Shamsah walking outside and squinting in the sun, probably searching for Abdo, her usual ride. At the sight of her father, the surprised Shamsah screamed with delight, then held her hand to her mouth.

Farid Fendil climbed out of his Rolls. Paying no attention to the surprised teachers, who obviously did not expect to see him there, he lifted his little girl by her waist and turned her around. He hugged her and kissed her cheek.

"What's the occasion, *Abuya?*" Shamsah asked her father. "Is everything okay? Is Abdo ill today?"

"No, Abdo is fine," he said, opening the door for his daughter.

She hopped in the car, and with her father's help, she freed her arms from the straps of her backpack. "Thank you, Father. But ... is everything all right?"

"Yes, of course," Farid said, putting Shamsah's backpack in the back seat.

"Aren't you working today, *Abuya?*"

"Am I not allowed to spend a little quality time with my own daughter?" Farid said with a smile and a wink.

After a ten-minute drive, he pulled up in front of the posh Triano outdoor French café.

"Father! This is wonderful!" Shamsah squealed as they were shown to a table under an umbrella.

"They just opened this restaurant. They used to be very popular in Alexandria, long, long before you were born. I have tried to get them to open here for five years. They just relocated, and I wanted us to be the first to try their specialty."

"You are the best in all the world!"

"I am going to see to it that I am a good father," he said, forcing a smile.

"And Mother, does she know I am here with you?"

"Mother does not need to know everything. They have your favorite chocolate éclair," he said. "They have fondants, you remember, like the ones in Paris? And petits fours. Oh my, they will have to roll us out of here," he chuckled, burying his face in the tall menu.

Inside the Fendil mansion, Yasmina went to the kitchen and out to the courtyard to greet Shamsah, who was expected home from school at the usual afternoon time. She found Abdo polishing yet another one of her husband's cars—a fire-engine-red Lamborghini Countach. Abdo had told her that *Abu* Farid purchased the sports car, which just arrived from Italy. But Yasmina couldn't care less about the car. She was puzzled.

"Where is Shamsah?"

"*Abu* Farid picked her up from school today. He wanted to surprise her," Abdo said joyously.

"Whaaaat?! And you let him because you had to polish his new car? You let him pick her up without telling me?!"

Abdo was surprised by her sudden outburst. He thought Yasmina would be happy that her husband offered to fetch his daughter from school and spend a little time with her. He had not expected her angry reaction.

"I'm so sorry," he said, looking abashed. "I am sure they'll be back soon," he added, glancing at his watch.

"Take me to the school right away!" she screamed, spotting the regular family white stretch limo. Abdo ran after Yasmina to open the door for her.

When the Fendil limousine arrived at Shamsah's school, all the children had been picked up, and the campus was deserted. Yasmina ran inside the school.

Abdo had never seen her in such a hysterical state. He began to sweat, and visions of the ordeal with Nageeb flashed through his mind. His stomach felt queasy.

Yasmina burst out of the front doors of the school, followed by two seriously worried teachers. They turned paler as Yasmina yelled louder.

"But Mrs. Fendil, it was her own father who picked her up, not a stranger ..."

"Abdo was supposed to pick her up and no one else! Don't you people follow instructions?"

Inside the limo, with the windows closed so that Yasmina's hysterical cries could not be heard, Abdo punched in Farid's cellular number.

"Sorry to disturb you," Abdo said to Farid, who answered his cell phone after the second ring. "Mrs. Yasmina would like to know if Shamsah is with you," he said rapidly, keeping his voice down. Listening to the receiver, Abdo nodded. "Mrs. Yasmina asked because there is a piano lesson she has to attend this afternoon ..." He listened, then smiled. "Thank you, I will tell her," he said, then closed the flap of his cell phone, just as Yasmina was running back to the car. Finding the doors locked, she became irate. Abdo pressed the unlock button and jumped out of the car to open the back door, but Yasmina climbed in the passenger seat. "Why did you lock the doors?! Why? What is going on? Oh my God!" she yelled, slapping her own face and banging at the dashboard with both fists. "Oh my God!" she screamed as Abdo ran to climb behind the wheel. Within seconds, he was speeding down the boulevard.

At the entrance to Triano's sidewalk café, with its bright blue-and-white awning, a limousine pulled to the curb in front of Farid's shady table. Clad in a gray western suit and red tie with the golden MOFHAJ emblem, a chauffeur jumped out of the car and ran to open the passenger door. Sheik Abdullah Kharoub proudly emerged, with his usual sense of pride, and in his traditional white *gallabeya* and headdress. He walked straight to Farid, while his men stood by the car.

Farid saw the sheik coming and frowned.

"We are pleased to see you and glad you kept your appointment," the sheik said.

"It is my pleasure to see you, Sheik Abdullah," Farid said. He rose and gave the man a kiss on both cheeks.

"It appears we have a difficult time keeping an appointment with you lately, Mr. Fendil," he said.

Farid returned to his chair, next to his daughter, but waited for the sheik to sit first. "I have been busy with the construction of the resort at Sharm El Sheikh, as you might imagine."

"Of course. I hear positive reports, *hamdallah*."

"*Hamdallah*, praise to God, it is coming along. But there is so much work yet to be done."

"Yes," the sheik nodded. "Of course. *Hamdallah*." He motioned to one of his men and a chair was pulled up next to Farid.

Without looking at Shamsah, the sheik continued to address himself to Farid.

A *gallabeya*-clad waiter rushed in and brought a demitasse of hot Turkish coffee and a tall glass of ice water on an ornate silver plate, then disappeared.

"If there is any uncertainty, due to the fact that you have postponed your appointments with us on several previous occasions, let me assure you, my first wife is quite good and experienced in the matter. The procedure, performed by herself, has been known to be painless. And quite successful, praise be to Allah. There is never to be a moment of concern. Allah is there to watch over the protection of our children, and the safety of your daughter is ours as well. We are looking forward to this initiation, God willing," he said with authority, even though his eyes were now blinking rapidly and he did not once look Farid Fendil in the eye. "It is a joyous occasion for the women. Of course, a relief for us, and without a doubt, an honor for your daughter's future husband."

"Of course," Farid nodded, straightening in his chair.

"I have to go on an extended trip soon," the sheik said. "I trust, as God wills, that it will be done upon my return."

Shamsah leaned over to look at the sheik and his entourage. "Are you talking about me, Father?" she asked with a degree of concern in her voice.

Farid squeezed her hand then patted it in a comforting manner. "Please. Enjoy your éclair, *ya benti anah*." He turned to the sheik. "I have news, Sheik Abdullah," he said, inching closer to the sheik's ear to make sure Shamsah would not hear what he was about to say. "My daughter has already been circumcised."

The sheik immediately stiffened and looked straight into Farid's eyes. "What do you mean?"

"It has already been done."

"*Done?*"

"Yes."

"And when might that have been?"

"When she was a little over a week old," Farid replied matter-of-factly.

The sheik appeared surprised, and in fact angry.

"It has been an automatic procedure for our newborn daughters," Farid said, looking steadily into the sheik's eyes.

"What do you mean, Mr. Fendil?" He straightened. "At birth?"

"Not at birth. Ten days after. In our family, it is done the same time they have their ears pierced."

The sheik leaned forward and glanced over at Shamsah, who wore tiny gold earrings with the traditional turquoise stone. "Who performs such a ceremony?! And I don't mean the piercing of the ears," he said, glaring sharply at Farid Fendil.

"My wife's mother, as I told you. Our midwife," Farid Fendil said. "The respected Madame Sultana, may Allah bless her soul, and may she rest in peace. My mother-in-law was the renowned midwife of her time."

"Perhaps as a midwife only. I was never informed otherwise."

Suddenly, Farid Fendil didn't care whether the sheik believed him or not. "She was actually an authority in the field of clitoridectomy," he said, nodding with a slight smile, "if you'll pardon my use of the medical term."

The sheik's face turned red. "I see," he said, putting a hand on the table and rising from his chair.

Don't you wish you could see, you filthy old man, ibn el kalb. *Hyppocrite.* Farid Fendil politely brought his palms together and rested his hands on his lap. "May your voyage be a good one and in good health, *inshallah.*" He made no attempt to rise or kiss the sheik's hand.

The sheik grunted, cleared some phlegm from his throat, and marched back to his waiting limousine.

"They make the best chocolate-covered marzipan," Farid said as soon as he heard the sheik's limousine drive away. He took a deep breath. "You know, besides éclairs, Noora loved chocolate-covered marzipans."

Shamsah looked shocked, and paled.

"What's wrong?"

"Mother said we should never mention her name in your presence."

"Why?"

"I'm sorry, Father. I don't know ..."

"It's all right to talk to each other about what we feel."

"I am not sure why we could not mention her name. I think because ... because it would bring ... grief."

"Why don't we order some chocolate-covered marzipan in honor of your sister ..."

"Yes," Shamsah said, smiling now. "Noora loved chocolate-covered marzipan. Thank you, Father ..." A frown returned on the child's face. "What did these men want, Father?"

"Business," Farid answered with a shrug.

"I thought they wanted something from me, Father."

"No, nothing from you, *ya benti.* They just want from me."

Abdo's limousine arrived with a screeching halt in front of the restaurant. Yasmina stormed out of the car.

"Shamsah! My baby. *Wa'a layah. Ya Allah! Ya benti anah!* It has befallen upon me. Oh God, my daughter!" She grabbed Shamsah, kissing her all over her head and crying "Thank God!" She threw her husband a hateful stare while pulling her daughter closer to her. She covered her daughter's head with her hand and pulled her back to the waiting car.

"But Mother, Father and I were having a nice conversation. I haven't finished my dessert. They're bringing us chocolate …"

"We have better pastries at home," she said with clenched teeth. Wrapping her arms around her child, she shielded Shamsah from any possible harm.

Abdo stood by the limo, looking at Farid. He shrugged his shoulders. "I'm sorry … I didn't know what to do," he said, silently articulating each word so that *Abu* Farid could hopefully understand him.

Farid nodded. "It's all right," he said.

Abdo nodded politely and climbed back in the car, leaving Farid alone to watch his family drive off.

Late that night, Abdo tapped at Farid's door.

"I'm sorry. Forgive me for coming to you at this late hour. But I am left with much confusion … I need to ask your permission," Abdo said.

"Come in," Farid said. He was sitting up in bed, reading a passage from the Koran, his bedside lamp burning next to him.

"Mrs. Fendil wants me to accompany her as a family member …" Abdo said.

"Where?"

"Well, I do not wish it, but she wants me to travel with her … She needs a man as an escort on her trip … with the children …"

"Where, Abdo?"

"Switzerland. She did not want me to tell you, but …"

"It's all right, Abdo."

"I'm so sorry. She says the best schools are there for Shamsah. And Kettayef. I could not leave without telling you," he said sadly.

Farid put the heavy book down on the nightstand. Sitting at the edge of his bed, he hung his head low, and remained in that position for a long time.

"Is there anything you would like me to do?" a very uncomfortable Abdo asked.

Farid Fendil slowly looked up at Abdo. "Do whatever Mrs. Fendil wants. They do have better schools for Kettayef. And it is safe there ... for Shamsah," he said. Then he whispered, almost to himself. "There, she should be safe."

"I beg your pardon?"

"Just be with them, always."

"I will never leave them; you have my word of honor," he replied. As Abdo turned to leave, Farid Fendil called him.

"Yes?" Abdo stopped at the door.

"Thank you, my son." He rose and shuffled over to Abdo, embracing him and kissing him goodbye, twice on each cheek.

CHAPTER 50
ANNETTE'S LETTER

"Look, you've got mail," Noora said, setting down the envelopes sent by Sam, Ian Cohen's butler.

He pushed the mail away, sending a few envelopes to the floor. "Get me outta here!"

He hated rehab and seemed to put all his energy into complaining, instead of getting well. But the physical therapists said he was progressing. However, he was still forgetful, and at times, he seemed confused. The doctors assured Noora that it was par for the course.

As she picked up the mail from the floor, she noticed a light blue envelope with French stamps. *It's for me!*

When a male nurse convinced Mr. Cohen to take a little walk down the hall, Noora was finally able to open the letter.

"It's from Annette!" she said out loud to no one, her heart bursting with excitement as she ripped open the envelope. It was a handwritten letter on pretty blue-and-white paper.

"*Ma très chère amie,* I am infinitely sorry for not having written for such a long time. A thousand thanks for your kind letters, and for the beautiful card from Hawaii!"

Noora's eyes filled with tears as she slowly sank to the edge of a plastic chair in front of the window.

"*Docteur* Alain opened a new clinic in Juan les Pains, and I am helping him," Annette wrote. "Alain has proposed. You must see the diamond ring he gave me. We plan to marry in six months. I would like you to be my maid of honor ..."

The Honolulu sun filtered through the tall window behind Noora, warming her back. She remembered the first time she met Annette. That dreadful day, when Noora had been washed on the beach.

"My poor dear, we can fry an egg on your back!" Annette's sing-song Parisian words rang in Noora's ears.

So much had happened since. Noora held Annette's letter to her heart. "Thank you, God," she whispered and ran out of the room, down the hallway, in search of the phone.

Turning the hallway corner, she heard Ian returning to his room from physical therapy. "Get me out of this Popsicle joint or let me croak!" he shouted. "Kelley? KELLEY?! Where the hell is she!"

This time, he would just have to wait, Noora thought. She had to call France.

"Mr. Cohen?" Noora asked that night, while Ian miserably tried to swallow a tablespoon of tomato soup.

"That soup's cold! We're not in Frogsville, and I sure as hell didn't order Vichyssoise!"

"How would you like to go home?"

"Home? Yeah, right. Quacks won't release me. They say they have to see improvement. Fuck 'em!" He pushed his food tray away.

"Remember the doctor who came to see you at the hotel in France? My friend, Doctor Alain Demiel?" Noora asked, trying to disregard his anger and putting on a cheerful voice.

"Spare me the gory details."

"What do you mean, Mr. Cohen?"

"You're gonna run off and marry him."

"Oh, no no, nothing like that. I called him and asked for his advice. I hope you don't mind, but he is a dear friend of my friend."

"Friend of a friend," he murmured, letting himself fall back on his pillow, and closing his eyes. "Very encouraging."

"Doctor Alain Demiel spoke to your doctor on the phone," she said, approaching his bed. "They agree that you would be better off in your own home than in the hospital ... *If* you have someone to care for you."

"No shit," he whispered, his eyes still closed.

"I should like to remain in your employ. Sam will be flying in to Honolulu. That is, if it's all right with you ..."

Ian popped his eyes open. "You called Sam too?"

"I ... I hoped you wouldn't mind. Sam will be here to help you, and ..."

"Just promise you won't run back to Frogsville."

"What if I promise to return you to your Bel Air home and be your caregiver?"

* * * * *   * * * * *   * * * * *

Less than four months after his quadruple bypass surgery, Ian Cohen had to admit he felt better than he had in the past few years. He no longer feared the possibility of a stroke, or worse yet, that he would be paralyzed and would have no one to care for him. Everyone in Hollywood knew that no matter how popular the producer, you were "as good as your last picture." And if you were the unfortunate one stricken by a serious ailment, your business was shot to hell.

It was uncanny how Kelley Karlton had popped into his life. At the right time, too. Like some angel, only he never would have thought that she would come to his rescue in the form of a French hotel chambermaid. Not that he ever believed in any of that psychic woo-woo stuff, and the word "spiritual" always annoyed him, but he actually prayed for someone he could trust to come to his needs. Through some kind of something he could not explain, the girl must have been sent to him by Bevvy.

He liked having Kelley around, especially when he came home in the evening, grouchy as hell. She always greeted him with a smile, never bitching, perfectly happy to have spent the entire day at his mansion, reading the scripts and manuscripts he gave her, or working in the garden, planting or tending to his roses. She had a thing about roses ... especially the peach-colored ones like they had in the South of France.

What he really liked most was that no one at the studio could figure out their relationship, and he was aware there was juicy gossip. He always liked keeping his personal life a mystery—especially his relationship with Kelley Karlton—and above all, a mystery when it came to his stepson. Always envious and jealous about anything Ian did, whether business or personal, Kenni was constantly trying to figure out what Ian was doing with such a young chick. Not that Kelley Karlton was either provocative or as glamorous as the parade of hopefuls at the studio; but from the plain clothes she wore to the way she carried herself, she still had a certain style and class, and she didn't suck up to anybody. Best of all, Kelley did not give a flying crap about Kennil-worthless.

Ian chuckled at the thought of how his stepson tried to make a pass at her at one of the recent Hollywood parties he had to attend one Sunday evening. He had brought Kelley as his guest. He was going to make a quick appearance, shake hands, and split. But their short appearance was long enough for Kenni to try something stupid.

"Is he getting fresh?" Ian had asked her after she walked away from Kenni and headed to the dessert table.

Kelley had smiled confidently, saying, "Mr. Cohen, I know how to handle myself."

Ian *wanted* Kenni to think she was his girlfriend. *Make the lazy bum think we're an item,* he thought.

"The desserts here suck," he whispered, quickly nudging Kelley toward the exit. "Tell me the Hamlet has better chocolate cakes."

"The Hamlet has better chocolate cakes," she said, smiling.

Ian hated the little hors d'oeuvres they served that invariably gave him heartburn, and he was itching to go back and dine at his habitual Sunday night hangout—and hide away in his cozy booth by the bar. He had missed that place, and he sure as hell did not miss those lame Hollywood parties where everyone wanted to be seen but no one really gave a shit about him.

Sitting across from Ian Cohen in the last booth of the restaurant, Noora toyed with her huge piece of chocolate cake on a plate large enough for four. "I need to return to France," she finally gathered the courage to say.

"You're not my prisoner. But uh ... if you want more money ... we can talk."

"Oh no, thank you ... It's not at all a matter of money. I would like to attend a wedding. And, since you don't really need an assistant ... or a caregiver now ..."

"Can't say that I blame you for leaving. I've been an asshole."

"Mr. Cohen, what I am trying to say is, I was asked to be maid of honor at my best friend's wedding."

He continued to chew, keeping his eyes on his plate. He looked up and gave her an "I don't believe you" look. "My best friend's wedding, huh?" He chuckled. "Haven't we heard that title before?" He poured more ketchup on his plateful of fries. He became serious and looked her in the eye. "I wish you'd stay."

"I didn't think you needed me anymore," she said.

"I need you even more."

"To nag you about nutrition?" she teased. "Certainly not."

"That don't bother me," he said, taking a big bite out of his rare burger.

"I ... I'm not sure I can continue being of service."

He reached for the salt shaker and caught her serious look. "See? Like now. You remind me about stuff that's bad for me." He put down the salt and sprinkled pepper on his fries. "You're also not afraid to tell me if a script sucks. You're a good story analyst."

Noora felt herself blushing. "Really?" She was never sure whether he liked her comments about the scripts—he argued and grumbled often enough.

"Yeah. Really."

They sat eating in silence until Noora finally raised enough courage to speak. "I have a confession to make."

"There's a Catholic church down on Santa Monica by the Beverly Hills flats."

"There is something I would like to tell you," she said seriously.

He didn't respond.

"The passport I came with ..."

"I know," he said, not looking up.

"I beg your pardon?"

"It's your friend's," he said, stuffing his mouth with fries. He took a big gulp of beer and wiped his mouth with a paper napkin. "I needed you to come back with me ASAP." He raised an empty bottle of beer to a passing waitress. "Another beer, Marj."

"Right away, Mr. Cohen," the waitress said, taking the empty beer bottle on her way to the bar.

"At that time, there was no time for legalities when I was about to kick the bucket," he said.

Noora stared at her dessert. *He knew all along! What else did he know? Would he have cared if he knew I was an Arab—a Muslim, no less?* She was certain he did not know her origins. If he did, he would stop referring to the Arab people as "ragheads" or "camel-jockeys" in front of her.

"So, when's that wedding?" he asked.

Air France flew Noora back to Paris. Nervously holding her passport at the arrival gate of Roissy Airport, Noora felt weak, and her hands trembled as she waited her turn at Customs. She had dyed her short blonde hair back to brown to match Annette's passport picture. She wore brown contact lenses. With a dark pencil, she had reshaped the contour of her lips to match Annette's. When her turn finally came, she could barely breathe—surely she would get caught this time. The official opened the passport and looked at her briefly. The thump of his stamp on the passport resounded in every nerve of her body. Her heart skipped a beat. She grabbed her carry-on and ran out to the baggage claim.

Noora was to meet with an attorney in Paris the next morning to arrange for "Kelley Karlton" to have her own passport—finally! How much did that cost Ian Cohen—and wasn't he running a major risk?

"Don't ask questions," Ian had warned her. "Just sign the documents that show you were born in Frogsville. You'll get yourself a passport so you can fly back with your own name. The only thing I ask of you is that you don't make me look like a horse's ass."

Noora wasn't sure she understood what he meant. But she knew this: She would never betray his trust. At least as far as Kelley Karlton was concerned.

"Just get back here as soon as you can."

Did he think she would run away with her new passport and he would never see her again? The only way she would prove him wrong was to simply return to Los Angeles. And she would immediately send a postcard telling him she had arrived in France and confirming her return date. No, she would not disappoint him.

*****   *****   *****

On a sunny Riviera afternoon, in a rose-filled outdoor restaurant called Le Beau Mirage, a rabbi chanted a Hebrew prayer. Beneath a white gazebo festooned with pink rosettes and lilies of the valley, Noora stood next to Annette, who looked radiant in a white-laced gown. Family and guests watched with anticipation as *Docteur* Alain Demiel smashed a glass wrapped in a white linen napkin.

At the sound of broken glass, everyone clapped and shouted "*Mazel tov!*"

While a violinist played a tune from *Fiddler on the Roof,* Annette turned to her maid of honor and smiled gratefully with teary eyes.

There were more than a hundred guests, a few relatives, and close friends mostly from Alain's side, along with other doctors and their wives. But the one who captured Noora's attention was Ahna Morgenbesser, Annette's grandmother, who sat next to Noora during the dinner reception. The woman watched Noora intently. Every time Noora met her gaze, Ahna smiled.

Noora began to feel uncomfortable.

"Annette was right," the old lady said in a German-accented English.

"Sorry?"

"Annette was right. You are a very special young lady. I think she said you are a writer."

"A writer? No," Noora said with a little chuckle. "Not me. I just like to write. I'm not very good. I also like to read ... Novels and such." *What did Annette's grandmother mean?*

"I would like to tell you my story. After the wedding. Most people don't believe it, but I have a feeling you will."

Noora put her napkin on her lap. What was she supposed to say?

"We have much in common," Ahna Morgenbesser said.

"Really?" Noora took a sip of water. What could they possibly have in common? They were decades, cultures, and continents apart.

"You are a survivor."

She knows, Noora thought. *Oh my God, she knows I am an imposter.*

"My eyes are not so good anymore, but I can still see. In a different way. In a different way, you understand."

Turning to the woman, Noora nodded and forced a smile. A shiver ran through her body. It seemed as if Um Faheema was watching her, through the eyes of Ahna Morgenbesser. *C'est très bizarre,* Noora thought, *as the French would say, very weird.* She excused herself and headed to the ladies' room.

Inside one of the bathroom stalls, she allowed her tears to flow. Her emotions were getting the better of her. Why now? Well, she tried to rationalize, weddings are an emotional event, and hers was a dream taken away ... *Michel* ... More tears flowed, cascading down her cheeks. She patted her face with toilet paper. Her makeup was ruined. She waited for the other ladies to leave the bathroom. Once alone, Noora made it to the sink and splashed water on her face, patting it dry. *Breathe, Noora, breathe. Everything will be fine. For now.* She had to hurry back to the reception so that no one would suspect how she felt. She had capped her emotions so well; she no longer knew why she felt such pain in her heart. Luckily, she had a little foundation, lip liner, and eyeliner, which she applied, hoping no one would notice that she had cried. *But it was a wedding; doesn't everyone cry?* When she returned to her seat, the old woman had not moved from her chair.

"I hope to see you again, my pretty. *J'espère*. And I hope I will have the opportunity to spend some time with you," the woman said, taking Noora's hand. "Please come to Paris before going back to America."

"I can't. I have to return to the United States, where I am employed ... I have a job waiting ..."

"Yes, I understand. But do come for a visit. You can stay with me. I have plenty of room. I can still make the best *kuchen*," she said, glancing at Noora's untouched piece of cake.

"Thank you. Perhaps another time I'll visit. With Annette," she offered cheerfully, hoping to pacify the lady.

"My time in life is becoming short."

"Oh, perhaps not, one never knows ... I enjoyed meeting you, and I'm sure we will meet again." Noora smiled, grateful to see the other guests starting to bid farewell to the bride and groom.

CHAPTER 51
THE CURSE

Zaffeera threw her Chanel and Gucci shopping bags and Louis Vuitton tote on her bed. After a visit to the gynecologist, she had gone on a shopping marathon at the brand-new, four-story Al-Balladi mall.

"It's another girl!" she said bitterly.

Gamelia, who had remained her personal maid, hurried to unpack Zaffeera's purchases. She laid the new clothes on Zaffeera and Michel's king-size bed, the way she had been instructed, carefully cutting off the tags, laying each item aside for Zaffeera to give the order whether they needed washing or dry-cleaning. Zaffeera never wore anything she brought home from the store. Each garment had to be cleaned or washed before she would wear it.

"*Hamdallah!* And what a blessing it is, Miss Zaffeera," Gamelia offered politely, while carefully smoothing down and admiring one of the new silk blouses. Zaffeera whirled around and slapped Gamelia hard across the face.

"You idiot! It's a curse!" Zaffeera hissed.

Shocked by the sudden blow, Gamelia fell to her knees, lowered her head, and hid her face in her hands. "Forgive me ... forgive my stupidity, Miss Zaffeera," she implored. "I am nothing. Nothing."

"Don't call me Miss Zaffeera! I am Mrs.! Mrs. Amir, MRS. AMIR! Do you understand?!"

"Yes, Mrs. Amir, I beg your forgiveness Mrs. Amir, please, *Mrs. Amir,*" she pleaded, crouching closer to the floor, her arms protecting herself from another possible blow.

Zaffeera stormed to her bathroom suite and slammed the door behind her.

She had to give Michel a son, honor her family, and show the men of Al-Balladi, and all the affluent families her father knew, that the Amirs were giving birth to sons. She knew she had passed every other test. She was a model wife and a woman of high position in the eyes of Al-Balladi, volunteering in children's hospitals, and serving meals to the poor in nearby villages.

She always wore the most exquisite clothes, as if she were the wife of a dignitary, and her hair was always in place. In rural areas, she always covered her head with the proper headdress. She knew that Michel was impressed with her intelligence and sense of organization. She kept organized files for her husband while he was designing their new house. Since he continued to be fascinated with Frank Lloyd Wright, she found everything ever written on the architect. She even became an expert in feng shui, the Chinese art of creating harmony in the home—theirs and the ones he was commissioned to build. She often accompanied Michel to Los Angeles when he worked as consultant to other architects, builders, and real-estate developers—she was there for him, never complaining, making him feel like a king. She had to present him with a son. She would stop at nothing to give Michel a son!

Zaffeera stood fuming in front of her floor-to-ceiling mirror.

The twitching of her left eyelid began to throb faster. Her first abortion in Italy and the second in Paris had been easy. This one would have to be in Los Angeles. It should be easy to get rid of that female fetus secretly, in that immense, anonymous city.

Michel was due to leave for Los Angeles in a few days to oversee the construction of a new house in Bel Air, and she was proud of him. After all, wasn't Bel Air one of the wealthiest residential areas in Southern California? He had invited her to accompany him. During takeoff on the Concorde, she was going to announce that she was expecting. She had it all planned. Of course, she would not have told Michel she knew it was a boy—just give him the wonderful news that she was carrying his baby! Now everything was shot to hell.

Instead of reveling in his joy, she would be forced to sit and watch him read books and magazines through the long flight and pay no attention to her, as usual. Misfortune had fallen upon her once again.

When they finally landed in Los Angeles, Zaffeera gave a deep sigh of relief. Soon she would get rid of that awful morning sickness that lasted three quarters of the day. Traveling long distances, of course, didn't help, not that flying ever bothered her, even if the flight was turbulent. This time, she had spent most of the trip vomiting in the bathroom. Michel didn't seem to have noticed, too busy reading books on architecture—mostly about Julia Morgan, the woman architect who built Hearst Castle in California. For the first time, she didn't mind, as long as he didn't suspect her condition.

Early the next morning, as usual, Michel did not show a single sign of affection—what a waste of opulence in such a lavish Beverly Hills suite and no lovemaking. But again, she didn't mind and didn't even have the desire to get close. She wanted him to leave so she could go on with what needed to be done. Fortunately, his first meeting was in the early morning. To her surprise, however, before leaving, he stopped at the door, came back to bed, and while she pretended to be asleep, he gave her a quick peck on the cheek. *Well, that was a nice surprise.* It was really a shock.

The moment Michel closed the door, she counted the seconds until the elevator bell, down the corridor, finally sounded. She waited to make sure he was gone, and when she was convinced he was, she bounced out of bed and called information for the American Medical Association. She was given a few names of reputable gynecologists.

The third doctor on the list she had jotted down had a clinic several blocks east of Fairfax on Santa Monica Boulevard, in West Hollywood. No one would know her there. But for the first time, she was scared. She had always been in control, afraid of nothing. Something gnawed inside her. She didn't know why.

Heading east on Santa Monica Boulevard, Zaffeera adjusted the rearview mirror of her rented car. Surely no one would ever recognize her in that dreary part of Hollywood, driving a little white Toyota.

She wore a long black skirt and white blouse with a fringed black shawl and a straw hat that fell down to the rim of her large, cheap sunglasses. As she climbed the dusty outdoor steps that led to the front porch of the women's clinic, Zaffeera felt her heart beating hard. She had been through this mess before. The procedure was not difficult. They inserted an object, and minutes later, she was no longer pregnant. She would menstruate again, and there would be nothing more. Why was she so uneasy now? After each procedure, she had been informed she was to have "no sex for ten days." No problem. Michel never made sexual advances anyway. She was always the one who started the seduction, at the break of dawn, when he was most vulnerable—in his sleep.

She sat in the doctor's small waiting room in a shabby wicker chair. The few other women in the waiting room did not look American. The magazine she picked up was printed in Russian. Zaffeera leafed through it and stared at the pictures, her mind elsewhere.

Who the hell was this doctor, making me wait for almost an hour? She was the last one left when the receptionist finally called, "Mrs. Jean Williams? We forgot to ask. Do you have an insurance card?" she said in a strong Russian accent.

"An insurance card?"

"Yes, so I can make a copy for our files. We can fill out your medical forms and mail them for you ..."

"Yes, I do have a great insurance plan," Zaffeera replied. "However, my medical insurance is from England. We moved here recently from London," she said, accentuating a British accent. "I will pay in cash, then send the paperwork to my insurance company. That will make it easier, I am sure."

"Please follow me," another nurse said, holding a file.

Zaffeera waited twenty more minutes inside a frigid, air-conditioned examining room, where she had to strip down and sit on a paper runner, wearing nothing but a thin paper gown.

After a quick tap on the door, a doctor wearing a baseball cap popped his head in. "Mrs. Williams? Sorry for the wait. I'll be right back."

That's it, Zaffeera thought. *I'm out of here!* She had done extensive research on that doctor. Board certified, he was supposedly one of the best and most respected gynecologists in Los Angeles. It was hard to believe it, with that shabby office. If he was so great, why was he not in Beverly Hills? Or at least in Century City!

Doctor Eugene Brandis finally walked into the examining room. He removed his baseball cap, revealing that he was nearly bald. But his face was young. John Lennon lenses rested on his prominent, angular nose. His eyes were a gentle blue.

"Hello, hello. I'm so sorry," he said, his voice soft and whispery. "What a day ... I've had one emergency after another ... Hi, I'm Doctor Brandis," he announced with a sigh, extending his hand to Zaffeera. The moment he shook her hand, his focus was completely on her.

"How do you do, I am Mrs. Jean Williams," Zaffeera said.

The doctor took a moment to read her application in her new chart. Zaffeera had written that the purpose of her visit was to "terminate pregnancy."

He reached for the wall phone and summoned one of his nurses to come in.

After a pelvic examination, the doctor said, "You can get dressed. Let's talk in my office."

Zaffeera felt uneasy as she sat across the doctor's dusty old desk, piled high with files. He finally looked up.

"I'm sorry, I cannot perform an abortion," he announced. He removed his glasses and rubbed his weary eyes before replacing the glasses on the bridge of his nose.

Zaffeera was shocked. Who was this idiot telling her what she could or could not do with her own body?! "Why not?"

"You're too far along," he said, sighing and shaking his head.

What kind of talk was that from a doctor! "It's been six or seven weeks, not more," she said, trying to stifle her rising anger.

"More like three months," he said, still shaking his head, "as you could see it on the ultrasound monitor. You heard the strong heartbeat."

Zaffeera's ears were buzzing, and she was almost shaking with rage. But she knew it was imperative to stay in control. She should have had that abortion done long ago, but she had undergone several tests to be absolutely sure it was a female fetus. She watched the shine of his bald head, wanting to spit at it. She wanted to slap him and bring the *homar* to his senses. She crossed her legs, pulled a few loose strands of hair from her face, and tried to remain composed. Her left eyelid started to twitch furiously.

"I don't think it's been that long."

"I'm afraid so," the doctor said.

"I will pay you triple the amount you usually charge. More, if necessary. In *cash*," she said, leaning closer to him, waiting to see him become impressed. "Looks like your office could use some remodeling."

Showing no emotion, he busied himself writing down information in her chart. "I'm sorry, Mrs. Williams," he said without looking up. It was obvious, as far as the doctor was concerned, that the consultation was over.

"But if I have it, I'll die .... I'll truly die!" She raised her voice, almost forgetting her British accent. She calmed herself and looked at him intently. "It is a matter of life and death, Doctor."

"Indeed, it is," he replied gravely as he finally looked up. "I am glad to announce that you are in very good health."

"No, I am not. You have misdiagnosed ..."

"You are welcome to seek another opinion. As far as I can see, you should have a perfectly normal pregnancy, a normal delivery, and a healthy baby."

Zaffeera rose and stormed out of the doctor's office. On her way, she briefly stopped at the receptionist counter. "Bill my insurance," she said and angrily ran down the stairs.

That night, Zaffeera lay awake in bed and stared at the ornate ceiling of the lavish Beverly Hills Hotel suite. Michel was sound asleep. Zaffeera wondered if she could get rid of this alien invader by pounding on her stomach. No, she would only injure *herself*. Silently, she rose and glided to the bathroom. She stared at her reflection from the dim nightlight.

"Bloody female fetus! You are not going to win power over me!"

Three days later, Michel eagerly announced to his father, his father-in-law, and his wife that he had been commissioned by a prominent family, a well-known investment banker, to design his home in Bel Air.

Although Zaffeera tried very hard to act pleased, she could not share his excitement.

"I am proud of you, Michel," she told him, hugging him and wishing they would celebrate over a night filled with passionate lovemaking.

But now his focus was on another house. Someone else's joy, instead of the house he was to build for them at Al-Balladi. The family who would live in the house Michel was to design had two boys, and the wife was expecting their third. How could that woman be so damned lucky?!

Zaffeera was becoming more and more anxious. She must get rid of that female creature inside her before it was too late!

As the hazy California early sun filtered through the hotel's sheer curtains, a light beam of her blue diamond wedding ring sparkled straight to Zaffeera's eyes. The diamond was beautiful and perfect.

She found the heavy phone book inside a nightstand drawer, threw it on the comforter, and kneeled by the foot of the bed, searching through the Yellow Pages.

Less than an hour later, Zaffeera drove herself to a clinic in the San Fernando Valley. She was never more thankful that Abdo had taught her how to drive when she was merely fifteen. Without her father's knowledge, she had acquired an international driver's license when she was in London. It would have been impossible to wait for a taxi or get a limousine and tell the driver to wait for her at an abortion clinic. Driving in Southern California seemed nearly as important as breathing.

Zaffeera laid out twelve hundred-dollar bills on the counter of the reception desk in a brand-new, small structure and was ushered into the examining room. She had found the right place. Finally.

Less than four hours later, Zaffeera drove back to Beverly Hills by the Ventura Freeway. Traffic became progressively heavier, bumper-to-bumper; at times it was at a standstill. She didn't feel much bleeding, and there was no discomfort at that time, but she was starting to feel anxious. Thirty minutes later, as she finally neared the freeway exit, she began to feel cramps similar to those of an oncoming menstruation. Luckily, Santa Monica Boulevard was free of cars, and she was able to zoom down the boulevard, catching green traffic lights most of the way to the hotel. She made a sharp right to the hotel and realized she still had to return the car. But the rental office was not that far, and the cramps had eased. She returned the compact Toyota to the rental office on Beverly Drive, and from there she took a taxi back to the hotel.

On the bureau of their hotel suite, Zaffeera found Michel's note.

"I hope you enjoyed shopping in Century City.
I am meeting with the couple whose house I will be designing.
Please join me in the restaurant downstairs.
Michel."

He did not even sign it "love"?! But he did honor her by requesting her presence in a business meeting. As she headed for the bathroom to change, she felt a pinch below her stomach that rapidly grew to an excruciating cramp, followed by another, then another. She really wanted to join her husband. She wanted to meet the couple who had commissioned Michel to design their house, wanted them to know she was Mr. Michel Amir's wife. But all she felt like doing now was crawling into a warm bed and holding her knees to her forehead. The pain was becoming intolerable. She barely managed to ring the restaurant downstairs.

"I am so sorry, dear Michel," she breathed, truly barely able to speak. "I must admit, I made a dreadful mistake."

"What happened, Zaffeera?" Michel asked on the phone, sounding genuinely concerned.

"I never thought I would admit such a thing to you, or anyone. But … actually, I … I shopped till I dropped!"

She heard him laugh. *It's not funny!* she wanted to shout and slam down the phone in his ear. Instead, she forced a chuckle. "Yes, I just need to rest."

"I'm sorry you're not feeling well," Michel said kindly, sounding more serious now, as if he knew he should not have laughed. "May I get you anything?"

"No, thank you. I'll be fine …"

There must be something wrong with Michel, Zaffeera thought, crouching beneath the down comforter, wishing she had a heating pad. *It is the man who determines the sex during conception. What* real *man does not want a son? Why on earth would he want a female? Surely he must want a girl—in order to name her… No. He could not still be thinking about* Noora! *Could he?* "Shit!" Zaffeera said out loud, forgetting her cramps for a brief moment until she was seized by another sharp pain.

She phoned the nearest drugstore in Beverly Hills and had the medicine prescribed by the clinic delivered to the hotel. That night, and for the next day, she lay in bed, doubled over in pain. Even the codeine-filled capsules did not do their work. For the first time, she wanted Michel to stay away. Luckily, she knew he was going to continue being busy with meetings. He was not due back until after dinner, and hopefully he would not notice how ill she was.

Quite often, Zaffeera searched through Michel's drawers. Even his luggage. She knew everything he owned. The day before her abortion, she had searched in his attaché case and there, to her fury, she found in a hidden pocket a picture of Noora. The photograph was taken in Alexandria at San Stefano Beach Club when they were younger. They had danced on the beach terrace, while Zaffeera remembered eating her heart out, watching them make eyes at each other. Noora's picture looked worn. Worn out! Could Michel be looking at that picture often? Every day? *Every night?!*

I am losing my mind. She's dead! Damn you, Noora! Damn you, in whatever HELL YOU'RE IN!

Zaffeera bit her knuckles hard while her cramps intensified.

CHAPTER 52
SUSPICIOUS MINDS

Who the hell was this chick barging into his father's life? Kennilworth wondered when he saw his stepfather and that young woman arrive together at a Hollywood function at the Beverly Hilton Hotel.

He heard she was nothing but a maid when Ian Cohen scooped her out of a hotel in France and brought her to the U.S. How did she get him to vacation in Hawaii when they were in the middle of pre-production? And he knew Roz had informed Ian about the attorney in business affairs who had sent a memo advising that the writers hadn't completed the shooting script!

It appeared the girl was often his stepfather's personal escort. Could Ian be that pussy-whipped? Did the old man think he could fool everyone just because he didn't put an arm around her and they didn't hold hands? But Kennilworth was glad they didn't show physical affection. That would have looked disgusting. And why would he choose that chick over the myriad movie stars in Hollywood? That girl was young enough to be his goddamned granddaughter! The hottest stars could barely get Ian Cohen's attention. Even *he* couldn't get a moment alone with Ian Cohen. At first, Kennilworth thought it was a possible ego thing—having a young French maiden. But that type of relationship should have been over by now.

The girl never wore sexy clothes, yet she exuded femininity. Every time he saw her, she wore either a classy pantsuit or a business suit where the skirt always reached below the knee. She didn't show cleavage like most actresses, yet she looked stacked. What if those two decided to—God forbid—get hitched? It would be a disaster. His mother should be rolling in her grave. *That bitch could get all his money.*

He had to put an end to it—fast! He had to think of a way.

Returning home from yet another ostentatious Hollywood awards ceremony in Beverly Hills, Ian Cohen shuffled into his office and dropped wearily on his brown leather couch.

It had been eight months since his quadruple bypass surgery, and even though he felt better, he was emotionally drained. Slumped over, he stared at his feet for a long moment. Finally, he raised his weary head. "Kelley? Kelley! Where the hell is she?"

"I'm here," she said, approaching his office door.

"Listen, I'm making a promise to myself, and you gotta make me keep it. Don't let me set foot in one of those fucking affairs again. They're not like they used to be," he said, staring sadly at the floor. "That time's gone," he complained. "As dead as Irving Thalberg. As gone as Vivian Leigh ... Unless I am nominated for an Academy Award, and that'll never happen ... not with the shit I produce ... Right?"

"Oh, Mr. Cohen."

"Yeah, well, I don't need to prove anything. I sure as hell don't need their awards ceremonies, shaking hands with phonies. And those parties. I don't need their catered foods that give me heartburn, and I sure as hell don't need Kenni watching over us, making stupid remarks."

Noora slowly approached Ian and sat on a chair next to the couch.

"Kenni." Ian shook his head. "He's nothing—*nothing* like his mother. Bevvy liked parties—intimate ones, where guests knew each other. And they didn't shake your hand while looking around for who else was there with a bigger name who might help their frickin' career. Bevvy was an angel. And she knew good stories. You know, she could predict a hot property or a flop, from the first few pages of a script. And she read everything. But Kenni, no. I spent a fortune on film schools for that kid. All a waste of money. He just wanted to nail actresses and show off his fancy Italian sports cars. He doesn't even know how to pronounce their names, let alone drive them! Loser, that's all he is. Spoiled rotten loser."

Ian continued to pour out his frustrations. "I encouraged him to go on his own. But as dumb as Kenni is, he was still smart enough to get me to make him executive V.P. Executive shithead ... Well, it's my company. My studio. I can fire his ass ..." He looked up at Noora. "Sorry ... I didn't mean to cuss ..."

Noora nodded. "It's all right."

"You be careful with that guy," he said, waving a finger.

"Yes, Mr. Cohen."

"Ian! Call me Ian already," he said, the crease of his frown line more pronounced.

"Yes, Ian," she repeated and smiled.

"I've seen him hovering around you like a dog in heat."

"I can handle myself."

"You know, I'm only keeping him around because of my promise to Bevvy. Ah, if only she hadn't died. Beautiful Beverly. So young ..." He groaned and held his head in his hands.

"May I get you anything? A glass of ice water?" she asked, rising.

"Go on up to bed. No need to get tangled up in my misery."

"I'm sorry. What may I bring you?"

"Ask Sam to bring me a glass of gin and tonic."

She stood there without moving. He looked up and met her eyes. She gave him a look—one he understood.

"All right, Nurse Kelley. Soda water. Spike it up with bitter lime, or something that makes me think it's the real thing. Put a little pepper even," he grumbled.

The next day, Ian returned to his office late in the afternoon, after spending most of his day watching dailies. As usual, "Kennilworth-less" could not have picked a worse time to barge into Ian's office.

Sitting behind his desk, Ian was busy jotting down notes on a legal-sized pad, while his stepson flopped on one of the leather chairs facing Ian's huge oak desk. From the corner of his eye, he watched Kennilworth as he opened the leather box on his desk and helped himself to one of Ian's expensive cigars.

"So tell me ... What's so special about that girl?" Kennilworth asked, running his nose along the cigar from end to end.

"I'm busy," Ian said without looking up.

"You'd have more time if you didn't have Frenchy."

Ian felt the hair on the back of his neck rise.

Staring at his stepfather's prized cigar, Kenni continued, "The girl's not only taking your time, and your health, everyone says she's after your money." He huffed the words all in one breath.

Ian had to control himself to keep from jumping over his desk and punching his worthless stepson in the face.

The discomfort in his left leg, where the scar still itched, and where the doctors had removed arteries for the bypass surgery, was a reminder that stress can kill. And Kennilworth-less was not worth dying for.

Ian took a deep breath and looked up at his stepson. "I've made some changes in this property," he said, and handed over a heavy box containing a 600-page unbound manuscript. "I'd like you to look this over ... uh ... read it, before I consider hiring a screenwriter for the adaptation. Let me know what you think."

Kennilworth set the cigar down on Ian's desk and remained silent for a moment. "Sounds good," he finally said. He hesitated a moment, then took the box.

"I've made some editing notes on some of the pages. You might want to add your thoughts in the margins." Ian looked down at his papers. "Let me know by Monday," he said. "Would be great help."

Kill that fucking kid with kindness, Ian thought. Or better yet, *get shithead out of his office!* Kennilworth's suggestions would probably be worthless. Ian had given up asking him to read screenplays, especially manuscripts, years ago. The kid did not like to read.

"Okay," Kennilworth said. He finally rose rather eagerly from his stepfather's chair and walked out, carrying the manuscript.

"Thanks," Ian said. As soon as his stepson was gone, Ian squeezed the pencil he was holding so hard, it broke in half.

The heavy rain that pounded Saturday night cleaned the morning air, leaving a fresh scent of blooming flowers from the manicured lawns of Beverly Hills and Bel Air—a perfect Sunday morning.

Kennilworth stayed home Saturday night until three in the morning reading the manuscript his stepfather had given him. He usually reserved Saturday nights for the posh Le Dome restaurant, where he hung out at the bar and later drove west on Sunset Boulevard, to the Beverly Hills Hotel's Polo Lounge. Depending on his mood, and also depending on the young starlet he had on his arm on Saturday nights, he would enjoy a late-night snack at Spago. He usually took the girl with stars in her eyes to his home up on Angelo View, where he enjoyed a night of fucking. Sunday mornings were reserved for more sex—in bed or in the shower, followed by a late brunch in Marina Del Rey or Malibu, whatever struck his momentary fancy. And if the girl really gave good head, he would take her to the Hotel Bel Air for champagne brunch. He didn't do that often; it was too expensive. But somehow, the atmosphere of that place, seeing movie stars sitting at nearby tables, made the weekend girlfriend even hornier. He would take her back to his place, and they would have great sex in the afternoon and lie around in bed until early evening. If the girl was still fun, he would keep her around if she made dinner for him.

Lately, he had a difficult time finding a young chick who would put out. But that weekend, he didn't mind being alone, because he had that manuscript to read. It was too long, and he was almost sorry for having gone to his stepfather's office. Kennilworth had never admitted to anyone that he hated to read. Especially lengthy things like manuscripts. He never had to read anything literary agents poured into their offices, because Ian Cohen Enterprises employed readers, or "story analysts," as they liked to call themselves. If Ian preferred to do his own reading, that was his problem. As if he didn't trust anyone's opinion.

He must have trusted my opinion, Kennilworth thought. *There had to be something special about that manuscript.*

By three o'clock in the morning, however, Kennilworth had to force himself to stay awake and make a few minor changes in the margins to prove he had read the thing. The story was actually good, full of action, titled, *The Battle of Mefisto.* Maybe there was a big celebrity name attached to this project. By Monday, Ian had better inform him as to who was going to be the female lead.

He must have fallen asleep after that thought, because the next thing he knew, he woke up feeling so horny, he wanted to bite his knuckles. He jumped in the shower instead. He realized he had not had a girl in over a week! Ejaculating in his morning shower was not enough. A man of his business stature should *never* run out of beautiful girls to satisfy him at any given moment.

He heard rumors that Francine Papillon, his ex live-in, had hooked up with some middle-aged screenwriter she met the day she moved to the

Chateau Marmont. *I should have set her up at a Holiday Inn in Torrance or Orange County,* Kennilworth thought bitterly.

Still wet from his shower, he scanned through his black book, but realized he was now more famished than horny. He threw on black gabardine trousers and a loose Hawaiian silk shirt. With the manuscript in his briefcase, he hopped into his red Ghibli Maserati and drove down to Nate N' Al's Deli, ten minutes away, where they served his favorite—mushroom and spinach omelet; lox, cream cheese, and thickly sliced onions and tomatoes, on perfectly-toasted bagels.

At least he lucked out with the perfect parking space in front of the restaurant. A crowd of admirers popped out of everywhere on the sidewalk, snapping pictures of his car. Kennilworth loved the attention.

At the restaurant, he was treated like a celebrity. Everyone recognized him, called him by name, and shook his hand. Soon, he should find himself a lovely young aspiring actress, he thought with a grin, eager to fuck his brains out.

Sitting alone in a circular corner booth for six, Kennilworth set his manuscript on the table and leafed through the Calendar section of the Sunday *Los Angeles Times.* He glanced up and noticed a veteran actor, smooching with a long-haired blonde a good thirty years his junior. Why, that old fart! He thought of his stepfather. He tossed the newspaper aside, picked up his manuscript, and left without finishing his breakfast. He cruised around Beverly Hills. He could drive his sports car down Sunset Boulevard, east to Hollywood, where he would surely find a hooker. But at this stage of his life, he should not have to pay for sex!

Here I am, the big shot—bored out of my wits with no one to suck my dick while those old guys are screwing young chicks! He shifted forcefully into high gear and the Maserati screamed up Rodeo Drive, heading north. He screeched to a halt because of the traffic light, and spotted a police car on his right. As soon as the light turned green, Kennilworth carefully drove ahead. Another speeding ticket he sure as hell didn't need. He made a sharp left, crossing Sunset Boulevard, toward Comstock Park. A familiar figure jogging toward the park caught his attention. Slowing down, he recognized the new office receptionist. He honked once.

"Hey!" he shouted, after pulling to the curb, giving a quick glance at his rearview mirror to make sure there was no police car around. He kept his engine humming. Sports car loud. "Want a ride?"

"Oh, hey! Hello, Mr. Kennilworth Cohen!" the young woman said.

"Hell-lowww!"

"Nice car, Mr. Cohen!"

Kennilworth shrugged a shoulder, raised a pretentious eyebrow. "Wanna ride?"

"A *ride?* Really? Oh, no. Thank you!" she replied, but she was obviously impressed.

"Get in." It sounded more like an order.

"Oh gosh, I'd *love* to. I can't. Such a gorgeous car. Is it a Corvette?

"No!" he said, almost angry. "It's a Maserati."

"What?"

"A Maserati Ghibli. I picked it up in Italy."

"Eee-talee? Hey, wow."

"Come on, get in."

"I'm all sweaty and I've got ..."

"I don't mind. C'mon!" he commanded. *Down boy,* he thought, as he pressed down on his crotch.

"My husband and my little girl are waiting for me at the park. Otherwise I would've loved to go with you. Oh gosh, such a neat car!"

Stupid chick! Why didn't she say she had a damn husband and a kid? If they didn't make those discrimination laws at work, he would have had his personnel department fire her ass. *Bitch,* he thought, waving a hand and flooring it, back up to Sunset. No need to get upset over a *nobody.* This reminded him of the girl who lived with his stepfather. Another "nobody." Ian always played tennis on Sundays at the Beverly Hills Country Club. What was *Ms. Nobody* doing today?

CHAPTER 53
ZAFFEERA'S DILEMMA

"No! Not again!" Zaffeera shouted at her reflection in the mirror. Sitting alone on the boudoir chaise while brushing her hair, she felt the familiar mild cramps signaling the onset of yet another menstrual period.

One year and two months after her last abortion, Zaffeera was still not pregnant. She shuddered, remembering the terrible ordeal she endured at that dreadful little clinic in the Los Angeles outskirts of the San Fernando Valley, where she was left nearly paralyzed with the worst cramps she had ever experienced.

If Michel had been in bed with her every night, there might have been a chance to conceive again. But no, he had to spend most of his time abroad, working on some Bel Air mansion instead of focusing on her! He designed intricate waterfalls and fishponds for his new client. Koi fish, he said. *Who cares?* she thought.

Michel committed his precious time to foreign clients, strangers, while he neglected his own wife. She yearned for his hard body. Every night and day, instead of days filled with emptiness—walking around the new Al-Balladi mall—shopping for things she didn't need or care to own.

Not pregnant, and never likely to be—if Michel continued to neglect his husbandly duties, she thought, brushing her hair. With each stroke, her anger intensified. Realizing she would surely ruin the extensions she had put in last week at the beauty shop, she switched to a comb. She had worked hard on looking good. *For him. For what? All in vain.*

"I am a neglected wife, sexually deprived," she concluded. "It's unhealthy." *Patience,* a voice said inside her.

Fuck patience! She tossed her comb across the room. She had waited long enough for Michel to show some affection! She scratched her itchy elbow. Why wasn't he more demonstrative? There had to be something wrong with him. Could he be ... interested in ... men? *Boys?* No! She pushed the ghastly thought away. Of course he was not a homosexual—he *was* attracted to Noora. She wondered if he would have treated Noora the same way. Of course he would have. Only Noora wouldn't have known the difference, she was so stupid. Zaffeera picked up the brush again, telling herself she mustn't think about her dead sister. Not ever.

She scratched the back of her knee. The skin behind both knees felt dry and itchy. The rash had started on one elbow, and it spread to different places. She wondered if it was eczema. Obviously, the result of nerves and having to live a lonely, sex-starved life. Michel was to blame. Other people's houses were more important than his, and *she* was the one who had to suffer?

Pain stabbed through her right temple. She took deep breaths and held her hands over her eyes to calm herself. She must not let the headache take hold. She fumbled for the pills she had left on top of her boudoir table. *Migraines.* That word never entered her mind before she married Michel.

Yes, there had to be something wrong with him, though he sure had all the proper tools. He had the gift of perfection, only he didn't know what to do with it! She was tired of having to plan every evening with him—slipping an aphrodisiac into his wine. The first few times, it worked. The last time, he fell asleep. But she was able to catch him aroused during the early morning. No foreplay.

Sooner or later, he would return to Al-Balladi and work on their dream home—at least that. He had already completed the designs for a modern mansion surrounded by pools and waterfalls. Their new house would be the envy of everyone at Al-Balladi, but he kept postponing it.

Zaffeera hated living in her father-in-law's house, a boring, sprawling three-story Mediterranean-style villa where she spent night after night without Michel. At least she didn't have to have dinners with Michel's father, because he was busy completing the world-class resort at Sharm

El Sheikh in Egypt, with her own father. The only servant who lived in the house was the family's cook, an unfriendly older lady who spoke only French and didn't appear too excited about having Zaffeera living there. The old hag had a room next to the kitchen—far from the bedrooms upstairs—and she never dared to intrude on the rest of the house. There were two housekeepers who came weekday mornings, and the chauffeur drove them home every evening before sunset.

She looked around the large suite she occupied. Boring beige and peach décor, relatively comfortable. The wide king-size bed was ridiculous. Perhaps she should replace it with a queen-size bed, like she wished she could have done it for their wedding night, so that Michel wouldn't drift so far from her. At least she could have the new driver take her back to the mall and buy new bed linen. Something more elegant, *more sensual.* Satin. Silky satin sheets. She smiled at the thought. Soft and slippery—she fantasized the two of them nude in bed. How wonderfully delicious that would be—whenever he decided to return to Al-Balladi!

The only solution was to live with him in Los Angeles. They would purchase a cute hacienda in Beverly Hills; perhaps a cozy bungalow, next to the Beverly Hills Hotel. Yes, she would do it, she sang to herself, bouncing up from her boudoir chair and breezing across the room to the huge walk-in closet. She punched in the combination to her little safe on the back wall behind hanging dresses, and removed her large and shiny penis-shaped vibrator. She stared at the device and flipped the button to the "on" position. The vibrating motion was weak. She needed fresh batteries.

A gust of wind threw the window open and the sheer drapes billowed out wildly like huge sleeves waving toward her. Zaffeera ran to the window and managed to close it. She tried to catch her breath, holding the vibrator to her chest. A cold shiver ran through her. The glass of the tall french windows rattled and shook as if a violent wind swept through the house, then moments later, all was quiet, except for the gentle hum of her vibrator. Quickly, she flipped it to the off position.

Just a little wind, she told herself. *But how did it materialize so fast, when it had been calm and even balmy outside? My imagination is running away with me,* she thought, closing the heavy beige brocade curtains. The silver-framed wedding picture of Zaffeera and Michel had fallen on the carpet. She picked it up and replaced it on the table next to the window, and as she did, she noticed the other picture of Mrs. Amir—a silver-framed photograph with Michel as a boy about ten years old. Zaffeera bent closer as she stared at the black-and-white photograph. She had never really paid much attention to it before. Another shiver ran through her, as if the ghost of Michel's mother was present—watching her. She jumped when she heard a knock. Zaffeera dropped the vibrator in the pocket of her peignoir, took her wedding picture, and crossing the room, she placed it prominently on Michel's bedside table.

Another soft knock.

"Who is it?" Zaffeera asked.

"Missus Amir?" Gamelia's whimpering voice could barely be heard. "Missus … Missus Amir, it is only me."

"Go back to your cottage," Zaffeera snapped. "Wait there."

Zaffeera kept her personal maid nearby. She hated to admit it, even to herself, but where Michel failed, the brainless little maid still knew how to satisfy her. It had been a terrible revelation. But what else could she do? Soon after her wedding, Zaffeera moved Gamelia from the Fendil mansion to Mr. Amir's guest cottage near the pool, a separate little bungalow. Zaffeera decided she would have to go to Gamelia and get some relief, away from the Amir mansion from now on. The haunting feeling that the ghost of Michel's mother was in the bedroom, *watching*, gave her the creeps.

The next night, in the maid's cottage near the pool, Gamelia performed oral sex on her mistress. Despite every orgasm Zaffeera reached, still she did not feel the type of satisfaction she needed.

She began to think about the new chauffeur. Not that she wanted to, but her mind kept drifting back to the young driver. She had noticed his shoes: enormous. His gloved hands on the steering wheel seemed large and strong, revealing he had to be well-endowed.

The Amir family's original chauffeur had suffered a stroke and was on a long leave of absence. Michel's father hired the young man while the old driver was recovering.

On her way back to her room, with curiosity getting the best of her, Zaffeera went to her father-in-law's office and found the new driver's employment file, below a small pile of papers on Mr. Amir's desk.

The new chauffeur had a German-sounding name: Friedrich Meinecke. How did one pronounce such a name? She would have to ask him, the next time he drove her to the shopping mall. Perhaps it would be a good way to start a conversation. A handwritten note on the bottom of his application said, "Nickname is Fred."

It appeared "Fred" had worked as the personal chauffeur to some British dignitary during the past eight years. His driving record, according to the second page of the application, appeared flawless. A photocopy of the young man's international driver's license was stapled to the file. Usually, no one looked good in their passport or driver's license photographs—yet in the copy of that picture, he looked like a movie star.

Excellent manners, excellent driving record. Speaks English and has moderate understanding of the Arabic language, Zaffeera read. She never paid attention to employees. But that driver—with the tailored navy blue uniform and crisp white shirt—was hard to ignore. It could be dangerous, of course, but it was nothing more than a fantasy.

Fantasies are fun and would make her frustrating life less boring, Zaffeera thought, carefully replacing the file exactly the way she had found it. Climbing the stairs back to her lonely suite, Zaffeera was glad the French cook had gone out that evening to visit a relative.

Alone in the house, she locked her door, breezed to the dresser by the window, and turned her mother-in-law's picture face down. Staring at the black velvet backing of the silver frame, she picked it up again and focused on the young Michel. He was so cute when he was a boy. Soon she would give him a son who would resemble him. She wished she could cut his mother out of that picture. She opened the dresser drawer, threw the picture inside, and banged the drawer shut.

CHAPTER 54
FALSE PRETENSES

Michel drove up to the house on Bel Air Road in the new black four-door Mercedes he recently leased. He was to meet with the owner of the property, along with the general contractor. He would need to rent a house for a year—a quaint hacienda perhaps, like the ones he saw south of Olympic Boulevard. Nothing too extravagant, just something comfortable for him and Zaffeera. The location would be close enough to the Bel Air mansion he was designing.

Zaffeera had expressed the desire to own a second home in Los Angeles, but that would depend on whether he got the job.

She returned to Al-Balladi because she had been ill, apparently experiencing some female problems. He noticed she had been pale and often tired. There were times when he could have sworn she was pregnant. She would put on some weight and then lose it. Perhaps it was from her female problems. Or dieting? She never talked about it, and he hesitated to say anything. Michel realized he did wish Zaffeera were pregnant. A baby would be a blessing. He liked his wife. But he could never love her. If she gave him a child, perhaps in time, he would grow to love her in some way.

The thought of having a baby girl made him smile. Contrary to what he had believed early in the marriage, he realized that he would not name their baby Noora. There was only one Noora, and she was forever in his heart. The baby should have her own name, her own identity. If they were to be blessed with a girl, and if Zaffeera agreed, maybe they would add Noora as her middle name, in honor of her aunt.

Why am I thinking about Noora now? I have to focus on this meeting, and I'm running late. Suddenly, he felt the need to drive fast—wherever his car would lead. He liked to speed down the Pacific Coast Highway with the windows down and loud music on the radio, to drive his grief away from his mind. He was glad Zaffeera was back at Al-Balladi. They had cried together for Noora before they were married, and after, but he had to stop grieving in front of Zaffeera. Soon after they were married, she had reminded him that it was against Muslim laws to mourn for those who were "done with this lifetime and back in Paradise." Obviously, she needed to get on with her life, and he was not helping. Lately, in fact, it seemed to make her jealous if he mentioned Noora's name.

The silver Jaguar ahead of him honked, jarring him out of his reverie. He realized traffic had been stopped for a while. What could stop traffic for so long on a normally quiet residential street?

Ahead of the Jag, a young lady was standing next to a bright red convertible, talking to the driver. Michel drummed his fingers on the steering wheel and glanced at the clock on the dashboard. Whatever was going on up ahead would delay him by a few more minutes. *Couldn't the driver have the courtesy to pull over to the curb? Wait. That young lady. With short blonde hair. Like the one in Honolulu ...*

He ran a weak hand through his hair. *It's not possible. This can't go on,* he thought. *I see Noora everywhere. I can't help myself. I must face it. I need psychotherapy.*

Sitting pretentiously in his gleaming Maserati Ghibli, Kennilworth Cohen ignored the honking.

"Why won't you say where you're going?" he asked.

"I'm going to the hotel."

"The Hotel Bel Air?"

"Yes," Noora said, glancing nervously at the honking car.

"By yourself?"

"I am delivering a package."

"Who for?"

"I believe we are stopping traffic."

"I'm sure you do that often. Hop in."

"No, thank you. I like to walk."

"C'mon. It's a fun car!"

"Ghiblis are great cars indeed, but I planned to walk. Good day." She turned away to resume her walk.

"Wait! There's no sidewalk. Very dangerous. You'll get run over!" He hopped out of his car, rushed around, and opened the passenger door. At least five cars were backed up now, all of them honking.

Michel found himself blowing his horn along with the others. He stopped. Just because the car in front of him was honking, and the one behind, and he was running late, didn't mean he had to be rude. He cracked his door open, watching out for oncoming cars. He craned his neck for a better look at the girl, who was climbing into the red convertible. The driver made a rapid and dangerous U-turn, passing Michel's Mercedes. His head blocked Michel's view of the girl.

Stop looking at girls, Michel chided himself and shifted into gear. The traffic was moving again.

At the parking entrance of the Hotel Bel Air, Kennilworth sat in his car and tapped nervously on the steering wheel while listening to Madonna on the radio. At least twenty minutes had passed. How long did it take to deliver a package? He should have gone with her. Ian had become so secretive about everything; perhaps the girl honestly didn't know anything.

Several tourists were jabbering about his car and taking pictures. *No, it's not a goddamned Ferrari! Idiots.* But how did his stepfather's maid—or assistant, or whatever the hell she was—know his car was a Ghibli? She couldn't have seen an emblem on the rear of his car, because someone stole it and he never got around to replacing it. His stepfather must have told her.

When Noora announced to the hotel manager that she was there to deliver a package for Mr. Gianni, from Mr. Ian Cohen, she was asked to wait in the lobby. She sat on a wing chair and watched the parade of people. She was told to deliver the package to the actor in person. Her attention was caught by the beautiful arrangement of peach-colored roses and pale pink lilies. The flowers' sweet fragrance transported her back to her grandmother's garden. *You have to live in the present,* a voice said, as Noora opened her eyes. She had almost forgotten about Kennilworth. She wished she hadn't accepted his offer to ride in his car. She remembered Nageeb had a similar red Ghibli Spider—their father gave it to him on his eighteenth birthday. It felt good to sit in Kennilworth's car, actually. She had, for a brief moment, closed her eyes and lost herself amid the distinctive smell of the leather seats ... Abdo would have been horrified to see how Ian's stepson shifted gears and how he handled that car—it was criminal.

Why couldn't she just call Abdo and let him know she was alive? Her eyes welled. She turned her gaze to the crackling fireplace nearby in the lobby. It would endanger Abdo if she tried to contact him. She could *never* get in touch with him. She would not jeopardize the caring relationship he had with his adopted family, and especially with her father.

"Are you Mr. Cohen's messenger?"

She looked up. "What? Oh, yes," she said, springing to her feet. She should have said she was Mr. Cohen's *assistant,* not his messenger.

"Follow me, please," the hotel manager said. They made their way through a long cobblestone walkway, bordered by the loveliest lilac and pale blue mums. They turned down winding, narrow paths where the bright sunlight played hide-and-seek through tall, leafy trees, and down another pathway; Noora was guided to a private bungalow.

The hotel manager knocked and waited. The door opened. A handsome young blonde man appeared. He wore a white terry robe with the Hotel Bel Air's logo embroidered on the breast pocket. Noora recognized him instantly from magazine covers, posters, and billboards.

"Hey! Great. How ya doin'?" He didn't wait for a reply. "I've been waiting for this package," the movie star said.

Noora removed the large brown envelope that concealed the heavy package, and glanced at the instructions written on top. "When you get to Gianni's bungalow, give the manuscript to him personally, ONLY. NO ONE ELSE!" he had printed with a black felt pen.

"It's from Mr. Ian Cohen," she said, handing the actor the thick envelope.

Now that the package was personally delivered and in the young man's possession, as per Ian's instructions, she would walk back to his house, eager to lose herself in some romance novel of a forgotten era.

"Thank you. I can find my way out," she said to her escort.

"My pleasure, madame," the manager said with a French accent, and walked away.

"Come in, come in," the movie star said to Noora, his robe slightly open, revealing that he was nude. "I have something for you," he murmured with a sly grin.

He walked back inside, picked up an eight-by-ten glossy of himself from the desk in the suite, wrote something on it, and inserted it in an envelope. Noora stood at the threshold and did not take one step further. The movie star returned to the door and took his time licking the flap of the envelope while lifting his eyebrows at Noora. He handed her the sealed envelope as if giving her a prized gift.

"I'll make sure Mr. Cohen gets it," Noora said and rushed off before he stopped her.

She wanted to toss the envelope in the garbage, but she couldn't find a trash bin along the pathway. It was just as well, because she would place it on Mr. Cohen's desk and say that the actor handed her the envelope, and she assumed it was for Ian. She folded it in half and put it in her pocketbook.

Noora made her way down to the pond. She had been there a month or two before, while Ian was attending a meeting. "Bevvy used to love high tea here. I'm sure you will too," he had told her, and said she should check out the swan pond.

She had indeed enjoyed the tea and petits fours, the quiet time alone. Most of all, she had especially loved sitting under the small weeping willow, far enough from the swans not to disturb them as they glided so smoothly and elegantly.

But today, as she made her way down the stone steps, she discovered a wedding was in progress. Quietly, she took a few steps across the lawn, far enough from the ceremony.

The fairytale setting left her breathless. Hundreds of pink roses adorned the gleaming white gazebo ahead. The bride wore a long, flowing white gown, and the dark-haired groom stood by her side. At least a hundred guests were seated on white folding chairs while the couple exchanged vows.

As she rushed away from the wedding, she thought she heard someone calling: "Hey, lady!"

She remembered her sunglasses on top of her head and quickly shielded her teary eyes.

"I ... am sorry," she stammered as Kennilworth approached a little too close. She brushed a tear from her cheek, pretending to remove strands of hair. "I was detained a bit longer than I expected."

"You all right?"

"Me?"

"Yes. You look upset."

"Me?"

"Who else?" he answered impatiently.

"I just want to take advantage of this beautiful Sunday and walk home," she said. "I like to walk." She turned away and headed back out to the parking lot through the covered bridge.

"Okay, I get it. You like to walk. But you know," Kennilworth said, chasing after her, "even in Bel Air, a pretty young woman walking alone ... it's not a good idea."

She stopped beneath the awning near the valet stand.

He touched her arm gently and gave her a warm smile.

"Thanks for your concern. I'll be careful," she said, turning away from Kennilworth and starting for the street.

"Let me drive you," he said, rushing after her. "I need to return something to my father anyway."

Kennilworth's sports car zoomed around to the parking lot and the valet hopped out, ran to the passenger door, and opened it. Kennilworth nudged Noora firmly to his car and helped her in.

"Allow me." He turned to the valet. "Just a moment." Kennilworth gave the valet a tip.

"These guys work hard," Kennilworth said, back in his car and shifting forcefully into gear. "They deserve a good twenty-dollar tip." He zoomed down the street. "It's nothing for me and it's a lot for them. I see you know a little bit about cars."

"Not really," she said, wondering how she allowed this guy to talk her into riding with him. "May I open the window?"

"Sure." He was going to show her where the button was, but Noora already knew and pressed an index finger above the dashboard.

"Not too windy for your hair?"

"I like the wind."

"How come you know so much about sports cars?"

"I really don't."

"Where are you from?"

"France."

"I mean originally."

"London. But I lived in France."

"Funny, you don't sound either British or French."

"Really? I believe you passed the street," she said.

"I was looking at you and forgot where I was going."

Noora gave him a look, thinking of one of Ian's favorite expressions—"full of prunes."

"You are very pretty," he said.

Really full of prunes, she thought.

"We don't see many classy ladies around here," he said. "If I seemed a little rude or pushy earlier, forgive me. I'll drop you off anywhere you say. I just need to pull over where you won't get run over." He maneuvered his car to the curb; he then pulled to a wide driveway, jumped out, rushed to the passenger door, and helped her out.

"Thank you."

"Pleasure. Again, forgive my forwardness."

She wasn't sure if he was full of prunes or just plenty full of hot air. One thing was for sure: He was full of himself.

Noora enjoyed the short walk back to Ian's house. She pressed the code buttons, and Mr. Cohen's wooden gate opened. She glanced over her shoulder across the street. Behind tall Italian pines that bordered the property, an ugly mansion would soon be built, Mr. Cohen had told her. He was not happy about having construction workers barging into what had once been a quiet cul-de-sac. He often complained about the neighborhood going "straight to hell because of all those rich ragheads invading the country."

Noora wished he would stop using that term—"ragheads." It certainly was not her place to protest. *You don't bite the hand that feeds you,* she reminded herself.

She rang the service doorbell. Cessi appeared, dressed in a pink suit.

"You look nice, Cessi," Noora managed to say in Spanish, stepping inside the immaculate kitchen that smelled like Pine Sol. "Your son, taking you to *iglesia* today?"

"*Si, señorita.*"

Noora chatted with Cessi for a few moments before she walked through the kitchen and across the vestibule to Ian's office. She placed the movie star's envelope on his desk next to the phone. "Why, I assumed the picture was meant for you, Mr. Cohen," she would tease him.

She felt a presence. Turning in her heel, she found Ian's stepson standing inches behind her.

"Oh, goodness!" she gasped, startled. "I didn't see you."

"Didn't mean to startle you," he whispered. "I'm also delivering something. My father gave me a manuscript to correct for him." Kennilworth put the thick box on his stepfather's chair. "I always put all the work I do for him on his chair so he doesn't miss it. The old man's eyesight is not so good anymore. He's also forgetful these days."

"Oh? Why, I wouldn't think ..."

"You might want to do the same," he interrupted. "For sure he'll miss it if you put it on his desk like that. What's in that envelope?"

"It's sealed," she said.

Kennilworth grabbed her in his arms, gave her a passionate kiss, taking Noora with such surprise, she lost her balance. He grabbed her tighter by the waist.

Once Noora regained her equilibrium, she tried to push him away. She struggled, but his arms were too strong. To her shock and embarrassment, she could feel him, hard like a stick, against her stomach, right through his black gabardine trousers. She felt trapped in his arms but still managed to push him away. He let go, stepping a foot away, only for a brief moment. He seized her again. Holding her tighter now, he whispered, "God, you are different. You know that?"

Noora remembered Ian's warnings. "*Beware of wolves. Especially Kenni.*" She always replied that she could surely handle herself. This time, she felt trapped and barely able to breathe.

"You feel so good ..." Kennilworth whispered.

She felt dizzy from the touch of a man—a touch she had longed for. Just to be held, to be loved. She could never allow such feelings to surface again. She almost moaned Michel's name, but caught herself. How could she allow this man to get so close? He was a phony. He was trying to find her lips. She should *slap* him …

As she was about to break away, a voice thundered, "WHAT THE FUCK DO YOU THINK THIS IS?!" Ian Cohen stood at the threshold of his office.

Kennilworth finally let go, and Noora put her hands to her flushed cheeks.

"I want you both outta my FUCKING OFFICE!" Ian Cohen growled. "And you!" He said, pointing a rigid index at Noora. "Get your shit out of my house."

"Mr. Cohen! It's not at all what you …"

"I'm gonna take a ride around the block so I don't *kill* you. When I get back, I want you GONE!"

"Please, Ian, absolutely, this was not …"

He turned and marched away, before Noora could explain the truth. Ian's words felt like icicles piercing her heart. A door slammed hard and walls vibrated like an aftershock.

Noora flew up the stairs. It didn't take her long to pack. *Leave the clothes he gave you money to buy. Leave everything!* He wanted her out. She would take Annette's sweater, cards, and letters; she should leave the few books she purchased and leave now! She grabbed a Neiman Marcus shopping bag from the chair nearby and ran to the bathroom. In a quick sweep, she threw her toiletries and stuffed the bag in her small suitcase. She had prepared for that moment, if he ever made advances. But she was not prepared to be thrown out for such an unexpected reason. How could she have allowed that manipulative stepson to kiss her? How could she have again been so weak and naive? She had kept the phone number of the Bel Air taxi company right by her bedside, in case of emergency. Now she couldn't find the piece of paper. Her fingers trembling, she dialed Information.

Finally, when she got through to one of the Beverly Hills cab companies, the clerk said it would take ten to fifteen minutes.

By then, Ian Cohen would surely be back. God only knew what he would do. She had witnessed his temper, but she had never been the cause. Until now. She flew down the stairs with her small suitcase, her purse, and two sweaters tucked under her arm. Kennilworth met her in the vestibule by the front doors.

"I'll help you," he said in a voice that sounded all too cheerful.

"Excuse me," she muttered and rushed toward the kitchen. *Haven't you caused enough harm?* She would leave from the service entrance, because he was blocking the front door.

"Let me do something," he said, pursuing her.

"Let me GO!"

"You can stay with me tonight. At my house. It's the least I can do," Kennilworth said.

She ran through the kitchen. Kennilworth did not follow her there.

Where was Cessi? She hoped Ian's housekeeper did not see what happened in Mr. Cohen's office. Maybe Cessi's son picked her up and they already left. She would not have the chance to say goodbye to Cessi, she thought, her mind racing with confused thoughts as she ran out to the courtyard, headed for the street. The gate was left open, but the taxicab was not there yet. Ian Cohen wanted her out of his house, *now*. No matter what, he would not believe her explanation. Why should he? *Where was that taxi?*

*****   *****   *****

Michel walked to the black Mercedes exhilarated after his meeting in the fifty-year-old cottage on Bel Air Road. He climbed in, closed the door, but couldn't start the car yet. He had to sit for a while and rewind in his head what just happened. It was almost too good to be true. He needed to take a deep breath, and most of all, plant himself back on earth. He reached over his shoulder and pulled down his seat belt. He stopped before buckling himself in, thinking God must have finally felt sorry for him and shone a ray of light upon his dark, cloudy life. He held the steering wheel with two hands. *Sublime... fantastique,* he thought in French. The meeting with his future client, a young man named Mr. Art Atta'ie, went better than he had imagined. *Il doit y avoir un Dieu après tout!* Mr. Atta'ie had approved Michel's proposal and designs. Indeed, there must be a God after all.

He reached for his cell phone to call his father and announce the good news. He stopped and stared at his phone, wondering about the time difference. His father was still at Sharm El Sheikh in Egypt, working on the hotel project with his father-in-law. He glanced at his watch. It was probably too late to call—or too early? He would have to wait a few more hours.

Michel had met Mr. Atta'ie in Paris, just the year before, where he had been introduced by one of his professors. The forty-three-year-old investment banker, who had purchased the two-acre lot in Bel Air, asked Michel to draw up plans for his family's dream home. Mr. Atta'ie was so pleased with Michel's proposal and drawings that he wanted to meet him in his Century City office the very next morning and get started on his house.

For the first time since he lost Noora, Michel felt a sense of hope. He would have to open an office in Beverly Hills, hire a staff. Ideas as to what he would name his company danced in his head. He was not an American citizen. He would have to seek counsel on the matter. He wanted to make sure everything he did was absolutely legal. So many plans—better things lay ahead.

His new client had twin boys—four years old. His wife was expecting another son, they told him, and the couple wanted to build a separate wing for their boys. Mr. Atta'ie wanted large windows and waterfalls. Michel came up with ideas that his client liked. He also proposed building a tree house with a small lift that would safely take the children up and down. The lift would be controlled by the touch of an electric switch hidden in the paw of a wooden bear statue that would be standing next to the tree. As a backup safety measure, the electric switch could also be controlled by the parents, from the house. He didn't think Mr. Atta'ie would like the idea, but he and his wife actually loved it. They said they had never heard of anything so "ingenious."

Mrs. Atta'ie especially loved the design of the main kitchen and adjoining den. She was so excited, she hugged her husband, and tears of joy appeared, welling up in her eyes. Mr. Atta'ie was beaming with pride.

Michel had discovered that from a specific angle of the property, where no one knew there was ever a view, there actually was a pretty good vista of Beverly Hills in the distance. He designed tall windows from that particular angle which also allowed, at night, the city's twinkling lights to show.

Michel rolled down the windows of his car. He pulled out of the driveway, his mind on the house plans, when suddenly he jammed his foot on the brake. A young woman was running right in front of his car. He could have hit her, he came so close. A taxi pulled up in front of the mansion across the street and she ran after it.

He swiftly pulled close to the curb, and stopped a few feet before the driveway of the open gates. She ran out of that house without looking if a car was coming. He could have killed her! It was that close.

"Hey!" he found himself shouting. "Watch it!"

What was he doing, screaming like a madman? Michel wondered, realizing his heart was pounding and his hands were trembling. The young woman turned and faced his car for a split second before opening the back door of the cab and hopping in.

He could have sworn she was the same person, the young woman he saw earlier, before his meeting. *Merde!* She was just someone who happened to look like Noora. And wearing the same dress as the girl he saw in Hawaii? *This coincidence is totally improbable, I am seeing things and I need help!*

Blinded by tears, Noora heard someone shout at her. Probably the driver of that black car. She wanted to say she was sorry, but she saw Kennilworth rushing toward the taxi.

"Where are you going? You don't need a cab!" Kennilworth shouted, rushing to open the taxi door.

Inside the cab, Noora quickly pressed the lock button. Kennilworth persistently tapped on the glass. "C'mon, don't be silly. He's just old and jealous! Stay with me!"

"Please, sir! Drive away!"

The cab made a fast U-turn and took off.

Seated stunned in his car, Michel crossed his arms on top of his steering wheel and dropped his head. *Everywhere I go, I think I see Noora.* He blinked back tears and shifted into gear. *Noora... Dear God, how I miss you.*

Inside the taxi, Noora checked her purse. She had her passport and the two thousand dollars she had managed to save. *It pays to be organized and think ahead,* she thought, something she never had to do growing up.

"Did you say the airport?" the driver asked.

"Yes, please," Noora said, closing her purse.

"None of my business, but is that guy your boyfriend or somethin'?" The taxi driver asked, peering at Noora from his rearview mirror.

"No."

"I think he just went through the red light back there, trying to catch up. Looks like he's tailing us. You wan' me to stop?"

Noora turned and saw the Ghibli gaining speed.

"No. I don't even know him ... Take me to the hospital."

"Hospital? Which one?"

"The Sinai ... I mean ... The one near the Beverly Center. Do you know where it is?"

"Cedars Sinai? You wan' me ta lose the Ferrari?"

"Just drop me off at the emergency entrance ... please."

"You okay, lady?" the driver asked, glancing curiously at Noora, adjusting his rearview mirror.

She touched her neck and gasped. "Oh, no!"

"All right, lady. I'm gonna pull over ..."

"No, no, please. I'm fine!"

"If you need to vomit, not in my car!"

"I assure you, I don't need to do any such thing."

"If you need medical assistance right away, I gotta know. I can dispatch ..."

"No! I'm perfectly fine. Nothing is wrong with me," Noora said impatiently, though indeed, something was terribly wrong. She had left Um Faheema's copper chain and blue bead under her pillow. *At Ian Cohen's house!* She was now without the crutch that she believed guided her and guarded her from evil. She couldn't go back, she realized, her heart sinking. How could she have forgotten Um Faheema's precious gift? The one thing that kept her close to her Bedouin friends and brought her a sense of security.

At the emergency entrance, Noora paid the driver and ran inside. She had to find another taxi, and try to lose Kenilworth. Why was he so determined to go after her? *Didn't he cause enough damage?* But the cab driver told her the "Ferrari" had made a turn a couple of blocks before the hospital. Maybe Kennilworth gave up the chase. He probably ran back to his stepfather and told him God knows what kind of a lie. She ran in the opposite direction, where she remembered taxis lined up outside along the curb. She pushed through the exit's glass doors and out of the hospital's main lobby, and hopped in a taxi van.

"The Los Angeles airport please," she said, closing the van's sliding door.

CHAPTER 55
MOUSTAFA'S DISCOVERY

Settled comfortably on an overstuffed pale yellow chaise, Ahna Morgenbesser watched the evening news. For nearly four decades, she had lived in a second-floor walkup on the Rue du President Wilson. Her cozy two-bedroom apartment was crammed with century-old furniture and bric-a-brac. An ornate upright piano stood in a corner by a tall window framed by sheer lacy curtains. A collection of old framed photographs and other memorabilia was displayed on the mantle of an old marble fireplace. A faded golden velvet couch, lamps in the style of *Doctor Zhivago,* and a well-worn oriental rug gave a sense of warmth and intimacy to the room.

"Mrs. Ahna Morgenbesser?" Noora's voice came through the receiver when Annette's grandmother picked up the ringing phone next to her chaise.

"Yes, yes!" Ahna said happily, recognizing the girl's voice.

"This is Kelley Karlton, Annette's friend. We met at her wedding ..."

"Oui, ah oui, bonjour!"

"I hope I am not phoning at an improper time."

"Au contraire," Ahna said, reaching for the remote and turning off the television. "*Comment allez-vous?* Oh, I do hope you are in Paris, yes?"

"Yes. Actually, I am at the airport ..."

"Wonderful. Welcome. You plan to take a taxi?"

"Yes."

"I'll give you directions. I just baked a Schwarzwalder kirsch torte. I hope you are hungry."

Moustafa felt an electric jolt from his brain to the pit of his stomach. He held his sandwich in midair, his mouth stuffed with food. He chewed slowly to make sure he did not miss one detail as he watched Noora through a crowd of travelers. She was standing by a row of public phones. She was on the other side of the walkway, too far for him to grab her. She was blonde now, with short hair—trying to disguise herself, but she could not fool him. He observed her as she picked up one of the receivers. She looked at a piece of paper, pressed the buttons on the phone, and began to talk, keeping her head down. He watched how she brought her head up and smiled. Without a doubt, she was talking to a man.

May Allah let me burn in hell if that is not the sharmouta. Moustafa had a sudden revelation: It was she who caused the helicopter crash that sent the future young doctor, the first son of Mr. Fendil, to his death. Her brother had to be the one who took her out of the pool, when they all thought she was dead, and then she killed him.

Moustafa crushed the sandwich in his hand and tossed it in a trash bin next to the food cart. He watched her as she hung up the phone, picked up her carry-on, and walked away—the sinful walk that belonged to her, like fingerprints.

He cursed his cousin Youssef for leaving him to watch their two carry-ons and attaché cases while he went to the men's room; of all times for the idiot to have to go and pee.

But Moustafa could still catch her. He rushed down the walkway through the crowded airport, straining to keep her in sight. She disappeared amid the fast-moving sea of travelers, but he spotted her again, heading down the escalators to the baggage claim.

Who had she been talking to on the phone? Was she to be picked up in a limousine? Someone was protecting her. *Who?*

"Stop!" Moustafa shouted in Arabic. He forced his way through the crowd. "Stop that girl!" he screamed in broken French. *"Arretez cette fille!"*

She walked straight ahead, through revolving doors, without looking back. Moustafa was surrounded by foreign faces giving him disapproving glances. *What are these European imbeciles looking at?!* "Let me pass. Let me through!" he shouted in Arabic.

He shoved his way down the escalator. As he was about to go through the revolving doors after the girl, he was stopped by strong hands that snatched him from the back of his suit collar.

"What are you doing?!" his cousin Youssef said furiously, pulling him away from a crowd of curious faces.

"I found her!"

"What?!"

"The Fendil girl!"

Youssef was a couple of inches taller than Moustafa, and stronger. He held Moustafa firmly by the lapels of his gray suit and said between clenched teeth, "Stop it this instant, or I'll report you to the sheik!" Youssef's eyes were fierce.

Moustafa stared at his cousin. He felt sweat immediately pouring out of him.

"Where did you leave our luggage?" Youssef's voice was icy.

"Let go of me."

"I will not tolerate this. You understand?"

Moustafa held up his hands. "*Aiwah,* I understand. Let go."

"How could you run and scream like a madman, chasing after some ... *girl?*" He pushed Moustafa ahead of him toward the escalator. "Where is our luggage?!" he asked as they were riding back up.

"Youssef, you have to believe me. That was Mr. Fendil's ... Mr. Farid Fendil's *daughter!*"

Youssef shoved him up the moving escalator. "You keep this up and I will no longer defend you! You've been obsessed with that girl too long! She is dead! That Fendil case is closed! People are staring at us. For the last time, where's our luggage?!" He stepped off the escalator and pushed Moustafa ahead of him.

"Next to the sandwich place. Youssef! Stop pushing me and listen!"

"I can't leave you for a second! Don't you know if you had gone through the revolving doors, you wouldn't be able to come back, because I'm holding your ticket?!" He growled. "*Hamdallah!* There they are. Looks like no one took anything. Anyone could've walked off with my laptop!" Youssef retrieved their attaché cases and their two black leather carry-ons. "Hold those two. One more misstep and you're deep in *khara.*"

Khara f'weshak! Shit on your face! Moustafa wanted to shout right back at Youssef. He took the two pieces of luggage and glanced back over Youssef's shoulder to see if there was a chance he could spot the girl, but Youssef continued to push him ahead. "Move!" They made it to the gate, where an agent waited for the last passengers to board the plane.

Moustafa took his assigned window seat in business class of the huge aircraft, while Youssef took the aisle seat. Moustafa squeezed a tight fist and rested his cheek against the window. He wished he could throw a good fist into the porthole and break it so they would have to deplane.

He had to analyze the situation carefully. Once they landed in New York, he would find a way to fly back to Paris. He could easily have seized her, if it hadn't been for his shit partner.

Youssef turned to Moustafa and shot him a suspicious stare. "I can't believe what you did!"

Moustafa remained silent. He watched the last few passengers as they made their way through the cabin aisles in business class, his mind on Noora.

"Don't you think our people have a bad enough reputation?" Youssef whispered angrily. "Not only in Paris, but in the world?"

Moustafa gritted his teeth, wishing he could shut Youssef up.

"Every time they see a dark-skinned man, whether Middle Eastern or Mexican, Sudanese or South African," Youssef went on lecturing, "especially a man with a thick black mustache like *yours,*" he gave it a sudden yank, "everyone assumes you're on a suicide mission, ready to explode in a public place!"

Moustafa never felt more humiliated. How dare Youssef touch his mustache in such an embarrassing manner! He moved his body closer to the window, but he was still too close to Youssef. Moustafa had to control his anger. Soon it would be Youssef who would be humiliated—they would all regret it—when the truth came out that they had been made fools! Fooled by a young woman, no less. He did not want her to roam around the world, enjoying life, that whore, doing more sinful things to other men! It still angered him every time he thought of how she had looked at him in that restaurant in London with such disdain. She had to die. First, he had to watch her on her knees, begging, pleading for her life. Shit, he realized he was infatuated. No! He just wanted to touch her! Then, he wanted to watch her beg. Then she would get what she deserved ...

"How many times I warned you!" Youssef went on, barging into Moustafa's furious thoughts. "And how could you leave our luggage in the middle of the airport!"

Moustafa waited for Youssef to finish his speech. Youssef always thought he was superior because he had more education, but *he* was the idiot. None of them had seen her body taken out of the pool. They had been criminally careless, and they had all failed in their duty to Mr. Farid Fendil.

He allowed a long silence before calmly turning to Youssef. "You are right. What I did was wrong."

Youssef picked the airline magazine from the seat pocket in front of him and started leafing through it angrily. "Fasten your seat belt, *homar*."

The flight to the United States seemed endless, but Moustafa kept calm, reminding himself that he had a plan. When he returned to Paris, he would hire the best private detectives to find her.

As they landed in New York, Youssef was still frowning. Before reaching up to the overhead bin and retrieving their carry-on luggage, Youssef looked down at Moustafa and said sternly, "I'll be watching you."

Moustafa remained silent.

At New York's La Guardia Airport, two members of the MOFHAJ greeted Moustafa and Youssef. They were clad in the same dark gray suits and red ties. Together and in perfect unison, they marched out the gate and waited at the baggage claim. When they retrieved their luggage, they filed out to the sidewalk, where a black stretch limousine waited.

Inside the car, Youssef finally spoke. "How is the sheik?"

"We are told the honorable Sheik Abdullah Kharoub is recovering well."

"*Hamdallah*, thanks be to God," a burly MOFHAJ member nodded.

"*Hamdallah*," everyone repeated.

They exchanged no further words until they arrived at the hospital in Manhattan and were directed to the oncology floor, where a few other MOFHAJ men were waiting.

One by one, they filed into the sheik's hospital room to pay their respects. Sitting on a high-back chair, the sheik looked pale as chalk. He had lost weight. His thick beard was so thinned out, there was hardly anything left. Moustafa noticed a tube going into his chest. The sheik was smiling and appeared genuinely glad to see his men. Moustafa saw that all of his headmen were present, including four of his eldest sons.

"It's a new approach," Moustafa heard the sheik explain. "There is no guarantee; it's all experimental, but I am in the hands of Allah now, and I am doing well, *hamdallah,*" he said. "I already had four weeks of this revolutionary chemotherapy," he added, pointing to the IV going through his chest. "I have twelve more weeks to go. They call it triple blockade. They won't have to poke me through the veins anymore." He looked down at his chest. "You can barely see it, and now I can barely feel it while they slowly drip the medicine that kills the cancer. It's a Portocath ... less than an inch in diameter. The size of an American quarter. They call it a port ..."

Moustafa was shocked to find out that the sheik had been diagnosed with prostate cancer two years before. Two years and no one told him? Cancer cells had ravaged the sheik's body and gone into his bones, he told them, and it was too late to operate. The more he spoke about his illness, the more Moustafa felt ill-at-ease.

"The prostate specialists in Paris said I had less than eighteen months to live. Allah guided me to the Egyptian oncologist who is right now in New York, that's why I had to come here. But he just announced he will be opening a special clinic in Jordan. So I will be in good hands. That doctor is in great demand. He is a genius. A Muslim. Right now he is lecturing at Harvard University. Imagine that. Because we have smart, educated men and Allah is on our side. *Hamdallah...*"

"Hamdallah," everyone chanted, standing with their heads bowed respectfully, their hands folded in front of them.

Moustafa stood behind his peers by the wall, next to the door. The IV going into the sheik's chest made Moustafa queasy. As long as there was no spilling of blood, he thought he could tolerate standing there. However, he was feeling progressively worse. If he fainted, it would be a disgrace.

The sheik said his "PSA" had gone back down to zero. *What did that mean?*

Sheik Abdullah Kharoub had been Moustafa's mentor. He provided him, and many other men, with respectable jobs they would never have had otherwise. Most of the MOFHAJ men came from poor families in rural villages throughout the Middle East. But how could Moustafa look up to the sheik now? He remembered reading in a magazine that a man with prostate cancer could not have an erection. A terrible revelation. A curse! With his facial hair nearly gone, his revered mentor was ... well, no longer a man.

Without wanting to, Moustafa had been staring at the IV, feeling more and more queasy. He bowed, praying to be dismissed and released from the hospital room that smelled like medicine and illness.

He drew a breath of relief when the MOFHAJ members were finally allowed to leave. Like a procession, the men marched to the exit—Moustafa feeling better with each step that took him away from the hospital room. Now that they had paid their respects to the sheik, Moustafa should receive a paycheck for his last assignment. He certainly deserved a vacation. After he brought back the Fendil girl, the sheik would assign him more important jobs; he was sure of that. And Youssef would be diarrhea-green with envy. Soon enough, that time would come.

Outside the hospital, Moustafa and Youssef waited their turn for a cab. Youssef suddenly turned to Moustafa. "I almost told the sheik about your irresponsible behavior," he said. "But I didn't want to agitate him at this time."

Moustafa was alarmed but tried to conceal it.

Riding in the cab, he was quiet. Youssef would do such a thing? Betray Moustafa, his own cousin? *When I catch the slut, you'll be on your knees, licking my balls!*

When Youssef and Moustafa reached their room at the Marriott near the airport, Moustafa turned to Youssef and looked him straight in the eye. "My behavior has been unforgivable," he bluffed. "I will give no further cause for concern. I have sworn to protect and obey," he said, looking steadily at his cousin.

Youssef gave a quick nod and said nothing further.

During the night, Youssef tossed restlessly in his bed while mumbling discernible words. "No ... not ... my time ..."

Youssef's mumbling gave Moustafa an eerie feeling; he lay awake wishing he could have his own room. At dawn, when Moustafa had finally fallen asleep, someone banged on the door. He jolted out of a deep slumber and wobbled over to answer it.

Youssef was sound asleep. *That son of a dog can sleep through a bomb,* Moustafa thought as he opened the door. A thick envelope was handed to him by a MOFHAJ member.

"Was that room service?" Youssef asked, lifting his head from the pillow, his eyes barely open.

"No," Moustafa said, praying it was their payroll checks and feeling the envelope. "Looks like airline tickets." Moustafa sat down at the edge of his bed. *If Allah is with me, they will be for Paris.* "There's a note attached," he said, holding the envelope toward the faint light coming from the window. "Says we are to open the envelope immediately and follow instructions." He handed the envelope and note to Youssef, who was trying to shake the sleep from his eyes.

"Turn on the light. Open it."

"You know it is my duty to give sealed envelopes to you first, as my senior partner," Moustafa said.

"I grant you permission. Read it," Youssef said, shuffling to the bathroom.

Moustafa switched on the lamp by his bedside. He opened the envelope. "Payroll checks," he said loud enough for Youssef to hear. With fury, he noticed that Youssef was compensated almost twice as much for the same assignment. He scanned the typewritten words on MOFHAJ letterhead. "We are to leave this afternoon." He looked away as Youssef urinated loudly in the bathroom. Moustafa felt his stomach churn.

"Going home, I hope, if it is the will of Allah," Youssef said from the bathroom. "We are due a little time off. I will be grateful to see my wife and all my kids."

Moustafa examined the tickets. "Cairo!" he exclaimed. His heart sank. *Cairo?* How could he be so unlucky, he wondered, reading the instructions.

"We are to leave New York ... and go to ... Cairo."

"Finally. Then where?"

"Wait at the gate in Cairo. There, we are to receive instructions for our next assignment," Moustafa said. He recognized the sheik's signature on the bottom of the paper, which was as good as God's final words.

Moustafa sat staring at the wall, nearly paralyzed.

"It must be for a very important government official. Otherwise, they would have given us more information," Youssef said. "Let me see those tickets."

Youssef and Moustafa arrived at La Guardia early. EgyptAir's gate opened its door for passengers to board the plane. Youssef handed over both tickets—his and Moustafa's—to the agent. He treated Moustafa like a kid who had misbehaved. Moustafa wished he could knock Youssef's teeth out.

Youssef settled on the aisle seat in business class. Passengers were starting to pour in and find their assigned seats. The moment there was a break on the aisle, Moustafa turned to Youssef.

"*Aii*, I have a bad case of diarrhea," he announced and unbuckled his seatbelt.

"What?" Youssef asked, annoyed.

"Must've been that sea bass last night," Moustafa said, rising and holding the seat in front of him for support. "Excuse me, but if I could just sit in the bathroom for a while," he whispered loudly as Youssef barely gave him room to squeeze out. Moustafa made his way through the busy aisles to the rear of the aircraft. He closed the door to one of the stalls in coach. Moments later, he emerged. An airline hostess had her back to him.

"Miss, oh miss," he said in Arabic to the young woman.

She turned to Moustafa with a friendly smile.

"I'm sorry, but I'm afraid I'll need to use the facilities often. I think I caught a serious stomach flu or food poisoning ..."

"I'm sorry to hear that."

As passengers were settling in before takeoff, Moustafa spotted Youssef peering over his shoulder from his seat ahead. "Is there an empty seat near the ... the toilets?"

"Mr. Youssef Sammek?" the hostess asked, bending to Youssef's ear and whispering. Then, louder, as she rose to give way to other arriving passengers through the aisle, she concluded. "If he doesn't come back to his assigned seat by the time we take off, I told him he can sit in coach. We have a few empty seats in the rear of the plane, near the lavatories."

"Thank you," Youssef answered, embarrassed. When she walked away, Youssef shook his head, mumbling curses to himself.

Inside the lavatory cubicle, Moustafa opened the door a crack and managed to slide the latch to "Occupied" with the tip of a long key. He closed the door. While two other airline stewardesses were busy helping passengers tuck luggage in overhead compartments, Moustafa swiftly ducked his way through an open rear door, tailing two mechanics who were deplaning.

With the crew and passengers all busy preparing for departure, it seemed no one saw Moustafa disembark. He meandered down the covered walkway. He sure as hell didn't expect it to be so easy. But if he were to change his mind, he would probably have a hard time getting back on board, he realized, because Youssef had kept his boarding pass stub.

He mounted a cement staircase that appeared to be heading back up to the gates.

"Hey! Where are you going?" a security guard challenged him at the landing.

Moustafa froze. Youssef's words rang in his ears. "*Every time they see a dark-skinned man … bushy mustache, like yours …*" He'd been caught. He'd get into more shit with Youssef.

"Where are you going?" the security guard queried again.

"Sorry. I am picking up my wife … and my family …" he managed to say, sweat pouring out of him.

"You need to go through that door. This area is *forbidden!* How did you get here?"

"I … I don't know. I was searching for the men's room. The agent upstairs told me to take the elevator. I don't know how I got down here. I am lost."

"You took the wrong elevator," the security guard said, shaking his head. He pointed to an elevator behind Moustafa. "Push the M button. It'll take you back to the mezzanine. Then turn to your left and follow the signs."

"Oh, thank you, sir."

Moustafa could hardly believe he was actually standing at the airport, back at the gate and looking out the window. His airplane was pulling away from the gate now. He waited a few more minutes and watched the aircraft taxi out to one of the runways. *I'd better not stand here,* he thought. What if Youssef could see him through the airplane window? No, that could not be possible. His seat was on the opposite side of the plane. *Better not take chances,* he told himself, rushing down one of the long corridors in search of the men's room. He chortled to himself. *Youssef probably thinks I'm still on the plane, shitting. Who's the* homar *now, Youssef?* Luckily, he had convinced his partner to stop at the bank before they got to the airport. With more than $5,000 in his pocket, and after exchanging his dollars to francs, Moustafa had enough to get around Paris for a while and hire a good detective. But how would he explain to Youssef and the sheik that he had deplaned just because he was ill? What else was he to do? He would justify that he had rushed to get back on the plane, but it left without him. Surely they would have to believe his story. However, the sheik no longer mattered—an impotent man. A man who was not man enough to grow a beard or mustache anymore. A dying man. He could no longer be his mentor.

Moustafa made his way to the men's room, entered a stall, and sat on the toilet so he could have some quiet time to analyze his complicated predicament. He rested both elbows on his knees. He would tell it like this: He had a terrible ... No, he had an embarrassing case of diarrhea. He thought he could make it to the men's room at the gate—because all the lavatories were occupied? No, because the stewardess didn't let him use the lavatories so soon before takeoff? He was in no condition to travel at that time, really. Yes, that's what he would tell them: He would say that he thought he had time to make it back on board the plane, and it left without him. He had to stick to a smart and simple alibi.

If the slut went down to the baggage claim only one day ago, he calculated, she still had to be in Paris. He reached inside the breast pocket of his jacket and pulled out his wallet. From a worn leather compartment, he removed three photographs of Noora—five-by-sevens he had folded in half and trimmed to fit in his wallet. He would scan those pictures in a computer and change hair colors for the detectives to see the many faces of the *sharmouta*. Perhaps he didn't need a detective. Why waste good money? Maybe she was at Le Crillon. Or the George V Hotel. Or the

Ritz? Where else would a girl like that stay? *Other than in bed with some rich* ibn kalb! "Slut!" he muttered, feeling a stabbing pain of jealousy.

Ten minutes later, Moustafa headed to the gift shop. He purchased a razor and mirrored sunglasses and returned to the men's room. Twenty minutes later, a clean-shaven Moustafa walked toward the TWA ticket counter.

He had not been without a mustache since he grew one when he was sixteen years old. His upper lip felt naked and uncomfortably cool.

He put on his sunglasses and started down the long walkway to the ticket counter, his mind on his lost mustache. There seemed to be some commotion. Women started screaming. People behind him were shouting, running back toward him. He turned. *I've been caught,* he thought. *But how? Did Youssef tell the pilots that his partner was missing?* Crowds were gathering in front of the airport monitors while other people were running to the huge glass windows surrounding the gates.

"Did you hear?" Moustafa heard one man behind him say to another.

"Oh my God!" a woman shouted. "It's not possible."

A few feet away from him, a Middle Eastern woman in traditional black robe and headdress fainted. While some people ran to her help, others were screaming and crying.

What's going on? I'd better get out of here, Moustafa thought. But suddenly, he couldn't move. His body felt like a clump of cement. He began to shiver furiously and his skin crawled with cold sweat. He stared blankly up at the monitor. His flight to Cairo flashed red: "See Agent."

He heard the news; he didn't need an agent to confirm it. The flight he was supposed to be on, the huge aircraft with all the people, hundreds of them, *with Youssef,* had crashed less than fifty miles out, into the ocean.

Remembering his red tie with the golden MOFHAJ emblem embroidered in the middle, he quickly removed it and thrust it in his coat pocket.

Trembling, he searched for another airline.

The agent at TWA's counter was kind to him and told him the flight to Paris now had several cancellations popping up on computer screens. Moustafa figured people would not want to fly soon after news of a plane crash. He told the attractive young ticketing agent that he had to join his family in Paris because his father died and he had to board the next flight. Due to the plane crash, the young agent was becoming more flustered, as the line of nervous travelers was rapidly growing longer and longer behind Moustafa. Busy printing out a new ticket and trying to figure out why her stapler was not working properly, she scarcely listened to Moustafa, and didn't ask for his passport.

At sunset, Moustafa's flight finally took off to Paris. Once they were airborne, most of the passengers were grasping their armrests, apparently uneasy about flying. Moustafa moved his lips in prayer. He was in the fifth row, in coach. *Khamsah,* five, was a good number. Traditionally, it brought protection, at times even luck.

When his flight landed in Paris at seven in the morning, Moustafa had a severe headache and was drenched in perspiration through the lining of his suit. He walked down the entryway and gateways, down the escalators where Youssef had stopped him only two days before—just outside the revolving doors leading to the baggage claim area.

He had cursed Youssef, and now Youssef was gone. Allah bless his soul. *Allah Akbar.* God is great. *Where are you, Youssef? Where I could have been!* Moustafa's entire body jerked from a severe shiver while he waited in the long line to have his passport stamped. He had to focus on the present and set aside Youssef's tragedy. He had other worries. What if the passport agent up ahead questioned him? What if someone on the plane did report him missing? What if they knew he had deplaned and suspected he had planted a bomb?! No. His passport was in order, and the names of the passengers on the flight could not have been announced so soon. Could they? Slowly moving forward in line, he wondered how many hours had passed since the crash. His partner was probably in the bowels of the Atlantic or maybe even parts of him were floating on the surface of the ocean—being devoured by sharks. Blood had gone up to the tip of his head, and he knew his cheeks were flushed. Drops of perspiration tickled as they flowed down his temples, and he wiped them with his coat sleeve. He probably had a fever. His entire body jolted at the sound of his passport being stamped.

He walked out and followed other travelers, his stomach practically in his throat. This time, he wouldn't mind having a tall glass of whiskey on ice. He breathed deeply and felt relieved to be out of there, until thoughts of Youssef returned. He shuffled down to the baggage claim with nothing to claim.

Making his way out of the busy airport like a sleepwalker, he stood gazing blankly at the cabs and shuttle buses lined along the sidewalk. Somehow, he found himself in a cab, heading for Paris.

He asked the driver if he knew of a small, inexpensive hotel, not too far from Le Crillon Hotel—if that were possible. Luckily, the Asian driver knew his way around Paris. He said that he used to be a professional chauffeur in Taiwan. Or was it Thailand? The cab driver stared at Moustafa through his rearview mirror. Moustafa probably looked pathetic.

"Are you okay, monsieur?" the cabbie asked with a thick accent.

"My French is miserable like me," Moustafa said, hoping to enlist sympathy. "Speak English?"

"I speak English. Oh yes, yes. Where you from?"

Moustafa had to reflect on that question for a moment. "I'm from ... London. My mother was British, actually," Moustafa lied. "My fiancée was ... she was on that airplane that crashed."

"No! The airplane that left from New York and ..."

"Yes, yes." Moustafa hung his head. "Alas yes, it is horrible."

"The one that happened just yesterday?"

"Yes," Moustafa said, starting to cry real tears.

"I just heard it on the radio. It's all over the stations," the cab driver said.

Moustafa wondered if anyone would describe him to the police and say he was a possible suspect. *Did anyone know what caused that crash?* Moustafa didn't dare ask the driver.

"I'm very sorry, monsieur," the cabbie said, glancing again at his passenger through his rearview mirror. "It is horrible!"

"She had money with her. A dowry ... to get us started ... My loved one and her money went ..."

Silence on the part of the driver.

"Don't worry. I have plenty to pay you. And I have credit cards, of course ..."

"Oh, no, no, I was not worried about that," the cabbie said. "Just very sorry. Very sorry."

"I need to go to a little hotel that doesn't cost too much. I want to shower and maybe rest a little before I see the family. I can't think too good right now." It was true; he felt like a clump of slimy flesh. "Her mother, her brother … they live near Le Crillon Hotel. But I just need to be alone and think …"

"I know a nice place. The manager is my friend. He's from my country. He give you good discount."

"I am most grateful, mon-see-oor …"

Moustafa checked into a hotel on a side street behind the lavish Meurice Hotel. A small bed-and-breakfast, sandwiched between newly renovated buildings in a narrow alleyway, the structure seemed to be awaiting demolition. The lobby was filled with incense smoke emanating from a miniature Thai temple propped on a stand near the check-in counter. Moustafa was in the right part of town, and the room was a good 70 percent cheaper than the luxury hotels. He was glad to be far from the airport.

Finally alone inside his dreary hotel room, Moustafa hung the "Do Not Disturb" sign on his door and sat down on the edge of the bed. Gripping the remote control, he stared at the tiny television set. It seemed every channel announced the crash. Didn't they have anything else to broadcast?

Why did Allah spare his life? Praise to Allah. *Allah Akbar,* God is great. He turned to the window. Through the yellowed lacy curtains, all he could see was a gray wall. He curled up in the fetal position on the frayed brocade comforter covering the saggy hotel mattress, and immediately fell into a deep slumber.

Moustafa's eyes popped open. All was dark in his room now, except for the flickering of the television set. He could feel he had a high fever. His throat was dry and sore. He glanced at the digital clock on the nightstand, displaying 7:30 in the evening. He peeled off his clothes, dropping everything on the floor. Wrapping himself in the comforter, he staggered into the bathroom to get a drink of water.

Shuffling back to bed, he slipped under the covers, trembling uncontrollably and wishing the hotel provided a terrycloth robe. Nothing was provided, no armoire, not even a dresser—just a chair and a small table. He glanced at the television set. Pictures of the passengers who had died on the crash were scrolling down at low speed, with the names below each photograph. A sad song played in the background. Why did they have to play that mournful music?!

He forgot about his fever and everything when he saw his own picture on television. He jumped out of bed and kneeled in front of the small screen. Dumbfounded, he watched the other faces as they scrolled down. Moustafa waited, holding his breath to see if his picture would reappear. Was it someone who resembled him? Perhaps he was delirious.

He found the remote and returned shivering to bed, pulling the covers to his chest. He flipped to another channel. Two television announcers were talking to each other about the crash. He flipped again, and the next channel was scrolling down photographs of the victims. There it was! Along with others, a copy of his own passport picture, on television, for millions to see! The announcer spoke rapidly in French, and Moustafa couldn't understand what he said. He switched to a Middle Eastern channel, but the announcers spoke Persian. He switched to an English-speaking channel and waited, watching the screen while his mind swirled with shock and questions. Awhile later, his picture appeared again, this time with his name.

Moustafa Abdel Gamal Samak (34)

It scrolled down fast, but fast enough for him to see that they even had the nerve to show his age, and they misspelled his last name.

They made a more serious error. He was alive. He must call and let them know! He looked around the four walls and held his head in his hands. *Am I losing my mind?* He reached for the phone. He had to contact the sheik in New York. He lifted the receiver, then placed it back in its cradle. *The sheik should be grieving for me by now,* Moustafa thought. *He must have heard the news. What about Youssef? They did not display his picture. Did Youssef leave the airplane too?* Did he chase after Moustafa when he couldn't find him on the plane? Moustafa's chest was heaving. No, Youssef was on that airplane. Youssef was dead. Moustafa barely made it to the bathroom before vomiting.

When he opened his eyes again, the sun had not yet come up. He automatically turned his head to the television screen, where names were scrolling down without pictures, in alphabetical order. He saw his name again, in black letters.

MOUSTAFA GAMAL SAMMEK

This time, they spelled Sammek correctly. Beneath his name, there was no mistaking. He read:

YOUSSEF ABDULLAH SAMMEK

It was confirmed. Youssef was on that plane.

They say that when people die suddenly, their soul cannot admit that they are dead. They continue to roam the earth, like ghosts.

"But I *am* alive!" he said, looking around his hotel room. "I left that airplane … I did not die!" He wanted to go out on the street and smoke a cigarette, drink something, eat, talk to people on the street, and see if they would respond—do the things men do when they are alive. But he was too sick to go out. He looked down at his arms, at his trembling hands, and weakly pinched himself here and there. *Ya satehr. I am not dead, God protect me, I* am *among the living.*

He chanted, "In the name of Allah …"

He kneeled on the floor and faced the window, putting his forehead to the musty old carpet. "*Allah Akbar!* Allah granted me life so I can find the wicked woman. For this, I am grateful. For this, I promise on my own life, I will see to it that the slut gets the punishment she deserves. God is great!"

*****   *****   *****

"It is terrible," Ahna said. "More innocent people dying. They're not saying what was the cause of that awful crash. Maybe it is too soon to tell."

Sitting in Ahna Morgenbesser's easy chair in her cozy living room, Noora held herself upright like a stiff plank, worrying that perhaps she knew someone on that plane. She had watched some of the names they scrolled on the screen. Instinctively, she checked for the name Amir, and luckily, no such name was shown. She waited until they scrolled down to the letter F, to see if any family member had been on that flight, and to her relief, there was no one she knew. *Thank God.* She prayed silently for the victims of the crash, and turned away from the television set.

Her own troubles were small by comparison to the latest news, but she could not stop thinking about what happened in Bel Air. She had betrayed Ian. Again, her life was in turmoil. Again she was on the run, wondering where she would live. She had felt the need to be loved, even for a brief moment, and the scent of Kennilworth's cologne broke down her defenses.

Only small-minded people blame others instead of themselves. How could she lose her head over something so silly, even though the scent reminded her of the man she would always love? The man she would never have again—without some miracle. She didn't deserve a miracle; she had kissed other men. Why had she done that? Was she given something stronger than champagne? *How naïve. How stupid could I have been?!* She must try to remember what happened that night, however painful. When she was in Eilat with Nageeb and recovering from her injuries, she knew he hadn't told her everything. He said there were photos of her. *What kind of photos and who took them? Did Michel know?* She betrayed Michel, she dishonored her father. Nageeb died protecting her. *Why do I hurt those I love most?* She remembered dear Um Faheema, who had given her hope; Noora missed her terribly. The lump in her throat grew larger and she fought back tears.

Could Michel still be in Paris? His hotel was near the Louvre, maybe a Metro ride away from Ahna's apartment at Levallois. *What was the name of that hotel?* she wondered, feeling dizzy. How could she have forgotten? *Michel must have graduated by now—and left Paris. He could have already met … and married someone else. Someone faithful.*

The velvet couch felt soft under her fingers. Could she sleep here tonight? Would it be wrong to impose on Annette's grandmother? She did invite her …

"You look so pale, my little dear," Ahna said.

Noora looked up. She did not see her when she returned from the kitchen.

"You don't have to watch that channel."

"Oh … That's fine."

"I keep the television on all day," Ahna said. "For company. But all they have today is news of the plane crash. I am so glad you are here." She smiled at Noora and waddled back down the narrow hall.

"Would you like a piece of cake?" Ahna asked, returning with a decorative silver tray.

"Perhaps a small piece, thank you. It looks wonderful. I really didn't come here to disturb you."

"Not at all. I am pleased you are here."

"How very kind of you. If I may be of any help," Noora said, wishing she could just curl up on the old soft couch and forget everything.

"You had a long trip," Ahna said, cutting her cake. *"Ah, J'ai oublié la carafe de chocolat au lait…"*

Noora understood. Ahna had forgotten the carafe of hot chocolate. "Allow me, please," she offered, standing up.

The kitchen was long and narrow, with a small gas stove and a fridge snuggled between the sink and counter. It also had a large, seemingly new oven. A small table with a chair next to the window that faced a courtyard told a story—of a woman who must do a lot of baking, but spends most of her time alone.

Noora returned to the living room with an ornate Limoge pot that emanated the inviting smell of hot cocoa, and she placed it on the coffee table. Ahna poured the beverage into matching cups that looked like small cereal bowls with handles.

Noora inhaled the warm aroma and closed her eyes as she sipped. The hot beverage felt good as she slowly drank. But she had to put the cup down. She set it on the delicate, crocheted doily in front of her. As she did, she suddenly burst into uncontrollable sobs—right in front of Ahna Morgenbesser, and she could not stop.

When Noora's sobs finally subsided, Ahna rose from her chaise with some difficulty and reached for a box of tissues on a shelf near the upright piano.

"Please … forgive me," Noora managed to say.

"It is good to cry," Mrs. Morgenbesser said, handing her the box of tissues. "It does not look like you have done that in a long time, *ma chère* Kelley Karlton."

"My name is not Kelley ... It is Noora ... Noora Fendil," she said miserably, and without really meaning to, she told the truth about herself. She could not stop talking until she had told Ahna everything she remembered—from the dreadful day her father tried to drown her, to the helicopter crash—the Bedouins, the man with the mustache who chased after her in Alexandria—about everything that had happened, until she met Annette on the beach. She also told Ahna about her relationship with Ian Cohen. "I didn't trust him at first, but after we returned from Honolulu, and he was recovering, I felt that Mr. Cohen and I had built a certain bond. A trusting friendship."

By the time Noora had finished pouring her heart out, Ahna's cake had been eaten, and another pot of hot cocoa had been poured. The old grandfather clock in the hallway chimed four times. Ahna Morgenbesser sat in silence, not once interrupting Noora's monologue.

Finally, when she was sure Noora was done, Ahna spoke. "Dear child," she said, "you have kept so much pain inside your heart. So much pain for so long. In the end, nothing can be more gratifying than to reveal the truth of our life."

Noora blew her nose and breathed deeply. "Sorry. I am so sorry."

"There is no need to ever be sorry, Noora ... Your name. Does it have a meaning?"

"In Arabic, *'noor'* means light. That's what my name was *supposed* to mean."

"Indeed it does. And now," she said, rising, "I have a hearty *poulet à la reine*. I think you need a little nourishment before you go to sleep."

"Oh no, I could no longer impose."

"It is my pleasure."

"Thank you so much," Noora said with another deep sigh. A heavy load seemed to have been lifted, and Noora was indeed famished. Ahna's delicious cake had been devoured hours before, and she was hungry again. But she was embarrassed for taking so much of Ahna's time and hospitality.

"The man you described with a mustache ..." Ahna asked, after Noora finished her chicken *à la reine*. "The one in Alexandria. You first saw him in London, you said?"

Noora nodded.

"Where do you suppose he is now?"

"Where? I … I don't know," Noora answered, surprised by the question. "I would certainly have no clue. I tried to forget about him after … after I went to America. Certainly he must have given up … It's been more than a year. He could never find me. He must think I'm still in the Middle East somewhere."

"One would assume so," Ahna said with a frown. She rose. "Come, I have something to show you."

Down the hall, Ahna Morgenbesser opened a door. Separated by a carpet with water lily designs, two single beds with flowered bedspreads stood on opposite sides along the walls.

"It was Giselle's room," Ahna explained, standing at the door. "Giselle, my daughter; Annette's mother. Annette grew up here. They shared this room. Annette could not stay here after her mother died. It was too painful for her. If you don't mind sleeping here, the room is yours."

Noora felt that she had stepped into a corner of a country French garden—like a Monet painting. "It's lovely," she said.

Several old books and porcelain statuettes were positioned on wall-mounted shelves. A tall, narrow window between the two beds was framed by floor-to-ceiling faded blue taffeta drapes tied back by brass hooks shaped like a rose.

A faint early-morning light was visible through the lacy curtains covering the window.

"Is it dawn? Already?" Noora asked, surprised.

"Yes."

"Goodness, I've kept you awake all night! I am so, so sorry."

"It was good … a time much needed for both of us."

How could that be possible? Noora wondered, when all she did was consume Ahna's food and talk about herself.

"Now we will both be able to get some sleep," Ahna said with a comforting smile. "Good night, *ma chérie,* and good rest."

CHAPTER 56
CITY OF LOVE AND DANGER

On a misty gray Parisian morning, Moustafa walked out of his dreary hotel. Miserably, he trudged along the narrow sidewalk on the Rue de something-or-other, a name he never bothered to remember, because he never imagined that after six months, he would still be looking for the Fendil girl! He didn't know how many fruitless days and nights he had spent walking the streets, taking the Metro from one end of Paris to the other. Moustafa was nearly out of money and out of hope.

Soon he would have no choice but to find a job. Who would hire him without a *carte d'identité*? Unless he worked in a Middle Eastern restaurant as a dishwasher. The thought of taking such a job sickened him. When he was a kid, he knew how to pick pockets. He was very swift and never got caught. But that was ages ago, and he was sure he had lost the touch. The one good thing about working in a kitchen was that he would surely get free meals. But while he was busy in a hot, greasy kitchen, the girl could escape in a limousine to the airport.

Moustafa trudged along the street, where wealthy tourists shopped. She had to still be in Paris. Allah would surely guide him. Otherwise, the Almighty One would have given him the need to leave the city. He was sure of that. He stopped at the window of a small bistro and stared at his reflection. If anyone he knew saw him, they would not recognize him. He had straightened his hair and had it dyed an auburn brown. But he was still bothered by the feeling of nakedness above his lip. He had to remain disguised. As soon as he found her, he would grow his mustache back again. He turned away and continued his walk, looking for a place to buy cigarettes.

At a magazine kiosk near the entrance of the Metro station not far from the luxurious Hotel Le Crillon, Moustafa nearly dropped his change when he spotted the slender figure, only a few feet away, heading toward the hotel. That same posture. Tall and proud. He was not mistaken. *It was the girl!* To his surprise, she was not accompanied by a man. She was strolling arm-in-arm with an old woman who had very white skin and yellow-white hair. The woman walked with a heavy limp and she supported herself on an umbrella that she used as a cane.

Moustafa followed the pair. *Why was the* sharmouta *with an old woman?* When he was not more than six feet behind her, he suddenly realized there was no way to catch the girl. He could not just reach out on a busy street and grab her. She would surely scream. He could say she was his wife who deserted him.

As he followed, the old woman suddenly turned and stared straight into Moustafa's eyes. He recoiled. There was something strange about that woman. She turned back to Noora and ushered her up the steps of the hotel. His heart racing faster, faster, he ran after them. A doorman stopped him.

"Are you a guest?" he asked in French.

"*Pardon?*" Moustafa watched the two women over the doorman's shoulder as they made their way into the lobby. "*Laissez moi passer.*"

"I'm sorry, sir, but if you are not a guest ..."

"Yes, yes! I'm meeting someone for tea!" he told the doorman in broken French. Since when did anyone have to be the guest of a hotel to enter its lobby?!

"Under what name?" the doorman asked.

"What do you mean? But that is personal, *excusez moi!*" Moustafa said, trying to imitate a Parisian accent. He was not wearing an expensive suit, but with his navy blue trench coat, he could very well look like an important actor or poet. "I am meeting with a very important person," he added with authority, wishing he had a handkerchief to wipe away the sweat above his lip.

"*Je regrette, monsieur,*" the doorman said. "Unless you give me a name of the person you are meeting, I can't let you inside."

Khara f'weshak! Moustafa wanted to spit at him. But he had to be careful. "It is obvious you don't recognize who I am."

The doorman appeared more suspicious.

"I am expected, and I am late. I am with *l'Alliance Française.*"

"If you give me the name of the person you are meeting, I will gladly have someone escort you."

"I have never been so insulted! I will call the Alliance. And you ... your job is in jeopardy!" Moustafa reached for his cell phone and pretended to dial while marching away down the sidewalk. His cell had been out of service for months, but it gave him a sense of importance.

What shit luck to have some idiot stop him! He ran around the corner, looking for another entrance to the hotel. He had never had such a problem before. He could hire someone to beat the shit out of that French bastard. He found the back entrance, and in minutes, he was inside the hotel.

Edging his way closer to the lobby, he saw the pretentious doorman out on the sidewalk with his back to him. He was welcoming a group of well-dressed men getting out of a limousine. Moustafa peered into the restaurant, where classical music filled the air and guests were being served tea. She was not there. Did she take the elevator upstairs?

At that moment, he could do nothing with all these people around. He had to follow her, find out her room number, if that's where she stayed. She was probably staying in a suite. *Bitch!* Surely she could not be registered under her own name, since she was supposed to be dead! He should have carried some chloroform. He should have been prepared. How expensive was chloroform and where could he get it? He began to imagine what he could do with her if she were unconscious—and he was alone with her in his hotel room.

For the very first time, he realized he had no desire to return her to her father. He would *keep* her. His body shuddered at the thought.

"What are we doing up here?" Noora asked as Ahna Morgenbesser guided her out of the elevators to the mezzanine.

"I wanted to look at one of the suites, in case we should stay here someday," Ahna said.

"Stay here? But why? Your apartment is prettier than any suite in this hotel."

"Well ..." Ahna chuckled, "it's just because it's home."

"Yes," Noora smiled. "Home is always better."

"But I'm still curious about those presidential suites. Aren't you?"

Noora shrugged.

"Dignitaries, presidents, celebrities stay here, you know," Ahna said, but she noticed that Noora's clear eyes were darkening. Perhaps her young companion had stayed here with her family. But it was not right to ask and evoke any more painful memories. "They know me here," Ahna explained. "Sometimes, when there is a special need, they hire me to bake some of their pastries, marzipan figurines, and *pièces montées*."

"*Pièce montée?* What's that?"

"The traditional French wedding cake."

"Ah, yes. I've seen them. Cream puffs mounted like a mountain and held together by a thick coat of hard candy, right?"

"Yes. Actually *enrobed* in luscious, delectable candy. You have to pull out the cream puffs without destroying them."

"It would seem rather difficult to cut into hard candy to get to the cream puffs," Noora said.

"*Ah, oui.* But that's the idea. First challenge of married life," she chuckled. "Once I had to bake three hundred cream puffs. What a chore that was. It took forever to assemble it. I had to bring all the cream puffs and assemble them right on site—at the Meurice Hotel in their grand ballroom. Well, I don't mean to sound vain, but it was the prettiest and tallest wedding cake I ever made."

Noora smiled. "You must have a special touch, for a luxury hotel to hire you for their wedding cakes."

"Yes, it is an honor. The money is good too," she said. "But my specialty is still the black forest cakes. Baking comes naturally to me. But I used to sculpt delicate roses and pansies ... Everything edible."

"Out of sugar?"

"Out of marzipan."

"I love marzipan."

"Well, I used to mold ballerinas and other marzipan figurines. I can still make them, but it's difficult now that I'm old. Arthritis, you know ... Too bad it's a forgotten art. I'm honored they still call me with cake orders. The head of food and beverage is an old friend," Ahna said, standing by the elevators, trying to distract Noora. "He invited me on many occasions to show me one of their presidential suites. They have three that they recently redecorated, I believe ..."

"The head of food and beverage invited you to see one of their presidential suites?" Noora asked, trying to understand Ahna's story.

"Yes, he's a wonderful man with impeccable taste. But perhaps we should do the proper thing. Let's go back downstairs," Ahna said, pushing the down button. "I'll see if he's not too busy. I knew his father since my husband A'iim was alive."

The elevator doors opened back down to the lobby. Ahna continued with her chatter, trying to keep Noora distracted, especially from noticing the man in the navy blue trench coat. Seeing him in front of another elevator, Ahna quickly pressed the button down to the lower level. The elevator doors never seemed so slow. She hoped the man had not seen them. He was definitely following them. The elevator doors opened. They stepped inside. The man had turned, and it was possible he spotted Noora, just as the elevator doors closed. He didn't have a mustache, like the man Noora described, and his hair was light brown, not black, but the intensity of his eyes alarmed Ahna.

They descended to the next floor. "I don't want to worry you dear," Ahna said, "but ..."

"What's the matter?"

"I'd like to go home, if you don't mind."

"What's wrong?"

"Just a little dizziness."

"Would you like me to take you to a doctor?"

"No, just take me home. I'll be fine. It happens." The elevators opened to the street level. Ahna rushed Noora to the rear doors and out to the sidewalk. She motioned to a passing cab.

Moustafa emerged from the elevator and looked out. Through the glass doors of the rear entrance, he spotted Noora on the sidewalk as the old woman was hailing a cab. He couldn't run after them, because he would attract attention to himself. A security guard stood by the revolving doors. Cursing under his breath, Moustafa made his way carefully, passing the security guard and heading through the revolving doors. When he stepped out on the sidewalk, Noora and the old woman had just gotten into the cab and it took off. Moustafa rushed after them.

When the traffic slowed at the corner of the main boulevard, Moustafa found a cab.

After a good half hour of inching through the slow traffic, the cab he followed stopped near the Levallois Metro entrance. Finally. He was starting to worry that soon he would run out of cab fare—enough money for a few dinners, he thought, but it was going to be worth it. He found the girl. He hopped out of the cab, paid the driver, and when he looked up, he saw the women's cab leaving. He lost sight of the two women in a crowd that spilled out of the Metro station onto both sides of the street. They must have gone in one of the shops—which one, he couldn't tell. *What was she doing in this part of Paris, with these working-class people?*

A group of thirteen or fourteen-year-old girls was coming out of the Metro. *Innocent virgins living in the area, probably ready to be corrupted,* Moustafa concluded. *The Fendil slut could very well be connected to a wealthy bordello, and the old woman could be a cover or maybe a retired owner.* He stood by the window of a bakery, pretending to peruse the display. He peered inside. Noora was not there, and neither was the old woman.

He checked every entrance on the block. *How could they have disappeared so fast, when the old woman looked like she could hardly get around?* Many of the buildings along the street had large wooden doors. They would open into courtyards and apartments. With his coat sleeve, he wiped the sweat from his brow. If he waited long enough, she would have to come out.

Where did she go? "NOORA!" Moustafa yelled. "Noora Fendil!" People were staring at him.

"What's the matter, *monsieur?*" a middle-aged woman asked, frowning at Moustafa.

"*Excusez moi,*" Moustafa blurted, out of breath. "I am looking for my wife ..."

"*Con de Pied Noir,*" he heard a man say behind him.

Moustafa understood the French slang "Black Foot," which stood for an Arab or North African. An Arab *cunt?* Was that what this stupid stranger, that French *ibn kalb,* called him? Moustafa turned on his heel. The man who insulted him was rushing to the Metro entrance and disappeared down the steps.

Parisians! He loathed them. Loathed them all! *Yeh-rak deenhom... kollohom!* May their religion burn! All of them! Moustafa cursed under his breath, feeling his blood rise to his head. Infidels! He wanted to chase after that man and knock his teeth out.

More people were staring at him. He sauntered across the street to escape their attention, and entered a *boulangerie,* closing the chiming glass door behind him. Past a long line of customers, he spotted the back of the old woman as she made her way beyond a tall glass pastry counter. What luck! Allah guided him there. *Shokran ya Allah.* Moustafa was not mistaken. Noora must have gone ahead of the woman.

"The line starts back there, *monsieur!*" sniffed a customer.

Why did they go through the door where workers were bringing out platters of breads and pastries? On top of the door was a sign: "Employees Only, No Admittance." Was the bakery a front for a bordello? He walked out, searching for the alley. There had to be an entrance behind the store, where they made deliveries, but he couldn't find the alley. They probably brought virgins through the service entrance in bakery trucks. Only Allah knew. Two older men smoking pipes at the edge of the street corner were staring at him. *There was no need to panic,* Moustafa thought. He would wait until nightfall. Now he knew where the Fendil slut was—inside that bakery front.

The bakery owner, Monsieur Daniel DuFour, drove Ahna and Noora home in his truck. He helped them bring up cartons of eggs, two large sacks of flour, sugar, and other ingredients. Ahna had most everything placed on the dining room table. She checked her list carefully before bidding Monsieur Dufour a friendly *au revoir* at the door.

Ahna, who reassured Noora that she felt fine again, returned to the dining room with a wide smile and the mail. "Tomorrow is a big baking day, *ma chérie.* I have four *schwarzwalder* kirsch tortes and three Hollander kirsch torte *blatterteig*... It's going to be fun! Piece of cake!" she laughed, checking her mail. "Monsieur Dufour is coming back tomorrow at eighteen hours to pick up the baked goodies."

"I want to help you in every way I can. Whatever you may need," Noora said, thinking that she never learned how to bake, her mother never taught her, and her grandmother only allowed her to lick the spoon ...

"I just need your company, *ma chérie*. I am so delighted you are here."

"Thank you," Noora said. Each passing day, Ahna reminded Noora how happy she was to have her company. Noora was grateful. She needed to do something to reciprocate—but she knew in her heart there was no way she could ever repay Ahna's compassionate and kind heart—and her hospitality.

"I have mail for you," Ahna sang, handing Noora a letter.

"Mail, for me?" *How could that be possible?* Noora wondered.

There was a sneaky gleam in the woman's eyes.

"Who is it from?"

"You'll see."

"Oh, it's from Annette!" Noora tore the envelope open.

"She called me with the news last night," Ahna said, putting both hands together and bringing them to her mouth.

Noora read in French: "First we were friends, now we are *une famille!*"

"A family?" Noora repeated, staring at the handwritten words. "*We would like you to be our baby's godmother! We hope you will say* oui."

"Yes! *Oui, oui, oui! Mais bien sûr que oui!*" Noora cried, hugging Ahna and jumping up and down like a ten-year-old.

Ahna cried happy tears and clapped her hands. "A baby! It's a *mitzvah*, a *mitzvah!* A blessing!"

Noora continued to read the letter out loud, then looked up. "Almost six months and she didn't tell us? 'I was spotting for the first four months and feared that I would lose the baby ...'"

"Annette never shared her burdens. She probably didn't want to burden you either," Ahna said. Happy tears escaped from her eyes.

"I don't want to know the sex of the baby," Annette wrote, "but if it's a girl," Noora read out loud, "we will name the baby after you ..." Noora lost her enthusiasm. "Name her *Kelley?*"

"We will tell her the truth. In due time. All in due time, *ma chérie*," Ahna said.

"I lied to Annette."

"Why don't we make reservations for Friday! We can catch the shuttle to Nice, and you can tell her in person. Annette will understand."

Noora sank on the couch, holding Annette's letter, wondering how she could possibly explain to Annette why she had not been truthful about her identity.

"I know Annette will be the first to say she knew it all along. You will see," Ahna said. "In the meantime, we must buy pink yarn."

"Pink yarn?"

"For the baby."

"What if it's a boy?"

"It will be a girl."

That night, after helping Ahna organize all ingredients for the next morning's big baking, Noora lay awake.

Ahna said she had baked those cakes since she was a child, and she was going to be paid generously. Noora wanted to help her. She would wash dishes, go on errands, and do whatever Ahna needed, even if she objected.

At first, Ahna was glowing at the thought of having a new grandchild. But later that evening, she seemed nervous, perhaps even a little anxious. Maybe she was feeling dizzy again? Noora tried to convince Ahna to see a doctor, but Ahna insisted that when it was her time to go, she would die at home, in her own bed.

What if Ahna did die in bed? I don't think I could handle that. She could not imagine staying in the apartment without Ahna. But where would she go? *You're being selfish,* Noora chided herself, tears welling in her eyes. Automatically, she reached for her neck to touch Um Faheema's blue bead. At times, she forgot she didn't have the necklace—it had become so much a part of her. Ian had probably tossed it in the trash—unless Cessilia kept it for her. For her return to Ian's world? Not a chance. Noora had thought of calling his house, but what if Ian picked up the phone?

She heard Ahna coughing in her bedroom. Her dry cough didn't seem to get any better. Perhaps *Docteur* Alain could convince her to get a chest X-ray or see a specialist. Ahna must live to see her great-grandchild, and hopefully see Annette's baby take his or her first step. *A baby girl?* Noora wondered, closing her eyes. "Michel," she whispered as tears filled her eyes. She turned her mind back to Annette. *Think of Annette and her baby. I have a family … people who care, who love me. I am going to be a godmother.*

***** ***** *****

The grandfather clock in the hallway chimed eleven times. Silently, Ahna Morgenbesser checked to make sure Noora was asleep, and tiptoed her way to the corridor, opened the front door, and locked it behind her. Downstairs, she tapped on the concierge's glass door and waited until a shadow appeared, heading her way. *"Bonjour Madame,"* said the concierge, standing stiffly at her door. She wore a housedress and rollers in her hair.

"*Bonsoir,* Madame Bucheron," Ahna said; after many years in Paris, Ahna could not get used to saying "good day" when it was night. "I would like to speak to your husband. He is not back yet?" she said, noticing that his bicycle was not parked inside the street door.

"He may have been detained. Is something wrong?" Madame Bucheron asked. "Wait!" she interrupted. "I have something in the oven." She never invited Ahna inside her apartment, and neither did the concierge's mother, who had occupied the same position in the same apartment since 1958, when Ahna first moved in. Ahna heard footsteps and the street door close. Jacques, Mme. Bucheron's husband, appeared, bringing his bicycle with him.

"*Bonjour,* Madame Ahna," he said removing his black gendarme cape and shaking away raindrops. "I didn't expect to see you at this hour."

"Yes, I know, but ..."

"Expect a heavy rainfall tonight," the policeman remarked. "But they said it will clear by tomorrow." He removed his hat and hung it on the coat rack in the foyer of his apartment. He turned to Ahna. "Is everything all right?"

"Yes. I would like to ask a favor of you."

Sitting in the kitchen, the gendarme and his wife were having their late-night supper.

"What did the Jewish woman want?" Madame Bucheron asked.

"Madame Morgenbesser prefers we call her Ahna."

"Is that what she wanted?"

"She thinks there's a stalker."

"A stalker?"

"Yes. She said a man may be following her."

"*Elle est folle.*"

"I don't think she's crazy"

"Who would care to follow her?!"

"She just asked me to keep an eye out. And since it is my job ..."

"Maybe they're after that girl."

"What girl?"

"In all these months, you haven't noticed the girl?" the concierge said, removing a pot roast from the oven.

"I work two shifts, in case you forgot," he said, pouring himself red wine in a tall water glass.

"She has a helper; apparently sent by her granddaughter. Now that she married a rich man, I guess she can afford it," she said, her words laced with jealousy and contempt.

"You mean her granddaughter, Annette?"

"Yes, Annette, who was a hotel maid in the South."

"She married that Italian? I thought he was a loser and a drunk."

"No, apparently she married some kind of a doctor."

"Annette married a *docteur?*" he asked, surprised.

"That's what the Jewish one, bragged about when she went away for a few days. But you know how she tells stories, that one. It appears that the girl who is staying upstairs is her caregiver. She shops for her, brings her groceries. And they go out every afternoon now. *La Juive* never did *that* before. The girl holds her by the arm so she doesn't fall. Probably cheaper than a nursing home. But if you ask me ..."

"I'm glad she has someone to help her. An old woman all by herself."

"No one is following them, and I would prefer you would stay out of her affairs."

"As a proud employee of the *Gendarmerie,* it is my job and my duty..."

"Oh, *j'ten prie!* Please! You don't have to recite to me. She has outlived us all, including my own mother, who was ten years younger! The concierge said. "You remember the stories she used to tell us about the Nazis and concentration camps? She was making it all up, of course. She should've been locked up long ago."

"It was Giselle who told you about her mother's experiences, not Madame Ahna."

"Poor Giselle thought if she made the girls think her mother was a war heroine, they would forgive her for being a Jew," she replied.

"I thought you two were friends."

"Not when I was old enough to realize what type of people they were, and after she started telling me those ridiculous stories."

"Well, now let's not speak ill of the dead."

"Whose side are you on?"

"Yours. Always on your side, *ma chérie,*" the policeman smiled, holding up his plate.

*****   *****   *****

When Noora saw people standing in line at the Customs counter at the Nice airport, she remembered the terror she felt when she presented Annette's passport. Her life in Los Angeles with Ian Cohen seemed like a distant dream. She felt a little pang in her heart. She realized she had been comfortable, and even happy, as happy as one could be under the circumstances of her ordeals. Was it possible she was missing Ian Cohen? It was true he had a miserable temper and was capable of being cruel with words. But he had a good heart and would not hurt anyone physically. Never. She remembered how ill and vulnerable he had been in the Honolulu hospital.

"Noora?"

"Oh, I'm sorry." Noora realized she had been absent-minded. "I'll get the luggage."

"Where are you, *ma jolie?*" Ahna asked.

"I'm here, Ahna," she said, pulling the luggage from the conveyor belt.

"Your mind left me awhile ago."

"I can't hide much from you," Noora said. "I was thinking about Ian Cohen."

"Yes. I am sure he thinks of you too."

"Oh, but not in a good way. I'm sure he would like to forget all about me," Noora said, rolling out their luggage toward the exit sign.

"I would not doubt he is missing you," Ahna said, walking with a cane and following Noora.

"Missing *me?*" Noora stopped and turned to Ahna. "I would doubt it very much after all ..."

"Yoo hoo!" someone called from the crowd.

"There she is, *ma petite Annette,*" she said, waving at her granddaughter, who was standing by the partition outside of baggage claim, with a round stomach and holding two huge bouquets of roses.

Annette and Alain lived in a renovated little villa in Saint Tropez.

"We have a room for the baby, but I am not going to furnish it, because I'm superstitious."

"Nothing will go wrong, darling; you are in good hands," Alain said, standing over the stove. He was preparing garlic shrimp for his wife and their guests.

"Alain is a very good cook. He makes bouillabaisse too. Even better than me!" Annette said as she and Noora set the table. "Would you believe we like the same *porcelaine* dishes? Same design. Alain bought a complete set before he met me. And I was buying one piece at a time of the same exact pattern!" she exclaimed happily. "Before we even knew each other. Was that destiny or what?!"

"Indeed, it is because you are a *clairvoyante,*" Noora winked.

Annette laughed with pleasure.

Later, as they stood in the unfurnished nursery, Annette said, "Look what you have done for me, for my *grand-mère*. You came into my life and brought light when I thought I was in a dark tunnel with no hope. Without you, I would still be cleaning hotel rooms and angry at Bruno. I forgive him and I even bless him. I wish him well because I have a good life of my own, all thanks to you."

"Annette ... listen ... there is something about me that you don't know..."

"I know," Annette said.

"You ... know?

"*Grand-mère* told me."

"What did she say?"

"She told me a little bit and said you can tell me the rest, in due time. I knew you would tell me when you are ready," Annette said. "I always felt you did not look like a 'Kelley,'" she said with a chuckle.

CHAPTER 57
IAN COHEN'S DISCOVERY

On a cold and damp Seattle night, Ian Cohen walked out of the theater, stunned. He watched the evening sky, lightly tinted in royal blue, a reflection of the million lights from tall office buildings in the distance, and silently, he thanked the heavens.

He did not expect such an enthusiastic audience response to the test run of his movie. He had had serious doubts about *Lord of Doom*. It did not have enough violent scenes for a much-publicized action-adventure film.

The young spectators, mostly between the ages of fourteen and twenty-four, had laughed at the right places and even cheered.

After the end credits rolled, Ian stood listening to spectators giving statements to reporters who thrust microphones at them as soon as they made their way out of the theater doors.

"I liked especially when Gianni at the end looked straight at Mick-the-Murderer and said, 'Don't tempt me, Kimosabe.'"

"That was great," another young spectator said.

"I really liked that movie," a father said. "Clever dialogue. We're gonna see it again. I think even my wife will too!"

"I'm going back to see it with my friends!" a teenage boy shouted on his way out.

"I loved it when he said at the end '*Don't tempt me, Kimosabe.*' I didn't expect that ..." someone said.

Neither did I, Ian Cohen thought, standing away from the crowd.

Bob Mercer, also known as "Bubba," the script doctor Ian had hired before his secret heart surgery, walked up to Ian. "Gotta tell you, I wasn't sure about the dialogue changes you sent us. I'm glad now. The audience loved it."

"Great response, huh?" Jake Goldenbaum, the head of business affairs at Ian's studio, slapped Ian on the back. He extended his hand to the screenwriter. "Hey, Bubba, great job. That last line … pretty much made the picture!"

"Well, I'd like to take all the credit," Bubba said, "but Ian's the one who made the changes."

"Not me," Ian said and pointed to the screenwriter. "It was the script doctor over here …"

"Hey, Ian, when did you suddenly get so humble?" Jake Goldenbaum said, laughing.

"Really … well, actually …" he said, the wheels of his mind starting to churn. *Did I really write that dialogue in the third act?* He thought it was Bubba who made the changes. Ian would certainly have remembered if he had written those lines. It was around the time they had cracked his chest open, and he was in even worse shape after the surgery. No one but Bubba could have made the changes—not Gianni the brainless lead star, even though he did a good job delivering the line after fifteen takes. And it could not have been the director, because Ian himself had to first approve the shooting script.

Numbly, Ian thanked people who walked up to him and shook his hand to congratulate him. He edged away back to the lobby and to the men's room.

Standing at the sink, he splashed cold water on his face and stared at the mirror.

Impossible. Who else? He remembered the homeless man … at the Honolulu zoo. The bum who kept repeating, "Don't tempt me." Kelley had said it was a monkey pod, and Ian had teased her: "Where are the monkeys?" And when the hobo said *Kimosabe,* Kelley had asked, "Wasabi?" He had made fun of her. He remembered how she looked at him, embarrassed at his teasing while he was being a jerk. In truth, he was feeling sorry for himself, moping and whining, being a major pain in the ass and a coward about having heart surgery. And all she was trying to do, the poor kid, was help him … She had even made him laugh that day. She had done more than that. She had saved his neck. She had fixed … yes, *fixed* what his own writers couldn't! She put herself on the line. All this, for him.

"Well, I'll be damned," he whispered to himself. He burst out of the men's room.

CHAPTER 58
AHNA'S LAST REQUEST

Two weeks after they returned to Paris, Ahna's nagging cough had not improved. She had refused to seek the pulmonary expert *Docteur* Alain had recommended. Ahna was stubborn. "This too shall pass," she insisted. She had too much to do, filling out many baking orders.

Monsieur Daniel Dufour and a young associate came to pick up the three *schwarzwalder* kirsch tortes, Ahna's specialty that no one could duplicate and the large chocolate cake with crème chantilly and cherries.

Noora hoped Ahna was finished with big orders for a while. She had made cream puffs for two hotel weddings, and countless apple kuchens, marzipan figurines, small castles, and flowers. She took special pride in her marzipan creations. "It's a dying art," she had explained. "That's why I'm still in demand."

Ahna seemed pleased with the check Monsieur Dufour handed her, and walked them to the door.

Noora knew that Ahna was well paid for her efforts, but was it really worth sacrificing her health?

Ahna seemed especially tired. The cough syrup and the mentholated ointment Noora rubbed on Ahna's chest night and morning helped her a little, but not enough.

"Now that all the baking orders are done, you have time to see a doctor," Noora said.

"*C'est d'accord*. I will see the doctor Alain recommended. I probably need antibiotics. You are such a treasure," Ahna said, shuffling wearily to her bedroom. "I could never have finished this job without your help, my angel."

Noora cleaned the kitchen, washed baking pans and dishes while listening for Ahna's cough from the bedroom. It was obvious she wasn't going to get any rest. Noora hung up a dishtowel and went to Ahna's room.

"Please let me take you to the emergency."

"Tomorrow morning we'll go to the clinic," Ahna said. "But it will probably take a week or two before I can see the specialist."

"You need medical assistance now," Noora urged.

"Let's leave the emergency doctors for more important cases."

"They won't refuse you, Ahna. At your age—and I don't mean that disrespectfully—you need to be careful with your health. Most of all, you need some relief from this stubborn cough," she said firmly, folding back the cover and helping her out of bed.

Ahna didn't resist. Indeed, it was clear she was feeling very ill.

Noora waited with Ahna behind one of the partitions of the emergency room. After a chest X-ray, the doctor returned to inform Ahna that they found fluid in her lungs. As a precautionary measure, she needed to stay overnight for observation.

"But surely I don't have to stay in the hospital."

"Ahna, you have a fever. I will stay with you. If you like, we can play cards, watch television. You didn't finish telling me your story."

"Oh, it is a long, sad one ... But you know, *ma petite chérie*, it has a happy ending ... At least when I was reunited ..." she said with a sigh.

Noora knew Ahna would be too tired to talk. What she needed now was to stop coughing and get some sleep.

While they wheeled Ahna to her hospital room, Noora phoned Annette from the nurses' station. "They expect to release her in the morning," Noora said, wanting to give Annette the good news first. "Just to be on the safe side, the doctor ordered Ahna to have intravenous antibiotics. The 'high-octane' type, he said. She should be able to fight this and get back on her feet in no time."

Annette wanted to fly to Paris, but Noora reassured her it was only a matter of time. "Annette, please don't worry. Your husband spoke to the pulmonary expert. Ahna will be fine. I'll be here with her."

"God bless you, Noora dear," Annette said. "You are an angel."

"Take care of yourself and your baby. Now, promise me," Noora said.

"Yes, I already have a doctor at home to nag me, thank you!" Annette laughed.

Noora was concerned about Annette. Her gynecologist recommended that she stay in bed and avoid lifting anything, or she might still suffer a miscarriage.

That night, as Noora watched Ahna in her hospital bed, something did not feel right. Ahna seemed exhausted. The coughing must have worn her out.

Ahna touched her chest. "It hurts," she said in French, then mumbled something in German that Noora didn't understand.

"Your chest still hurts?" Noora asked. Ahna's eyes were closed and her head was turned away from Noora. Besides the antibiotics, the nurses had given her something to suppress the cough, as well as a light dose of morphine to kill the pain.

Shouldn't she feel better by now?

Noora rushed out into the corridor, to the nurses' station. She had gone through the same thing with Ian Cohen, but his case was a lot tougher, a great deal more challenging, she reminded herself.

A nurse returned with Noora to check on Ahna, who was asleep.

"She's fine," the nurse said after listening to Ahna's chest.

"But it sounds like she is having some difficulty breathing."

"The wheezing is normal," the nurse said impatiently and left the room.

Noora pulled her chair closer to the bed. She felt a deep sense of sadness as she watched Ahna in her sleep. But why should she feel sad, Noora wondered, when Ahna was on her way to recovery?

"Ghizella ..." Ahna murmured.

"What?" Noora bent closer to hear. Ahna mumbled a few words in German. Was she having a bad dream? Perhaps it was the medicine. "Ghizella ... I hear the music ... I hear it now ..." Ahna whispered in her sleep. "It is ..."

What music? A pleasant dream, apparently.

"Beautiful ..." Ahna whispered. She was even smiling, while a teardrop oozed out of her left eye.

Gently, Noora patted her wet temple with a soft tissue. At last she was sleeping soundly. She hoped the nurses wouldn't wake her to check on her, the way they used to do with Ian.

Noora was startled out of her sleep when she heard Ahna. "You're still here?" Her eyes were wide open.

"Ahna!" Noora smiled, so happy to see her awake and even looking calm and rested. She even had rosy cheeks. Noora glanced up at the clock on the wall—almost two hours had passed. "How do you feel? Better?"

"Yes," Ahna replied. "My chest doesn't hurt as much."

"Oh, thank heavens," Noora said. The morphine was finally working.

"Go home, *ma chérie,* you need your rest," Ahna whispered. "What time is it?"

"Almost midnight."

"You are such a dear. But you must go home and sleep in your own bed."

"I wanted to stay with you."

"There is no need. I am fine."

A nurse walked in and mumbled something in French that Noora didn't quite understand.

"They want to check my vital signs," Ahna explained. "Ask if they can get me a bedpan; I don't think I can get up."

"*Excusez-moi, mademoiselle,* there's not enough room ..."

"Oh, sorry," Noora said. She could speak French pretty well now, but she didn't know how to say "bedpan."

Ahna spoke to the nurse.

"Yes, I will get it, but if she's not a relative, she can't stay," the nurse said decisively in French.

"She is my goddaughter," Ahna responded firmly.

"*Bon, d'accord.* I'll be back," she said and left the room, mumbling again. "*Mais quand même, 'ya pas assez d'place pour tant de monde...*"

"Parisians. They always have to complain. But she is getting me what I need. And you, *ma petite,* get some sleep. Do bring me my pink housedress. I think it's hanging behind my bedroom door."

"Yes, of course. Is there anything else I can bring?"

"Inside my armoire, in the bottom drawer, you will find underwear. The blue cotton ones we bought at the Printemps."

"Yes, good idea. But I am not sure I should leave you alone tonight."

"Yes, darling," Ahna answered, smiling gently. "It is already so late." She waved a hand. "Go home, *ma jolie*. Oh ... one more favor. Inside my armoire ... on the bottom drawer, under the lingerie, you will find my diary. Would you bring it? I have been wanting to talk to you about it," she said. "And take a cab. Don't walk alone at this hour."

"Yes, all right. I love you, Ahna," Noora said at the door.

The nurse returned, entering the room, brushing Noora as she passed her. Swiftly, she lifted Ahna's backside and placed a bedpan beneath her. Noora turned away at the door, to give Ahna her privacy.

"I love you, *ma chérie*," Noora heard Ahna say. Noora left reluctantly. She made her way down the corridor to the elevators, feeling an urgent need to return to Ahna's bedside. She saw another nurse open Ahna's door and walk inside. It was obvious they would not let her stay. She would call early in the morning and ask Ahna if there was anything else she could bring her.

CHAPTER 59
A SHADOW ON THE RIVER SEINE

As Noora walked down the hospital steps and out onto the sidewalk, she breathed the warm night air. The weather report had predicted rain, yet the sky was clear and she did not remember seeing such brilliant stars in Paris. She was satisfied that Ahna was in good hands—even if the nurses were rather stern—and it was all right for her to go home and sleep for a few hours. The pulmonary specialist was due back at eight in the morning.

There were no taxis. Since the hospital was only a few blocks past the Pont de Levallois, she decided to walk. It would do her good. Reaching the bridge, Noora passed a pair of young lovers, holding each other and kissing. They appeared so in love. As she walked on, Noora felt weighed down by sadness—and envy. A little anger even. "Michel," she whispered.

She stood in the middle of the bridge and watched a small boat chug along the Seine, passing below the bridge, slowly disappearing. She breathed in a gentle wave of sweet perfume—possibly from the young woman she just passed with her lover. The couple had walked away, the sound of their footsteps disappearing with their shadow into the darkness. "Michel," she whispered again, and turned to resume her walk, eager to get away from her thoughts and memories. She heard rapid footsteps and turned. A dark figure loomed above her.

"At last you're *mine!*" the swarthy man said, grabbing her by the shoulders.

She was paralyzed. It was that man who had attacked her before … in Alexandria! *The man from London!* She pushed him away and tried to flee. He grabbed her again, pinning her against the low cement wall of the bridge and pushing himself against her so hard, she felt trapped.

"Aah, I knew you didn't die," he whispered excitedly, his foul breath nearly asphyxiating her. "You fooled them *all!* Even your father. You did not fool me! They think I'm dead like you, and now you're MINE!" He pulled at her hair so hard, she cried out in pain. She struggled to push him away, but he pressed her harder against the cement railing, the weight of his body imprisoning her. "You won't get away this time!" he breathed in her face. She tried to scream. He put his hand to her mouth and squeezed hard. "If you scream, I'll stab you. I have a knife."

She slammed her knee up hard against his groin. He stumbled back, cursing. Furiously, he threw himself at her again and grabbed her neck. She managed to pull one of his hands away and bit it as hard as she could.. He screamed and let go long enough that she was able to climb over the railing and let herself fall into the river. Moments after she reached the surface of the cold water, Moustafa was right on top of her, grabbing her. They thrashed about in the water. She kicked him, desperately trying to free herself and get to the surface to breathe, while he held on to her for survival. They both sank under the water.

The memory of the day her father attempted to drown her flashed—she saw Moustafa glaring and nodding along with the other men. "*I denounce you!*" her father's voice of the past rang back through her brain …

In a sudden rage, Noora kicked her assailant, who was struggling to climb over her, to get to the surface. Breaking free and reaching the surface, she gulped some air.

NO MORE! she cried through the core of her soul.

She saw his hand reaching out to her. She grabbed his head as if it were a ball and thrust it down. Underwater, he took hold of her and desperately attempted to pull himself back to the surface. Noora kicked and shoved him away with a thrust of both feet.

Reaching the surface again, she swam in rapid strokes, downstream with the current. When she turned, she saw beneath the dimly lit bridge, a hand grabbing at the air above the surface, then his head. "Help me!" he begged in Arabic. His voice echoed as the current pulled him away. For a few seconds, she heard him coughing and gasping for air. Then nothing except the rippling sounds of the river.

The current grew stronger, pulling her downriver. She swam sideways until she could make it closer to the edge of a dock. She held on to a metal bar to catch her breath, and realized it was the bottom rung of a ladder. She struggled to climb, but the steps were too far apart and she didn't have enough strength to pull herself up. Trembling fiercely with exhaustion and cold, she held on to the steel step, to catch her breath. She looked around. Ahead she saw cement steps rising from the bank. Above, on the dock, she spotted a stumbling figure waving a large, gleaming bottle—probably a homeless drunk. Slowly she swam to the steps and managed to lift herself and climb up to the dock.

The drunk came closer to Noora. She wanted to run but he was barring her way. Her chest was heaving and she could barely feel her legs.

"Hey, whore, got a cigarette?" the drunk said in French, approaching close enough that she could smell him. When he reached out to touch her, she smacked his face with the back of her hand. He stumbled backward but didn't fall. Laughing loudly, he began to chase after her.

Noora managed to make it to a dark corner where she could catch her breath.

"Where are you?" the drunk sang. "Yoo-hooo! *Ta jolie chatte, montre-la moi!*" He chortled as if playing hide-and-seek.

Noora understood he said something about her... whaat? Pretty pussy...cat? *He wants me to show him what?!* Noora found an empty wine bottle right by her foot. She picked it up, ready to smash it over his head if he dared to venture a tad closer.

Searching for her, the drunk turned around like a dog chasing its own tail until he stumbled and fell, his wine bottle rolling down the dock, and off it went, splashing into the river. The drunk pulled himself up, screaming, "*Ma bouteille!*"

While the drunk cried over his lost wine bottle, an approaching barge cast enough light for Noora to make out steps leading up to the street.

When she finally reached the pavement, Noora remembered her purse. She must have dropped it when she was attacked on the bridge. She didn't think it fell in the river. It should still be there on the bridge, unless someone took it. Clutching her heaving chest, Noora made it back to the bridge, thinking how crazy she was to return to the same spot where she was attacked. But her wallet and the keys to Ahna's apartment were in her purse. *Courage*, the words of Um Faheema, rang back to her mind.

She searched beside the railing. There it was! Because it was zipped up, nothing fell out. *Thank you, God,* Noora thought.

The bridge was dark now. Some of the streetlights must have automatically been turned off. If she ran, she would warm up, she told herself. But she was exhausted and feared she might faint right there on the sidewalk. She managed to make it back through the deserted streets, and finally found herself a little more than a block away from Ahna's apartment building. Raindrops rapidly grew to a downpour. When she finally reached the front door, Noora leaned against it. She coughed and gagged; she had to get inside and get warm. With luck, she could make it up the stairs to the apartment without being seen. With trembling hands, Noora fumbled to find the keyhole in the dark. The lock resisted. She took a deep breath. *The door will open if I relax and take it slow.*

There were no pedestrians on the street and only a few cars swishing by on the wet pavement. She jiggled the key again, trying hard to hold her hand steady, and the door finally opened. Noora had lost her sweater downriver. She also lost her shoes after she fell off the bridge. *Or was it before?* Silently, she closed the street door and climbed the stairs, breathing as quietly as possible, but her teeth were stubbornly chattering.

Luckily, there were only two apartments per floor, and the neighbors in the apartment across from Ahna were hardly ever seen. She could barely fit the key to Ahna's apartment because she was trembling so hard. Her vision blurred. *Oh God, please, help me open that door!* Noora prayed, and the words of her assailant rang in her ears: *"Help me!"* he had screamed. Did anyone sober see them? The door opened, and Noora stumbled inside. Ahna and Noora had left the heater on, expecting to return from the hospital that afternoon, and now the apartment felt toasty. "Oh, thank you, God!" Her body continued to tremble fiercely now. She locked the deadbolt and placed the chain on the groove. She let herself drop, exhausted, on the vestibule rug. But her clothes were wet and sticking to her. Ahna's knitted afghan looked inviting, hanging on the coat rack by the console. With great effort, Noora managed to remove her wet clothes and grab the afghan. She wrapped herself in it and curled up next to the heater by the door, her body refusing to move one more muscle.

When Noora opened her eyes, her body was like a blob of jelly. *Did I faint or fall asleep?* she wondered, mustering enough strength to lift herself up. She picked up her wet clothes and hung the afghan back on the rack. She stumbled her way to the bathroom, only a few feet down the hall, and patted rubbing alcohol on her cheeks. It stung where she had been scraped, but she kept on. She gargled with diluted alcohol. She wished she could sterilize every part of her body that the man had touched. She poured some more alcohol on a clump of cotton balls and breathed in deeply, forcing herself to tolerate the sharp sting that ran down her nostrils to her throat. She had bruises all over her body. "This too shall pass, this too shall pass, you'll see," she repeated to herself. The grandfather clock on the hallway chimed twice. The small clock in Ahna's room followed, also ringing twice. Noora turned on the bathtub faucet, but she couldn't wait for the warm water to fill the tub. She hopped in the hot shower and allowed the steam to warm her aching muscles.

Wrapped snugly in two thick bath towels, Noora stopped in Ahna's room. Checking behind the door, she found the *robe de chambre* Ahna had requested. She picked the soft pink cotton housedress from the hook, folded it, and placed it on the small table by the front door, so she would not forget it.

In her room, Noora turned on all the lights and the little heater by the bed. She quickly dressed in a warm sweater and slacks. She wanted to crawl into bed and sleep away the horrible ordeal she just experienced, but suddenly she felt unsure. What if that man followed her home? But he couldn't have. He begged for her help. He held on to her as if he could not swim. Did he fall off the bridge or dive after her? Why?

The concierge's husband was a policeman. The building should be safe, she told herself. Fully clothed, she crawled into bed and pulled the covers up to her chin. She turned to the clock on the nightstand—2:30 AM. *"At last you're mine"*—his words rang eerily in her ears. That man who had chased her in Alexandria was *still* after her. Even Ahna had asked about him, but Noora thought naively that he had given up. She had sailed the Mediterranean, nearly killing herself reaching the French Riviera. She had traveled to Paris, New York, and Los Angeles. And to Hawaii ... How could he have found her? Was he actually searching for her, hunting her down? She tried to think. Where? On a crowded street somewhere? After all this time? All these years? She drifted off to sleep.

I'm proud of you, a voice said in Arabic.

"What?" *Oh my God, is somebody here?* She clutched her blanket. She had locked and chained the front door. Ahna's pale visage appeared briefly at the foot of her bed. Wearing the pink housedress, she was smiling down at Noora. Her skin and the dress rapidly grew darker, darker ... It was Um Faheema!

Noora woke with a start. She turned to the digital clock on the bedside table. Six twenty-five? She jumped up, her heart racing. Could she have been asleep for four ... four and a half hours? Did the phone ring awhile ago or was she dreaming? Ahna always kept the ringer low, so it did not disturb them in their bedrooms.

Noora felt weak, and her entire body ached as if she had been whipped. She wished she had enough strength to fix herself a pot of *café au lait.*

She would have breakfast and something hot to drink at the hospital.

Thank God she found her purse on the bridge, she thought, smoothing out the blanket on her bed. The assailant did not want her money. He wanted her! Quickly, she slipped on her socks and tennis shoes.

She had to tell Ahna what happened. No, she should wait. Then again, perhaps it was best not to say anything at all. She packed Ahna's robe, toothbrush, toothpaste, and a change of underwear. Was there anything else Ahna needed? She punched the buttons on the phone and dialed for a taxi.

When Noora ran down the stairs to wait outside for her ride, she ran into the concierge, who was mopping the wet floor, mumbling to herself. The woman looked up at Noora. "*Bonjour, Mademoiselle,*" she said firmly.

"*Bonjour, Madame,*" Noora replied.

"*Ou est Madame Ahna?*" the concierge asked, barring Noora's way.

"She had to stay in the hospital for one night," Noora said, wishing the woman had not asked. "She's doing much better."

"What's wrong with her?"

"She just had a nagging cough, but she is better. She'll probably come home today."

"Are you a caregiver or are you a relative?"

"I am a friend of the family," Noora replied.

"Are you Jewish too?"

Noora was stunned by such an unexpected question. She looked out and spotted her taxi, pulling in front of the building. "Well, no, but we are cousins," Noora replied and rushed outside.

Noora walked into the lobby of the hospital before seven o'clock and rode the elevator to the third floor. The air conditioning made her sneeze several times. She would not catch a cold! She would keep warm, drink a hot beverage as soon as she saw Ahna. She had to be strong and remain healthy to take care of Ahna. Before reaching the nurse's station, a young nurse stopped her.

"Oh, ah, *Mademoiselle* ... just a moment," she said. "Please, wait here."

Noora thought, *What now? I can't even walk down the corridor? Was it too early for visitors?*

Another nurse appeared and rushed up to Noora. "We tried to phone you ..."

The news was too hard to bear. The hospital official had to take Noora to another room. Noora sank into a chair and broke into sobs.

Ahna had passed away during the night.

"*Non, NON! Ce n'est pas possible!*" she wept.

CHAPTER 60
THE DIARY OF AHNA MORGENBESSER

They buried Ahna in Nice, in the same cemetery as Uncle Khayat. Not far from his grave, in fact, beneath an old olive tree, and not more than a half hour from Annette and Alain's home, so that Annette could visit her grandmother anytime she wished.

But Annette could not attend the funeral. She had received strict orders to remain in bed, for fear she might miscarry.

A week after the burial, however, Annette insisted that she had to pay her respects to her beloved grandmother. She felt stronger and said she would not lose her baby if she went to visit Ahna's grave. Alain had the morning off. "Please, come with us," she asked Noora.

"Of course," Noora said, wishing Annette would wait perhaps another week or two, when she felt stronger, or better yet, after her baby was born, but Annette was determined.

"I was fourteen years old when my mother died," Annette said, sitting at the edge of her bed, dressed in a lovely spring maternity dress. "*Grand-mère* would not allow me to go to the funeral. She told me it was only her remains, not her. In my heart, I knew she was right, but I still feel bad she never told me where my mother was buried."

The three of them got in the car. Noora climbed into the back seat, as Alain helped buckle his wife in. She dug in her purse and pulled out a white, embroidered handkerchief. "That was my mother's *mouchoir,* by the way," Annette said to Noora while wiping her tears with it. "Alain, please, we must put yellow roses on *Grand-mère's* grave, *je t'en prie.*"

"Bien sûr, ma chérie," he said, rubbing his wife's cheek gently with the back of his hand. "In the Jewish religion, we don't put flowers," Alain explained to Noora. "But Annette and I still prefer flowers to placing stones on a grave."

It was thanks to flowers Alain placed on my uncle's grave that I met him that day, Noora thought with a sigh.

"*Grand-mère* loved yellow roses. She used to say they had a special significance. For every yellow rose that bloomed, it was nature's message that someone made it back home. Home to the light."

On their way to the cemetery, Noora tried to listen to Annette. But she had other matters on her mind. The man she may have drowned who cried out in Arabic for her help. If she had kept her hair very short and bleached blonde, he might not have recognized her. "*You fooled them all ... Even your father ...*" His words rang in her ears. Had he known where she was all along?

"That's why it would be best, if you don't mind, to go back to *Grand-mère's* apartment ..." Annette's words brought Noora back from her thoughts.

Ahna's apartment? I can't go back to Paris! But how could she refuse? Annette would know there had to be a serious reason ... She would want to know ...

"Alain will meet you there this Thursday," Annette continued. "I'm sorry I am putting you through all of this," she said, turning to Noora from the front seat.

Noora! Focus on what Annette is telling you! "Please, it's fine ..." Noora said, leaning over and patting her friend on the shoulder while Alain pulled into a parking space in front of a flower shop. But Noora knew she had to leave, be on the run again. She could put Annette and her family in danger if she stayed with them while a dangerous man was still on the loose. "I'll do whatever is needed," Noora found herself saying.

When Alain went to the florist, Annette said she wanted Noora to donate all of Ahna's things to charity, except for the sweaters Ahna had knitted for her mother, Giselle, and the piano.

"*Grand-mère* worked in a bakery at night so she could purchase that piano for my mother. She gave it to her on her fourteenth birthday. You should have heard my mother play. Like a dream ..." she said. "But me, I was rebellious. By the time I was fourteen, I wanted to run off with my boyfriend! I was selfish when I was younger. If I'd known what I know now ..." she said, her eyes welling. "I ... can't repair the mistakes. I'd like to believe, after the worries I gave *Grand-mère*, that I made her proud. I know she was happy to see me married. To a Jewish man, too! The last time she came to see me, you know, she told me she was ready to leave ... now that she knew I was in good hands."

*****   *****   *****

Noora returned to Paris early Sunday morning, knowing that the concierge, Madame Bucheron, would be at church. She unlocked the door to Ahna's apartment.

In the vestibule, she put down her suitcase and turned the lock securely. She could still hear the flip-flop of Ahna's house slippers, could feel Ahna coming forward to give her a welcoming hug and a kiss on each cheek. She could have sworn something was still baking in the oven, because the apartment still smelled of her fresh-baked *kuchen*. Tears began to flow.

"I am sorry, dear Ahna," she murmured. "I will miss you so much." Every time she loved someone, that person was taken away.

She walked to the cozy little living room. *I must be strong*, she thought, pulling a tissue from the box on top of the piano. She sat on Ahna's chair, reflecting on the night she came to this apartment and poured her heart out to Annette's *grand-mère*, who had welcomed her with open arms. Noora remembered Um Faheema and Dweezoul, and even Saloush ... and then she thought of Nageeb. "How I miss you all," she cried.

She turned to the phone next to the chair. She stared at it for a moment, picked it up, and turned the volume up to its highest, then set it back down. If she could just call her mother ... *If I could just tell her I'm alive.*

She heard a sound.

Oh my God, someone is in the apartment?! Didn't she lock the door? She knew she did not hook up the chain. She jumped from her chair, her heart racing. *What if ... that man ...* She wanted to make her way to the kitchen and get a knife or a hammer from the little pantry behind the door. Too late, she couldn't make it that far. She hid behind the living room door. She heard footsteps approaching down the hallway. From the crack between the hinges, she saw a shadow. *A woman? "Madame la concierge!"*

"Oh mon Dieu, vous m'avez effrayée, mademoiselle!" the concierge said, turning and facing Noora.

"I frightened *you?* I live here, Madame!" Noora replied in French. *Just because she managed the building did not give her the right to sneak into one's apartment,* Noora thought angrily. *But thank God it was not that man …*

"I came to make sure everything is all right."

You came here to snoop, Noora wanted to say.

The concierge handed Noora a stack of newspapers.

Noora chided herself for not locking the door with the chain. The concierge had a passkey, she realized, and she could still unlock the deadbolt.

As she turned to leave, Madame Bucheron said, "Are you going back to England now that *la Madame* Ahna is gone?"

"England? Why would I want to go to England?"

"That's where you are from, *non?*"

"Non, Madame," Noora said walking the concierge to the front door. The woman waited for Noora to volunteer more information, but she remained quiet.

"I have people interested right now in the apartment. When will you vacate?"

Noora could not believe how cold the woman was. She had known Ahna for many years—decades! Ahna had lived there since the late fifties, and Annette's mother, Giselle, had gone to school with the current concierge. Why was she so cold, and even contemptuous? Ahna used to bring her fresh-baked cakes and cookies. Noora thought Mme. Bucheron probably threw away everything that Ahna gave her.

"Thank you for bringing me the mail," Noora said, standing at the door.

"I cancelled it."

"You … cancelled? What did you cancel?"

"The newspaper. No sense in having all those newspapers accumulate at the front door. After all, she won't be reading them anymore," the concierge said with a suggestion of a smirk.

"I would suggest you do nothing until we advise you. Ahna's family will be here in a few days. You may address your questions to them.

Excusez-moi. I would appreciate a little privacy. *Bonsoir, Madame,"* Noora concluded sharply and closed the door behind the woman.

"Ah ben ça alors," she heard the woman mumbling behind the door. "Who does she think she is? *Rien qu'une employée. Petite servante de rien dutout!"* the concierge said loudly.

Staring at the closed door, Noora felt sad. She turned and walked wearily to Ahna's chair and sank into it. *Nothing but an employee? Little for-nothing servant? Is that what they think of me?*

She thought of Ian Cohen. What did *he* think of her?

Well, she wasn't going to sit around moping. She went to the kitchen to make herself a pot of hot chocolate. Ahna would have liked that. *What did it matter what small-minded people like the concierge thought?*

Noora put the stack of newspapers on the kitchen table. She would need at least that much paper to pack the china and some of the glasses that Annette wanted to keep. Perhaps she could call Ahna's friend, the baker, who might bring her some boxes, Noora thought, pouring milk in a pan and lighting the stove. Waiting for the milk to boil, she picked up the top paper and leafed absent-mindedly through the printed sheets.

On the second page, a small headline caught her attention. She gasped and brought the paper closer as she read the bottom column with the heading:

BODY OF A MAN FOUND IN THE SEINE.

The body of a man with no proof of identity was found floating in the river outside Paris ...

The description fit her attacker—dark hair, dark skin, white shirt ... possibly a suicide, the article said.

Noora looked up. *Oh my God.* Behind her, on the stove, the milk boiled over the edges of the pot.

That night, Noora tossed in bed, unable to sleep. She checked the clock on the nightstand—3:10 AM. She had left all the apartment lights on; the electric bill would be sky-high. She rose out of bed and put a sturdy chair against the locked and chained front door. She left the television on—"for company," as Ahna used to say. Ahna liked to watch the news. Noora chose a channel where old movies played.

But her mind was on that man—Moustafa. Again and again, she reminded herself that the description in the newspaper fit her attacker, who had been found the morning after the struggle in the river. Unfortunately, too many people committed suicide by jumping off bridges into the Seine. How could she be sure it was the same man? How could she be sure she would ever be free of him?

She had to stop worrying and start packing. She might as well put her insomnia to good use, she thought. She should start making a list of what Annette wanted, and what would go to charity ... Annette had called the women from the Hadassah, the Jewish women's organization where Ahna Morgenbesser had been a lifetime member. They were going to come in two days to take the boxes to charitable organizations.

Could it really be that man ... Moustafa ... that man who stalked her since Alexandria? Since London! But he drowned! Didn't he? Stop torturing yourself, she thought, making her way to Ahna's room.

She remembered that Ahna had asked her to bring something else in the hospital, the night before she died ... *What was it? A journal?*

Looking in the armoire, inside a bottom drawer and beneath folded undergarments, Noora found a leather-bound book. As she carefully pulled it out, it fell open. It was a manuscript, handwritten in German. Holding the book with great care, she sat at the edge of Ahna's bed and stared at the weighty volume. The smell of old leather, mixed with a light fragrance of Je Reviens perfume, brushed her brain, evoking the memory of her college days in London and the familiar smells of her classroom—her professor, Dr. Pennington—and Noora's own forgotten ambitions to become a writer.

On the back of the cover, Ahna had written "1955." On the first page, a paragraph was written in German, in a different handwriting.

"To my beautiful wife," she read. Above the signature, in the same handwriting, the words were written in French: *"De la part de ton mari, AIIM. Ma femme, mon amour, pour toujours."*

It was legibly signed by Adolph Isaac Israel Morgenbesser. Noora looked up. "Aiim," she murmured to herself. Ahna used to refer to her deceased husband as Aiim.

Carefully, she leafed through the thin, musty pages. The first two pages seemed to be an introduction. Then an empty page; Noora turned it. On the back of the third page was a child's drawing of a woman—a simple circle filled with two large eyes colored in blue, two black dots for a nose, and a wide red smile. A little poem was written below the drawing.

> *Ma jolie maman aux cheveux blonds. Elle est belle comme une chanson.*

The little rhyming words were signed,

> *Giselle, ton enfant.*

Beneath the signature, in bold letters, Noora read:

> ***Pour ma maman que j'aime tellement.***

She wondered if Annette knew about this journal.

"No," Annette told Noora when she called the next morning. She had no idea her grandmother had left a journal. "It must be a little *calpain* … a booklet. *Grand-mère* was more interested in baking—I never saw her write."

"It is a little more than 500 pages," Noora said.

"Whaat?"

CHAPTER 61
"Annou"

Annie Noora Giselle Demiel arrived in the world on a warm and breezy July morning—two days before Noora's birthday. It was a relatively easy birth, considering that Annette's pregnancy had been difficult. Noora received permission from Annette's gynecologist and nurses to assist in the delivery.

Noora knew how to coach Annette, because she had assisted midwives at the Bedouin village, as well as her grandmother, Sultana, on a few childbirths when she was a teenager.

When Noora returned to the hospital two days after Annette gave birth, and with a cluster of pink balloons for Annette and her newborn, she was surprised to find a huge chocolate éclair in Annette's hospital room and balloons that said *"Bon Anniversaire!"*

"Bon Anniversaire, nos voeux les plus sincères!" Everyone sang the French birthday song. A champagne cork popped, and gifts were brought in by Alain. Even some of the nurses stopped to celebrate Noora's birthday—July 22.

Four years and four months since the tragedy of her personal life, and today they were celebrating her day. Noora swallowed hard and tried to hold back her tears.

What would her father do if he knew she were still alive? She could no longer control her emotions, and she burst into tears. "I'm just ... I'm not used to people fussing over me," she apologized.

"It's your birthday," Alain said, offering her a glass of champagne.

Taking the clear plastic cup, Noora watched the bubbles rise. For a brief moment, she was transported to the disco in London. She shook her head. "No! I ..." She was about to say that she did not drink, but Alain interrupted, putting an arm around Noora and giving her a kiss on the temple. "Annette and I are grateful. Deeply grateful."

Noora blushed.

On a sunny morning, not far from one of the beautiful seashores of the Riviera, a gleaming white limousine waited at the curb. Wheeled out of the hospital and holding her baby, Annette looked up at her husband.

"We're going home," he said. He could not have looked prouder. He turned and looked to the sidewalk.

Annette followed her husband's gaze and gasped at the sight.

"Surely my princesses must be brought home in style," Alain said, with a wink at Noora. A uniformed limo driver opened the door.

Alain and Annette snuggled up together with their tiny baby in the back of the plush, soft limo seats, while Noora sat opposite, snapping pictures of the new parents.

I wish Ahna were here, Noora thought, holding back a tear.

"*Grand-mère* is with us, you know," Annette said to Noora. "I can feel her presence."

"How did you know I was thinking of her?"

"Because she's psychic, remember?" Alain said. They all laughed. He reached over the baby's car seat and kissed his wife on the lips. Annette responded, keeping her lips on her husband's, their baby curled up, sleeping between her proud parents.

Noora snapped a last picture. "Perfect," she said, looking down at her camera, realizing she used the last exposure. When she looked up, Alain and Annette were still locked in their kiss. Noora turned to the window, then back down to her camera. "I think I should buy more film," she murmured, embarrassed. *The little family should be alone,* she thought. *This was their own private time.*

The baby fussed.

"Oh, oh, *petite Annou, Comme elle est mignonne,* she is so cute ..." Annette cooed. "I just fed you, my little angel."

"Are you sure you don't want me to hire a nanny?" Alain asked.

"Yes, my darling, I am certain, and I don't want a stranger taking care of our baby. Noora and I will be fine."

"We can't impose on Noora."

"It's not an imposition," Noora was quick to say. "*Bien au contraire,*" she added.

God keeps closing doors, but somehow, he opens a window, Noora thought, staring out the window. With every crushing sense of loss Noora had experienced, she somehow found resignation. When she lost Nageeb, she found Um Faheema, Dweezoul, and her other Bedouin friends. When she lost Uncle Khayat, she found Annette. When she lost Ian Cohen, Ahna Morgenbesser opened her home and her heart. When Ahna left this world, Annou arrived, bringing light and hope. And now, Annette and *Docteur* Alain ... But she could put them in danger as well, if that stalker was still out there, and if he did not drown ... If he did drown, and it was reported in the newspaper, then she was responsible. She would have been the cause ... The cause for... *Murder? No! Please, God, forgive me. It was self-defense! But in the eyes of the law...* She would still be considered a ...

"Noora. I only want Noora with me ... She knows all about newborns," she heard Annette tell her husband. "I trust her. She is the best friend I ever had."

The days and nights fell into a rapid rhythm. When Annette slept, Noora took care of the baby. After the first week at home, Annette began to grow weak and needed sleep more than ever. Noora said it might be postpartum depression and suggested they talk to Alain about it. Annette refused. "*Non,* he will drop everything and run home," she said. "It will not be fair to his patients." But Annette had daily fits of depression. A new round of crying started every afternoon.

Annette was blowing her nose when Noora came to her room.

"I never cried that much when I lost my mother," she said, sitting up in bed. "I was in love at that time with Bruno, and my world was around him. I was too young to realize. I was so foolish, so selfish."

"Time to pump your breast, Annette. I want you to get some rest today."

Noora waited while Annette pumped her left breast. Most women experienced a certain degree of depression, sometimes an inability to relate, and even withdrawal—possibly due to lack of sleep. *Thank heavens for breast pumping,* Noora thought. The baby had taken to the bottle well; Noora was sure glad about that.

"It's a blessing you are here. But where she is ... I feel her ..."

"Who?"

"My mother."

"Oh?"

"I feel the presence of my *maman.* I woke up two nights ago after Annou was born, and I saw her. In a vision. There. Where you are standing." Tears rolled down her cheeks again. "She said, 'I am proud of you.'" She handed the baby's bottle and breast pump back to Noora.

"Eight ounces?" Noora said, holding up the baby bottle. "You pumped eight ounces already?" She handed her friend a box of tissues. "You are Wonder Woman!" she teased, trying to add a little light to Annette's mood. "Four ounces when she wakes and another four ounces in three hours ... Right? But we cannot force her ..."

"Feed her only when she demands," Annette said with an exhausted wave.

"Good. I shall feed her on demand. I like that."

"She was beautiful."

"Of course," Noora said.

"I'm talking about my mother."

"I know."

"On the other side, they are happy. There is no negativity there. No wars. No revenge. No anger. There is only forgiveness ... Forgiveness and deep love and compassion. They show sadness only when we grieve for them. Did you know that?"

"No ... No, I did not know that." Noora turned away. "Sweet dreams," she whispered, closing the door behind her. She made her way down the hall to the baby's room.

No negativity in heaven? Wherever that may be. She wanted to believe. Why wasn't she receiving messages from "the other side," as Annette called it? *Nageeb! Was he happy?* Was he with their grandmother? Why didn't she feel their presence? Her hands full, she quietly pushed the door to the nursery with her elbow, where baby Annou was starting to fuss in her crib.

Nights had become her favorite time, alone with the baby. And now she would have an entire day. She enjoyed feeding Annou, changing her, and rocking her to sleep, singing Arabic lullabies her grandmother sang to her and her siblings, and songs she had learned from Um Faheema. Out of habit, Noora reached for her neck to touch the necklace. She missed it and wondered yet again if Ian Cohen's maid, Cessi, found it under the pillow … Did she give it to Ian? She would never know.

A week later, Annette's eyes were bright and she appeared to have gained her strength. "Today, we are going to take *ma petite* Annou out," she said.

"I had no idea this manuscript existed!" Annette told Noora as they sat at their favorite sidewalk café. The baby was snoozing in her English buggy, beneath a soft pink satin-and-lace comforter. "We must find someone to translate it. You know, the last few nights ... while you were taking care of Annou, and in the morning, when I was supposed to be sleeping?"

"Yes?"

"I have a confession to make. I didn't go back to sleep. I went downstairs to Alain's study and read my grandmother's manuscript. I feel guilty I didn't stay up with you, but I could not stop reading and … I am sorry …"

"You know how I love to spend time with Annou … But I had hoped you'd get some sleep …"

"I am sorry. I had to … I had to read what *Grand-mère* wrote … I needed to understand. I know a little German; I grew up hearing it, but I still had a difficult time comprehending the parts she wrote in German. Luckily, toward the end of her journal, she wrote more in French. Did she ever talk to you about a girl named Ghizella? She named my mother after her."

"Yes, actually, your grandmother mentioned her name the day before she died."

"What did she say?"

"Something about music. *The* music." Noora looked off, trying to recollect that night at the hospital. "'I hear the music,' she said. Yes, that's right. That's what she said, now I remember; she said, 'I hear the music.'"

"Apparently, Ghizella was the girl she could not save. She rescued many children," Annette said, picking up Annou and holding her close to her heart. Tears welled in her eyes. "She wrote that ... one night she undid the gas pipes and the Germans could not fix them to gas a group of prisoners ... they were all children. They made them walk in the freezing rain to the next concentration camp that had a bigger gas chamber. It was then that they escaped. Except for Ghizella, a sixteen-year-old girl ... When they had a chance to run, she told *Grand-mère* that she had to stay behind because she heard *the* music ... Like it was a specific music ... 'It is time for you to go and for me to go on and follow the music,' she told *Grand-mère* ... And a long time ago, when I was in school, I blabbed it all out to one of my dearest classmates, who told everyone in school, *et elles m'ont blasphémée!* They cursed me. All of them. They said I was a liar and the Jews killed their Jesus. We had it coming, they said."

Noora thought of the killing in Israel and the Middle East. She wished she could somehow have the power to stop all this hatred. "So much violence. In the end ... we are all the same."

"Isn't that what *Grand-mère* used to say?"

"Yes," Noora said. "She wrote it in her manuscript. 'In the end, we are all the same ...'"

"I never knew she killed two German guards and ... a cook. A woman."

"She ... *killed?*" Noora was stunned.

"Yes. She killed a German woman in the kitchen, a woman who suspected her and was going to denounce her, and my *grand-mère* took her place as the cook. She smuggled scraps of food the Nazi guards left behind every night when she served them their dinner, and fed the scraps to the children in the camp. These details that she described ... It was hard for me to read. I was tired, but I wanted to understand. More than anything, I want to know what she wrote in the first three hundred pages, the ones she wrote in German."

"Ahna worried she had nothing to leave you and her new grandchild ... All her paintings and family jewelry were taken by the Nazis."

"She left the type of treasure no one could ever take away," Annette said, gently rocking her baby. "Things I didn't appreciate when I was younger. Her story. It must be told—for the next generations and for those who still believe it never happened ... and for Annou."

The next morning, Annette's eyes were bright and she was filled with excitement. "I showed Alain *Grand-mère's* manuscript. It looks like she started writing it almost forty-five years ago. He is taking it to a translator."

That night and in the early morning, Noora thought about that manuscript. Annette was right. Ahna's story must be told. But how?

Chopping vegetables in Annette's kitchen, Noora couldn't believe how time had flown. More than two months elapsed, and baby Annou was growing cuter and more enjoyable every day. But Noora had that certain anxious feeling that there was something missing with her own life. She was happy living with Annette and her family, of course, but still it was not her home. She knew in her heart there was another plan. Yet she had not come up with anything.

That evening, when Alain arrived home for dinner, he walked in the kitchen, gave his wife a kiss, and handed her an envelope. "We're invited to the doctors' ball—at the yacht of the *Prince de Monaco* ..."

"Very funny."

"No, really," Alain said with a grin.

Annette opened the stylish envelope etched in gold, and her eyes lit up as she read the card. "Oh, *mon Dieu!* Oh, *mon Dieu, mon Dieu!* It's the yacht I have admired forever ..."

"And now you are formally invited. Along with a few selected doctors and their wives, to His Majesty's yacht. I suppose they figured I was important," he said with a wink.

Noora noticed the change in *Docteur* Alain after the baby's birth. When Annette was pregnant, he seemed concerned and preoccupied. Quite possibly because he had lost his first wife and feared he might lose Annette during her difficult pregnancy. Now he appeared happy and at ease.

"Is Annou asleep?"

"*Oui, mon chéri.*"

"Already?" he asked.

Annette was engrossed in reading the invitation, holding the card as if it were some kind of a priceless piece of jewelry.

"We just put her down," Noora answered, bringing the large bowl of *salade Niçoise* to the dining table.

Annette turned off the fire under a simmering pot of bouillabaisse. "The party at the yacht is only a week from now. What will I wear? It's not enough time for me to lose ten pounds!"

"You look perfect the way you are, *ma chérie*." He put down a few large euro bills on the counter. "You may want to check out the designer dress in the window of that boutique you like so much."

Annette looked at the money. "It's too much!"

She wrapped her arms around her husband and kissed him passionately. Noora turned away, blushing. She occupied herself putting the silverware on the table.

"We can't go," she heard Annette say.

"Why?" Alain and Noora exclaimed simultaneously.

"I can't leave Annou." She set the invitation on top of the money on the counter.

"But I'll be here with the baby. You wouldn't want to miss such a wonderful opportunity. You've always dreamed of being invited on board one of those yachts ..." Noora bit her lip. It wasn't up to her to barge into their private life.

"But that's when I nurse Annou. That's our bonding time together, since the rest of the time I just pump ..."

"She's almost three months old," Alain interjected. "It's only for one night," he said, looking genuinely disappointed.

"What time does the party begin?" Noora had to ask.

"Eight. Just when I nurse her."

"The party will go on until dawn," Alain said. "We can be fashionably late."

"It's always a pleasure to take care of Annou. She's used to me at night," Noora offered.

"I cannot impose on you every time I need to go out."

"You never go out! I am your friend and Annou's godmother. We are family. You have been wonderful to me; you gave me a lovely room, a home ..." But at times, Noora felt like she was a freeloader.

"I like you to be here," Annette said. "I couldn't have managed without your help. And Alain wants you here as well."

"Absolutely," Alain chimed in. "Annette, you'd better try on that dress as soon as the store opens tomorrow—before somebody else buys it!"

"How do I look?" Annette said, modeling her new strapless cobalt blue chiffon gown, while her husband waited at the front door.

"*Fantastique*, of course." Alain said. He turned to the window by the door and peered outside.

Clad in a tux, he looked like a young Alain Delon, the French movie star who was especially popular during the fifties and sixties.

"That's our limo pulling up," he said, and wrapped a shawl around Annette's shoulders.

"You both look fabulous," Noora said, holding the sleepy baby in her arms. "Have a wonderful time. I want every detail, Annette," Noora whispered as the couple left. Annette stopped midway, rushed back to Noora, gave a gentle little kiss on the baby's forehead, and ran back to join her husband.

Noora dimmed the vestibule lights and pulled the lacy curtains next to the front door. She watched Annette and Alain as they were whisked away in a black stretch limousine.

"Well, Annou," she whispered, "it's girls' night in." Baldo, the old Bouvier, was still at the vet's after a hip operation and needed to stay one more night for observation.

"We sure missed that big furry pup, didn't we?"

The baby wiggled in her arms. Noora carried her to the nursery and laid her gently in her crib. Annou stretched out on the soft sheet and produced tiny moaning sounds as she sucked on her pacifier.

"Sleep tight, little angel," Noora murmured.

Making her way to the kitchen, Noora smiled, thinking how much she loved the quiet of the night. She wished Alain and Annette would go out more often. She put a few last dishes away and tidied up the kitchen, then dimmed the lights lower and sat on the rocking chair by the breakfast nook. She realized she had craved sanctuary, and while she had found it temporarily in Paris with Ahna, tonight, she really felt safe and cozy in Annette's home, alone with Annou. In a lovely villa in the South of France, no less. Noora imagined Annette and her *Docteur*

Alain boarding the luxurious yacht. She hoped Annette would dance until dawn and not feel rushed to come home.

Through the lacy curtains, a shadow passed outside. Out of that window was the carport. There was no car parked there; Alain's Jaguar was in the shop. It had to be her imagination—or the headlights of a passing car making shadows.

She had planned to watch an old movie, keeping the sound low so she would hear the baby. She rose out of the chair and picked up the remote she had left on the kitchen counter. Again, she saw a shadow—this time passing from the other direction. The shadow of a man, Noora realized, her heart immediately starting to pound.

She dashed out to the corridor. Holding the television remote to her chest, she slowly peered back toward the kitchen. Everything appeared normal and the curtains were glowing from the light outside. Alain had probably left the exterior light on. That's when she saw the silver doorknob of the kitchen door next to the laundry room turn. Someone was trying to open it! The door had a deadbolt above the knob. The doorknob slowly turned back to its original position. She heard rapid footsteps. *Oh my God, quick,* she had to make it to the baby's room! As she dashed down the long corridor past Annette's room to the nursery, she heard the rattling of a window in the master bedroom. *Please God, let it be the wind,* she thought, trying to still her pounding heart. But there was definitely someone there. Noora snatched the portable phone in the vestibule. *The baby!* The corridor to the nursery next to the master suite never seemed farther to reach. When she finally made it to the baby's room, her heart drumming harder yet, she saw that all was dim, just as she had left it, and the baby was sleeping soundly in her crib. She heard the dreadful sounds of shattering glass. She screamed. The baby jumped and immediately began to howl. She grabbed Annou. *Must run! Where? Not the front door!* Too close to the kitchen where she heard the shattering window. Quickly, she switched all the lights on, in the nursery, while screaming loudly in French: "I have a gun! I HAVE A GUN!" She heard footsteps running down the driveway. *Had he entered the house?* She heard a car screeching away. The phone in Noora's hand rang, jarring her even more and it nearly slipped out of her hand.

"Allo? ALLO!" she answered, while trying to console the howling Annou.

"Is everything okay?"

"Oh … Annette …" *Thank God!* "She just … heard the ringing of the phone," Noora huffed, out of breath.

"*Ah non,* I'm so sorry, but I had to call you … I imagined Annou was in her crib and couldn't hear the phone, and … Can you imagine I wanted to be invited on board a yacht all my life, and now that I am a guest … an *honored* guest if you please, all I am thinking about is my baby! I miss her!"

"Annette, Annette, listen." *Was that prowler gone? Was it that evil man?! Could it have been …*

"I don't care about yachts and parties," Annette continued, totally unaware of Noora's trauma. "Unless I have *bébé Annou avec moi!* I'm crazy! Can you believe that? Can you hear me? *Allo-allo?*"

Holding the phone between her ear and shoulder, with the baby snugly in her arm, plugged to her pacifier, Noora turned on as many lights as she could find in the house while making her way down the hall. It seemed that who ever tried to break in was gone. *Oh God, what if it was that man, Moustafa?*

"Noora … Are you there? Is something wrong?"

"Baby's fine. Someone tried to break in … But he ran away. Everything's fine now. Everything's fine … I'm sorry …"

The next morning, after the police dusted for fingerprints along the windowsills, Alain was informed indeed there had been prowlers—two local young hoodlums had tried to break in.

"But we have an alarm," Alain said.

"It wasn't turned on, *mon chéri,*" Annette said. "We turn it on when we all go to sleep …"

The thugs had been caught, they were told by the gendarmes, but Noora was not convinced. *"At last you're mine… this time, you won't get away…"* A strong shiver ran through her body.

Had he really drowned? How could she know for sure?

Later that afternoon, Annette assured Noora that indeed, the young prowlers had been caught. "They were two teenage boys who break into homes when they think no one is home. They must have seen us leave in the limousine. And of all the times, Alain's car was in the mechanic shop, so they thought no one was home …"

During the next few nights, Noora lay awake, thinking about the incident.

Annou was now sleeping through the night. Annette's once-weekly housekeeper had grown so fond of the baby, she asked Annette if she could work for her more often, and take care of baby.

Noora knew it was time to leave.

"It's not that I'm not happy here," Noora told Annette several days later, while they were strolling along the *croisette* with Annou in her stroller.

"It would be selfish of me to ask you to stay. We will miss you very much. But you know ..." Annette stopped and stared out at the sea. "We all have our destiny. You must listen to your heart."

"My heart tells me I should take a copy of Ahna's manuscript with me. Would you mind?" Noora asked.

CHAPTER 62
ICE MELTS

I am now an American, Noora thought, landing at the Los Angeles airport. Out of habit, she brought a strand of hair down to her right temple, where the scar from her father's ordeal was still a reminder. But it was barely visible, especially with the concealer and foundation she religiously applied every morning. Her hair had grown a little longer than she wanted, and her blonde streaks had faded. But she still looked like her passport picture, so she knew there would be no problem. She was *Kelley Karlton.*

Her passport stamped, Noora took the shuttle to the nearest hotel. The Hilton on Century Boulevard was huge and crowded. The odds of running into anyone who would recognize her should be very slim.

She took a cab to the Beverly Center and had her hair cut and streaked—the same style as the evening with Ian Cohen and the Japanese family, and the first night she met Kennilworth. *Kennilworth!* The thought of that man made her cringe. She would handle Kennilworth quite differently if she ever ran into him again.

The real challenge was Ian. She wanted to talk to him without risking another unpleasant confrontation.

In her hotel room, she sat most of the night with a cup of hot cocoa from the all-night café in the lobby and stared blankly at the television screen. *Saturday Night Live* was on, but her mind was on the next night. How would she handle that situation? Certainly she was not going to call Ian Cohen and invite him to join her. She had to think of a clever way to run into him.

The next day, hoping Ian would arrive sometime after 7:30 in the evening at the Hamburger Hamlet, Noora made reservations supposedly for two, at 7:15 PM. When she arrived at the restaurant, she was shown to a booth. Perhaps she should have thought of hiring a lady companion, just to sit with her. Noora had made no friends while in Los Angeles. Her focus had been on Ian, and his Bel Air mansion had been a sanctuary for Noora during the three years and four months she had spent with him. Time had flown. Her sorrow had gradually eased until that dreadful afternoon when he ordered her out ... She could not think about that now.

She had brought two extra copies of Ahna's manuscript with her, professionally translated into both French and English, thanks to Alain's generosity. He would not tell Annette how much the translations had cost. It was a gift for his wife and for Noora as well.

Noora spotted Marj picking up drinks at the bar. The waitress who usually waited on Ian would certainly recognize her. Marj worked the bar area in the rear of the restaurant, and Noora sat keeping her back to that section. Sipping a tall glass of Coke with lemon and munching on chips and salsa, Noora began to feel anxious and even a bit nervous. Perhaps it was not the right way to approach the situation. That's when she heard his voice. She picked up the menu and held it an inch or two higher than eye level, her heart starting to pound. But why should she feel so vulnerable? If she were smart, she would put twenty dollars on the table and leave.

"Hellooo ..."

She glanced above the tip of her magazine.

"Oh ... Hello."

"What're you doing here?"

"I came for the chocolate cake," she was quick to reply.

His eyes were bright and there was a smile forming from the corner of his lips. "I came for the caesar salad," he said.

"Caesar salad?" She knew he didn't like salads, called that dish "frog food for rabbits."

"I try not to eat rare hamburgers and fries anymore," he said with a wink.

"Ian, they have our table," a man said, farther away.

"I'll be right there, Max," he said, but remained planted there, looking down at Noora. An awkward moment passed.

Noora noticed he had lost weight and looked fitter.

"Looks like you're waiting for someone," he said.

"Yes … Uh, no … "

"Well, it's nice to see you again," he said.

She nodded and smiled, and then he left.

She set the tall menu down beside her. She hoped he had not noticed her hands were trembling.

He made his way toward the booths by the bar—his usual table. They had made contact. She looked down at her hands. *Stop shaking!* Just because he was a big-shot Hollywood producer and she needed something from him did not mean she should feel intimidated. They had been through too much together for her to feel awkward or embarrassed. She had a serious mission.

"May I join you?"

To her surprise, he was standing less than three feet away. "What about … " She pointed toward the opposite side of the restaurant.

"Oh, Max? He's busy with a friend at the bar. Where's that chocolate cake?"

"I was wondering the same thing …"

"Mind if I sit for a bit?"

"No … I don't … mind."

"Kennilworth isn't working for me anymore," he announced as soon as he took a seat opposite her.

"What you saw that afternoon was not what it appeared …"

"I know," he said, shifting his weight.

She wanted to shout *You know?!* but she remained silent. Another awkward moment passed. "There was something I left in your house."

He dug in the pocket of his suit jacket. "You mean this?"

By the candlelight on the table, the blue bead with the copper chain glowed brighter than she remembered. He handed it to her.

She held it in the palm of her hand. "It was given to me by a dear friend," she revealed, staring at Um Faheema's necklace.

"I kept it in my pocket ..." he said, then added in a lower voice, "In case ... I should run into you again."

She wanted to cry. Of course, she would not allow herself. How she wished she could have shown it to Ahna. She looked up. *What did he say?* Surely she could not have heard him right. She couldn't bring herself to ask him to repeat it.

"Where are you living now?"

"France," she said, pronouncing it the way the British do: "Frauhnns."

"Are you visiting friends? You don't have to answer."

"I came for two reasons. Now I have one left."

CHAPTER 63
IAN COHEN'S DECISION

Noora sat in the tastefully decorated alcove not far from Roz's huge desk piled with scripts, stacks of mail, and two computer screens. She busied herself reading the *Hollywood Reporter,* but found the featured articles dry and boring. What else was there to do? She checked her watch. A half hour had passed.

Roz appeared genuinely happy to see Noora when she arrived at eight o'clock sharp for the meeting scheduled with Ian Cohen. But now he was late, and Noora had waited long enough. The office phones rang, one after the other, incessantly.

"The receptionists downstairs pick up after the first couple of rings," Roz explained, but when another phone rang with a different chime, Roz immediately picked up.

At least ten minutes must have passed, and Roz was still on that particular phone, listening attentively while taking notes. When she finally glanced up with a look of apology, Noora rose and motioned a little hand wave. She was leaving. She had come to get her necklace back—Um Faheema's necklace. This much she had accomplished. She had left Ahna's translated manuscript with Ian. Hopefully, he would take the time to read it, so if she were to return to France that day, she would not consider her Los Angeles trip to have been in vain.

"She's leaving ..." Noora heard Roz say. "I'll tell her," Roz concluded before hanging up. "He wants you to wait," she said, quickly adding, "We missed you, you know."

"I beg your pardon?"

"*I* missed you."

"I missed you too, Roz. Thank you. Obviously, Mr. Cohen is too busy ... Perhaps I should come back another time."

"He'll be crushed if you go, but you didn't hear it from me." She turned her attention to one of her computer screens and began clicking away at the keyboard.

"I didn't mean to sound rude. I know he's a very busy man ... Wait a minute, Roz, what do you mean, he'll be crushed ...?"

The keyboard stopped clicking. "Is that what I said?"

"What's going on?" Noora asked, taking another glance at her watch. Mr. Cohen was almost an hour late.

Roz motioned to Noora to come closer, and whispered above her computer screen, "He stayed up last night reading your manuscript and he overslept."

"It's not *my* manuscript. I ... just added the introduction about the writer."

"Can I read it?"

"Can you read what?"

"The manuscript."

"Of course. But ... if I remember correctly, you didn't read the scripts they sent to his office because they were too violent. This story is heart-wrenching."

"He said it almost brought him to tears. That, I gotta read."

"Wait a minute ... You mean he read the whole manuscript ... last night?"

"Traffic was the pits," was Ian's way of apologizing. He walked Noora to his office. "Sit down." He made his way around his desk, slumped in his leather armchair, and reached for a fat cigar from a carved wooden box.

Kelley Karlton gave him a disapproving stare.

Ian closed his eyes and ran his nose along the length of the cigar, slowly inhaling its aroma. "You're not my nurse anymore," he said, but still replaced the unlit cigar in the box. "Sit down. We need to talk."

She sat.

"Regarding that manuscript ... *Ahna's Coat.*" He picked up a legal-sized yellow pad next to his three phones. "I decided to green-light it," he announced without looking up, busy writing something.

"I'm not sure I understand."

"The foreword you wrote was good. Well-written. Good description of the woman, and since you knew her, I'd like you to co-write the script ... And you can be the associate producer," he said, words pouring out of his mouth like the wind. "First I'd like you to move back with me ... and ..." He stopped, looked up and into her eyes. "Say yes."

"Yes?"

"Good."

"No, wait. I didn't mean to say yes ... I need to think ... I couldn't just ..."

"I never went to your room. Cessi's the one who gave me your necklace. That was your room. Still is."

For the next six months, Kelley Karlton immersed herself in Ahna's story, while Ian Cohen was busy in his studio, working on the development of a feature film titled *The Battle of Mefisto.*

Noora hardly left her room, except for an occasional swim in Ian's pool, or Sunday nights, when they had dinner at the Hamlet restaurant.

The journal contained more than five hundred handwritten pages about survival and the human spirit—the true account of the heroic woman who managed to outsmart Nazi officers in order to save children. But Noora was still not satisfied with the screenplay adaptation. Something was lacking. Somehow, the essence, the life of Ahna's story was lost in the translation.

To make matters more difficult, Ian Cohen urged Noora to find the key people who could project Ahna Morgenbesser's story to the screen. The key is to find "the right director," he had said. How could she tell one from the other? And David Lean was dead. How about finding the actress who would portray Ahna?

Noora knew nothing about the art of moviemaking, let alone the process itself. *Didn't Ian realize that?* Just the night before, he had made a comment that surprised her: "I'm not a writer. That's why I hire them. The truth is, I've always been a better businessman than an artist."

Noora screened everything from D.W. Griffith to Charlie Chaplin to the latest modern-day directors known for their different styles.

The more she learned about the making of movies, from pre-production to post-production, the less she knew, and the harder it seemed. A crash course in film school would certainly not do it, and she wanted to get the project off the ground without constantly asking Ian for advice.

The possible directors she had interviewed had major egos. The men regarded her as a sex object—even though she was careful about her appearance, always dressing in conservative business suits. As for the women directors, to Noora's surprise, there was a sense of resentment. They each scrutinized her and tested her knowledge of moviemaking, even asking trivial questions about the history of movies, as if they were interviewing *her*. She knew they wondered how she had gotten so far in Hollywood.

But of all the men and women she had met, the last potential film director had to be the worst. He had not read the screenplay version of *Ahna's Coat*, because he said he waited for his story analyst to finish reading it. *Why didn't he read it himself?* According to Ian, before committing to anything, or even wasting their precious time to take a meeting, famous directors did not have *time* to read.

"That's what readers are for," Ian said.

"Readers?"

"In my days, they were *readers*. Now we have to give them fancier titles. But a good reader will write a good synopsis. Then the 'key' people decide if they want to take on the project or not."

"But you read all the scripts that come to your office," she said.

"I'm from the dinosaur era," he replied sadly.

As time flew by, all her efforts proved fruitless.

On another restless night—one of many—Noora woke again at 2:00 AM feeling she had to let go of her dream of making a movie, a venture that became more overwhelming with each passing day—and night. If Ian Cohen tried to convince her that making a movie was much more difficult than she had imagined, he succeeded.

One morning during the first week of August, Noora woke up with a dream song. Ahna used to hum a specific German melody when they took their afternoon walks around the little garden square across from her apartment in Paris.

Something about that melody ignited a certain feeling in Noora. If she could find a composer who would come up with that melody... *Ahna, I wish you could guide me...*

By the seventh month of Noora's attempt to write a screenplay adaptation, she thought she might have something to show Ian.

"It's a rough draft, very rough," she told him one Sunday morning, after spending the entire night worrying about what he might say. She was sure he was going to laugh at her, and advise her to stick to reading scripts, or forget about this project. But instead, he took the "property," as he called it, to the professionals, who broke it down and came up with a budget.

When Noora read the numbers, all she could do was sigh. "Obviously, too expensive." Ahna's manuscript was not the movie genre his company invested in. It was not only a World War II story, it was also a love story. The third act was about Ahna finding her husband, the man she had believed the Gestapo had killed.

"We're not shooting high-tech special effects," he said, to her surprise. "Ian Cohen Entertainment can raise the money. I know I gave you the responsibility of finding a director, and that wasn't fair."

She was about to object and say it was all par for the course, part of the learning, but he continued.

"I may know someone. He's German or something. Unfortunately, he retired from the film biz a long time ago. He wrote a couple of the best scripts I'd ever read. He was a film director too. That kid was a talent ... back in the seventies. A real visionary. But then one day, he quit. Just like that. I don't know if he'd ever want to direct again. He hated Hollywood. I'm sure he loathed me. I think he'll love *you*."

CHAPTER 64
CASTING CALL

Eight o'clock in the morning was the first audition for the part of Ahna Morgenbesser. The casting director Ian recommended was a large, no-nonsense woman in her early forties who, strangely enough, went by the name of Twinkie. When Noora arrived at the small stucco structure on Cahuenga Boulevard, only minutes from Universal Studios, she was shocked. The hallway and waiting room were packed with young women holding "sides," a few copy pages of a script. *Were they all there to audition for the part of Ahna?* None of them was right for the part.

In the office, Noora sat near Twinkie on a leather couch and checked the piles of eight-by-ten glossies and attached résumés that were stacked on the coffee table in front of them. There had to be at least a hundred candidates. "They're all modern California girls with a tan," Kelley Karlton remarked.

"That's why we have directors, to tell the costume designer to tell her people how to make the actress look like Morgenbesser. That's why they're actresses," Twinkie said, rolling her eyes. "We've got a big day ahead," she added hurriedly. She turned to her assistant, who approached timidly, carrying a manila folder.

"Ginger! Where's the coffee and doughnuts?"

"On their way. Here's the list you wanted," she said, placing the folder in front of Twinkie.

"Next time, don't send no gofer. Go for it yourself. By the time we get our breakfast, it'll be lunch."

"I'm sorry, Twink. I'll see what I can do," Ginger said, rushing out and closing the door behind her.

"I don't drink coffee, and I would rather not eat doughnuts at this time," Noora said, feeling an immediate distaste for the casting lady.

"I'll get you tea. Ginger!" she yelled. Her voice thundered like a bear's growl.

The young assistant popped into the office immediately.

"Thank you Ginger, there is no need ..." Noora started to say.

"Well, whatcha want? A latte?"

"Nothing, thank you," Noora said, rising. She went around the table and extended her hand. "How do you do, I am Kelley Karlton."

It was obvious Ginger did not expect the friendly gesture from a person attached to a big Hollywood name. She immediately turned to Twinkie, as if to ask her boss's approval to shake hands.

"How do you do, Miss Karlton," she said, shaking her hand uneasily.

"Okay, let's start already!" the casting agent said.

By the day's end, an exhausted Noora had interviewed some forty girls. None was right for the part of Ahna.

Twinkie, however, was very excited. "I like this one and this chick. Callback pile ... Ginger! Oh, that one, if she accepts the offer ... What's her name? Ginger! Get in here."

As soon as Ginger appeared, Twinkie waved an eight-by-ten black-and-white glossy. "Why isn't there a name on this headshot?"

"Sorry, Twink. But ... everyone knows who she is," Ginger ventured.

"Maybe some people *here* don't know who she is. Where's her fuckin' bio!"

"Coming right up," Ginger said, rushing back out to her desk. She returned with a thick manila folder and ran back to Twinkie. The name Francine Papillon was written in bold black felt pen.

Twinkie turned angrily to Kelley Karlton. "She's the first one who came to meet you and talk about the project. You asked her to read for you. Do you know how embarrassing that was? Don't you know who she is?" the casting director said, slamming the actress's picture on top of a new small pile.

"I know who she is," Noora said, remembering the first time she met her, with over-inflated lips and breasts, an arm hooked around

Kennilworth's, at the Beverly Regent Hotel, when she and Ian Cohen were having dinner with the Japanese family.

"How do you know? You acted rather clueless."

"We've met before."

"Not in person."

"Yes. We've met."

"Where, at the UNICEF party last week?"

"No."

"Yeah, okay, Ice's house, I'm sure."

"No."

"You know, I had to butter up her agent's ass just so she could take time off to come and see you. And she went for it. I'd say that was pretty white of her."

Noora had heard enough. She rose to leave.

"What're you doing? We're not finished."

"Yes, we are."

"No, we're not."

"I believe we are."

"Great. I'll call her agent."

"No."

"Excuse me?!"

"No one got the part," Noora said, walking to the door.

"Excuuuse me, hell-low?!" Twinkie shrieked. "This is not the way we do business here."

"I agree."

"I don't think you get the point, Missy. If you want star quality, she's got it. If you want bigger-name celebs, they'll laugh at your face. We don't have that kind of budget."

Noora stopped and turned to Twinkie. "Who is *we?*"

"Who's *weee?!* After all I've done for you? We've worked our asses off, putting ourselves on the line for your bullshit!"

Noora sighed. She had to turn away. Those words were like icicles hitting straight to her chest.

"Who the fuck do you think you are?!"

"Nobody," Noora replied.

"Exactly. I gave you lots of extra time just because Mr. Cohen and you ..."

Noora turned and faced Twinkie. "Mr. Cohen and I what?!"

Twinkie stared at Noora defiantly, pressing her lips tight. She turned and stomped furiously back to her office.

Noora walked outside. She needed to breathe. It was a smoggy day in the San Fernando Valley, yet the air felt fresher than the air-conditioned casting office.

An old beige Chevrolet driven by a young woman pulled into the parking lot as Noora walked to her car. The smoke from the carburetor made her cough. The young woman parked her smoking car a slot away from Noora's. A boy, about nine, was sitting in the passenger seat, looking unhappy. The young woman got out of her car, rushed around to open the passenger door, and sat at the edge of the seat, apparently trying to appease the troubled boy.

"I don't care anymore!" the boy shouted.

Noora looked around the parking lot. Somehow, the boy's behavior made her uneasy. Whatever was going on was none of her business, she thought, unlocking her car. As long as the boy was not being abused. *At least the smoke from that woman's car had dissipated,* Noora thought, glancing over her shoulder. The young woman was hugging the boy, who was crying.

Once behind the wheel of her leased Mercedes, Noora rolled down her window. "I'm sorry!" she heard the young mother say; she then retrieved a black portfolio from the back seat of her car and rushed toward the office building Noora had just left.

The boy ran after her. "Mom! I'm sorry too."

The woman turned and ran back to him. "It's the last time. I promise."

"That's what you always say. Why can't I go with you?"

"They don't want kids. Keep your whistle handy."

The boy pulled out a large silver whistle hanging from a string around his neck.

"Stay in the car! Read your book."

"You're wasting your time!" he shouted over his shoulder. Pouting, he returned to the car and slammed the door shut.

Through the rearview mirror, Noora tracked the woman as she ran to the building. She was thin, and not very tall, had to weigh less than a hundred pounds. Her stringy, pale blonde hair fell to her shoulders.

The young woman returned to the car, shouting. "Where's my lipstick! Oh God," she said, frantically searching in her purse.

The boy climbed out of the car and pulled out a lipstick and a compact case from his pockets and handed them to her.

"Don't do this, please! It's not funny," she said, taking her makeup. "It's hard enough! I'll lose this chance if I can't try this audition one last time. Please. And stay in the car!"

"Why can't you get a real job?!"

The young woman's face dropped. She turned away, shoulders slumped, and disappeared around the bend to the casting building. Standing alone, the boy kicked a few imaginary rocks and walked back to the old Chevrolet.

Noora started the engine and switched it into reverse. She started to pull away but stopped and pulled back into her parking spot.

She watched the boy. Sitting in the car, he was juggling two oranges. His mother certainly didn't have "star quality." She was probably going to the second floor, where she knew they were casting for a new diet drink commercial. She looked like a washed-out blonde who could come to life if she wore the right makeup ... No wonder she was begging for lipstick. She was so pale, so blonde ... So ... *AHNA!*

"Her name is Shoshanna Teresa Kahn," Noora said, placing an eight-by-ten, black-and-white glossy headshot on Ian's desk. "Setchka for short."

"Setch-what? What kind of a name is that?" Ian asked, studying the young woman's headshot.

"A name we'll need to get used to."

CHAPTER 65
A DIRECTOR FOR AHNA

Where did I get the crazy notion that Ian Cohen would want to make a movie based on Ahna's life? Noora remembered when she had first met him, he had said, "I don't do *Sophie's Choice,*" which she later realized he was talking about the World War II movie. No, he did not do movies that dealt with the Holocaust or anything close to that.

What was really behind it all? Was it because she wanted to escape France altogether? Because she feared Moustafa was still out there, in Paris? Of course not; one had *nothing* to do with the other! But she *did* still feel unsure and needed to get out of France. The newspapers said an unidentified man had drowned in the Seine—it could have been anyone. If he didn't drown, then he could have followed her. But the prowlers at Annette's house had been caught, she reminded herself for at least the hundredth time—eighteen-year-old delinquents. Nothing to do with Moustafa—or any of those dreadful fundamentalists.

Still, Noora was not convinced. And all she could do now was toss and turn with a pounding heart and a tormented mind.

The bright green numbers of her alarm clock displayed one o'clock. She had an early-morning appointment with yet another possible director. This time, the meeting would be held at Ian's office. Hopefully, whomever they were interviewing would take Noora more seriously, but she wasn't going to get her hopes up.

For some reason, and especially at night (since returning to California), thoughts of Michel seemed to be returning more often. *What are you doing right now, and where are you? And, dare I ask … with whom?* She tried to push the thought away. *I MISS YOU SO MUCH!* She punched her pillow and sank her head into it.

The land line on her bedside table rang, startling her. *Who could that be at this hour?* Hoping Ian was not calling to say he was ill, she lifted the receiver.

"Hello?"

"Hello … uh …" a male voice she did not recognize said on the phone.

She hoped it was not a prank call.

"May I speak to … Kelley Karlton?"

"Who's calling, please?" She pushed the covers away and sat up in bed.

"My agent, Riley Basser was contacted by a producer, Ian Cohen … He asked me to call someone by the name of Kelley Karlton," the voice on the phone said. "Is Kelley a man or a woman?"

Noora was ready to hang up, run straight to Ian's room, knock on his door, and ask how he could possibly give out her personal phone number instead of the regular one at Roz's office!

"I'm sorry," the man on the phone said. "I … I wasn't informed who … Oh, I'm sorry, I just realized … you're now three hours ahead. We don't do that daylight saving stuff here. My name is Jaqui Amstern. I live in Hawaii … Kauai. I'm a retired film director."

"This is Kelley Karlton speaking. A woman."

"I'm so sorry …"

"Did you say Mr. Ian Cohen gave you this number?"

"Yes. I apologize because … I realize it's late there … But they wanted me to contact …"

"Perhaps you'd like to call back in the morning, during business hours," she hinted. "Do you plan to be in Los Angeles in the near future?"

"Well, no … I have an art gallery here in Hanalei, and I don't travel to L.A. much … But I received quite a few messages on my answering machine from my ex-agent, and from Mr. Cohen himself. Something about a film in development and that they wanted to talk to me …"

Noora wondered if he wasn't drunk. Or … *stoned?*

"Fact is, I'm really retired now," the man on the phone repeated. "I don't work in Hollywood anymore ... but I understand there was an original ... an original manuscript?"

"Yes."

"Written by a woman ... A woman by the name of ... Ahna Morgenbesser?"

Noora thought his slight accent was German. He said "Morgenbesser" the way Ahna pronounced her name. "Perhaps we can send your agent the screenplay adaptation. Tomorrow morning. During *business hours,*" Noora said, pressing on the last two words.

"I would prefer to read a copy of the original manuscript."

Noora bounced up, paced for a moment, and sat back at the edge of her bed. "It's a diary over 500 pages, handwritten, mostly in German. And French." She flicked on her bedside lamp in search for a pen. *What was his name again?*

There was a long pause at the other end of the line, then finally he said, "I can read German. Can you send me a copy of the original diary?"

"The *original* diary?"

"Yes, you said there's an original diary?"

"Yes."

"And ... You said there's a copy translated to English?"

"Yes, there is."

"Okay. I'd prefer to read them all myself ..."

"You're kidding."

"Pardon?"

"Oh ... I mean ... If you would give me your name again, and address, I'll have Mr. Cohen's office overnight the copies to you tomorrow."

"Overnight to Hawaii takes two days. Mr. Cohen said there's a script adaptation?"

"Well, there is ... but ... actually, a rough draft."

"I would like to read that too."

Noora was speechless.

CHAPTER 66
LIMOUSINE LUST

Where had the time gone? Summer had rolled in, then came September. Since her new diversion, it had been easier for Zaffeera to remain in Al-Balladi rather than Los Angeles, where Michel remained, designing that complicated house she had loathed and cursed every day. But she wasn't too upset about that anymore.

Zaffeera had started the seduction of her young chauffeur. Not that she had expected her fantasy to materialize. She was just having a little fun. Every time he drove her to the new shopping mall, she kept her legs apart a little more. Sometimes she asked her driver to take the "long way," around the city, through the desert road. And so, two lonely, sex-starved souls found each other.

On a few occasions, she had caught his glance over the rearview mirror, but he never said anything. Finally, one afternoon, from that mirror, she had spotted beads of sweat on his forehead. It wasn't hot in the car with the air conditioner blasting, but he removed his cap and wiped his brow and the back of his neck with a handkerchief before putting his cap back on. That day, she had shaved her pubic hair and felt tingly clean like a young virgin bride. And that day, he took a different turn along the desert road. That was also the day she wore no underpants. She had casually kept her legs wider apart, bringing her skirt a bit higher than her knees.

He stopped the limousine at the edge of a hill, in the shade of a huge, droopy mango tree. There, he killed the engine, climbed out of the limousine, and opened the left passenger door, opposite from Zaffeera's usual seat. She wondered what he was doing, excited at the prospect that he might rape her.

For an endless moment, he stared at her very seriously. He was breathing hard as if he had just jogged a few kilometers. Finally, he parted his lips.

"Oh … ah, hm … listen, Mrs. Amir, I can't take it anymore," he huffed breathlessly. "I am only human and you are beautiful."

"*Beautiful?*" she asked, trying to control her own breathing.

"Yes. *Beautiful.*"

Well, that was all she needed to hear. Those words were enough to shatter any rules or religious beliefs. Michel had never spoken to her with such hunger, lust, or desire. That man wanted *her*. Was he actually shaking with desire? Yes! He *needed* her … He said she was beautiful. He said it *twice*. How could she resist such a man?

"Please, do with me as you wish," she murmured, closing her eyes, wetting her lips.

"But Madame … that is not possible," he said.

Zaffeera's eyes popped open. How could he turn cold at such a heated moment? She could have slapped him. "You have my permission!" she ordered and locked all the doors.

He pulled her to him, stared at her glossy cherry lips, for what seemed like a never-ending minute.

"Do me. Now!" she commanded.

He kissed her like she had never been kissed before, thrusting his tongue deep into her throat. On the stretch limousine floor, where the sheepskin carpet was thick and soft, her handsome chauffeur made love to her, kissing every part of her body, and fulfilling every fantasy a woman could imagine enjoying with a young man who could easily pass for a movie star. With every thrust, she screamed with pleasure, and never did she expect him to last so deliciously long.

CHAPTER 67
MAKING A MOVIE

The first day on the set, Noora stared at the grim world Jaqui had created.

"Good morning," he said and gave Noora a kiss on the cheek.

"Good morning," Noora replied, trying to conceal her shivering. *Who would have expected it to be so cold in Poland in the middle of June?* She should have brought warmer clothes.

"Something wrong?" he asked.

"It's ... just that ... it's very realistic."

"Good," he said and rushed back toward the main camera, which had been positioned and ready to roll. On his way, he stopped for a brief moment and patted the art director on the back. "Good job, Albert," she heard him say. "Very realistic."

Noora understood why the director chose to shoot in a European locale like Poland, but for Noora, such a dreadful scene was just too real. A low, stark building façade on bare, muddy grounds outlined against a gray sky: a pathetic crowd of children, their faces smeared with dirt, clad in rags, gathered two by two, facing several uniformed German guards—a landscape of horror.

In adapting the story, Noora had focused on Ahna's courage and cleverness in saving the children—not on the concentration camp and the experience of the children themselves.

A smoke machine behind the realistic camp façade the art director had designed was now blowing with full force, which gave the idea of bodies burning. Noora's chest tightened, and she was experiencing difficulty breathing. She was starting to feel unsteady and slightly ill.

She had to remain calm and remind herself that no one was about to be carried away, no one was about to be beaten and killed—not herself, not these children, not now ... Not at all!

But ... *where did all these children come from?* There were so many. If Ian Cohen were present, he'd be screaming, "Too many extras! I'm not paying for all this!"

Realizing she was standing too close to the set and probably in the film crew's way, Noora stepped back. The crewmembers all seemed to know who she was. She had been introduced as the associate producer who had brought the property to Ice (as everyone seemed to call him). She was really an imposter lucky enough to have found Ahna's manuscript.

"Quiet on the set!" she heard the assistant director shout.

The children were crying on cue, it seemed. She heard Jaqui's voice: "Let them cry while we're rolling!"

"Speed!" came the shout from another angle.

"ACTION!"

Her stomach became queasier while she watched, all the while trying not to watch, as the camera rolled.

Children were crying louder now. German guards were yelling. There was a gunshot, followed by another. More yelling, more cries. *Enough!*

She turned and walked away, careful not to step on the sea of electrical cords. Once clear of the movie set, Noora made her way to the long craft services tables laden with coffees, teas, and an array of snacks. She picked up a Styrofoam cup. Maybe she should make herself some tea. She studied the variety of little tea packets, trying not to pay attention to what was happening on the set. Quietly, she filled her cup with hot water, but she felt queasier. *Chamomile tea might help,* she thought. She started searching for honey.

"*CUT...*" Jaqui's voice came from a loudspeaker, echoing through her brain.

My God! What have I done? She tried to breathe deeply, and turned away from the food. *They're making a movie out of a horrible time, reliving it ... It's insane. These children.*

Noora had adapted that terrible scene from Ahna's manuscript. But then she had crossed it out, saying it was "too much." As Ahna had explained earlier in her writing, the Germans liked order above all, and would not usually beat people unless they caused "trouble." Their strategy was to use deception to get cooperation. Through cunning, they were able to lure their victims naked into gas chambers voluntarily, making them believe they were going in to take a shower. But as Ahna described it in her journal, young Ghizella, about sixteen years old then, had caused tumult, screaming that she had seen the ghost of her grandfather at the entrance to the showers, warning that it was a trap! Children were crying and screaming ... Ahna never finished describing that horrible moment. She mentioned an empty cornfield and a train station not far from that area. Because of the confusion, some of the children had been able to slip out during the transfer to the gas chambers. The German officers went after dozens of victims who were trying to escape. There were gunshots, she said. Years later, Ahna had learned that some—although very few—of the escaping prisoners actually had survived.

It wasn't worth putting the children through such a scene, just to make a movie. Holding the steaming hot cup close to her face, Noora made her way back toward the camera, where Jaqui was now conferring with Setchka Kahn, who had been awarded the lead role. Even though the actress was much younger than Jaqui, there seemed to be a strong connection between the two of them. Noora suddenly didn't feel right about disturbing their meeting. She would have to wait until later, she thought, breathing in the steam of her chamomile tea.

Working with Jaqui day after day on rewrites, she saw his determination to keep the script as close as possible to Ahna's original manuscript. Jaqui was a perfectionist, probing with so many questions about Ahna Morgenbesser herself—especially during the time Noora lived with her in Paris. He wanted to make every scene accurate, every moment as true-to-life as possible. He'd gone too far! This frightening set and violent scene would make the audience feel as if they were literally right there, in the prison camp!

But wasn't that what a movie was supposed to be? *Realistic?* How could she complain? Jaqui's perfectionism and eye for detail would make for an honest, high-quality film.

So what was the problem?

The long morning hours passed. The same scene was shot, re-shot, and shot again. Finally, the director of photography conferred with Jaqui on the following setup for another scene, while the crew and cast members drifted toward the long tables the caterers had prepared.

After the terrible scene in the concentration camp, Noora was relieved to see the German "officers" and costumed "prison guards" laughing with the children. They were teasing each other good-naturedly. It was obvious that genuine camaraderie had developed, once they were not acting in front of the camera.

The children gravitated eagerly toward the tables loaded with large platters of cooked chicken and other meat, cheeses, fruit, breads, and pastries. A number of the children appeared to have some physical deformity. Their eyes wide, it looked as if they were not used to seeing so much food; but they all kept their arms down at their sides, as if trained to wait, until they were each handed their own food tray.

"Hello!" she heard Jaqui say behind her.

She turned. "How's everything going?"

"Very well," he said, beaming. "These kids are amazing, aren't they?"

"Yes … But that's what I wanted to ask …"

Jaqui interrupted her to announce something in Polish.

"Pardon me?"

"Lunchtime!"

"Yes, lunchtime," Noora murmured, grateful for the break from filming. She looked past his shoulder. Outside one of the vans, Setchka was being shown a few prison garments by one of the costume ladies.

Noora and Jaqui walked toward the last empty table and sat down with their lunch trays. "Where did you find these children?" she had to ask.

"The orphanage. It's only two hours from here," he said, gulping down his turkey salad sandwich.

"You … used real orphans?"

"Yes. It's sad to see how many of them were maltreated," Jaqui said, his mouth full.

"What?"

"Most of the children you see here have been abused by their own parents. Many were abandoned ... or just dumped at the orphanage door."

Quietly, they both sat and ate. Jaqui looked up and pointed to a young boy about eight. "See that one over there?" The boy's right eyelid drooped conspicuously. "His father used to burn him with cigarettes. How a father can do that to his own child is beyond me. I couldn't even imagine ..."

Noora had to look away. Her father's words resonated in her brain: "*I denounce you!*" Numbly, she picked up her fork and poked it around in her salad.

Jaqui went on eating. If he expected a response from her, he wasn't pressing her for it.

Noora took a deep breath and glanced at the nearby tables where the dozens of children were eating hungrily. "I'm glad you thought of using an orphanage," she said at last. "Perhaps I could visit ... help in some way."

"More than you already have?"

Noora looked up, surprised.

"Mr. Cohen told me you gave a big chunk of your fee to the orphanage. That was wonderful of you ... I know it's confidential, but I was involved in the budget."

She managed to fork a piece of lettuce into her mouth. She had not returned from France to profit from Ahna's story! Ian's company had paid a million-dollar fee for the manuscript, which she divided with Annette (who put it in a trust fund for Annou). Noora did not feel it was right to accept another fee for the adaptation, especially when Ian Cohen was virtually supporting her. She had a lovely room in his Bel Air mansion, rent-free, and as the associate producer, she was being paid a good salary, with insurance benefits, plus her per diem while she was on location. Ian had claimed that if she didn't accept the fee for the screenplay adaptation, he would have to donate it to "a good cause." It was a business matter to him, but not to her. She wished Jaqui had not been told.

"... And he matched it," she heard Jaqui say.

"Beg your pardon?"

"He matched it. So now finally they'll have not only a new kitchen and new beds, thanks to you, they'll practically have a new facility."

"Oh ... good ... Yes ..." was all she could say.

"I thought you knew ..." he said, glancing into her eyes, realizing her surprise.

"Mr. Cohen must have been so busy with other things ... How many kids in that orphanage?"

"So far, about two hundred or more."

Noora nodded and stared at her salad.

Jaqui finished off his lunch. "Excuse me," he said, picking up his tray. "Another scene coming up."

Noora sat on a high folding chair, far from the set. *Would he ever finish with these violent scenes?* she wondered, trying to proofread the latest rewrites approved and faxed by Ian Cohen's office. It was already late afternoon, but Jaqui kept on shooting the "day" scene. The dark gray clouds, although still visible, had moved toward one part of the horizon, and the sun, still shining right above the land, painted the sky a dominant orange hue.

The children's cries became more intolerable, even though she knew they were acting, and the screaming segued into sickening waves of sound until she felt as if she were drowning. *"I denounce you!"* His words echoed in her heart. She put her hands over her ears and closed her eyes. *"I DENOUNCE YOU!"* She heard her father's voice again. The screams from the movie set became her own. She opened her eyes. *Had she screamed aloud?* She looked around. It didn't appear that anyone heard her. The production people were all engrossed behind the camera, watching the intense scene unfold. Dumping her script and pen in her canvas bag, she slipped out of her chair and walked away, toward the row of trucks and cars, where drivers sat reading newspapers and playing cards. A couple of security guards stood several yards away from the grip truck and the "honey wagon" that housed the bathrooms. She thought perhaps she could hide in one of the bathroom stalls.

"Miss Karlton," a large, husky man said as he approached her, "are you all right?"

"Is there someone who could drive me back to the hotel?"

Dizzy and ready to vomit, Noora didn't think she could make it down the endless corridor to her hotel room.

Later, when she stumbled out of the bathroom, her stomach at war with her mind, she crawled into bed. *How could Ahna have managed to survive such horror?*

"To be alive again, one must learn to forgive ..." Ahna Morgenbesser had written in her manuscript. But how could Ahna forgive those who had so horribly persecuted her people and killed their children? Ahna had told her, on one of their afternoon walks in Paris, "We must be strong enough to learn to forgive the past ... Not to condone or forget. But *forgive.*"

But he's my FATHER! He had kicked her in the face. He had tried to kill his own daughter.

She stumbled to the bathroom and again vomited, barely hitting the toilet bowl.

She made it back to the room and searched frantically for the bottle of Roger & Gallet she had packed somewhere in her carry-on. It was Ahna's. There was still more than half of the cologne left in her toilette table when she passed away, and Annette told her she should keep it. Ironically, the lemony fragrance had always reminded Noora of the Chabrawishi cologne of Egypt. Finally, she found it tucked in a back pocket, and splashed the cool *eau de cologne* over her forehead, her cheeks, and her nose. It stung her eyes a bit as she did, but it helped her breathe in deeply and feel a little relief.

She had left the bathroom light on, and the door open a crack, in case she needed to make another fast dash.

She lay on the king size hotel bed, staring at the dark ceiling, her body like a clump of cement. She remembered lying in Um Faheema's sand-filled bed, when she was badly injured and in horrible pain—afraid she had been buried alive. She began to experience that terror again. Calm down, Noora. *Calm down,* she whispered to herself. *It's over.*

She recalled Ahna's words: "When you are ready, you will be able to feel your pain... Without fear."

When I am ready? "I'm still fearful, Ahna," she said, staring toward the dagger of light that crossed from the bathroom door to the foot of her bed.

Ahna had also told her, "You must learn not to be afraid of your own feelings."

"Ahna, you taught me so much," she whispered. "You and Um Faheema …" Yet she had nearly forgotten those words of wisdom, and realized she had never tried to face her greatest fear: that horrific experience at the pool.

I must face my terror! She cried, tears now cascading like water. Every time she thought about what happened that day, every time she came close to her feelings, she pushed her fear away. She worried that if she faced the fear, it would make her *insane!* She would want to die! She sobbed into her pillow.

Noora woke up with a start. Somehow, she must have fallen asleep, exhausted from her emotional ordeal. Her stomach felt raw. She knew she couldn't throw up any more. There was nothing left. She turned to the window. The sun had set awhile ago, apparently. She turned to the alarm clock next to her bed. It was nearly nine in the evening.

"*Forgiveness is not easy,*" Ahna had written, "*but it is something we must practice every day of our life, if we are to live again.*"

God had given Noora the chance to live again. And again …

Ahna had written: "*You can only reach forgiveness through gratitude … Gratitude for your life … And compassion for those who have done evil. And from that comes the strength to never let it happen again.*" Although Noora had carefully edited this passage in Ahna's manuscript, she had not understood the powerful meaning of those words. She had never taken the whole of that message into her heart.

More tears streamed down her face. She pulled herself up and sat at the edge of the bed, then grabbed a tissue and took a deep breath.

But it was not about German soldiers, Nazis, and murderers filled with hatred for other religions and races, she thought, staring up at the oversized gilded mirror on the wall. It was about one man—*her father* … She grabbed the box of tissues and tossed it against the mirror with full force. "MY OWN FATHER!" she shouted at the mirror that had tilted from its hanging position. She grabbed her head with both hands and paced. Staring down in the dark at the carpet, she sobbed.

Yes, YES! It was true, she must have committed an immoral crime … For that, she must accept responsibility. She remembered the disco … the loud music … drinking champagne like water. How many glasses? Had she kissed a man? There was another young man she thought was

Michel ... *He was kissing her!* Why did she allow it? Nageeb had said there were pictures. Of *her?* What could the pictures have shown to affect her father in such a way that he became enraged enough to want to murder his own daughter?

There were several men that day in their living room—in gray suits, surrounding her father ... One of them was that man with the mustache! She gasped. He was at the pool! And she remembered him at the disco. Holding a camera. Staring at her! And he held it up to one eye ... Oh my God! It was *him!*

Those men had deceived her father, plotted to destroy him through ... *her!*

She stumbled, weaving her way from wall to wall, to the bathroom. She threw up some acid from her stomach. *I must calm down.* She made it back to the room, and with trembling hands, pulled a bottle of soda water from the little refrigerator. Twisting off the cap, she drank slowly and tried to control her pounding heart.

She realized the shame her father must have felt, how it pained him. How it made him suffer enough to turn his humiliation into such anger, causing him to commit an act he would never have committed otherwise: murder—followed by further bad consequences ... Nageeb's death. And the punishment their entire family endured.

A family that had once been filled with nothing but love.

She began to weep. It was not her father who was to blame for what he had done. Those men in gray suits ... and that other, older man—the sheik. His eyes, filled with such intense hatred ... and anger.

They probably hated the fact that her father was not like them. He was wealthy, famous, and powerful, admired and respected by everyone, including Westerners. They tried to destroy him by taking away his most precious possession: his family!

The fundamentalists wanted to control the people and were against freedom, especially women's. She had noticed the changes around their homeland. Slow but sure. They were there, those changes, small at first, creeping in like cancer cells. It had been happening, right in front of her, but she had been too naïve to see, to understand what it meant. And now it was too late. And so she wept.

She wept for her father, she cried for her mother, for Nageeb ... and for Zaffeera, for Kettayef, and for sweet little Shamsah. And for Abdo too. She wanted to cry until she would finally fall asleep. Because there was nothing she could do to change the past. It hurt so much to realize that there could be such evil. The only thing she could do now was learn to bear it, and begin to forgive.

It was the same evil that killed the children in concentration camps, the same evil that was killing children all over the world.

When she opened her eyes, Noora found herself stretched out in bed beneath the comforter, a pillow sham on top of her head, and perspiring profusely. Her face felt warm, and she knew her eyes were swollen from crying. She turned to the window and tried to focus. A crescent moon began to shine brightly, then disappeared behind a cloud. Slowly, it reappeared. Clouds were moving rapidly, as twinkling stars played around the dark post-midnight sky.

Noora removed her clothes and slipped under the sheets. Lying calmly in the dark, she let her thoughts drift.

The next time she glanced at the clock by the bed, it was 2:28 AM. The moon, shining brightly now, had moved to the far left of the window. Resting her head on two propped-up pillows, Noora began to feel something in her mind breaking and releasing. There was a sudden sense of calm, a sense of peace. The burden she had felt for so long, one she had so desperately tried to avoid, was gone. Noora realized, in fact, that she had forgiven her father.

As she stared at the moon, studied its silver crescent shape, she wondered about Michel.

CHAPTER 68
THE MAN WHO KNEW AHNA

"When you watch stars long enough, they become a part of you ... and you are never alone ..."

Sitting by the airplane window in business class, Noora thought of Dweezoul's words. She gazed at a universe dotted with thousands of stars ... perhaps millions, like diamonds, on black velvet, similar to the magnificent desert sky above Um Faheema's Bedouin village. To her surprise, Noora realized one of the larger stars she had been watching was actually pulsating to the rhythm of her own heartbeat, reminding her of what Dweezoul had said: "We are a part of them ..."

She wondered what he was doing. Stretching above the highest dune, on his magic carpet—stargazing? No, Dweezoul did not gaze at stars. He spoke to them, as if indeed there was a connection. What else did he tell her? At times, in the middle of the night, when she fell asleep on his soft blanket, sandwiched between Dweezoul and Saloush the goat, and with the desert sand still warm from the day's heat, he recited words like poetry—melodious, enchanting words, lulling her to sleep. She wished she could remember his poetry.

She had experienced episodes of many lifetimes since she left the Bedouin village. Meeting Annette ... Ian Cohen ... Ahna Morgenbesser. Then Ian Cohen, again—a new man. He no longer screamed —at least not around her.

He didn't lose his temper when she informed him that the production was running over budget. He approved most of the footage sent to him daily in Los Angeles. He had dictated memos, transcribed by Roz, that he found the rough-cut scenes moving. He even used the word *passionate*. His suggestions and the few changes he had made were good ones, and Jaqui had even agreed.

They were finally flying home to Los Angeles, where Jaqui had scheduled the other difficult task: post-production.

Jacqui was sitting several seats in front of Noora, with Setchka and her son.

For Noora, making *Ahna's Coat* had been a gift from "The Source of All There Is," as Um Faheema would have said. It had changed Noora's life in ways she could not have imagined. There were moments when she had wondered if she could survive the emotional ordeal. At first, she had been frightened, not just because she was a neophyte in the situation, but she had been generally anxious, even imagining that the man who had attacked her in Paris would return. Or any one of those men who would, no doubt, show no mercy. Somehow, after she had spent a night battling her personal demons, after she lost her anxiety on the set and no longer looked to the security guards to keep her safe, she found she had become much more confident. She had been able to get through the difficult sixteen weeks of filming in Poland, without total exhaustion.

The crew had been pushed to the limit, at times working seventeen-hour days, six days a week. But somehow, everyone seemed to remain in high spirits and didn't appear to resent Jaqui, the "slave driver" director who was putting them through it.

To everyone else involved in the project, it had been what Ahna would have called a *mitzvah*. Jaqui had said it too. It had been a good omen—even though many described it as the hardest job they ever had.

Jacqui Amstern had been tireless, and demanded accuracy in every scene described in Ahna Morgenbesser's original manuscript. He also seemed intent on finding out from Kelley Karlton everything she knew about Ahna herself.

Jaqui was nothing like the Hollywood directors Noora had interviewed in Los Angeles, or those she had heard about who screamed and embarrassed the cast and crew on location. When a scene wasn't working, for whatever reason, Jaqui walked away, took time for himself, and returned ready to shoot the next scene. When someone forgot his or her lines, Jaqui calmly took the actor aside and returned later, ready to start again.

According to his bio, Jaqui Amstern was born in Poland in 1938, and had spent some of his younger years in Paris, where he studied with prominent film directors in the sixties. He was considered to have been a part of the "*Nouvelle Vague*," the nostalgic era of the "New Wave." She noticed throughout the production, how passionate and dedicated he was to his work. It was uncanny how beautifully he captured Ahna's story from her writing. And Setchka too; watching her, Noora could almost believe that the younger Ahna was standing before her.

Noora closed her eyes. Her job was pretty much done, she figured. It felt good to just relax. She checked her watch. Almost seven more hours before they would land in Los Angeles. With luck, she could get some sleep. She pulled up the armrest of the vacant seat next to her so that she could stretch out.

"Hello … is someone sitting next to you?"

Noora looked up. There was a childlike essence to Jaqui, a boyish look to his demeanor. Removing the small pillow and blanket from the empty seat, she smiled. "Please, sit down."

Together, they sat in silence. She should perhaps ask him how he felt now that the location shoot had finally ended, but she remained quiet. He seemed to want to talk, yet he too remained silent. He gave a few deep sighs, and appeared on the verge of saying something. But he didn't.

She turned to the window. "Look at that star. Isn't it beautiful?

"Looks like an airplane," he said.

"Is it?"

They watched together for a while. "My goodness, it is a star," he said, leaning closer to her, to get a better look out the window. "It's beautiful."

He leaned back in his chair and looked up. "You remember the scenes when Ahna poisons the food of the guards who had tortured the children?"

"Yes, of course," Noora replied, turning to him, puzzled. How could she not remember them?

"And you remember when the prisoners are talking about the death of the guards?" His slight musical German accent had become more pronounced.

"Yes," Noora said. She also remembered that he had insisted on adding something to the screenplay at the last minute.

"The Germans believed both guards died of heart attacks," Jaqui said. "But we, the children ..." He stopped.

In the dimly lit cabin, Noora watched the shadow of his profile. He appeared more intense, as if trying to shake away something on his mind.

"But *we*, the children," he said firmly, "we believed it was an act of God."

For a moment, she thought that making the film had driven him temporarily insane. It was quite a few minutes before he spoke again. As most of the passengers around them slept, and the plane cut across the night sky, 39,000 feet above the Atlantic, Jaqui told his story.

Jacqui Stern, born July 8, 1935, was one of the children Ahna had saved from the concentration camps. "I added the A-M in the beginning of my last name, in honor of my savior, Ahna Morgenbesser," he told Noora.

In 1944, Ahna Morgenbesser had killed the woman cook in the kitchen and managed to smuggle food to the children. Jacqui was nine years old. In her diary, Ahna had described poisoning the two prison guards who had tortured several of the children. Their death remained a mystery. No one knew it had been the heroic act of Ahna Morgenbesser herself.

After Jaqui became silent, Noora realized her mouth was still agape. She turned to the window and rested her knuckles beneath her chin, for her mouth refused to close on its own.

There had been some subtle signs that Jaqui had been somehow connected to, or had known Ahna Morgenbesser. But Noora had not considered the possibility of such a coincidence.

The faint morning light had begun to show, and from the airplane's porthole, she watched the formation of the clouds below—pale violet, fluffy, cotton-candy clouds. As the plane flew west, catching up with the sun, purple and hot pink hues began to form on the horizon.

"Well, I'd better get back to Setchka. She'll wonder where I am," he said with a smile. He unbuckled his seatbelt and gave her a kiss on one cheek and then the other. Noora responded with a warm hug. They sat sharing a warm, friendly embrace. She wanted to say something, but couldn't find the proper words. Closing her eyes, she felt almost as if he were still the child he had spoken about, the child Ahna had saved.

"Thank you ..." she managed to utter. "Thank you so much ..."

When they broke away, he looked at her, blinked away a few stubborn tears, and smiled. "Try and get some sleep. Thank *you*."

When the sun rose and the flight attendants came down the aisles to check that seatbelts were buckled in preparation for landing, Noora remembered Dweezoul's words: "There is no coincidence ... There are no accidents ..."

CHAPTER 69
AN INVITATION

"Yes ..." Michel replied after Zaffeera ended their phone conversation saying, "I love you."

"I'll call you back as soon as I find my way back to the hotel," he said, and added rapidly, "I do too, thank-you-goodbye." He pressed the "End" button on his cell phone.

How was he to respond? He didn't really *love* her.

He drove out toward the exit gate of the Burbank Studios. He had just attended the most positive meeting he'd ever hoped to have. An in-house studio attorney who was referred by Mr. Attai'e (the client whose Bel Air house Michel had nearly completed) had referred the potential client to Michel. He was grateful for the opportunity. The house he was to bid for was in the posh "Beverly Hills Flats," where Zaffeera wanted to live.

Perhaps it was time to leave Al-Balladi. He had nothing left there—except sad memories. Perhaps Zaffeera would not mind moving to Los Angeles.

It wasn't fair to leave Zaffeera alone in his father's mansion, far from her family. She never complained about that. She never complained about anything, which sometimes concerned him. There was something about her that he couldn't quite comprehend. She was always so quiet. And perhaps ... secretive? He never really knew what Zaffeera was thinking—unlike Noora. Maybe she was just very shy. But more than that ... What? He didn't know. He did like her intelligence—she had a great sense of logic too, and organization. She took care of him, bought his clothes, sent them to the cleaners, and she even took care of his business files. At first, he thought she could assist him in his new business. But no, now he didn't think that would work. Living together, working together ... sleeping together. Definitely wouldn't work. When they were in bed, he could tell she wanted affection ... a great deal of it. She wanted sex; perhaps because he had been traveling so much. But it was difficult for him to make love to a young woman he didn't love! They had never really talked about having children, but he knew it was time ... Time to start a family, and focus on their future. Perhaps then, after they had a baby, he could learn to love her. They say love grows. He hoped so.

Only recently Michel had found out that Zaffeera's mother had gone to Switzerland several months before with the two younger children, Kettayef and that darling little Shamsah. When Michel asked about her family, Zaffeera explained that her mother wanted to be close to her children, even if they were in the best boarding schools in Switzerland. Who could blame her? She had lost her two oldest children. But still, Michel couldn't help but wonder why he wasn't told that Zaffeera's mother had left Al-Balladi. If he had known, he would not have let her stay alone. He didn't know if Zaffeera had friends; she never talked about any girlfriends. Apparently, she was only close to her family.

It appeared she had been close to Noora. The real reason Michel had wanted to build a home at Al-Balladi was because Noora was buried there.

After making a left out of the Burbank Studios, he screeched to a halt at the red light. He had to be more careful and not allow himself to become too emotional, especially when he was behind the wheel. Every time he thought of Noora, a deep feeling of anger churned inside him. He couldn't help it. But he had to learn to control such feelings. In the beginning, he had felt grief. How long did he grieve? Was it three years? No, four ... Now he was angry. But anger would get him nowhere, and he needed to focus on his business. That always took him away from thoughts of Noora.

The potential client, Mr. Meyer, had given him the directions, saying it was best to take a left, and two long blocks later, he would find the freeway, unless he wanted to take the Cahuenga Pass. *Where was that?* He was stopped at another red light before the freeway. Mr. Meyer had invited him to join him at a screening of a World War II movie that had not yet been released. Perhaps he should have accepted the invitation, but Michel wanted to call his father, who was at Sharm El Sheikh overseeing the major celebration for the opening of the new hotel and spa. He and Zaffeera would definitely attend. He knew she was looking forward to it. They could vacation at their father's new hotel for a few more days. He hadn't seen his father in ... how long? Too long, if he couldn't remember. And he missed him. Afterward, they would fly to Los Angeles and begin their search for a house to lease in Beverly Hills.

So many good plans lay ahead, but it was wise not to keep his hopes too high. So far, even though Mr. Meyer expressed interest, he had not yet signed or confirmed anything.

CHAPTER 70
A SMALL WORLD ... AFTER ALL

One early morning in late November, Noora received a call from Annette. Alain had been invited to attend a medical convention in Los Angeles in January, and she and Annou would accompany him. They were looking for a hotel near UCLA, but Ian Cohen would not hear of it. The granddaughter of Ahna Morgenbesser was going to stay at his house with her family. He had plenty of room. The bungalow next to the pool was a large studio apartment with kitchenette and all the amenities.

At the Los Angeles airport, Noora's heart skipped a happy beat when she spotted Annette, Alain, and Annou—her "Triple-A family," as she called them.

Little Annou looked up at Noora and raised two little chubby fingers. Trying to keep a third finger halfway down, she squealed. "I am two ... a half," she said in English.

"We are teaching her to be bilingual," Annette said, fighting back her tears of joy. "Oh, *ma chère amie*, how I have missed you!" she cried, hugging Noora.

When Noora and the family arrived at Ian's Bel Air mansion, Annou ran inside the house. As her parents looked around the entrance in utter awe, Annou spotted the open doors to his office and ran over to Ian, who was sitting behind his desk, finishing a phone conversation. Before he could hang up and rise to greet his guests, Annou had climbed up on his lap. From that moment on, Ian Cohen was smitten with the adorable child.

Noora always felt a deep sense of happiness when she was with Annette. And today, together with Annou, they were on their way to the happiest place on earth. As they neared Anaheim, the traffic on the freeway was at a near crawl. But with so much catching up to do, Noora and Annette barely noticed.

Sitting in the back, buckled up in a child's seat, Annou was busy playing with a new doll Noora had given her. "Why can't Papa come to Disneyland too?" Annou whined while Noora maneuvered her car through the heavy freeway traffic.

"Papa is busy today," Annette explained patiently. "He is a good doctor, *ma chérie,* and he was invited to a special medical convention at the big *Université qui s'appelle UCLA*. Can you say UCLA?"

"Ew—See—Elle ai!" repeated Annou.

"Oui, ma petite Cocotte!" replied Annette.

"Is that language Franglais?" Noora asked, laughing.

"Yes, it seems that's how we talk these days!"

"Maman, Maman, we have to come back with Papa," Annou said in English. "I want to show him all I will see *aujourd'hui!"*

"Bien sûr, ma petite chérie," Annette said.

No sooner had they parked the car at the huge parking lot and headed down Disneyland's Main Street, than Annou announced she had to see "the dolls" first! To Noora's relief, the line to the "Small World" ride was unusually short. It was a good time to come—midweek, mid-January, when most children were back in school, after the winter break.

While they waited in line, Noora's cell phone jingled. "I won't answer it," she said to Annette, but when she saw the lighted numbers, she said: "It's Ian! He never calls at this hour ..."

He barely waited for Kelley Karlton to say hello. "You done with Disneyland yet?"

"No, Mr. Cohen," she said. "We just got here. The traffic was horrendous."

"*Ahna's Coat* has been nominated!"

"What?"

"WE WERE NOMINATED! They just announced it! Cessi saw it on television, on her Spanish channel, if you can believe, and called Roz, who just called me in the car when I already reached the freeway!"

"Oh goodness! It's wonderful."

"Four categories!"

"What do you mean, four categories?" she asked as their line moved faster. Soon they were next to climb on the boat.

"Best Actress ... Best Direction ... and get this! Best Picture! That means ME! Oh, and I thought I'd let you know, also best screenplay adaptation ... You know what that means?"

The music of "It's a Small World" became louder.

"Oh, my God!" Noora murmured, following Annette and Annou, who were climbing onto the boat.

"WHAT? Are you still there? Are you already at the Small World ride? I can hear the music!"

"Yes, we just started and ..."

"You're supposed to start at Main Street."

Noora turned to Annette, who had a questioning look on her face: "*Qu'est-ce que c'est?*" she asked while Annou began poking at her mother to look at the pretty dancing dolls at the beginning of the ride.

"Your *Grande-mère's* film has been nominated!"

"Nominated?"

"Yes! For the awards!" Noora turned back to the phone. "Did you say *four* categories?"

"*Oh, mon Dieu!*" Annette exclaimed, nearly jumping out of her seat.

"What did you say?" Ian asked on the phone.

"Annette and I are saying, *OH, MON DIEU!*"

"Oh my Gawd, indeed! Remember when I said I never wanted to attend Hollywood events? This is different. Forgive *my* French this time, but shit, WE'RE FUCKING NOMINATED!"

"I forgive you!" Noora said laughing, tears of joy filling her eyes.

"I want you to walk with me on that red carpet, so I don't say anything indecent to that woman with the ten facelifts, asking stupid questions ..."

Noora laughed as she watched little Annou's face, her eyes wide, her mouth open. The child was captivated by the dolls jerking around under colorful lights that created dazzling reflections on their jeweled costumes.

"We're starting to go inside now. I hope I don't lose reception …"

"Call me when you get out of the Dolls. I'll be waiting outside!"

"You're … here? At the park?"

"Yes, and I know the traffic was horrendous, I was following you girls all the way, but you were too busy jabbering in your frog language," Ian Cohen said. He had never sounded happier. "Get ready to get written up all over the place, Ms. Kelley Karlton," Ian said before hanging up.

Noora stared down at the cell phone. *Written up?*

"It's a small world after all …" Annou sang along with the music.

CHAPTER 71
THE DISCOVERY

3:00 AM—Noora was unable to sleep. How would she explain to Ian Cohen that she could not accompany him to the awards ceremony? Under normal circumstances, being nominated would be a great honor and a most exciting time in anyone's life. But the circumstances of her life were not normal, and instead, she felt depressed. Such an event would be televised all over the world, no doubt, but perhaps not in Jordan. It was possible the fundamentalists no longer allowed American television to be shown there. She wasn't an actress, for heaven's sake. Who would want to bother wasting their film on her? Except for the fact that she would be right next to Ian Cohen.

Kelley Karlton was nominated for the screenplay adaptation. Noora Fendil was dead.

Her hair had grown down to below her shoulders, and her blonde streaks had grown out. She had been so busy with the movie production and entertaining her dear friends Annette, and sweet little Annou, she had not bothered to take the time for her hair. Kelly Karlton could bleach her hair a Marilyn Monroe blonde, and have it cut much shorter. No one would be paying attention to her, and she could wear sunglasses like Jack Nicholson. *Oh no, that might bring more attention.* She could wear tinted glasses to be on the safe side!

She remembered that every year, her father liked to watch the American film awards on television. Would he recognize his own daughter if he saw her on television? Even with her disguise? Impossible. But if she were to ever let her father know she was still alive, it would be by her own choice, not by having her deception suddenly revealed to her family in public.

The next day, she waited until she knew Ian would be at his office. She dialed his number while standing in front of a store on Rodeo Drive, admiring an exquisite black evening gown in the window. It had a low neckline, but not plunging, and delicate golden straps.

When she apologized, saying she would not attend, Ian laughed. "Last-minute jitters, huh?" he said. "Honestly, I hate all that Hollywood hoopla. This is different! You're being honored for your work!"

"If I could ask you to please understand," she said. But she knew she would have to give him a solid reason.

"Roz just brought our lunch ... I have my accountant here ... Let's talk about it tonight, okay?"

"Yes ..., of course," she replied. She had called at a busy time. She should have waited until that night to explain.

She went inside the store to ask the price of the gorgeous black gown. She would tell Ian she would meet him at the post-awards party and maybe she would wear that dress. *Let's see if it looks right on me first,* she thought.

Five thousand dollars? Noora thought, walking out, minutes later. *That's insane.* The saleslady bragged about the designer. Noora had never heard the name. The gown was certainly well-made, but a price that high belonged on a wedding dress. She couldn't imagine purchasing a pricey dress for a party, and certainly not when so many people in the world were starving.

She was about to walk to her car in the indoor parking garage down the street, when her cell phone jingled.

"Aloha!" Jaqui's voice chimed the moment she answered. "How're you doing?"

"Fine ... And you?"

"Great. What're you going to wear?"

"For what?"

"The Awards!"

"Oh ... Yes, well, as a matter of fact ..." She wanted to say she wasn't going, but didn't think it was the right time. "I'm ... not sure ..."

"All the best designers are pouring in, calling on Setchka's agent constantly. They want her to wear their creation. Only a year ago, if she dared to even ask for the price of their gowns, they'd laugh at her. Now they're begging her to wear their designs for free! Isn't that ironic?"

"Yes, it sure is, Jaqui. Where are you?"

"We're still on Kauai ..."

"Who's we?"

"Setchka and Alan, her son."

Thank God, Noora thought. *Are those two getting ... serious?* "That's wonderful, Jaqui; say aloha to them for me."

"I'd let you talk to her, but she ran to the beach with Alan to catch some waves and hopefully get a little tan. We're flying back to L.A. tomorrow. She's getting excited about attending the Awards! It's not my thing, but I guess I'll have to go too!"

"You might win!"

"I already did! We have much to be thankful for."

"Indeed ... How does she like Kauai?"

"She loves it! It's a good thing, because she's going to spend more time here with me! Alan too. There's a nice little school here in Hanalei ..."

"Wait a minute, Monsieur Jaqui, what are you trying to tell me?"

"We were both going to tell you before anyone ..."

"What! Tell me what?"

"I proposed right on the beach last night at sunset, facing Bali Hai. And they both said YES!"

"Oh my God! I am so, so happy for you! All three of you!"

"Thank you! You're our angel, you know that ... Listen, Setchka saw a dress at that corner boutique store between Rodeo and Wilshire. You know where it is, right?"

"Of course."

"I'll give you the style number. I can e-mail a picture ... Would you mind going to see it? She put it on hold, it's under her name, but that was a week ago. She wants you to see if you like it before she decides to buy it."

"It would be my pleasure. But it's not up to me. If she likes it, she should have it!"

"She wants you to see if first, because she trusts your opinion, and if you think it's the right dress for that type of event, I'm buying it for her. Please don't tell her!"

The evening gown Setchka had chosen was indeed beautiful—classy, yet simple, an azure vision in delicate silk. She punched in Jaqui's cell phone number but there was no answer. She left a message on his voicemail: "Hey, Monsieur Jaqui, about your fiancée ... I have to say ... she's not only a gifted actress, she has a pretty good sense of style! I put it on hold for you. Call me. Aloha, you devil!"

She walked back up the sidewalk on Rodeo Drive, toward her parked car. On her way, she stopped at David Orgell's, to admire the crystal Lalique swans in the window. She had seen them at the Lalique store in Paris. She looked up, and someone inside the store caught her eye. The young woman stood at the counter, talking to a salesman. *Zaffeera?* Her heart began to pound. She felt unsteady. It couldn't be ... Next to her was ... *Michel?* Impossible! *Steady, girl, just inquire about the crystal swans and look closer. It's not them. This guy's hair is longer than Michel's,* she thought, venturing cautiously into the store. She removed her sunglasses.

They were both leaning on the long glass-top counter, looking at porcelain china. The man—*could it be Michel?*—wore a black butter leather jacket and dark trousers. *It was Zaffeera!* She stood next to him, to his right, wearing a perfectly fitted navy blue suit. She lifted her left hand and gently caressed his back. Perfectly manicured fingernails, that same pink-mauve polish that she always wore—Zaffeera's signature, long acrylic nails and polish!

Noora recognized the ring. Her "Forever"-shaped, ribbon-design ring with the diamond that glinted under the store's recessed lighting. The motion of her hand on his back, proclaimed he was... *hers?*

She approached the couple, ready to say something: *Zaffeera! Is that you?*

Something like a loud nervous chuckle got stuck in her throat, and she couldn't utter a sound. An explosion of feelings rocked her. Her heart hammered, as she watched the couple talking to the salesman. She fled, hurrying out of the store. A moment later, she returned, knowing she had to be sure, one way or the other. They were now walking away from her, guided by the salesman toward the back wall, where a large selection of bone china was on display, beneath bright recessed lighting. She saw Zaffeera's profile as she briefly turned her chin up to Michel and smiled at him. The way she moved her head ... The way she looked at him ... Her hair was thicker, longer, a richer color of brown ...

Noora jerked away, turning before Zaffeera could spot her from the corner of her eye. They shouldn't recognize her from the back ... She had been through so much, they would not know or suspect it was her ... She began to walk toward them, where they were looking at porcelain platters on the back wall. The salesman picked up a hand-painted platter.

Zaffeera exclaimed, "*Michel, chéri, il est superbe ce motif!*"

Zaffeera's voice! The same affectation—the fake-sophisticated way she used to imitate the Parisian accent.

Noora rushed out of the store. She hurried away, down the sidewalk, crossing the street, just as the light changed, nearly getting hit by a honking car. She retreated to the sidewalk.

"*Michel chéri?*" Zaffeera had said. *Since when?! Since ... since she got rid of me!* Noora turned back toward the opposite side of the walkway where the pedestrian light blinked red. She kept walking, down toward Wilshire Boulevard.

Something inside had ignited, and her heart pounded faster. Her blood rushed to her head, and she felt ready to explode.

The fog that had enveloped her mind began to burn away. Everything that had remained hidden for almost seven years became as clear as the bright lights illuminating the store's displays, and as crisp as her vision of the two of them!

How could I have been so blind?!

The past came crashing before her eyes. That night in London ... the disco. The girl in the blonde wig! Manicured nails—stroking the wig ... Same pink mauve polish ... The London taxicab, Zaffeera telling the driver to take them to ... *Where ... Where? What was that name? Noora! You must remember!* All this time ... It was ... ZAFFEERA! Zaffeera who ... must have ... *drugged me?* The *Velvet Cave!* That's what it was called! The chocolates she gave her earlier that day! They had an aftertaste, but she didn't want to disappoint her sister, and she ate them anyway ... How odd she'd felt soon after ... She remembered Zaffeera's behavior on the plane going home ... Oh my God, *Zaffeera wanted Michel!*

As she quick-stepped her way back to her car, her hands shaking with anger, Noora picked up her cell and dialed Ian's phone. "Mr. Cohen ... Ian!" she said the moment he answered.

"Whatsa matter? You okay?"

"I shall definitely accompany you to the Awards, if the invitation stands."

"Atta girl!"

"Can we go to the Hamlet tonight?"

"What's goin' on?"

"I've got a story to tell you."

"Really? Whose?"

"Mine!"

CHAPTER 72
THE REVELATION

Zaffeera lay in bed, staring at the bedroom ceiling of her father-in-law's Al-Balladi mansion. Her menses were three days late, and she hoped this time, this time ... *Don't get your hopes up!* she warned herself. Thoughts of what she would name him danced around her. She could name him Nageeb Michel Amir. Or Gabriel Michel Amir? Gabriel had been Nageeb's middle name. Perhaps she should name him something that rhymed with their last name ... How about Zaffir Amir? Zaffir Michel Amir?

Michel was already downstairs in his father's office, still in his robe after his morning swim, working on some kind of a blueprint, no doubt. For someone else's house. That's all he seemed to be doing these days—designing homes and studying blueprints, instead of playing in bed with her! It wasn't as if he needed the job or the money. His father was a very successful man, and his mother had been a wealthy Egyptian woman who had left her fortune to her only son.

But she shouldn't complain ... too much. Last night, he had *made love* to her. He had actually, and finally, made the first move! It wasn't exactly what she would call acrobatic, long, and lustful sex, but it was better than his previous attempts, when she had been the one making advances. She could tell he was trying to please her. Poor guy, he was so shy in bed. She finally admitted to herself, he just didn't know much about pleasing a woman! Although it was true he had gone to school in Paris, the most romantic city in the world, he had spent his time probably surrounded by dull professors, studying architecture instead of the art of sex.

One thing was for sure: She wasn't going to torment herself, worrying whether he loved her or not. He had *married* her! She knew he didn't have a mistress. She checked and rechecked his appointment book, his receipts, dreading the possibility that there might be another woman. He was so handsome. Everywhere they went, especially in Los Angeles—where there seemed to be more beautiful women than men—they all stared at him. She could see them from the corner of her eye, from stores to restaurants, from Beverly Hills to New York! If they only knew that her handsome husband, with the hard bronze body, was better at choosing jewelry than performing in bed. She stared at the Tiffany tennis bracelet he had given her in Beverly Hills last week. He had also chosen the most exquisite and delicate fine French porcelain china for the new home they were going to lease for a year. When he took her to that store, David Orgell, and showed her the china he had liked, Zaffeera almost had an orgasm right there. Michel had impeccable taste. He was the one who had found the right house for them: a simple but functional five-bedroom house with a pool; near Rodeo Drive, practically walking distance to her favorite designer stores and popular restaurants. Oh, but if he could just fuck better! And didn't anyone ever tell him that there was something more than the archaic position—and something called *foreplay?!* If she could just run downstairs, right now, and rape him! The thought alone gave her a sudden, uncontrollable shudder. To have sex right on that soft, hand-woven Persian rug in his father's office, or better yet, on Mr. Amir's butter-leather couch! Perhaps Michel felt uncomfortable having sex with his wife in his father's home. She couldn't blame him for that. *I'll bet that's what it is,* she thought, floating across the room to her puffy boudoir chair. She sat in front of the mirror, fluffed up her hair, and applied lip liner and strawberry-flavored gloss. But what about when they were at the hotel in Beverly Hills? And Hawaii? She wasn't going to analyze that now. Because right now, she might be pregnant.

She tossed her lip liner on her boudoir table and rushed to her walk-in closet. Punching in her personal combination, she pulled out a box with packages of pregnancy tests. She heard shuffling outside. Quickly, she replaced the box back in her safe, and walked out to their bedroom, in her satin nightgown.

"Guess what?" Michel said, tightening the belt of his bathrobe. His eyes were bright, and he looked like a little boy who just won his first trophy for some ballgame.

Why don't you remove that dumb robe so I can pull down your bathing suit, if you still have it on, and lick your body, Zaffeera thought, *while you finally kiss my poor, neglected vital part!*

"Well… *Ma jolie,* I can't believe it!" he said in French. "*C'est fantastique.*"

Zaffeera put both hands to her mouth. He called her his… *pretty?*

"Well, what?" she asked, excited.

"I got the job! He accepted my bid!"

"*Fantastique!*" She repeated his word in French. It was awful. Now he'd be working while she sat alone in that house in Beverly Hills? *What if she was pregnant and needed him at home near her?*

"I heard the fax machine in my father's office just now. There was a letter from the new client I told you about, Mr. Meyer …"

"Yes," Zaffeera said, removing her white satin robe, tossing it at the foot of the bed. "You mean the executive at the movie studio in Burbank?"

"That's right. You remember," he said, visibly impressed.

"Of course I remember." She was now clad in a delicate silk and lace, barely blush, lightly transparent thousand-dollar négligée she had purchased recently from Neiman Marcus.

"They want me to meet with them first thing Monday morning. If I leave early enough in the morning, I can make it back to L.A. by tomorrow night …" He stopped, paced for a moment, and stroked the morning stubble of his chin, thinking. "Oh, but we were scheduled to leave next weekend, weren't we …"

"Yes, we were," she replied, trying to conceal her disappointment.

"I'm sorry, *ma chérie* … Would you mind … finishing packing? I know there isn't that much more to do … right?"

"That's right. I can finish organizing. Don't worry, Michel." She loved the fact that he called her his darling.

"You're wonderful," he said, walking up to her. "I'd better take a shower … so much to do," he mumbled, and holding her face gently with both hands, he smiled.

That same smile. The one he had given her the first time she saw him, in Alexandria. So many years later, that smile had not changed. He gave her a quick peck on the lips. "*Merci, merci!*" He turned and walked to the bathroom while undoing the belt of his terrycloth bathrobe. As she started to float after him, ready to join him in the shower, he had already entered the bathroom, and closed the door behind him.

***** ***** *****

Zaffeera was furious. *It was Sunday morning, for heaven's sake.* She needed him in bed, their bodies locked in each other's arms. *Why did he have his old alarm clock set for five in the freaking morning!* And why didn't he use the gentle wave sound of the new alarm she had purchased for him? "Get rid of this alarm! Sounds like a pig being strangled!"

"Sorry," Michel mumbled as he reached for the alarm clock by the bed.

"I wish you didn't have to go," Zaffeera said, lowering her voice, putting an arm around him, just as he was about to pull the twisted sheets away and hit the shower. "It's Sunday. The sun isn't even up yet," she purred.

"I'm sorry," he said, turning off the button and clumsily replacing the alarm clock on his nightstand.

"Stay with me. Make love to me." Zaffeera jumped up, catching herself. "I'm sorry," she said, rubbing her face. "I … I was having a dream."

"What kind of a dream?" he asked, stretching his body before rising out of bed.

"I'm not sure … It was all … mumbo jumbo."

"I've had those. Didn't mean to startle you. I should've slept in the other room so I wouldn't disturb you …"

"You don't disturb me, Michel. I like sleeping next to you."

"Thank you …" He mumbled, sitting up in bed, stretching his back. "I had a sudden leg cramp in the middle of the night, and I didn't sleep much after that, and when I finally did, there went the alarm … of course …"

"I'm sorry, let me massage it. You probably need more calcium in your diet."

"Really?"

"Yes. And a good massage," she said, pulling herself closer to him, gently caressing his right shoulder.

"I wish I didn't have to go. I should've told him I could meet him on Tuesday instead of Monday morning in his office …"

"I'll miss you," she said.

"You'll join me in Los Angeles soon. Which reminds me, I'll tell the pilot you'll be flying next Saturday, right?"

"Yes," she sighed, returning to her pillow. *There goes my morning fuck,* she thought.

"I have a feeling you're going to be happy there," he said, rising.

"Did you need the chauffeur this morning? I ... I'm sorry, I didn't call him," Zaffeera said, acting a bit sultry.

"Oh no, that's fine. I'm taking my father's Jag. It needs to be driven."

"Michel?"

"Yes?"

"Looks like I'll still need my maid ... in Los Angeles."

"Of course," he yawned, padding to the bathroom. "I'll advise the pilot today ... Two passengers ... Next week ..." He closed the bathroom door.

The road leading to the Al-Balladi airport was almost an hour away, unless Michel floored it to ninety miles an hour. But at that speed, the car started to shake. He would have to tell his father's mechanic. The car hadn't been driven in a few months, since he had it checked when he was in Los Angeles. He had enjoyed taking it for a spin with Zaffeera, a few days ago. He slowed down to seventy and put it on cruise control. The sun in the horizon began to show a brilliant orange glow, slowly lighting the indigo desert sky into purple and hot pink hues, while the stars faded, leaving a few to still sparkle before daylight. "Beautiful," he whispered, glad now that he was up early enough to catch such a stunning sight ... *A feast for any weary eyes ... and soul,* he thought. His cell phone jingled.

"Monsieur Amir, we regret to inform you, there's been a slight delay ..."

"Delay?"

"There's nothing to be concerned about, but we won't be able to leave for another two hours," the pilot said.

"Something wrong with the plane?" Michel asked.

"No, mechanically, everything is in perfect order, ready to take off. But we can't land in Cairo until two hours later than our scheduled time. The good news is, you still have plenty of time to make your connection in Paris, for the nonstop to L.A."

Two hours? Michel thought he could drive back home, but by then, it would be almost time to turn right around. Zaffeera would want him to come back to bed, and he might fall asleep and miss his flight. He would just wait at the airport and start to work on the new plans. His mind drifted to Zaffeera. She had been a little too rough lately during their lovemaking. Last night especially was the first time she appeared so ... demanding in bed. "More!" she had said, as if commanding him to perform better. He felt obligated to try harder and please her. Not that he couldn't ... But not when he felt pressured, even obligated. When he climaxed, she shouted, "Oh no, not yet!" He pulled away, feeling embarrassed. He felt the pain on his back. She had cut into his skin with her fingernails. Why had she been so rough? Maybe she wanted to be sure to conceive? No, that could not be the reason. It was more than that. Whatever the reason, he didn't like it.

It was possible she was upset that he was leaving her to finish doing all the packing, even though she told him she didn't mind. But he could tell she was disappointed. He would offer to arrange for people to assist her, if she needed more help.

How would their life be when she moved to Los Angeles? So far, he had been away from her a great deal, traveling, and it worked out fine for him. But that did not help their relationship. He really didn't know her, and he felt stifled at times by having her around for more than a week ... How could he stay married to her if he started resenting her? It all came back to Noora. At times, he even started feeling anger toward Zaffeera ... Anger that she wasn't Noora. It wasn't fair, but there it was.

He was going back to Los Angeles to work on his second love: architecture. He should focus on the Monday morning meeting with the studio executive. It was going to be a complicated house on a small lot. His new client wanted a pool and koi pond, water lilies, and a cabana, plus an office facing the pool ... a large master suite upstairs with a view to the southwest, and a theater with a *Gone with the Wind* theme. Challenging, all right, but it could be done—if he worked hard enough to figure it out.

Up ahead on the deserted road, Michel spotted a dark figure. As he approached, he could see it was a peasant woman selling flowers at the edge of the road. Beautiful roses ... peach, yellow, and red. He slowed down and stopped several feet before her. He turned off the ignition and got out of the car, keeping the car keys and his cell phone in his coat pocket.

Clad in a long black dress and veil that covered her entire face except her eyes, the woman was accompanied by two young boys, one about five and the other not more than seven. "Please buy my flowers," she said. "Very cheap."

Michel opened his wallet, and as he did, the small picture of Noora he had hidden in his wallet fell to the ground. As he bent to pick it up, the older boy ran up to Michel. "Please buy our flowers!" he shouted, as if ordering him. "Not much traffic today and we are hungry!"

"How much?"

The boy mentioned a number Michel could barely understand. Did he mean the equivalent of fifty cents for each rose? Or the whole bouquet?

He cautiously pulled out a twenty-dollar bill, while darting his eyes around to make sure no one was hiding, ready to rob him. But the area was deserted. He tucked Noora's picture back in his wallet. "I only have American dollars right now," he said in Arabic to the boy, showing the paper bill. "Twenty dollars ..."

"Okay!" the boy shouted excitedly. "Twenty Amrikan dallah!" he cried out. He ran back to his mother and picked up half their stock.

Michel took a bouquet of the prettiest peach-colored roses and handed the boy the money.

He looked around again. It was probably miles to the next rural town. He walked up to the woman and gave her an additional bill, a hundred dollars, before rushing back to his car. As he did, he heard her cries of joy. "May Allah bless you!" she shouted, looking at the money, her eyes bulging. *"Allah ye naouehr aleikum!"* she cried, raising her hands to the sky. The two young boys ran after him, jumping up and down, wanting to give him all their flowers, shouting in their native tongue: "Allah will bless you! Allah will bless you!"

"Yes," Michel nodded, pulling back to the road. "May the Lord bestow light upon you, too." He said, waving at them. "*Shokran!* Thank you! He drove off.

Michel had nearly forgotten about the old picture of Noora he had hidden in his wallet. He checked his watch. He had enough time to take a detour and visit her grave. He had never been back since that first time with Zaffeera. It had been too painful. Now that they were going to be gone so long, possibly even for good, he wanted to visit her grave. Perhaps then, he would finally have some closure ... perhaps.

He remembered where it was. Several miles away from downtown Al-Balladi, not far from the souq and market of flowers—at the edge of town, and at the foothill of that particular mountain.

When he arrived, he saw trucks and cranes parked around the area. Obviously, the construction of what was going to be a commercial building. Had he made a mistake? No, he recognized the entrance to the souq. The little flower market was still there, where Zaffeera had purchased the roses for her sister. He turned to the bouquet of flowers he had set down on the passenger seat. He felt a tightness in his chest at the memory of that dreadful day, when Zaffeera and he had gone to visit Noora's grave ... So many years ago now. But what was going on? They were building on top of a ... *cemetery?*

Holding his bouquet of flowers, he approached one of the construction workers. "What are you doing here? This is a cemetery!"

The worker turned to Michel and stared at him as if looking at a madman. Other men approached him, some exchanging glances. Michel began to feel awkward.

"Do you have a general contractor on site?" he asked the men in Arabic.

"He's in his office, over there," one of the men replied, pointing to a trailer a few yards away.

Moments later, after Michel had spoken to the general contractor inside the trailer, and learned the truth about this site, he never felt more embarrassed. He hurried back to his car, stopped before opening his door, stared at his flowers, and angrily tossed them aside. He climbed in his car, and as he pulled back to the road, he floored the gas pedal. The blood had risen to his head, and he was burning with anger. He opened all the windows. He had been fooled, he thought, punching once at the steering wheel. Fooled by Zaffeera! Stricken by his grief, he had been too numb, too naïve, too stupid to know about burial customs. He had believed her ... He had trusted her! He started toward the road to the airport, but decided to turn right around and confront her. Where was Noora buried? Why did she lie? He dialed Zaffeera's cell number. There was no answer. No, he needed to confront her in person. He made a U-turn and headed to his father's house. He would have to cancel the meeting. He was not in a position to meet with anyone, no matter how much he had wanted that opportunity. No matter how proud his father was when he gave him the good news the night before.

When he arrived at the house, he jumped out of his car and ran inside. "Zaffeera!" he shouted, searching for her. He climbed the stairs two at a time to their bedroom. He nearly bumped into Gamelia, who was just leaving the room, holding a breakfast tray.

"Oh! I ... I beg your pardon, Mr. Amir," Gamelia said, immediately lowering her eyes.

"Where is Zaffeera?!"

"She ... Mrs. Amir went out, monsieur."

"Out where?"

"Oh ..." she answered, finally looking up at Michel.

"Where did she *go?*"

"D...Doctor. Doctor's appointment."

"Why did she go to the doctor? It's Sunday."

"Yes, they ... they are open only in the morning on Sunday. She's ... just an examination before ... Before trip to America ..."

Michel could see he had frightened her. Her hands trembled as she stood before him. The small crystal vase holding a single short-stemmed rose clattered against the half-empty demitasse of coffee on the tray. "Sir ... may I ask her to call you upon ... her return?"

"No. Thank you," he said, toning down his voice level. He should not have yelled at her. "I just came back to pick up something I forgot ... There's no need to tell her. I'll call her later ... Later tonight ... Thank you. Sorry... I didn't mean to... All's well. Thank you."

"Yes, sir."

Tightly grasping the breakfast tray that her mistress Zaffeera had barely touched before leaving the house, Gamelia watched Michel run down the circular stairway and out the front door. She had to set the tray down on the nearby console in the hallway, because her entire body shook uncontrollably. "Allah, please forgive me for lying," she mumbled.

He knows. He knows something is wrong, Gamelia was sure of it. How could she tell Zaffeera's husband where her mistress really was?

She heard Michel's car drive away. Suddenly she wasn't frightened anymore. She was angry—angry because Zaffeera was cheating on her good husband. Sick of Zaffeera treating her like a slave. Sick of Zaffeera *raping* her; sick and tired of living in fear that Zaffeera would beat her again at any time, for any reason. She touched her cheek and put her hand against her ear. She could still feel the ache where her mistress had struck her so hard and knocked her to the floor, kicking her like a beast.

CHAPTER 73
JUSTICE

For more than a half hour, Gamelia ran. She stopped for a moment's rest and squinted up toward the hill.

During the first few times when her mistress engaged in her illicit affair, Gamelia had to hide in the dry bushes a few yards away from the limo and guard the area near the cliff. She had to keep Zaffeera's cellular ready to press the automatic dial button that would ring straight to the mobile phone in the limousine, in case any passing cars or occasional nomads would be spotted from a distance. But the area proved to be always deserted, and Zaffeera no longer needed her maid to be her guard.

Gamelia hiked up the hill, panting and exhausted, but exhilarated. She was going to seek justice one way or another, even if it cost her her life. As she approached, careful not to breathe too loudly from the hard climb, she saw the black stretch limo, parked near the edge of the cliff, swaying.

Slowly, she approached the car and peeked in the back window. Inside, Zaffeera was intensely engaged in sex with her chauffeur. Gamelia silently crawled her way along the endless black gleam of the stretch limo and approached the driver's side, praying they had not locked the door. It clicked open. She climbed in the car, which was idling with the air conditioning on, full blast. She did not shut the door, for fear that they might hear it, although it appeared that the lovers in the back were too engrossed to notice the intruder.

Gamelia looked at the dashboard and gearshift for a brief moment. The couple behind her panted louder and faster in their passion.

She remembered watching Abdo shift into gear, whenever she sat up front when he took her out on errands for Zaffeera. He had shown her how a car moves forward, and how to make it stop. She thrust the gearshift into the "Drive" position.

Slowly at first, the limousine began to roll. She noticed the emergency brake light on the dashboard and remembered seeing Abdo reaching below on the left side of the steering wheel. She released the lever. She also remembered when Abdo pressed down on the foot pedal, the car rolled faster. She pressed the toes of her right foot on the pedal a bit, and stopped. She tapped once again on the accelerator. She pulled her foot back, unsure of what she would do. The car was nearing the edge of a cliff that overlooked a vista of the desert below. Gamelia's toes rested upon the gas pedal again, this time with a definite intention. The couple did not hear the tires as they crackled on the dry gravel, and gained momentum. Panting louder in the back, as the lovers were apparently reaching climax, the wheels rolled faster. Zaffeera gave her devilish howl of ecstasy—and screamed again, realizing the car was in motion.

Forward the limousine went. Zaffeera's eyes grew their widest ever when she saw Gamelia was at the wheel. "The brakes!" she shouted, horrified. "Slam on the brakes NOW!"

Gamelia threw back a determined glance over her right shoulder. "*La'a, setti ya Sharmouta!*" It felt so good to finally say those words out loud. "No, my lady the Whore!" And with a smile of defiance, keeping her hands firmly on the steering wheel, Gamelia added: "Make me!"

Naked, Zaffeera lunged forward and tried to jump over to the driver's seat but the glass partition between the front and the passenger area had limited space. Zaffeera still managed to slide herself forward, trying to push her maid out of the way, while in the back, her lover fumbled desperately to slip his pants back on.

"Let justice be done!" Gamelia cried, pressing on the gas pedal.

Zaffeera pushed her maid as hard as she could toward the driver's door, in an attempt to get a hold of the steering wheel and take control of the car. The driver's door swung open, and Gamelia fell out of the car. She hit the gravel hard, her right shoulder first; she rolled once and stopped. For a split second, the limo appeared to be suspended in midair, as if time had stood still. And then it tilted ...

Down the sleek limousine *dove* over the cliff, crashing onto the rocks below, tumbling further, rolling and smashing against rocky ledges until it flattened on a massive boulder at the bottom of the ravine.

Zaffeera's last screams of terror echoed through the rocky precipice while Gamelia watched from the edge of the cliff in utter horror. Smoke from the car began to sizzle upward. "*Allah, ya Allah,* what have I done?!" Gamelia cried as pieces of rocks began to give way beneath her; down they went, down until they hit metal of the crashed car below, causing eerie-sounding echoes. Little by little, Gamelia crawled backward, unable to watch the grisly sight.

Why did Zaffeera push me out of the car, Allah? I was supposed to dive into hell with her. Gamelia was trembling too hard to risk standing. Once again, Zaffeera's dreadful last cry of terror rang back in Gamelia's ears, and dissipated with the sound of her breathing and her pounding heart. She turned away from the crash and continued to crawl further inland, far from that dreadful cliff, as far as she could from that horrific scene—for how long, she would not remember—and soon found herself back on her feet. She looked at her hands; they were badly bruised and bloodied. Her chin was also scraped from the fall, and she felt a sharp pain on her right shoulder. But her long black dress had protected her body. The soft brown leather slippers Zaffeera always made her wear, because they were noiseless, were still on her feet, thanks to the tight elastic band.

"Why did you spare me? *A'alashan, Allah* ... Why, God?" Gamelia sobbed. Holding on to her bruised shoulder, she stumbled painfully ahead, walking as fast as her body would let her, far enough from the road that led to the crash site, and a good two miles toward the area of gated mansions in the posh community where Zaffeera lived. Beneath the shade of a huge lone mango tree, Gamelia took refuge, falling to the ground by its trunk, wanting to disappear in its shadow. She wrapped her arms around her knees and crunched her trembling body into a ball. When the pounding of her heart began to subside, Gamelia raised her head. Under the tree, she watched the mango leaves, like spears, and rotten mangoes on the ground, some with only their pointy seeds left, picked nearly clean by birds. Above her, she gazed at the little green mangoes starting their new life, hanging on long stems. Was it possible Allah wanted her to live? But for what purpose? She thought of her mother and her grandmother. A voice inside urged her to return to her village—where she was born—where she had promised herself never to return. She had not been there to help her mother tend to her ailing grandmother. She had shut the door to that past completely. But they were her loved ones. Shamefully, she had left them. She had been raped by the devil man who violated her young body. For the first time, she realized that other girls in her village could have suffered the same predicament. A sudden burst of energy came over her, and nearly running now, she understood in her heart that Allah had given her the chance to live so she could go back to help others, so she could protect ...

Unless someone saw the accident? *What if Zaffeera survived?*

No one heard or saw the car crash. No one knew until before dawn, when Zaffeera did not return home that night, and rising smoke from the burning car was spotted.

When Michel landed at the Los Angeles airport on Sunday evening, two security guards met him at the exit gate.

"Are you Mr. Michel Amir?"

"Yes." Michel watched the men, puzzled. "Something wrong?"

"There has been a serious accident ..."

CHAPTER 74
AWARDS NIGHT

"Five minutes!" Ian Cohen said nervously. "Why did they have to send us a limo? We could've taken our own car," he complained. "What's wrong with my Rolls-Royce?!" He adjusted his uncomfortable cummerbund. As he loosened the bow tie around his neck, he looked up. Noora stood at the landing of the stairs, wearing a proud smile and the classy black gown with the delicate gold straps.

Cessi and Sam walked up behind Ian and clapped their hands. Ian just stared, his mouth open.

She began to come down the stairs.

"We have a problem," Ian said seriously. Noora stopped, her smile fading. "You're gonna outshine 'em all."

"As long as I don't outshine the future Mrs. Jaqui Amstern!" Noora replied, laughing.

It had happened like a dream. When Noora heard Kelley Karlton being called, she remembered floating down that aisle and flying up to the stage. If the cliché 'Cloud Nine' meant anything, Noora was on Cloud Countless! She made a speech, one she had not prepared. Her words flowed out of her lips like sweet water, and she managed to say it all in the short time they allowed before the orchestra played. She had thanked the heroic Ahna Morgenbesser first. "She taught us love, she taught forgiveness ..." Then she thanked Annette, Alain, and Annou. She took a brief pause and thanked "The exceptional producer, Mr. Ian

Cohen." She knew all the cameras were now on him! "And don't call him ICE! He's got the warmest heart!"

Everyone in the audience laughed. She thanked Jaqui and Setchka, and her son, and then she stopped and said: "Thank you, Um Faheema. And to you, Dweezoul!" She touched her bead proudly worn around her neck (which did not take away from her glamorous gown). She was escorted backstage by two exquisitely-clad models. When she floated back down to her seat, she gave Ian a warm hug. She waited for the lights to dim for the commercial break and the next presentation.

She waited long enough to watch him walk up and accept his award. Then she made her way quietly outside and slipped out through one of the back doors. She crossed the street and caught a taxi. She returned to Ian's house and grabbed the one carry-on that Cessi had kept for her.

"I saw you on tele-beezion, Miz Karrl-tone; you look beautiful!"

"Thank you, Cessi!" Noora said and gave her a hug. She ran upstairs to change, and minutes later, she hopped back in the taxicab and was driven to the airport.

Noora took the redeye from L.A. to Paris. Once she arrived at Orly Airport in Paris, she waited at the airline's private lounge. *What time was it at Al-Balladi?* Ahna had said, "The opposite side of anger is courage." At this time, she felt neither. She was on a mission. Moments later, she heard Kelley Karlton being paged through the loudspeaker. The representative at the lounge was able to book her on a nonstop to Cairo, boarding immediately, with a transfer to Al-Balladi. However, there was just one seat left in coach class on the flight to Cairo. Would she mind? What did it matter where she sat? As long as she got there.

As the plane soared into the cloudy sky, so did Noora's heart. She leafed through a magazine, and a line caught her attention: "*This period of incubation will soon make way for illumination.*" She rubbed Um Faheema's blue pearl. She pressed the talisman to her chest and closed her eyes.

Um Faheema appeared in her mind's eye. The vision of her wearing her black veil draped around her head was vivid. Slowly the face dissolved into a younger Um Faheema with a clear, unwrinkled face. And she was wearing white. *White?* White silk covered her head and floated around her, below her shoulders. She could smell the sweet aroma that was hers only, of herbal teas—mixed with the fragrance of rose water and lavender, tangerine and lime ... Noora welcomed and inhaled the scent of her memory. The old woman's lips began to move, the one tooth sticking out just a bit. *Courage,* she said in French. *Cour-ahj, Noora ...* With every word in every passing moment, Um Faheema's eyes brightened. *Cour... age!!* She repeated in French. *Court,* meaning run! *"Rabbena ma'aki ya benti,"* Noora heard her clearly now in Arabic. The Lord is with you, my daughter.

When the plane touched down on the Cairo runway, Noora was jolted from sleep. "I'm almost there." She should board the next plane back to the States—for where could she find the courage to confront her father? What would she say to him?

She was unprepared. First, she needed to show up. *Alive!* Was there a death certificate? There had to be.

He had denounced her. *You don't denounce your flesh and blood, Father,* she thought as she followed the other passengers out of the gate ... *You don't!*

Moments later, a haze of dizziness overcame her. *I can't do this ... But I must.* Fear was a paralyzing disease. She would not fall into that trap again.

Noora stepped out of the plane and breathed in the warm air—the fragrance of her past. *Take your courage with both hands,* she thought, looking around. She took a deep breath ... How different the Al-Balladi airport seemed now—more buildings in the distance. More cement, marble, and limestone buildings, everywhere.

There were more airplanes—private and commercial jets—more people milling about. Most of the women were veiled. Some were completely covered, from head to toe!

Following other passengers, she walked to the gate and straight to Customs. She waited in a line that seemed to have materialized in a matter of seconds. She looked around, wondering when they had built this stark building. Security guards were posted everywhere. She kept her large sunglasses on, and her head covered by a black silk shawl. The line moved quickly. Noora felt the blood rush to her head as the security official checked her passport and visa. He looked up. "Remove your sunglasses," he said impatiently. She did. She knew everything was in order; but she felt uneasy. She should have brought a male traveling companion or a bodyguard to accompany her. *How could she have neglected such an important detail?!* Women in that part of the world did not travel alone. In the form distributed on the plane prior to landing in Al-Balladi, she had written the purpose of her trip was to visit her family. After routine questionings, most of which she had written down on the passenger questionnaire prior to landing, the official finally stamped her passport. She followed other travelers through an exit leading to the conveyor belt where travelers were to retrieve their suitcases, some of which were being searched thoroughly.

Noora had brought only the small carry-on. She would not need more than a change of dresses—long black skirts, black blouses, a pair of black pumps—two long scarves to conceal her head and neck—and a long white chiffon dress with a white silk scarf to match.

"Miss Karlton?"

Noora whirled around, startled. *Calm down,* she chided herself. Her heart was still hammering and she was perspiring.

"How do you do? I am Khamis, of Oasis Travel and Tours."

"Ah, yes! I am so ... glad to see you!"

"Thank you, welcome. May I carry your bag?"

"No, thank you. It's not heavy."

"The luggage of your flight should be coming through here at any moment ..."

"I don't have luggage. Just this."

The chauffeur was surprised. "Very well," he said. "The car is right over there." He pointed across the passageway, where a row of gleaming black limousines awaited.

"So many limousines ..." Noora said before she could catch herself.

"Pardon, Madame?"

"Oh ... it all looks so new."

"A lot of construction going on these days. I'll bring the car around. If you don't mind waiting right here."

"Thank you," she said, adjusting her sunglasses and wrapping her black shawl tighter around her, completely concealing her hair.

The limousine pulled up and the chauffeur ran to open the back door for Noora.

As they drove away from the airport, onto the familiar road, Noora spotted a glass skyscraper in the distance.

The structure loomed in the hazy horizon and reminded her of a Las Vegas hotel she had seen in a magazine, with dozens of trimly cut trunks of royal palms planted in perfect succession along a stretch of manicured lawns.

"I've changed my mind," she said.

"Excuse me?"

"Do you have to get back to the airport as soon as you drop me off?"

"No, madame," the driver replied, seeming confused.

"I may need your service for the rest of the day."

"I am at your service."

"I just need to check in at the Hyatt Hotel first, then could you … Could you take me to 27 Nassehr Street?"

"27 Rue Nassehr?"

"Yes. After I check in."

"Of course." There was a pause, then: "Would that address on Nassehr be the … the developer's house, Mr. Fendil?"

"Yes."

Inside the hotel lobby, there was a long line at the check-in counter. Noora made her way to the ladies' room, and moments later, she returned to her waiting limousine. Dressed in the long white skirt and long-sleeved cotton blouse she had brought with her, white leather pumps, and an extra-long chiffon scarf she wrapped around her head, Noora wore no trace of makeup.

The tall filigree gates leading to the Fendil mansion were open—as they had always been.

The façade of the house and the Tiffany front doors seemed smaller than she remembered.

"Drive inside, please," Noora said.

The royal palms lining the driveway waved in the wind. One could swear they were waving at Noora, welcoming her. Only she knew better. This was no welcoming return. The trees were much taller now. The lawn was impeccably manicured, but her grandmother's rose bushes bordering the driveway were gone. Other than that, not much had changed.

The limousine made its way to the marble front steps. One of the Tiffany front doors opened. A young houseboy dressed in a white *gallabeya* appeared holding a portable vacuum. He was obviously surprised by the unexpected guest and watched the pretty lady who got out of the limo and climbed the steps.

"I'm expected," she announced decidedly in Arabic and brushed by him, entering the house.

Her ease in speaking Arabic again surprised even herself.

The young houseboy watched the attractive figure clad in white from head to toe, her heels echoing gently on the marble floors, as she made her way through the corridor.

Noora marched ahead, through another long corridor, adorned with columns and archways—straight to the men's wing.

Farid Fendil had returned from work early. The quadruple bypass surgery three years before had been a success, and he had recovered rapidly. But that afternoon, he felt heavy, perhaps from the desert heat that had blown in from the south, and this morning, he had experienced some shortness of breath. He decided to go home for a refreshing swim in his remodeled pool.

Wearing a bathing suit and long white terry robe, Farid made his way out through corridors of the men's wing. He decided to take the shortcut through the courtyard shaded by the huge mango tree.

On the opposite side of the house, Noora's heart pounded as she made her way to her father's office. He was not there. Right outside of the double doors, a houseboy was sweeping the floors. He was obviously stunned at the sight of a woman in the men's wing.

"Where is Mr. Fendil?" Noora asked in Arabic.

"He ... I think he ... went to the pool ..."

"Thank you." She walked on.

The houseboy ran a hand to his chest. "*Ya satehr,*" he said. He ran in the opposite direction, through Mr. Fendil's bedroom suite and to his bathroom, which resembled the interior of a Turkish bath. An older houseman clad in a white *gallabeya* was hanging fresh golden monogrammed towels.

"I … saw a ghost. *Wallahee,* a woman ghost … In the men's wing," the houseboy said, his face pale.

"You've been smoking hashish again?"

"No, I swear … she had blue eyes and … I … aiii … she went to the pool …."

"Go to the mosque and pray. Finish your work later."

Noora stopped at the tall glass double doors with etched designs of tropical birds and hesitated. *I cannot do this! I must, I must! My love for my father has never faltered. I cannot allow fear to stop me now … He must know the truth. Just do it!* She pushed one of the doors, and it swung open. She stepped inside the sunny atrium housing the Olympic-sized pool. A pair of life-size bronze statues of lions (that were not there before) greeted her on either side of the narrow marble walkway, bordered by a dense array of palms and other plants. The lush tropical setting radiated beneath an enormous glass dome.

As she walked down the path, the white veil that covered her head slowly loosened and fell to her shoulders. She could hear the swishing sounds of water. She ventured closer where the pathway cleared to the pool.

With each stroke Farid Fendil took, a vision seemed to form up ahead, above the steps of the pool. A tall young woman appeared. She radiated beneath the bright sunlight emanating from above. A sudden pain gripped his chest, and he swallowed pool water. He coughed, and his eyes blurred from the water. But he tried to focus on the woman who stood there. He waited for his cough to subside. The pain in his chest eased a little. Slowly, he swam forward, but he had not yet reached the shallow end of the pool. He could see her now.

He gasped and started to choke. He tried to swim to the edge by the handlebars for support, but he couldn't. "Help …" he managed to utter and sank for a moment, swallowing more water. He was still in the deep end of the pool and his chest pain was excruciating.

The fifty-seven years of his life flashed before his eyes. He saw himself back in his wife's room, the morning Noora was born. The aquamarine pool around him metamorphosed into the color of Noora's eyes. His arms were too weary to reach the edge. Again, the vision of Noora appeared. He felt heavy, heavier ... He could no longer float, and could barely breathe.

"Help! Help me, Allah!" he pleaded.

Noora watched her father in disbelief. Could he be drowning?

She felt his desperate struggle and she began to choke as well. He was begging for *her help*.

She threw her veil aside, kicked off her shoes, and dove in.

She pulled him to the surface but he was too heavy. With sudden strength, Noora managed to pull him to the shallow end, and dragged him up to the steps. Breathing hard, Noora held her father in her arms.

"*Abuyah.* Father," she cried, dripping wet hair strands falling to her eyes, mixing with her tears.

He gagged and coughed. And then he stopped.

Gently, she rocked him. "I love you ..."

"*Arusah, ya arusah anah,*" he whispered. "Doll, oh doll of mine ..."

He touched her face. She put her hand over his.

"*Shokran ya Allah* ..." he whispered. Thanking the Almighty God, Farid Fendil took his final breath and allowed a tear to fall.

EPILOGUE

Michel opened the door to the limousine before Abdo could switch off the engine. He wanted this day to be over. He wanted to return to his father's private jet as soon as possible. He wanted to be whisked away, back to L.A.—where he could be engrossed in his work. Where he wouldn't have to think about his life—the mystery, the grief, and the drama surrounding it. He needed to forget ...

He ran up the stairs to the Tiffany front doors of the Fendil house. Mrs. Fendil had returned from Switzerland with Abdo and her two children. Michel wasn't sure why she had summoned him. Perhaps she thought that being with the family of Zaffeera would help ease his grief. He prayed they had not invited the whole town to offer their condolences. Sympathy he did not need—or want.

A houseman opened the door and nodded politely. Another ushered him down the long corridor, then stopped. "This way," he motioned. "They are waiting ..." he said and turned back to greet Abdo at the front door.

As he made his way down the marble halls that seemed endless, Michel thought he should have more compassion. They had become his family as well. Mrs. Fendil certainly did not deserve all this suffering. How could he refuse her invitation? He had to come back ... for her ... Having lost two of her children was bad enough, but now to lose another daughter, Zaffeera, and her husband, in such a short amount of time ... It must be unbearable. Indeed, he needed to be present, at least to help comfort what was left of the Fendil family. Eventually, he would get over the tragedy of his marriage—and Zaffeera's strange death ... But Noora? He could never get over Noora. He entered through the wide-open doors to the great room and saw Mrs. Fendil hugging someone tightly, her shoulders moving up and down in a heavy sob. At first, he thought it was Shamsah, for he only saw her brown hair, which was shorter now and reached down to her shoulders. Mrs. Fendil had her arms wrapped around the girl's back. But she was taller, and when he looked around the room, he saw Shamsah, her hair up in a ponytail, sitting with Kettayef on one of the couches. He could tell that both had shed tears, but the odd thing was, they were smiling. Shamsah was the first to see him. She gave a little gasp, jumped up from the couch, and rushed to her mother. She gently placed a hand on the woman embracing Mrs. Fendil. "Look, look who is here," Shamsah said with excitement in her voice.

When she turned, the first thing Michel saw were her eyes. They were swollen and red, but they were the same aquamarine eyes which had haunted him for the past seven years.

Before he knew it, he was holding her. Everything was exactly the way he remembered. Her skin, her smell, how she fit in his arms so perfectly. He closed his eyes and took in this miraculous moment, a part of him wondering if it were all true, the other not really wanting to know. Because at that moment, Michel was holding his angel.

Fifteen months later—May, 2001

Moored off the coast of Antibes in the South of France, the ninety-foot yacht now christened *The Nageeb* gleamed on the horizon.

Inside the yacht, a very pregnant Noora floated in the yacht's lap pool, while little Annou splashed happily nearby with her mother, Annette.

"*Viens, ma chérie,* come. You have been in the pool long enough," she said to her little girl, who was now four years old.

Michel dove in from behind and kissed his wife on the neck. Noora turned and smiled broadly at him.

He pulled her close to him and they kissed. As he suddenly picked her up in his arms and twirled her around in the water's surface, she threw her head back and laughed. He said something close to her ear that made her laugh harder.

"What could he be telling her that makes her laugh so much?" Kettayef asked his mother. Speaking well now, Kettayef had grown into a young man.

"Young lovers. You know how that is," Yasmina answered, watching Noora with a smile.

"No, I really don't. Someday maybe I will."

"Yes, you will. But don't get any ideas before you finish college."

"Yes, Mother," he said, with a sneaky twinkle in his eye. "I can't wait for Noora to see her surprise."

"I can't wait either," Shamsah said, pulling a chair next to her mother. She had grown into a lovely sixteen-year-old. In a bathing suit and sarong tied around her waist, Shamsah had the same straight ballerina back as Noora, and rich brown hair that fell in waves, below her shoulders. Annou ran up to her and sat on her lap.

"It might be too much of a shock," Yasmina said, taking a sip of her lemonade.

"Yes, at first. But ... you don't suppose she'll have the baby when she sees him?" Shamsah asked, putting her arms around Annou and kissing her head.

Yasmina Fendil laughed. "Oh please! She's not due for two more months ..."

"Anyway, we have Annou's papa on board ... just in case," Kettayef said, winking at little Annou.

The roar of a small taxi boat was heard by everyone except for Noora, who was busy splashing with her husband in the pool.

The taxi boat cut its engine and came aside the yacht. Abdo stepped on deck first and motioned behind him to the guest, not yet visible, to wait a moment.

"Come on out, Noora. Lunch is ready," Michel said, glancing quickly toward the area where Abdo stood. He nodded.

Noora climbed up heavily and Michel helped her out, wrapping a bath towel around her. Slowly, his hands on her shoulders, he turned her around.

The red fez was the first thing that came into view as he climbed on deck. Noora had to blink a few times. Surely it had to be a vision.

"Oh my God." She put both hands to her mouth. It *was* a vision. Years had passed and he had grown … *so tall!* It couldn't be … But he had not changed. She remembered the train station … the last time she saw him … before her tears blinded her last view of him.

"It's me!" He opened his arms wide. "I never saw so much water in my life! A vast desert of liquid … and you. In the middle!"

"Dweezoul?"

She stepped forward unsteadily. "Oh my dear God!" Michel held a steady arm around the small of her back. "Oh my dear God, tell me this is not a dream!"

"*Bent el Noor,*" he said.

Who else would call her "Daughter of Light"? He was now more than three inches taller than Noora.

"Dweezoul! It *is* you!" Tears began to flow.

He ran to her and wrapped his long arms in a warm hug.

"How? How did you find me?"

"You have a very clever husband," he said.

THE END

About the Author

Born in Alexandria, Egypt, Lucette Walters grew up in Paris and later, Chicago. She moved to Los Angeles where she began a career in film. She lives in Southern California and Hawaii.

Printed in the United States
By Bookmasters